THE CHILDREN'S BOOK

THE
CHILDREN'S
BOOK

A NOVEL

A. S. BYATT

ALFRED A. KNOPF · NEW YORK · 2009

THIS IS A BORZOI BOOK
PUBLISHED BY ALFRED A. KNOPF

Knopf, Borzoi Books, and the colophon are registered
trademarks of Random House, Inc.

Originally published in Great Britain by Chatto & Windus,
the Random House Group, Ltd., London, in 2009.

The poem "Trench Names" originally appeared in *The New Yorker*.

Library of Congress Cataloging-in-Publication Data
Byatt, A. S. (Antonia Susan), [date]
The children's book : a novel / by A. S. Byatt.—1st ed.
p. cm.
ISBN 978-0-307-27209-6
1. Women authors—Fiction.   2. Children and adults—Fiction.
3. Runaway children—Fiction.   4. Country homes—England—Fiction.
5. Family secrets—Fiction.   6. World War, 1914–1918—England—Fiction.
I. Title.
PR6052.Y2C48 2009
823'.914—dc22
2009016334

Manufactured in the United States of America
Published October 6, 2009
Reprinted One Time
Third Printing, October 2009

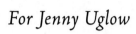

For Jenny Uglow

I
🌿 Beginnings

Two boys stood in the Prince Consort Gallery, and looked down on a third. It was June 19th, 1895. The Prince had died in 1861, and had seen only the beginnings of his ambitious project for a gathering of museums in which the British craftsmen could study the best examples of design. His portrait, modest and medalled, was done in mosaic in the tympanum of a decorative arch at one end of the narrow gallery which ran above the space of the South Court. The South Court was decorated with further mosaics, portraits of painters, sculptors, potters, the "Kensington Valhalla." The third boy was squatting beside one of a series of imposing glass cases displaying gold and silver treasures. Tom, the younger of the two looking down, thought of Snow White in her glass coffin. He thought also, looking up at Albert, that the vessels and spoons and caskets, gleaming in the liquid light under the glass, were like a resurrected kingly burial hoard. (Which, indeed, some of them were.) They could not see the other boy clearly, because he was on the far side of a case. He appeared to be sketching its contents.

Julian Cain was at home in the South Kensington Museum. His father, Major Prosper Cain, was Special Keeper of Precious Metals. Julian was just fifteen, and a boarder at Marlowe School, but was home recovering from a nasty bout of jaundice. He was neither tall nor short, slightly built, with a sharp face and a sallow complexion, even without the jaundice. He wore his straight black hair parted in the centre, and was dressed in a school suit. Tom Wellwood, boyish in Norfolk jacket and breeches, was about two years younger, and looked younger than he was, with large dark eyes, a soft mouth and a smooth head of dark gold hair. The two had not met before. Tom's mother was visiting Julian's father, to ask for help with her research. She was a successful authoress of magical tales. Julian had been deputed to show Tom the treasures. He appeared to be more interested in showing him the squatting boy.

"I said I'd show you a mystery."

"I thought you meant one of the treasures."

"No, I meant *him*. There's something shifty about him. I've been keeping an eye on him. He's up to something."

Tom was not sure whether this was the sort of make-believe his own family practised, tracking complete strangers and inventing stories about them. He wasn't sure if Julian was, so to speak, *playing* at being responsible.

"What does he do?"

"He does the Indian rope trick. He disappears. Now you see him, now you don't. He's here every day. All by himself. But you can't see where or when he *goes*."

They sidled along the wrought-iron gallery, which was hung with thick red velvet curtains. The third boy stayed where he was, drawing intently. Then he moved his position, to see from another angle. He was hay-haired, shaggy and filthy. He had cut-down workmen's trousers, with braces, over a flannel shirt the colour of smoke, stained with soot. Julian said

"We could go down and stalk him. There are all sorts of odd things about him. He looks very rough. He never seems to go anywhere but here. I've waited at the exit to see him leave, and follow him, and he doesn't seem to leave. He seems to be a permanent fixture."

The boy looked up, briefly, his grimy face creased in a frown. Tom said

"He *concentrates*."

"He never talks to anyone that I can see. Now and then the art students look at his drawings. But he doesn't chat to them. He just creeps about the place. It's sinister."

"Do you get many robberies?"

"My father always says the keepers are criminally casual with the keys to the cases. And there are heaps and heaps of stuff lying around waiting to be catalogued, or sent to Bethnal Green. It would be terribly easy to sneak off with things. I don't even know if anyone would notice if you did, not with some of the things, though they'd notice quickly enough if anyone made an attempt on the Candlestick."

"Candlestick?"

"The Gloucester Candlestick. What he seems to be drawing, a lot of the time. The lump of gold, in the centre of that case. It's ancient and unique. I'll show it to you. We could go down, and go up to it, and disturb him."

Tom was dubious about this. There was something tense about the third boy, a tough prepared energy he didn't even realise he'd noticed. However, he agreed. He usually agreed to things. They moved, sleuth-like, from ambush to ambush behind the swags of velvet. They went under Prince Albert, out onto the turning stone stairs, down to the South Court. When they reached the Candlestick, the dirty boy was not there.

"He wasn't on the stairs," said Julian, obsessed.

Tom stopped to stare at the Candlestick. It was dully gold. It seemed heavy. It stood on three feet, each of which was a long-eared dragon, grasping a bone with grim claws, gnawing with sharp teeth. The rim of the spiked cup that held the candle was also supported by open-jawed dragons with wings and snaking tails. The whole of its thick stem was wrought of fantastic foliage, amongst which men and monsters, centaurs and monkeys, writhed, grinned, grimaced, grasped and stabbed at each other. A helmeted, gnomelike being, with huge eyes, grappled the sinuous tail of a reptile. There were other human or kobold figures, one in particular with long draggling hair and a mournful gaze. Tom thought immediately that his mother would need to see it. He tried, and failed, to memorise the shapes. Julian explained. It had an interesting history, he said. No one knew exactly what it was made of. It was some kind of gilt alloy. It was probable that it had been made in Canterbury—modelled in wax and cast—but apart from the symbols of the evangelists on the knop, it appeared not to be made for a religious use. It had turned up in the cathedral in Le Mans, from where it had disappeared during the French Revolution. A French antiquary had sold it to the Russian Prince Soltikoff. The South Kensington Museum had acquired it from his collection in 1861. There was nothing, anywhere, like it.

Tom did not know what a knop was, and did not know what the symbols of the evangelists were. But he saw that the thing was a whole world of secret stories. He said his mother would like to see it. It might be just what she was looking for. He would have liked to touch the heads of the dragons.

Julian was looking restlessly around him. There was a concealed door, behind a plaster cast of a guarding knight, on a marble plinth. It was slightly ajar, which he had never seen before. He had tried its handle, and it was always, as it should be, since it led down to the basement storerooms and workrooms, locked.

"I bet he went down there."

"What's down there?"

"Miles and miles of passages and cupboards and cellars, and *things* being moulded, or cleaned, or just kept. Let's stalk him."

There was no light, beyond what was cast on the upper steps from the door they had opened. Tom did not like the dark. He did not like transgression. He said "We can't see where we're going."

"We'll leave the door open a crack."

"Someone may come and lock it. We may get into trouble."

"We won't. I *live* here."

They crept down the uneven stone steps, holding a thin iron rail. At the foot of the staircase they found themselves cut off by a metal grille, beyond which stretched a long corridor, now vaguely visible as though there was a light-source at the other end. The passage was roofed with Gothic vaulting, like a church crypt, but finished in white glazed industrial bricks. Julian gave the grille an irritated shake and it swung open. He observed that this, too, should have been locked. Someone was in for trouble.

The passage opened into a dusty vault, crammed with a crowd of white effigies, men, women and children, staring out with sightless eyes. Tom thought they might be prisoners in the underworld, or even the damned. They were closely packed; the boys had to worm their way between them. Beyond this funereal chamber, two corridors branched. There was more light to the left, so they went that way, negotiated another unlocked grille, and found themselves in a treasure-house of vast gold and silver vessels, croziers, eagle-winged lecterns, fountains, soaring angels and grinning cherubs. "Electrotypes," whispered the knowledgeable Julian. A faint but steady light rippled over the metal, through little glass roundels let into the brickwork. Julian put his finger to his lips and hissed to Tom to keep still. Tom steadied himself against a silver galleon, which clanged. He sneezed.

"Don't *do* that."

"I can't help it. It's the dust."

They crept on, took a left, took a right, had to force their way between thickets of what Tom thought were tomb railings, surmounted by jaunty female angel-busts, with wings and pointed breasts. Julian said they were cast-iron radiator covers, commissioned from an ironmaster in Sheffield. "Cost a packet, down here because someone thought they were *obtrusive*," he whispered. "Which way now?"

Tom said he had no idea. Julian said they were lost, no one would find them, rats would pick their bones. Someone sneezed. Julian said

"I told you, don't *do* that."

"I didn't. It must have been *him*."

Tom was worried about hunting down a probably harmless and innocent boy. He was also worried about encountering a savage and dangerous boy.

Julian cried "We know you're there. Come out and give yourself up!"

He was alert and smiling, Tom saw, the successful seeker or catcher in games of pursuit.

There was a silence. Another sneeze. A slight scuffling. Julian and Tom turned to look down the other fork of the corridor, which was obstructed by a forest of imitation marble pillars, made to support busts or vases. A wild face, under a mat of hair, appeared at knee height, framed between fake basalt and fake obsidian.

"You'd better come out and explain yourself," said Julian, with complete certainty. "You're trespassing. I should get the police."

The third boy came out on all fours, shook himself like a beast, and stood up, supporting himself briefly on the pillars. He was about Julian's height. He was shaking, whether with fear or wrath Tom could not tell. He pushed a dirty hand across his face, rubbing his eyes, which even in the gloom could be seen to be red-rimmed. He put his head down, and tensed. Tom saw the thought go through him, he could charge the two of them, head-butt them and flee down the corridors. He didn't move and didn't answer.

"What are you doing down here?" Julian insisted.

"I were hiding."

"Why? Hiding from who?"

"Just hiding. I were doing no harm. I move carefully. I don't disturb things."

"What's your name? Where do you live?"

"My name's Philip. Philip Warren. I suppose I live here. At present."

His voice was vaguely north country. Tom recognised it, but couldn't place it. He was looking at them much as they were looking at him, as though he couldn't quite grasp that they were real. He blinked, and a tremor ran through him. Tom said

"You were drawing the Candlestick. Is that what you came for?"

"Aye."

He was clutching a kind of canvas satchel against his chest, which presumably contained his sketching materials. Tom said

"It's an amazing thing, isn't it? I hadn't seen it before."

The other boy looked him in the eye, then, with a flicker of a grin.

"Aye. Amazing, it is."

Julian spoke severely.

"You must come and explain yourself to my father."

"Oh, your *father*. Who's he, then?"

"He's Special Keeper of Precious Metals."

"Oh. I see."

"You must come along with us."

"I see I must. Can I get my things?"

"Things?" Julian sounded doubtful for the first time. "You mean, you've been *living* down here?"

"S'what I said. I got nowhere else to go. I'd rather not sleep on t'streets. I come here to draw. I saw the Museum was for workingmen to see well-made things. I mean to get work, I do, and I need drawings to show . . . I like these things."

"Can we see the drawings?" asked Tom.

"Not in this light. Upstairs, if you're interested. I'll get my things, like I said."

He ducked, and began to make his way back amongst the pillars, crouching and weaving expertly. Tom was put in mind of dwarves in mine-workings, and, since his upbringing was socially conscientious, of children in mines, pulling trucks on hands and knees. Julian was on Philip's heels. Tom followed.

"Come in," said the grimy boy, at the opening of a small storeroom, making a welcoming gesture, possibly mocking, with an arm. The storeroom contained what appeared to be a small stone hut, carved and ornamented with cherubim and seraphim, eagles and doves, acanthus and vines. It had its own little metal gate, with traces of gilding on the rusting iron.

"Convenient," said Philip. "It has a stone bed. I took the liberty of borrowing some sacks to keep warm. I'll put 'em back, naturally, where I found them."

"It's a tomb or shrine," said Julian. "Russian, by the look of it. There must have been some saint on that table, in a glass case or a reliquary. He might still be in there, underneath, his bones that is, if he wasn't incorrupt."

"I haven't noticed him," said Philip, flatly. "He hasn't bothered me."

Tom said "Are you hungry? What do you eat?"

"Once or twice I got to help in the tea-room, moving plates and washing them. People leave a lot on their plates, you'd be surprised. And the young ladies from the Art School took notice of my drawings and sometimes they passed me a sandwich. I don't beg. I did steal one, once, when I was desperate, an egg-and-cress sandwich. I were pretty sure the young lady had no intention of eating it."

He paused.

"It isn't *much,*" he said. "I'm hungry, yes."

He was rummaging behind the tomb in the shrine, and came out with another canvas satchel, a sketch-book, a candle stub and what looked like a roll of clothing, tied with string.

"How did you get in?" Julian persisted.

"Followed the horses and carts. You know, they turn in and drive down a ramp into these underground parts. And they unload and pack things with a deal of bustle, and it's easy enough to mingle wi' them, wi' the carters and lads, and get in."

"And the upstairs door?" Julian queried. "Which is meant to be locked at all times."

"I came across a little key."

"Came across?"

"Aye. Came across. I'll give it back. Here, take it."

Tom said

"It must be horribly frightening, down here alone at night."

"Not near so frightening as t'streets in t'East End. Not near."

Julian said "Please come with me now. You must come and explain all this to my father. He's talking to Tom's mother. This is Tom. Tom Wellwood. I'm Julian Cain."

Major Prosper Cain, of the Royal Engineers and the Department of Science and Art, had an Elizabethan manor house, Iwade House, in Kent. He also lived in one of the small dwelling houses which had grown up round South Kensington's monstrous steel and glass Boilers. (The purpose-built, cast-iron building, designed by a military engineer for the Museum, had three uncompromising long rounded roofs, which were mockingly known as the Brompton Boilers.) The dwelling houses were largely inhabited by the successors to the sappers who had originally constructed the Boilers after the Great Exhibition in 1851. Major Cain had what was not exactly an official residence, slightly larger than those of his men. There were ambitious projects to extend the museum buildings, and murmurings against the military presence. A competition had been held. Precise visions of palaces, courtyards, towers, fountains and ornaments had been scrutinised and compared. Aston Webb's project was declared the winner, but no work had taken place. The new Director, J. H. Middleton, appointed in 1894, was not a military man, but a reserved ascetic scholar, who came from King's College Cambridge and the Fitzwilliam Museum. He was at odds with Major-General Sir John Donnelly, secretary of the Science and Art Department. Moves had been made by keepers and scholars to demolish the inner dwellings, on the grounds of fire hazard and leaking flues. Twenty-seven open hearths, with chimneys, had been counted. The art students complained of soot and smoke rising into their studios. The military pointed out that the team of Museum fire-fighters was composed of the sappers who inhabited the buildings. The argument continued and nothing was done.

Prosper Cain's narrow little house had elegant hearths, both on the ground floor, and in the first-floor drawing-room. They were decorated with delightful tiles by William de Morgan. He had offered Olive Wellwood a French gilt chair, carved in an ornate style detested both by the Arts and Crafts movement, and by the Museum keepers. His eye was eclectic and he had a weakness, if it was a weakness, for extravagance. He took pleasure in the appearance of his visitor, who was dressed in dark slate-coloured grosgrain, trimmed with braid, with lace at the high neck and fashionably billowing sleeves above the elbow. Her hat was trimmed with black plumes and a profusion of scarlet silk poppies, nestling along the brim. She had a bold, pleasant face, high-coloured, eager, firm-mouthed, with wide-set huge dark eyes, like the poppy centres. She must have been, he judged, around thirty-five, more or less, probably more. He deduced that she was not in the habit of wearing such tight corsets, kid shoes and gloves. She moved a little too freely and impulsively. She had fine flesh, fine ankles. She probably wore Liberty gowns or rational dress, at home. He sat opposite her, alert and fine-featured, like his son, his hair still as dark as Julian's, his neat little moustache silver. His wife had been Italian, and had died in 1883, in Florence, a city they both loved, where their daughter had been born, and christened Florence, before the fever struck, and the place became tragic.

Olive Wellwood was the wife of Humphry Wellwood, who worked in the Bank of England, and was an active member of the Fabian Society. She was the author of a great many tales, for children and adults, and something of an authority on British Fairy Lore. She had come to see Major Cain because she had a project for a tale that would turn on an ancient treasure with magical properties. Prosper Cain said gallantly that he was delighted she had thought of him. She smiled, and said that the most exciting thing about her small success with her books was that she felt able to disturb people as important and as busy as he was. It was something she could never have expected. She said his room was like a cavern from the Arabian Nights, and that she could barely resist getting up and looking at all the wondrous things he had collected. Not much Arabian stuff, actually, said Prosper. It was not his field. He had served in the East, but his interests were European. He was afraid she would find no scholarly order in his personal things. He didn't believe that a room needed to be set slavishly in one style—most particularly not when the room was, so to speak, a room within the multifarious rooms of the Museum, as the smallest eggshell might be in a Fabergé nest. You could set an Iznik jar very well next to a Venetian goblet and a lustre bowl by Mr. de Morgan, and they would all show to advantage.

"I hang my walls with mediaeval Flemish needlework, next to the small tapestry my friend Morris wove for me at Merton Abbey— greedy birds and crimson berries. Do look at the very satisfactory strength of the twist of the leaves. He never lacks energy."

"And these?" enquired Mrs. Wellwood. She stood up impulsively, and ran a grey-gloved finger along a shelf of incongruous objects with no apparent relation to each other, aesthetic or historical.

"Those, dear lady, are, as it were, my touchstone collection of *fakes*. These are not mediaeval spoons, though they were offered to me as such. This nautilus is *not* a Cellini, though William Beckford was led to believe it was, and paid a small fortune for it. These baubles are *not* the Crown Jewels, but skilful glass replicas of some of them, which were exhibited at the Crystal Palace in 1851."

"And this?"

Mrs. Wellwood's soft finger ran lightly over a platter containing very lively images, in pottery, of a small toad, a curled snake, a few beetles, some moss and ferns, and a black crayfish.

"I've never seen anything so lifelike. Every little wart and wrinkle."

"You may or may not know that the Museum came to grief through the *very* expensive purchase of a dish—not this one—by Bernard Palissy. Who is immortalised in mosaic in the Kensington Valhalla. It was subsequently realised to our embarrassment to have been made—as this one was—as an honest replica by a modern French pottery. Sold as souvenirs.

It is in fact—without incontestable artists' marks—*very* hard to distinguish a fake Palissy—or a copy, I should say—from the seventeenth-century thing itself."

"And yet," said Mrs. Wellwood, quick on the uptake, "the detail, the precision. It looks unusually *difficult*."

"It is said, and I believe it to be true, that the ceramic creatures are built round real creatures—real toads, eels, beetles."

"Dead, I do hope."

"Mummified, it is to be hoped. But we do not know precisely. Maybe there is a tale to be told?"

"The prince who became a toad and was imprisoned in a dish? How he would hate watching the banquets. There is a *half*-stone prince in the Arabian Nights, who has always troubled me. I must think."

She smiled, catlike and content.

"But you were consulting me about gold and silver treasures?"

Humphry Wellwood had said "Go and ask the Old Pirate. He'll know. He knows all about hiding places and secret transactions. He haunts markets and antiquaries, and pays pennies, so we are told, for ancestral heirlooms that get onto street stalls after revolutions."

"I want something that's *always been missing*—with a story attached to it, naturally—and that can be made to have magic properties, an amulet, a mirror that shows the past and the future, that kind of thing. You can see my imagination is banal, and I need your precise knowledge."

"Oddly," said Prosper Cain, "there aren't so many gold and silver treasures that are very ancient—and that's for a very good reason. If you were a Viking lord, or a Tartar chief—or even the Holy Roman Emperor—your gold and silver things were part of your treasury, and always—from the point of view of the artist and the storyteller—in danger of being melted down, for barter, or soldiers' wages, or quick transport and hiding. The Church had its sacred vessels—"

"I don't want a grail or a monstrance, or that sort of thing."

"No, you want something with a personal *mana*. I see what you need."

"Not a ring. There are so many tales about rings."

Prosper Cain laughed aloud, a sharp bark of a laugh.

"You are exacting. What about the tale of the Stoke Prior Treasure—silver vessels buried for safety during the Civil War, unearthed in our own day by a boy hunting rabbits? Or there is the romantic tale of the Eltenberg Reliquary, which was purchased for the Museum by J. C. Robinson in 1861. It came from the collection of Prince Soltikoff— who had bought it with about four thousand mediaeval objects from a Frenchman after the 1848 revolution.

"It was hidden in a chimney after Napoleon's invasion by the last canoness of Eltenberg, Princess Salm-Reiffenstadt. And from the chimney somehow it reached a canon in Emmerich who sold it to a dealer in Aachen—Jacob Cohen of Anhalt—who called one day on Prince Florentin of Salm-Salm and offered him one small walrus-ivory figure. And when Prince Florentin bought that, Cohen returned, with another and another and another—and in the end the reliquary chest itself, black with smoke and reeking of tobacco. Now, Prince Florentin's son, Prince Felix, persuaded him to sell the pieces to a dealer in Cologne, and *there,* we believe, clever modern fakes were substituted for some pieces— the Journey of the Magi, the Virgin and Child with St. Joseph, and some of the Prophets. *Very clever* fakes. We have them. This is a true story, and we are convinced the original pieces are squirrelled away somewhere. Would this not make a great tale, the tracking and restoration of the pieces? Your characters could go on the trail of the artisan who made the fakes . . ."

Olive Wellwood had the feeling writers often have when told perfect tales for fictions, that there was too much fact, too little space for the necessary insertion of inventions, which would here appear to be lies.

"I should need to change it a great deal."

The scholar and expert in fakes looked briefly displeased.

"It is so strong as it is," she explained. "It has no need of my imagination."

"I should have thought it calls upon all our imaginations, the fate of those lost works of art and craft . . ."

"I am intrigued by your toads and snakes."

"For a tale of witchcraft? As familiars?"

At this point the door opened, and Julian led Philip Warren in, followed by Tom, who closed it.

"Excuse me, Father. We thought you should know. We found— *him*—hiding away in the Museum stores. In the crypt. I'd been keeping an eye on him and we tracked him down. He was *living* down there."

Everyone looked at the dirty boy as though, Olive thought, he had risen out of the earth. His shoes had left marks on the carpet.

"What were you doing?" Prosper Cain asked him. He didn't answer. Tom went to his mother, who ruffled his hair. He offered her the story.

"He makes drawings of the things in the cases. At night he sleeps all alone in the shrine of an old dead saint, where the bones used to be. Amongst gargoyles and angels. In the dark."

"That's brave," said Olive, turning the dark eyes to Philip. "You must have been afraid."

"Not really," said Philip, stolidly.

He had no intention of saying what he really felt. This was that if you have slept on one mattress, end to end with five other children— a mattress moreover on which two brothers and a sister had died, nei- ther easily nor peacefully, with nowhere to remove them to—a few old bones weren't going to worry you. All his life he had had a steady crav- ing for solitude, hardly even named, but never relaxing. He had no idea if other people felt this. On the whole it appeared they did not. In the Museum crypt, in the dark and dust, briefly, this craving had been for the first time satisfied. He was in a dangerous and explosive state of mind.

"Where are you from, young man?" asked Prosper Cain. "I need the whys and the hows. Why are you here, and how did you get into a locked space?"

"I come from Burslem. I work in t'Potteries." A long pause. "I run off, that's it, I ran away."

His face was stolid.

"Your parents work in the Potteries?"

"Me dad's dead. He were a saggar-maker. Me mum works in th' paint shop. All of us work there, one way or another. I loaded kilns."

"You were unhappy," said Olive.

Philip considered his inner state. He said "Yes."

"People were hard on you."

"They had to be. It weren't that. I wanted. I wanted to make some- thing . . ."

"You wanted to make something of your life, of yourself," Olive prompted. "That's natural."

It may have been natural, but it was not what Philip meant. He repeated

"I wanted to make something . . ."

His mind's eye saw an unformed mass of liquescent mud. He looked around, like a baited bear, and saw the flaming de Morgan lustre bowl on the mantelshelf. He opened his mouth to comment on the glaze and decided against it.

Tom said "Won't you show us your drawings?" He said to his mother "He used to show the lady students, they liked them, they gave him bread . . ."

Philip undid his satchel and brought out his sketch-book. There was the Candlestick with its coiling dragons and poised, wide-eyed little men. Sketch after sketch, all the intricacies of the writhing and biting and stabbing. Tom said

"That's the little man I liked, the elderly one with the thin hair and the sad look."

Prosper Cain turned the pages. Stone angels, Korean gold ornaments for a crown, a Palissy dish in all its ruggedness, one of the two definitely authentic specimens.

"What are these?" he asked, turning more pages.

"Those are just my own ideas."

"For what?"

"Well, I thought salt-glazed stoneware. Or mebbe earthenware, that page. I were drawing the metal to get the feel of it. I don't know metal. I know clay. I know a bit about clay."

"You have a fine eye," said Prosper Cain. "A very fine eye. You were using the Collection as it is intended to be used, to study design."

Tom drew a sigh of relief. The story was to have a good ending.

"Would you like to study in the Art School?"

"I dunno. I want to make something . . ."

He was suddenly at the end of his resources, and began to sway. Prosper Cain was still studying the drawings, and said, without look-ing up,

"You must be hungry. Ring for Rosie, Julian, and tell her to bring fresh tea."

"I am always hungry," said Philip, suddenly loudly, with twice the force of his earlier remarks. He had not meant it to be funny, but because he was truly about to be fed, they all took it as a joke, and laughed merrily together.

"Sit down, boy. This isn't an interrogation."

Philip looked doubtfully at the flame and peacock silk cushions.

"They'll clean. You look all in. *Sit down.*"

. . .

Rosie, the parlourmaid, made several journeys up the narrow stairs, bringing trays with porcelain cups and saucers, a cakestand with a solid block of fruitcake, a platter of various kinds of sandwich, delicately designed both to appeal to a lady and to nourish growing boys (cucumber slivers in some, wedges of potted meat in others). Then she brought a dish of tartlets, a teapot, a teakettle, a cream jug. She was a wiry small person in starched cap and apron, about as old as Philip and Julian. She set everything out on occasional tables, put the kettle on the hearth, bobbed at Major Cain and went downstairs again. Prosper Cain asked Mrs. Wellwood to pour. He was amused to see Philip raise his cup to his eye to study the shepherdesses on flowered meadows around it.

"Minton porcelain, Sèvres-style," Prosper said. "An abomination in the eyes of William Morris, but I have a weakness for ornament . . ."

Philip put the cup down on the table at his elbow, and did not answer. His mouth was full of sandwich. He was trying to eat daintily, and he was *horribly* hungry, he was ravenous. He tried to chew slowly. He gulped. They all watched him benignly. He chewed, and blushed under the dirt. He was close to tears. They were aliens. His mother painted the borders of cups like these, with fine brushes, day after day, proud of her repetitive faultlessness. Olive Wellwood, smelling of roses, stood over him, handing him slabs of fruitcake. He ate two, though he thought it was probably impolite. But the starch and the sugar did their work. His unnatural tension and wariness gave way to pure fatigue.

"And now?" said Prosper Cain. "What shall we do with this young man? Where shall he sleep tonight, and what should he do with himself?"

Tom was put in mind of David Copperfield's arrival at Betsey Trotwood's house. A boy. Coming to a real home, out of dirt and danger. He was about to echo Mr. Dick—give him a bath—and managed not to. It would have been most insulting.

Olive Wellwood turned the question to Philip

"What do you *want* to do?"

"Work," said Philip. It was an easy answer and it was largely right.

"Not to go back?"

"No."

"I think—if Major Cain agrees—you should come home now, with me and Tom, for the weekend. I imagine he has no thought of prosecuting you for trespass. This weekend is Midsummer Eve, and we are having a midsummer party at our house in the country. We are a large family, and friendly, and one more or less makes no difference."

She turned to Prosper Cain.

"And I hope that you too will come over to Andreden from Iwade, for midsummer magic, and bring Julian, and Florence too, to join the young folk."

Prosper Cain bent over her hand, mentally cancelled a card party and said he would—they all would—be delighted. Tom looked at their captured boy, to see if he was pleased, but he was staring at his feet. Tom was not entirely sure about Julian coming to his party. He found him intimidating. It would be good to have Philip, if he would consent to enjoy himself. He thought of adding his voice to his mother's, and was embarrassed, and did not.

2

They took the train to Andreden, in the Kentish Weald, and took a fly at the station. Philip sat opposite Tom and his mother, who leaned against each other. Philip's eyes kept closing, but Olive was explaining things to him, to which he knew he should attend. Andred was the old British name for the forest. Andreden meant a swine pasture in the forest. Their house was called Todefright. In fact they had changed it from Todsfrith, but the change was etymologically sound. Fryth, in the old language of the Weald, was a word for scrubland on the edge of a forest. The local Kentish word for that was "fright." They supposed Tod meant toad. Philip asked stolidly, were there any toads, then? Lots, said Tom. Big fat ones. Spawn in the duckpond. Frogs too, and newts, and tiddlers.

They drove between hawthorn and hazel hedges, along curling lanes between overhanging woods of beech, and birch, and yew. Philip had felt the shift in the air as the train pulled out of the London pall. You could see the edge of the darkness. It was not as bad as the thick dark air full of hot grit and melted chemicals that poured from the tall chimneys and bottle ovens in Burslem. His lungs felt nervous and overdilated. Olive and Tom did not take the fresh air for granted. They exclaimed ritually about how good it was to get out of the dirt. Philip felt dirt was engrained in him.

Todefright was an old Kentish farmhouse, built of stone and timber. It had meadows and a river before it, woods rising uphill behind it, and a wide view to the high edge of the Weald across the river. The house had been tactfully extended and modernised by Lethaby, in the Arts and Crafts style, respecting (and also creating) odd-shaped windows and eaves, twisting stairs, nooks, crannies and exposed roof-beams. The front door, solid oak, opened into a modern version of a mediaeval hall, with settles and alcoves, a large hand-crafted dining-table, and a long dresser, shining with lustreware. Beyond this were a (small) panelled library, which was also Olive's study, and a billiard-room, which was Humphry's, when he was at home. There were many outhouses—kitchens, sculleries, guest cottages, stables with haylofts, inhabited by scratching hens and nesting swallows. A wide, turning staircase rose out of the hall to the upper floors.

A large number of people, adults and children, came running and strolling to welcome Olive and Tom. Philip took them in. A short, dark-haired woman in a loose mulberry-coloured dress, printed with brilliant nasturtiums, was carrying a baby—maybe a year old—whom she handed to Olive to be kissed and hugged, even before Olive had taken off her coat. Two servants, one motherly, one girlish, stood by to take the coats. Two young ladies in identical indigo aprons, long hair falling over their shoulders, one dark, one tawny, younger than Philip, younger than Tom, but not by much. A little girl in a robin-red apron, who shoved past the others, and grabbed Olive's skirts. A little boy, with blond curls, and a Fauntleroy lace collar, who clung to the mulberry lady's skirts, and hid his face in them. Olive buried her nose in the neck of the baby, Robin, who was reaching for her poppies and hat-pin.

"I am like a tree with birds in it. This is Philip, who has come to stay for a little while. Philip, the two big girls are Dorothy and Phyllis. This is my sister, Violet Grimwith, who makes everything work here—everything that *does* work, that is. This little demon is my clever Hedda, who cannot keep still. The one being bashful is Florian, who is three. Come out and say hello to Philip, Florian."

Florian held on to Violet Grimwith's skirts, and was distinctly heard to say, into the cloth, that Philip smelled bad. Violet picked him up, shook him, and kissed him. He kicked at her hips. Olive said

"Philip has left home, and come a long way. He needs a bath, and some clean clothes—and a bed made up in Birch Cottage, if Cathy could see to that. And Ada might perhaps fill a bath for him—go with Ada, Philip, first things first—and when you are refreshed, we will see about supper and plan-making."

Violet Grimwith said she would look out something for Philip to wear. She thought he was too big to get into anything belonging to Tom. But there might be a shirt, in Humphry's weekend drawer, and even maybe breeches . . .

Philip mutely followed Ada, who was the cook, into the servants' part of the house, and then through the back, into the stable-yard and across to the guest cottage, which had a downstairs room with a sink and a pump, and an upstairs loft, reached by a ladder, where Cathy could be heard, thumping bedclothes. Philip stood awkwardly. Ada fetched a tin bath, two jugs of hot water, a jug of cold water, soap and a towel. Then she left him. He took off the top layer of his clothes, and tentatively mixed some of the hot and cold water in the bath. Then he took off the remaining protection of his underpants and singlet. He was not used to baths. He was used to a quick sluicing under a cold communal pump. He lifted a leg to straddle the rim of the bath. Violet Grimwith came in without knocking. Philip reached for the towel to cover himself, and stumbled with a splash into the water, barking his shin on the edge. He made a choked, wailing cry.

"You don't need to mind me," said Miss Grimwith. "Let me see that scrape. There's nothing I haven't seen. I've nursed all their little wounds, all their lives, I'm the one they turn to, when they *need* to, and so I hope will you, young man."

Much to his alarm, she advanced on him, bearing the soap, and a cannikin of warm water, which without warning she poured over his thick hair, so that jets sprang into his eyes and over his shoulders.

"Shut your eyes," she advised him. "Keep 'em tight shut, I'll get to the *roots* of it, I will."

She applied soap and water to his hair as she spoke, pommelling and twisting and then massaging the skin of his scalp, probing with thin fingers for the taut muscles in his neck and shoulders.

"Let go," said the surprising woman. "We'll have every cranny clean and lively, wait and see."

She spoke to him as though he was a baby, or just possibly a fully grown and complicit man. Philip decided to keep his eyes shut, in every sense of shut. He tightened his sphincters, pushed his chin into his chest, and felt the fingers and palms slap and maul him. Under the water they came, accidentally or on purpose, briefly fluttering against what he thought of as his whistler.

"Muck of ages," said the sharp voice. "Surprising how it accumulates, muck. Now you're a nice pinky-pig-pink, not elephant-hide. You've got a fine thatch of hair, now the dust's out, and the other stuff. You can open your eyes. I've wiped the soap off, it won't sting."

He didn't want to open his eyes.

He was encouraged to dry himself whilst Violet Grimwith held up various garments against him, for size. He struggled, still damp, into some patched long-johns, and chose a plain dark-blue twill shirt out of the three presented to him. Tom's breeches were too small. "I *knew* it, really," said Violet. A pair, presumably belonging to the master of the house, in brown cord, sagged a little, but could be, as Violet suggested, hauled in with a thick belt. She produced a truss of needles and bobbins, told him to stand still, and took in a pleat on each side over his hips, sewing fast and precisely. "I know how young folk are, they are ashamed to look *odd* and hate things *not fitting right*. This is only makeshift, but it'll hold for the duration. You'll forget they're too big, this way. One thing less to bother yourself about." She put one hand on each of his hips and turned him round like a mannequin. She gave him a stout pair of new socks, but none of the shoes she had brought fitted, and he had to put on his old dirty boots—after she had given them a brush over. A tweed jacket with leather trim completed the outfit. She even gave him a clean handkerchief. And a pocket-comb, made from white bone, with which she tugged at his hair before inserting it into his jacket pocket. There was no mirror in Birch Cottage, so he couldn't look at her handiwork. He wriggled; the underwear bothered him. Violet ran her fingers round inside his waistband, and straightened him. She rolled his old dirty clothes into a bundle. "I'm not stealing them, young man, they'll come back darned and laundered."

"Thank you, mam," said Philip.

"If you want anything at all, *I'm the one*. Remember that. There's a nightshirt on your bed, and a pot under it, and a toothbrush by the pump. I'll give you matches and a candle when you come back. You'll sleep deep in the good Kent air."

Supper was ready in the dining-hall. The table was laid with pretty earthenware plates and mugs, glazed in yellow, with a border of black-eyed daisies. Robin and Florian had been put to bed, but Hedda, who was five, was still there, as they ate early. Olive summoned Philip to sit at her side, and said he was handsome. Humphry Wellwood nodded to him from the other end of the table. He was a tall, thin man, with a fox-red beard, neatly trimmed, pale blue eyes and a dark brown velvet jacket.

There was cauliflower soup, followed by a lamb stew, and a vegetable and pumpkin pie for the vegetarians (Olive, Violet, Phyllis and Hedda). Philip took two bowls of soup. Prosper Cain's fruitcake was a long time away; he had two weeks of near-starvation and a lifetime of perpetual hunger to feed. He had supposed Mr. Wellwood, who worked in the Bank of England, would be like the factory owners in the Potteries, stiff, grand and condescending. But Humphry told the children what was clearly an instalment in a running tale of secret naughtiness amongst the bank clerks in the depths of the Bank, who kept tethered bull terriers attached to the legs of their desks, and divided sides of meat from Smithfield before going home for the weekend. Phyllis and Hedda shuddered dramatically. Humphry recounted a jape in which one young man had tied the laces of another man's boots to his high desk-stool. Dorothy said that wasn't really funny, and Humphry agreed immediately, saying with half-mock sadness that the poor young creatures were confined in the shadows with no outlet for their animal energies. They are like the Nibelungen, said Humphry, they go to the bullion-vaults to stare at the machines that weigh the gold sovereigns—like half-human creatures that swallow the good coins and spit out the light ones into copper vessels. Tom said they had seen an amazing candlestick which Major Cain had said might be made out of melted-down gold coins. With dragons on it, and little men, and monkeys. Philip had made some wondrous drawings of it. Everyone looked at Philip, who stared into his soup. Humphry said, as though he really meant it, that he should like to see the drawings. Violet said, don't embarrass the poor lad, which embarrassed him.

From time to time, during the meal, Olive turned gracefully and impulsively towards Philip, and urged him to tell her all about himself. She elicited, slowly, the information that his dad was dead in a kiln accident, and that his mam worked at painting china. He had worked himself, carrying full saggars to the kilns. Yes, he had sisters, four. Brothers, asked Phyllis. Two, both dead, said Philip. And a sister, dead.

And he had felt he had to get away? said Olive. He must have been unhappy. The work must have been hard, and maybe people weren't kind to him.

Philip thought of his mam, and found his eyes, to his horror, hot and wet.

Olive said he didn't need to tell them, they understood. Everyone stared at him with warmth and sympathy.

"It weren't," he said. "It weren't . . ."

His voice was unsteady.

"We shall see you have somewhere to live, and work to do," said Olive, her voice full of gold.

Dorothy asked rather abruptly if Philip could ride a bicycle.

He said no, but he'd seen them, and thought they must be real exciting, and wished he could try one.

Dorothy said "We'll show you tomorrow. We've got new ones. There'll be time to show you, before the party. We can ride in the woods."

She had a rather fierce little face, not pretty, and looked cross most of the time. He did not wonder why. Exhaustion was overcoming him. Olive asked him two or three more probing questions about the ill-treatment she was convinced he had undergone. He answered monosyllabically, spooning blancmange into his mouth. This time he was rescued by Violet, who said the boy was dead on his feet and she proposed to find him a candle and see him to his bed.

Violet said "You mustn't mind my sister. She's a storyteller. She's making up stories for you. I don't mean lies, I mean stories. It's her way. She's fitting you in."

Philip said

"She's been—so very kind. You all have."

"We have our beliefs," said Violet. "About what the world should be like. And some of us have experience—like yours—of what it *shouldn't* be."

The moon was caught in the branches of the trees round the cottage. He was solaced by learning the lines of the network of twigs, which was both random and ordered. He didn't point this out to Violet, but thanked her again, as he took his candle, and made his way into his cottage. He feared she might try to kiss him goodnight—he could not predict what these people would do—but she simply stood, and watched him take his candle up the ladder.

"Sleep tight," she called.

"Thank you," he said, yet again.

And then he was alone, with a brave candle, in a cottage. This was what he had wanted, or part of it. There was a nightshirt, laid out on the clean sheets of the wooden bed that was temporarily his. He looked out of the window, and there were the branches, lit by the moon on a dark blue, cloudless sky, with their fish-shaped leaves overlapping, and just trembling. He translated the shapes into a glaze, and puzzled over it briefly. It was too much. He wanted to cry out, or to weep, or, he understood, to touch his body—his body washed clean—as he had only ever been able to do furtively, in dirty places. He must not leave marks, that would be shameful. He finally contrived a safety-pad of the handkerchief he had been given or lent. He could rinse it, subsequently, under the pump.

He lay back, and took himself in hand, and worked himself into a rhythm of delight, and a soaring wet ecstasy.

Then he lay still, listening to the sounds in the silence. An owl called. Another owl answered. A big branch creaked. Things rustled. The pump below dripped in the stone sink. How could he ever sleep, in such a roar of silence, how could he forgo a conscious moment of the bliss of solitude? He stretched arms and legs to all points of the compass and fell asleep almost immediately. He woke and slept, woke and slept, time after time before dawn, each time taking possession again of the dark and the silence.

The next day, they prepared the Midsummer Party. Violet gave Philip a breakfast of eggs, toast and tea, and told him he was co-opted to make lanterns. The garden would be full of them. He was to go up to the schoolroom, where the lanterns were being made.

The imposing staircase took an interesting turn as it went up. In an alcove, at the turning, standing on an oak coffin stool was a jar. It was a large earthenware vessel, that bellied out and curved in again, to a tall neck with a fine lip. The glaze was silver-gold, with veilings of aquamarine. The light flowed round the surface, like clouds reflected in water. It was a watery pot. There was a vertical rhythm of rising stems, water-weeds, and a dashing horizontal rhythm of irregular clouds of black-brown wriggling commas, which turned out, inspected closely, to be lifelike tadpoles with translucent tails. The jar had several asymmetric handles which seemed to grow out of it like roots in water, but turned out to have the sly faces and flickering tails of water-snakes, green-spotted gold. It rested on four dark green feet, which were coiled, scaled lizards. Or minor dragons, lying with closed eyes and resting snouts.

This was what he had come to look for. His fingers moved inside its contours on an imaginary wheel. Its form clothed his sense of the shape of his body. He stood stock still and stared.

Olive Wellwood came up behind him and put an arm about his shoulder. She smelled of roses. Philip resisted shrugging. He disliked being touched. Especially at private times.

"It's an amazing pot, don't you think? We chose it for the pretty tadpoles—they go with our idea of Todefright. The little ones love to stroke them."

Philip could not speak.

"Benedict Fludd made it. He works in Dungeness. He's invited to the party, but he probably won't come. His wife will. She's called Seraphita, though she was born Sarah-Jane. The boy's Geraint, and the girls are Imogen—she must be about your age—and Pomona. Pomona's Tom's age and lucky enough to be as pretty as her name—so dangerous, don't you think, giving romantic names to little scraps who may grow up as plain as doorposts. Pomona isn't very appley—you'll see—more a pale narcissus."

Philip was interested only in the potter. He managed to mutter that the pot was extraordinary.

"He has religious fits, I'm told. They have to hide the pots, to prevent him smashing them. And he has anti-religious fits."

Philip made a strangled, noncommittal sound. Olive ruffled his hair. He didn't flinch. She led him up to the schoolroom.

"Schoolroom" to Philip meant a dark chapel annexe with long benches, and a heavy atmosphere of unwashed bodies, baffled thinking and prickling fear of the cane. Here, in a room full of light, with pimpernel chintz at the windows, everyone was at work in his or her own space. The girls wore bright aprons, like coloured butterflies, Dorothy butcher-blue, Phyllis deep rose, Hedda scarlet. Florian had a cowslip-yellow smock. The long, scrubbed table was covered with coloured papers, glue pots, paintbrushes, paintboxes, jars of water. Waste-paper baskets overflowed with crumpled, rejected efforts. Violet presided, helping with a snip here, a finger on a knot there.

Tom made room for Philip to sit next to him. "No," said Phyllis, "next to *me*."

Phyllis had hair the colour of butter, slick and shiny. Philip sat down next to her. She patted his arm, with a gesture that belonged to a child younger than she seemed to be. Or a gesture you might use to a pet, Philip thought unjustly. He remembered his sister Elsie, who had never had her own space in any room, and fought a constant battle with nits in her pale hair.

They showed him their lanterns. Tom's had hunched crows on flame-colour. Phyllis had put simple florets, daisies and bluebells on grass-green. Dorothy had made a pattern of skeletal hands (not human, Philip thought, maybe rabbits) on violet. Hedda was slowly cutting out a silhouette of a witch on a broom. Phyllis said

"We *told* her that witches are for Hallowe'en not Midsummer. But she got good at Hallowe'en witches, she got the knack of the hat and bristles—"

"Witches don't stop *being,* in midsummer," said Hedda. "I *like* witches."

"Help yourself to paper, Philip," said Violet Grimwith, "and to scissors and paste and paint. We are all curious to see what you will do."

He felt better the moment he had his hands on solid things. He took a large piece of paper and covered it with the pattern of tadpoles from the master pot, which he needed to remember. Then he made another with the long sly snake flickering round it, grass-green and gold on blue. Violet took these away to make into lanterns. Philip had another idea. He painted a dull red horizon, with shadowy grey forms rising high above it. There were squat cylindrical forms, and tall bottle-shaped forms, and shapes like hives and casques. There was a flowing festoon of flame and tongues of pewter-grey smoke from the summits, the skyline of Burslem, made elegant as a party lantern.

"What's that, what's that, then?" asked loud Hedda.

"That's where I come from. Chimneys and bottle ovens, and furnace flames, and smoke."

"It's beautiful," said Hedda.

"Aye, on a lantern," said Philip. "In a sense it is beautiful, as it is. But horrible, too. You can't breathe rightly."

Dorothy took the lanterns and ranged them with the other finished ones. Phyllis said

"Tell us about that place. Tell us about your sisters. Tell us their names."

She nestled closer to him, so he could feel the warmth and weight of her body, almost leaning on him, almost cuddling.

"They are Elsie and Nellie and Amelia and Hope," said Philip reluctantly.

"And the dead ones? Our dead ones are Peter, who died just before Tom was born, so he's fifteen, and Rosy, who was a dear little baby."

"Be quiet, Phyllis," said Tom. "He doesn't want to know all that."

Phyllis insisted, moving closer to Philip. "And *your* dead ones? What are their names?"

"Ned," said Philip flatly. "And Robert Owen. And Rosy. Well, Mary-Rose." He tried very hard to remember neither their faces nor their bodies.

Dorothy said "After lunch we're going to take Philip out and teach him to ride a safety-bicycle." She told Philip "We've all got one. They've got names, like the ponies. Mine's called Mona-Bona-Grona, because she creaks. Tom's is just the Steed."

"And mine is Tiptoes," said Phyllis. "Because my legs are almost too short."

"It is the most wonderful sensation," said Dorothy. "Most especially running away downhill. Have some more paper, make another, we have to hang them from all the trees in the shrubbery and the orchard."

I were begging scraps of paper in South Kensington, Philip thought. And here they throw away whole sheets with one gone-wrong bird in one corner.

He looked up and had the disconcerting sense that Dorothy was reading his mind.

Dorothy had indeed, more or less accurately, followed Philip's thoughts. She did not know how she had done that. She was a clever, careful child, who liked to think of herself as unhappy. Faced with Philip's hunger and reticence, she was forced, because she had been brought up in the Fabian atmosphere of rational social justice, to admit that she had "no right" to feel unhappy, since she was exceedingly privileged. She was unhappy, she told herself, for frivolous reasons. Because, as the eldest girl, she was treated as a substitute nanny. Because she was not a boy, and did not have a tutor, as Tom did, to teach her maths and languages. Because Phyllis was pretty and spoiled, and more loved than she was. Because Tom was *much* more loved. Because she wanted something and did not know what it was.

She was just eleven—born in 1884, "the same year as the Fabian Society," Violet pointed out. They had been the Fellowship of the New Life, in those days, and Dorothy was the new life, drawing in socialist ideals with her early milk. The grown-ups made further pointed and risky jokes across and about her, which irritated her. She didn't like to be talked about. Equally, she didn't like *not* to be talked about, when the high-minded chatter rushed on as though she was not there. There was no pleasing her, in fact. She had the grace, even at eleven, to know there was no pleasing her. She thought a lot, analytically, about other people's feelings, and had only just begun to realise that this was not usual, and not reciprocated.

She was busy thinking about Philip. He thinks we are being *kind* out of condescension, whereas actually that isn't so, we are just being friendly, like we always are, but it makes him suspicious. He doesn't really want us to know about where he comes from. Mother thinks his home is unhappy and his family are cruel—that's one of her favourite stories. She ought to see—I can see—he doesn't like that. I think he feels bad because they don't know where he is or how he is. He feels *more* bad now we're making all this fuss of him than he did hiding under the Museum.

I wonder what he *wants,* she asked herself, without finding an answer, since Philip was silent on that subject—as, indeed, he was silent about almost everything.

The safety-bicycle lesson took place in the afternoon, as promised. Philip was lent Violet Grimwith's cycle, a solid machine, painted blue. Violet had named it Bluebell. The Hanger Woods were full of bluebells. Nevertheless Tom and Dorothy felt it was a weak name.

Tom, on the Steed, rode round and round the grassy clearing between the back door and the woods, demonstrating balance. Dorothy helped Philip, holding his saddle, whilst he balanced precariously.

"It's much easier if you're *going,*" she told him. "No one can balance at a standstill."

Philip set off and fell off and set off and fell off and set off and pedalled halfway round the clearing, and fell off, and set off and rode, a little wobbly, right round the clearing. For the first time since he had come to Todefright, he laughed aloud. Tom was wheeling figures of eight. Phyllis appeared and executed some neat circles. Tom said Philip was now good enough to go out into the lanes, so they went out, Tom in the lead, then Philip, then Dorothy, then Phyllis. They pedalled along Frenches Lane, which was flat, between hawthorn hedges, and then turned up the wooded hillside, up Scarp Lane, between overarching trees which made deep wells of shadow, interspersed with dazzling blades of brightness. Philip had an idea for a dark, dark, cauldron-like pot, with shiny streaks on a matt surface. When he thought of the imaginary pot, and not of the metal construction that carried him, his balance improved, and he accelerated.

Behind him, Dorothy also went faster. She had the passion for speed which is strongest in girls of eleven or twelve. She dreamed of riding a racehorse along a beach, between sand and sea. Since she had had the bicycle she had dreamed frequently of flying, quite near the ground, skimming the flowerbeds, seated like a fakir on an invisible carpet.

At the brow of the hill they rode along a glade, and Tom said "Shall we swoop down Bosk Hill?"

"It's steep," said Dorothy. "Will Philip be all right?"

"I'm doing finely," said Philip, grinning.

So they turned into Boskill Lane, which had both a sharp gradient and crooked-elbow corners. Dorothy was now in front of Philip, behind Tom, who was speeding away from them. Dorothy felt the usual, delightful tightening in her insides. She looked back to see if Philip was all right. He was nearer than she thought, and she wobbled across his track. He shuddered, skidded, and went through the air, more or less over Dorothy. She fell over on the track, scraping her shins, wheels and pedals spinning. Phyllis sailed past, gripping her handlebars, primly upright.

Dorothy picked up Mona-Bona-Grona, and went to look at Philip. He was sprawled on his back under an oak tree, deep in a mass of wild garlic, crushed by his landing into extraordinary pungency. He was lying still, staring up through the leaves.

"My fault," said Dorothy. "All my fault. Are you hurt?"

"Don't think so, no. Winded."

He began to laugh.

"What's funny?"

"There are things in the country that smell quite as foul as things in the town. Only vegetable foul, not smoky. I've never smelt anything in the least—like this."

"It's wild garlic. It *isn't* very nice."

Philip could not stop laughing. "It's horrible. But it's new, you know."

Dorothy crouched down beside him.

"Can you get up?"

"Aye, in a minute. Gimme a minute. I'm out o' puff, as we say. Is the machine damaged?"

Dorothy inspected it. It was unharmed.

Philip lay in the disgusting and fascinating smell, and let his muscles go, one by one, so that the earth was holding up his limp body, and he could feel all its roughness, the squashed stalks, the knotty roots of trees, pebbles, the cool mould under. He closed his eyes and dozed for an instant.

He woke because Dorothy was shaking him.

"You *are* all right? I could have killed you. You aren't concussed or anything?"

"I'm quite happy," Philip said. "Here."

Dorothy said, taking it in,

"I could have killed you."

"But you didn't."

"If you want," said Dorothy, speaking out what had been going round in her mind for some hours, "just to send a postcard to your mother, just to say you're all right and not to worry, you know— I could get you one, and post it for you."

Philip was silent. Things turned over in his mind. He frowned.

"I'm sorry," said Dorothy. "I didn't mean to upset you. I wanted to help."

She sat hunched, with her arms around her knees.

"You didn't. Upset me. An' you're right. I ought to write to our mum. If you do get me a card, I will write. And thank you."

They rode back more soberly. Dorothy fetched a postcard and stamp from Olive's bureau. Philip held the pen awkwardly and stared at the blank rectangle. Dorothy—not overlooking him—waited by the window. Once or twice he seemed to be about to set pen to postcard, but did not. Dorothy decided he might get on with it if she went away. When her hand was on the door-latch, Philip said

"Promise you won't read it?"

"I wouldn't. Letters are private. Even postcards. I could get you an envelope to put it in, that would make it private. Would you like that?"

"Aye," said Philip. He said "It's partly I'm a bad speller."

He wrote

Dear Mum and all,
I am well and Ill rite agen soon. Hope you are well. Philip.

Dorothy brought an envelope and Philip addressed it. He was grateful and also irritated, that Dorothy had noticed his duty and his need.

3

This was the Wellwoods' third Midsummer Party. Their guests were socialists, anarchists, Quakers, Fabians, artists, editors, freethinkers and writers, who lived, either all the time, or at weekends and on holidays in converted cottages and old farmhouses, Arts and Crafts homes and workingmen's terraces, in the villages, woods and meadows around the Kentish Weald and the North and South Downs. These were people who had evaded the Smoke, and looked forward to a Utopian world in which smoke would be no more. The Wellwoods' parties were not Fabian teas with solid cups and saucers and a frigid absence of entertainment. Nor were they political meetings, to discuss the London County Council, *Free Russia* and Russian starvation. They were frivolous, lantern-lit, silk and velvet fancy-dress parties, with masques, and dancing to flute and fiddle.

The children mingled with the adults, and spoke and were spoken to. Children in these families, at the end of the nineteenth century, were different from children before or after. They were neither dolls nor miniature adults. They were not hidden away in nurseries, but present at family meals, where their developing characters were taken seriously and rationally discussed, over supper or during long country walks. And yet, at the same time, the children in this world had their own separate, largely independent lives, as children. They roamed the woods and fields, built hiding-places and climbed trees, hunted, fished, rode ponies and bicycles, with no other company than that of other children. And there were many other children. There were large families, in which relations shifted subtly as new people were born—or indeed, died—and in which a child also had a group identity, as "one of the older ones" or "one of the younger ones." The younger ones were often enslaved or ignored by the older ones, and were perennially indignant. The older ones resented being told to take the younger ones along, when they were planning dangerous escapades.

The parents—and the Wellwoods were no exception—found it hard in practice to do what they believed in theory they should do, which was to love all the children equally. A man and a woman with eight, or ten, or twelve children spread their love differently from the way in which they might have concentrated on a singleton or two infants. Love depended on the spaces between infants, on the health of the parents, on death, on the chances of which child survived an epidemic or an accident, and which did not. There were families in which the best-loved child had died, and remained the best-loved. There were families in which, apparently, the dead had disappeared without trace, and were not spoken of as realities. There were families in which an unborn child was dreaded and shrunk from, only to become, on emerging alive from blood and danger, the best-beloved after all.

Most of the parents of these favoured children had not themselves been so fortunate. If they had run wild, it was because they were neglected, or being hardened for life, and not because freedom was good for them.

Much of the freedom, both of parents and of children, depended on the careful work of servants, and of dedicated aunts, who had been old-fashioned sisters, in stricter days.

The Wellwoods appeared to be one of these open and pleasantly complicated families. Humphry Wellwood was the second son of a Quaker wool merchant, himself the younger brother of a Quaker banker. The family home was in the North of England, where Yorkshire meets Lancashire, south of Cumberland. Humphry was born in 1856 and his brother, Basil, was two years older. Basil was sent into an uncle's broking business, in 1873, as a stockbroker's clerk. He did well in the City, moving to an Anglo-German bank, Wildvogel & Quick, and marrying, in 1879, a Wildvogel daughter, Katharina, when he was twenty-five and she was twenty-seven.

Humphry was a very bright schoolboy, and the masters at his Quaker school persuaded George Wellwood to send him to Oxford. He entered Balliol in 1874, and came under the influence of Benjamin Jowett and T. H. Green, who believed that they were educating leaders of men, but also felt strongly what Beatrice Webb, as a young woman, described as a growing "class consciousness of sin" or guilt. This sense of sin led this generation of young men and women to go out and do good to the poor, in person. They went to the East End and managed tenement buildings. They conducted university extension classes for workers. H. M. Hyndman, who founded the Social Democratic Federation in 1882, was sceptical about the motives of these high-minded people. They came in waves of fashionable concern, he said, having discovered that there was a brick and mortar wilderness just beyond the Bank of England with two or three million inhabitants, many of them in woeful distress. Hyndman was a cynic. He remarked that "many a marriage in high life was the outcome of these exciting excursions into the unknown haunts of the poor."

Humphry graduated in 1877, two years after the Christian Arnold Toynbee, whose devotion to the needy, and early death, were commemorated by Canon Barnett's founding of Toynbee Hall, designed as a community of graduates, who would, themselves, live and teach amongst the poor. Humphry, full of excitement, gravitated naturally to the East End, and lived in two rooms in College Buildings, a model tenement. He gave classes in all sorts of places on all sorts of things: the English, the Ideals of Democracy, Sanitation, Henry V, the Gold Standard, and English Literature. At Oxford, like everyone else, he had studied dead languages and maths. Literature excited him greatly. He taught Shakespeare and Ruskin, Chaucer and Jonathan Swift, Wordsworth, Coleridge and Keats. He was good at it. He acquired a following of students of all ages. He read aloud, with fire and clarity. He was helpful to eager women, after the class was over.

In 1879 he put on *A Midsummer Night's Dream* in a church hall in Whitechapel. The cast was a daring mixture of real workers and idealistic visitors. It was also a daring mixture of men and women. Humphry thought almost constantly about women, whatever else he was thinking of. He dreamed waists and ankles, unwound hair and the haunches that moved under the staid skirts. The *Dream* is a good play for women, but this project was (he knew it) entirely inspired by two particular young women who came to all his classes and sat at the front, asking clever questions. They were out of place amongst the Cockneys, Irish, Polish and German Jews. They spoke broad Yorkshire. Humphry's own accent was educated Yorkshire, with some flat vowels. They wore plain, well-cut dark dresses, with very pretty little hats, decorated with gay silk flowers, anemones and pansies, poppies and violets. The elder was strikingly lovely, with huge brown eyes and coiled mahogany hair. The younger had the brown eyes, but lesser, and usually cast down, and nut-brown hair scraped subtly tighter. They were certainly not condescending lady visitors. They were the deserving poor—their gloves were threadbare, their shoes creased and worn—but there was something loose and wild about them under the respectability, that appealed to something wild in Humphry.

He had made friends with a young Cambridge man, Toby Youlgreave, who was writing a dissertation on Ovid, in the hope of a Fellowship at Peterhouse, and lecturing to the East End audiences on English Fairy Mythology, his real passion. Toby's Christianity was fraying, but he believed there were more things in heaven and earth than most people dreamed, and told Humphry, seriously, over a beer, that he had seen uncanny creatures, not only in woods near Cambridge, but passing between market stalls, or peering out of windows, in the Mile End Road. Our world was *interpenetrated*, he said. We had known it in the past. We have lost the knowledge. He was a large-shouldered man, of middle height, with impressive buttocks and calves, and a thick head of lion-coloured curls. His eyes were as blue as the Pied Piper's, candleflames where salt is sprinkled. His lectures were popular, for various reasons. Craftsmen came for ideas for brooches and carvings of English little people or haunting spirits. The religious dissatisfied came in search of the spilt spiritual content of their lives. Mothers came for tales to tell children, and teachers for information. And then people came because word went round that you could never quite tell what Mr. Youlgreave would say, or what he would claim to know.

It was some time before the two friends realised that the Misses Grimwith were sitting in the front row of both the lectures on Literature and those on Fairy Mythology. They also realised that both were smitten by the elder Miss Grimwith.

Toby said to Humphry "It's you she prefers. You have *gravitas*. You impress her. I'm a buffoon."

Humphry didn't disagree: it was what he thought himself. He said "We could put on the *Dream* and she could be Titania. I'm sure she could do it. We could combine our classes."

Naturally, Humphry directed. In the end, he couldn't bear the idea of anyone else playing Oberon. He offered Toby Puck, but Toby said he had always wanted to play Bottom, and that way he would at least lie in Miss Grimwith's arms. They borrowed a Church Hall in Whitechapel, and auditioned Miss Grimwith, whose rich, light voice rang out, perfectly. Miss Violet Grimwith, offered Hermia, or Hippolyta, said she had no ambition to act but would make the costumes, as she was a dressmaker. They found a wiry cockney barrow-boy, who was a perfect Puck, and a tall blonde lady librarian for Helena. The Athenians were a pleasant mix of visiting gentlemen and indigenous workers. The costumes were generally judged to be aesthetically brilliant. Olive

Grimwith was dressed in floating moonsilver with peacock feathers, silken flowers and naked feet. Humphry wanted to get to his knees and kiss the feet. He tormented himself with detailed thoughts of other things he wanted to do. At the end of the fairy dance at the end of the play, he whirled her into the wings, and took her into his arms.

They were married in the Whitechapel Register Office in 1880. Violet came, and Toby Youlgreave, and witnessed the marriage.

Humphry did not immediately tell his family that he was a married man. He was living on an allowance from his father in Yorkshire, who believed that Humphry was preparing for a university teaching career, and did not mind—indeed approved—his charitable enthusiasms. A son, Peter, was born two months after the wedding. Some months later, Humphry took his bride and his baby, and introduced them to his brother. Katharina Wellwood was by then herself expecting a child (Charles, born later in 1881). The baby Peter was irresistible, at the confident, smiling stage. Olive was elegant and ladylike. Basil lectured Humphry on improvidence, and on responsibility, and found him a regular job, as a clerk in the Bank of England. It was not what Humphry would have desired, but it was a steady, if modest, income. Humphry, Olive, Violet and Peter moved into a little house in Bethnal Green. Humphry turned his sharp mind to banking. He needled Basil by joining the arcane bimetallism dispute siding with those who proposed a double monetary standard. Silver and gold, both, should be basic monies, to the obvious advantage of our Empire and traders in India. Basil, with most of the City, staunchly supported the Gold Standard. Basil felt, but did not say, that Humphry was shifty and ungrateful, as well as irresponsible.

The year 1881 was a year of beginnings. A number of idealist, millenarian projects and groups were founded. There were the Democratic Federation, the Society for Psychical Research, the Theosophical Society, the Anti-Vivisection movement. All were designed to change and reinvent human nature. The younger Wellwoods looked into them all and joined some. Toby Youlgreave, who was almost part of their small family, immediately joined the Theosophists, and took his friends with him. All three also attended the early meetings of the Democratic Federation, which was mostly attended by German and Austrian socialists and anarchists, some disgruntled English workingmen and some university idealists. William Morris defended the Austrian dissident Johannes Most, who wrote what Morris described as a song of triumph at the assassination of Tsar Alexander II. Most went into a British prison, and Hyndman demonstrated in public. Basil begged Humphry not to involve himself.

In October 1882 Edward Pease founded the Fellowship of the New Life, and the younger Wellwoods went to its meetings. They discussed, there and at the Democratic Federation, organisation of unemployed labour, the feeding of board schoolchildren, nationalisation of mines and railways, the construction, by public bodies, of homes fit for the People.

In the winter of 1882, in Christmas week, Peter came down with croup, and died. In the same week, Thomas Wellwood was born.

In 1883 Olive Wellwood was seriously ill. Violet managed the little house. Karl Marx died. Attempts were made to explode local government offices, *The Times* newspaper and underground railways full of people coming from exhibitions in South Kensington. Basil took Humphry to his club, and told him very firmly that anarchism simply *would not do*. A Bank of England officer could not be seen hobnobbing with anarchists.

Humphry responded by taking his wife—to give her a change of air, he told Katharina—to Munich, where they had various secretive meetings with freethinkers and socialists. They visited the Alte Pinakothek, and were present at the opening of the Löwenbräukeller, complete with napkins and tablecloths, and the music of four military bands. Olive recovered sufficiently to dance at Fasching. Tom was left behind with Violet for the first, but not the last, time.

In 1884 the Fabian Society branched out of the Fellowship of the New Life. Humphry and Olive—now restored to a pale loveliness—joined. So did Toby, though his attendance was irregular. Olive knitted through the meetings, head bowed, clicking her needles.

Dorothy was born in the late autumn of 1884. Phyllis was born in the spring of 1886. In 1888 a girl was stillborn.

In 1887 Olive wrote some stories for children, and sold them to various magazines. These were conventional tales of children suffering hardship—an orphan rescued by a nabob, miners' children fending off starvation, a sickly child restored by a talking parrot.

Hedda was born in 1890 and Florian in 1892.

In 1889 Andrew Lang's *Blue Fairy Book* appeared. Tales for children suddenly included real magic, myths, invented worlds and creatures. Olive's early tales had been grimly sweet and unassuming. The coming—or return—of the fairytale opened some trapdoor in her imagination. Her writing became compulsive, fluent and daring. She took ideas from Toby's ethnological books. She invented dangerous hidden elfin and dwarfish folks. She wrote *Elfinia and the Forest Beasts, The Sandals of the Salamander, The Queen of the Ice Caverns, The Hidden Knife-Box People, The Boring Borehole,* and *The Shrubbery, or the Boy Who Vanished,* which made her name, and earned her a considerable sum of money. She was now writing small books, and longer ones, as well as magazine stories.

The younger Wellwoods decided to move to the country, bought Tode-fright in a dilapidated state, renovated it, and settled there at the time of Florian's birth, at midsummer 1892. In 1893 another girl was born and lived for a week.

It was in that year that Humphry Wellwood also began writing for the Press. He wrote a few articles for the *Economist,* under his own name. He also began a series of anonymous reports on dubious financial dealings, published in a satirical weekly called *Midas.* His pseudonym was The March Hare. He wrote about the Kaffir Circus and the activities of the Randlords, who dealt in South African gold. He took an interest in the new Westralian mines, some of which were as fictitious as Olive's imagined Borehole. The Wellwood children played games in which they chased gnomes and great Worms through Jumpers Deep, Nourse Deep, Glen Deep, Rose Deep, Village Deep and Goldenhuis Deep, or through Bayley's Reward, Bird-in-Hand, Empress of Coolgardie, Faith, Hit or Miss, Just in Time, King Solomon's, Nil Desperandum and The World's Treasure. Tom had clear imaginations of many of these places. Rose Deep was glittering caverns of rosy quartz, with flushed rivers winding into the mountains. Nil Desperandum was black and slippery with sullen fires in hidden crevices, and funnels opening to the sky. He knew you could see the stars by daylight from the depths of mines, and tried to imagine how this would look in reality. Would the sky that held the visible stars be blue, or black, and why?

Basil Wellwood made money in the Kaffir Boom. He made suggestions for small investments to Humphry, who instead invested early, on principle, in bicycle shares. Upon the flotation of the Dunlop Tyre Company, Humphry suddenly found himself more than financially comfortable. He engaged a maths tutor, with a view to entering Tom for Eton. Toby was helping with the classics.

There was champagne at the 1895 Midsummer Party.

4

The Wellwoods' Midsummer was a slightly movable feast. Humphry explained to Philip that midsummer day—that is, the longest day of the solar year—is in fact June 21st. But the European Feast of St. John is the evening of June 23rd leading to St. John's Day on June 24th and that also is called Midsummer. "In practice," said Humphry, who believed in talking to the young as though they were fellow men, "in practice, we have been somewhat eclectic with our own celebrations, choosing true midsummer, or St. John's day, depending on the convenient day of the week for holding a party. Today is Friday 21st which is *true midsummer,* although midsummer eve was yesterday, and we shall be embarking on the declining days at dawn on Saturday, though still in advance of Europe . . . Saturday is full moon, so we will celebrate—if we are lucky with the weather—by the light of a waxing gibbous moon. 'Gibbous' is a good word," said Humphry, who was a word-savourer. Philip had been alarmed at the number of words flying round the table that he had never before encountered. But he now had a mental image of a waxing gibbous disc, and his ever-active mind's eye began to decorate a large bowl with waning gibbous, waxing gibbous, and truly circular discs. It could be interesting. Silver and gold on dark cobalt.

"Friday is a good day for friends to join us," said Olive. "They are all gathering here for the weekend away from the city. We shall keep you very busy with preparations, Philip."

"Good," said Philip.

The household, family, staff and Philip, was set to frenzied work. Olive and Humphry had both already completed their writing stints, around dawn, before breakfast. The kitchen was full of smells of cooking, and no one was to have anything for lunch except bread and cheese, for the stove, and most of the crockery, were pre-empted. Philip was assigned to help with the decoration of the garden and orchard. He helped set up trestle tables on the lawn near the house, and then to arrange little cosy, or conspiratorial, groups of chairs in picturesque places. All chairs were requisitioned—wicker chairs, deckchairs, schoolroom chairs, the nursery rocking chair, cane and metal garden chairs. They were placed in arbours, in the clearing at the centre of the shrubbery, even in the orchard. Then the lanterns were swung from branches, and half-concealed in clumps of tall grasses and decorative thistles in the herbaceous borders. Philip was sent with Phyllis to hang lanterns in the orchard. It was an unkempt, raggedy place with moss and lichens on the twisted branches of old fruit-trees, and brambles snaking in from the wild and in places smothering everything. Some of the trees had odd structures in them made from planks and bits of rope. These were good places for illuminations, Phyllis said. She attached lanterns to ropes and sent Philip climbing up to the platforms. "These are old tree houses," said Phyllis. "From when we were little. Even Hedda can get into these. We've got a much better one—out in the forest. But it's a secret," she added, doubtfully. Philip was picking up hard windfall apples. Phyllis told him to watch for wasps. "You get all sorts of worms in them, popping their little black heads out at you. It's a horrible idea, biting into something wriggly—"

They wandered into the orchard. Phyllis pointed.

"These two trees are the magic trees from the story. The golden apple and the silver pear. You can only see the gold and silver in certain lights, you have to believe. These two are the centre. Their branches touch the ground, and their heads are in the sky. And all this—stuff—the bryony and the wild roses—grows over them to make them lovely—"

They were old, neglected, beautiful trees. Philip looked at the shapes of the snarling of their branches and wished he had a pencil. Phyllis took his hand and pulled him forward.

"This is where Rosy lies. See this circle of white stones. Rosy is under these, under the apple and the pear."

A kitten, a bird?

"We bring her flowers on her birthday. We pour out libations of apple juice for her. We don't forget her. We will never forget her."

Her voice was solemn, and creamy with warmth.

"She lived for a week, just one little week, that was all she lived. She had the most perfect little fingers and toes. Now she sleeps here."

She bent her head reverently. Philip, without putting it into words, detected play-acting. He wondered unkindly if Phyllis even thought about what was really under the white stones, amongst the roots. He said vaguely and falsely

"That's good."

He threw several of the hard little apples into the bramble patch.

Then he hung a lantern with a crescent moon and a black bird-shadow in the branches of the pear tree, over the white stones.

Phyllis took his hand. She pushed her little body against his side. He had the sense that her flesh had always been clean and pleasant, and that, by contrast, his own *never had*. This was a feeling, again not in words. He pulled away.

After the decoration of the garden, and the bread and cheese lunch, the business of dressing-up began. Violet dressed the children—including Philip—in the schoolroom whilst Humphry and Olive went to put on their robes, which were a gesture towards "their" play, *A Midsummer Night's Dream,* not rigidly Elizabethan, not yet Athenian, but more flowing Arts and Crafts silks and linens, silver and gold, flowery and floating.

There was a large painted chest in the schoolroom, an imitation of a Renaissance marriage-chest, with woodland scenes of dark glades, pale ladies, hounds and a white stag painted on the sides. This was the dressing-up chest, and it was unusually well stocked with silken shifts, frilled shirts, embroidered shawls, fillets for veils and coronets for princes.

"It helps," Violet said to Philip, "to have a dressmaker as an auntie, who can turn a toga into a ball dress and back, or magic silk flowers out of old stockings. I think we should dress Hedda as Peaseblossom. Here is a lovely pink and violet shift."

Hedda had her arms deep in the silks, rummaging.

"I want to be a *witch,*" she said.

"I told you, dear," said Violet. "Hallowe'en's for witches. Midsummer is for fairies. With pretty wings, organdie, look."

"I want to be a *witch,*" Hedda repeated. Her small face was an angry frown.

Olive had come in with a sparkling buckle she needed Violet to stitch to a sash. She ruffled Hedda's hair.

"She can be a witch if she likes," she said easily. "We want them to be comfortable, don't we, so they can run about and have fun. Have you found witch clothes, darling? Here's my old black shawl with a lovely fringe and a fiery dragon on it. And here's Phyllis's old black dancing-tunic—if you just put a few stitches, Vi, so she doesn't spring apart. And here's a glass beetle-brooch, just the thing. And Philip will make you a hat with black paper. Not too big, Philip, so it stays on—"

"And a broomstick," said Hedda.

"You must ask in the kitchen for the loan of a besom."

Violet's face had a mutinous look, not unlike Hedda's, but she did as she was asked, or told, and the little girl was soon spinning in a whirl of black batwings and floating fringe. Violet did up the unresisting Florian in yellow and green, with a scalloped jerkin, as Mustardseed. He had a pointed felt cap, which he kept patting uncertainly. Phyllis accepted the rejected Peaseblossom, and was lovingly hung with silk gauze, mauve, rose and ivory; she had a silver cloak, like folded dragonfly-wings, and a wreath of silk flowers on her hair.

Dorothy was Moth, in a grey velvet tunic with a cloak with painted eyes. Violet tried vainly to persuade her to wear wired antennae.

Tom had to be Puck. He went barefoot in brown tights and a leaf-coloured jerkin. He too rejected a headdress and said he would put twigs in his own hair. Phyllis said Puck didn't wear glasses. Tom said "This one does. Or he'll fall into the pond and get trapped in brambles."

They came to the question of Philip. He said he couldn't dress up, he would feel silly. No one wanted to suggest he should be a rude mechanical. It would be insensitive. Tom said "Can't you put on a sort of toga and be one of the Athenians?"

Philip did not know *A Midsummer Night's Dream* and was totally baffled by the costume selection. He said he didn't think he could wear a toga. He was not, in fact, sure what a toga was.

"I don't like to be looked at," he said, strangled. All the children, even those who were prancing about flaunting their disguises, understood the need not to be looked at. Dorothy had an idea, and took down the butcher-blue painting smock Tom wore for crafts lessons.

"You could go as an artist. You might wear this anyway, to make pots and things."

The smock had a high neck, full sleeves, deep pockets. It was a coverall. It was in many ways less of a disguise than the borrowed clothes he had on. Philip looked down at his legs.

"You could go barefoot," said Dorothy. "We do."

"You could just stay as you are," said Tom.

Philip put on the smock. He felt comfortable. He allowed Violet to change his boots for sandals. Everyone who was not barefoot wore sandals.

"Now you can run and jump," said Dorothy.

His feet under the straps were whitish but not white. He felt a moment's pleasure at the idea of running and jumping.

· · ·

The guests began to arrive in the midafternoon. They came at intervals, from far and near, in carriages, pony-traps, station flies, on foot, and, in one case, on a tandem tricycle.

Humphry and Olive stood on the steps to receive them. They were dressed as Oberon and Titania. Humphry had a silk jerkin embroidered with Florentine arabesques, black breeches and a voluminous velvet cloak, swinging at a daring angle from a silken cord across his shoulder. He looked absurd and beautiful. And amused. Olive wore pleated olive silk over pleated white linen, with a gauze overcloak, veined like insect wings. Her hair was dressed with honeysuckle and roses. She looked warm and wild. Violet, beside her, wore a dress stitched with ivy-leaves on satin, and held her head girlishly on one side, heavy with silk ivy and white feathers. The children were running around. They would be called to order when other children arrived.

The firstcomers—they had only to walk across the meadow from their farm cottage—were the Russian anarchists. Vasily Tartarinov had escaped from St. Petersburg in 1885. He gave lectures on Russian society, and received generous assistance (including the cottage) from English socialists. He had two sets of clothes, his working smock and the dress suit in which he gave his lectures. He had come in the dress suit. He was a dramatic figure, inordinately tall and thin with a long pointed white beard like a wizard. His wife, Elena, wore the better of her two dresses, which was brown poplin with black braid and black buttons. Her hair was scraped back. They had made no concession to fancy dress. The children, Andrei and Dmitri, both around Phyllis's age, wore their usual aprons, red and blue. They mostly pretended they could not speak English.

The tricycle rolled in, vigorously pedalled by Leslie and Etta Skinner, fellow Fabians. Skinner worked on human statistics and heredity at University College, London. He had sleek black hair, white skin and blue eyes. Etta Skinner was older than Leslie. They had met in the Men and Women's Club, at the college, in the 1880s. They had discussed the Woman Question, birth control, animal passion and the sexual instincts. Skinner was very serious and had a beautiful voice. He aroused a great deal of animal passion in colleagues and students. The Wellwoods agreed he had married Etta to protect himself from frenzied maenads. Etta was a dedicated Theosophist, attended gatherings on esoteric and astral matters in Albemarle Street, lectured on vegetarianism, and taught reading, writing and arithmetic to the London poor. She had a round face, tight lips and pepper and salt hair with a fuzz of broken ends. She looked as though she had once been expectant and greedy, but had learned better. She was distantly related to the Darwins, the Wedgwoods and the Galtons, which, Humphry pointed out, must have been attractive to a specialist in heredity. But the Skinners, married for ten years, had no children. Humphry said it was odd that people interested in ancestry often were not ancestors. Olive replied that she didn't like Etta's clothes, which were home-dyed and sacklike. The usual dress appeared, in an unsteady plum colour, as she divested herself of her cycling skirt and veil.

Close on their heels came Toby Youlgreave, also on a bicycle. He had a tiny weekend cottage in the woods. He and Etta began a discussion of folk customs at midsummer.

Prosper Cain came from Iwade House in a carriage, with Julian, and his daughter, Florence. They wore fancy dress. Prosper was disguised as Prospero in a sumptuous black robe covered with signs of the zodiac. He carried a long staff, made of a narwhal tusk, with a pommel stuck with moonstones and peridots. Julian was Prince Ferdinand, in theatrical black and silver. Florence, who was twelve, was very prettily dressed as Miranda, in a flowing sea-coloured shift, with her dark hair flowing, and a necklace of pearls. Julian and Tom eyed each other cautiously. They had shared an adventure, but were not sure they wanted to be friends. Olive came smiling forward and Prosper kissed her hand. He said in her ear

"I borrowed this fantastic object from the collection, dear lady, but tell no one."

"I don't know whether to believe you."

He was still holding her hand.

"No one ever does. I encourage uncertainty."

Julian caught sight of Philip in the smock.

"I didn't recognise you."

Philip shifted from foot to foot. Tom said "He's made topping lanterns. Come and see."

They went off, and Florence followed.

The Dungeness party were in a kind of brake; the ladies had brought their party dresses in wicker baskets, because they had come a long way. Benedict Fludd, as Olive had predicted, had not come. Seraphita, in the days when she was a Stunner from Margate called Sarah-Jane Stubbs, had been painted by Burne-Jones and Rossetti. Now in her forties she still had the fine bones, the knot of black hair, the huge brow, the wide-spaced green eyes and calm mouth of the paintings, but her body was heavier and her expression less mildly beneficent. She was travelling in a loose Liberty robe, but had brought a grander one, with a confection of veiling to throw round her head and shoulders. Her children were Imogen, a child of sixteen embarrassed by breasts, Geraint, a little older than Tom, who had inherited his mother's eyes and hair, and Pomona, who was Tom's age, had flowing chestnut-coloured hair and had brought a home-woven gown, embroidered with crocus, daffodils and bluebells. Both girls had also brought beaded and embroidered Juliet caps. Geraint had a kind of handwoven smock, not unlike Philip's.

The Fludds were accompanied by a solemn young man whose name was Arthur Dobbin. Dobbin saw himself as Benedict Fludd's apprentice. He hoped to found a commune of craftsmen in the salt marshes round Rye. He was smallish, and plump, with slicked hair and an anxious, determined look. He would have liked to come dressed as Oberon, or Sir Galahad, and he knew it would not do. He was dressed in the knitted Jaeger woollen garments, popularised by G. B. Shaw, which were a little sweaty in flaming June.

Dorothy was waiting for the next carriage. So was Humphry, who drew in a breath as it pulled up smartly in front of the house. The other Wellwoods were here. They had driven over from Vetchey Manor, their country house. They were soberly dressed in travelling costumes, and had bandboxes with them. Basil and Katharina sat looking forwards; their son and daughter, Charles and Griselda, sat behind the driver, looking back.

Dorothy was waiting for Cousin Griselda. Cousin Griselda came into her mind when she had to use the word "love" which she tended to be careful with. Griselda was the same age as Dorothy, and was closer to Dorothy than her sister Phyllis. Dorothy, a realist, rather thought she did not love Phyllis, though she knew she ought to. Perhaps because of this she loved Griselda—whom she did not see very often—a little more emphatically. Dorothy was sometimes afraid that she had started out with a smaller capability for love than most people. Phyllis loved everything—Mother, Father, Auntie Violet, Hedda, Florian and Robin, Ada and Cathy, the ponies, the fluffy kitten, dead Rosy in the orchard, the Todefright toads. Dorothy had varying feelings for most of these people, some of them loving. But she did love Griselda, she had fixed on Griselda to love.

Frieda, Katharina's lady's-maid, had the seat beside the driver. She came down to oversee the unloading of the bandboxes.

Basil Wellwood was shorter and more muscular than his younger brother. He wore a well-cut pale grey suit, which he did not intend to change, and had a diamond ring and a multiple watchchain of complicated links. He did not quite suppress a frown when he saw Humphry's bright garments which he thought were absurd. He complimented Humphry on the hot sunlight, as though Humphry had found someone to procure it, which Humphry in turn found absurd.

Charles, aged fourteen and preparing for the Eton scholarship exams, resembled both brothers, with red-gold hair, sandy lashes and strong features. He too wore a suit, with a cravat with a pearl tiepin.

Katharina was thin and pale, her head on its slender neck dwarfed by a hat with dove-wings on its rim, and a closely tied spotted veil. Her hair was between faded grey and mouse-blonde. She had large, mixed-coloured eyes in slightly ravaged sockets of bruised skin, finely wrinkled and folded.

Griselda was very thin, with fine silver-blonde hair, plaited round her head, like a true *Mädchen,* Humphry thought. She wore a mushroom-coloured travelling costume. Her mouth was thin and unsmiling. She was tall, and did not look strong. Dorothy ran to greet her.

They went inside, to change their clothes. Phyllis, attaching herself to Dorothy and Griselda, said

"Have you got a lovely costume, Cousin Grisel?"

"You are all in fancy dress."

"It's midsummer," said Dorothy. "We always are. Aren't you?"

"I am not. I have got my new party dress. You will see."

The dressing took time. There were endless laces and buttons. When mother and daughter emerged from Olive's bedroom they were lovely to look at and completely out of place. Katharina was in mauve and white shot silk moiré and Valenciennes lace with huge leg-of-mutton puffs above the elbow. She wore kid gloves and had a confection of lace and fresh rosebuds, like a giant pincushion, on her head. Griselda was in shell-pink satin, with a lace yoke, decorated with all sorts of little darker pink bows, around her puffed sleeves, around her hem. Phyllis said it was lovely. Dorothy said "It might get dirty if we go in the orchard."

Griselda said "It's completely inappropriate. Charles calls it Little Bo-Peep."

"You do look like a china doll," said Dorothy, "one in a fairy story, standing on a shelf, that's loved hopelessly by a tin soldier or a presumptuous mouse."

"It would not be remarkable in Portman Square," said Griselda, quite flatly. "I shall just have to endure."

A pony-trap arrived, which appeared at first sight to be carrying a troupe of ghosts and ghouls, white-faced and staring. The driver was Augustus Steyning, who lived in Nutcracker Cottage on the edge of the Downs. He stepped down on long long legs, pointing elegant toes like a dancer. He had a small silver beard, and an elegant moustache, and thick, well-cut silver hair. He was wearing a country suit, but turned out to be also dressed as Prospero, having brought a cabbalistic hooded gown and a knobby walnut staff. He was a theatre director and occasional playwright, whose best-known works were productions of *Peer Gynt* and *The Tempest,* although he had written a historical drama about Cromwell and Charles I. His ideas were advanced. He was interested in the new German drama and in German tales and imaginings. (His house, though it had nut trees in its garden, was not named out of English whimsy so much as for Hoffmann's sinister tale of the Nutcracker and the Mouse King.) His trap was full of large theatrical masks.

"I brought an ass's head, my dears—Midsummer is incomplete without one and this one had the distinction of having been worn by Beer-bohm Tree himself. We may take turns to disappear inside it and be metamorphosed. And I brought these delicious disguises from Venice—here are Pierrot and Columbine, here is a vulture who is really a plague doctor keeping away from bubos, here is a black enchantress with sequins. Here is the Sun, with flaming rim, and here is the Moon, with cloudy mountains and silver tears . . ."

He turned to Olive.

"I took the liberty of bringing my guest. He is driving himself, as he needs space. He is just behind me—"

A shadow of irritation passed over Olive's face. It was her party. She was the giver. And then the second trap arrived, with one man, and an inanimate company—in this case hidden in black boxes and brass-hasped cases.

"He is an old friend of yours, I believe—" said August Steyning. (He liked to call himself August, in honour of the clowns.) "I hope I did well." He had noticed Olive's little grimace.

Olive looked at the newcomer, hesitated and then swept forward with outstretched hands.

"Welcome to our house. What an unexpected delight—"

The stranger stepped down. He was small, thin and dark, clothed in black drainpipe trousers and a long black jacket, and a black felt hat with jay feathers in the band. He had a theatrical pointed beard and groomed moustache. His feet did not crunch on the gravel. He bowed briefly over Olive's hand.

"This is indeed an old friend, whom we met in Munich. Major Cain, let me introduce Herr Anselm Stern, who is an artist of a most unusual kind. Herr Stern, this is Mr. Wellwood, my brother-in-law, and Katharina Wellwood . . ."

She did not introduce the children.

Cathy was instructed to help Herr Stern with his boxes. Hedda touched them, and asked what was in them.

"You shall see in good time," said August Steyning. "With your mother's permission, we hope to show you."

Herr Stern, supervising the stowing of the boxes, suddenly found his voice, and said, in halting English,

"I have brought a gift for the little girls."

He looked uncertainly from Dorothy to the befrilled Griselda to pretty Phyllis, to the small black witch with the beetle-brooch.

"The box with the red string," Herr Stern told Cathy. "Please."

"What can it be?" said Phyllis.

"Open it, please," said Anselm Stern.

It was in parchmentlike paper, and the size of a shoe-box. Violet cut the string, Phyllis undid the paper. Hedda darted forward and took the lid from the box inside, which was very like a shoe-box if not a shoe-box. She peeped in.

"There is a *shoe,*" she said.

Violet lifted it out.

It was a very large shoe made of stitched leather, dark russet-red, with a large tongue and a big steel buckle with a sharp spike.

Inside were what Dorothy at first took for mice. She took a step back.

"They are babies," said Phyllis uncertainly.

The shoe was crammed full with little stuffed dolls, each with a round head, and staring beady eyes.

They wore either small lederhosen, or small enveloping aprons. Phyllis laughed uneasily. The dolls stared out. Hedda said

"It's the Old Woman Who Lived in a Shoe. Only there's no Woman, the children are on their own in there."

She grabbed the shoe and held it to her chest. The other girls felt relief.

"It is a most *original* toy," said Violet.

"You like it?" said Herr Stern to Hedda.

"It's a bit scary. I like scary things."

August Steyning explained that Anselm Stern was a puppetmaster. He performed enchantments with glove puppets, and with marionettes. As a surprise gift for the queen of fairytale, he said, bowing to Olive, they hoped to perform a version of Cinderella for the guests. The cast were safely enclosed in the black japanned boxes they saw. And if the curtain-raiser pleased them, he hoped they would all come next day to Nutcracker Cottage to see something more elaborate. "I say *we* shall perform," he explained, "because Anselm has been instructing me in the mystery of the marionettes. I am to be Sorcerer's Apprentice. I shall animate the Ugly Sisters."

Olive smiled. Humphry invited them all to refreshments.

"First, food and drink. Then the performance. Then further refreshment and dancing. We have talented musicians—Geraint on the flute, Charles with the fiddle, and Tom, who does what he can with a tin whistle."

They gathered on the lawn. Steyning, just returned from meeting Anselm Stern, had brought shocking news from London. The Liberal government had unexpectedly fallen. A routine vote on the army estimates, the supply of small arms, had unexpectedly become a Vote of Confidence. Lord Rosebery had resigned, and Lord Salisbury was now Prime Minister, until an election could be held, in the autumn.

Prosper Cain said this change might affect the Museum badly. It was still waiting for Sir Aston Webb's winning plans for the new front and courtyard to become solid *things*. "We are a builders' yard," he complained. "This can at best delay things further."

Basil Wellwood saw no one with whom he could discuss the effect of the events on the Stock Exchange. He thought he was amongst a curious clutch of people, all tinsel and fake gilding.

Leslie Skinner spoke in an undertone. He believed Lord Rosebery's name had been mentioned in the sad events surrounding the recent trials. It had been rumoured that the sad death of Lord Queensberry's eldest son—not Lord Alfred Douglas, but Lord Drumlanrig—had been not a shooting accident but an act of self-destruction, designed—they did say—to protect Lord Rosebery's good name? And there had been concerns about this during Mr. Wilde's unsuccessful libel suit against Lord Queensberry? Skinner had a look of pure academic enquiry. His grave face expressed a desire for precise knowledge.

Violet Grimwith made a clucking sound and gathered together those children who were listening, leading them away to taste fruit cup. Julian and Tom did not follow. Julian beckoned to Tom, and they sauntered in hearing distance behind a trestle table, sampling tartlets. It was less than a month since Wilde's third court appearance, his second trial for indecency, after a first jury had failed to agree. Everyone discussed it endlessly. Julian, like his schoolfellows, had read the press reports. He wanted to hear. Leslie Skinner said to August Steyning that he believed he had been in court.

"I was," said Steyning. "I was indeed. The poor man stood in need of a friendly audience. I was compelled to bear witness. It was a true tragic fall. With uncanny aspects. Did you hear the story of the palm-reader's predictions?"

No, they all said, though Humphry at least knew the tale very well.

Steyning told them, holding out his own long, pale, exquisite hands, one after the other, in illustration.

"It was at a supper of Blanche Roosevelt. The chiromancer was in obscurity behind a curtain, and the guests thrust in their anonymous hands. The left hand, it appears, shows the destiny written in the stars, and the right hand shows what its owner will make of that destiny. Oscar's left hand—they were *much* plumper than mine—showed huge, brilliant achievement and success. The right showed *ruin*—at a precise date. The left hand is the hand of a king, but the right that of a king who will send himself into exile. Oscar asked the precise date, was given it, and abruptly took his leave. The prophecy appears to be fulfilled."

Skinner asked Steyning's impression of the trial.

"He bore himself with dignity and stood like a sacrificed beast. He allowed himself to be trapped into witticism. He spoke bravely about the love that dare not speak its name. He was applauded. But it was no triumph. And his present state is desperate. They have removed his name from the theatres where his plays are performing—not for much longer, I suspect. It is said prison is killing him. He had some idea of treating it as a monastery, or Prospero's study, but he sleeps on a board, has neither books, nor pen, nor ink, and is made to work the treadmill. His flesh is fallen into folds. He cannot sleep."

Humphry, who moved in the world of press gossip, remarked lightly that Lord Rosebery had been sick, very sick, for months, and had suddenly recovered at the end of May. Only for his government to fall, it appeared, today. He exchanged glances with Steyning and suddenly saw Tom and Julian.

"You don't need to stand around listening to political chatter. Go and arrange seats for the marionettes."

Tom and Julian wandered away across the lawn.

"You are always told you don't want to hear things precisely because you do," said Julian.

"Do you?" Tom asked.

"They think we don't know these things. They ought to know you learn in school, just by being a boy. You learn them along with Greek and cricket and rowing and drawing. And sniggering and poking and passing messages. They ought to know we know. They must have known themselves."

Tom did not know. He lived at home and was home-tutored, though Basil and Humphry were planning for him to do the Marlowe scholarship exams next spring. Basil had intervened when Humphry had spoken of sending Tom to the newfangled newly founded Bedales where boys mucked out farm animals and swam naked. Basil would help, he said, with his nephew's fees. Tom was very bright, good at maths, good at languages. He did Latin and Greek with the anarchists, who liked teaching, and were grateful for the income. He did maths with a tutor, whose lessons would increase after the summer. Tom walked through lanes and meadows to his lessons. He lived wild, much of the time. He was not sure he wanted to know what Julian was talking about. He was not sure he wanted to be friends with Julian. He was often unsure what he wanted, and as a result, being amiable, he had many acquaintances and no close friends. He was thirteen, and still all boy, whereas Julian was fifteen, and could on occasion be a serious young man.

Tom's spectacles made him look owlish. His fine fair hair sprang all ways, and asked to be ruffled. His skin was young, unspotted, and golden brown with outdoor living. He had his mother's eyes and long lashes. His cheekbones were high and wide, his mouth gentle. He was the sort of beautiful boy, quite unconscious of his beauty, who was much discussed and courted both in Julian's prep school, and at Marlowe. Julian had asked himself whether Tom was pretty, or a possible object of passion, and had seen that, in theory, he certainly was. Pretty boys at school became rapidly self-conscious. Tom seemed unconcerned, and it lent him charm and distance. Julian expected to be full of love and lust, and consequently usually was. He had an inconvenient habit of watching himself from a distance, and wondering whether the love and lust were strained and faked. He was afraid of being isolated and solitary, which he feared was his fate. He was certainly not himself an object of desire to other boys, as far as he knew—and he was knowing. Also he was constantly concerned by pustules, and the craters of past pustules. He was not sure whether Tom, despite being pretty, was not so simple that he was boring.

Tom was assessing Julian in his usual terms. Was he, would he ever be, someone who could be invited into the Tree House? It was too early to tell, but he rather thought not. He said, blandly and meaninglessly,

"Grown-ups always think we don't know things they must have known themselves. They need to remember wrong, I think."

The audience were gathered for the marionettes like a flock of hens. They sat in a half-moon, in the blue daylight, on chairs, stools, grass. Griselda and Dorothy sat together on embroidered footstools, to safeguard Griselda's skirt. They both thought they were too old for puppet shows.

August Steyning stepped out from behind the booth that he and Herr Stern had erected. It had star-spangled midnight-blue curtains. He bowed, profoundly, and announced

"We welcome you to *Aschenputtel, or Cinderella*."

He went back, behind the dark box.

A trumpet sounded, and a tapping drum. The curtains swept open. A funeral procession crossed the stage, to a slow beat: black-coated mourners, carrying a coffin, the sombre widower, the decorous daughter, cloaked in black, her face shadowed. The coffin was lowered, to sad drumbeats. A green mound, and a gravestone rose in its place. Father and daughter embraced.

The next scene was in the house. The stepmother and stepsisters arrived to strutting violin music. The marionettes were delicate creatures, with fine porcelain faces, real human hair twisted or plaited into elaborate coiffures, and a frou-frou of finely stitched skirts, crimson, lilac, amber. The sisters were not ugly. They were fashionable beauties, with pearl necklaces and haughty little faces with sneering mouths and plucked and painted eyebrows. They and their mother were like peas in a pod, from the same mould. Aschenputtel had long golden plaits, and a simple sky-blue dress. The step-family indicated imperiously chairs she should dust and arrange, silver tureens she should carry, the hearth she should sweep, the fire she should tend. She moved as they commanded. A puff of real smoke came from the fireplace.

Aschenputtel shuddered, sat on a stool, put her sweet china face in her fine china hands. The shudder was human and disturbing, as the little limbs swayed and folded.

The father returned, booted and caped for a journey. He kissed their hands and asked what they would like as a gift on his return.

There were few words in this production, but this ritual question was spoken in August Steyning's high, light, reedy voice, which seemed proportionate to the tiny actor. He lifted it to counter-tenor. Silk and velvet, said the crimson sister. Rubies and pearls, said the violet. A branch of whatever tree touches your hat, said Aschenputtel.

She was next seen kneeling by the green mound and the grey stone, smoothing the grass, planting the twig. Slowly, wonderfully, a tree unfolded from beneath the stage, a wiry trunk uncurling branches, hung with a haze of leaves. Two white doves, fluttering and swooping, stitched from feathers and silk, with jet beads for eyes, pink toes and iridescent ruffs, settled in the tree. The violin twittered. The doves flew to Aschenputtel's fingers. She lay down and embraced the mound, and they strutted and preened in her hair.

Dorothy blinked. The little creatures had taken on a sinister life, which perturbed her. She set herself against giving in to the illusion. Griselda beside her was staring, engrossed.

The stepmother set Aschenputtel to sorting lentils from cinders. The doves sifted the ashes, and deftly threw the lentils into a pan—a rain of tiny clatterings could be heard.

The sisters were fitted with ball-gowns, by a new marionette, a sub-servient dressmaker, her painted mouth full of pins. One sister had puce bows. One had purple pom-poms. Aschenputtel sat by the hearth, head in hands.

The weeping daughter stood by the mound, her hair now loose, a mass of gold threads, under the dancing tree, which waved its arms and produced, like a descending angel, a fine gold dress, a coronet, a pair of gold slippers.

The Ball was done behind gauze, with whirling figures, and dance music in a music box, twanging waltzes, prancing polkas. The prince had shining white hair, tied back, a long dark coat and knee-breeches. He danced with the golden girl. The clock struck. She fled. The tree and the birds made a second dress out of thin air, silver as the moon. And a third, caught like the starry sky in the pointy branches. The counter-tenor sang.

Shiver and shake, little tree
Throw gold and silver over me.

The prince appeared, with a pot of pitch, and cunningly painted the steps of his palace. They danced, the chimes sounded, Aschenputtel fled, the little gold shoe was left shining on the tar.

The final scenes were gruesome. One disdainful sister, her proud expression unchanging, aided and abetted by her mother took a kitchen cleaver to her big toe, splat. "When you are queen, you will not need to go on foot," said the mother, falsetto. The bride and groom set off on horseback, on a finely caparisoned horse made of real hide. The gold shoe brimmed with blood. Several of those children remembered, well into their future, that they had seen the red liquid dripping from the shoe.

Dorothy blinked and refused to imagine.
The pirouetting doves called to the prince

Turn around, look behind
Blood in the shoe.
Turn around, change your mind
She's not the bride for you.

So they turned back. And the stepmother, learning nothing, following her fate, took the cleaver, slap, to the second sister's heel, and crammed her porcelain toes into the golden shell.

"How horrible," said Hedda, audibly. "When it's already all bloody."

The doves sang, the prince turned back.

Aschenputtel's father called her from the cinders where she sat in drab rags. She came and put her dainty toe in the slipper and was embraced by the prince. She ran off, and reappeared, radiant in her starry dress. Puppet father and puppet daughter clung to each other, centre-stage, her china cheek on his shoulder, as he stroked her golden hair.

The backdrop became a candlelit choir. The wedding procession came back from the altar. The doves flew down, at the church door, cooing and shrilling, and mobbed the haughty sisters, beating their white wings about their heads, topping their headdresses, obscuring with commotion faces that were then revealed to be eyeless, with bloody sockets.

Griselda closed her lips. Dorothy shuddered crossly. Phyllis said that it was all wrong, there had been no pumpkin, no godmother, no glass coach. No rats and mice and lizards, cried Hedda, overexcited, unnerved by cruel doves. Florian said, More, having understood nothing, mesmerised by the moving miniature world.

Griselda said to Dorothy that it was interesting, how different the story was. Dorothy said she herself wasn't very interested but that if Griselda wanted to know, she should ask Toby Youlgreave, he was always going on about fairytales.

Griselda, looking like a lost china shepherdess in a swarm of raggedy fairies, pulled timidly at Toby's arm. She said she really wanted to know why the story was different. "Dorothy said you would tell me." Toby sat down beside her on a garden seat. He said that the version she was used to was the French one by Charles Perrault—whose stories were written for young ladies, and usually had fairy godmothers. Whereas Anselm Stern's version was German, out of the Brothers Grimm. Griselda said that she herself was half-German, but that she did not have German fairytales at home. She wished she did. Toby said those were only two of the endless versions from many, many countries from Finland to Scotland to Russia—with varying combinations of some or all of the events—wicked stepmother, selfish sisters, friendly animals, magic dresses, shoes, with or without blood in them. The Grimms believed that what they were collecting were part of the very old beliefs and magic tales of the German *Volk*. There are English fairytales, too, said Toby. Mrs. Olive Wellwood uses them, very cleverly.

Griselda said that her aunt's fairy stories frightened her. So did Hans Andersen, he made her cry. But not this sort of tale. She didn't know why. It should be scary, there was a lot of blood. Toby said these were memories of some other time, long ago, and he agreed, they weren't scary.

"They are just *like that*," said Griselda, feeling for what intrigued her, not finding it.

Toby looked at the serious thin face. He said he would send her a book of the Grimms, if she was allowed to receive it. Griselda said she didn't think her family had anything *against* the Grimms. They just didn't know about them. Toby wanted to stroke her hair, and say, *don't worry,* but he didn't think that was a good idea.

Everyone, old and young, now gathered for a kind of sumptuous picnic. As happens in such gatherings, where those whose lives are shaped, fortunately or unfortunately, are surrounded by those whose lives are almost entirely to come, the elders began asking the young what they meant to do with their lives, and to project futures for them.

They started, naturally, with the older boys. Prosper Cain said Julian had a fine eye for antiques, and could tell the real thing from a fake. He had a collection of valuables he had found in flea-markets, a mediaeval spoon, a very old Staffordshire slipware beaker. Julian said easily that after Cambridge he might indeed like to work in museums, or galleries. Seraphita Fludd said she hoped Geraint would be like *his* father, an

artist, and *make* lovely things. Geraint said she knew really he was no
good at that kind of thing. He was good at maths. An astronomer! cried
Violet. Geraint said he should like to make a *comfortable* living. He smiled
amiably. Basil said he should go into business, in that case. Like William
Morris, said Arthur Dobbin, who hoped to introduce business practices
in the artists' workshops in Lydd. Geraint went on smiling, and eating
jellied ham mould. Basil Wellwood said Geraint was welcome to join
Charles in his family firm. Charles made a strangled noise, blushed, and
was heard to mutter that that was yet to be decided. Etta Skinner said it
was odd that nobody in this forward-looking community had asked any
of the girls what they wanted to be. She hoped some of them had ambitions. Prosper Cain, simultaneously, asked Tom what he hoped to
become. Tom had no idea. He told the truth.

"I don't ever want to leave here. I want to go on being in the
woods—out on the Downs—just being here—"

"And to be boy eternal," said August Steyning, inevitably, with a
theatrical hum. Olive said Tom had all the time in the world.

Leslie Skinner took up Etta's point. He addressed Dorothy, almost
pugnaciously.

"And you, young woman. What do you hope to be?"

"I am going to be a doctor," said Dorothy.

Violet said that was the first that had been heard of *that* idea. It was
indeed, the first time it had formed in Dorothy's mind, and she had spoken spontaneously. Doctors and nurses was not a game they played. But
she heard herself answer, and suddenly in her head there existed a
grown-up Dorothy, a doctor. Not sweetly benign, but wielding a
scalpel. Skinner said that was a fine ambition, though the way was hard
still, and he hoped she would come to University College.

"But you must want to be married, Hejjog," said Phyllis, using a
nickname Dorothy disliked. "I do. I want a lovely wedding, and a house
just like this, with a rose garden, and I want to bake bread, and wear
lovely dresses, and have seven children . . ."

Phyllis knew she was pretty. She was always being told she was. The
young Fludds, Imogen and Pomona, could have been described as beautiful, but they were beautiful in a subdued and uncertain way, certainly
unlikely to be Stunners. They were both graceful and awkward in their
home-woven linens and hand-enamelled bracelets. Imogen had full
breasts, and wore no supporting underwear. She looked plump. She said
she had from time to time thought of studying embroidery at the Royal

College. Pomona said she might like that, too, or she might like to stay and make tiles in Dungeness. Hedda said she wanted to be a witch. Violet slapped her wrist.

They turned to Florence Cain. Florence had had a governess who had borne in upon her that she had caused her mother's death, and must devote her life to caring for her father. Florence had not mentioned these admonitions to her father, who was quite unaware of them, and was also well looked after by housekeepers and sappers. He liked to play games with both Julian and Florence, filling brass trays with miscellaneous buttons, beads, bottles, snuffboxes and so on, and asking his children to remember them, describe them and identify them. He took quite as much delight in Florence's acuity as in Julian's. Florence did, indeed, look like his lost Giulia, but he thought of the likeness in terms of a Van Eyck angel, serene amongst its crimped hair.

"Well," he said, "Florence. What will you do?"

"I shall keep house for you," said Florence, who thought this was understood.

"I hope you won't. I hope you'll have a home of your own, and before that, an education. I hope Julian will go to Cambridge, and I hope you will too. Newnham College offers a great deal. I hope you will want to go there."

Florence was confused. They had never discussed this, and now firm statements were being made, in the middle of a large party. She did not know anything about Newnham College. It was just a name.

"She doesn't want to be a maiden lady," said Julian. "A bluestocking."

This annoyed Florence, who said she didn't see why she shouldn't learn something. Julian was going to. She would do so. She fell over her words, and fell silent. She couldn't imagine what she might try to learn.

That left Griselda. Basil and Katharina were clear about her future. She would be Presented at court, become a debutante, and make an advantageous match. Katharina said she hoped Griselda would be as happily married as her parents.

Griselda twisted a puce bow rhythmically round and round. Her mother tapped her fingers. Griselda had been shocked—deeply shocked—when Dorothy said she wanted to be a doctor. She had not thought of wanting anything beyond release from puce bows. She had an intense secret life, which consisted of reading novels about women reduced to silent attentiveness, full of inner rebellion, or of the effort of resignation. Jane Eyre, Elizabeth Bennet, Fanny Price, Maggie Tulliver.

But all these had really wanted love and marriage. None had wanted anything so—so destructive—as to be a doctor. Why had Dorothy never said anything of this intention? Griselda loved Dorothy as Dorothy loved Griselda. She loved Todefright with a passion she dared not admit to, even in Todefright. She came to stay there, and was immediately released from her good clothes and set loose to run wild in the woods. There were books everywhere. She had it in her pale head that she and Dorothy might live in the country together, and never bother with stays and hatpins and button-hooks. That was all she had thought of. And now suddenly Dorothy's world was black bags, and blood, and sickbeds, and grief and drama, and Griselda was nowhere. Dorothy had a secret. Griselda, her face white, said

"I mean to study. Like Florence. I learn German and French. I mean to study languages."

Katharina said that Griselda had the best possible teachers, and her progress was exemplary.

Basil remarked to the surrounding bushes that women's education simply made them dissatisfied. He did not say with what.

Griselda twisted another bow, and her mother tapped her hand. Humphry Wellwood picked up Florian.

"And what do you want to be, Florian?"

"A fox," said Florian, with total certainty. "A fox, in a foxhole, in a wood."

5

Olive believed she was a wonderful party-giver, and the belief was infectious, though not entirely well founded. It rested on the charm of her presence, and where she was, her parties were lively. She liked to be at the centre. She liked to charm, and to charm those she was excited to entertain—in this case leaders of culture, Prosper Cain and August Steyning, both of whom stood, champagne glasses in their hands, laughing at her self-deprecating jokes. She relied on others to do what was needful—introduce people, feed people, change the structure of groups. To a certain extent Violet could do this—she saw to bodily comforts, but was uneasy with bright talk. And Humphry could normally be relied on to amuse both men and women, but he had become ominously locked in argument with his brother. Children flickered and flitted along the flowerbeds and in and out of the shrubbery as the light thickened.

Vasily Tartarinov was performing his party piece to the Skinners and the young, Tom, Julian, Philip, Geraint, Florence and Charles. His party piece, which also formed part of his London lectures, was the story of a horse. The English cared about horses. It was the way to hook their attention. This horse, a noble black beast, Varvar the barbarian, had played an essential part in a series of daring escapes from Russian prisons and police surveillance, including Tartarinov's own. Varvar had been waiting when Prince Kropotkin flung off his immensely heavy green dressing-gown, in a movement practised for weeks, and simply *ran* out of the prison hospital courtyard and into a waiting carriage, where one conspirator was waiting, whilst another distracted the guards by showing them how to see parasites under a microscope. Varvar had galloped out of sight with Sergey Mikhailovich Kravchinsky, known universally as Stepniak, and now a much-loved member of English socialist and anarchist groups, advising on the translation of the Russian classics, looking like a great, amiable bear in his thick beard. Tartarinov, in his turn, had been on his way down from his apartment, with a small bundle of essentials, to rush away behind Varvar, when he met the secret police coming up.

"I dissembled," he told them, in his high-pitched voice. "I said to them, we are too late, I am on the same errand, the bird is m-m-m-*flown*. The trail is cold, that is how I put it. We all descended together, and I got into the carriage, and we walked sedately to the corner, and then away flew the great Varvar, like the wind. He took me back to Cherkasov's estate, where he lived, and I disguised myself as a seaman, and worked my way, via Sweden and Holland, to my refuge here. Others were less fortunate." He touched a handkerchief to his eye.

The English socialists were embarrassed to ask certain questions. Three years ago an anonymous article in the *New Review* had described the cold-blooded killing of a certain General Mesentsev. He had been stabbed with a blade, a kitchen knife wrapped in a newspaper, exactly the method subsequently used to assassinate the French president, Carnot, only last year. The article had implied that Stepniak was the killer. His English friends were deeply moved by his writings on the torture, imprisonment, and execution of Russian nihilists and objectors. But they were troubled to imagine the laughing man they took tea with waiting on the pavement, with the knife and the newspaper. They had become increasingly nervous about random acts of violence. Last year, an unknown man had mysteriously blown himself to bits outside the Royal Observatory in Greenwich. The grown-ups remembered the spate of attacks ten years ago—on government offices, *The Times* newspaper, underground stations, railway stations, Scotland Yard, Nelson's Column, London Bridge, the House of Commons, the Tower itself. They understood that suffering caused rebellion. They tried to understand covert, isolated attacks on ordinary people. They tried to inhabit the minds of bombers. It was hard.

"Tell me, Mr. Tartarinov," said Etta Skinner, who was a Quaker and a pacifist, "would you resort to blowing things—and people—up, to help your cause? You yourself, would you do such a thing?"

"We have to be prepared. There is certainly nothing we will not blow up, if it stands in our way. We must look steadily to the *end* and choose the appropriate means. Without flinching."

Etta pulled her shawl tight around her shoulders.

"And you yourself? Could you kill someone in cold blood?"

"I do not know. I have never been faced with the necessity. None of us know of what we may be capable, when we are called."

The group was joined by August Steyning, who wanted to introduce Anselm Stern, who brought greetings from socialists in Germany, several of whom were, as German socialists often were, given the Kaiser's loathing of them, in prison for *lèse-majesté*.

The boys asked themselves, naturally, if they could kill someone. Geraint had been brought up on tales of knights-at-arms and Icelandic warriors, but he did not imagine blood. Charles had disappointed his father by taking no pleasure in foxhunting or shooting. He rather thought he could not. Philip was not really listening to the conversation. He was looking at the juxtaposition of textures in the grass, the flowers, and the silks, and the very rapid colour changes that were taking place as the sky darkened. Browning and vanishing of red, efflorescence and deepening of blues. Tom imagined the thud and suck of a bomb, the flying stone and mortar, and could not quite imagine the crushing or burning of flesh. He thought of his own skull and his own ribs. Bone under skin and tendons. No one was safe.

Basil and Humphry Wellwood had begun to argue about Bimetallism and the Gold Standard. They came across the grass, breathing wrath and rhetoric, pointing decisive fingers into the evening air. Basil was a member of the Gold Standard Defence Association. Humphry supported the Bimetallic League.

That summer of 1895 was the height of the Kaffir Circus boom. Shares in real and fictive seams of gold were feverishly traded. Basil dined with the Randlords and had made a fortune, in gold and in paper. Humphry publicly used the jibe that a mine was a hole in the ground owned by a liar. He also said in public that the financial press took underhand *douceurs* to promote or condemn prospectuses. Basil suspected Humphry of being responsible for pseudonymous articles in satirical journals, mocking Croesus, Midas and the Golden Calf.

He also suspected him of using confidential knowledge from his employment in the Bank of England to attack that institution. In 1893 it was rumoured that the Chief Cashier, Frank May, had made huge, unauthorised advances to his son, a speculative broker. Worse, he had made advances to himself. Through 1893 and 1894 rumours seethed and bubbled. May had made advances to the City Editor of *The Times*. The Bank's governors were genteel amateurs, could not produce a balance-sheet, had no independent auditors. Basil thought he detected Humphry's style in some of the attacks. He was himself not happy with the state of affairs. But he believed the Old Lady should put her affairs privately in order. What Humphry was doing, if he was doing it, was treachery to the Bank, and treachery to Basil, who had put him there. Moreover the writings endangered Basil's own dealings, and even his reputation.

They joined the group in time to hear Tartarinov's remarks about blowing up obstacles. Basil muttered to his brother that he kept odd company for a man in a responsible position. Humphry said with even-toned bad temper that his beliefs were his own business.

"Not if they include condoning explosions and skulduggery. Where your activities are not ludicrous, they are murderous."

"And gold-grubbing and wage-slavery are not murderous? Do you know how goldminers live? Or the poor creatures who stitched your fine shirt, and bled onto it?"

"You will not better their condition by parading along the Strand in your frock-coat and silk hat, selling pamphlets."

Humphry began to speak the speech he made at meetings. He described the three *million* people swarming in the fetid wilderness beyond the Bank, without food or clothes to keep them in health, or beds to sleep in. The Social Democrats had claimed, in their despised pamphlets, that 25 per cent of workers earned too little to subsist without hunger and sickness. Mr. Charles Booth had challenged this figure and done his own meticulous survey of the poor. And he had revised the figure—*upwards, Basil, upwards*. Not 25 per cent but 30 per cent of working families tried to survive on less than £12 0s 0d per month. Think, said Humphry provocatively, tilting his champagne glass at his brother, how much of what you regard as personal necessities can be purchased for £12 0s 0d.

Basil did not feel able to mention the considerable moneys he disbursed to charities.

Humphry went on. He described the furious decline of the state of an injured worker—a man with a crushed hand or foot, or an eye blinded by splinters. In *no time at all* he had no house, no food, his children starved, their clothes were pawned, they slept in the workhouse or in the streets, his wife had to sell herself for bread. Mr. Booth and Mr. Rowntree had looked into schooling. At times of *no special distress,* they found, there were 55,000 children in London schools alone who were too weak from hunger to be expected to learn *anything*. "Fifty-five thousand is a large number. Now, imagine them one by one, child by child . . ."

Basil said that he was not a meeting, to be worked up. He would like to find practical solutions to the problem of poverty. He did not think it would be solved by fomenting revolution, or blowing up public buildings and injuring innocent bystanders.

Humphry said, as he had said before in meetings,

"I once walked through Poplar behind two ragged men. They bent continuously to the pavement, picking up orange peel and apple cores, grape stems and crumbs. They cracked the pits of plums between their teeth for the kernels inside. They picked single undigested oats out of horse dung. Can you imagine?"

Florence Cain, who was lifting a shrimp patty to her lips, dropped it on the grass.

Violet said "Really, Humphry, I see no need to disgust and upset the children."

"Don't you?" said Humphry. "I hope they will remember, and remember again when they are choosing how to live."

The boys and girls listened. Tom tasted the plum kernels and oats in his dry mouth. He knew he would sleep badly. Philip wrinkled his brow and backed away. Those lives held up to horrify were his life. He was one of the many who were poor. And he had left his poor mother, and made his sisters poorer. He felt dully angry—not with Basil, the rich man, but with Humphry, who had made him into an object, had appropriated his hunger.

Charles Wellwood was truly affected. He had a logical mind and a Christian upbringing. In school chapels and Sunday services, chaplains and parsons in speckless surplices repeated Christ's injunction. "Sell all thou hast and give to the poor." Charles thought this was quite clear, and his mentors and family were either foolish or sinful not to understand. The Christian message was levelling and anarchic. Nobody appeared to hear it. Except possibly his uncle Humphry, who was possibly also writhing with discomfort about the creature comforts that lay about him. He thought he might ask Humphry, one of these days, what was to be done. Out of earshot of his parents. His mother was a good and fearful Lutheran, who gave away both time and money, visiting hospitals for the poor, organising bazaars and clothing collections. But she ate from Meissen porcelain with silver spoons. There were hideous inconsistencies.

Dorothy said to Griselda "Let's go away and look at the lanterns in the orchard. You'll have to mind your nice shoes."

"Silly shoes," said Griselda, following her cousin.

Geraint automatically sympathised with anyone who was not shouting. He admired Basil's self-restraint. He loved the sheen on his waistcoat and the sparkle of his studs. There was a mystery in correct dress. There was a mystery in money. He was sick of homespun and home-made. He had secreted a glass of champagne behind the black lacquer puppet-boxes, and thought it was delicious and complex, cold bubbles bursting on his tongue, the mist on the glass, the transparent gold liquid. Some people had this every day. Some people did not sleep under a leaky roof in an old mansion with a cold wind blowing through it, for the sake of mounds of clay and visions of glazed vessels. Money was freedom. Money was aesthetic. Money was Arab stallions, not rough cobs. Money was not being shouted at. (Even though Humphry was shouting at Basil.) Money was freedom. Money was life. Something like that, Geraint thought. The brothers had always stepped back from the brink of a real rift. They sparred, and grumbled, and spoke of something else. No one supposed, when Humphry provocatively mentioned Barney Barnato, that this time would be different.

Barnato was a genial, smooth-talking East Ender, who had made a fortune in the diamond fields of Kimberley. He was a founding member of a club in Angel Court, off Throgmorton Street, which was jokingly known as the Thieves' Kitchen. Barnato had moved from diamonds to gold mines, and was in the process of founding his own bank. He generated a fever of greed and excitement and risk. Basil had invested in his enterprises, and was uneasy about it. An article had appeared in a satirical paper, the *Domino,* over the pseudonym, The March Hare. It represented the Thieves Kitchen as a gambling Hell in which a recognisable Barnato appeared as a demon croupier, raking the stakes into a fiery pit. It compared him also to Bunyan's "Demas (gentleman-like)" who "stood a little off the road against a little hill called Lucre, and called to the pilgrims Ho! turn aside hither, and I will show you a thing. Here is a silver mine and some digging in it for treasure; if you will come, with a little pains you may richly provide for yourself. Christian asked Demas Is not the place dangerous? Hath it not hindered many in their pilgrimage? Demas said Not very dangerous, except to those that are careless. But withal he blushed as he spake."

The March Hare had played elegantly with that giveaway blush. Humphry made the mistake of quoting Bunyan in the argument with Basil. This reminded both of them of The March Hare's accusations. But Humphry quoted further into *Pilgrim's Progress,* passages not in the *Domino* attack. Barnato led people into rashness and loss, said Humphry. "Whether they fell into the pit by looking over the brink thereof, or whether they went down to dig, or whether they were smothered in the bottom by the damps that commonly arrive, of these things I am not certain . . ." People perish like Mr. By-Ends, said Humphry.

Basil said "You know your text very well."

"We all know the *Pilgrim's Progress,* from childhood. And you must know it is apt."

"We do not all have it at our fingertips, to quote in libellous articles, to which we dare not put our name."

The accusation had been made. Humphry could neither bluster, nor deny.

"You cannot deny the argument has weight? That the warnings in it need to be heard?"

"A man should not do one kind of work by day, and stir up mud by night, to stick on his colleagues. And to harm his family," Basil added.

Humphry sneered. He did not feel like sneering—he felt he was himself on the brink of a pit. But the form of the quarrel required him to sneer.

"You cannot have been so foolish as to implicate yourself—or your family—in any of Barnato's gambles?"

"You do not know what you are talking about. You purvey malicious chatter which can *do real harm*—"

"I do what my conscience leads me to do."

"Your conscience is a will o' the wisp, leading into a bog," said Basil, rather cleverly, twisting the metaphor his way.

Violet said "Let us talk about something else. Let us make peace."

Basil said "I think I cannot stay in this gathering any longer. Come, Katharina. It is time to leave."

Katharina said "Very well." She was conscious that it was hard to sweep out when your spare clothes were in your host's bedroom. She said to Charles

"Fetch Griselda."

"She'll not be happy," said Charles, *sotto voce*.

Dorothy and Griselda were fetched back from the orchard. Katharina told Griselda they were going home.

"Why?"

"Never mind. We are going home. Put on your cloak, please."

Griselda stood in her party dress, white, like a pillar of salt. She had not a defiant nature. But she had not a compliant nature, either. Tears brimmed in her eyes. She swayed. Dorothy said

"We have been looking forward to midsummer for ever. We have not had the fire, or the music, or the dancing. How can we have them without Griselda and Charles? How can we have the music without Charles? Their beds are made up . . ."

Basil said to his wife "I really cannot stay."

"Perhaps we might leave the children with their cousins. It is a time that they have been looking forward . . ."

"As you wish. I simply do not want to stay."

"Then we will go," said Katharina, signalling to her maid, putting out her hands to Olive, who had come to see what was happening. She did not feel she could apologise for Basil, indeed, she felt he was justified, but she had no wish to ruin the party. Violet appeared at her side, murmuring sensible things about the later return of the children. The carriage came and was loaded. No one went to wave goodbye. Humphry went and refilled his glass, drained it, and refilled it again. He was full of an electric sense that everything was at risk. For the moment, there was the party. He called for music.

Dorothy said to Griselda

"The *first* thing is to find you a dressing-up dress, like ours."

Griselda was still white and stricken. Violet took her hand to lead her into the nursery. Violet instructed Philip and Phyllis to light the lanterns.

Griselda stood in the nursery and undid the buttons on the pink dress. She stepped out of it, and it subsided, Miss Muffet reduced to a tuffet. She ought to put it on a hanger. She left it where it lay.

Violet said that the Rhine-maiden dress was the thing. It would look pretty on Griselda.

This was an old evening dress of Olive's, cut down by Violet, and securely stitched into a girl-sized fancy dress. It was sea-green pleated silk over a grass-green underskirt, with a gilded girdle. Violet adjusted it. Griselda put up her hands and undid the tight coils of her hair. Violet brushed it out over her shoulders. Griselda had eyes which would normally be called grey, or hazel, which became, when she was dressed in green, suddenly emerald. Dorothy said "You look lovely." Griselda wriggled. "I can move, at least."

When she rejoined the party, everyone clapped. Humphry took another glass of champagne and proposed a toast to Greensleeves. Violet said it was the Rhine-maiden dress, and Anselm Stern began suddenly to sing a version of the opening music of *Rheingold,* bowing over Griselda's hand. He had a clear, high voice.

They danced. The music was a trio: Charles on the fiddle, Geraint on the flute, Tom on a mixture of a small drum and a penny whistle. They played "Greensleeves" for Griselda, and "O du lieber Augustin" for August Steyning and Anselm Stern. It was a developing tradition that the old danced with the young. Humphry whirled Dorothy, her small squarish feet racing to keep time, whilst Prosper Cain revolved calmly with Florence. Olive danced with Julian, who was neat and graceful. August Steyning led out Imogen Fludd, and then danced with her stately mother. Humphry released Dorothy, who was breathless, at the request of Leslie Skinner, who handled her as though she was breakable and hopped over tufts in an odd way. Anselm Stern danced with Griselda, humming to himself, capering like his own puppet prince. The Tartarinovs danced together, moving like one whirligig. Anselm Stern bowed to Dorothy, who backed away, and said she did not want to dance any more.

Violet Grimwith insisted that Philip dance with her. He flushed crimson in the lantern light, and shambled to and fro, staring at his feet, until she released him, and took her turn with Humphry. He backed away into the shrubbery, where he found Dorothy, sitting on a bench in the near-darkness, in a kind of nook in the hedge. Both of them were in search of solitude and felt constrained to be polite. Dorothy said, with Fabian truthfulness, that you could have too much dancing. Philip agreed, with a kind of snort.

They sat in silence. Dorothy said

"No one asked you what you wanted to be."

"Just as well, probably."

"I said I wanted to be a doctor. I didn't know I did, until I said it, that was what was odd. Because I do."

Dorothy believed that if you told someone something truthfully, and honestly, you were giving them something, a kind of respect. Philip said

"Can women be doctors?"

"There are some. It's hard, I think, to get the training." She paused. "People don't think women should work."

Philip wanted to say "My mum works, she has to." It wasn't the right thing to say. He said "My mum works, she has to."

Dorothy gave him her attention.

"And you? What *do* you want? Why did you run away?"

He said, sounding cross because he was desperate, "I want to make *something*. A real pot." He always saw it in the singular. "It might seem odd, like, to run away from the Potteries, to make a pot. But I had to."

"I think you will find a way," said Dorothy, serious in the dark. "I hope we can help."

"Everyone has been very kind."

"That isn't the *point*."

There was a silence. They were aware of each other's unspoken thoughts, the form of Dorothy's apprehensiveness about her newly discovered ambition, and what it might do to her life, the inarticulate shape of Philip's need. It grew darker. They stood up at the same time, and went out of the shrubbery, back to the dancers.

August Steyning and Anselm Stern had relieved the musicians so that they could dance. Steyning took the flute, and Stern the fiddle. They improvised waltzes and Bavarian folk dances. Geraint, daring, asked Florence Cain to dance, and they took a few tentative steps, treading on each other's toes, before Humphry swept her off, and signalled to the players to go faster. He held Florence very close, his hot dry hand hard in the small of her back. She felt him controlling and teaching her body rhythms she hadn't known she knew, swaying and intricate, her face held on his embroidered chest. Her feet were suddenly skilful, as though she was one of Herr Stern's puppets. She caught her breath. Violet applauded. Olive came circling past, dancing with Tom, as they had danced in the nursery, holding both hands at arm's-length, swooping round, and round, and round, Tom's feet scampering on the periphery,

Olive smiling and rotating in the centre, so that when they stopped the whole sky went on hissing in a circle, the planets and constellations, the great wheeling moon, the whipping branches of the trees, the blurry flame of all the lanterns.

After the dancing, when they were all breathless, came the now almost traditional tableaux from *A Midsummer Night's Dream*. August Steyning produced the ass's head said to have been worn by Beerbohm Tree, and Toby Youlgreave reenacted Bottom's enchanted sleep, lying on the rising mound that led to the shrubbery, whilst Dorothy, Phyllis and Florian hovered as Peaseblossom, Moth and Mustardseed. Toby was not in fancy dress apart from the papier-mâché and horse-hair mask he was inside. He lay in Olive's lap, his modern legs in flannels looking both thick and vulnerable. Olive stroked the mask. Toby could feel her heartbeat, somewhere lower in her body. He snuggled up to her, as a child might, empowered by the drama, remembering with regret the earlier performances, in which he had been in a torment of erotic pricking and pulsing. Just there, under the skirt, was the desired place. His hot cheeks were on it. Or not on it, on a smoothly lined boot with ears, which encased his head. He sang damply into it. "The finch, the sparrow and the lark, the plain-song cuckoo grey—" She was trembling a little. She stroked his mask. She stroked his living shoulder-flesh. Humphry advanced in his cloak, and squeezed juice on her eyelids, and she started dramatically away. The enchantment was over. Oberon had won, and claimed the changeling boy.

The other passage they always acted was the end of the play, the blessing of the house. Tom stood at the entrance to the shrubbery, and began

> Now the hungry lion roars
> And the wolf behowls the moon—

He spoke lightly, clearly, in time. Everyone was still.

> And we fairies that do run
> By the triple Hecate's team
> From the presence of the sun
> Following darkness like a dream

Now are frolic; not a mouse
Shall disturb this hallowed house:
I am sent with broom before
To sweep the dust behind the door.

Philip was caught in the common stillness. The lion roared and the wolf howled in his unaccustomed head. Glamour was sprinkled over humans and bushes, and for the first time he saw house and garden as their makers saw them, with love. It was both wild and tame. Magic flickered inside the hedged and walled circumference. Humphry and Olive, fairy king and fairy queen, spoke the golden speeches of blessing on married men and women, on children born and unborn. (Olive had begun to suspect she was pregnant again.) The watchers had contented faces.

Hedda came running in her witch dress. She cried "Fire! Fire!" portentous and gleeful. The audience streamed back towards the lawn.

Philip's lantern, with its painted flames and smoke, and elegant, sinister forms, had been given a place of honour in a herbaceous border, standing on an uneven terra-cotta pillar. As its candle burned down, it had wavered and flared. Then it had fallen into the surrounding vegetation, which was a mixture of ferns, brackens, fennels and poppies, both the great silky Shirley poppies and self-sown wild ones. It was a very English piece of semi-wildness, at the centre of which was a huge alien clump of pampas-grass, including last year's growth, which was dry and burned fiercely, with a crackle. Poppies shrivelled in the heat. There was a smell of roasting fennel. Sparks rose against the curtain of the dark, and tiny floating tissues of blackened leaves and seeds. Violet said she would go for a bucket, but Olive said, no, it wouldn't spread, and it was a magical midsummer bonfire, like the ones made by Stone Age people and mediaeval witches on the Downs.

When it died down, they should leap over the ashes. It was a real Midsummer bale fire, a propitious sign. Lovers should leap together over the ashes. Burned branches—or stems—should be saved. Toby Youlgreave could tell them all about bale fires.

They stood round her, watching the flames catch, hearing the sap hiss in the stems. She smiled recklessly at Prosper Cain, August Steyning, Leslie Skinner, Tartarinov. She said to Toby "There is even fernseed, look."

Fernseed, Toby said, was almost too tiny to be seen. It had the power of making you invisible, if gathered at midsummer. You need to gather it with a forked hazel bough, over a pewter plate. It is said to be fiery in colour, and folklorists think it is the seeds of the burning light of the sun. There is a German story of the hunter who shot at the sun on midsummer day, and collected three hot drops of blood on a white cloth, and this became fernseed. It is said to reveal buried treasure if you throw it in the air. One of the most potent charms there are.

The fire diminished, and became a glow amidst floating grey leaf-ash.

"We must jump," said Olive, charming and beckoning. She took Tom's hand, pulled him forward, ran and leaped with him, laughing, beating the dying sparks from her skirts. Humphry took Griselda's hand, and they jumped together. Soon everyone was running and jumping, anarchists and Etonians, the tall playwright swinging the diminutive Hedda by the waist.

Someone was singing. It was Anselm Stern, leaning against an elder, clear and reedy, Loge's song of the fruit of eternal youth,

> *Die goldenen Äpfel,*
> *In ihrem Garten . . .*

It was magical. Everyone agreed, it was magical.

The Wellwoods disrobed in a lamplit bedroom, the curtains open to the moon and the starry sky. They bickered, in a customary way. Humphry stood in his velvet breeches and embroidered jerkin, leaning against the bedpost, looking at his wife, divested of her wings and robes, standing in bodice and bloomers, still with the honeysuckle and roses in her hair.

"I saw you enchanting those men. You can't help it. The German and the don, the playwright and the soldier from the Museum, you gave them all a look—"

"There's no harm in that. Whereas it really isn't proper to tell little girls like Griselda, that green dresses were for prostitutes, because they were tumbled in the grass."

"Did I do that? I have seriously drunk too much. I shouldn't think Griselda knows what a prostitute is. She doesn't live in reforming circles."

"Well, Dorothy knows, she can hardly help it. So I imagine Griselda does."

"Etta Skinner will be enrolling them to promote pro-prostitute leaflets."

"You have drunk too much."

She was plucking the wilting wired flowers, one by one, from her hair. He stepped out of his clothes and stood naked, slightly aroused, reaching for his nightshirt. This was white cambric, embroidered by Violet with bulrushes and arum lilies. She had made him a nightcap, with gold chrysanthemums. He never wore this, but it hung on the bed-post, and perhaps Violet supposed that he wore it.

"I drank too much because of Basil. He knows, now. He always knew, I suspect, but it wasn't in the open. According to his lights what I wrote was not honest."

Olive said, easily, "You did what you thought right."

"I don't know. I did what I felt I must do. Now, you know, I think I shall have to resign from the Bank. For noble and ignoble reasons, both. I think I must. I don't know how we shall pay Tom's school fees."

"And what will you do?" said Olive, pausing in the act of unbuttoning.

"I shall write. I shall use my pen. I shall write for journals. I shall write books. I can get things done, in the world."

Olive resumed her unbuttoning. She stepped out of her underwear.

"I shall write harder. I am doing better than adequately. I shall work harder."

"You like that idea. The woman as breadwinner."

"I do like it, yes. We both do, I think."

"We make a good partnership. Fortunately."

Olive had put on her nightdress, white and not embroidered by Violet.

"Maybe too good. This is the wrong moment, but I have to tell you. There will be another little open mouth. I am almost sure."

Humphry tilted his beard up, laughed, and embraced his wife. She could feel him erect, under the bulrushes.

"Clever girl. Clever Humphry. How good we are at what we do, isn't it so, creamy Olive?"

"You needn't be smug. You know it has dangers. You know it will be an expense. It won't be so easy for me to win bread."

"We've love enough for another. We'll find a way, we always do."

He stroked her flanks, smiling.

"I expect you're so pleased, because you're still drunk. How shall we manage?"

"Violet will take over. You will rest and write. And I shall change the world, one of these days."

From his moonlit room, leaning on the windowsill, Philip could see their forms, moving across their window-pane, graceful, obscurely occupied. He did not know them. He was outside, peering in. That suited him. He watched their lamp go out, and stood still for some time, looking at the moon. Then he took his towel, and lay down, and pleased himself again, shivering with brief delight in his solitude. Then he was limp, and drifted into sleep.

6

Nutcracker Cottage, like many English things, appeared at first sight to be an instance of pure whimsy, but was in fact more complicated. It was a restored labourer's cottage, with new thatch, and small recessed windows in thick white walls. The front garden had long beds along a flagged path, thick with flowers—hollyhocks, delphiniums, foxgloves and pinks, sweet williams and bachelors' buttons, with a haze of self-sown forget-me-nots. The front door opened directly into the parlour, with walls covered by what William Morris had called "honest white-wash, on which sun and shadow play so pleasantly." The parlour had been made by knocking two rooms into one. At one end was an alcove-study papered with Morris's pink and gold honeysuckle, and containing a plain table. There was little furniture—a heavy dining-table, some heavy, mediaeval-looking chairs, a modern box piano. The plainness was contradicted, to an extent, by a scattering of incongruous pots, on the mantelshelf, in the hearth, on the windowsill. There were lunatic mugs with smiling faces, a piece of fine Italian gold and indigo majolica, decorated with arabesques and maenads, an imposing piece of Sèvres-style Minton, in that violent dark sugar-pink, with Pierrot and Columbine on an oval plaque amongst roses and clematis. Standing in a corner, four feet high, was an object that amazed Philip and was immediately identified by Prosper Cain as a version of the Prometheus Vase shown by Minton at the Paris Exhibition in 1867. Prometheus in fleshy earthenware sprawled on the gleaming turquoise dome of the lid. A green-gold eagle perched on his thigh and belly, and tore at his crimson liver. The tall handles were blond-bearded chained Titans in mail shirts. The body of the vase was painted with fury, a whirling scene of mounted, turbaned oriental hunters and hounds, spearing a hippopotamus at bay, its painted mouth wide open, displaying tusks, molars, and a coral tongue and throat. At the foot of the vase snakes were coiled and intertwined with acanthus leaves. Philip stared. He could not begin to comprehend the glazes, let alone the subject-matter.

The puppet theatre was already set up on the dining-table, which had been displaced to make room for the audience. It was a large, black lacquered box, veiled by black velvet curtains, with imitation onyx pillars and a gilded architrave. The table itself was covered by a velvet pall, underneath which the puppet caskets were stacked.

August Steyning offered everyone tea in the garden. His house-keeper, Mrs. Betts, was arranging sandwiches and an urn on the round stone table on the lawn. The garden was surrounded by trees—a walnut, an ash, hawthorns, sloes—and fenced, with a wicket-gate that led to the wild, a little wood on a rising hillside, in which, Steyning said, he had hidden surprises for children bored by adult talk.

Anselm Stern was wearing a soot-coloured, not-entirely-British Norfolk jacket over his dark drainpipe trousers. He stood with his teacup (Minton, Dresden shape, painted with pansies) and spoke in German to Vasily Tartarinov. He was hesitant in English, but became rapid and passionate in German. Tartarinov, much taller, wearing his working smock, bent over him, speaking softly and insistently. The English formed an impression of conspiratorial secrets, partly because the only words they understood were the names of the recently assassinated French President, Carnot, and the guillotined anarchist, Vaillant, who had thrown a nail-bomb into the Chamber of Deputies. Yet a few moments later, Tartarinov joined authoritatively in a discussion about royal treasuries between Olive Wellwood and Prosper Cain with some knowledgeable observations about the gold and silver objects in the possession of the Tsar. Etta Skinner, wearing a shapeless flowing apple-green tent, took her teacup gingerly and stared critically at the sandwich plate, which had the Three Graces dancing on a floral meadow, surrounded by sugar-pink. August Steyning smiled at her. He said she probably thought he should have earthenware plates, bearing the marks of the fingers that made them, was that not William Morris's diktat? Etta said that was indeed her preference, but everyone had a right to his own taste. August said he liked things absurd and fragile, and that the skill of the painter and gilder was as much skill as that of the moulder. Philip stood, looking sullen, taking in the argument, thinking of his mother. Prosper Cain said he had a weakness for Minton who had designed some bold pieces—including the ceramic pillars—for the museum. Olive Wellwood described how, as a small child, she had made up stories about people on teacups.

"We had some precious ones that only came out on Sunday, and feast days, with girls in pink floating petticoats clinging to craggy ledges with bushes with roots in the air. I gave them all names, and worked out how they got stranded on those stony places, and how they were rescued by eagles, just as the North Wind set about to blow them over . . ."

When Olive spoke, she made an electric silence around her. She was looking lovely, in a tea-gown of cream Liberty lawn, covered with field flowers, cornflowers, poppies and marguerites. She had a straw hat with a scarlet ribbon. When she saw they were all listening, she laughed, and said

"I still do that. People on plates, sipping from glasses they will never empty, plucking roses they never put in their hair. I imagine them escaping, out of their flat circle. I had an idea about two-dimensional beings trying to locate themselves in a three-dimensional world. And then the three-dimensional beings would enter another dimension in just the same way. Catch glimpses, of other life-forms—"

Anselm Stern said something to Tartarinov about Porzellan-sozialismus.

"Ah, yes, m-m-m," said Tartarinov. "Fyodor Dostoevsky's definition of utopian socialism, m-m-m, the pleasant and frangible vista on a teacup. Porcelain socialism."

"Maybe that is all we are," said Humphry, ruefully. "Porcelain socialists, or in the case of Etta, earthenware socialists. When the just society comes, we will have quite other ideas of beauty. I agree with Morris, Sèvres is an abomination. I am shocked at you, August."

"To be frivolous is to be human," said August. "To be pointlessly skilful is to be human, as far as I can see. I hope you would not consider legislating to prevent me from having a Sèvres vessel."

Humphry frowned. "We must hope to make a society where nobody wants anything so absurd."

Etta nodded vehemently. Leslie Skinner said that a new society must produce new patterns, as yet not thought of. Made by craftsmen, not by wage-slaves. Humphry looked round for Philip, but he had sidled away to go back and look at the Prometheus Vase.

The children, most of them, had wandered, as instructed, into the wood. In it they found creatures squatting in hollows, perching on roots, warty toads, scaly lizards, an owl with matted clay feathers and amber glass eyes, a pair of malevolent crows. Tied to their necks and claws were shiny scarlet boxes of sugar flowers, and burnt toffees. They wandered, nibbling, along a rapid little stream, over a wooden bridge. Hedda had brought the shoeful of manikins, from which she would not be separated.

Philip stayed behind. He wanted to stay inside and study the vase, but came out to be given tea and cake, and found something just as interesting. This was a fountain, which was, like the two-faced jars and mugs indoors, and the grotesque creatures in the wood, the work of the Martin Brothers, which appealed to August Steyning's theatrical imagination. It was shaped in a series of thick dishes, glazed in muddy greens and browns and occasionally vivid ceramic emerald slime. The stem of it was intertwined roots, serpents, worms and creeping ivies. The dishes were inhabited and clung to by toads and newts and fish with legs.

Behind the column, blending into it, was a figure of Pan, knob-horned, bearded, squinting and grinning, with water pouring down his smooth torso and into the shaggy hide of his haunches and over his cleft hooves. He brandished his pipes, through which water and green vegetable threads dripped, slowly.

Philip pretended to be absorbed in it, and then was.

Someone put a hand on his shoulder.

"I am told you are an expert on pots."

It was Arthur Dobbin, who had accompanied the Fludd ladies. Philip shrugged and shook his head. He muttered that he come from Five Towns, that was all.

"And what do you make of this monstrous creation?"

Philip said it was clever. It was interesting. It was difficult, he should think. Dobbin gave him a little lecture on the Martin Brothers and their strange craft. He said he had been told Philip wanted to make pots. Was this right? Was this why the fountain intrigued him?

Philip said guardedly that yes, he did want to make pots.

"Not like this, exactly. This is—alive and very clever—but I want— I want—"

He remembered that Dobbin was associated with the aqueous pot at Todefright.

"I work with a potter," Dobbin informed him. "I work with Benedict Fludd, the husband of that lady. I try to help, but he finds me inept. I believe in hand-crafts, but my talent isn't—isn't for working with clay. Mr. Fludd is not a patient man. I do believe he is a genius. I should like to encourage a community of artists—that is my dearest ambition—it would be easier if I were more skilful with my hands."

His tone was a strange mixture of cheerful enthusiasm and stolid gloom. He squeezed Philip's shoulder. Philip said

"I should like to see Mr. Fludd's work. I saw the pot—back at the house—I saw it—I've never seen anything better—"

Dobbin squeezed again, and relaxed.

"Where do you go from here?"

"I dunno. They seem to be thinking about it."

"I might be able to help."

August Steyning came out of his house with a large drum, and beat a tattoo, proclaiming in his high, clear voice, that the show was about to begin.

When they were all indoors, and seated, he stood before the curtained box, and spoke to them.

They were about to see the Sternbild Marionettes, from Munich, perform E.T.A. Hoffmann's *Der Sandmann*. August wanted to offer a word or two about marionettes. Many of those present would know Punch and Judy. He himself had his own Punch and Judy. They, and their German cousin, Kasperl, were honest artists, with ancient traditions. They were glove puppets, and glove puppets were of the earth, earthy. They spring up from below, like underground beings, gnomes or dwarves, they belabour each other with cudgels and go back into the depths, of their booths, of our human consciousness. Marionettes, by contrast, are creatures of the upper air, like elves, like sylphs, who barely touch the ground. They dance in geometric perfection in a world more intense, less hobbledehoy, than our own. Heinrich von Kleist, in a suggestive and mysterious essay, claims daringly that these figures perform more perfectly than human actors. They exhibit the laws of movement; their limbs rise and fall in perfect arcs, according to the laws of physics. They have—unlike human actors—no need to charm, or to exact sympathy. Kleist goes so far as to say that the puppet and God are two points on a circle. The earliest shadow puppets were in fact gods, the presences of gods. "I found in Amsterdam some exemplars of the oriental shadow-figures, the Wayang Golek, whose movements were made by trained priests. Herr Stern and I have studied these marvellous beings, and introduced some refinements into his German figures."

He bowed. His pale hair flipped over his face. He stepped behind the box.

. . .

An illusion is a complicated thing, and an audience is a complicated creature. Both need to be brought from flyaway parts to a smooth, composite whole. The world inside the box, a world made of silk, satin, china mouldings, wires, hinges, painted backcloths, moving lights and musical notes, must come alive with its own laws of movement, its own rules of story. And the watchers, wide-eyed and greedy, distracted and supercilious, preoccupied, uncomfortable, tense, must become one, as a shoal of fishes with huge eyes and flickering fins becomes one, wheeling this way and that in response to messages of hunger, fear or delight. August's flute was heard, and some were ready to listen and some were not. The curtains opened on a child's bedroom. He sat against his pillows. His nurse, in comfortable grey, bustled about him, and her shadow loomed over him on the white wall.

She told the small Nathanael about the Sandman. "He steals the eyes of naughty little children," she said, comfortably, "and feeds them to his own children, who live in a nest on the moon, and open their beaks like owlets."

There was a heavy tap-tap of slow feet ascending the stairs. The backcloth showed the shadow of the turning of the banister, and the rising head and shoulders of the shadow of the old man, hook-nosed, hump-backed, claw-handed, stump, stump, his coat-skirts swinging.

The puppet-child pulled the blankets over his head, and the stage darkened.

In the next scene Nathanael's father, the alchemist, and his horrible visitor, Dr. Copelius, bent over their secret work in a cauldron. The stage was full of shimmering firelight. Nathanael hid, and was discovered. Copelius waved his ebony stick. The father fell dead and crumpled into the flames. Smoke rose.

Happier scenes followed. The grown Nathanael, his friend Lothar, and Lothar's sister Clara, met and embraced in a garden. Clara had spun-gold hair and a blue silk dress. The garden was full of roses and lilies and blue light. They danced to flute music.

Then Nathanael was in his study in Rome, surrounded by tiny books, a globe, an astrolabe, the articulated skeletons of tiny creatures which danced furiously together when the room was empty of humans. Snakes, rats, lizards, cats. They gave the pleasure that the miniature gives, the tiny perfect replica of something that arouses an inexplicable delight in the onlooker. Nathanael in this pleasant place was visited by the Copelius-puppet in disguise, wearing a cloak, a brimmed hat and an eye-shade, carrying a pedlar's tray of glinting glass eyes and tiny tubes which were spyglasses. Nathanael bought a spyglass. When he looked into it, holding it to his eye in his white china fist, a circle of rosy light appeared, moving as he moved his head.

And then, on one side of the stage, there was a female figure in a window, in a rosy halo, and Nathanael at the opposite side, staring through his glass. She wore a plain white silky dress, which the light filled with pink flares and sanguine folds. She moved very little—she raised her little hand to her calm round mouth, to cover a yawn, she turned her head modestly down.

The ball scene, which followed, was a triumph. A musical box played, invisible. Couples whirled across the stage, gliding smoothly in a waltz, capering extravagantly in polka and hornpipe, curtseying and bowing. Nathanael danced with Olimpia. The puppetmaster, with extraordinary skill, created simultaneously the agitated movements of his hero, and the mechanical glide of his beloved. The male puppet rushed busily around the female, ushering, supporting, interrogating, bowing over her hand, trembling with emotion. She repeated her series of restricted gestures, the graceful inclination of the head, the raising of the elegant hand to the pink, round mouth.

The curtains closed, and reopened. Nathanael burst into the room where Olimpia's princely father was quarrelling with Dr. Copelius. They menaced each other with ebony canes. Copelius leaped into the air like a furious frog. They laid hands on Olimpia, who lay still, draped over a satin chair. They grasped her, one by the neck, one by the feet. They tugged. Olimpia trembled, but did not struggle; the representation of her minimal movement was very fine. Suddenly and terribly she came apart in their hands, exploding all over the stage, her head flying upwards with floating hair, her trunk flying sideways, extruding a coil of metal wires. The prince and the doctor menaced each other with an arm and a leg. Hedda clapped her hands, and an infant anarchist began to cry and had to be comforted. Nathanael collapsed in despair.

Lothar and Clara reappeared, lifted him, restored him to life. They went walking on a church tower, against battlements. Nathanael had his arm around Clara's blue waist. And then Nathanael's shadow rose huge in the limelight as the blue sky darkened and began to menace him, independent of him, larger than life. He turned to face it, and began a gyratory, jerky dance of shadow-boxing, like a hanged man on the end of his strings. Lothar took hold of Clara and led her away from the maddened whirl. Nathanael's movements became wilder, jerkier, less and less human, and his shadow clawed at him out of the backcloth. He leaped up, cycling his legs in emptiness, for a moment in flight and weightless, and then plunged over the parapet to his doom.

Everyone applauded. Tom felt winded, as though he had been in a fight, and lost. He looked furtively at Julian, Charles and Geraint, to see how they had responded to the play, and saw that they were all smiling and clapping enthusiastically, so he too clapped. Philip clapped. He had been interested above all by the china faces of the characters. How did you decide, when a character went through so much, and could have only one expression, what that expression should be? He could see how Dr. Copelius could do well with a mouth that both smiled and sneered, but Nathanael was exactly right, serious and not strong, delicately thin and not quite smiling. His mad dance at the end had showed more of the shadow than the solid face. That was clever. And the *difference* between the "real" puppet and Olimpia the puppet-automaton was wonderfully done. To glide with a caricature of the gliding all puppets did—that was something. He clapped.

Dorothy hadn't liked *Cinderella,* and didn't like this. Her head was full of the idea of spiders, and strings, and stings. She thought of the clever fingers controlling the story and its characters, and she thought, only half-consciously, of all such control as dangerous and to-be-resisted. She enjoyed the disintegration of Olimpia. She told herself she couldn't see the point, but she could, and didn't like it.

Griselda did like it. She felt a freedom in the otherworld inside the box, where things were livelier, more beautiful and more terrible than the mundane. Clara's blue silk robe was magical in its tiny pleats where her own Miss Muffet dress was a monstrosity. Olimpia was an excellent parody of, and commentary on, the world of calling-cards and teacups. There were better things in the world than she was being offered. The puppetmaster knew that.

He came out, Anselm Stern, with August Steyning, from behind the velvet box that now concealed his creatures, and bowed to his audience, shyly, without meeting their eyes. Mrs. Betts brought more refreshments. Anselm Stern disappeared again. Griselda looked at Dorothy, who looked cross.

"I'd like to look at the puppets. Shall we?"

"I'm sure he'd be pleased if you did. I don't really want to."

Griselda hesitated.

"Go on," said Dorothy. "He'll be pleased."

Griselda went and stood beside Anselm Stern, who was sorting and winding the wires, and putting the little figures, now inanimate, into their boxes or beds. They stared out of their pale faces with black intense eyes, in no particular direction. Griselda said

"*Ich danke Ihnen, Herr Stern, ich danke Ihnen für eine grosse Freude. Das war ausgezeichnet.*"

The puppetmaster looked up and smiled.

"*Du sprichst Deutsch?*"

"*Meine Mutter ist aus Deutschland. Ich lerne nur, ich kann nicht gut sprechen. Aber die Sprache gefällt mir. Und die Märchen. Ist es möglich,* Der Sandmann *zu lesen?*"

"*Natürlich. Es ist ein Meisterwerk von E. T. A. Hoffmann. Ich schicke dir das Buch, sobald ich nach Hause komme. Deutsch mit Hoffmann zu lernen, das ist etwas.*"

He stood up, and rather formally offered her his hand. Then he took a small notebook and a pencil from his pocket, and asked her to write her name and address in it. Griselda was elated, both because she had had a real conversation in German, and because she was to receive a book of fairytales.

Arthur Dobbin was thinking about Philip. He wanted to suggest to someone that Philip should go back with the Fludds and himself to Purchase House. Benedict Fludd was in need of an assistant. Dobbin had hoped to be that assistant, and had failed. The clay squirmed to shapelessness under his fingers. His kilns aborted. Fludd had told him, when he left for Todefright, not to bother to come back. He wanted to go back. Fludd had genius, and Dobbin wanted to be near it. He wanted to take Philip as a peace-offering. He considered asking Seraphita Fludd, but she was not in the habit of making decisions; she endured, stately and smiling. Her daughters appeared to be like her. Geraint might listen, but Dobbin sensed that Geraint did not like him. And Geraint was afraid of his father's moods, like everyone else. There was also Prosper Cain, who came to Purchase House for advice on ceramics, since Fludd would not go to him. Dobbin found decision-making hard. He watched Philip watch the puppets, intent and thoughtful. Dobbin wanted to be part of a wider group, a fellowship. He looked at Philip with a preliminary love. Lydd in the Romney Marshes was a perfect place for a community, even if Fludd was a difficult figurehead. Dobbin could smooth things. He thought that might be his vocation.

He had come to Lydd by accident. Like many of his kind he had changed his life as a result of a visit to Edward Carpenter at Milthorpe. Carpenter, with his working-class friend George Merrill, lived a life of studied simplicity, cultivating the earth, wearing homespun and homemade sandals, sunbathing and windbathing naked to the elements. Dobbin had heard Carpenter lecture, in Sheffield, on the evils of civilisation, and the way to cure them. Dobbin had responded violently to the anarchist saint's reasonable charisma.

He was the plump son of a doctor's widow. He was dutifully studying medicine, as his father would have wished, and continually failed the medical exams. He imagined, timidly, passionate friendships with fellow students, but was almost pathologically dumb with embarrassment. When he heard Carpenter, he knew that the only answers were a complete change of life, or self-slaughter. He thought he was not imaginative. He had no idea where to look for a new life.

Some of this he managed to mutter to Carpenter, over the convivial beer and smoke after the lecture. Carpenter recognised him for what he was, and invited him to visit Milthorpe.

There he enjoyed George Merrill's salmon pie, and watched the two men quietly knitting. The house was occupied by a shifting population of seekers, idealists and the lost. There were Cambridge men and farmworkers, emancipated women and unsatisfied clerics. Dobbin gave up medicine and got a job in a pharmacy. At Milthorpe one summer he bathed naked in the stream with a gipsyish wanderer called Martin Calvert. Calvert had trained for the priesthood and given it up. He had been a lay member of a religious community in Glamorgan. He had learned to weave at a Crafts community in Norfolk. When Dobbin met him, he had decided to be a potter. To work with the stuff of the earth itself, he said. Dobbin was immediately taken with this idea of an art of the earth. They noticed, blushing and laughing as they bathed, that their members were erect and swaying in the water—"like charmed snakes" Martin laughed, and Dobbin was charmed.

They went on a walking tour, in search of a master of ceramics. They went to the South Kensington Museum and saw vessels made by Benedict Fludd. Martin Calvert said that this man was a master, and they might try to find him. Dobbin saw the perfection of the pots, through Martin's eyes, as Martin described them, the proportions, the subtle glaze, the authority.

They walked south, in search of Fludd. They found him in Purchase House, a partly derelict Elizabethan manor, hidden in woodland in the flat marshy plain beyond Lydd. Martin spoke for both of them, with engaging enthusiasm. Fludd was in an expansive mood, and accepted their offer of help with a firing. The firing was a disaster. Fludd's mood darkened. He cursed them. Dobbin was almost sure that he uttered a formal curse, out of a commination service. The next morning, Martin was not there. He had taken his pack, crept out before dawn and disappeared.

Dobbin stayed where he was, and waited for a message, which did not come. He avoided Benedict Fludd who was now in semi-retreat— and tried to be helpful to Seraphita and her family. He couldn't make pots, but he could cook. He cooked fresh fish, and vegetable pasties, and custard tarts. The Fludd women could not cook, and they were at the time too poor to employ a cook. They accepted him. His heart was broken, but he was too genuinely humble to make much of it.

This continued for six months or so. Fludd mostly pretended not to see Dobbin, and Seraphita gave him small sums of money to do shopping and repairs. One day, he went into the village church. The marshes are spread with imposing churches, built for rich farmers and seafarers before the sea receded and the waterways silted up. This church was dedicated to St. Edburga. To Dobbin's surprise it had a small Burne-Jones window, showing the saint in a graceful white gown, barefoot amongst flowery meadows. Dobbin knelt down under her grass-and-golden light, put his head in his hands, and found himself weeping, with tears spouting between his fingers.

Someone came up behind him, touched him gently, and offered help.

That was how Arthur Dobbin met Frank Mallett, the curate at St. Edburga's. He was thin, blond and skinny, with a pretty little moustache, and a Shakespearean pointed beard. He was a bachelor and lived in a cottage in the village of Puxty. He was not Martin, and not Edward Carpenter. In some ways—shyness, lack of self-respect—he resembled Dobbin, so that he easily abandoned the roles of counsellor or rescuer, and became a friend. They talked of the dream of a community or fellowship, of the new life that could start in the draggled barns and out-houses of Purchase House to the benefit of everyone.

Dobbin decided that the only thing to do was to ask Geraint. Geraint was talking to Julian and Florence Cain about boarding school and les-sons at home. Geraint would have liked to be at Eton or Marlowe, he thought, but was coached in Latin and History by Frank Mallett, and shared a maths tutor with the sons of the local squire. He was not pleased to be interrupted by Dobbin, earnestly asking about Philip.

"Go and ask Mama," he said.

Dobbin looked depressed. Both of them knew she would give no answer. Florence said she had seen Philip's drawings, which were amaz-ingly good. Geraint said if he was that good, they were not doing him a kindness to bury him in the marshes with no one to talk to. Florence said he had been sleeping in a tomb in the basement. Florence's interest roused Geraint. He said that he thought his father might be pleased to think about Philip if Florence's father were to recommend him—send a letter or something. So Prosper Cain was consulted, and he spoke to Seraphita, who smiled pacifically and said she was sure it would all turn out well.

7

Humphry left on Monday morning to resign his post at the Bank of England. He was full of nervous excitement. He told Olive, who was resting in bed, that he would speak to the Secretary and ask for his resignation to take place immediately. He said he should miss the Old Lady. He thought he might stay in Town and see a few people. He would go to the *Yellow Book* evening in the Cromwell Road, and have a word with Harland. He would call on Henley at the *New Review,* and drop in at the *Economist.* And perhaps take the train to Manchester and talk to the *Sunday Chronicle.* Olive remarked mildly that at some point he would need to settle and *actually write* something. And added that she hoped Oscar's arrest with a yellow book under his arm had not finished the magazine.

"It was only a French novel. Not Harland's *Yellow Book.*"

"Nevertheless, they had their windows smashed by a nasty crowd."

Humphry in his city suit bent and kissed his wife. She was never responsive in the early days of pregnancy, another reason for taking a trip elsewhere. He said he would get breakfast sent up.

"And send Tom, if you see him."

"Of course."

In the hall Violet held out his overcoat and his hat, with his briefcase. He wondered if Violet knew Olive was expecting. He knew remarkably little about what the sisters knew about each other. He said "Look after the house, Vi."

"You may be sure I shall."

Tom came up with the breakfast, which Ada had put on a tray. Olive said, as she always said, "Come to my arms my beamish boy," and they both laughed. Tom put the tray on the bedside table, and bent into Olive's embrace. She was flushed. Her hair was a dark pool against the pillows. In earlier days Tom had snuggled into bed with her, and she had told stories of the inch-high warriors who marched through the counterpane's hills and valleys. Later, both he and Dorothy had been invited to curl one at each side, but Dorothy was gawky and the whole thing became less cosy. He had for some time been too big to get into the bed.

But he sat on the edge, and patted the unseen limbs under the covers, and said he was sorry she didn't feel well. She smiled, and said it would pass. She thought she would have a working-in-bed day. Perhaps he would fetch the story books? She had had a few new ideas. Tom kissed her again, slid off the bed and went downstairs.

The story books were kept in a glass-faced cabinet in Olive's study. Each child had a book, and each child had his or her own story. It had begun, of course, with Tom, whose story was the longest. Each story was written in its own book, hand-decorated with stuck-on scraps and coloured patterns. Tom's was inky-blue-black, covered with ferns and brackens, some real, dried and pressed, some cut out of gold and silver paper. Dorothy's was forest-green, covered with nursery scraps of small creatures, hedgehogs, rabbits, mice, blue-tits and frogs. Phyllis's was rose-pink and lacy, with scraps of gauzy-winged fairies in florid dresses, sweet-peas and bluebells, daisies and pansies. Hedda's was striped in purple, green and white, with silhouettes of witches and dragons. Florian's book was only little, a nice warm red, with Father Christmas and a yule log.

The project had begun with Tom's discovery, in his story, of a door into a magic world that appeared and disappeared. The imaginary door was in a real place, in a Todefright cellar full of coal and cobwebs. It was a small, silver trap-door, that would take a child, but not an adult, and it could be seen only by the light of the full moon. It led into an underground world full of tunnels, passages, mines, and strange folk and creatures, benign, maleficent and indifferent. It turned out that Tom's hero, who was sometimes called Tom and sometimes Lancelin, was on an apparently endless quest to find his shadow, which had been stolen by a Rat, when he was in his cradle.

This tale had been so successful, that Olive had invented other doors, in the fabric of their daily reality, for the other children. Dorothy's alter ego, a stalwart child called Peggy, had found a wooden door, with iron bolts, in the root system of the apple tree in the orchard. This proved to be a way into a strange country populated by half-beasts, people and creatures who could change their skins and sizes, sometimes by choice and sometimes by accident, so that you might find that you were a human child one moment, and a hedgehog the next, hiding in dead leaves. There were wolves in this land, and wild boars. Phyllis's character, a princess who had been changed for a little servant girl, found a crack in a teapot she was being made to wash, in the middle of a picture of a pretty glade, in which ladies danced, with flutes and tambourines. You could make yourself small enough to slip through the crack by chewing a certain kind of Chinese tealeaf, known as gunpowder, which came in hard little pellets and unrolled into leaf shapes in hot water. In Phyllis's story there were princes and princesses all waiting in castles, frozen or sleeping, for the redeemer to find the clue, and release them. Hedda's way in was inside the grandfather clock in the dining-hall. You could see the gateway whilst the clock was striking midnight. It led to a world of witches, wizards, woods, cellars and potions, with children roosting in cages like chickens in need of setting free, and wondrous contests in shape-shifting between magical dwarfs and wizards, black ladies and blue gnomes. Florian's story had hardly begun. It was possible his door was in the chimney, where he claimed to have seen a hefty scarlet figure with a sack. It was also possible that he would grow out of that, and make another world. In the interim, his story was peopled by his stuffed toys, a bear called Furry, a white cat called Snowy, and a stripy knitted snake called Ringary. In the world through the portal they were figures of power, sleek and glossy, Bear, Cat and Snake.

Tom looked into his book. The story had advanced a page or two. A group of seekers were descending a dark tunnel—they were the shadowless hero, a gold lizard the size of a terrier with garnet eyes, and a transparent, jellylike formless being who poured along the ground and constantly changed shape. A new figure had appeared, who ran in front of them, leaving soft footprints in the dust. There was some question as to whether it was the lost shadow, who had taken on substance. Or it might be another seeker, a friend or an enemy or simply a stranger, in the dark.

The stories in the books were, in their nature, endless. They were like segmented worms, with hooks and eyes to fit onto the next moving and coiling section. Every closure of plot had to contain a new beginning. There were tributary plots, that joined the mainstream again, further on, further in. Olive plundered the children's stories sometimes, for publishable situations, or people, or settings, but everyone understood that the magic persisted because it was hidden, because it was a shared secret.

All of them, from Florian to Olive herself, walked about the house and garden, the shrubbery and the orchard, the stables and the wood, with an awareness that things had invisible as well as visible forms, including the solid kitchen and nursery walls, which concealed stone towers and silken bowers. They knew that rabbit warrens opened into underground lanes to the land of the dead, and that spider-webs could become fetters as strong as steel, and that myriads of transparent creatures danced at the edge of the meadows, and hung and chattered like bats in the branches, only *just* invisible, only *just* inaudible. Any juice of any fruit or flower might be the lotion that, squeezed on eyelids, touched to tongue or ears, would give the watcher or listener a way in, a power of inhuman sensing. Any bent twig might be a message or a sign. The seen and the unseen world were interlocked and super-imposed. You could trip out of one and into the other at any moment.

Tom delivered the heap of books to his mother in her nest of quilt and counterpane. She asked him if he had peeped. Of course, said Tom, of course he had peeped.

"Who do you think is running in front of them?"

They made the plot between them, some of the time.

"A lost boy. A boy who fell in by accident, down one of the shafts?"

Olive considered. "Friend or enemy?"

Tom was not sure. He said he thought the intruder was not sure. He could turn out to be either. He still thought he could get out quickly, Tom told his mother, he hadn't learned how hard it was to get out.

"I'll work on it," said Olive. "Now go and do your Latin."

Olive was sometimes frightened by the relentlessly busy inventiveness of her brain. It was good and consoling that it earned money, real bankable cheques in real envelopes. That anchored it in the real world. And the real world sprouted stories wherever she looked at it. Benedict Fludd's watery pot on the turn of the stair, for instance. She looked casually at the translucent tadpoles and had invented a whole water-world of swimming water-nymphs threatened by a huge water-snake, or maybe by that old terror, Jenny Greenteeth, lurking in the weeds and sifting them with her crooked fingers, before she reached the landing.

Yesterday's events had also transmuted themselves into story-matter, almost as fast as they had happened. She had watched Anselm Stern's version of E. T. A. Hoffmann's tale with glee—her response to any performance, any work of art, was the desire to make another, to make her own. She was in *that* world, watching, not in flat dailiness. The gliding movement of the puppets, the glitter of the limelight on their silk organza dresses, the half-visible strings, like spider-silk, had transmuted into other figures in other lights in her head, almost before they had performed their own sequence of movements. Suppose a puppet managed to free itself and come to life, and strut and nod amongst clumsy humans, with their thick, fleshy fingers? It wouldn't be like Pinocchio; the creature would have no desire to be a "real child," just a desire for independent life. For a moment, at the terrible point when Olimpia disintegrated into a whirl of severed limbs, Olive had done Anselm Stern the justice of simply responding to his art, of feeling simple shock. But then she was away again. Supposing a puppet become a real creature met a doll who refused to be real, who was inert, waxy, complacent? There were dolls who somehow had souls—or characters, or personalities anyway—and there were dolls who resolutely refused to come into being, who simpered and sat like suet. Dorothy didn't like dolls. Phyllis had a whole cot full of both kinds, the living and the lifeless. Suppose the newly freed puppet walked into a nursery and was attacked by a flannelly array of simulacra—of course, she had got this idea from Olimpia, in the first place, how *clever* Hoffmann was—you could make a truly eerie tale for children, but you must be careful, she knew, not to overstep some limit of the bearable. She often came close to overstepping it. Indeed, her success as a children's writer had begun with *The Shrubbery,* which did come very close to the impermissible, indeed, according to some percipient critics, crossed the boundary. But children liked to glimpse the unbearable, in manageable doses. She herself had had a book, as a child, Hans Andersen's *Tales.* Her mother had read to her, "The Princess and the Pea," "Thumbelina." She had been filled with horror for the inch-high girl, in the care of the stupid kindly mouse, who was promised to a stout, blind, black Mole who would take her underground to bourgeois comfort where she would never again see the light of day. It was probable, Olive thought, that the whole complicated wanderings of Tom underground had started with her own childish fear of Thumbelina's mole-tunnel.

She spread honey on her toast, and sipped her tea. Tom had put a little posy of wild flowers on the breakfast tray, heartsease and bluebells, and a few fronds of fern. She felt a movement of nausea as she bit into the toast, which the sugar of the honey alleviated. An unbidden image of the unborn child inside her came into her mind, something coiled in a caul and attached, like a puppet, by a long thread to her own life. She tried very hard to feel neither hope nor fear for the unborn. If she thought of them, it was more in terms of the waxy stillborn, with their closed faces, than in terms of a potential Tom or Hedda. She feared for them, and their presence disturbed her peace. Also, she cared for them, she took care. She bit into the honey and butter and bread, nourishing herself and the blind life she had not exactly invited to settle in her. She turned her mind to the shadowy fugitive underground.

Olive Grimwith was a miner's daughter. Her father, Peter Grimwith, had been a buttie, hacking away at the coal-face in his stall, under the very ground she walked over, to get to school, or the Goldthorpe shop. Her mother was Lucy, who had been born Lucy Appledore, a draper's daughter, in Leeds. Lucy was a small, thin, exhausted creature, who hoped to be a schoolteacher, and knew things like the meaning of the name Lucy, which was "light." There were five children, Edward, Olive, Petey, Violet and Dora, who had been an unexpected baby, and had died with her mother, of pneumonia, when Olive was twelve. Edward and Petey had both gone down the mine at the age of fourteen. Olive Wellwood told no stories about Goldthorpe, or the Gullfoss mine. She had packed away the slag-heaps and winding-gear, the little house in Morton Row, with its dark uninhabited parlour, its animated kitchen and pocket-sized garden, the ever-present stink of the ash pits across the yards, and the grime that floated onto the strips of lace curtain. She had packed it away in what she saw in her mind as a roped parcel, in oiled silk, with red wax seals on the knots, which a woman like and unlike herself carried perpetually over a windswept moor, sometimes on her head, sometimes held before her on two arms, like the cushion on which the regalia lie at coronations. This vision was not a story. The woman never arrived, and the parcel was never opened. The weather was grey and the air was turbulent. When Olive Wellwood found her mind heading in that direction, she was able to move imaginary points on an imaginary rail and shunt her mind away from "there" and back to Todefright, with its penumbra of wild woods and flying elementals.

Olive Grimwith persisted in Olive Wellwood, not least because of the steady presence of Violet Grimwith, who had been little at the time of the disasters, and nevertheless felt the pull of roots, wanted to remember *things,* would say suddenly "Do you remember bread and dripping on Sunday? Do you remember greasing pit boots?"

It was Olive who, when she could not avoid it, could remember Peter and Petey, Lucy and Dora. Or so Olive thought.

The storyteller was not Lucy, who taught them their letters, and tried to teach them manners. It was Peter, who came home for his tea, his clothes stiff and black with coal dust, his eyes and lips red in his coal-black face, his fingernails broken and engrained with jet. He took Olive on his knee, after his bath, and told her tales of the world underground. He told her about the living creatures down there, the soft-nosed ponies who trundled tubs of coal along the tunnels, the mice and rats who whisked in and out of the ponies' nosebags, ate the miners' snap and chewed their candles, if they were not careful. He told her about the bright yellow canaries, trembling and hopping in their cages. They were a living alarm-system. If they suddenly fell dead, it was a signal of the approach of one of the invisible terrors, choke damp, white damp, fire damp. These were gases released from the deep slumber of the coal by the hammers and pickaxes of the miners, or by the collapse of a section of pit-props. For the coal, Peter Grimwith told his daughter, had once been living forests—forests of ferns as high as trees and brackens as fat as barrels and curling things that were scaly like snakes. And they were sunk and compacted into ancient mud. You could find the ghost of a leaf, millions of years old, or the form of a thirty-foot dragonfly, or the footprint of a monstrous lizard. Most wonderful was the idea that their vegetable death had only been suspended. The three damps were the exhalations of the gases of their interrupted decay. He told her the names of the dead plants which now smouldered and flared in their kitchen grate. Lepidodendron, sigillaria. He told her the scientific names of the gases that were the "damps." Carbon dioxide, which smothered you fast. Carbon monoxide, which crept up on you, peacefully so to speak, smelling of violets and other sweet flowers. And methane, "which is what comes out of the back end of cows, Olive," which was the fire damp. There were tales that rats sneaking off with smouldering candles had sparked huge explosions. "Perhaps you could put a match to a cow, Olive," said Peter, and Lucy said "Hold your tongue, that's not a nice thing to tell a girl."

There were stories too of invisible inhabitants of the mines—beings known as knockers who could be heard tapping, a creature called Bluecap, who was clothed in a flaring light-blue flame, and sometimes helped to push the tubs, a mischievous bogle-thing, called Cutty Soams, who delighted in cutting the soams, or traces, by which the ponies and the workers pulled the tubs and trams. You did well to put out a ha'penny for them, if you knew they were there. His tales of kobolds were as practical and as vivid as his tales of rats and canaries.

He brought home in his pocket, from time to time, a coal with a fernleaf apparently incised in it. And twice he brought one of the "coalballs" for which the Gullfoss mine was famous. A coal-ball is a preserved knot of once-living things, compacted together, leaves, stems, twigs, seed-pods, flowers and sometimes even seeds, millions of years old. Olive Wellwood still had these petrified lumps, but she showed them to no one.

Edward, a big boy like his father, had gone cheerfully down the mine, or so Olive thought, if she thought about it, for she had never "known" Edward, who was too big to notice her. Petey, on the other hand. Petey. He was a year older than she was, and took after the mother, rather than the father, a slight little person, though wiry, with his mother's fine mouse hair. (Olive's raven abundance came directly from Peter.) He was a boy who wrote poems, and knew the names of flowers and butterflies, and said to Olive that he knew he must go down the mine, but it was not what he wanted. What? Olive whispered into his ear, in the dark, in bed, where they clutched each other for warmth and comfort. What do you want? And Petey said, it's hardly worth me thinking to want anything, since I can't have it. And Olive said, *I* would think, if I was a boy. And Petey said, isna that t'same thing, really? Tha knaws tha mun be a girl, an I knaw I mun go down t'pit.

Petey went down the pit, as he must, and because he was little, was set to watch a gate, as a trapper. The tunnels' ventilation, and the containment of fire damp, depended on a series of low gates that were operated by small boys, squatting in holes scooped out of the pit-wall, holding a string, which they pulled, to let the trucks pass. They sat for twelve-hour shifts in the dark, under the low roof, waiting for the sound of approaching trucks. Petey told no one how frightened he was both of the dark, and of the shifting narrowness of his hole, with miles of earth, and coal, and stone pressing on it, and somehow on him. But the night before he went down the first time he gripped Olive tightly and said "What if I canna? What if I darena?"

And Olive had an imagination of herself, asked to go down there, and of how she would begin to scream and flail in the descending cage, howling to return to the surface. For she could not imagine bending her neck under that threshold, creeping willingly into that dark. They held each other and trembled, and there were tears on both faces, hot and wet.

When he came up, the first time, Petey said, it wer non sa bad. But the next morning, Olive could feel him rigid with terror.

He got used to it. He had been tugging his string in the dark just under a year, when far above, the bed of the River Gull trembled, quaked and boiled with bubbles, which were observed by an interested farmhand. This man saw, to his amazement, the river begin to pour away from both sides, through a gaping chasm under its banks. He began to run. He understood that the earth between the bed of the river and the roof of the mine had given way, and water was pouring into the workings. He ran two miles to the pithead, and men went down with messages, and others came back, who had managed to sidestep the rolling torrent, which was filling up tunnels and shafts, cutting off communications with outlying passages.

Petey's little hole filled up. Olive did not know if it filled up fast or slowly, if he had tried to escape, or been immediately overwhelmed. Bodies of boys—six of them, and seven men—were sucked along and spat out by the coil of filthy black water. A rescuer fell into an unexpected pothole and was also drowned.

There was a service in the Chapel and a collection for a memorial stone near the site of the disaster. Peter Grimwith seemed smaller. He walked hunched, looking at the ground. He took Olive on his knee still, after tea—she was almost too big—but he had little to say, no stories, no pocketed secrets. Lucy did not weep in front of the other children. She was pregnant, she coughed perpetually, the rims of her eyes were scrubbed and red. She too, despite her swollen belly, seemed to be shrinking.

Six months later the whole village was shaken by a series of booms and cracking sounds. They knew what it meant, they lived in dread of it. Everyone left what he or she was doing—a pie half-covered, a boot half-cleaned, the newspaper squares torn up for the ash pits—and went quickly, a few running, most walking fast, very fast, to the head of the shaft, where flames and cinders and hot grit were flying in the evening air. Men came up, and tried to say where the damage was, where men must be trapped. Olive stood holding Violet's hand, because Violet had grasped her. She would have preferred to have no human contact, *not to be,* to be in abeyance altogether. Not knowing was intolerable. He was alive, he would come up, they would cling to him and weep. He was dead. They would bring up his body. Or not, if it was consumed, or buried too deep in the treacherous carbon swamp.

They never found him, nor any of those who had been working with him. The waiting was as long, and as bad, as could be imagined.

Once Olive woke at night with the idea that Peter and his mates were still alive down there, in a pocket of air behind palaces of rubble, waiting for rescue that couldn't, and didn't, reach them.

These two stories were folded away in the oiled, roped package. The knots were sealed. The woman walked across the moor, in the wind, with the closed, calm parcel, containing the obscene things.

When Lucy took to her bed and began to die, with the new baby who refused meekly to take milk, or begin to live, Olive stood by her bed, still as a stone. Violet was wonderful. She made beef tea, having begged the beef from the neighbours, she spooned it into Lucy's cracked lips, she wiped her face, she stroked her hands, she bent over and pulled back the red eyelids, peering under and in. Lucy's sister, Ada, came from Batly and urged Lucy to live. Auntie Ada and Violet were not friendly to Olive. Stir your stumps, cried Ada. Violet whimpered, and shook the dying woman, compulsively. The person who saw how it was with Olive was Lucy herself, who said in her own mind, struggling less and less often to consciousness, she's taken too much, she's all done in. But she found she couldn't lift her hand to beckon to Olive, or get her mouth to form words. Her last real emotion was anxiety over Olive's stony stare. Don't be hard, she wanted to say, and couldn't. Well, if I can't, I can't, she said to herself, and closed her eyes for ever.

Auntie Ada's husband, George Mablethorpe, had had an accident in the pit five years earlier. His hip had been crushed by a fall of rock. He sat at home and mended things—boots and shoes, broken china with invisible rivets. There was a son, Joe, who worked down the pit and brought home some of his wages, but the family's income, and standing, were precarious. Ada was a dressmaker. She sewed pit clothes in heavy cloth, servants' uniforms, skirts and petticoats. She set Violet, who was good with a needle, to helping her and learning her craft. Olive was good with books, but not with a needle. She had won a scholarship to the high school, and Peter had been proud of her. Auntie Ada let her go on going to school for a year. When she came home at teatime she worked. She scrubbed the wooden closet seat. She knelt on the cement floor to scrub it and she scrubbed the floor, in its stink. She cleaned boots, she peeled potatoes, she polished knives, she scrubbed the front doorstep. Auntie Ada decided she couldn't be kept in clean pinafores and tidy boots and took her away from school. She didn't like Olive. She decided to send her into Service. That way, she would not need feeding, and could send back some of her earnings.

Olive went first to be a housemaid for the owner of a vegetable shop in Doncaster. She wore a black stuff uniform and a heavy pinafore, and an ungainly starched cap like a helmet. Her legs were too thin for the black cotton stockings which hung in folds round her ankles. She was an object of disgust to herself, and her employer felt her presence as baleful. She was sent back to Auntie Ada, and said not to give satisfaction. Auntie Ada bent her over her own sharp knees and beat her with a hairbrush.

She was sent off again, after consultation with the minister at the Chapel, to be maid of all work to two maiden lady schoolteachers in Conisborough. The Misses Bean had a bookcase full of books, and were genteel. Olive had to pretend to be two maids—a scullery maid enveloped in a mob cap and a thick apron, a parlour maid who brought tea in a starched lacy crown and a frilly apron, with a bib. She hated these clothes. When she looked at her face in the mirror in the morning she imagined a lady, in a ball-gown and a coronet sort of thing. She was growing prettier, and could see it.

If Olive had been nicer, or more pliable, or more pathetic, the Misses Bean would have discovered that she had been made to give up a scholarship, and might even have lent her some books, or sent her out to lectures or evening classes. But she continued to look haughty and baleful, and they continued timidly to criticise her ironing, or darning, or silver-polishing. There was a day of hideous embarrassment for all three of them when Olive came into the breakfast-room and said she would have to give notice, as she believed she was dying.

"Dying of what?" asked Miss Hesther Bean.

"Of an issue of blood," said Olive, quoting the Bible, cramped by her first period, bleeding profusely, completely uninformed. The Misses Bean could not bring themselves to explain. They sent for next-door's Cook, who explained, roughly, not kindly, and showed Olive how to cut up, and wash, strips of old sheets.

She told herself stories. She had told stories to Violet, when they were little. "There was a green cow and it *would not* go into its shed, no matter how hard it got hit. It *would not,* because it didn't want to, and they got dogs to bark at it, and they got ropes to pull it, and, and, and, they put hay for it in its shed, but it *would not.*"

"Why wouldn't it, Olive?"

"I dunno," said Olive, whose vision of the cow's extremity was clear, but who saw no reasonable outcome.

She lived in two stories when she was in Service. One was conventional enough. There was once a noble lady who had been stolen from, or had to flee, her true home, and was living in disguise, in hiding, as a kitchen maid. Riddling the ashes, after all, was what such heroines had to do, they were all smeared and bleared with ash on the path to their epiphany in ball dress and jewelled slippers. There was need of a prince, and she looked for him, as maidens did in folk-magic, swimming out of the darkness behind her candlelit face in the mirror (she was going to be beautiful, that was something, the ugly duckling was qualified to be a swan, the ash-girl to be a bride). Only there was no substance to the shadow. There were words. Handsome, dark, dangerous, wild (she read romances). But no solidity. He was faceless. And worse, he did nothing, so there was no story, only the significant ash-riddling. Once she found a real little jewelled pin in the ashes, hot gold, with tiny blue stones and enamelled leaves. She took it out, and hid it behind a brick in the wall of the backyard. It was a talisman. But the magic it would work was not yet brewed.

The other story was, as storytelling, more satisfactory. Once (only once) Peter and Lucy had taken their children by train to the seaside, to Filey, where they had taken lodgings for a week, and played and paddled in the great sandy bay. Filey had been *clean*. The sea had been vast. You went down a steep hill, and into a tunnel under the promenade and the road, and you came out on the blowing soft sand, beyond which was the hard, wet sand, with its rippled surface and its pools of salt water. She began to tell herself a story of a boy, Peter Piper, imprisoned in an orphanage, a boy alone in the world, with no one to love, and no one who loved him. And this boy formed a plan, which he carried out with meticulous patience, to escape at night and *walk* to the sea, away from the soot and the sludge and the sulphur. This tale was as precise in the telling as the other was loose and vague. Everything had to be imagined, and worked through—the staircase in the orphanage, the bolt on the inner door of it, the great locks on the outer, the stolen key that released them, the oil that silenced the grinding of the mechanism.

Step by step, literally, as Olive Grimwith performed her household tasks, Peter Piper marched into liberty, along long city roads with lurking beggars and coal-delivery men, onto a highway, through villages (not real villages, she knew the names of none, but villages with greens, and ducks, and geese, and shops with jangling bells on springs over the door). Peter developed blisters, and Olive limped across the Beans' kitchen. Peter was hungry, and turned aside into a field, where a kindly shepherd gave him a sandwich—no—gave him cheese, and an apple— delicious, crumbly cheese and a *hard, sweet* apple—her mouth watered.

There were pursuers, of course—the authorities, the master to whom Peter was to be apprenticed—Peter lay hidden in a ditch and saw their boots go past—

It was in fact Violet who suggested, one Christmas, when Olive was on a brief visit to Auntie Ada and her family, that perhaps they should run away.

Violet was covered with bruises which Olive had only half-noticed. Her mind on Peter Piper, and the road to the seashore, she asked Violet where they should run to.

"London, I should think," said Violet. "We could get work of some sort there. I've saved up enough for one train ticket. We'll have to take the money for the other out of her purse."

And so they came to be in the audience of Humphry Wellwood's English Literature lectures, dressed in blouses, skirts and hats made by Violet, who had found a good job in a dressmaking shop, and had found work for Olive, too, in plain-sewing, nothing fancy.

Violet had thought this might be a good place to find, as she put it to herself, a step up and out.

Olive found Humphry, and the rhythms of Shakespeare and Swift, Milton and Bunyan, which she thought she had craved all her life without knowing it.

They stepped up, and out.

Whilst Olive wrote her stories, Violet instructed the smaller children on the lawn. It was a hot, bright day. The servants were finishing clearing the end of the party. Violet was settled in a sagging wicker armchair, her workbasket beside her, darning socks, pulled neatly over a wooden mushroom, which had been painted like a fly-agaric, scarlet with white warts. Phyllis, Hedda and Florian were doing "nature study" with a collection of flowers and leaves they had collected. Tom and Dorothy, Griselda and Charles, were lying around on the lawn, half-reading, half-listening, half-making desultory conversation. Tom was supposed to be doing his Latin. Robin slumbered under a sunshade in his perambulator. A cuckoo called, from the orchard. Violet told them to listen.

"In June he changed tune," she said.

"Cuck," cried the cuckoo abbreviated.

Violet told about cuckoos.

"They make no nests. They borrow. They lay their eggs secretly in other birds' nests, among the other eggs. The mother cuckoo picks the foster mother carefully. She lays her eggs when the foster mother is fetching food. And the foster mother—a willow-warbler, maybe, a bunting perhaps, feeds the stranger fledgling as though it was her own, even when it grows much larger than she is, even when it is almost too large for the nest, it cries for food, and she answers . . ."

"What happens to her real children?" asked Hedda.

"Maybe they leave early," said Violet vaguely.

"It pushes them out," said Dorothy. "You know it does. Barnet the gamekeeper showed me. It pushes the eggs out, and they go splat on the ground, and it pushes the fledglings out. It goes round and round and shoves with its shoulders, and tips them out. I've seen them on the ground. And the parents go on feeding it. Why don't they know it isn't theirs?"

"It's surprising what parents don't know," said Violet. "It's surprising how many creatures don't know their real parents. Just like Hans Andersen's ugly duckling, which was really a swan. Mother Nature means the baby cuckoo to survive and fly away with the other cuckoos to Africa. She takes care of it."

"She doesn't take care of the willow-warblers," said Dorothy. "If I were the willow-warbler, I'd let it starve."

"No you wouldn't," said Violet. "You'd do what comes naturally, which is feed what's crying out for food. It's not so easy to decide who are your own real children."

"What do you mean?" said Dorothy, sitting up.

"Nothing," said Violet, retreating. Then, almost *sotto voce,* she said to the mushroom-stocking "Who is a child's real mother? The one who feeds it, and cleans it, and knows its little ways, or the one who leaves it in the nest to do as best it can . . ."

Dorothy could hear Violet's thoughts, as she had heard Philip's. This was not the first time Violet had spoken this way. She said, turning to science for help,

"It's just natural instinct. For the cuckoos, in their way, and the willow-warblers in theirs."

"It's the kindness at the heart of things," said Violet. She stabbed at the sock with a needle. Charles said, in an audible undertone,

"Lots of people aren't really their parents' children, don't really know who their real parents are, you hear about it all the time—"

"You shouldn't be listening to such things," said Violet, with a return of force. "And folk shouldn't be telling you."

"I can't help having ears," said Charles.

"Then you'd better wash them," said Violet.

Hedda took up her shoe-dolls. "All these have no father or mother, only a shoe. They are *mine* to look after."

Something had become very uncomfortable. Tom put his nose in his Latin. Griselda proposed to Dorothy that they go for a walk in the woods. Charles said he would come, and Tom.

"Cuck," said the cuckoo in the wood. "Cuck, cuck, cuck."

"It's funny," said Dorothy, "how it knows it's a cuckoo when it comes to flying to Africa, it goes with the cuckoos. I wonder what it thinks it is, when it goes. It can't *see* itself."

They went into the woods, two by two, two boys, followed by two girls, all four clothed in shabby, serviceable Todefright clothes in which trees could be climbed, and brooks could be forded. They were going to the Tree House, which was a secret, hidden place, which very few people knew about or could find. It was woven into the tentlike lower branches of a Scots pine, which was the central roof-tree, stitched together with cord and strings, thatched with heather and dead bracken, disguised with more random branches. It had two rooms, with spy-hole windows. It was possible to lie out on its roof, amongst the arms of the tree, and there were couches of heather, and wooden box tables inside. It was Tom's favourite place on earth. Inside, and wholly hidden away, he was himself. He thought of the Tree House as his place, although the designing intelligence, the solidity of the construction, were Dorothy's. Dorothy liked to bring things to it, to study them—small skulls, and unusual plant forms. She also liked to go into it with Griselda and talk intensely for hours. Tom assumed that they talked, for he had the grace not to go with them. And because he left them together, they in turn left him his long periods of solitude, when the house was his hiding-place. There was always the problem of Phyllis, who insisted on tagging along, if she noticed they were going there, and was unwelcome both because she tried to "play house" in it, with mummies and daddies, and because Tom, Dorothy and Griselda knew that she was the weak spot in their tissue of silence. She might tell, she might enjoy telling, and had to be both threatened and bribed.

Charles was allowed to come because he was not *very* interested in tree houses—he was urban by nature—but suitably admiring of the constructive skills that had gone into the building. Tom had wondered whether Philip would like the house. He thought he might, since he had been found in a hidey-hole. But Philip had already gone to the marshes in the carriage with the Fludds and Dobbin. Tom had also wondered whether to show it to Julian. Julian might not see how special it was. And Dorothy might not like Julian's dominating presence. It was altogether too early to have views about Julian.

They sat down on the heather couches, which were covered with blankets, and Tom offered them all apples and toffees, from a store he kept in a box.

"What did you mean," Dorothy asked Charles, "when you said lots of people aren't their parents' children?"

Griselda said that her friend Clementine Burt was always being teased because she didn't look anything like her father, and then people pointed out that she *did* look very like Lady Agnes Blofeld, and her mother had said that was natural, because they had an ancestor in common. But her brother Martin had overheard their parents talking, and had told Clementine he was sure her father *was* Lord Blofeld. Charles elaborated. Lord Blofeld and Clementine's mother had to have adjacent rooms at big country-house parties. It was well known by everyone. Dorothy asked if Clementine was very upset. Griselda said she wasn't sure. She didn't want to talk about it. Dorothy was distracted by wondering whether Clementine was more Griselda's friend than she was. Griselda added that Clementine had said she was sure she wasn't the only one. Charles said Agnes Blofeld was quite put out, because Clementine was prettier and nicer than she was, the same sort of girl, but much more attractive. Tom did not like talk about whether people were attractive. He said, musing,

"If you found out your parents weren't your parents, would you be a different person?"

"I think so," said Griselda. Dorothy said it went back to what Auntie Violet had said, about your real mother being the one who took care of you and fed you and so on. She had always known that Violet believed, in some way, that she *was* their real mother. She saw why, but she did not think of herself, or want to think of herself, as Violet's daughter.

Griselda said that Clementine had heard her parents shouting at each other, and her mother weeping.

Tom said everyone's parents shouted at each other, didn't they? Dorothy remembered being with Tom on the landing, overhearing a violent parental argument. "I have always looked after your children," one had yelled, and the other had said, "And I may say the same." Tom and Dorothy both knew that parents in rage referred to *the* children as "your children." It was never pleasant for children to overhear such things, it could not be, they had become objects, bones of contention.

Sometimes they played a game of "Who would you like for parents if you didn't have your real ones?"

You wouldn't want to play that game if you were Clementine.

Tom thought of his life, the woods, the garden, the books, the human voices, the presences of family in and out of the house, the wonderful movement from comfort to freedom and back.

"We are a happy family," he said, vaguely and gently. "Have a bull's-eye? Or a pink fizz?"

Charles asked Dorothy if she was really going to be a doctor, or was it just something she had said?

"I just said it, and saw it was true."

"I should like to do something like that. I don't know if I could face all the mess of people being sick, let alone having to carve them up. But I think one should try to do something to make things better. Your father understands that. Mine doesn't."

THE SHRUBBERY

THERE WAS ONCE A MOTHER, *whose husband had gone on a long voyage, and had neither come back, nor sent any news, for a long time. Consequently, the family had fallen upon hard times, though they lived in a pleasant house in the country, with gardens and orchards. Mothers in stories, in general, are of two kinds. There are mothers who are warm, and devoted, and self-sacrificing, and resourceful and endlessly good-tempered and loving. Then there are the other kind, who are often not mothers, but only stepmothers, who are unkind, and proud, and love some children (their own) better than others, and treat children like kitchen-servants, and will not let them play, or dream. If you had to choose, the mother in this story is a good mother, not a bad stepmother. But she is not perfect, as real human beings are not perfect. She has so many children that they call her Mother Goose, or Old Shoe-Woman, when they are teasing. She does her very best for them. She darns their clothes and turns sheets sides-to-middle, and makes nourishing food out of inexpensive—no, let us say honestly—out of downright cheap things, carefully simmered, made tasty with herbs that cost nothing. She makes sure that those who go to school have waterproof shoes. She scrimps and saves so that each child has some little gift to open on his or her birthday or at Christmas. She has sat up all night sometimes, making a pretty blouse out of an old dress, or a furry toy out of an old jacket of her own, that has worn so bald that she cannot go out in it. And anyway she has nowhere to go to. She has no time for visiting, nor friends to visit.*

Most of her children were good-natured and helpful. They had their tasks—polishing spoons, fetching milk, watering the herb garden. The little ones ran about the kitchen and the yard like a flock of goslings and were of course often in the way, or underfoot. But there was one—neither the smallest nor the biggest, but perhaps the largest of the very little ones who were not yet at school—who caused trouble. His name was Perkin, but nobody used his name. They called him Pig. This nickname had a kindly origin. One of his sisters, peering into the cradle when he had newly appeared amongst them, had observed that he was shiny, like an "icky pinky pig." And everyone had laughed, and ever so lovingly, they had called him Pinky Pig, when he was a plump baby, and just Pig, when he began to run about independently.

I think we all know someone who has an embarrassing nickname that would have been better discarded or not thought up in the first place. Pig found his natural enough, when he was very little, and even had a toy piglet, made of pink flannel, from whom he would not be separated. He took an interest in pigs he met on walks, or on visits to farmyards. But as he got older, he noticed people using his name reproachfully or mockingly. "What a little pig," they said, when he ate too fast. "What a grubby little pig," they said when he got muddy, which he often did, because he liked playing in earth, uncovering roots, studying earthworms. So somewhere he began to think his name meant that he wasn't liked, perhaps wasn't loved.

I am not saying that his nickname made him a naughty boy. Naughty boys are born every moment, and all mothers know that naughtiness is like curly hair, or blue eyes—it just happens. Pig was in fact a pretty boy, with yellow curls and bright blue eyes, sparkling with mischief. But he was most ingeniously naughty.

He brought things into the house, and stored them in odd places. He made a nest of worms in the flour bin, and the worms suffocated, and the flour had to be thrown out. He fed a whole seed-cake to the birds on the lawn, and the children had to go without cake for tea. He got in amongst the canisters on the dresser and mixed lentils with tealeaves, mustard with sugar, peppercorns with raisins. "My own cooking," he called this, and wailed most dolefully when Mother Goose spanked him, which she did to teach him a lesson, which he refused to learn. He came in from the garden covered with mud and made himself a nest amongst the clean laundry in the basket, where he fell asleep, looking innocent and charming, like the Babes in the Wood. All the clean bedclothes and towels and shirts had to be washed again and mangled again and dried again and ironed again. And then he fell over, carrying a jar of paintbrushes in water, and landed head-first in the washed-again clothes and soaked them with painting-water. He hid things—he hid teaspoons in mouseholes, and buttons in drains, and scissors in the pickle-jar, and forgot where he had put them. His long-suffering mother—and she was long-suffering—said that having him in the house was like living with a boggart or a naughty imp. Once, when he cut up his new collar to make it look like lace, she called him a changeling. What was that? asked Pig. But he got no answer. He was always asking questions, that was another thing. What was the wind, and why was this beetle dead and this one wriggling, and who growed the grass, and who were the little people in the roots of the shrubbery, and why did pigs snuffle, and what tapped at his bedroom window at night and why did people have to sleep when they could be awake? He got no answers because his mother was exhausted, and because most of his questions were asked in a shrill voice when one of the other children was already talking and saying something sensible moreover, about school homework or holes in stockings.

He liked collecting things. He had a bag of dead insects and a bag of special twigs and a bag of glass marbles, and a bag of personal pebbles, which were the collection he most loved. He knew them all, their knobs and smooth surfaces and rough places. Most of all he loved a piece of white limestone with a hole running through it, a self-bored stone he had found in the shrubbery. He would put it to his eye and say he could see things through it that were invisible. He said he saw little women trotting about on the draining board. He said he saw his mother's hair full of spiders spinning long threads to make her a veil. He said he saw a mouse holding out a hank of gold thread on the ends of its tiny paws, for another mouse to wind into a golden ball.

There came a day when Mother Goose was particularly tired, and particularly sad, for she had received a letter in the post, and thought it might be news of her husband, but found that it was after all a forgotten coal bill. She was making pastry, to make a big pie for the children's supper, with a little meat eked out with a lot of vegetables and herbs. It happened that the only child in the kitchen was Pig, as all the others were at school, or running errands, or playing with friends, or taking naps if they were little. Pig was playing with his marbles and pebbles, by the fender in front of the range. Mother Goose was suspicious because he was so quiet. She knew she ought to be pleased that he was quietly playing, but she was unhappy, and she was right to be unhappy, of course. She sifted the flour and fat through her fingers, and heard a faint clicking sound. She said, without looking round,

"What are you doing, little Pig?"

"Playing at marbles," said Pig. "The marble army is fighting the pebble army. The marbles is quicker and the pebbles is thicker."

"You mustn't let them roll around the kitchen floor," said Mother Goose. "It's dangerous."

Pig didn't reply. She was always saying things were dangerous, and no harm had ever come to him. When she turned back to her flour he sent out an advance party of marbles, the little green and rose ones he called "punies," and they scattered satisfactorily round the hearth. The pebbles had to go after them. They made a solid formation in a square, and then, click, clack, crunch, they flew into the punies, and there was mayhem. Pig sent out a platoon of brown marbles, in support of the little ones, and the pebbles responded with a furious assault.

Mother Goose turned round. She said "I told you not to let them roll on the floor," and Pig was startled, and dropped the whole bag of marbles, which went every which way. He started to scramble away to hide behind the coal-scuttle, for he saw he would be smacked, and he ground his knee on a marble, which hurt, and caused him to see that it was a bit dangerous.

Mother Goose came across the kitchen, intending to grab Pig by the ear and spank him. But she slipped on a rolling clutch of marbles and pebbles, and fell with a crash, knocking over the pastry-bowl as she fell. Her hair came unpinned and she hit her head on a table-leg and hurt her cheek and blacked her eye. Her hair was full of flour and her cheek was bloody, and she glared at Pig, she did glare. Pig decided she looked funny. It was better than deciding she looked frightening, though in fact she did look a bit like a wild witch. He laughed.

"That's enough," said Mother Goose. She began to gather up the pebbles and marbles and throw them into the waste basket. Pig shouted "Don't" and Mother Goose said

"I have had enough of you. Go out into the shrubbery and don't come back."

Pig felt that the whole kitchen was turning round and round like the coils of smoky glass inside the see-through glass of the big alm-marbles. He snatched at his self-bored stone—he couldn't save any of the others—and scrambled to his feet, and ran out of the kitchen door. He pulled it shut after him as best he could—he wasn't tall enough to reach the latch. And he stood for a few minutes in the yard, waiting to be called but he wasn't. So he trotted round the side of the house, and across the garden into the shrubbery, which was a big shrubbery, and overgrown, with things that shouldn't be there, the snaking brambles and clumps of nettles and wandering tresses of bryony, for Mother Goose had had to tell the gardener she couldn't pay him. For a person as small as Pig, the shrubbery was the size of a forest. Or at least, not to exaggerate, of a dense little wood. It had mazy paths, and things were reaching out to infest them, and obscure them, and cover them over, pennywort which runs riot, and periwinkle, plants which are pretty but need a firm hand, and untidy trailing plants with sticky burrs.

Pig didn't usually go far into the shrubbery. He got his worms and his pebbles from the flowerbeds in front of the house. But he thought he would just show Mother Goose, so he marched in, and went on marching in.

As he got further into the trees and bushes, and further away from the house, he had the feeling that the bushes, and the undergrowth, were getting bigger, and that he was getting smaller. He went a little more slowly—he didn't really know exactly where he was, by now, for the shrubbery was laid out like a maze, and Pig was far too small to see over the top of anything. He might be going in a circle that would lead to the mouth of the first path he had entered, or he might be pressing further and further to a hidden centre. It was late afternoon, and the shadows of the leaves were long on the other leaves and the gravel path, shadow on shadow, like a grey web over the green. At the same time all the things in the shrubbery appeared to be more solid, and more full of the deep greens and tawny browns of the things that grew there. He stopped to look at a holly. A holly is a living creature in any case but this holly seemed to him to be full of almost too much life, of a different kind. The shiny leaves almost seemed to be giving out a green light, and the few berries seemed to be redder and rounder and glossier than any berry he had ever seen before. And yet at the same time, they were caught in the thick net of almost solid shadows. Pig said to himself, I am not afraid, which meant, of course, that he was. He clutched his white stone tighter, as though it was a talisman. He saw a little clump of toadstools with silky fawn surfaces and the most lovely pleated frill of very pale flesh-colour whorled round above the pearly damp stems. He had the odd idea that he wanted to be the holly-berry, or the toadstool, not only to see. He went slower still—he had all the time in the world, he had been told never to come back—and felt time had stopped all around where he was.

He came to a place where there was a little wooden bench in a diminutive clearing. The bench was covered with a very bright green slime that was growing on it. Pig sat down on it without even thinking of how the slime was going to stain his legs and his socks and trousers. It was suddenly quiet. There had been sounds of things in the undergrowth—a bird chirping like two pebbles rubbed together, and once a rustle of unseen feet in the leaf-mould. Now there was nothing. Pig put his stone to his eye, and looked through it at a tangle of brambles and ferns. Sitting on the ferns was a very small woman, a nut-brown woman with a brown skin, and long brown hair under a brown hat, and sharp brown eyes under bushy eyebrows. She was neither old nor young, and she was wrapped in a brown cloak, veined like a leaf. She had a neat litle basket, and was gathering something—Pig could not see what, it was too small. He sat very still, said nothing, and went on looking through his stone. After a moment or two, the woman closed the basket, climbed down off the fern fronds she had been sitting on, and walked away down the path. He watched her go, until she came to a gnarled root of a thornbush; she ducked under it, and seemed to disappear into the earth.

Pig stood up and trotted after her. He knelt down on the path, on his green-stained, mud-stained knees that would so have upset Mother Goose, and he looked under the root. There were a few fine white bones, from some long-dead fledgling, and a carpet of leaves, rotted to skeletons. No sign of any little woman, though there was a kind of mousehole, going in and down, under the tree. He looked in, and saw spiralling mud, and shadow. He put his self-bored stone to his eye, and put his eye to the hole and peered down.

It was beautiful. It was a hall, with a bright gathering of people, some all earth-brown, like the woman he had followed, but some all gold with bright hair and yellow garments of a very old-fashioned kind, and some all silver, with moony-white hair and dresses with glancing lights in them. They were all very busy—some cooking at a bright hearth, some weaving on tiny elegant looms, some playing with tiny children the size of ants or beetles. The whole room was brown, with brown tables and brown velvet chairs and hangings, but there were gold and silver plates and cups on the tables, and little lamps burned in silver lampholders in crannies and on shelves.

"Oh!" said Pig. "How I wish I could come in."

There was a shrill chattering sound, like a flock of disturbed starlings, and all the brown and gold and silver faces were turned up to him, and everyone froze motionless.

Then a slender man, one of the gold people, with a gold jerkin, and pointed gold shoes, came to the foot of the tunnel, down which Pig was peering. He wore a most lovely cloak, made of the soft blue and soot-black and lemon-yellow feathers of blue-tits and great-tits, and a kind of high-crowned hat, with a feather in its ribbon.

"You can come in," he said. "You are welcome."

"I am too big," said Pig, who had always been too small for anything he tried to do.

"You must eat fernseed," said the little man. "Do you know where it is to be found?"

"Underneath the leaves' fingers," said Pig, who was observant. He looked about him, and there were pale ferns, glimmering in the shadow of the thornbush. He was an impulsive child. He did not think, is this safe? Or, how will I get back if this works? He picked a fernleaf, and scratched the seeds from underneath the fronds, and put two or three on his tongue, and swallowed them. Then he turned back to the tunnel under the roots and picked up his stone and looked through.

It is very difficult to describe his sensations during the next few moments. He was, at exactly the same time, looking at a small mousehole, or wormhole, into which two of his plump fingers might have fitted with difficulty, and balancing himself on a kind of ledge above a broad, deep, rough stairway with huge steps cut in mud and leading steeply down. Worse, his lovely stone was at the same time fitted as it always was into his little fist, and become as heavy as a tombstone.

"Courage, Pucan," said the voice of the little man, whom he could not see, for the tunnel had grown very long and was full of a kind of mist.

"My name is Perkin," said Pig.

"Amongst us, it will be Pucan. Everything is different here."

There was a moment when Pig, or Pucan, thought of drawing back.

But his body felt full of the mist which was in the earthy hole, and he could hear the little voices calling through the mist, and the fair folk leaping and singing, like tiny musical hammers on glass. So he lifted a foot, which was at the same time as heavy as lead and as light as a feather, and dragged it over the rim of the hole. And when that was done, there he was, a tiny manikin, lithe and wiry, running easily down and down into the hall. And when he made his way into it, there was the golden man, now taller than Pucan was, and a silver lady, and they welcomed him ceremoniously and with laughter. They said they were the king and queen of the Portunes, Huron and Ailsa, and he was welcome to their midst. And everyone joined in a circular, mazy dance, capering and pointing their toes, and Pig found that he knew the step as well as the next dancer, and that he could sing the tunes with the best of them.

In the world outside it was getting dark, and Mother Goose had tidied her kitchen, put away the marbles and put the pie in the oven, where it was giving out a tasty smell. She had washed and dressed her wound and brushed and knotted her hair. And for a time she had enjoyed the silence. It was quiet and orderly. And then, because she was a mother, she had begun to wonder what had happened to Pig. So she went to the door and called him, softly, in the evening air, and then louder, with a note of irritation and alarm in her voice. But everywhere was silent. There were none of the usual noises, no owl screeching, no wing flapping on its way to a roost. The air felt thick, like jelly setting. She thought Pig must be hiding to annoy her, but she wasn't sure she believed herself. She caught up her shawl and went out to look for him. By then, all the other children were back in the kitchen, so she told them to look after each other, and to look out for Pig, and shout to her, if he came back.

And then she walked, in the dusk, hurrying and calling, like a hen whose chicks had wandered away. She walked faster and faster, in wider and wider circles, and the silence thickened round her voice. At first she called, Pig, Piggy, and then, to make it more enticing, Little Pig, and finally, because Pig sounded suddenly bad in her ears, in the dark, she called Perkin, Perkin. But there was no answer and darkness fell, and the giant silver-gold moon rose over the shrubbery, shining blindly, making different shadows. And she had to go in again, for she had many many *children to feed and put to bed, and it was late, and Perkin-Pig did not answer.*

The next day, he had not come back, and she resumed her search. She searched, and kept the house distractedly, and searched again, day after day, her voice more and more weary and forlorn. She ranged widely, in lanes and fields where Pig had never been. She went through and through the shrubbery, which had resumed its usual life and noises, birds, mice, snail-shells under her feet. And one day—after a long time—she noticed little Pig's self-bored stone, shining whitely, half-buried under a root. And she picked it up and began to cry, and put the stone's opening to her weeping eye.

She was simply looking around, not searching for anything, when she saw the opening of the hole, or tunnel. And for some reason she felt she must look into the hole through the stone—reminding herself as she did so of Pig's irritating little ways, which seemed more charming with hindsight. And she saw the warm brown hall, and the gold, silver and brown people, all at their work, weaving and stitching, polishing and broiling, and a gathering sitting at table, amongst whom she saw Pig-Perkin, comfortably clothed in a nut-coloured jerkin and leggings.

She tried to speak but could only make little wailing sounds.

Pig looked up. What he saw was a huge single eye, veined with red, brimming with salt water, surrounded by long wet hairs, blocking the way out through the tunnel. He dropped the gold beaker he was drinking from. Then she heard her voice, as she found it, and said "Pig, little Pig, where are you?"

"You can see," he said. "I'm on a visit. To my friends the Portunes. I have a new name. I have work to do, down here, and I shall go out and look after growing things, with the others—"

He was swimming around in front of her tear-filled eyes. She thought he seemed to have become ageless, neither boy nor man. She said

"Come home."

He replied that she had told him not to.

"You know I didn't mean it," she said.

"Words have their own life," said King Huron, coming to the foot of the tunnel. "Go home, woman. Pucan is in a good place here."

She said something about getting a spade, about digging them out, like ants.

There was a terrible buzzing in the hall, then, more like angry hornets. The King said

"You will do no good. He will not come back, and you will bring down ill luck on yourself and all your family."

She was afraid. She sat like clay, staring through the hole in the stone.

"Go home," said Pucan. "I'm around and about. I'll come to see you, one of these days, quite soon."

"Promise?"

"Oh yes," he said, and took up his beaker, and drank whatever was in it.

She put the self-bored stone carefully in her apron pocket, so as no longer to hear the buzzing and the laughter. He had said he would come, quite soon.

As she hurried out of the shrubbery, and saw the sunlit windows of the house, and her eldest daughter with the smallest child, looking out of the door for her return, she remembered the tales of those who visited the friendly folk, and for whom seven years passed like a day and a night.

8

The Fludds drove slowly along the North Downs, and then south-east towards Rye and the Romney Marsh. Seraphita and her children sat in their shabby carriage, and were alternately followed and preceded by Arthur Dobbin, with Philip, in the pony-trap. They came across the Low Weald, skirting the eastern arm of the Downs, through Biddenden and Tenterden, across the Shirley Moor and onto the road that divided the Romney Marsh from the Walland Marsh, heading towards Lydd and Dungeness. The first part of the journey was over rich country, fields full of cows and festooned with hops, along lanes that wound under thick green branches, and along banks of gnarled roots, clutching. Dobbin tried to talk to Philip, and Philip stared around him, distracted. Once they came to the marshes the air changed—it was cooler, and salty, Philip thought, and less still. There were all sorts of small canals and cuts and runnels to be crossed. There were trees that had been shaped by steady blasts of wind, stunted and reaching sideways. Philip wanted to draw them. They were a stationary form of violent movement. Things croaked and whistled and wailed. There was no soot.

They drove south through Brenzett and Brookland. Dobbin, who might have been expected to point out landmarks, became silent and brooding. He fidgeted the pony's mouth, and it shook itself crossly. They went along a lane with high hedges and a green, murky ditch, and turned through a gate, into a driveway. There was a house, behind beech trees, with Elizabethan chimneys. They drove in through a gateway, into a yard full of outbuildings, stables, a midden. Philip smelt burning. It extinguished the smells of salt water and blown grasses. It was woodsmoke. It hung heavy in the air.

Dobbin told Philip to hold the pony, and went in, through a latched door, to what looked like a dairy, or a milking-shed. Philip stood with the pony. Someone came out of a door on the other side of the yard, a short, heavy man, moving fast, shaking his head, waving his arms and shouting.

"I told you expressly *never to come back*. Get out of here. Go away."

Philip stood. Benedict Fludd took in the fact that Philip was not Dobbin.

"Get along with you. Put the pony in his stall, and scarper. Where did he go?"

Philip had no idea where the pony's stall was. He stood mute. Fludd cursed him in mediaeval English and strode in through the door through which Dobbin had gone. The carriage rolled into the yard. Geraint climbed down and started to see to the horses. There seemed to be no servants to help him. Fludd came out of the dairy building, more or less dragging Dobbin, and still swearing. He had a thick, upright head of dark hair, a heavy, curling black beard and muscular arms and shoulders. He wore a workman's smock, heavy cotton trousers and fisherman's boots. "Get out," he said, repeatedly, to Dobbin. Geraint led the carriage horse into the stables, and came back for the pony, without speaking to his father or to Philip.

Imogen said to her father

"Don't be angry. We're back in time to help with the firing. We can all help."

"No you can't. We fired it, Wally and I fired it, while you were gallivanting. Total disaster. Total."

"Why didn't you *wait*?" asked Imogen. Her father said curtly that he'd wanted to control his own firing whilst the disastrous Dobbin was absent, and couldn't muck it up. But Wally had dozed off in the night, and the fire hadn't been fed right, and not only the firing but the kiln itself was in rack and ruin. And the carter had come with the clay and had had to be paid.

Seraphita stood in the yard, stately and gloomy, and asked whether there was any food in the house. Fludd said no, there wasn't, he had had neither time nor inclination to go into Lydd, and Wally had been needed in the pottery, and the money had been needed for the new clay, and he had not had the slightest idea when they might condescend to come back, had he? She should have thought of that, shouldn't she?

The three Fludd women stood like calm statues, and looked at each other and Dobbin, for help. Dobbin said nervously that he could ride over to the farm and get bread and milk, and something for supper, cheese or bacon, and some vegetables. If that seemed a good idea. But he would need money. Seraphita peered into her handbag, and found a few coins, which she handed over to Dobbin. Geraint came out of the stable and said the horse had had enough for one day, and the provisions must be got on foot. Dobbin asked Philip if he would like the walk to the farm. Philip said maybe he could make himself useful with the kiln. Fludd glowered at him.

"Who's he?" he asked Seraphita.

"Arthur thinks he may be able to help you in the workshop."

"One clumsy oaf is enough."

"He's not clumsy," said Dobbin. "I grant I am—" Benedict Fludd growled—"I grant I am, but he's not. He comes from the Potteries. He's worked in kilns. He wants to work with you."

Seraphita said, staring into the distance, that if no one could be got to help with the work, no work would be done. Fludd said it might all just as well go to rack and ruin. Philip said

"I saw your pot, at that house, at Todefright. I do *want* to work for you. I do know my way round."

He began to walk into the pottery, which had been the dairy. He knew enough about the evil-tempered to know that you had to walk away from them, or they couldn't give up their wrath, even if they needed to.

The pottery was in chaos. There was a small kiln, at one end, its doors hanging open, revealing slumped shelves, and a mess of ash and shards of exploded vessels. There were pots drying on shelves along one wall, and floating ash and grit was settling on them in an undesirable way. There were bins of water, and bins of slurry, not properly covered. There were all sorts of dishes of glaze and brushes, not neatly ranged, but dangerously slopping into each other. In the middle of the floor was a heap of broken biscuitware that looked as though someone had been jumping on it. Philip thought carefully. Don't touch a man's tools, unless you have permission. Don't empty his kiln, he needs to note what went wrong where. Inside the door he found a broom, with which he began to clear the surface of the tiled floor. He saw a tin bath in which some of the broken pieces had been put to make grog, and added a few, as he worked, the clean ones. Benedict Fludd followed him in. He stood gloomily in the doorway, and watched him sweep. Finally he said

"You can help me get all this stuff out of the kiln. It's got to be done. I need to find my test pieces."

It had been a glost firing, with a load of glazed vessels in what Philip could see to be mostly greens and honey colours, all scorched, blistered, scarred and shattered. He helped Benedict Fludd in total silence, putting the pieces in a clothes basket, sweeping up the debris. Everything had collapsed in towards the centre. Right at the top, Philip found an intact small saucer, and then another. They were still warm, about blood-heat. He blew on them softly, to move the ash. One was the same gold and turquoise colour as the Todefright pot, and one was a very striking brilliant red that he thought he'd never seen before, a kind of rich cochineal crimson. Both had been painted with a swirling cloudy grey, a smoky web through which a tiny creature peered up through the veiling. The creatures were little demons, with nasty, snarling expressions, full of life. Philip broke the silence.

"There's some little'uns here as aren't smashed. Glaze has held pretty well."

He handed them to their maker, who turned them over, humming tunelessly. Philip ventured to say that he'd never seen that kind of red.

"We all try to rediscover the *sang de boeuf*. This was meant to aim at the Iznik red, but it's nearer *sang de boeuf*. I hadn't a lot of hope of it."

Philip said that the other glaze—the blue-green-gold one—was like the Todefright pot.

"That's another hit-and-miss. More miss than hit. Have you done glazing work?"

"I worked in th' kilns. Packing the saggars at the top of the bottles. But me mother is a paintress. She's sick, with the lead and the dust. They all are. But she knows colours, and I've watched her."

"Hmm," said Benedict Fludd. "Hmm."

They continued to clear up, in a now reasonably companionable silence.

Pomona came timidly to the doorway, and said that there was supper, if they wanted it. Fludd said, amiably enough, that he was ravenous, and Philip noted the loosening of Pomona's muscles, in face and shoulders, where she had braced herself for rage. He noticed the same thing in the rest of the family—even Geraint—who were sitting round the kitchen table, on which were soup bowls, honey-glazed, with burnt umber snakes coiled inside them, a large platter of cheeses, a loaf of bread, and a dish of apples. Fludd sat at the head of the table, and patted the seat next to him for Philip. He bowed his head, and began to say Grace, rapidly, in Latin. *"Gratias tibi agimus, omnipotens Deus, pro his et omnis donis tuis . . ."* The family bowed their heads, and Philip copied them. Then Imogen served steaming vegetable soup from an iron pot, and they ate.

Nobody said anything. Everyone watched Philip, who had a confused sense that much depended on him, and that he was perhaps not equal to his task.

When they had finished, Fludd said he was considering employing Philip in the workshop. Dobbin said "Oh, *good*" and attracted another series of snarling remarks about his own uselessness. Dobbin said bravely that if only Mr. Fludd had reliable assistance in the workshop, it would be possible to rebuild the big kiln, and . . .

"And save ourselves from starvation," said Fludd. "It's a long prospect, with little hope."

He seemed almost pleased with this prognostic.

Imogen said her father should see Philip's drawings, which he had made in the South Kensington Museum. These were fetched out again, with his pad of paper, and everyone admired the lithe dragons and helmeted gnome-men from the Gloucester Candlestick. Philip kept the pad, and his pencil, and began to draw. Fludd watched him. He drew from memory, the underwater forms on the Todefright pot, the way the tadpole creatures floated between the rising strands of weed. He found he remembered remarkably accurately. He knew that for the first time in his life, maybe, he was deliberately *showing off* his talent. Fludd should know he could see, and keep proportions, and remember. His hand skated over the paper. The fish-forms, the swimming embryos, flickered into life. Benedict Fludd laughed. He said he had forgotten how good that pot was. He was surprised he had parted with it, that charming lady had cajoled it out of him. Dobbin wondered if he had been paid at all for his work, but this niggle—anyway pointless—about past insouciance was swallowed in his relief and delight that the potter was smiling. He had been at Purchase House long enough to know that Fludd's mood moved in repeated—though unpredictable—cycles, from rage to geniality, from grim, inactive despair to superhuman efforts of work and invention. Between the extremes, things got done, pots got made, even, with luck, sold to keep off starvation. The family sat round in the lamplight, looking like a family, the laughing father, the graciously attentive mother, the two lovely daughters handing out apples, even Geraint admiring the drawings. Geraint was thinking that Philip could be really *useful* and would be worth cultivating. He needed help, to make it possible for him to get out of this house. He had given up any idea that the ineffective Dobbin might be help. But Philip—possibly—might be.

Purchase House had many rooms. More of them were empty, and in a state of decay, than were inhabited. There was an uncarpeted stone staircase, with a metal banister, leading to the first floor: it must once have been imposing, but now wound gloomily up into the dark. Imogen led Philip up with a candle, and showed him into a bare little room, with a bed, and a washstand, a small chest of drawers and a high window, too high to look out of. It was a little like a monastic cell. There were sheets and a woven bedcover, embroidered with a bunch of lilies. Imogen seemed undisposed to talk to Philip, and almost embarrassed by finding herself alone with him. She showed him the water-closet at the other end of the landing, past several closed doors. Then she left him, with a matchbox, and his little flame.

He lay down, composedly enough. His incoherent plan had brought him to a potter, and possible work. He thought about the Fludds as he lay on the edge of exhausted sleep. He had not much to compare them with—the family at Todefright, perhaps. Violet had packed him a nightshirt, and the borrowed clothing, now a gift. That family was running, and laughter, and hugging and reciting nonsense, and he did not know how to behave with it, but felt a kind of grief that he was not part of the charmed circle. Here everyone was unnaturally still and watchful, apart from the potter himself, who had moods, a state Philip recognised from the temperamental master-craftsmen he had seen from a distance. He thought he didn't like Geraint, but was not sure. Geraint had a nice face, as though he would have talked, if he had had anyone to talk to. Arthur Dobbin meant well, but Philip had unthinkingly accepted Benedict Fludd's and Geraint's assessment of his uselessness. Dobbin, too, had a bedroom somewhere in the house. If he had particularly enraged the potter, he sometimes slept in the parsonage, with Frank Mallett. Seraphita had once said she was always glad if he stayed overnight, but it was always "overnight" however long it went on. He was a guest, not part of the family, something Philip had understood without reflection. He had also understood that there was little money, and that Dobbin was the only person who had any sense about provisions.

In the middle of the night, something odd happened. The latch on his door lifted, and the door creaked open. His eyes were used to the dark, and there was enough moon- and starlight for him to see. The person who came in was female, with flowing hair loose on her shoulders. She was white like bone china in the moonlight, and naked. She walked barefoot, with delicate little steps, across the rug on the floor, and stood by his bed. It was Pomona. She had new little uptilted breasts, and—he saw clearly—a little bush of soft gold private hair. Her mouth was relaxed, and unnaturally calm. She breathed as though she was sleeping, and Philip thought she was, she must be sleepwalking. He kept his eyes open, and his body quite still. Her eyes were open, and unseeing. He knew from hearsay and gossip that you must not wake sleepwalkers. It could kill them, it was said. Maybe she would go away. In the interim he looked with aesthetic pleasure and moral distress at the naked form, and the white skin. Quite suddenly, she bent down, lifted the blanket, lifted a knee, and slid into bed beside him, putting a surprisingly solid arm across his neck, and curling up to him. Her leg was over his thigh. He held his breath. He had not the slightest idea where she had come from, so could not carry or lead her back to her own room.

He waited. He almost dozed, with keeping still and breathing shallow and even. What if she woke? But she did not wake, and finally, after a lapse of time, she swung her legs out of the bed again, and moved like an automaton towards the door. Philip padded after her, and opened it wide, to let her through. Perhaps he ought to have gone after her, to see that she came to no harm. But he was embarrassed and fearful.

9

Arthur Dobbin sometimes stayed overnight in the Puxty vicarage with Frank Mallett. He did this both when Benedict Fludd had threatened him with violence, and when he and Frank had cycled into Rye, or Winchelsea, for a lecture. Frank's vicarage was a pleasant old stone house, thick-walled against the wind and weather, with small windows, and deep fireplaces. It stood by the side of Frank's Norman church, built in the twelfth century when there had been a harbour, and great waves driving in from the Channel. The church dated from the draining of the Walland Marsh, and was built on land taken from the sea, and enclosed by mud dykes. In the thirteenth century the land was battered, ravaged, and reshaped by monstrous storms, and the sea carried silt into the harbour of Romney and piled it there, so that many prosperous ports found themselves slowly moved inland, and no longer able to trade. The farmers died of the Black Death in the fourteenth century, and the congregations dwindled. Sheep were everywhere on the marsh, cropped the rich grass, wandered along the flat horizon. The wall of St. Edburga's Church could be seen from the windows on one side, alongside its small, grassy graveyard, with flagged path, lych-gate, and stunted yews. From the other side, where Frank Mallett had both his study and his breakfast-room, there was a view of the marshes: grass, sheep, clumps and long stands of reeds moving in the air, plovers and gulls. This room was the room where Dobbin had passed the happiest moments of his life. Breakfast at Purchase House tended to be burned, or raw, or in short supply, or all of these at once. Breakfast in the vicarage was bacon and eggs, precisely fried with soft centres, warm toast wrapped in a linen cloth, freshly churned butter, honey and plentiful strong, newly brewed tea. Dobbin particularly liked eating these things in bad weather, when squalls raced across the reeds, and the sky was pewter, and the sheep huddled grimly. He felt it was a sacramental meal, but had not dared to say so to Frank, who presided at real sacraments, however exiguous his congregation.

They talked, a lot of the time, about what went on in Purchase House. Frank had found it difficult to understand why Arthur Dobbin had not long ago been discouraged by Benedict Fludd's temper, and even by his own increasingly obvious unfitness as a helper. Dobbin had a cult of genius. Benedict Fludd was a genius, the only one Dobbin knew. Dobbin himself had no artistic talent but he wished to serve it, and seemed to feel, against the evidence, that he had been *led* to this place, and this task. The poverty of the landscape and the people led him to think this was the right place for a community centred on genius, making beautiful, wholesome things. And then, he had found Frank Mallett. And then, in moments of despair he did not have any idea where to go next. Frank—who was also lonely—thought Dobbin was obsessed and irrational, but joined in his vague projects because he liked his company, and because the Fludds were by far the most romantic and problematic of his parishioners.

One day, some weeks after Philip's arrival at Purchase, Dobbin and Frank were taking breakfast together, before riding their bicycles into Winchelsea, to find out about a new series of lectures, set up by the local Theosophists. Dobbin spread butter, and spread honey, and remarked that the honey was particularly well-flavoured, he could taste clover, he thought, very delicate. Frank replied, as Dobbin had known he would, that it was his own honey, from his own bees. He had sent some pots, with Dobbin, to the Fludds, with his compliments. He had received a note of thanks from Seraphita, in round, childish handwriting.

Dobbin said that Benedict Fludd had been transfigured by Philip's workmanship. They were rebuilding the little kiln, in the outhouse, and talking of building a big one, with a bottle chimney, and a revolving flue grate. Philip had drawn his idea of the flue grate for Fludd, who had been truly interested. If there was a big kiln, of course, said Dobbin, more helpers would be needed. He himself did his best, and could use his shoulder-strength to feed a kiln on spent hop-poles—"under supervision," he said ruefully. But it was, he said, chewing the crisp toast and the soft, sweet honey, a case of chicken and egg. There was no money to increase production, and there was no produce to earn more money. And pottery kilns, which he had always thought of as stable, down-to-earth, *solid* no-nonsense means to art-works, turned out to be both violent and temperamental, like Fludd himself. You could lose months of designing and throwing, and decorating, in one flare of fire, or gas, or explosion of a blister of water in an ill-made vessel. He thought that now Philip was there, Fludd might be induced to make some saleable small pots—or tiles perhaps—which could help to feed the family. Seraphita and her daughters had their looms of course, but they worked slowly and stiffly, and their work depended on Fludd being in the mood, and having the energy, to design patterns for them. They didn't do too well, left to their own devices. There was a conversation the two friends always had, at this point, going over the same ground, making the same baffled, owlish points, as though they were newly perceived discoveries, about the curious lifelessness and inhibition of the three female members of the Purchase House family. Dobbin, since the Tode-fright party, was able to bring new observations to this discussion—he had observed the three at both Todefright and Nutcracker Cottage, half-hoping that out of sight and smell of Benedict Fludd they might relax or chatter. But they had not. "It is as though they have sleeping sickness, or are under a spell," said Dobbin, as he often said. He added that Geraint had got on very well with the other young people, the Wellwood boys, Charles and Tom, young Julian Cain, and his sister, Florence. He felt happy to be offering all these new persons to Frank, to be solemnly discussed. Frank knew, or should have known, Geraint, of course. He gave him lessons in classics and history and nature study, which were most of the education Geraint had received. Geraint was good at maths, and Frank was not. He tried to teach Geraint, and Geraint laughed at his mistakes. Geraint did not confide in Frank, though Frank had initially hoped he would. He was bored and bitter, Frank was sure of it, and had a basically agreeable and outgoing nature, Frank was also sure, though he could not quite say why. Unlike his sisters Geraint had made friends with local youths, and went out as crew in fishing-boats, or helped to pick apples and harvest onions. He ran wild on the marshes, chatting to poachers and gamekeepers, and listening to the tales of smuggling, which everyone told. Frank and Dobbin discussed all this, too, and tried to think what would become of Geraint, without coming to any clear vision or prospect. They were not very good planners, that was why they were where they were.

Frank Mallett, however, knew more than a little more about Benedict Fludd than he ever disclosed in his pleasant coil of discussion with Dobbin. He had once been asked—urgently, desperately beseeched—to hear Benedict Fludd's confession. This would be two years past, now, when Frank had been more Anglo-Catholic than he now was, had had moments when he yearned for the mysteries and solidities of sacraments and the presence of saints and angels who might answer his need for the larger life, and make his spirit less lonely and meagre. His church, like most Marsh churches, had been despoiled at the Reformation. The Virgin had been smashed, and the stone angels bashed and beheaded, though the ghosts of a fresco in which they played on trumpet and psaltery at the Creation, still stained the east wall, under the oval textboards which had replaced them with Puritan admonitions. "Except the Lord build the house, they labour in vain that build it." And Solomon's saying "Sand and gravel are very heavy things, yet the anger of a fool is much heavier." And Job: "As the waters fail from the sea, and the flood decayeth and drieth up: So man lieth down and riseth not: till the heavens be no more, they shall not awake, nor be raised out of their sleep." Marsh Puritans were obsessed with the shifting dangers of masses of water and sand.

Most of the Norman windows had been smashed and Frank had had the idea of raising money in the diocese and commissioning a window from the great artist living in the parish. He had called on Fludd, and put the proposal—as a very vague beginning—to him, and Fludd had said he had many ideas, the spirit of God brooding on the waters, maybe, or a Tree of Life with gold and crimson fruits. For a few weeks these images had been discussed enthusiastically, over mugs of beer, and drawings had been produced, in chalk, and ink, and watercolour. Frank Mallett still had one or two. The rest had been destroyed by Fludd in an excess of despair. Frank had called one day, as usual, and found the potter sitting in his great chair and staring at nothing. He seemed almost unable to speak, almost catatonic. He had muttered "I can do nothing," and "Leave me," and Seraphita had come into the kitchen and said— tonelessly—placidly?—that her husband was unwell, and would not be ready to do anything for some time, she knew this well, and could assure Mr. Mallett that there was nothing to be gained from visiting, until Fludd was well again. Mallett had ventured the opinion that artistic powers perhaps ebbed and flowed like the tides. (He would not now dare to utter any such platitude.) Seraphita had agreed, flatly, that this might be so, and had stood, statuesque, waiting for him to take his leave. He knew, as her spiritual advisor, that he should offer her help, or comfort, or a chance to share her burden. But she looked at him, dully, patiently, waiting for him to go, and he went. Another time might be better, he told himself. This was all before Arthur Dobbin and the vanishing Martin Calvert had turned up at Purchase House.

· · ·

And then, one winter afternoon, when Frank Mallett was in St. Edburga's Church, kneeling in fact, in prayer in the chancel, trying to combat the seeping away or silting up of his faith, Fludd had come in search of him. He had flung open the door, letting in a roiling gust of wind, which rattled papers and briefly disturbed the altar-cloth. He stood in the nave, his bull-shoulders jutting forward, his large head hunched between them, paying no attention to the fact that the priest was kneeling. He said

"I am in mortal need. Will you hear my confession?"

Frank had got up, not gracefully. He was afraid. He was a young man, and innocent, despite his pretty pointed gold beard on his chin. He had lived a sheltered life, and had so far encountered no real horrors in his brief ministry, only the present fact of death, and the destructive bad temper of competitive churchwardens and hassock-embroidering ladies. He said mildly that this was an Anglican church, and that confession was not a sacrament. Fludd laid a hand on him, tugged at his sleeve, made him sit down in a box-pew and sat next to him, his breath laboured. He was wearing a black smock, which had a parodic look of a cassock.

"God," said Benedict Fludd, "your God, that is, strides in and out of my life with no warning. One day he seems impossible—laughable, laughable—and the next, he is imperious." He stopped. He said "It is like the phases of the moon, maybe. Or the seasons of the sphere we live on, rolling in and out of the light, skeleton trees one day, and then snow, and afterwards the bright green veil and after that the full heat and shining. Only it is neither regular nor predictable. And there are—others—who stride in, when he takes himself off. Who seem persuasive. Like Hindoo demons who are gods in their own terms."

Frank listened. He thought in his young head that the rhetoric was practised. He murmured something about the tenacity of faith in the dark times of the soul, in the lean years of the spirit.

"I have no will," said Fludd, with a note of satisfaction. "I am a battleground simply, and yet I live and walk about in the world. But there is—are—chinks of light, moments of stasis, between one state and another, between the victories of the Pale Galilean and the multiform Life-force. If you take my meaning. Times when I look before and after."

"Yes," said Frank.

"I am at such a cusp. Your God has removed his presence as though it had never been. He sheds no light, he illuminates nothing, all is thick grey cloud, or empty night full of pointless points of brightness whose order is nothing to do with me, but not yet menacing. It will be. Today I am lucid."

"Yes," said Frank.

"I tell you, young man, of things you cannot really imagine. I must unburden myself. I wish to tell you the tale of my werewolf-changes, so that perhaps the telling may release me. Do I make myself clear?"

"Yes," said Frank, who was physically alarmed by the big body trembling beside him. "So far, yes."

"I may be what you may call mad, tomorrow," said Fludd. "It will not seem so to me then, but from here I see it with nausea. Each visitation is worse. There was no hint of it when I was a child. I was a choir-boy with his head separated from his little body by a great pure white starched collar. If I flicked my own tiny pudenda no one knew and it was all innocent. And the sun shone all the time, round and bright like my collar. And then I began to become a man, and my voice broke, and my collar was taken from me, and my body—you understand—grew a life of his own, not under my control. I had terrible imaginings. I liked to hunt things. Creatures. Frogs and rabbits. I made clay images of them with love, and I destroyed them ingeniously, also with love. Do you understand? I see you do not. I have chosen my confessor intelligently. For you are a person of integrity, and will not speak of this. I went to Art School, and made drawings of the naked—men and women both— and imagined, aha, *drawing* them in quite another sense, like chickens. I made private drawings of drawing. I walked up and down the Haymarket like Rossetti you understand—looking at the flesh for sale, and slid into my double life in the end with ease. I found a young woman whose trade it was to understand men like me, and gratify their imaginings. I visited her—more and more frequently—and imagined hurting her, more and more ingeniously—and loved her, with my sunny self, more and more deeply and innocently. There was nothing, nothing we could not talk of, and in her presence—in her cheap bed, young man, Father, I became whole, and cleansed. She was called Maria. She was a Maria Magdalena who washed away sins, and she was Venus Anadyomene to me, though she was ill-nourished I think since birth, my artist's eye saw she was puny, though my lover's eye saw her breasts as globes of milky marble, and the tuft between her legs as the bushes surrounding the gate to Paradise Lost—and Regained." He stopped. Frank thought, this is practised rhetoric, he has told this tale before, and polished it. It may be a fiction, or simply a *version*. He wondered how he knew these things.

"Do I embarrass or excite you, young man? Father?"

"No," said Frank, though he was both embarrassed and minimally aroused in his own flesh. "No, I am here to listen."

"I know, naturally, that I was not her only lover," said Fludd. "She had her trade, it was part of her Self. Or so I thought. Maybe she was only a lost, impecunious young creature, driven by pure hunger and cold to offer heat and hearing which I took for understanding. I think differently of it from day to day, from phase to phase of my own moon-cycle. I did form the intention of making her my wife. I needed her so abjectly. It was when I found her that I found my vocation—fingers in clay running with water, fingers puddling in divine female flesh— I made vessels that were metaphors for her and our dealings with each other, coiled mermaidens and fern fronds uncurling—oh, it was all innocent enough, despite her trade and my madness."

He stopped. Frank had a crazy moment when he wondered if this Magdalen had become Seraphita Fludd, and if that explained her inhib-ited stiffness.

Fludd was doing something which Frank saw was wringing his hands; he thought he had never seen it done before. Fludd said

"The next bit is nasty. You are the first person to whom I have told this—this thing. I went to see her at my fixed time—I had a key, but we had agreed when I should and shouldn't visit—and I went up the stairs, two at a time."

He stopped again. Frank waited, his own hands folded.

"There was a stench. I noticed it, I think, before I opened the door. She was on her bed. She was quite dead. She was a mass of raw, open wounds and blood, and blood. The edges of the pools of it were con-gealing, like glaze, on the surface of her thighs, and on the linoleum."

"Yes," said Frank, to interrupt the flow.

"She had run about, all over the room, pouring blood, grasping at things with bloody fingers, the marks were everywhere. I couldn't look at her face—it was simply a mass of bloody *knobs*—"

"Yes," said Frank, more firmly. He said "What did you do?"

"I stepped back, and closed the door, and went home to my lodgings. What else could I do?"

"Called the police?"

"Vengeance is mine, saith the Lord. It was too late for help. And I became—ill, sick, debilitated."

He came to a stop.

"This is all?" said Frank.

"All? It is a horror."

"But not a horror of which you are—by your own account— guilty."

How to find the voice of a confessor, or a judge. It slipped across Frank's mind to wonder whether Fludd had really killed the woman, in a brainstorm, and was either lying or had forgotten. And it slipped into his mind to wonder whether the story was *made up,* either to hurt him, Frank, with, or to feed Fludd's appetite for horror. Fludd said

"I am not lying, you know." Then he said

"I am faithful to her, involuntarily. I do not love my wife, as I promised to do. There are thick walls between us. She is a beautiful woman, who expects to be desired, and I do not—often—desire her. I should not have married her."

"It is very late to say that," said the priest.

"She is a stupid woman. A plucked chicken in a serge carapace. Sometimes I think she has no soul."

"You promised to love and cherish her."

"I have tried. I may sneer to you, now, but I have tried. There is no love in our house. I am not the only one guilty of that."

"I cannot judge, there."

"I am not asking you to judge. Or to interfere. If I thought you had the *nous* or nerve to interfere I wouldn't talk to you. Look at you shaking. You will pretend this—confession—has never happened."

"I expect it was partly your intention to make me shake. What do you expect me to do?"

"Nothing, nothing, nobody can do anything. I shall go home and slide for a time into my private compartment of Hell. I am horribly afraid—always—of never finding the way out or of—"

"Or—?" Frank prompted. But Fludd had come to the end of his confession, just as abruptly as he had begun it. He stood up, and stumbled out of the church without a backward glance.

Frank Mallett had thought to himself that what had been "confessed" was not what Fludd had come to confess. He lived for a few weeks in fear of Fludd doing something to harm himself, or his family, or some outsider—he had been afraid of something in the future, and had confessed something far in the past. Fludd did indeed enter a black period, alternately swearing and breaking pots, or taking long solitary marches along the shingle beach at Dungeness, waving his arms, and shouting at the sky. Frank Mallett made timid attempts to visit Seraphita and "bring her out" and Seraphita, remorselessly, made minimal tea-party comments on the weather, or the jam, or the servants, and waited for him to go away. Geraint's schoolwork suffered when Fludd was in a black mood. His arithmetic deteriorated. So did his Latin translation. And then one day—or so Frank imagined it, for he was not, naturally, present at the time—Benedict Fludd shook himself, and went back into his studio and began beating out wedges of clay.

The two friends cycled into Winchelsea on a very hot summer day, to discuss the preparation of a series of lectures, in Lydd, for the darker months in the autumn. They took paths across the Walland Marsh and along the Camber Sands, which covered the drowned town of Old Winchelsea, as though it had never been. They skirted Rye Harbour, and wheeled past Camber Castle along the flats, with the hill on which Winchelsea had been rebuilt in the thirteenth century, a mediaeval planned town, in front of them. They were visiting Miss Patty Dace, who lived in a small house facing the part-ruined church of St. Thomas the Martyr, across peaceful turf, marked by ancient leaning gravestones. Like many Winchelsea houses this one resembled the white clapboard houses of New England. It had a small, well-tended front garden.

Miss Dace was waiting, and opened the door before they could knock. She was in her forties, and made of bone and muscle, with a fierce face, hooked nose, high cheek-bones and deep-set dark eyes under brows like bristling caterpillars. Her hair looked as though it had undergone intense applications of the curling-tongs, but in fact coiled itself naturally, as though she had African ancestors. She liked to be busy. She was the acting secretary of many groups: the local Theosophists, the local Fabians, the Winchelsea and District Dramatic Society, the Circle of Watercolourists, and a group which worked for women's suffrage. She had taught at a London girls' school in her time, and had worked briefly as an assistant almoner in a hospital. She had been very active in the agitation to extend the franchise for local authorities and Poor Law boards to married women, and women who were not home-owners. Last year the Liberal Government had abolished the property qualification for Poor Law boards and had made it possible for married women to stand for election. Miss Dace had rejoiced. She had stood for election herself, and had been defeated by a married woman, Mrs. Phoebe Methley, the wife of a writer, Herbert Methley, who had bought a smallholding near East Guldeford. Miss Dace had had a good Christian upbringing. She tried to feel neither disappointment nor resentment, and turned her attention to the cultural life of the community. She was the custodian of the Fabian book-boxes, which were despatched from London full of challenging and improving reading. She arranged lectures, both for the Fabians and for the Theosophists, and for combined groups of both. Until recently, she had also, through something called the Christo-theosophical Society, tried to arrange discussions of esoteric spiritual life, and especially the female aspect of Christian spirituality. Patty Dace wanted *more life* and thought it might reside in Theosophy. She had been put out to read, in the pages of *Lucifer,* a passionate denunciation of Christianity's attitude to women, written by Blavatsky herself, studded with quotations from the Bible and the Church Fathers about woman as the organ of the devil, the hissing of the serpent, the most dangerous of wild beasts, a scorpion, an asp, a dragon, a daughter of falsehood, a sentinel of hell, the enemy of peace. Mme Blavatsky noted that in the New Testament "The words sister, mother, daughter and wife are only names for degradation and dishonour."

Patty Dace the feminist, Theosophist and socialist sat down and argued with Patty Dace the vestigial Christian, condemned her nostalgia for the Church, and renounced it. This had led to a certain amount of embarrassment over what she felt to be duplicity in her dealings with Frank Mallett, with whom it was such a pleasure to collaborate in choosing lecturers and publicising lectures. She would, oddly, not have been comforted to know that Frank himself often felt that his faith was erected on shifting and slipping sands. She liked the Church to be *there,* like the overlarge, ancient solid mediaeval buildings in the marshes, a reality, even if she had to relinquish her connection to it.

She welcomed the young men, and gave them cups of tea, and homemade shortbread biscuits after their ride. They had, as a committee, secured a series of Thursday evenings in a community hall in Lydd, where audiences of local writers and teachers and shopkeepers were augmented by officers and men from the military camp near the town. She put on her spectacles, and said to Frank that they should perhaps find a title for a series. Dobbin said he thought they should find exciting speakers first, and then make up a title. Although Dobbin had been shy and ill at ease at Todefright he felt in retrospect that he had been privileged and delighted to meet the glittering folk in their fancy dress. He wanted to hear them again—Humphry and Olive, Toby Youlgreave and August Steyning, the anarchists and the London professor who worked with Professor Galton on human statistics and heredity. He said that he had heard some very interesting ideas about folklore and ancient customs whilst in Andreden. Maybe she could think of those.

Miss Dace said she was interested more in *change*. She wanted lectures on *new* things, the New Life, the New Woman, new forms of art and democracy. And religion, she said, looking bravely at Frank.

Frank sipped his tea and said thoughtfully that in fact there was only an apparent contradiction. For many of the new things looked back to very old things for their strength. The Theosophists looked back to the wisdom of Tibetan masters, for instance. William Morris's socialism looked back to mediaeval guilds and communities. Edward Carpenter's ideas about shedding the stultifying respectability of Victorian family life looked back also, to human beings living in harmony with nature, as natural creatures. And the same was true of the vegetarians and the anti-vivisectionists, they required a wholesome respect for natural animal life, as it was before technical civilisation. In the arts too, Benedict Fludd, for instance, wanted to return to the ancient craft of the single potter, and to find the lost red glazes, the Turkish Iznik, the Chinese *sang de boeuf*. The Society for Psychical Research had rediscovered an old spirit world, and lost primitive powers of human communication. Old superstitions might furnish new spiritual understanding. Even the New Woman, he said, venturing a half-joke, sought freedom from whalebone and laces in Rational Dress but also in free-flowing mediaeval gowns. Women's work in the world appeared to be new, but in the old times abbesses had wielded power and governed communities, as principals of colleges now did. Maybe all steps into the future drew strength from a searching gaze into the deep past. He would almost dare to propose himself as a lecturer on this theme.

There is a peculiar aesthetic pleasure in constructing the form of a syllabus, or a book of essays, or a course of lectures. Visions and shadows of people and ideas can be arranged and rearranged like stained-glass pieces in a window, or chessmen on a board. The committee considered what it would like to hear, and how the contributions should be balanced. Dobbin proposed that August Steyning be asked to expound his ideas about the new theatre, which would go beyond realism into the ancient skills of marionettes and puppets. It was agreed that Toby Youlgreave should be asked to speak on the relations between modern folklore and the ancient fairy faiths of our ancestors. They decided to invite Edward Carpenter to speak on his hopes for men, women, and his "in-between sex," newly described. Names were brought up: Bernard Shaw, Graham Wallas, Beatrice Webb. Annie Besant, who had spoken persuasively, intensely and successively for secularism, birth control and Fabian socialism, had taken on the disputed leadership of the Theosophists since Madame Blavatsky had, in 1891, "abandoned a physical instrument that could no longer be used," the "worn-out garment that she had worn for one incarnation." For two or three visionary moments the three made models of what Mrs. Besant might have to say. But Patty Dace said, reluctantly, that she felt that Mrs. Besant would be too implicated in the current problems of the society to want to come and talk in Romney Marsh.

Miss Dace proposed a lecture on prostitution and the injustice in the differing ways in which women and men were treated. It was not, on reflection, a good idea to give such a lecture to an audience including so many military men. Maybe Mrs. Wellwood could talk about modern children, and modern children's literature; that was safer. It was agreed, rapidly, that Mr. Fludd was not temperamentally suited to lecturing. Maybe someone from the South Kensington Museum could speak about crafts and their future.

All of them knew, even Dobbin, that no lecture series conforms to its ideal elegance and depth, as first mooted. Lecturers refuse, lecturers fail. The same people, who can be relied on, turn up, and say the same things. There would have to be a lecture on vegetable-growing, and Mrs. Wolsey would have to give it. Bernard Shaw would be replaced by some thin and nervous student, who would have no idea how to speak to soldiers. They went on to the second stage of planning, which is the secondary list of reliable performers.

Patty Dace said she thought they should ask Herbert Methley. He had decided opinions and was an inspirational speaker. She had heard him, once, in Rye, which was an indication that he might be willing. She could not remember exactly what he had said, but she remembered it as being mesmeric. It had been to do with freeing the instinctual self, something like that. Everybody present had been stimulated and excited.

Frank said that he had never met Mr. Methley but he had been very impressed—very impressed indeed—by the copy of *Marsh Lights* which Miss Dace had kindly given him. He had gone on to read *The Giant on the Hill,* and *Bel and the Dragon,* which he had also admired. He would be delighted both to meet Mr. Methley, and to hear him speak.

Patty Dace looked searchingly at him. He smiled mildly back. He was unaware that the gift of the novel had been a test of his faith on her part. It had tested his faith. But he felt obliged not to reveal to Miss Dace how much it had done so. In fact, he thought about it, quite hard, every day. It had given him solid images of his doubt.

It was a novel about someone in his own position, the solitary priest in a made-up Marsh church, with a dwindling congregation. The priest in the book, who was called Gabriel Medcalf, had been bewitched by, or had fallen in love with, or had deceived and disappointed, a woman called Bertha, whom he met mostly when he was walking along the brook in the countryside. There was a kind of *greenness* about this character, which was rather cunningly done by flickering references to the lights in her pale hair, or her eyes, or the shadows on her fine skin. Frank was not very responsive to female charm, and Bertha corresponded to no fantasy of his own. He rather thought she might be an embodiment—symbolic or actual—of a kind of elder-tree witch, a guardian of flowers and berries. She had no blemishes, and was evasive. What Frank responded to was a something in Methley's description of the relations between the church building and the landscape. In this world, the church was gaunt and skeletal, a solid shell around a lifeless space. The spiritual energy had leached into, or returned to, the earth and the marsh and the water around the church. Trees appeared to walk, and moved angry arms, or spoke in inhuman voices, creaking and groaning. The marsh lights flittered and gathered in dancing circles, and split again into snakes of light, running errands across the evening darkness. Frank had been impressed as a boy by Wordsworth's sense of the ancient force—not measured by human time—in crags and boulders. Methley had learned from him—huge stones lurched like primeval scaled beasts, from the lips of brackish lakes to dry land and back.

Hillocks heaved with slow, slow energy. Cracks opened into traps. The whole earth was possessed, and either indifferent or inimical, unless the inadequate Bertha was meant to be a way to enter it, or find harmony in it. Gabriel Medcalf failed the test, and ventured less and less frequently outside his church, and its walled graveyard. Gabriel in the novel lost his sense of the divinity of Christ, and saw him as "a kindly Jew, slaughtered long ago in Palestine." This phrase had got under Frank Mallett's skin. He recognised it, and resented his recognition. At times he felt his own church, like the one in Methley's novel, to be surrounded by inimical elementals, crowding in, peering through keyholes, muttering and waiting. He wasn't sure he wanted to meet the author. But he didn't like failing tests. He suggested that he and Arthur should call on Mr. Methley and discuss their project with him.

Patty Dace said that that was an excellent idea. She thought for a moment or two, and then said that the Methleys were very keen on their smallholding and were enthusiastic gardeners. If they didn't answer the doorbell, they could usually be found by walking round into the garden at the back.

They pedalled the East Guldeford road in a companionable silence, and found their way to Wantsum Farm, which was hardly large enough to be called a farm, but supported a few sheep, some ducks, a pair of goats and a small orchard. The farmhouse was squat, with small windows and an ill-fitting door. They rang the bell, and when no one answered, did as Miss Dace had suggested, and went along the path round to the back of the house, across a rough lawn with a diminutive duckpond, and through a gate in a wall into the kitchen garden.

They made their way to the centre of this space between high rows of peas and beans, growing up poles with supporting netting. These screening plants explained why they came upon the Methleys, quite suddenly, in a sheltered spot at the centre of the radiating paths. They were sitting side by side upon the grass. Herbert Methley was holding up a book and Phoebe Methley was shelling peas and broad beans into a colander on her lap.

Both of them were naked. Both wore spectacles.

Everyone stared.

Neither Arthur Dobbin nor Frank Mallett had seen a naked woman during his adult life, though Frank had visited sweaty sick or dying ladies in dishevelled nightgowns.

Both Methleys had sun-roughed and reddened noses, necks and wrists. Both were otherwise lean and pale. Herbert Methley was dark, with flopping fine hair, and a luxuriant black growth under his armpits and round his relaxed member. He was quite sinewy, with thin but muscular arms and legs, and a spattering of wiry hair on his chest. Phoebe Methley had sandy hair tied up in a knot with a broad band. Her breasts—they saw her breasts first, to the exclusion of the rest of her—were flattening mounds, hanging over her rib-cage, with nipples the colour of dog-roses, not sticking out, but retracted. They saw that she too had a lower bush of hair, a brighter ginger than her head, and averted their eyes. She had a long neck, and the skin on it was just beginning to crease into folds. She had big eyes—very big behind the glasses—which if she had been clothed might have been the first thing they would have noticed. They startled her into upsetting the colander, which had been resting on her thighs, so that hard bright green spheres of peas, and grey-green kidney-shaped broad beans rolled everywhere on flesh and earth.

Neither Frank nor Dobbin, curiously, felt urged to back off, or retreat in disorder. Herbert Methley said, easily,

"You have caught us taking the sun. Sun-worshipping, in fact. It is our habit, when we can, and this is truly flaming June."

Frank Mallett murmured that he had been told they would find them in the garden. Innate caution led him not to say by whom he had been told. There had been a glitter in Miss Dace's eye.

Phoebe Methley rolled on her hip to gather up the peas and beans. Dobbin felt impelled to help her with this task, and impelled to turn his head away. He did neither, but continued to study her naked flesh. Frank Mallett said

"Perhaps we should return another time. We came to ask about a lecture series in the autumn. We hoped you might . . ."

Herbert Methley stood up, stolid on his naked feet, and reached from a camping stool some folded garments that turned out to be two embroidered gowns in the form of kimonos. He held one out to his wife, who stood up, in a practised movement, and held out her arms for the sleeves. She did up her sash, and went down on her knees to continue the gathering of the peas and beans. Herbert Methley said

"The original couple in the original garden were in a happier state before they learned shame. Come into the house. Tell me about your lectures."

His voice had a northern tang, which Frank, a child of the Home Counties, could not place. Dobbin knew it came from somewhere quite a way north of his Sheffield.

They padded back in single file, into the house through the back door, Phoebe Methley in the rear with the colander, like some saint's attribute in a painting. She went into the kitchen, to make tea. Herbert Methley offered the two friends seats in low, slatted Arts and Crafts armchairs. The room was full of a smoky darkness, after the blaze of light in the garden. There was a vase of field flowers on a carved table. Dobbin explained the lecture plan to Herbert Methley, and Frank withdrew into his own mind for a moment, wondering whether to thank Methley for *Marsh Lights,* or at least to tell him how it had moved him. He decided against this. He found he was annoyed that this robed person, with his electric black hair, was more the owner, so to speak, of the imagined rocks and stones and elder bushes than he, the reader. Readers ought not to meet writers, he thought. They are *meant* not to.

He came out of his brief reverie to hear Methley proposing a lecture on "something like 'Elements of paganism in modern art,' or even 'Elements of the pagan in modern art and modern religion.'" Frank said that that was exactly what they had hoped for. He then added, with a fake casualness, that he had enjoyed Mr. Methley's work very much. Mr. Methley said he was delighted. He asked if Frank had read his latest book, *Apple-bobbing.* He would be happy to present a copy. He found one, and inscribed it, in a neat hand. The man in the dog-collar smiled cautiously at the man in nothing but a robe splashed with crimson peonies and gold and silver chrysanthemums.

As they rode back home, Dobbin said

"The odd thing is, how much more bad-mannered it seems it would have been, to run away. It is really *odd* that courtesy seemed to mean we had to stand and stare."

Frank said the world was changing. And he agreed, it would have been much ruder to withdraw than to stand their ground. Dobbin, remembering his brief visit to Edward Carpenter, and his naked air-baths and river-baths in the Derbyshire countryside, asked whether Frank would ever be tempted to take the sun, in that way. Frank said, no. He said, after further thought, that the human body was not lovely, seen uncovered. His face was flushed with the energy of his pedalling. The marsh sheep moved slowly across the marshes, grazing the salty grass. Dobbin said it had been a successful day. Frank said it had, indeed.

II

THE GOLDEN AGE

10

The old dairy was a good shape for a pottery studio. The kiln was separated, in a room that had been a scullery; its chimney protruded through
the slate roof. The dairy had slate shelves, with drawers under them, and
various cupboards in the wall, as well as an inner larder, where once butter and whey had cooled, and now the pots were left to become leather-
hard, or to wait for a glaze to dry. The windows were small and deep-set.
There were two, and a wheel stood underneath each of them, one a large
wheel with a treadle motor, one a simple hand-turned wheel, with a
milking stool and bucket beside it. There were little stained-glass
roundels set in the windows. One showed a maned and horned sea
serpent on cobalt waves, and one a white sailing sloop, skimming or
foundering, it was not clear which. Pinned to the door was a life-size
coloured drawing of a Renaissance man, in doublet, hose and gown, all a
dark crimson, and a flat velvet cap. He stood beside a large urn.

Philip, very cautiously, set about ordering things. He swept up the
debris, and made a neat heap of the reusable parts of the exploded kiln.
He was tactful: he knew what things he could rearrange, and what he
might need permission to touch. There were drawers containing tangles
of metals, used for experimental glazes, which he left as they were. The
new clay he put in bins, in a kind of coal-shed, pointed out by Fludd,
who at first stood in the doorway, poised and watchful, to see what
Philip would do. Philip wiped the wheels, and found cloths to cover the
slurry. Fludd said "Well, we might take a look at the kiln. We need to
take care with the mortar. The last was too coarse. It exploded here and
there, and marked the pots." Philip nodded. He knew about explosions.
He even offered advice as they rebuilt the firing-holes and the spy-holes
for the pyrometric cones. He went up on the roof—Fludd held the
ladder—and repaired the chimney, where it came through the slates.
From up there across the yard, he saw the fat-necked shape of what he
did not know was an oast-house. He came down again and asked Fludd
what it was. It was too fat to be a kiln, he said, though at first, when he
saw them in the countryside, he had thought they were bottle kilns.
Fludd explained about the hop-growing, hop-picking and brewing in
Kent. He fired his kiln, he said, with spent hop-poles, which were plentiful and easy to get. Philip said he thought you could make a whacking

big kiln in one of those. Fludd said "We might. You'd have to make some pots yourself." Philip grinned with pleasure, and Fludd grinned back.

Over the next weeks, cautiously, the two of them made pots. At first Philip simply did apprentice-work. He wedged the clay, a process akin to kneading bread, which battered every air bubble and water drop out of the solid mass. Otherwise, as Philip knew very well, a duck-egg bubble could expand, and burst, in the firing, causing large or small explosions, which could lose the whole kiln-full. The clay was mostly local. There was clay dug from Rye Hill, which was a strong red, and clay dug in the marshes, which was sandier. Fludd pointed out one sackful—reddish—and remarked drily that that was the clay to which we all returned, and had been excavated from the graveyard, which had a particularly rich layer of it. He looked at Philip to see what he thought, and Philip grinned again. It was, as Fludd said, good strong clay.

Fludd did import, by train, a pale, creamy clay from Dorset, which he used to make pouring slip, or engobe, and mixed with the red clay to lighten it. Philip learned to pound and sieve this clay, and mix it in water. He learned to revolve clays in the bladed pug-mill which stood where the butter-churn had been. He learned to mix clay bodies and later to mix glazes. Like most potters, Fludd was secretive about the recipes for both these things. He had leather-backed ledgers, locked in a drawer, written in a code, based on Anglo-Saxon runes and Greek lettering, which Philip could not read. He did not use conventional weights, but had his own spheres of dried clay, numbered from one to eight. Philip mixed tin glazes and lead glazes, and was given mugs of milk to counteract the poison in the lead. He mixed antimony and manganese and cobalt. There was a substance called pin-dust, made of the copper powder left over from the manufacture of pins, which made green glazes.

There came a day when Fludd invited him to sit at the wheel and throw a pot. Fludd centred the ball of clay for him, and Philip put his wet square hands on it, and depressed the centre. Brown clay ran over his fingers as though they were becoming clay, smooth and homogeneous, or as though they were clay becoming flesh, with living knuckles and pads. The clay under his hands rose and grew into a thin cylindrical wall, higher and higher, as though it had its own will. It whirled evenly round, lined with the movement of the fingers—up, up, and then suddenly it flapped and staggered, and form slumped into formlessness. Philip was breathless and laughing. Fludd laughed too, and showed him how to finish the rim, how to recognise the form to which the clay aspired. He said that many master craftsmen never threw a pot, but confined themselves to the decoration. Philip said, how can they not want to know the *feel* of the clay. Fludd said, Philip had potter's hands. He took Philip's place, and threw a tall crane-necked jar, a wide deep dish, a useful beaker, a squat jug with a ludicrous lip. Philip tried all these, and after a time succeeded more often than not. He kept laughing, soundlessly. Fludd smiled, benign. His bad temper seemed quite gone. He gave Philip a fat sketch-pad, and said in his ear, as he circled and smoothed the wet earth, that he must feel free to come in and model whenever he wished to.

Philip did not quite trust the genial mood that had come over the artist. He did not presume. He had noticed—without having analysed—the perpetual quality of watchful fear, or at least anxiety, in the curiously inert female members of the family. He had noticed Geraint's scornful wildness, and whatever lay under it, though he could not have told anyone that he had noticed. Fludd appeared, even in a good mood, to have no small talk. The family, very unlike the Todefright gaggle, seemed to expect to eat in near-silence, and disperse after meals. On one occasion Fludd announced that Philip must have more clothes, so that those he was wearing could be washed. He seemed to assume that his vague request would be carried out. In fact, a parcel of clothes was put together—but it was put together by Dobbin and Frank Mallett, some things from both of them, some from members of the parish, fishermen's socks and a jacket, workingmen's shirts, blue and grey. Another working smock, so that Tom Wellwood's could be washed. Philip found Pomona, sitting on the terrace in front of the house, altering cuffs and replacing buttons for him. He protested. She said "You can believe it's a change from embroidering crocus and daisies." Her voice was breathy and too quiet. Philip said he could sew, and Pomona said, be quiet, and let me measure this against you. Imogen came out through the door with glasses of barley water, and said to Philip "If you can help him—so that work is done, and things are made—and sold—we shall all be *greatly* in your debt." Philip said he hoped there would—reasonably soon—be enough for a trial firing.

Fludd and Philip were taciturn, in different ways, and for some weeks they discussed only the weight of clay, or the best place to dry a platter, or the colour of glazes, or why Philip's pots had gone wrong. Fludd did not think to ask his apprentice about his past life, or his family, and Philip volunteered nothing. Philip himself rarely asked questions, and only after some time asked about the figure in the drawing pinned on the door. He said he thought he might have seen it, in South Kensington, was that possible? Fludd said indeed it was. This was the figure of Palissy, the great French potter, from the Kensington Valhalla in the South Court. Ah yes, said Philip. I saw a dish—with toads and snakes— in Major Cain's house. He said it was a fake. Fludd said that the Museum had made a horrible error, buying a modern imitation of a Palissy dish, worth at most £10 0s 0d, for thousands of pounds. He added that it was a mistake easily made—the fakes resembled Palissy ware quite astoundingly accurately. Was Philip interested in the potter? Oh yes, said Philip, who was interested in pots.

Fludd began to tell Philip the heroic life history of Bernard Palissy. He told it in vivid, intense instalments, to the rhythm of the wheel, or the slap and thud of the wedging, or the scratch and slush of the sieving. It felt almost like an initiation rite—this was the exemplary tale of what it was to be a true worker with clay, a complete artist. Fludd's voice was deep, and he left gaps between his sentences, as he meditated on what he was saying. Philip meditated too. He was learning.

He learned that Palissy had been, like Benedict Fludd, an inhabitant of salt marshes, a workingman who painted portraits and had also learned to paint on glass. He was poor and ambitious, and one day someone showed him "an earthen cup, made in Italy, turned and enamelled with so much beauty" that he had been driven to learn how to do such work—"regardless of the fact that I had no knowledge of clays, I began to seek for the enamels, as a man gropes in the dark."

Fludd stopped, and said "Something like that happened to me. It's not *reasonable,* how a choice is made, of this or that craft, this or that life. In my case it was an Italian majolica plate, gold and indigo, covered with arabesques, and a kind of shadow in light—"

Philip said "I saw your watery pot at Todefright. I was looking already of course, I grew up, with the clay, but I *saw* that pot."

It was the most personal thing he had ever said. Fludd, who was painting a jar with a stripped goose-plume dipped in manganese, looked up and smiled straight at Philip, seeing the serious square face.

"It's a form of madness," he said. "Palissy was a madman, and in my book supremely sane, and you'll come to see—if you stay here—that I too am a madman. When the wind's in the wrong quarter, I'm driven the wrong way. So to speak. You'll see, I'm telling you in advance. A good gale in the right direction—and some solid earth—and I'm driven to be a perfectionist."

He told how from seeing *the one cup,* Palissy had narrowed and intensified his search for perfection to the discovery of a *pure white* enamel to put on earthenware. He had a wife, and many children, and lived in poverty, for years upon years, experimenting with mixtures of metals and tinctures he'd learned from glass on hundreds and hundreds of shards of pot, which he took to local potters, or glaziers, to be fired. And he failed, and failed. Fludd gave a bark of laughter, and observed that failure with clay was more complete and more spectacular than with other forms of art. You are subject to the elements, he said. Any one of the old four—earth, air, fire, water—can betray you and melt, or burst, or shatter—months of work into dust and ashes and spitting steam. You need to be a precise scientist, and you need to know how to play with what chance will do to your lovingly constructed surfaces in the heat of the kiln. "It's purifying fire and demonic fire," he said to Philip, who took in every word and nodded gravely. "*Very* dangerous, very simple, very elemental—"

Palissy had given up his search, for a time, and turned his attention to other things—the nature of salt, or salts, the way plants used salts, the way plants used manure, and the way it was connected to salts—and the construction of artificial salt marshes—"on earths which are tenacious, clammy, or viscid, like those of which are made pots, bricks and tiles."

He loved the *earth,* said Benedict Fludd. He worked with the earth and he loved it. He got his hands dirty, and improved his mind.

Another day, he told the heroic story of the initial discovery of the white glaze. He enacted Palissy's four-hour wait at a glass furnace for the three hundred broken pieces of clay, each numbered and covered with a different chemical mixture. The furnace is opened. One of the shards has a melted compound on it, and is taken out, dark and glowing. Palissy watched it cool. His thoughts were black. But as the black shard cooled it whitened—"white and polished"—a white enamel—"singularly beau-tiful." Palissy is a new creature, reborn. The glaze contained tin, lead, iron, antimony, manganese and copper.

Palissy ground a quantity of it—he tells *no one* the proportions, of course—coats a kiln-full of vessels, relights his own kiln and tries to raise it to the heat of the glassmaker's kilns. He works for six days and nights, heaping in faggots, and the enamel will not melt or fuse. "He lost the first firing," said Fludd. "He went out and bought new pots, and reground his glaze, and relit his furnace, and laboured another six days and nights. In the end, he had to feed his furnace with his own floor-boards, and smash up his kitchen table. And still the firing failed, and he was thought of as a mad alchemist or forger, and reduced to extreme poverty. He worked for another eight years, built a new kiln, and lost a whole firing of delicately glazed pieces because the mortar had been full of flints which splintered, and spattered his pots."

"But in the end," said Philip. "In the end, he found the enamel, and made the pots."

"He worked for kings and queens, he designed a Paradise Garden, and an impregnable fortress. He hated alchemists—he knew they were looking for something simply mythical. He liked to watch plants grow, and speculate about how hot springs, and fresh-water springs, rise in the bowels of the earth. He had a theory of earthquakes, which wasn't unreasonable—he was thinking cleverly about earth, air, fire and water moving mountains—"

"What happened to him?"

"He was a Protestant. He didn't accept the doctrines of the Church, and he wouldn't compromise his beliefs. They put him in prison, and condemned him to death for heresy. He should have been burned to death for refusing—in his own words—to bow down to images of clay. He died in the Bastille, tough as ever. He was seventy-nine. I will lend you Professor Morley's book, you can read it in there."

Philip said he was afraid that would be no use. His reading was not up to it. He added, reddening, "It's not up to much, to tell the truth. I can make out simple words, that's all."

"That won't do," said Fludd. "That's no good. Imogen shall teach you to read."

"Oh no—"

"Oh yes. She hasn't enough to do. You won't get far if you can't read. And you'd like to read about Palissy."

. . .

Docile Imogen agreed to give Philip daily lessons in reading. She said she had never taught, and did not know how to teach, but would do her best. She sat with him at a garden table in the orchard, or in the kitchen if the wind was blowing in from the Channel. She wore the same two or three lumpy linen dresses, with uneven necklines and embroidered lilies and irises, on whose petals Philip could *feel* the tiny spheres of blood from pricked fingers. He noticed—he was young and male—that she had a strong and well-proportioned body under the sacklike folds. He thought with the tips of his potter's fingers about the contours of her breasts, which were round and full. He did not notice any female atmosphere around her—no scent in the hair, no hint of the smell of her skin, no hidden damp, breathing—and he was too young to know how odd this absence was. He did think, as she sat with her head of heavy hair bent over the pages, that she resembled some of the ceramic madonnas in the Museum. Sweetly calm. That was not quite an accurate way of putting it.

For the first two lessons she wrote words on a paper pad in flowing calligraphy. Words like "apple" and "bread," words like "house," "studio" and "garden." She then decided Philip would do better with joined-up stories, and brought out a handsome book of fairytales, illustrated with line drawings by various artists, including Burne-Jones and Benedict Fludd. The stories were an eclectic collection from the Grimms and Andersen, from Perrault and the poets, including Tennyson's "Lady of Shalott." The illustrations calmed Philip's sense that he was being asked to read something babyish. This was the world of the Dream scenes enacted at Todefright. He was experimenting with modelling clay snakes and dragons to make handles for pots and he was impressed by Fludd's wicked imps. He read "Cinderella" and "The Sleeping Beauty," "The Princess in the Glass Mountain" and "The Princess on the Pea," "The Little Tailor" and "The Constant Tin Soldier," and finally "The Lady of Shalott" and "The Snow Queen." He practised writing—which he was good at, since he was already precise with pen and pencil. He practised drawing imaginary persons, following the flowing lines of Burne-Jones's garments and hair.

This was not quite what he had wanted. This wasn't his style. Fludd had illustrated "The Snow Queen." His Queen had a long, sharp face and a *sad* smile in a whirlwind of snowflakes over a lake of ribbed ice.

She was attended by deformed imps, and tiny Kai was curled at her feet, like a sleeping snail. The pattern of lines was mesmerising and frightening. Philip wanted to learn from it, and do something different.

The stories—for better or worse, for insight or danger—gave him ways of describing the people around him. Imogen was the Sleeping Beauty, she had pricked her finger and was sleepwalking. He alternated this image with a half-dream image of her as a figure half-baked, fried in biscuit, not yet glazed or coloured, a pale first attempt at a living creature. Geraint—who was at home as little as possible—was some version of the Ashlad, careering about the outside world looking for his fortune. Pomona was all the Cinderella daughters in the hearths, woebegone and unregarded. She had come to his bed twice more, and frightened him terribly. What could he do, if she woke and found herself there?

Imogen never touched him, even accidentally. Pomona pulled at him constantly, fingering his smock, his clay-covered hands, standing behind him at table and ruffling his hair. No one commented on this behaviour, and Philip put a lot of energy into pretending it was not happening.

He made two more dangerous analogies, more or less simultaneously. In his daily work he was slowly making order in Fludd's storerooms, arranging crocks and sacks, sweeping and mopping. When he could write fluently he would label everything, he told himself. The pottery had colonised much of the servants' quarter of the manor house—which didn't matter, because there were no servants, only an old woman who came in from the Marsh and cleaned, slow and creaking, and her daughter, who helped out with the laundry. Philip found a pantry that was locked. He asked Fludd if there was a key, and Fludd replied curtly, no, there was not. Philip remembered this when he read "Bluebeard." He noticed for himself that people in stories always did what they were told not to do, and went where they were told not to go. He couldn't see why, and had no intention of trespassing. But, perhaps because of Bluebeard, he thought the pantry was *odd*.

One day, putting his book together in the kitchen where he had been reading, he saw Seraphita coming in from one of her rare excursions outside.

She came with little skimming steps across the grass and across the gravel path, very slow, very rhythmic. Unlike her daughters, she paid a lot of attention to her dress. She wore white muslin decorated with violets, and a violet shawl. The muslin flowed from a high yoke: she was uncorseted, with a simple violet sash. Her gleaming hair was coiled on her head, and pinned with silk violets. She looked straight ahead, dreamy and distracted, her mouth composed in a pretty, unchanging half-smile. Philip thought it was as though she was skating on unseasonal ice—or rolling along on invisible balls or wheels. She came in through the door and progressed past him, still smiling fixedly, acknowledging his presence with an inclination of her long neck so transient that he wondered if he had imagined it. She reminded him of something. He remembered what it was. It was the puppet Olimpia, from the brilliant performance of Anselm Stern, Olimpia who was an automaton—a puppet *playing* a puppet, where the other characters had been lifelike.

He did not know what ladies did—he supposed they called on each other, went to parties, went shopping, went riding, played tennis. Not Seraphita. She walked, sat in her chair and stared pleasantly forwards till lunch, stitched a little, operated a loom a little, waited a little more, and arrived at supper-time. He thought she passed whole days without speaking. When he read about the Lady of Shalott, who was under a curse, and saw the world only in a mirror, he thought of Seraphita Fludd, and her large, glaucous, luminous eyes. But the Lady was awash with desire and discontent. The Lady rushed across a room and opened a window. Mrs. Fludd rushed nowhere.

Another peculiarity of the family was that they all went for walks in the countryside, but no two went together.

Geraint associated with gangs of young men on the marshes. These local youths, when Philip encountered them, tended to avoid him, or, if they were in groups, to gather and mock at a distance. Geraint made no attempt at all to introduce Philip to the boys he knew, and indeed barely spoke to him. Fludd went out for whole days, wrapped in a caped oilskin, carrying a gnarled walking-stick and wearing a brimmed hat pulled down over his brow. He never invited Philip to join him. Imogen went into Lydd, and occasionally, by bicycle, into Rye or Winchelsea, to buy food and sewing things. Sometimes Pomona went with her. They did not invite Philip—not, he thought, because they did not want him, but because it did not occur to them. He waited a few weeks until his writing had improved, and then wrote a careful letter home. He waited a little longer, and asked Dobbin, who had called in, about posting it. Dobbin explained about the post office in Lydd, and gave Philip a postage stamp. He asked Philip if he would like to walk with him to Lydd—or borrow a bicycle from the Fludds. Imogen said of course he could borrow hers. Dobbin asked if Philip had seen much of the countryside and Philip said he had not left Purchase House.

"Not seen the sea?" said Dobbin.

"No," said Philip. He said "I don't exactly have working hours, or wages . . . So I keep doing what I can."

Dobbin said Philip must walk with him and the vicar to see the sea. He could not be wanted *all* the time in the studio, encouraging though his work was. Dobbin asked Seraphita, who said she was sure Philip should go out now and then, they should ask Mr. Fludd. Fludd, when asked, said of course Philip should see the sea. He was a canny boy. He would know when he could go. And when he could not, of course, he would know that too.

So he walked, with Frank Mallett and Dobbin, to the seaside village of Dymchurch. Dymchurch has a seawall to keep back the ever-encroaching stormy salt water, and the seawall has to be climbed in order to see, or get to, the beach. The three went up the narrow steps, and Frank and Dobbin watched benignly to see their artistic protégé from the Midlands take his first look at the sea. It was a still, sunny day, and waves wrinkled in peacefully, one after the other, and soaked into the sand. Philip felt the mass of the water in his bones, and was changed, but found nothing to say, and stood there looking stolid. Frank and Dobbin waited. Philip said, after a time, that it was big. They agreed. He remarked on the salt smell, and the sound of the gulls screaming. It was a very long time, he felt, since he had been expected to *say* what he did or felt, as opposed to simply doing or feeling. He knew he needed to make acquaintance with the sea on his own, by himself. Children were paddling in the edge of the water. He wondered what it felt like, but his body shrank from it. Frank and Dobbin walked with him along the beach, and he got better at making the required exclamations of interest and amazement. He picked up a piece of seaweed, interested in its texture and little bursting cushions of water. He picked up some fragile pink shells and a razor shell. Frank and Dobbin were delighted. They walked him back into the village, bought him a good lunch in the Ship Inn, and told him tales of smugglers, in whom he was less interested than in the texture of the sea-surface and the seaweed. It was Frank Mallett who asked if he had a sketch-pad and pencils. Philip said no, he had used up the one he had had in South Kensington. Mr. Fludd had given him one and he had used that too. Frank bought him a new one in the general store in Lydd—the paper was not very good, it was greyish and too porous, but it was paper. They took him home.

On the way back to the vicarage at Puxty Frank Mallett asked Dobbin if he felt worried about Philip's position at Purchase House. He seemed to be doing a lot of work, for no reward, said Frank. No one thought of providing things for him, personal necessities. Dobbin said that Fludd *liked* Philip. He thought for a moment, and then said he thought maybe Philip was the only person Fludd liked. He said he hoped Philip could make things workmanlike enough for the pottery to earn some money. And then he could have wages. They must just keep an eye on his welfare.

In the studio Philip told Fludd he had been to see the sea. He said he hoped to go again. Fludd said, why not, and that Philip should go to Dungeness, Dungeness would interest him.

Philip made his way to Dungeness, on foot, one hot day when the broom was shining gold and the seakale was covered with spherical seeds, turning from pale green to bone. Dungeness is bleak and rich, the longest shingle stretch in the world, swept by winds from the sea, westerlies and easterlies. It is inhabited—boats are drawn up on the pinkish bleached pebble banks, and there are strange, soot-black wooden huts, in which fishermen live, and round which lobster pots, anchors, broken oars, nets, accumulate. You walk out, over the stony surface, which is in fact full of strange life, plants and creatures, which prosper and suffer in extremes of weather. At the end of the promontory pebbles are banked high above a shingle beach which is constantly sucked back into the dark wake, churned and thrown up elsewhere. Between the pebbles, ochre-pink, seakales sprout with fantastic fringes of frills or leaves that are purple or rich green or blue-green. Philip saw viper's bugloss, spiky blue and sinister (maybe only because of its name) which he knew from meadows in Staffordshire, but which here seemed bluer and livelier. He saw cotton lavender, and scarlet poppies and clumps of pink valerian. All this was both bright and provisional: in winter it all disappeared as though it had never been.

Philip walked almost ceremoniously along the shingle towards the bank of pebbles at the edge of the land. The first time he came—he came many times—he was eager to reach the water edge, and only took in the human clutter and the tenacious vegetables with sidelong glances. He met no one. It was his adventure, and felt like his place. When he came to the end, he scrambled up the bank with the pebbles rattling and rushing below him, pulling him down with them, so that he went up slowly and with effort. There was the sea, to be seen from the unstable summit. He stood under a sunny sky and saw that it was dark and deep, with patches of wind, and contrary currents, pulling this way and that, and the waves coming in, and in, and shifting and grinding the stones. He thought it would be good to see it in a storm, if he could stand up. He was at the edge of England. He thought about edges, and limits, and he thought about Palissy, studying salt water, and fresh water, springs and runnels on the earth. He hadn't ever considered the fact that the earth was round, that he stood on the curved surface of a ball. Here seeing the horizon, feeling the precariousness of his standpoint, he suddenly had a vision of the thing—*a huge ball,* flying, and covered mostly with this water endlessly in motion, but *held to the surface* as it hurtled through the atmosphere, and in its dark depths, blue, green, brown, black, it covered other colder earth, and sand and stone, to which the light never reached, where perhaps things lived in the dark and plunged and ate each other, he didn't know, maybe no one knew. The round earth, with hills and valleys of earth, under the liquid surface. It was pleasant, and frightening, to be alive in the sun.

He sat down on the pebbles, which were warm, and ate the bread and cheese and apple he had brought. He thought he must take a stone back with him. It is an ancient instinct to take a stone from a stony place, to look at it, to give it a form and a life that connect the human being to the mass of inhuman stones. He kept picking them up, and discarding them, charmed by a dark stain, or a vein that glittered, or a hole bored through. He held them, and looked at them, put them down and lost them, gathered up others. The one he finally chose—almost irritably by now, feeling anxious about the huge accumulated bank of rejects—was egg-shaped, with white lines on it, and narrow little bore-holes that didn't come all the way through. Hiding places for tiny creatures, sand-spiders or hair-thin worms.

He spent time drawing things—the leaves of the seakale, a ghostly crab-shell, a piece of bleached driftwood, just for the pleasure of look-ing and learning. Now and then he looked furtively at the water, to see if it had changed—it always had. He felt changed, but there was no one to tell.

He returned often, and extended his exploration also across the Marsh, discovering the Norman churches perched in sheets of marshy water, kept from foundering by dykes and ditches. Once he saw, from the height of the pebble bank, on a windy day, the bent figure of Benedict Fludd, struggling along at the water's edge, shuffling his feet amongst the stones, gripping his hat. He appeared to be shouting at the sea. Philip did not hail him, and did not mention later that he had seen him.

He drew, and drew, and drew.

He went to Benedict Fludd, when his sketch-book was full, and showed him designs he had made from his drawings, which he thought might perhaps be worked into tiles. He had an idea for a series. An allover pat-tern of seakale leaves, and one of tangled seaweed, with keylike forms and plump bladders. A very delicate, lacy pattern, formalised one day when he had seen, outside the lonely church of St. Thomas Becket in Fairfield, that the dykes and the marsh grass were completely infested with crane-flies, long-winged, angular-legged, fragile.

He made a geometric web of their touching bodies. He made another with the pale little balls of the seakale seeds on their separate stalks, and one with fronds of fennel. He got interested in a principle of design that used the underlying geometrical structure of the natural forms to make a new formalised geometry. He marked them out as best he could with soft pencil on greyish furry paper. He said to Fludd that he knew some-thing about pricking out paper designs which could be used to repeat patterns in biscuit, before glazing. But he didn't know how to make glazes. He knew about pin-dust, which made pea-green, and various things that could be done with manganese. But he didn't know how to get that grey-blue-green of the thicker kales. Or the ghost-colour of the crane-flies, which, he said daringly, it would be good to trace over cobalt colours, or maybe a sort of marshy green?

Fludd said he had an eye. He said his paper was rubbish, and was ruining his designs. Philip said it was all he had. Fludd opened a cupboard and thrust several sketch-pads into Philip's hands, and a box of variegated pens and pencils. He said he thought they might make the tiles. They could try out glazes.

When they had a batch ready for firing, they reloaded the kiln, and sat up all night, feeding it with driftwood and sawn hop-poles. Geraint offered to help, which was unusual. He liked the drama of the cavern of flame and was interested in the product. The firing and the cooling were surprisingly successful. The kiln produced a row of tiles, blue, gold, green and scarlet, with the Dungeness patterns in webs of grey and charcoal and burnt umber over the colours, and another row, in a creamy glaze, with the patterns in crimson and blue and coppery-green. Philip was entranced. Pomona said they were very pretty. Geraint asked if they could make more—a lot more?

"It's not too hard," said Fludd.

"You could sell them. Supply them. To architects and people. They'd make lovely hearths. It could be a steady income."

Geraint was only fifteen, but he was in a perpetual anxiety, bordering on rage, about the absence of a steady income. He mentioned the tiles to Frank Mallett when he went for his history lesson. He asked Frank if he knew anyone who might need tiles to decorate a house, or a church. He said that if only there was a place to show the tiles—in Rye, in Winchelsea, in London, how did he know? But he knew it must be *possible* to find a way. My father is so impractical, said Geraint. He's an artist, he doesn't make things people can buy. But these tiles Philip has made look very nice and can be repeated, they say, over and over. Papa says they are very original. They may be, I don't know. But I do know people will *like* them. Only how will they see them?

Frank and Dobbin discussed the matter with Geraint over luncheon. It was Dobbin who had the bright idea of enlisting Miss Dace. She would know people who might be prepared to display a few tiles—very elegantly—in a bay window, or in the window of an art shop, or even a shop that sold fashions. In the end, they might make their *own* window.

Maybe even a London showroom. Dobbin thought back to the Tode-fright midsummer. He said that Prosper Cain had been there, from South Kensington. He himself had seen Benedict Fludd's work in the Museum, a wonderful vase, and a kind of dish. Maybe Major Cain might help? When he first came to Purchase House himself, he had hoped to be able to suggest a community there—like Edward Carpenter's, but different, centred on the art of ceramics. If all went well, he said, delicately skirting the question of Fludd's problematic temperament, might not Major Cain send funding, and students who would assist, and provide knowledge about buyers for a new range of ceramic work?

Geraint said it all depended on Philip Warren, whether it would last, this time. He had got the kiln going, and designed the tiles.

Dobbin said he was sure Philip would stay, if there was work for him.

And food, said Geraint, and even a living wage. Nobody seems to have thought about *that*. My family thinks it is vulgar to think about money, they think it is too low a thing for them to attend to—but *I know* there isn't any. There really *isn't any*. They can't buy clay, and they're in debt to the farmer for milk and eggs, and I have to charm the shopkeepers in the most disgusting way to have tea, or coffee, or meat. He brightened. "We might offer the butcher some of the tiles, for his display, in exchange for meat. I am not a vegetarian by choice. I *like meat*."

11

In November 1895 Olive Wellwood was great with child. She sat at her desk in her usual flowing robes, which still concealed her condition from visitors and small children, and tried to write. She found it hard to write when she was "expecting"; the stranger inside seemed to suck at her energy and confuse the rhythm of sentences in her blood and brain. Part of her wanted simply to sit and stare out of the window, at the lawn, flaky with sodden leaves, and the branches with yellow leaves, or few, or none, she thought, taking pleasure at least in Shakespeare's rhythm, but also feeling old. She took pleasure, too, in the inert solidity of glass panes and polished furniture and rows of ordered books around her, and the magic trees of life woven in glowing colours on the rugs at her feet. She never got used to owning these things, never saw them simply as household stuff. They were still less real than the ash pits of Goldthorpe. They still had the quality Aladdin's palace must have had for him and the princess, when the genie erected it out of nothing. She kept trying to write a story with the title "Safe as Houses," which would be ironic, because houses were not safe, like the Three Little Pigs' foolish constructions of straw and wattle, or the house in the Bible builded upon sand. Houses were builded upon money, and Humphry had quarrelled with his rich brother, and abandoned his solid job amongst the ingots in the Bank in Threadneedle Street. Her ever-inventive mind played like light over Banks and turf banks, straw, sand, wattle and square-cut quarried stone, but the story would not come, it was not ready, and she was not ready to inhabit her fear of dispossession.

She loved Todefright as much as she loved any living being, including Humphry and Tom. When she thought of it, it had always two aspects, its carved and crafted presence, doors, windows, chimneys, stairs, and the world she had constructed in, through and under it, the imagined, interpenetrating world, with its secret doors into tunnels, and caverns, the otherworld under the green fairy hill. She imagined her home standing on terrifying strata of underground rocks and ores—flint and clay, coal and schist, basalt and grit, through which snaked rivers and branching tributaries of cold water and gleaming ores—liquid silver and gold—she always imagined them liquid, like quicksilver though she knew they were not.

All writers perhaps have talismanic phrases which represent to them the force, the intrinsic nature of writing. Olive's was from the ballad tale of True Thomas, who had been taken under the hill by the Queen of Elfland.

> For forty days and forty nights
> He wade thro red blude to the knee,
> And he saw neither sun nor moon,
> But heard the roaring of the sea.

She wanted to write that—the wading through blood—the absence of sun and moon, and the roaring of the sea—but she had never done so, for her tales, though they were getting darker and stranger, were meant to be for children. There was a proliferation of Christian stories at that time, about the exemplary deaths of little children, looking upwards to the skipping little angels in the fluffy clouds of heaven. But there was nothing like red blood to the knee. She thought briefly about the coming birth, the blood that would flood, the pain that would gripe, the possibility that the emerging stranger on the flood of blood would be mottled, waxy and inert, a tight-lidded doll, like Rosy. She knew about amniotic fluid—the unborn creature did not *really* float in blood—but blood went to it, her blood, down a livid rope that could give life, or could strangle. These things were not spoken of, or written about. They were therefore more real, and more unreal, intensely, simultaneously.

She needed to keep writing. Todefright's continuance depended on it. Humphry had sold several articles, on the Randlords, on poverty in the East End, on the desirability of the public ownership of all land. He was giving courses of lectures in Manchester and Tunbridge Wells and Whitechapel, one of them with Toby Youlgreave on Shakespeare's England, one on local government and one on the history of Britain. He was happy, but he was earning much less than his salary at the Bank. And he was away for days and weeks together. Olive imagined young women staring at him from hard chairs in municipal halls, as she and Violet had stared. She was of two minds about this. She did not like to be touched, when pregnant, and felt practically that there was something to be said for Humphry being distracted. But there was always the risk of a little more than distraction, a public scandal, a wavering of his love, a threat to the safe house.

. . .

When she had no ideas for stories, she turned, half-reluctantly, to the secret tales that belonged to Tom, Dorothy, Phyllis and Hedda, rewriting bits of them in easier, public forms, rounded-off and simplified. There was no stated understanding that the secret and private should be inviolate. Tales are tales, Olive told herself, endlessly retold and reforming themselves, like severed worms, or branching rivers of water and metal. The children's tales contained things taken from other storytellers—her own True Thomas met the Queen of Elfland in her skirt of grass-green silk, and a sinister Mole in Dorothy's world of shape-shifting animals owed much to Olive's own excited childhood fear of Andersen's "Thumbelina." There were passages she wrote and rewrote, sometimes changing them radically, sometimes hardly altering a word. One of the beginnings of "Tom Underground" had been written some time after the original beginning, which had been the meeting with the Elfland Queen. Maybe she could use it to make a saleable tale and Tom would grimace, and she would say it was not the *same* tale, and would confide in him, woman to man, about the terrors of the Cash Flow.

She took up her pen and began writing, on a new sheet. Blood flowed from heart to head, and into the happy fingertips, bypassing the greedy inner sleeper. She would begin with the baby. Sometimes the baby in the tale was a royal prince, and sometimes a sturdy son of a miner. Today, she settled for the prince.

There was once a baby prince, much longed for and much loved, who, perhaps because he was so slow to arrive in the waiting palace, was believed by everyone to be flawlessly beautiful and wonderfully clever. He had a pleasant disposition, though he could easily have been spoiled, and was good at amusing himself when left alone, which of course was rare, except at night. There was a guard outside his night-nursery, for the usual malign fairy had said that something would be stolen from him. His name was Lancelin, Olive wrote, and crossed it out and wrote it again as she could not think of anything better, or different.

. . .

At night, Lancelin's nursery transformed itself (as most nurseries do), into a cavern of shadows. Shadows are mysterious things. They are real and unreal, they have colour and no colour. When the moon shone in through the stone windows she lit up certain things, partially. Lancelin had a rattle in the form of a horned and bearded godling below whose waist a line of carved goatskin became a mother-of-pearl handle, which Lancelin clasped. The godling's arms were outstretched and at his fingertips dangled strings of little bells—gold and silver like metal bubbles, and in the moonlight these became quite other metals, moonmetals, glinting and slaty. Lancelin liked to hold up the manikin and twist him to and fro in the cold light, and the little bells rang out, and Lancelin saw the shadow of his own arm, on the four walls, with the shadow of the toy in its insubstantial fingers. He would make this other self bigger and smaller, longer and shorter, against the white quilt, or wavering over the rails of his crib. He could make a thicker, darker figure, drawing all the dark into itself, squat on the counterpane. Or an elongated, ash-grey, gesticulating demon, holding the room in its arms. It was eyeless, mouthless, sliced into strips by the bars of the cot. He could multiply himself and wave his hands to his shadow hands, which waved back.

There were other shadows in the night-nursery, with which the fearless baby often offered to play. Shadows lurking in dark hollows between pieces of furniture which could be imagined—if you twisted your head so the moonlight caught on a gilt drawer-knob—to have shining eyes in the dark. Or there were tall, still forms who stood in corners and could be seen, and seen through.

You may think it is unusual for a boy not to be frightened of shadows. We all see dangerous faces in knots of wood in wardrobe doors, and witches in the shadows of branches on the ceiling, waving in the wind, stretching out long grasping fingers.

But he was not frightened, which makes what occurred all the more shocking.

Something moved in the dark of the corner of the room, by the skirting board. Lancelin watched it and laughed, but he could not change its shape by moving his head and after a bit it began to move forwards and he saw that the dark was solid. It was sleek and it was shining, it had colourless *dark fur that reflected the moonlight. It had small pale feet with sharp claws, and a quivering snout, with whiskers. And a long pale hairless tail, that thumped and slithered behind it. Its eyes had little crimson centres, that glowed.*

It came on, and on, and Lancelin prepared to welcome it. He liked new friends. It stood up on its haunches, and made a little leap between the bars of his crib, and squatted at his feet. Lancelin made a questioning noise. The creature opened its mouth, showing rows of needle-sharp yellow-white teeth. It lowered its head and began to bite and to rip. It was ripping away, not at the pretty white quilt with its embroidered flowers, but at the invisible seams where Lancelin's shadow touched the soles of his feet, and the tips of his fingers. He could have touched the soft fur of its busy head, but he was afraid of the sharp teeth, and afraid of the scissoring sound they made. It paid no attention to Lancelin himself. When it had worked its way all round the shadow, it rolled it up, with little kneading and rolling movements of its paws, into a tiny bundle. Then it took up the bundle and jumped softly out of the crib and into the dark. Lancelin raised his arm in the moonlight. It cast no grey shape, anywhere. It was as though he himself was not there.

. . .

Here Olive came to the point where she had stopped the last time, and could not think what might happen next. She needed neat narrative, as opposed to the endless flow of Tom's underground river. The baby could not follow the rat into the dark. What would the king and queen and court make of a child without a shadow? She vaguely remembered that there were existing fairytales about lost shadows. *Why* was it frightening to have no second self, to cast no shade? She saw vaguely that she had made the baby so smiling and self-confident because that was an image of shadowless singularity. He might become one of those protected beings who weren't allowed out because they were vulnerable—like Sleeping Beauty, who must not see spindles, like the Buddha, protected from disease and death. He lived in perpetual noonday, which was intolerable. He would *have* to go down the rathole, no two ways to it, he would have to go into the world of shadows and retrieve his own. She imagined a kingdom of rats with human shadows, mocking a questing infant. A Helper was needed—a dog, a cat, a worm (no, though it was subtle and subterranean), a magic snake, maybe, snakes ate rats . . .

She could not think what to write next. And at that precise moment— a relief, and a terror to writers—she heard the wheels of the station-fly on the gravel. Humphry was back. She wrote a sentence

"At first the king, queen and courtiers noted only that Lancelin was even more beautiful, sunny and smiling than they remembered. And then this singularity of grace began to be alarming."

Always leave writing *in medias res* was a rule she had learned. She put away her writing pad, and went downstairs to greet her errant husband. As often happened, Violet had got there first, was helping with his over- coat, had taken possession of his bookbag and umbrella. He kissed Olive, and made a joke about her girth, which did not please her.

He went into his own study, to look at his letters. There was a consider- able heap of them, some a week or two old, some arrived yesterday. Olive sat in a rush-backed chair in the corner of his study. She was dis- inclined to go back to her interrupted work, and mildly resentful of the interruption.

Humphry read the letters, smiling to himself. He put them back in the envelopes—except the bills. Then he came to one, out of which a press cutting fell. Humphry read, and was frozen. Olive asked what was the matter, and Humphry handed her the cutting.

"Slit throat at train terminus. Financier found dead." For a moment, Olive thought Basil had killed himself—Humphry's violent reaction suggested something as grave as that. It was not Basil—it was "Freder- ick Oliver Heath (38) a member of the Stock Exchange who had been unable to sleep for the past 3 weeks owing to trouble caused by heavy monetary losses" . . .

Olive said "Did you know him?"

"No, but I know he was in trouble with Kaffirs. I know several things that most people don't yet know. I am sure—I have always been sure— that Basil is too deep in Barnato's muck except that 'muck' is too solid a word, it's *murk,* a murky cloud of obfuscation and prestidigitation and rope tricks and promises never meant to be kept. Basil won't have sold, partly because he won't want to admit I might have been right—I *know* Basil. I must telegraph him. I'll take the pony-trap. Forgive me, my dear, when I've only just come in . . ."

Humphry was both genuinely distressed, and taking energy and pleasure from the drama. He strode out, calling to Violet to get the man to harness the pony, to fetch his coat . . .

Olive sat in Humphry's study, and pondered the useful words, muck and murk. Rats were mucky and murky. Briefly her mind revisited, and shied away from, Peter's and Petey's tales of rats in mines, eating candles, and the men's snap. She began to tidy Humphry's papers, and cast an eye over the letter he had been smiling to himself over. It began "My Very Dear."

She looked at the signature. "Your (no longer a maid!) Marian."

I am not a fool, Olive said to herself. It is *much more* sensible not to read this, which is not addressed to me. She read it.

My Very Dear

You have been gone for so short a time, and yet already everything, the whole world, is quite another place, emptier and fuller. I truly do not know who I was, or how I lived, before I first saw and heard you. The woman I now am came into being as you spoke about the lovely equality of the bantering lovers in Much Ado About Nothing, *about how a man and a woman can love, and not know they love, and how very rarely lovers in plays and stories are at ease with each other. I thought I would teach my students that wisdom, and did not see, until too late (blessedly too late), how my deepest desire was to be at ease in that way with you, you your very self. If I fought your ideas in public it was only in search of that ease where anything may be said. And when you said other things—when I felt myself personally valued and for the first time (however illusorily, however guardedly) to be beautiful and desired—I became your slave, and will remain your slave. Though I cannot imagine you wanting to play master, you are a friend first, and a lover second, and I, I am shining with joy.*

I wrote as far as this, yesterday, my darling. I did not say I was feeling unwell, while you were here, for I wanted not to waste one moment of our secret and precarious time. But I was unwell, and now I know the cause,

*the most natural of all, and truly a matter of rejoicing, for me at least. I am
to be a Mother. I ask for nothing—no help, no advice—I am an
independent woman, and trust to remain so. If all goes well, and if we can
continue to be at ease with each other in these new circumstances, I should
like my child to know his father in some way—though never to ask for any
material thing. Oh, my Very Dear, of course I am afraid, but I am also
resourceful, and will put no burden on you, believe me—only a prayer
that, if it can conveniently happen, we may continue to see each other.*

Your (no longer a maid!) Marian

Olive refolded this document, and said Damn, several times. This was
bad, very bad. This was a woman who was somebody, not a frivolous bit
of skirt. This was a person not unlike Olive, to whom Humphry was
real, and who was, as she said, *at ease* with him, which must mean that he,
in turn, was *at ease* with her. Some sort of teacher, who had heard him
talk on Shakespeare. Someone to whom he indubitably owed something, despite her disclaimers and his financial position. "Damn," said
Olive again, beginning to be angry, stoking an inner flame. "Damn and
damn." She was quite sincerely worried about the predicament in which
this strange woman found herself. Humphry must *of course* offer help, it
was his duty. She knew only too well the special feeling he gave of being
comfortable and at ease with women—it was what she loved in him,
herself. She thought it went with one kind of promiscuous love-
making, rarer than the Don Juan with his sequential conquests, the man
who found women truly interesting. If Humphry had come home at
that moment, she would have embraced him, perhaps, and smiled ruefully, and made sure of her own charm and her own central place in
his affections—which she had never, really, had cause to doubt. But
Humphry did not come home, and Olive's mood veered into grievance.
She began, almost vindictively, to read the other letters on the desk, and
discovered two rejected articles. "A very clever analysis, but so opinion-
ated that I can't quite see it as an expression of the beliefs of our journal."
"Very interesting, as always, but I am afraid we have no room for articles
of such limited appeal to the general public." Olive felt threatened—she
should be *earning money* with her little prince and her sinister fat rat, not
standing here waiting to discuss peccadilloes, or worse. Todefright was
threatened. Olive said Damn.

. . .

By the time Humphry came in, she was like a humming top, spinning with wrath. He was followed by Violet, gathering up his coat and hat.

"I have sent a telegram," he said. "I think I must go and see Basil, I am absolutely certain I know dangerous things he does not know. I'll wait for an answer to my telegram and then set off. This will have far-reaching and terrible consequences, if Barnato's nets are unravelling—and I know it is not *if,* it is *when*—"

"You can go and see Marian," said Olive.

"Don't be silly, she's in Manchester," said Humphry, preoccupied with gold mines and brothers.

He saw what he had been led to betray, and took in his wife, and the dissipated heap of letters. He smiled his foxy, intent smile, *interested* in Olive's reaction.

"*Touché,*" he said. "You of all women should know better than to read private papers. It's not serious, you know that. Nothing to do with you and me, which is why you shouldn't stoop to reading private papers."

He put out a hand to caress her, and Olive slapped it down.

"It is to do with me, it is *deeply* to do with me, we shall lose Todefright unless we earn some money, and don't do things which create more dependent mouths. I work and work, I have to keep Todefright going *by myself,* and I am sick and anxious and should be resting—"

"Money," said Humphry. "Money, or sex relations, which comes first, which is more certain to cause arguments and harm marriages? An interesting problem."

"It isn't an interesting problem, it's *my life*—" cried Olive. Up to that point, it had not been clear to either of them whether a monstrous row was going to happen, or could be avoided. Now it was clear that it was to happen, it had to be gone through with. Olive clasped her hands round the unborn infant, and began to shout, like an operatic fishwife. Humphry could have tried to calm, or apologise—in any case he had to abandon his attitude of detached amusement and calm certainty. He was never defensive. When threatened, he attacked. "Listen to yourself," he said. "How can a grown-up woman make such a racket? I thought you had become a civilised being, but no such thing, you rant like a skivvy, like a washerwoman—"

There were various shapes the rows took, various cycles of reproach and counter-reproach, various sabre-slashes at the whole fabric of the marriage. This row was long, and bad.

Tom and Dorothy and Phyllis stood on the stairs, listening, ready to scurry up to the bedrooms before they were caught. They heard the sentences they always heard.

"I have always tried to love all your children equally, you cannot say I have not. It has not been easy, though you may think it has. You do not thank me."

"I might say the same. You cannot claim I distinguish your children from my own. All of them have their place, equally, equally, you must admit that."

Dorothy put her face in her hands. She was the one interested in the human body. She had a clear idea of how children came into the world. It was easy not to know who your father was. It was much harder not to know who your mother was, though it could happen, Griselda had suggested ways in which society women slid changelings into families. Some village families had complicated structures where grandmothers, mothers, aunts and elder sisters were indistinguishable, where children grew up supposing their mother was their sister, and their grandmother their mother. People had babies at ages hardly older than she herself now was, this she knew. But here, who, how? Violet liked to say she was their "real mother" but as far as Dorothy could work out, she liked to say this precisely because she was not, she offered free mother-love from the position of not-mother, of maiden aunt. You could see who was somebody's mother, you could see the unborn child growing.

It was odd, it was certainly odd, that there was a family habit of sending everyone away before the arrival of new babies. She hadn't been at home *at the moment of* anyone's birth. She had been with Griselda, or on holiday at the seaside with friendly families. Dorothy did feel threatened. Whose child was or wasn't she? Almost unconsciously, she detached herself a little from love. She would be canny. She would not invest too much passion in loving her parents, her *acting* parents, in case the love turned out to be disproportionate, unreturned, the parent not-a-parent.

. . .

Tom did not think clearly. He felt his world was threatened, and his world was Todefright, woven through and through with the light from the woods and lawns, summer and winter, golden and frosty, and also woven through and through with the web of his mother's stories, stories whose enamelled colours and inky shadows, hidden doors and flying beasts made the real Todefright seem briefly like a whited, plaster-cast sort of a place, a model of a home merely, which propped up the constant shape-shifting of the otherworld, whose entrance was underground. He didn't—he *couldn't*—even begin to imagine Olive not his mother, and it did not occur to him to try. And Humphry was Humphry, who had always been there. What he feared was that everything might turn out to be cardboard and plaster of Paris, though he feared this in the depth of his gut and behind his eyes. He could not have put it into words.

Phyllis did not hear all the words of the shouting parents. She watched Tom and Dorothy, for a clue to how to react. They were upset. Why? They were excited. By what? As usual, she was left out, too stupid, too innocent. She pulled at Tom's arm—he was kinder than Dorothy—to ask "What is it, what is it?" a meaningless question that went unanswered. Dorothy said "We'd better scarper, we'll get found out," and began to tiptoe, rapidly, up the stairs. As she did so, silence fell inside the study. They had never stooped to peering through keyholes, and so did not see Humphry and Olive, entwined, her heavy womb pressed against his trousers, her head burrowing into his shoulder, his hand stroking and stroking her descending hair, a small smile on his sharp mouth.

The next day, Humphry ordered the yard-boy to bring the dog cart early, and drive him to the station. Olive appeared, fully dressed, in coat and hat, long before her usual time of rising. She said she intended to visit Prosper Cain. She needed to resurrect her museum adventure story. John Lane the publisher was interested in it. Humphry smiled, and helped her up, and they drove off together, chatting amiably. Humphry fully understood that it was necessary for Olive to reestablish the balance between them, by visiting a man who clearly admired her. He understood, more ruefully, that her financial anxieties, and the sense that the household depended on her writings, and her fear that these were threatened by the coming birth, were real concerns, even if she was half-teasing him with her independence and importance.

Tom and Dorothy and Phyllis watched them go.

"*That* seems to be more or less patched up," said Dorothy.

"Is it, is it?" said Phyllis, and got no answer.

"If he makes it up with Uncle Basil, I shall certainly get sent away to school," said Tom.

"You might like it," said Dorothy, who knew Tom was appalled at the idea of sleeping and eating with hundreds of what she thought of, and was sure he did, as savage boys.

"I might not," said Tom, digging her in the ribs. "Let's go to the Tree House."

Its secret enclosure was calming and energising, even in wet late autumn, even in the beginning of winter. It was easier to find, now the leaves were fallen, but still protected by clumps of natural-looking bracken, pushing into crannies, and by the low sweep of the evergreen branches. Phyllis walked, as usual, three steps behind the others. None of them spoke. Part of Tom's mind was watching a supernatural horse, in the next coppice, with a cloaked rider. Dorothy examined gateposts on which a gamekeeper had pinned rows of stiff little corpses, bedraggled crows, and stretched stoats, and the small, pathetic shrunken velvet of moles. It was unfortunate for Olive, who had no idea of this, that Dorothy associated her "own" story of the anthropomorphised furry creatures in and under the woods and meadows, with these slaughtered pests and predators. Dorothy carried a leather satchel, into which she pushed carefully unpinned specimens, who could be dissected and examined. She didn't ask herself if Olive knew she didn't like "her" story. She was taciturn by nature, and observed drily to herself that Olive was so excited by her own inventions that she hardly needed a response from the designated audience. Dorothy wasn't a very reading child, though she was very bright, and read fluently. She had one book which she carried in a pocket because it amused her darkly. It had been sent to Olive to review in *The English Illustrated Magazine,* along with a heap of children's tales and fairy stories, although it was no such thing. It was called *Mother Nature's Little Book of Bedtime Rhymes,* and was by Herbert K. Methley. It contained prancing, jaunty little rhymes about creatures which, if anthropomorphised at all, must appear evil in that human guise. The spider and the praying mantis, crunching up the living, nutritious limbs of their mates. The cuckoo, that great deceiver, laying her camouflaged egg (Nature was so *helpful,* the blotches were indistinguishable from the willow-warbler's own eggs) and flying off to sing in the branches, whilst her industrious skinny offspring, with its blind, fleshy head, evicted the little warblers, one by one, and grew into a monster that dwarfed the nest. The ichneumon fly, laying its exquisite eggs under the skin of grubs, who were walking larders, slowly sucked dry. Dorothy had showed it to Tom, who waved it away. He was not a boy who pulled the legs and wings off things. Dorothy said

"It's a good book because that's how the world *really is*. And it makes it funny, which is clever."

"*What* is it, how is the world, what do you *mean*?" asked Phyllis, and got no answer.

12

Prosper Cain was happy to be distracted, by Olive Wellwood, from the problems of the Museum. Various papers and magazines were on the attack, criticising the circulating exhibitions, expressing shock at the imprudent purchase of fakes, including the Palissy platter, and most of all complaining that the art education of the British had "idiotically and inexplicably become vested in the hands of soldiers." The Museum was nothing more than an almshouse for the army. The present Director, Professor Middleton, was not a soldier, but a reclusive scholar from Cambridge, who was greatly ill at ease with Major-General Sir John Donnelly, head of the Department of Science and Art, and was also persecuted by the irascible aesthete James Weale, keeper of the Art Library. The atmosphere was sour, and Prosper Cain spent much of his time shuttling between incompatible people with unacceptable proposals. He had no one in whom to confide, and felt lonely. It was pleasant to be greeted by Mrs. Wellwood's warm smile of admiring respect, to be asked for anecdotes and practical information that were easy and pleasant to impart. He noticed her condition, under her swinging Liberty dress. In some curious way it allowed him, safely, to recognise that she attracted him. She was like a lovely carving or painting, though he could hardly say so. She fixed her liquid dark eyes on him, and he relaxed, and smiled back. He asked how the tale of the child detectives was progressing. She said that the construction of a detective story was interesting.

"You know, Major, a story, especially a mystery story, is all topsy-turvy. It works *backwards,* like tunnels of mirrors. The end is the cause of the beginning, so to speak. I need my resourceful children to find hidden things, and *therefore* I need to know who hid them, and where, and why. But really they were hidden in order to be found."

Prosper Cain said he hadn't thought of it that way. He asked if her own children helped her to write about child characters. He was not sure he knew how young people thought or felt, despite having two of his own.

Olive dropped her voice, and leaned towards him.

"You know, it's a truism that writers for children must still be children themselves, deep down, must still feel childish feelings, and a child's surprise at the world."

"You write from your own inner child? I don't know if my own still exists. Military life and museums do not encourage spontaneity."

"I will share a secret with you. I don't *really like* making up imaginary children. I get most frightfully bored by their little disputes and their innocence. I think the persisting child in myself inhabits Elfland—not pretty gauzy Fairyland but a more dangerous and wilder place altogether. I like watching invisible beings and strange creatures who creep into the real world from *elsewhere,* so to speak. I would like to write the *Morte d'Arthur* or 'Goblin Market,' not *The Adventure of the Hidden Casket*. But readers have an insatiable desire for these clever little persons who detect and have comic adventures. So I try to oblige them."

She laughed. She said she was talking too much about herself, she was sorry, she would go back to her list of questions. Prosper Cain said he liked to hear about herself. Indeed, he said, he found her work—and her—fascinating. He hoped she would continue to treat him as a friend, and talk to him freely. "Most of my conversations," said Prosper Cain, "are dull, formal and difficult."

Olive said she could not believe that, and if it was really so, it was a pity, and should be remedied.

What they would next have said remained uncertain, as they were interrupted by Florence, who had found Geraint Fludd wandering in the South Court, all by himself. She had invited him to tea. He had said he had indeed hoped to come across her, there was something he was trying to get up the courage to ask her father . . .

Tea was called for, and brought. Olive studied Geraint. He was fifteen, two years older than Florence, who was demurely dressed as a young lady, in a serge skirt and a striped shirt, and looked older than she was. Geraint was dressed shabbily in worn breeches and a Norfolk jacket. His wrists were outside his cuffs. His skin was tanned like a gipsy, Olive thought, and he had dark red cheeks amongst the tan, and an elegant mouth. His hair was very curly and all over the place—a kind of Pan figure, Olive thought, a wild boy disguised as a real, ordinary boy, who would be interesting to insert into a story. He was both ill at ease and full of determination, she saw, watching him frown, watching him watch Major Cain over the rim of his cup. He did not know how to say what he had come to say, Olive saw, and Florence also saw. Florence said "Geraint has something he wishes to ask you, Papa. He came on purpose."

"Ask away," said Prosper, full of an unusual benign goodwill, pleased by Olive's presence and also by the interruption—and therefore the safe prolongation—of their intimate moment.

"It's hard," said Geraint. He meant to ask Major Cain to help to sell his father's work, to help to get the pottery on its feet again. But he could not plead, and should not betray the family's appalling poverty—not least because that would be self-defeating. Major Cain would think very ill of him if he did that.

Olive watched him seeking inside himself for the right words. She was already turning him into one of her detecting children—that sense of adult responsibility in a child was a *useful* emotion to study. Also the blush, and the reticence. She said

"I believe you have—or your family has—been able to help the lost boy I met when I first came here—the runaway boy Julian and my Tom pursued in the cellarage? How is he doing? His drawings were delightful. Is he still with you?"

"Yes, he is. Yes, that's partly why I've come. He's been helping my father—working with my father—and they've got the kiln going and made a lot of ware that my father seems really pleased with. I wanted to ask you—to ask you—if you would come and look at what they are making." He hesitated. "My family isn't *practical*. It must be the most unpractical family in the country, I sometimes think. Nobody thinks—"

Geraint looked desperately round the room. Prosper, Olive, and Florence were all looking at him with courteous encouragement.

"Nobody thinks, sir, about how to sell anything, or get anyone to come and look at what's been made. My mother and sisters are very *artistic*." Despite himself a note of pure contempt crept into this adjective. "We had that man Dobbin, you know, who was at the Midsummer party and the puppet show—he wanted to help my father, and he wanted to set up some sort of school, or community in Purchase Hall—there's plenty of room, it could work. But he couldn't help my father—he hasn't the aptitude, they said—and my father kept getting angry, and Dobbin went to live with the vicar. But he said you said my father has genius, and that the Museum has some of his work and I thought—I thought you might understand what should be done next. Or anyway come and look at the new work. My father really *likes* Philip—I've never seen him work like this before."

He hesitated. He blushed again. Olive thought his blush was delightful.

"The thing is—nobody has even thought of paying Philip. It isn't really *right*. I seem to be the only one who thinks about these things—

who will buy the pots, where the—the clay, and the chemicals—and—and *our food,*" he said in a rush, "will come from."

"I'm sorry," he said, very red indeed now, wishing already that he hadn't mentioned the food.

Prosper Cain looked appropriately serious. Florence cut a piece of cake for Geraint.

"I shall come to Rye. I shall bring Florence and Julian, who has a holiday, and I shall come to see this new work, and think what may best be done. Your father is indeed a genius, and is indeed impractical, like many great men. Should I write to him, or simply appear?"

"Write," said Geraint, "in a general sort of way. Don't say I came."

"Of course not. I shall come next weekend, which is Julian's holiday. It will all appear quite casual."

"May I come?" said Olive impulsively. "I should dearly like to see the new work, too. I may be able to help. Or Humphry may, he knows all sorts of financial people. I could bring Tom and Dorothy, it will be a pleasant excursion . . ."

Prosper said he would be very happy if she came. Geraint thought of saying that *large numbers* of visitors might have a bad effect on his father, and then thought he had achieved all he could have hoped, and should let things be. Olive read his mind in his face.

"I don't think we should all necessarily bother your father, not all at once. We will linger in the background and see if we can be helpful. And look at the sea, it will be wonderful to see the sea again."

Geraint smiled at her. She smiled back. "And you? What do you mean to do with your life? Are you artistic?"

"Good Lord, no," said Geraint, with excessive vehemence. "It got left out of me altogether, anyone would think I was a changeling. I'm clumsy with my hands, and my family say I have no taste."

"So what do you hope to do, then?"

"What I want," said Geraint, relaxing after his huge effort, "what I want, is to make a lot of money and be *comfortable.* I'd like to be in a bank, or something. I don't know where to start."

"You start by asking my husband," said Olive, who loved giving people things. "He gave up his bank position, but he knows exactly how to set about finding one. When you are quite sure that is what you want."

"Oh, I am. I think and think about it. I am quite sure."

13

The Cains and the Todefright Wellwoods came to Rye, and stayed in the Mermaid Inn. The weather, which had been stormy and chilly, was suddenly bright, clear, and even warm. St. Martin's Summer, said Benedict Fludd, who was invited to lunch in a private room in the Mermaid, with Seraphita and his children. There is often a false summer in the third week of November, a pleasant enough delusion. Prosper had made military arrangements. He had ordered a roast goose, with onion sauce, and heaped roast potatoes and buttered carrots, to be followed by a huge apple pie with thick cream. They had come by train; the Todefright party included Tom and Dorothy; Violet remained in charge of the lower half of the family. After lunch, Prosper had explained to Florence, all the young folk would go for a ramble—maybe along the beach at Dymchurch, since the weather was so mild and tempting. He needed to talk to his old friend, and he needed to do it quietly. The Fludds were hungry: the food was plentiful and comforting. Geraint talked to Julian, who was sitting opposite Tom, at the youthful end of the table, studying his face. Dorothy talked to Florence, about schooling. Florence was going to Harley Street College in the next academic year. Dorothy did not know what would become of her though she did know that Tom was to be crammed for entrance to various schools.

Seraphita, Imogen and Pomona smiled serenely. Fludd spoke about St. Martin, St. Martin of Tours, that was, who had been a Roman soldier and given his cloak to a beggar. He was often depicted with a globe of fire, or with a goose, since they flew over round about his feast. There was a good window in St. Martin's Church at Puxty, which used the glass very effectively in the ball of fire.

Philip had not been included in the party, and had not expected to be. He had taken some bread and cheese and set out in the strangely unseasonal weather on a long ramble. He walked to his favourite Marsh church, the diminutive, brick-built church of St. Thomas Becket, near Fairfield. Philip thought of this church as his own particular church; he knew little about Thomas Becket, and did not know that the church was built on Becket lands. He had never seen a church so isolated. It stood amongst water-meadows, stretching flat and far, on which for miles the fat sheep busily cropped the salty grass. There was no road leading to it, and from it no village, no high road could be seen, only the marshes and the weather. The marshes often flooded in the winter, and then the church appeared to float mysteriously on sheets of floodwater, reflected in the dark-bright surface on calm days, blustered and beaten by howling winds and spray on stormy ones. Philip made his way from tuft to tuft of the marsh grass, for it was sodden underfoot and water welled up between tussocks. When he got to the church, he looked around at the endless sky, the flat horizon, the apparently endless sheep-studded meadows, and felt peaceful. He didn't think exactly in language. He noticed things. The dabbing movement of a duck. The awkwardly beautiful, almost crippled look of the trailing legs of a flapping heron. Fish squirming in mud. Patterns made by the wind.

He sat for a long time on a stone in the churchyard, not even thinking. Time was so slow, there was no reason ever to stand up, or to move on.

A figure appeared on the Fairfield path, at the limit of vision. A woman in silhouette, in a skirt, with her hair bound in a scarf, and what looked like a small suitcase in her hand. She stopped to lean on a gate, and then walked a little way, and then sank to the ground, like a kind of hummock, and stayed down. Philip stood up, and set off across the marsh, feeling that this other person, who now shared the emptiness with him, was both an intruder and perhaps in need of help.

It took him some time to reach her. During his striding, leaping, occasionally bogged approach, she did not stir.

She appeared to have fainted or died. She had crumpled quite compact, her body in a ball, her face on her outstretched hand, the cardboard suitcase on the wet dust, within reach. Philip knelt down. He did not want her to be dead. He took her shoulder, and turned her face slightly towards him. The face was grimy, the lips slightly cracked, the eyes closed. Her nostrils and lips trembled: she was breathing. A breeze tugged at the edges of her gipsy-scarf, which was more animated than she was. She was wearing a felted coat, bunched over a grey skirt. Her ankles were swollen, and her shoes cracked and dusty. She had walked a long way.

Philip squatted beside her amongst the wayside grass, and took her hand, which seemed the politest thing to do. He bent over, and said in her ear, gently,

"Can I help?" and then, "How do you feel?"

She trembled a little and stirred, and opened her eyes, briefly, staring out past Philip's occluded head at the sunlight. What she said, however, was his name.

"Philip Warren."

Philip stiffened.

"I'm looking for Philip Warren," she said. "I keep getting lost."

Philip pushed back the scarf and the hair from her face, rearranged her features in his mind's eye and saw she was his sister Elsie. Elsie, a year older than Philip, was the sister he loved, had found it hardest to leave. He said

"Elsie. It's me. I am Philip."

"I can't see your face because of the sun. I got lost. I walked and walked and walked, and there were no people or places. What are you doing out here?"

Philip felt briefly very annoyed.

"What are *you* doing is the question. Can you sit up?"

He pulled at her, no longer with respect, but with the intimacy of family. She sat up, and smoothed her skirts, stretching her horrible feet in front of her. She had always been, as far as was possible, fastidious about her person and clothing.

"Mum died," said Elsie. "I came to tell you."

"No one wrote."

"You don't put any addresses on your postcards, do you? Probably you don't want to be *bothered*. But I thought you ought to know Mum died. Auntie Jessie took the others, except Nellie, who's gone into Service. I didn't think I could last, I didn't think I could see the year out in a house with Auntie Jessie."

"What did she die of?"

"Lead poisoning. That's what was always coming, and it came. She asked for you. A lot. She wanted me to give you her brushes and the Minton cup, and I've got them in that suitcase. I said I'd find you. She *knew* I couldn't abide to be with Auntie Jessie. And I *have* found you, though not where I'd have expected."

She spoke with a kind of determined vehemence, her voice thick with dust and thirst. She said

"You ought not to have . . ."

She began suddenly to weep, hot little tears bursting out through her eyelids, spattering on her grey cheeks.

Philip was partly trying, and partly refusing, to think about his mother. He half saw her, thin and stooping, and crossly shut the picture out.

Elsie heard the next question.

"The postcards said Romney Marsh, and Winchelsea. I walked to Winchelsea, and someone said if I was looking for potters there was a madman out at somewhere called Purchase. So I set off walking there, and got lost, as you see."

"You'd better come back wi' me. Can you walk?"

"I *was* walking."

"Aye, and you fell over, I saw you. Can you get on your feet?"

"I shall have to."

It took a long time, a rather painful time, to walk back to Purchase House. Elsie leant on Philip, briefly from time to time, and then limped on, erect and full of will. She was a thin, wiry girl, with high cheekbones, blue eyes, and a set mouth, not sulky, but ungiving. That was new, the hardness of her look.

Philip was ashamed of his most powerful feeling. This was that he had *lost* something—and he was not thinking of his mother. He was thinking of his solitude. He had, through sheer willpower, broken free of the Five Towns, and come to an unlikely place where no one knew who he was, or what he felt, and all that mattered was that he was good at doing what he had always known he *must* do, making pots with his hands. If he had a sister—who would spread her disparaging opinions, or just as embarrassing, her loving opinions, of him, amongst these people who helped him, but weren't interested in his self or soul—he would have *lost* something, he thought. Then he thought at last, as he trudged along the lane, between hedges now, of his poor mother, who had always *lost* almost everything, except the skill at painting that had killed her, and the brood of children who might die, or become horribly ill, and were too many for her small wage to feed, so that they grew thin and grey-skinned like Elsie. Who had a will, he said to himself, thinking furiously as he didn't often think. Elsie had a will, and it looked quite as strong as his own.

He thought also, no one paid him any money, he had nothing to *give* Elsie, he was going to have to beg on her behalf. It was a bad business.

. . .

When they arrived back at Purchase House, they were both shocked to find the kitchen full of people. The whole lunch party was there, Prosper Cain and Humphry Wellwood, Benedict and Seraphita, Olive. The young people had gone on a beach ramble, and were back with things collected from the shore, shells and seaweeds, razors and angels, crab-claws and carapaces, bladderwrack and leathery bladed fronds, bronzed or bleached. Arthur Dobbin and Frank Mallett were there, having been invited to tea though not to lunch. Seraphita had bestirred herself to make some insipid tea, which she served in a variety of faience cups and saucers, no two the same. Imogen had made a cake, which had sunk towards the centre, and crumbled on the plates. Everyone was standing round the kitchen table, peering at it, so that the two Warrens, coming quietly in through the door, saw only bent backs and heard the murmur of voices. Elsie thought, erroneously, her head swimming, that Philip had become part of fashionable society. They were perceived by Pomona, who hurried towards them, crying "Here he is, here he is," and stroking Philip's arm. Everyone turned round. The party surveyed the two Warrens.

Benedict Fludd said "Ah, there you are. We are looking at your handiwork. At what you have made."

Philip said "Excuse me, this is my sister Elsie, from Burslem. She come to look for me. She walked. All the way from Burslem."

The gathering took stock of Elsie. Elsie was intimidated by Olive's hat, which was black and ample, decorated with scarlet bows and fruit. Olive said "Extraordinary." Seraphita said "Really?" Frank Mallett observed that the young woman looked ready to faint with exhaustion and should be given a chair, and some tea, perhaps, or a glass of water. Dobbin brought a chair which he set down near the back door. Elsie collapsed onto it. Everyone went on staring. Seraphita absently poured a cup of tea, which Dobbin gave to Elsie. Elsie handed it back to him: she was shaking too much to hold on to it genteelly.

It was somehow clear that Seraphita had no idea of what to do, and did not propose to do anything.

That left Olive, who was a grown woman, and Frank Mallett, who was a clergyman. He consulted Olive, and it was agreed that Miss Warren should be found a place to rest, and perhaps some temporary fresh clothing. Olive bent over Elsie and said it was very odd to be present at the discovery of *two* runaways in one family. She was thinking what a good story it would make, the girl who had walked across half England to find her brother. She smiled at Elsie, absently, studying her intently. Elsie said later to Philip that there was something witchy about the woman with the hat. Somewhere under the gratified storyteller in Olive stirred a memory of her own flight from indigence in the north. Philip had no intention of telling the assembled gathering that his mother was dead, so Olive had no clue that Elsie was, in some ways, close to her own younger self. But she sensed it, she sensed something, of which she would not speak.

A display had been arranged—it was Geraint's idea—of some of the new vessels, and one or two different layouts of Philip's newly designed tiles. Fludd called Philip over to talk to Prosper Cain about the glazes, and about how he had chosen the designs, the Dungeness flora, seakale and bladderwrack, crane-flies and fennel. Prosper spoke knowledgeably about the glazes, and admired the steely blue-green, and the rich red, with surprising pinky-white wings in it. Humphry said—as it was hoped he would say—that a fortune could be made, if these were properly marketed. He had been to the Martin Brothers' showroom in Brownlow Street. Something like that might help. Geraint said "There are lots of little shops in Rye showing all sorts of crafts. There could be a *better* shop, for *better* work." Humphry said Geraint had the right ideas—was he a potter? No, said Geraint, no, he should like to work in a bank, or some such place, he was interested in that sort of life. Humphry smiled. He had just become reconciled with his brother Basil, who had, after all, heeded his warnings about Barnato's bank and the Kaffir shares, and was indeed, as his friends were ruined, or committed suicide, prepared to show gratitude to Humphry, and had offered to pay all Tom's fees at public school. Humphry told Geraint that he should ask advice of his brother the banker. He would take him to see him, when they were both in Town. Basil would advise, might even find a suitable position, in due course. Geraint flushed, and thanked him.

Tom had told Julian that he was to take the exam for Marlowe next summer. He said it had looked as though he might not go there, lately, but now they were looking for tutors, or tutorial colleges. He wasn't sure that was what he wanted, at all. Julian looked at Tom, and thought he was the most beautiful boy he had ever seen. Marlowe would love him. He was not sure Tom would love Marlowe. He thought he, Julian, could easily, easily fall in love with Tom. All he said was, non-committally, that Marlowe wasn't too bad, as schools went. Not too bad, really.

Prosper Cain said that the pots were the work of a master, and a master working at the height of his powers. He admired a peacocky platter with scattered gold and silver fruit all over it, and said he would certainly like to have it, for the Museum if he could bear to part with it, for himself, in all events. Olive picked up a small red vessel—part pot, part sculpture, which was a curled black demon, tailed and stubby-horned, holding a flame-coloured, incurving cup which was at once a fire and a cauldron. "This I must have," said Olive to Benedict Fludd. "He has the most *wicked* face, he means mischief."

"The luck of the firing," said Fludd. "There's one over there whose face doesn't come through the glaze. You have a good eye." He bent gallantly over her hand. He told Philip to wrap it, but Olive was reluctant to let it go, turning it in her hand, near the window.

Frank Mallett had asked Imogen to find something, perhaps, for Elsie Warren to wear, since she was so dusty. And maybe some water? he said, wondering why exactly the Purchase women were so languid and inept. Imogen did as she was asked, and Elsie appeared timidly in the doorway in a trailing black skirt and a kind of woven overblouse with orange and brown chrysanthemums. Neither of these garments fitted her. Imogen had not thought of pins, or needles. Elsie still had her cracked and dusty shoes, and still wore her dusty scarf, which she had refused to relinquish, because she knew her hair was horrible. Frank said he hoped she was comfortable. She stared defensively round the room, and then hitched up her skirt, and began to clear away the used cups and plates. She found the scullery, and the sink. The company went on talking. Elsie came back and asked Philip in an undertone about hot water and dishcloths. She had found something to do, and understood that there was a need for it. Frank Mallett smiled at her, and thanked her, since no one else appeared to think of doing so. Prosper Cain and Humphry were talking to Benedict Fludd about showrooms and students. Julian was talking to Tom. Dorothy found Philip, and said she liked his work. She said that it was amazing that his sister had found him. How was his mother?

Philip looked at Dorothy's sharp, practical, interested face.

"She came to say she is dead," he said.

Dorothy said she was sorry, and was. She imagined Philip receiving this news, and thought he must feel bad not to have been there.

"You couldn't *know,*" she said.

"I could've sent an address. I didn't."

"She probably understood, you know."

Dorothy was not sure how much mothers understood, in fact, but a bleak look had come into Philip's face, and she wanted to change it.

"I don't know as she did. Elsie's mad at me. She's brought me my mother's brushes. My mother said to give them to me."

"You see, she understood." That was a good thing to say, whether or not it was true. She said

"Of course, Elsie's mad at you. But she's there to make it up to."

Philip looked gloomy. Dorothy remembered how much she had liked him, before. She said

"Those tiles. They're very good, you know that. The way you make patterns out of real things. So that you see the flies and fennel, you can really see them."

"I *did want* to make pots—"

"And just see what luck you've had. It feels as though it's a kind of *fate,* you know. You must go on making pots, that's for certain."

14

The winter that followed St. Martin's Summer was sodden and severe. The end of golden 1895 was struck with gloom. On Monday December 23rd the whole Tartarinov family rushed uphill to Todefright, brandishing a telegram. The Wellwoods gathered in their hall already decorated for Christmas with green boughs, holly and mistletoe. Stepniak was dead, said Vasily Tartarinov. Humphry had visions of bombs, or furtive stabbing. Tartarinov was in tears. Stepniak had indeed died violently, possibly accidentally, possibly not. He had walked onto a railway line, near his home in Bedford Park, and had been cut down by a train, and killed, more or less instantly. It was a local train, on a single track. The driver had whistled and braked, whistled and braked, in vain. It was hard to understand, said Tartarinov, waving expressive hands, mopping his face, how Stepniak could have failed to get out of the way. Maybe his foot was caught. Maybe he had been overwhelmed by personal sorrows and the sorrows of the world, and had decided to end his life. We shall not see his like again, said Vasily Tartarinov, whilst the Wellwood family ordered tea to be brewed, and tried to help him compose himself. No, we shall not see his like again, Humphry agreed, wishing the Tartarinov children would stop howling, and Mrs. Tartarinov would cease to look as though she might choke with emotion.

Olive held on to the back of a chair—it seemed rude to sit down, but her muscles ached all over. She kneaded her distended flanks, surreptitiously, with her fingers. Tartarinov's vivid imaginings of Stepniak's torn body reminded her that soon, soon she would herself face pain, and possible death, of one, or two people.

Tom had been about to walk down to the Tartarinovs', to read Virgil with Vasily. He was clutching his *Aeneid,* and his exercise book. He tried to take his mind away from Stepniak's fate before he had really imagined it, and failed. He saw the shining rail, stretching before and after, and the black, thundering weight, in its shroud of steam, bearing down, a final dark rushing. It would have been quick, it must have been quick. A moving wall of black, a solid tunnel opening. *Facilis descensus Averno.*

. . .

Stepniak's funeral was on the 28th. Christmas came between, and the Wellwoods put up a tree, hung with baubles, bright with candles, and sang together, "The First Nowell," "Silent Night." They carved two geese and ate Christmas pudding, spherical in eerily flaming blue sheets, like a captive will o' the wisp, Olive thought, inventing a story about a flame-imp set to work in a suburban kitchen, causing chaos. After Christmas, before the imminent birth, the larger children were sent to spend New Year with the Basil Wellwoods, in Portman Square. Humphry took them to London, delivered them, and went on to join Stepniak's funeral cortège, which processed slowly from Bedford Park to Waterloo Station, from where the coffin would travel by train to the crematorium at Woking.

It was a day of steady, smutty London drizzle. The coffin was covered with a blanket of brilliant flowers, tied with red ribbons. Radicals and revolutionaries from all Europe marched behind it. Hundreds of people gathered at Waterloo. Speeches were made in German, Italian, Yiddish, French and Polish. The crowd stood for over an hour and listened to the socialist and anarchist leaders, Keir Hardie, Eduard Bernstein, Malatesta, Prince Kropotkin, and John Burns, the workingman, unionist, Fabian and Radical MP for Battersea, who had organised the proceedings. Eleanor Marx spoke as she always did, passionately, lucidly; she said Stepniak had loved women, and women would grieve for him. William Morris, hugely fat and breathing badly, spoke for English socialists and condemned Russian oppression. This was Morris's last speech at an open-air gathering. Humphry Wellwood went by train to Woking Crematorium with the mourners, sitting discreetly at the back, watching with almost technical curiosity as the coffin passed through folding doors into the flames. Later he wrote a moving description of the event for a magazine, describing international grief and solidarity, confusion and a baffled sense of loss in the soaked, patient crowds on the railway platform, and the heartstruck weeping mourners before the furnace.

The next day, December 29th, was the Feast of St. Thomas à Becket, the turbulent priest and wilful politician, bloodily cut down before his own altar. Another proud and wilful politician, Joseph Chamberlain, was Colonial Secretary in the new Conservative Government. He secretly encouraged Cecil Rhodes, Prime Minister of the Cape Colony in South Africa, to send his friend, Dr. Starr Jameson, with 500 men to invade the Boer republic of the Transvaal. President Kruger, of the Transvaal, was resolutely refusing voting rights to the inflooding speculators and miners, the uitlander in search of Kaffir gold. Humphry, on his way back to Todefright, heard the rumours that were coming in by telegraph, and would dearly have liked to stay in London, to follow events, and to write something wry and witty about the jingoistic mood, so different from the international grief for Stepniak, that was overtaking much of English public life. The Fabians were divided about questions of empire—some, including socialists like Ramsay MacDonald, hated the whole idea. Some believed in planning for the greater good of the many, which included the farflung inhabitants of the colonies. Beatrice Webb, one of the moving spirits of Fabian socialism, had been in love with Joseph Chamberlain as a young woman, and wrote in her diary at the beginning of 1896 that the whole mind of the country was absorbed in foreign politics, that the occasion had found the man, and Joe Chamberlain was today the National Hero. "In these troubled times, with every nation secretly disliking us," she wrote, "it is a comfortable thought that we have a government of strong resolute men, not given to either bluster or vacillation, but prompt in taking every measure to keep us out of a war and to make us successful should we be forced into it." Little England, Great Empire. In 1896 Humphry Wellwood was interested in the relations of armies and gold mines, diamond merchants and Stock Exchange dealers. The dead Nihilist jostled the piratical Starr Jameson in his busy mind. But Olive had made him promise to go home, immediately, so he went.

When he opened his front door he was greeted by a full-throated howl of pain, followed by wild sobbing, from upstairs. It had begun. Violet appeared on the stairs, took his coat, patted his shoulder, said "She's having a hard time. The child is fast in the passage, and cannot come out. And they are both weak, I think."

"Shall I go to her?" Humphry asked. Olive liked to be left alone at these times. Violet kissed him and said she would tell her he was back, that would settle her a little. She would talk to the midwife, and then she would make Humphry a cup of tea, or a bowl of broth, after his journey. All the little children had been taken to the Tartarinovs' by Nurse. She was looking after the Tartarinov children too, as the couple were away at the funeral.

Violet went back to her sister's bedside, and returned to say that Olive could perhaps see Humphry later, the doctor and the midwife were busy. Another scream echoed across the landing: Humphry and Violet crept downstairs. There was frantic, agitated moaning, and smooth hushings and calming noises from the attendant medical people.

Olive thought she had forgotten what pain could be. She was a railway tunnel in which a battering train had come to a fiery halt. She was a burrow in which a creature had wedged itself and could go neither forwards nor back. She was arch after arch of electric pain and the imagination of geometry could not create an issue—the immovable object and the irresistible force were *one thing,* and could neither advance nor retreat, so that bursting seemed the only way out, like the eruption of a volcano. Something would drown in there, something would be engulfed by flame. The doctor begged her not to fling her head from side to side, not to waste her breath on shrieking and wailing, but to make an effort, for the sake of the child who could not come out, and expel it.

She arched herself, howled and bore down.

Red and angry, black-lipped and uttering a desperate whimper, the child shot into the world. He was a boy. They cleaned his face, and cut his cord, and he wailed again, and again—"He has a good voice," said the doctor. "And strong limbs," said the midwife, circling a puny thigh with one hand, wiping the crimson male organ. Blood and water were everywhere. Olive felt it well out. And the afterbirth, so all was well. The midwife bundled up the bloody sheets, and mopped the floor, and washed the mother, and arranged her under a pretty counterpane, tugging a comb through her sweat-tangled hair. She tickled the swathed child under his chin. "Now we'll fetch Daddy, now you're fit to see." She put him in the cot—not new, but prettily decorated with starched sheets and ribbons. She went to look for Humphry who was consuming his bowl of broth, watched intently by Violet, to whom he was describing the funeral, the weather, the music, the flowers.

Humphry tiptoed into the bedroom, in the traditional manner. Olive looked at him from far away, her hands inert on the counterpane.

The midwife showed him the boy, who had reddish hair, not very much, and strong features, a brow, a big mouth. What shall we call him, Humphry asked Olive. She shifted the bleeding sack of her body. You choose, she said. Humphry was thinking of Shakespeare, for the article he would write about the Transvaal. He was thinking about England. He hesitated between Harry and George. "Cry God for Harry, England and St. George." Harry was more dashing. Harry was a good no-nonsense English name. "Harry," he said, and Olive smiled, and said Harry was a good choice, she too had been considering Harry. Harry Basil, she suggested, thinking of Basil's forthcoming generosity with Tom's school fees.

15

In the New Year of 1896, Humphry went to Portman Square to take home his two eldest children. Phyllis, Hedda, Florian and Robin had been taken by Cathy the maid to visit her family on a farm near Rottingdean. Phyllis had looked plaintive, and sulked a little. She preferred being the youngest of the big children to being the eldest of the small children. Violet tried to suggest that the Basil Wellwoods might find room for her, it would do her good to be more independent, but nothing came of that. Dorothy was grim and tense during these discussions. She wanted to be with Griselda, and having Phyllis around was quite exactly *not* being with Griselda. Tom would rather have stayed at home; he did not have interests in common with Charles, who was a year older than him, but they did not quarrel, either.

It was decided that Humphry should approach his friend Leslie Skinner, who worked with Karl Pearson in the Department of Applied Mathematics at UCL, to find a good tutor to take both Charles and Tom, and coach them for the entrance exams of Eton and Marlowe. Toby Youlgreave had agreed to help them with history and literature. Tartarinov was doing well with Tom's Latin, and Humphry was happy to suggest that he reciprocate his brother's hospitality by offering space to Charles in which he could come and polish his classics. Basil and Katharina felt that what young women needed was accomplishments—music, manners, painting and drawing. They offered to invite Dorothy to share Griselda's art lessons. Griselda had been reading *The Mill on the Floss* and had persuaded Dorothy to read it too. They sat in Griselda's bedroom, indignant Maggie Tullivers, for whom maths and Latin and literature were not considered.

They all went to tea with Leslie and Etta Skinner, in their narrow parlour in Tavistock Square, to meet the maths tutor Leslie Skinner thought might do the job. They all went, because Humphry combined the tea with a visit to the British Museum, and he enjoyed Dorothy's company on such outings. He took them to see Viking gold and the Elgin Marbles, and made them all shudder in front of the Egyptian coffins with dead men and women bandaged inside them.

The parlour had dark green Morris & Co. wallpaper, spangled with scarlet berries, and a Morris set of spindly Sussex settle and chairs, with rush seats. There were woven rugs on a dark floor, and high shelves of orderly books. The possible tutor was already present, a young German, from Munich, Dr. Joachim Susskind, in a threadbare suit, and wearing a red tie. Dr. Susskind had flowing, hay-coloured, dry hair, and a fine, waving moustache to go with it. His eyes were blue and mournful, not clear, glassy sky-blue like Dr. Skinner's but a clouded, faded blue, the diluted blue of an almost-white Small Blue butterfly, Tom thought. He looked mild and harmless. Leslie Skinner presented him by saying that he was not only a first-class mathematician, but also a first-class teacher, which many mathematicians were not. Dr. Susskind smiled mildly. He said he should like to know whether Tom and Charles *enjoyed* mathematics? Yes, said Tom. No, said Charles. Dr. Susskind asked both of them, why? Tom said it wasn't arithmetic he liked, he often got that wrong, it was the way things fitted together in geometry, the sense of finding it out. Charles said he didn't like feeling a fool, which was the effect maths had on him. Leslie Skinner asked which subjects Charles *did* like, and Charles said, none, really, they didn't tell him what he wanted to know.

"And what do you want to know?" asked Skinner, Socratic.

"Things about life. Why are the poor poor? What is wrong with us?"

Humphry laughed, and said he was afraid Charles would not get much information about poverty at Eton. Charles said he didn't want to go there, but nobody cared what he thought. Skinner said it was always useful to be taught *how* to think, and Dr. Susskind said, almost inaudibly, looking at no one, that that was a good question to ask, a good question.

The two girls sat side by side, one dark, one pale gold, their long hair brushed out over their shoulders. Etta Skinner turned to them briskly and asked in a principled and slightly combative tone where *they* were to get their education. Leslie Skinner turned his blue look on Dorothy and gave her his complete attention.

"You are the young lady who is to be a doctor."

Dorothy said she was.

"Then it is high time you were seriously studying science."

"I know," said Dorothy, incurring a sharp look of reproach from her father.

"Well, I do know," she said, answering the look.

It turned out that Etta had an answer to propose. She herself did some teaching at Queen's College, in Harley Street, which gave classes to females of any age over twelve years, either to prepare them for a teaching career, or to improve their skills and knowledge if they were already teaching. Dorothy and Griselda might attend—part-time even—together. Griselda said she would go to science classes with Dorothy if Dorothy would go with her to classes in German and French. And Latin, said Leslie. They would need Latin if they were to think of university, as he hoped they would. UCL made provision for women to study science. Skinner told Humphry that a good Fabian should consider his daughters' education as seriously as his sons'. Humphry said that Dorothy—and Griselda—were still only little girls. Hardly, said Skinner, smiling at the two serious young faces. Hardly. They would be young women any moment, he could see. His look made Dorothy feel unexpectedly heated, on her skin, and also inside her. She wriggled a little and sat straighter. Griselda said she didn't think her parents saw any need for her to be educated. Skinner said, it should be enough that she *wanted* to be educated. Etta took Humphry's arm, and said surely he could explain to his family how much it might mean, how much it should be a right . . . Griselda said Dorothy could stay with her, and they could go to the lessons together, if only the families agreed. Humphry said he would miss his girl, and Dorothy said he might not notice, he was so much away, now, himself.

Tom and Charles began immediately to go to University College to do maths with Dr. Susskind, who shared a poky little office in a mews behind the main building, with another statistician, who was collecting data on human heights, weights and ages. They went on Monday and Tuesday afternoons, and were given work to take home. They were measured themselves, as a statistic. Then, some weekends, they travelled to Todefright to work with Vasily Tartarinov, and to read with Toby Youlgreave in his cottage.

Tom liked the maths well enough, and tried not to think of the consequences of getting the Marlowe scholarship. He felt unreal in London, as though his flesh and blood were in abeyance, as though he was a simulacrum of a boy, floating along Gower Street with its prim houses, dodging cabs in Torrington Street. The maths, especially the geometry, intensified his sense of abstraction. He waited to be back in Todefright. He thought continuously of the woods and the Tree House. He read

William Morris's new book, *The Well at the World's End,* and also *The Wood Beyond the World,* and *News from Nowhere.* Charles read these books, too, but they did not discuss them much, except to make a joke, when their homework was hard, of the fact that William Morris appeared to believe that boys could educate themselves as and when they chose, with no more chalky effort than they had put into learning language as babies. Joachim Susskind delighted in teaching Tom, for he was indeed quick, and instinctive, and did not need lengthy explanations.

Charles was slower and less apt. He was given extra lessons, in Dr. Susskind's lodgings in a house just behind the Women's Hospital, between Euston and St. Pancras. It was true that Susskind was a good enough teacher to see not only *what* Charles didn't understand, but how and why he didn't understand it. He explained, in his soft German voice, just what was blocking enlightenment. At first he didn't talk to Charles about anything other than maths. Then, one day, he said

"You asked, why are the poor poor. I was struck by that."

"What I can't see—what I really can't see—is why *everyone* doesn't ask themselves that, *all the time.* How can these people bear to go to church and then go about in the streets and see what is there for *everyone* to see— and get told what the Bible says about the poor—and go on riding in carriages, and choosing neckties and hats—and eating huge beefsteaks— I can't see it."

"I have brought a book for you to read. I think probably you should not let it be seen in your home. But I think it will speak to you."

So Charles Wellwood read Prince Kropotkin's *Appeal to the Young,* which called on young doctors, lawyers, artists, to consider how they would live and work in the light of the horrors of starvation, disease, and desperation in the world of the poor. Its prescriptions for the good life were vaguer than its fierce calling-up of the bad. It called on the young to organise, to struggle, to write and publish about oppression, to be socialists. It did not say how the desired revolution could be brought about. Charles went back to Dr. Susskind and asked if he had more such books. The two looked at each other, the German gentle and quietly excited, the English boy tense with abstract need, his face white, erupting on brow and cheeks, his eyes hungry.

He asked Susskind if he was a socialist. Susskind replied that he was an Anarchist. He believed the world would be better if all authority, all hierarchy, all institutions were abolished. There would come a revolution. After that, harmony, all giving to all and accommodating all.

Something in Charles was wary of the prophetic enthusiasm of this. If goodness were really easy and natural, how had authority ever come about? He had read *News from Nowhere* with a certain scepticism. He was not sure it was possible to return to mediaeval pastoral and abolish the machine. He was coming to believe that the Todefright Wellwoods were not *real* socialists, were not confronting the problem head-on. For one thing, their house was full of things made in small quantities by poor men for rich ones. He had heard his own father sneer at Morris & Co. for selling vastly expensive fabrics and tapestries with golden age and paradisal foliage on them. Somehow they slid away from the horrors they should be confronting.

He said as much, as best he could, to Susskind, who said how wise he was, that Mr. Morris himself had called himself a dreamer of dreams, born out of his due time. Peter Kropotkin believed in the printing-press. Maybe Charles would not believe this, but not far from where they were was just such a press, producing a monthly revolutionary paper called *The Torch of Anarchy*. It might interest Charles to know that the paper had been founded by three young people—still children really—from a famous poetic family, by Olive, Arthur and Helen Rossetti, when they were younger than Charles was now. The press had recently moved to a stable loft in Ossulston Street—but had produced powerful revolutionary literature from a room in the basement of Mr. William Rossetti's house—a basement in which *everything* was painted blood-red, said Joachim Susskind, smiling over the absolute enthusiasm of the young Rossettis. He said, timidly, that he could give Charles some copies of this pamphlet, and even take him to see the press at work, if he felt he could go there. He himself helped out when he could. He loved mathematics as much as revolution, so he could not give up his college work. Statisticians and mathematicians would be welcome in the new order. Professor Pearson was not unsympathetic, though he inclined more to Karl Marx's socialism than to Kropotkin's anarchism. Indeed he had changed his name from Charles to Karl, to show his respect for the thinker.

Charles wanted to see the press. He wanted to see work being done, to change things. No one thought to question him at home, if he said he was going to visit Dr. Susskind. And so, one afternoon, the two of them set off for Ossulston Street.

Ossulston Street stank. The gutter ran with yellow horse-piss, and the road was almost solid with caked dung. Charles walked gingerly, trying to keep his shoes clean, and wondering whether clean shoes should be of any concern. The offices of *The Torch of Anarchy* were in a loft above a stable, behind the "jugs and bottles" door of a dingy public house, The Bay Tree. Joachim Susskind and Charles had to negotiate a kind of midden to get to the wooden stairs that led to the loft. As he went up, Charles suddenly remembered Humphry's midsummer speech about the poor man who picked and ate undigested oats from stuff like this. This was what he *ought to know about*. He followed his tutor through a ramshackle door into a long wooden shedlike room, full of dust, floating in the air, thick on the heaps of literature and pamphlets which covered almost all the floor. There were strong smells in this dusty air—tobacco smoke and tobacco juice, human odours of thick sweat and excrement, a pervasive smell of sour milk, and another of rancid fat. And the smell of dog, though he could see no dog. There was also a smell of sour beer. A man in a greasy jacket was scoffing fried bread and bacon scraps from a newspaper on what appeared to be the plate of the printing press, at one end of the room. There were two or three little groups of people, none of whom appeared likely to be the young Rossettis. One group was talking fast and intently in Italian. One consisted of three people on a bench, against which leaned a hard placard. "The Day of the Beast Is Upon Us." At one end of the room was a mattress, where someone—or more than one person—was snoring thickly under a heap of tattered cloth and a bundle of flags. Susskind said to the eating man that he had understood that Comrade Bartlett would be printing. He had brought his promised article on the German anti-socialist laws. He had brought a young man who was interested in anarchist ideas. Comrade Bartlett said his hand was too black with ink to shake the new Comrade by the hand, and asked his name. Charles said his name was Karl. He said he would like to help. Comrade Bartlett swept his meal off the press and began to ink it. Charles/Karl found himself worrying intensely about his clothes, at which the inhabitants of the loft appeared to be staring. His shirt was clean and starched, his jacket was pressed and expensive. He looked *wrong* and moreover he was going to get dirty, and be in trouble at home. He was saved by Joachim Susskind, who produced a workman's apron from his bookbag and gave it to Charles, with a smile of complicit understanding.

Charles was not sure if he would go back to Ossulston Street, after that first visit. No one paid him much attention. He worked as hard as he could, and came away with a sheaf of leaflets and pamphlets to read. But he did go back, again and again in the early part of 1896, as much because he respected Joachim Susskind, as because he felt he was meeting the real working class. He was not sure that these people *were* the real working class. He was sure that Herr Susskind—who now addressed him as Karl—was concerned about the working class. And he liked *The Torch,* when he read it. He was given various issues, which were illustrated by moving drawings of despairing women, by Lucien Pissarro. It contained writings by Leo Tolstoi and Peter Kropotkin, commemorations of the martyrdom in 1887 of the Chicago Anarchists and a debate between Quaker pacifism and the advocates of violence and propaganda by the Deed. It advertised reprints of Morris's *Useful Work vs. Useless Toil* and attacked the Prince of Wales for the size of his clothes bill. It also carried tales from *The Arabian Nights,* and German fairytales by Otto Erich Hartleben. Karl read the instructions on HOW TO HELP.

> Take a Dozen copies of each issue of THE TORCH and try to sell or distribute them.
> Leave copies of THE TORCH and other literature in railway carriages, waiting rooms, tram cars, refreshment houses and other places for the public to read.
> Get newsagents to sell THE TORCH.
> Turn up at meetings to support the speakers and assist with the literature.

He acquired a set of clothes for Ossulston Street, which he kept in Joachim Susskind's rooms—some old leggings, a frayed jumper, a jacket from a pawn shop, a workingman's cap, which he pulled over his eyes, enjoying the feeling both of disguise and of becoming some other person. All this was conducted most discreetly by the tutor and his pupil—they didn't discuss, or plot, these refinements, they simply *happened.* They did discuss whether it would be "a good thing" for Karl to go out into Hyde Park, or anywhere else, to sell bundles of *The Torch,* and they decided that he could do so, if he kept away from places near Portman Square. Susskind and Karl wandered many London streets at times when Charles was thought to be doing homework, or joining in rambles, mildly discussing imprisonment and execution, and whether the planting of bombs was a duty or an act of irresponsibility. Those who had gone to the scaffold in Paris and Chicago were brave martyrs. They had had "no alternative" Susskind said, and Karl agreed. But they agreed also that they were not, themselves, natural killers. Susskind said, padding along Baker Street, that he should like to believe reasonable persuasion was enough.

One evening, at a meeting in Ossulston Street, to discuss this very issue of the requirement of a violent response to the violence of oppression, Karl had a shock. There were more people there than usual—some new Comrades had arrived, having been smuggled out of Russia. When they came in, Vasily Tartarinov came with them, wearing the suit he always wore to teach Latin and Greek to the boys. Charles/Karl sat in a dark corner with his cap pulled down. He did not know what his parents might do to him if they found out how he spent his time. He did know that Joachim Susskind would be treated as a traitor, and probably lose his job.

The meeting eddied about. Long speeches were made, and the man with the placard said that since the Day of Judgement was coming almost immediately there was little to be said for bothering to kill people. They would all soon be overwhelmed. A kettle of tea was provided, and poured into cracked and greasy cups. Tartarinov came past Karl. He said "Good evening," formally and distantly. Karl looked up at him. Tartarinov winked, and refroze into formal strangeness.

At their next tutorial meeting Tartarinov greeted Tom and Charles as usual, and as usual, tartly, praised Tom's translation at the expense of Charles's. They were still working on the Sixth Book of the *Aeneid,* where the hero, having broken off the golden bough, descends to the Underworld to interrogate his dead father. They had reached the passage where the Sibyl and Aeneas come to the vast elm, where false dreams hang from the branches like bats, and shadows of imagined monsters hiss and gnash their teeth. The Sibyl prevents Aeneas from turning his sword on the bodiless, flitting lives, their forms only transitory and vanishing. Tartarinov chanted the Latin in a lusty Russian accent.

et ni docta comes tenuis sine corpore vitas
admoneat volitare cava sub imagine formae,
inruat et frustra ferro diverberet umbras . . .

Tom saw in his mind's eye gradations of shadowy matter, thicker and thinner irreality, coiling like steam from a train or smoke from a chimney, but in the dark, under dark branches, *cava sub imagine formae.* Charles was annoyed by the enthusiasm of Tartarinov's declamation. Charles saw nothing. Nothing was in his head. These things were unreal things, Gorgon, Harpy, Chimaera, things from childhood. No-things. He wanted another sign from Tartarinov, another wink for his secret self from the anarchist who had perhaps blood on his hands, who was far from his homeland because of his belief in his cause. But Tartarinov appeared to be truly obsessed with this old dead poetry in an old dead language. This man was *double,* Charles thought, a man with two faces and two minds, however whole-hearted he looked. And so was he, Charles/Karl, becoming double. His secret made him think of himself as invisible, a subtle being who thought his own thoughts and had his own purposes, whilst the outward boy said the banal things boys do say, about cricket and prep, about birds' nests and punishments. This led him to wonder whether Tom was double, and if so, what was in the secret Tom. He thought perhaps Tom was not double. Tom appeared to take Tartarinov—and Charles himself—at face value, gently.

Once the idea of secret selves had begun to spread little roots in his mind, he began to look at everyone differently, half as a game, half as a dangerous piece of research. After the morning with Tartarinov he walked with Tom along the road past the woods and onto the Downs, where Toby Youlgreave had his cottage, which, he insisted, had once belonged to a swineherd. Toby was coaching the boys for the general essays they would have to write. It was a cold crisp winter day, with frost on the ground and snow in the air. They wore caps and mufflers and woollen gloves. Toby gave them mugs of tea, and toasted them crumpets at his inglenook hearth. The floor of his small sitting-room was populated by uneven pillars of stacked books, on some of which previous mugs of tea had stood, and butter had been smeared. He had set them an essay on "Dreams" and told them to take that word any way they liked—

dreams, nightmares, daydreams, hopes for the future. He had said they would need to find vivid examples of whatever they chose. He made them read out what they had written, as though they were in a university tutorial. Tom read well, clearly, without expression, a little too fast. Charles paced himself, listening to his own argument. He liked to argue, even about dreams. Tom had chosen to write about real, night-time dreams, what they felt like, what they meant. Charles, who knew Tom would do that, had deliberately chosen the moral and political meaning of the word, the dream of justice, the dream of a future life, Utopia. Tom wrote about the sensation of dreaming, and distinguished between those dreams in which the dreamer is neither actor nor watcher but a kind of *looker-on,* like the voice of a storyteller in a story. Almost commenting, but not quite, because all the same you were sort of helpless, you couldn't *make decisions* in dreams, but you did know you were in them, and that you would wake to the real world. Sometimes you tried to stay asleep, to see what would happen. Then there were the dreams you were *really in* and had the sensation that you couldn't get out— dreams of being buried alive, or told you were to be hanged tomorrow (he had that one often) or dreams where you were being pursued, and the beast you thought was behind you turned out to have gone about and around, and was waiting for you at the end of the corridor. It was odd that the dreams you were completely inside were almost all *bad* dreams.

Not all, said Toby Youlgreave. You might dream—he hesitated delicately—that you were loved by someone—or that someone dead was living after all, it was all a mistake.

In that case, said Tom, waking would be as dreadful as dreaming the bad dreams.

Charles wondered if Toby's secret was to do with love. With the sex instinct. He kept coming back to it, though that might be because he got so wound up in poetry all the time. There was an awful lot of love, and sex, in poetry. It made Charles's skin prick, but he wasn't sure he cared for it. Flather, he thought, using one of his nanny's old words. Flather. Toby's secret is some sort of flather.

His own essay had been a rather perverse, but certainly clever, demolition of the dream of the good life in William Morris's *News from Nowhere,* and the kind of communities associated with it, who wore hand-printed skirts and ate vegetables. He wrote that the dream of Heaven had always worried him because it was so boring—there was nothing to *do*—and the dreams of Heaven on Earth, going back to the land, living in vegetable gardens and little plots of flowers, with no machines to be seen anywhere, struck him as a sleepy refusal to look at real problems and make real plans about what to do. He quoted Morris against himself

> Dreamer of dreams, born out of my due time
> Why should I strive to set the crooked straight?

He was indeed, wrote Charles/Karl censoriously, "the idle singer of an empty day."

His anger stirred in his sentences, making them alternately blunt and incoherent. Toby Youlgreave set about benignly to sharpen and point them. He said these points were perhaps best not made in a scholarship exam for a very privileged school.

Toby waited for a comment—from Tom, not Charles—and Tom said, thoughtfully, that he feared that was what he was, a dreamer. Toby Youlgreave looked at the darkening cottage window in the late afternoon, and said, almost to himself, that that was what they all were, living so pleasantly, dreamers. Have some treacle tart, he said, mocking himself gently. I made it specially for you two. How do we get out of dreamland? *Hic labor, hoc opus est,* he said.

Tom took the entrance exams, that July, in a kind of dream. Olive was worried for him, but he was himself unworried: maths was maths, Latin was Latin, he knew what he had to do as he knew how to throw a cricket ball or steer a bicycle. He wrote an essay on Keats—"My Favourite Poet"—for Marlowe, and an essay on "The Characteristics of the English" for Eton. Marlowe accepted him: Eton rejected him: both schools accepted Charles. It was faintly disturbing to Tom to be rejected. He was not used to it. Charles's parents decided he would go to Eton. They bought him a new bicycle. Charles slid away, in some anxiety, to consult Joachim Susskind. He said it had to be against his principles to go to Eton. Susskind, surprisingly, encouraged him to go ahead. The world was imperfect, he said. One boy could not change it by refusing to be educated. He should go to Eton and learn to argue, and observe the ruling classes at their most absolute, and consider how to thwart their purposes. We must be wise as serpents, he said, quoting Jesus Christ, who was, he claimed, the first Anarchist, and not adding the corollary, harmless as doves, because he was still thinking of the propaganda of the Deed, and whether or not it was right to strike symbolic blows. Susskind was excited by the banishment of the Anarchist groups from the Socialist Second International, meeting that summer in London. The Anarchists refused political action. Susskind was not sure where he stood on this, either. Bakunin had said Germans made bad anarchists because they wanted simultaneously to be Masters and Slaves. There was a German kind of orderliness to Susskind's anarchism, at war with a German liking for carrying things to extremes.

Both Tom and Dorothy had been reading Kenneth Grahame's *The Golden Age,* published a year ago. Grahame had given the book to Humphry: they had once been colleagues in the Bank of England, where Grahame still worked—he was grander than Humphry had been, and was already promoted to Acting Secretary of the Bank. Like Humphry he wrote for the *Yellow Book* and like Humphry busied himself bringing culture to the East End. He had published a work called *Pagan Papers* in 1893, a tribute to the goat-god Pan, with a frontispiece by Aubrey Beardsley, which contained the stories of childhood which were continued in *The Golden Age.* Dorothy asked Tom if he thought going away to school would change him, like Edward in the book. Tom said, vaguely, of course things wouldn't be the same, and suddenly, for the first time, focused his dreaming mind on what this new beginning was bringing to an end, on what he had done to himself by passing an exam. He was filled with fear and grief, which were impossible to impart to sharp Dorothy.

Olive, despite her preference for legend and fairytale, had herself published two books, that year, about imaginary children, written fast, and easily, and compulsively. Money had been needed because Humphry had had to "help out" with the confinement of Maid Marian in Manchester. He looked sidelong at Olive, before he asked for help, but he made no wild speeches of contrition, did not beat his breast, said, almost man to man, "She's a good creature, you know. She's got a good brain. She's brave." Olive said he should have thought of all that earlier, and Humphry said, with a kind of satyr-grin, that he *had thought* he had thought of it, but clearly not well enough. He was inviting Olive to grin with him. Much of his success as an errant husband lay in this whiskered grin of collusion—there were women out there whom, briefly, he couldn't resist—but she, Olive, his wife, was the one he shared things with, the one to whom he spoke truthfully, from himself. She took a curious pleasure in the power of independence when she gave him a cheque to meet the Manchester bills. You did not so much mind being—conventionally—betrayed, if you were not kept in the dark, which was humiliating, or defined only as a wife and dependent person, which was annihilating.

Olive's two stories were *The Runaway* and *The Girl Who Walked a Long Way,* and were based, in part, on the way Olive imagined the tale of Philip Warren and the tale of his sister Elsie. She had been able to use her own memories of escaping from the coalfield, and from the industrial smoke, to find oneself in the Garden of England amongst orchards full of apples, and gardens full of wholesome, clean vegetables. Her two characters were preadolescent children, escaping a cruel aunt and a drunken uncle. They settled, not in anywhere like Purchase, but in a farming community of orphan children and runaways like themselves. She had invented a kind of guru for this community, a Pied Piper who vaguely resembled Edward Carpenter in idealism and sandal-making. But she could not prevent this figure from being either domineering or sinister, and realised that this was because what children liked to read about was a world without adults, in which they themselves produced their food, and decided how to run things. So she replaced the Carpenter figure with a fourteen-year-old boy called Robin, who was camping in a derelict barn, and took in other fugitives. They called themselves the Outlaws, and learned how to pick mushrooms and berries, and entice runaway hens to lay eggs in their outhouse. She was rather pleased with this concept, and did not know whether to be annoyed or amused to find that Marian in Manchester had called her son Robin. She told Humphry that it was negligent—or invidious—of him to have two sons called Robin, and Humphry smiled his satyr-smile and said that only proved that he had little or nothing to do with Marian and her child, apart from making sure they had enough to live on. Olive didn't point out that it was she who had made sure. They both knew that.

That summer, before Tom left home, they all went together, big children and tinies, and in-between Phyllis and Hedda, on a seaside holiday in a village called Selstrood, which had a wild beach that looked across the Channel to France, which was sometimes visible as a shadowy strip in the sky, and sometimes hidden in mist or cloud, and now and then a lit, creamy line of solid rock, just distinguishable from bright cloud and wavecrest. They took an old vicarage, furnished only with minimal wooden chairs and tables, and iron bedsteads, and they camped in the way the English like to camp. Tom and Dorothy, and Charles and Griselda who came with them, had workmanlike tents in the orchard. Violet hired a donkey cart, and drove the little ones along the quiet lanes. Olive wrote furiously. They had beach picnics, carrying hampers of delicious things through the sea-holly onto the washed sand. They swam. They visited Purchase House, of course, which was still shabby, but had a look of polish and darning and clean crockery, no doubt contrived by Elsie. Olive studied Philip and Elsie. Elsie noticed this, and Philip didn't. He was learning his craft, and Benedict Fludd was still in a reasonable temper, and still producing work.

Other people came. Toby Youlgreave came, and lodged with Miss Dace in Winchelsea. He talked to Griselda about literature, and Charles confirmed his idea that Youlgreave's secret other self was Olive Wellwood's knight errant, or maybe something else. The Cain family came, and stayed in a comfortable inn, near Winchelsea. Prosper Cain was in need of rest and distraction. It was proving to be a horrible year at the Museum. The Director, Professor Middleton, had been found dead in June, with a laudanum bottle and a glass at his side. He was known to have taken laudanum regularly since he had had "brain fever" as an undergraduate, and a verdict of death by misadventure was returned. But most people, including Prosper, suspected that he had taken his life, in an excess of despair over battling scholars, soldiers and librarians. The campaign against the military presence in the Museum in the art newspapers had intensified: in July, at the time of Tom's exams, the parliamentary debate on the Budget had produced scathing criticism of the management of the Museum, led by the socialist John Burns. Cain wanted to be able to forget all these things. He thought he might try to interest Benedict Fludd's aimless daughters in finding places at the new Royal College of Art, formed from the old National Art Training School. Pomona was still just about a child, but Imogen was seventeen, and nobody seemed to care what happened to her. She didn't talk to Julian, who was a year younger than she was, and in a mood for sauntering sardonically away on his own. Some of her embroidery was quite promising. Vapid, Prosper thought truthfully, but technically promising. He wondered, not for the first time, what was wrong with Seraphita, and remembered the empty laudanum bottle.

. . .

There were many picnics on the beach, under umbrellas with bleached stripes, where Olive sat in a graceful swirl of muslin and a cotton sun-hat, holding court, Prosper thought, as he became a courtier. He liked the free movement of the many Wellwoods, up and down the sand, in and out of the salt water, collecting things in nets and buckets, riding away on bicycles. He confided in Olive Wellwood as a figure of mother-hood, but he knew that she knew that his eyes were on her waist, and the eager movements of her hands, and the curl of her haunch and thighs under her. He said he was afraid his Florence had too much *gravitas* to run freely with Dorothy and Griselda. She had been forced into grown-up seriousness before her time. Look at her now, sitting on a rock, staring out to sea like a mermaid. He did not know how to make it up to her. Olive asked, looking down at his solid fingers playing with the sand, if he had ever thought of remarrying—even perhaps for Florence's sake? And Julian's. Prosper said he had wondered if he should, but had never yet met any woman he could—take to in that way. Or if he had, he said, they were already spoken for. He knew there were things he could not discuss with Florence, that she might need to discuss with someone. Olive said she thought he did very well on his own; he was a percipient person. She said Julian was a young man, now, he had almost nothing of the little boy left in him. She did not like, she confessed, the thought of Tom going away to Marlowe. She did not believe Tom was as strong as Julian. "He is ludicrously *innocent,* I sometimes think," she said confidingly. "Life will deal him blows. He has run wild, delightfully, but he will find it hard to adjust to discipline."

So they talked on quietly, sharing things, in a rather pleasant electrical prickle of unactivated sex. It was like dancing. Olive enjoyed it. She had a right, she thought, considering Maid Marian. There needed to be *balance,* if balance was the word, latitude for latitude, excursion for excursion. Humphry's vagaries meant she had a *right* to take pleasure in being admired, looked at, confided in.

Toby loved her too much. He waited, perpetually dumb, he didn't know for what, and everyone could see it, she thought, and she herself had to be circumspect and watchful, for the truth was, she couldn't do without Toby, she needed Toby to talk to about fairy mythology, about plots and tales. Every now and then she paid for conversation— she didn't feel commercial, it was *loving,* as she loved Toby—with a silent, passionate embrace, mouth to mouth, skin to skin, her laughing face close to his bemused one. He had understood from the beginning that these encounters could only happen if no one spoke, and they were never referred to. He had been awkward at first, blushing, clumsy, but he had grown adept at clutching and letting go, at fierceness followed by lassitude and a kind of consequent indifference. She guided his fingers into hidden places, her body at first immobile and then quivering a little. She did not know what he *thought* of all this. It didn't matter, as long as they were not discovered, and he did not become overexcited, indignant, or morose.

Toby had been lecturing in Winchelsea and Lydd, in the winter and spring, speaking about the Saxon fairy-faith, and the Paracelsian elementals. He had become a great friend of Patty Dace, Frank Mallett and Arthur Dobbin. The inner group of the Theosophists had held discussions of Edward Carpenter's *Love's Coming of Age* in Miss Dace's parlour. This group included Herbert and Phoebe Methley, who were resolutely outspoken about the fact that sex-love and its expression were natural and necessary to both sexes. If Patty or Frank or Dobbin directed a curious look at their bodies as they said these things—and these looks were almost inevitable—they stared back, amiable and unabashed.

Olive wanted to meet Methley, and commanded Toby to bring the Methleys to Sunday lunch in the vicarage. She wanted to meet Methley because, like Frank Mallett, she had been greatly perturbed by one of his stories. He had a book of inconsequential tales of the sighting of fairies, or people of the hills, or the kind folk (who were not kind). These tales were written in a pragmatic first person by a naturalist who saw and observed these creatures as other men observed rare bugs or birds. The introduction to this book pointed out, persuasively enough, that there were indeed more things in heaven and earth than humans could usually apprehend with their limited senses. We cannot see radio, or molecules. We can receive an electrical shock from an apparently inert wire. We see clouds form and unform—where is what made up that bulging grey muscle a minute ago, where now is the grey-blue veil of mist that hung over the marsh poplars? How can it be that our species so steadily and persistently and consistently reported sightings of the fair folk, and occasional dealings with them, if they do not exist? In the beginning of the Bible men talked and walked with God: then with Angels: then with invisible voices. Some humans—of whom I myself am one, wrote the narrator, whose name, he wrote, was Nathanael Carter—have the trick of vision that lets us see these people, which is perhaps no odder than knowing where a trout lies under the shelf of a stream, or where honey is hidden in a tree-trunk.

"Nathanael Carter" claimed to have seen the fair folk from early childhood, and to have thought nothing of it, as a boy, until a teacher reproved him for lying when he told what he had seen. So he did not tell, any more. He understood that he saw because he did not tell.

Olive had never supposed for one moment that fairies or spirits existed. She lived most intensely in an imagined world peopled by things and creatures that drew their energy and power from other human imaginings, centuries and centuries of them. But she didn't suppose that these creatures were tangible—or alive and going about their purposes when she was not "making them up," or watching them in her mind—did she? Did she? She read Methley's tales and was half-convinced that the storyteller must indeed have seen what he said he had seen—it felt like sober fact, to read, and did not run into the usual groove of the fantasy-tale. Did he really know something she didn't? Or was he simply an extraordinarily competent writer? Either way, she needed to meet him.

His creatures were not exactly pleasant. One story began

I came upon one of these folk when I was out with my butterfly-net on the moors. I saw a wriggle of grey flesh in the heather, and believed I had startled a young rabbit, and then my eyes came into the right frame to see the other, and he came clearly into my vision as though I were adjusting a binocular glass. He was sitting with crossed legs in a clump of gorse, and his flesh was silver-grey like an eft, but duller, like pewter. He must have been about two feet high, if standing. He was all the same colour—he had long, rather coarse, pewter-coloured hair, and pewter eyes in his cobweb-grey face. They weren't human eyes—nor cats' eyes neither, and didn't resemble the eyes of any beast or fish I have ever seen. I don't think he saw me. His bony mouth was pursed with effort, and his long sharp fingers were busy. He was skinning a fat slow-worm—which was still alive and writhing—with a triangular stony knife, chipped to the thinness of a leaf. He was quite naked. All the fair people I have seen have been quite naked, except for a female walking unobserved in Smithfield Market, who wore a skirt made from a single cloth, like a Malay, and a necklace of pearls.

Olive mentioned this tale to its author, who sat next to her at lunch. She asked him quite directly if he saw the things he described.

"They ring true, do they? I don't think I could make them up. Sometimes I embroider a bit, or add a bit—but I must see them, to begin with. Don't you? Your splendid stories are so full of authentic powers, I imagined . . ."

After the visit, Herbert and Phoebe Methley took to walking in the direction of the old vicarage, or joining the games of cricket and rounders on the beach. Methley wore cotton shirts and a floppy sunhat. His legs were long and brown and wiry. He was a good bowler—too good, he demolished the younger batsmen too quickly—and an indefatigable fielder. Olive sat with Phoebe, or with Prosper Cain, and watched them all run. Herbert and Phoebe went bathing with Toby and the children. Phoebe wore a bathing cap which made her face look gaunt, Olive thought, and a bathing dress with a bunched little skirt round her thin hips.

When Methley was alone with Olive he spoke to her with a different intentness. He consulted her about writing, about editors, about literature. What did she make of Bernard Shaw? Had the man a heart, when all was said and done? And Kenneth Grahame, did she succumb to his charm? Was it not all a little bloodless? He was a man who looked a woman in the eye and did not look away. What did she make of John Lane's new magazine, *The Savoy*? He said he envied Olive the fullness and complexity of her life. The boys and girls and their different characters. He did not know how she could stretch her love so far—though he saw very clearly that she did so. He had no experience of it. They were sitting on the beach, picking at a dish of strawberries. Olive said that children connected you to the earth, and therefore weighed you down, a little. She felt, she said, like a farmyard hen, clucking. (Though it was Violet, at a little distance, who was wiping Florian's sandy face after a fall, and sponging Robin where he had dirtied his pants.) Methley said the family must be of inestimable value when it came to writing tales for children. She wrote with such insight into the hopes and fears of childish minds. Olive said that she did not believe having children was necessarily helpful. It was enough to have been a child . . .

"I do not know," said Methley. "I am childless, and sometimes, these days, I lose touch with the child I once was. Do you think there is an age when we become completely *adult,* Mrs. Wellwood, with no child left in us? When is that, do you think? I am not referring to second childhood that comes to all of us who don't die early enough."

His voice was dropped and very serious. He spoke to a thought Olive had had. She wrote for the child she had been, the child she was. In a kind of flurry she asked Methley whether he regretted having no children. The moment she had spoken she regretted the question. There were many reasons why marriages were childless. They were best left unmentioned.

He bent towards her.

"I have observed that there are childless marriages in which the unique pair are everything to each other, everything. They enact the absent children, they love the child in each other, they have a capacity for play and innocence which often—I have noticed—disappears from more fecund relations. Though they can also be—to use Blake's term— *experienced* with each other, uninhibited by any watching presence . . ."

Olive could not think of a quick answer. Herbert Methley went on

"It is not quite true that my marriage is childless. I feel I can trust you, Mrs. Wellwood—like all good writers, you let your private self be seen in public, and I know you are wise and kind. I myself have no children. My wife has three daughters. She was the wife of—a vicar in Batley— happily married but unawakened. Living in a dream world of good deeds and pretty dresses. We met—she and I—and tried to deny for two years what had struck into us and struck us down. She was ill. I could not write. She had a mysterious fatigue, she could barely stand or walk. I went to tell her that I was leaving Batley—I thought of emigrating to Canada—and I took her hand—and we saw, together, *as one,* that I could not leave, not alone, not ever again. So she came with me, and we live happily here, and are, as I said, everything to each other. We do not tell most people of this. Her husband refuses to divorce her. Or to allow her to see her daughters—which may be as well—she has chosen another life, and any step back into the old one would be painful, very painful."

Two or three days later, Herbert Methley came alone to the old vicarage. He found Olive in the orchard, sitting at a folding table, writing. She was wearing a simple straw hat and a loose, butcher-blue dress, not unlike her daughters' aprons. He stood easily before her—his body was always at ease, even if his voice was not.

"Do not let me disturb you, dear Mrs. Wellwood. No one knows better than myself the horror—the vein-freezing unpleasantness—of having the flow of writing disrupted. I came merely to bring you a little present—here it is—I have taken the liberty of writing in it—it is possibly the best of my work—but you shall be the judge."

He handed her a wrapped book, and went away. Olive was moved. Almost nobody knew how painful it was to have the inky thread of sentences snapped by others. He was a considerate man.

The book was *Daughters of Men* by Herbert Methley. Inside, he had written

"For Olive Wellwood, a wise woman and a gifted writer. From her good friend, Herbert Methley."

Olive finished her writing stint, and began to read *Daughters of Men* as she rested in a hammock after lunch.

It was the tale of a young man in the provinces who liked women. It began by making the point that very few men admitted to liking women, in the plural. A good man should be in search of the One Woman who would partner his soul, but how was he to recognise her if he did not explore, compare, investigate what women were?

The first part of the novel detailed the hero's relations with various young girls, classmates at school, girls who sang in the church choir, girls like solid dryads met when he was wandering through the woods in search of peace and quiet, girls who were quizzical behind haberdashery counters. His name was Roger Thomas. The descriptions of his relations with the girls were coded, but somehow the nature and variety of extensive sexual experiment was conveyed. There was enough description of skin and electricity, of hands grasping petticoats, of long young throats and the eye travelling downwards, or lovely young legs, going upwards from fine ankles. There was hair—curly black like blackberries, shiny brown like chestnuts, pale like flax. About halfway through the book Roger Thomas noticed a melancholy woman, a married woman, his elderly headmaster's young, lovely wife. He felt her intelligent eyes on the back of his head. He began to fear her judgement of his innocent and less innocent flirtations. He was now working as an apprentice teacher. She and he sat side by side at her kitchen table, drawing up lists of exam results, making papers. One day she put up her hand, with the pen still in it, and traced the shape of his mouth with her fingers.

They became lovers. They lay tragically in each other's arms on blankets in the woods, on the carpet in front of the little heater, with its red glow, in his rented room. They planned a clandestine weekend in a pub, and loved each other with abandon, grieving over each passing moment as they took delight in it. That was meant to be the passionate farewell to sin, but the story ended in the same way as Methley's confided tale of his relations with Phoebe.

Olive thought it must be autobiographical. She thought Herbert Methley was very good at writing about flesh and its stirrings, and was surprised that the book had not been banned by the Lord Chamberlain, or seized by the police. She was interested in the way descriptions of sex incited sexual stirrings in a reader—in this case, herself. The word made flesh, she muttered to herself, half-amused, half-irritated. He had meant to do this to her, she knew it. But her response was confused by the image of Phoebe Methley, whose solid flesh and sensible face came between Olive the reader and her entry into the world of the book. She kept seeing Phoebe's rather large knuckles, the beginnings of wrinkling on her neck, the slight sag of her stomach and breasts in her bathing suit.

What did Methley *want* her to feel? She thought about the relation between readers and writers. A writer made an incantation, calling the reader into the magic circle of the world of the book. With subtle words, a writer enticed a reader to feel his or her skin prickle, his or her lips open, his or her blood race. But a writer did this on condition that the reader was alone with printed paper and painted cover. What were you meant to feel—what was she meant to feel—when the originals of the evanescent paper persons were only too solidly present in flesh and bone and prosaic clothing? A gingery tweed jacket, a faded cotton skirt with lupins on it, and an elastic waist that clumped oddly?

Herbert Methley came and sat beside her on the beach a few days later. Tom, Charles and Geraint were swimming. The girls were walking barefoot at the edge of the sea, in their swimming costumes. Julian was reading a book. Methley said to Olive

"Did you read my book?"

"With great interest," Olive said, substituting the word "interest" for the word "pleasure" at the last moment.

"You are a shrewd reader. You will see that parts of it are taken from life. More than is usual in my work. I wanted you to have read it, to know me."

"Ah—" said Olive, looking down. He put his hand over her hand, on the sand. He gripped a little. She did not withdraw her hand.

"A love like that—a history of such—such pain, and such fulfil-
ment—is a sacred history. It changes a man. Like Roger in the book, I
used to take myself lightly, I was consumed with what I believe is *normal*
widespread curiosity about the sex-feelings. But once a man has truly
given himself—and sacrifices have been made—there can be no further
question . . ."

Olive thought, rather sharply, I do not need warning off. She
extracted her hand, and used it to rearrange her hair. It was probable, of
course, that he was not warning *her,* but shoring up himself, against his
own inclinations, which he seemed to be only too much aware of. She
said, demurely, with a little smile, that what he said was very right, very
honourable. She thought to herself that this kind of conversation was
altogether more perturbing than Toby's devotion, or Prosper's courtesy. She would be glad when Humphry came back from wherever he
had gone—he had said it was Leeds, but it could well be Manchester.

Olive Wellwood was thirty-eight. She came from a class where many,
perhaps most, women did not live much beyond that age, where what
was in women's minds was diminishing strength and the looming of real
death. Yet here she was in the magical Garden of England, with a good
body, and a face that was, she thought, more interesting, more defined,
yes indeed, more *beautiful,* than when she had been a green girl. And
spider-webs of sexual attraction floated everywhere, and touched their
skins, like dandelion seeds on white spiralling parasols, like ozone waft-
ing in from the sea. It was still *her* time, she thought, looking out at the
Channel and the children—and Toby who was leaping with them, and
Violet camped with nanny and pram—and Prosper who was striding
towards them in a smart panama hat. The children were children,
blessed children, not yet formed. Though she saw that Herbert Methley
had detached his attention from her, and was staring with a pleased
expression at the gaggle of girls, pale, fine Griselda, brisk dark Dorothy,
dreamy Pomona and inhibited Imogen, pretty Phyllis and composed
Florence, the only one in whom could be seen a shadow of the woman
she would be. "Aren't they lovely?" she said to Methley, who gave her a
sharp look, smiled conspiratorially, and agreed.

The boys were coming out of the water, onto the sand. They were
like sealfolk, Olive thought. Sleek creatures of the deep, beaching them-

selves and taking human form. Shaggy Geraint and precise-gestured Charles, and behind them, riding in prone on a wave, then standing thigh-deep in the moving water, his hair streaked and streaming with it, Tom. He seemed reluctant to come out. He bent and stirred the surface of the water with his golden arms. He was the most graceful creature she had ever seen. It was noon. The sun was high and shone directly down on her golden boy, who was not reflected in the moving surface of the sea, which he had broken into shining particles, myriads of slanting glassy fragments, a mosaic of surfaces, as there were myriads of glittering water-drops catching the light and making rainbows along his shoulders and in his long hair. He had fine gold hairs all over his body, too, she saw. Fine gold hairs long enough to cling together and make dripping patterns on his chest and thighs. Olive saw—it was the effect of dandelion-plumes and ozone—that his thin rod (she had no familiar word for it) was half-upright along his stomach. She loved Tom. She could not keep him. Tom loved her—this was still *her time,* with him, too—but he would go away, and be changed.

She started making-up, in the other world. The queen in the clearing, on the horse with fifty silver bells and nine at every tett of its mane—whatever a tett was. The woman and the boy, in the clearing. A story. She smiled, at a safe distance now, and Herbert Methley wondered what she was smiling at, and misconstrued it, as was natural.

Dorothy went to the pottery workshop, to see how Philip was.

Philip was at the wheel, his wet hands inside the moving, growing clay wall of a pot. Dorothy stood in the doorway and watched him. She touched the tips of her own fingers with other fingers, trying to imagine, in her skin, how this work would feel. It was precise, and extraordinary. Philip came to the end of turning, finished his rim, smoothed the sides with a wooden baton, and lifted the bat from the wheel. He said to Dorothy "Hello, then," without turning round. She hadn't been sure he knew she was there. He said

"Would you like to make a pot?"

Dorothy said she would. Philip found a smock for her, and ceded his seat at the wheel. He took a ball of clay, and slapped it on the wheel, and centred it for her. "Now," he said, "press down, so, with both hands— use your thumbs—and feel it come up."

Dorothy pressed. The clay was wet and clammy and dead, and yet it had a motion of its own, a response, a kind of life. The wheel turned, the clay turned, Dorothy held her fingers steady inside the red-brown cylinder which rose, with narrowing walls, to the rhythm of the turning. Dorothy was delighted. And then, suddenly, something went wrong—the rhythm faltered, the clay walls frilled, slipped and collapsed inwards, and where there had been a tube there was a flailing blob. Dorothy turned to Philip to ask what she had done wrong. She was half-laughing, half-crying. Philip was laughing. He said "That always happens." He took the lump in his hands to re-form it, and at that moment Elsie came in from the storeroom door, carrying something, unaware of Dorothy's presence, holding it out to Philip.

"Look what I found. Did you ever see the like?"

Then she saw Dorothy, and blushed crimson. Dorothy wondered why she had alarmed her so—they knew each other, a little, not very well—and then began to understand what she was holding. Philip had understood immediately, and the blood was also rising in his face.

"It was in a box at the very back of a kind of gloryhole," said Elsie.

It was white and shining. It was a larger-than-life, extremely detailed, evenly glazed model of an erect cock and balls, every wrinkle, every fold, every glabrous surface gleaming.

"I didn't do it," said Philip.

"I didn't think you did," said his sister. She said to Dorothy "I'm sorry." She wasn't sure if she was on first-name terms with Dorothy or not.

Dorothy advanced, with her hands covered in wet slip.

"Can I have a look? I'm going to study anatomy. Do you think it's for use in hospitals?"

"No," said Philip. "I think—I think it's a phallic *Thing*."

He had learned that word from Benedict Fludd's talk. Neither of the other two knew what it meant.

"Religious, sort of," said Philip, half-embarrassed, half on the edge of hysterical laughter.

Dorothy took the phallus and brandished it. She said "It's very *big*," and also began to laugh uncontrollably. Elsie joined in the laughter.

"Do you think—do you think"—Dorothy asked—"it's a self-portrait, so to speak?"

She had left brown clay fingerprints where she had clasped it.

"You'll have to wash it," she said to Elsie, and collapsed again into laughter.

"Give it me," said Philip. "I'll run it under the tap. And then Elsie shall put it quickly back where she found it."

His fingers recognised just how well it had been made, how its maker's fingers had felt it out, and followed its swelling veins.

When they had given up laughing, they did not know what to say to each other, and yet felt very close. Dorothy said she had better be off. She asked if Philip would give her another lesson. She asked Elsie, in a voice still thick with laughter, if Elsie made pots.

"Aye," said Elsie. "Tiny little 'uns, when there's no one watching. I like 'em thin and small."

"You never told me that," said Philip.

"You never asked," said Elsie.

16

Olive rewrote the beginning of Tom's story yet again.

TOM UNDERGROUND

IT WAS A CURIOUS FACT *that when the young prince was a small child, with a sunny nature, and a normal quantity of childish curiosity and naughtiness, the absence of his shadow appeared more to amuse and enchant those who noticed it, than to cause them any alarm. But as he grew older, and began to show the first signs that he must put childhood behind him, his family and courtiers began to murmur when they thought he was not listening, and to consult wise men, without his knowledge, about what the meaning of this singularity was. They began to cover mirrors in rooms where he was, as though he might become aware of his absence, or partial absence, at the least. The boy himself noticed other people's shadows, which he studied intently as they fell across courtyards, or were suspended on walls, stretching and contracting, visible human-shaped intangible nothings. He could not see his own shadow, and for some time assumed that no one could see his own shadow, but only other people's shadows. Then he saw a little girl, playing a laughing game of making her shadow climb a wall, and making shadow-rabbits with her fingers against a light. There were no rabbits and no dragons in his fingers, or if there were, they were invisible. He did not know who to ask about this problem. He felt his parents would have spoken to him, if they wanted to, or were able.*

He took to going for long walks in the grounds of the palace, which were extensive. He was not allowed to ride out of the gates because of the fear of kidnapping, by lawless bandits, or foreign schemers. But there were little woods, within the walls, and pretty semi-wild clearings, and long rides, overhung with trees. He noticed he was going out more and more either in grey weather, when everything was the same colour as the shad-

ows, or at noon on bright days, when nothing cast a shadow, under the high sun.

He had a favourite place, where a clump of birch trees surrounded a small mound, where he would sit, and watch the busy insects going in and out of their holes under the earth, or read a book, or look at the sky through the leaves. He called it a magic place, in his mind, and always felt that the air had a different quality there, was full of movement and sparkles, in the stillness.

There was a stone bench, but he didn't sit on it. He sat on the turf, which was warm, in summer, and cool in the autumn.

Sometimes he dozed. He must have been dozing, for he found his eyes were closed, and there was a sound of very faint bells ringing, very large numbers of very small bells, as though the trees were full of them. And there was a sound of rushing, as though a large bird were alighting in the clearing. He was reluctant to open his eyes. The bells became still, and he felt he must look up, or time would be suspended.

There was a fine lady, on a white horse, in the clearing, where no one and nothing had been. The horse was both creamy and silvery: it had ivory-coloured hooves, and a proudly arched neck, with a flowing, heavy mane of fine hairs, into which were woven myriads of tiny silver bells, on crimson threads, that glinted in the sunlight like raindrops, and rang when the horse tossed its head, or turned to look at Thomas. Its saddle was crimson leather, and the sweeping skirt of its rider was grass-green velvet, with a sheen on it like a green field of tall grasses, rippling in the light. She had fine green leather boots, and silver spurs, and he lifted his eyes upwards and finally took in her face, which was the most beautiful thing he had ever seen. It was fine and pale and pointed, with high cheekbones, and a sharp mouth. The lady had a mass of pale gold hair, which was caught in a silver snood under her brave cap with a curling green feather from no bird he had ever seen or imagined. She had long gloved fingers, and carried a little whip, with an ebony stock and a silver pommel. Her eyes were green. They were green like a great, watchful cat, not like any woman, or any man he knew. She looked neither kind nor unkind, and it occurred to him that perhaps she could not see him, perhaps she was in some other world that had become briefly visible in his. He saw, then, that neither she nor the lovely horse cast any shadow. They rippled with lights and light, from the bells and the gleaming coat of the horse, and the lady's hair and her velvet skirt, but they cast no shadow.

She looked down on him, and smiled, neither kindly nor unkindly. He stood up, and gave a little formal bow, which seemed the right thing, and stood shadowless next to the shadowless pair. He meant to say something like "Greetings," or "My lady," but he said

"You have no shadow."

It was, he realised, the first time that word had crossed his lips.

"I am an Elf," said the lady. Her voice was like fragments of fine ice in the wind, like the silver bells in the horse's mane. "I am the Queen of Elfland, and we cast no shadows. You are True Thomas, a human, and you should cast a shadow, and do not."

"It seemed a small thing," he said, "at first. A curiosity. But now it is not so amusing."

"You were not born without a shadow," said the Elf Queen. "It was taken from you, in your cradle, by a great rat, who cut it away with his sharp teeth, and carried it carefully down a rathole. There are ratholes everywhere, even in palaces, and they lead underground, underground, into the world of shadows, where the queen of the Dark Elves weaves them into webs, to trap mortals and other beings. Your shadow is folded away in a chest in her dark house, where the rat took it, running through tunnels and corridors, clutching it softly in his sharp teeth. He is her friend and servant. They can use a human shadow to trap the man or woman to whom it belongs, to snare them in darkness and use them to work their will. All this kingdom, when you are king, can be ruled by them, through the manipulation of your shadow in the shadows. Bit by bit they can draw the whole land into the shadows and take it from under the sun."

"This appears to be my fault, but I have done nothing," cried Thomas.

"Harm can come about without will or action. But will and action can avert harm."

"What must I do?" asked Thomas, for he saw clearly that the Elf Queen had come to tell him to do something.

"They cannot use your shadow until you, and he, are men, and not boys. So you must go underground, now, whilst you are still a boy, and the shadow is harmless, and find it, and bring it back to the upper air."

"How can I do that?"

"I will take you some of the way. You must mount behind me."

"I am not ready," said Thomas, thinking of his life in the palace, the things in his room, his books, his games, his anxious mother and father, his old nurse.

"You are as ready as you will ever be," said the Elf, and bent low, and held out her hand, with the whip in it.

He had the thought—he was a canny boy, even if honourable and straightforward—that she might herself be a malign force, come to do him harm.

"If you do not trust me, this will be the worst day of your life," she said, and he seemed to know, inside himself, that this was so. So he stretched up, and took her hand, which was cool and dry, and swung easily into the saddle behind her, and put his arms around her fine waist, and bent his face towards the velvet gown.

"Now," she said, "we ride, with the wind, into the waste lands."

And the horse leaped out of the mound, and went like a wind (there are creatures that do move like the wind) towards the high wall that surrounded the palace. There it collected itself, and stood back on its haunches, and rose, and leaped, and cleared the wall with space to spare, and the green cloak flying, and the wind in Thomas's hair.

And they rode away fast, across that kingdom, and into strange lands, and stopped for a while by the gate of an orchard. The Elf Queen told Thomas he must not pluck the fruits, which hung invitingly on the boughs, because they looked fair, and were foul, and would poison him. But she gave him a milky cake from a bag at the saddle-bow, and a flask of clear water to drink. And the sky began to darken, not as it did at home, but as though a curtain was being pulled over it, or they were entering an invisible cave.

"This is the border of Elfland," said the Queen. "This is a shadowland where the shadowless travel." The rocks, and the grass, were grey, and a little river that ran beside the track was grey, and thickets they passed were grey, rat-grey, shadow-grey, and there was a sound of rushing and roaring, like breakers on the beach. And the grey stream went faster over the grey pebbles, breaking with little crests of grey foam. The skirt of the lady still shone green, and the coat of the horse still gleamed ghostly-white, and

Thomas's own hands were still pink with the human blood that circled under his skin.

The river opened out onto a pebbly strand, where a tide of water lapped, and rose and fell, quietly enough, a pink and grey frill. Thomas could not see the other side of the tide, whose surface shimmered endlessly before him, but he did see that it was not grey, but red, like blood, or perhaps was blood. There were neither sun nor moon in that evenly slate-grey overarching roof. The horse stepped forward without hesitation into the bloody tide and walked on, lifting its proud feet delicately. And soon it was in knee-deep, and occasionally breast-deep. And Thomas saw that the blood appeared to stain the white coat, and then dripped off fetlock and silver hoof, leaving no permanent mark. And they went on in this way for what seemed to Thomas not hours, nor days, but weeks, with a sullen water-roaring in his ears, and flat grey and crimson ripples before his eyes.

They came to another strand, in the end (or I should have no further tale to tell) and the horse stepped out on the fine sand. It shone golden, and before Thomas's eyes was a long beach, and cliffs of white chalk, covered with fine green turf, and white gulls swooping and crying, and a few woolly sheep balanced on the cliff-edge, munching the low bushes that grew there. The cliff-walls were riddled with caverns, out of some of which little rivulets ran, cutting edged tracks in the sand, meandering round pebbles. Thomas looked back, and there, a space out at sea, was a red line which was the edge of the blood, and a great wall, like a looming sea-fret, which was the edge of the grey world, through and beyond which nothing could be seen at all.

"This is my own country," said the Elf, dismounting and helping down Thomas. "And here we must part, for although I live under the hill, I cannot go with you underground, where you must now go. I will give you my satchel of food, and the water bottle which was filled at the spring in my orchard, where I hope in time you will come. The right way in—one of the ways in, for there are many—is through the central one of those three slits you see in the cliff-face. You must wind your way in and down, in and down to where the Dark Elf and the rat are waiting. The way is long— walking, scrambling, climbing, crawling. The mine-tunnels down there are populated with all sorts of creatures, human and inhuman, ancient and very young and lost. You will find help and companions—so much I can see—and you will meet dangerous things, and wild things, some of which She will have sent, and some of which have their own concerns, nothing to do with Elves, or rats, or shadows. You will do well to travel with others, but you must choose your companions wisely for there are wicked things down there that seem reasonable and friendly at first sight.

"I have three gifts for you. The first is a light which will shine in the darkness—it is made of elvish fireflies, enclosed in a glass, which will spin into flaring brightness, briefly, if you shake them and whisper to them the words 'Alfer Light.' I advise you most earnestly to let no one know that you have this glass—or any of these things. The second is an imperfect map of the tunnels that lead to the dark court. It has been made by Light Elves, many of whom perished in the passages, and we do not know—for no one has survived who knows—how accurate it is, or how many major branches are not recorded. If you could mark on it where it goes wrong, and where it is of help, other later travellers will be grateful.

"The third thing is another thing even I do not perfectly understand. It is a little brass case in which is suspended—we do not know how, or by what physics, or magic—a needle of crystal, that spins around and shows the way to the centre. It is said, also, that it gives out a strange light, blue like a gentian, when it comes near enough to Herself, but this I cannot vouch for.

"Do you have a question?"

"One question? I have a thousand."

"One. You must go quickly, not looking behind you, before the tide comes in and cuts off the mouth of the cave."

"What is the worst thing I can meet down there?"

"The worst? The Dark Elf, and the great rat, are bad things. But the worst may be your own shadow, when you see him, if you recognise him."

"That is bad, since I must seek him out."

"It is bad. Go quickly now, and watch your steps."

17

In September 1896 Tom put on his spanking new uniform, and got into the train, at King's Cross, with crowds of other Marlowe boys. The family—Olive, Violet, Dorothy, Phyllis and Hedda—Violet carrying baby Harry—had come to see him off, and already he saw that they were an embarrassment. They were too many, too loud, too female, too agitated. His mother's beauty made her remarkable in the wrong way. Dorothy's scruffiness made her remarkable in another wrong way. They had had long discussions about how much of his hair must be cut off. It had been trimmed, once, and cousin Charles had said it wouldn't do, it would be thought girly, and now it was trimmed close to his head, so that he felt exposed, and saw himself as a condemned felon. He wore a cap, sewed in segments of wine and gold felt, with a tassel and foolish little brim, that made his lovely face egg-shaped. He wore a blazer, in the same rich wine-red, with a unicorn embroidered in dull gold on the breast pocket. He was not allowed, as a new boy, either to do up the buttons of this garment, or to put his hands in his pockets. He had a wine-red tie with small unicorns on it, which he would be allowed to exchange for a knitted tie in two years, and a bow tie when he was eighteen. He had a stiff white rounded shirt-collar, which had to be buttoned—later again, it would be allowed to be unbuttoned, and later still he could wear a shirt with a pointed collar, like a man. His mother said she thought the presence of the imaginary unicorns might be a sign of imagination. Tom did not think so. When he got into the train, Hedda started to howl, and had to be taken away.

And so he went North. Marlowe was in the Yorkshire dales, just outside a market town called Fosters. It was hideous, built in grey stone slabs, imposing and imprisoning, with all sorts of anachronistic turrets and portcullis gates. Tom saw Julian Cain, and called out to him, across a quadrangle. Julian sauntered over—the boys cultivated a kind of vulpine lope—and said *sotto voce* that Tom must *never* use his first name, and must *never* speak to older boys unless he was spoken to. Tom said how could he *know* all these things? And Julian said he would learn them pretty quickly, or the archets would take it out of him. Boys who at Eton would have been prefects and fags, were at Marlowe archets and butts. Julian asked what house Tom was in, and was told Jonson

House—the Houses were named for seventeenth-century dramatists, the heirs of Marlowe, Dekker and Jonson, Middleton and Ford, Webster and Turner (anglicised from Tourneur). Tom said he was to be Hunter's butt. Hunter was the head archet of Jonson, blond and muscular, with a face like a knife. He was captain of the Second Eleven, and rowed stroke in the Jonson boat. Tom had formed an unfavourable impression of him, but dared not ask Julian what he was like, in case he was breaking some complex tabu. Julian knew what he was like, but dared not tell Tom. Tom would find out soon enough. Julian was in Ford House, whose head archet was a mild boy called Jebb, who was the best slow bowler in the whole school, and therefore did not have to keep proving himself. Julian looked at what had been done to Tom's loveliness, to cram him into cap and blazer, and saw that it still shone out. The shaved nape of his neck was elegant and vulnerable. For Hunter's butt, this presaged horrors. Keep out of Hunter's way, Julian wanted to say, keep out of his way, my dear. Tom's innocent mouth was perfection. It said "There is so much to learn, and no one tells you what it is."

"They knock it into you," said Julian. "As it was knocked into them."

Julian, at sixteen, shared a study with two other boys. Tom, as a new bug, had no private place. Not even the jakes, where the boys stood and sat at a long open stool with regular holes in, and considered each other's privates, furtively or openly. Not in the dorm, where he lay two feet away from a boy called Hodges and a boy called Merkel, both of whom had that smell both cheesy and acrid which permeated the whole school. Hodges asked him if he liked touching or being touched best, and Tom went fiery-faced and said, neither. He was, of course, being touched, by Hunter, who had his own gang of bloods, solid members of the rugger scrimmage, who played a kind of game of forfeits with the newbutts, which consisted of tearing off their garments, one by one, as they tested them on arcane school lore. "What do we call a creep who smarms at the archets." "A sucky-bum," said poor Tom, who knew that one. But they went on and on until they found things he didn't know— that you must never say bacon and eggs, but always pigs and shelly, you must not say prep, but bogroll. What must you do when we beat you? Say thank you, because it's good for you, or we'll beat you a lot more. His underpants were taken before his socks and shoes, and they all handled him, one after another. The whole code of such places insists that it is foul and dishonourable to tell anyone of such happenings. Tom didn't.

He bumped into Julian on a cross-country run in the Dales, for a short distance, and thought of speaking to him. But he looked at Julian and saw both that Julian knew what was happening, and that Julian, like everyone else, expected him to grin and bear it.

His letters home said that he was settling in, and had various duties like making the archets' beds, and bringing them things from the tuckshop. He imagined a stolid, unimaginative small boy writing, and wrote what he imagined such a boy would write. Humphry remarked to Olive that his letters were dull for a boy with two writers for parents, and Olive said that it was just protective camouflage, she was sure, boys at school were not encouraged to show their feelings. He always wrote at the end

"Thank you, Mama, for sending the story. It makes all the difference."

Considering that there were six other children in the house, and Humphry of course, Olive missed Tom appallingly. He had something to do with her power to write good stories—real stories as opposed to pot-boilers—and she needed him. He was neither audience nor muse, exactly, but he was the life of the story. She went on writing *Tom Underground* for him, compulsively. She hoped he didn't mind her having changed her hero's name from Lancelin to Tom. Names are things over which writers sometimes have little control. Tom underground would neither act nor think, without his true name. The plot sprouted all sorts of delectable, frightening complications as Tom underground made his way inwards and downwards, along rushing underground rivers, along ledges beside plunging black funnels whose end could not be seen—or heard; if you dislodged a pebble, no sound of landing came back. Sometimes there were caverns lit by encrusted glittering jewels, which someone unknown had cut free of the rock and polished. Sometimes at a distance there were sounds of activities—whisking things that might be rats, or larger animals, trundling wheels of trucks in adjacent galleries, passing trains and troupes of gnomes and salamanders, from whom Tom concealed himself in a crevice, fearing their alien dark faces and spiked, filthy fingernails.

Time went on, and Tom's stolid little letters continued to come. Thanks, Mater, for the delish fruitcake, which was much appreciated by the archets. Can you send more treacle cake, the Head Archet likes it.

(So do I, when I get any.) Yesterday we went on a cross-country run in the Dales, by a trout-stream. It was soggy weather, we got soaked and covered in mud, but it was nice to be out in the open, and I put up a respectable time, coming third. I am trying to improve at rugby and have a mass of bruises to show for my efforts. Fawcett Major said my running was creditable but my tactical sense nil. I shall work on the latter. Thank you for sending the story. It makes all the difference. Your loving son, Tom.

The story was an embarrassment. How does a suddenly little boy, deliberately deprived of privacy, read dozens of pages of typed paper, without drawing attention to himself? How and where could he hide? The story was a necessity. Tom reading *Tom Underground* was real: Tom avoiding Hunter's eye, Tom chanting declensions, Tom cleaning washbasins and listening to smutty jokes was a simulacrum, a wind-up doll in schoolboy shape.

He went underground. The school was heated by a bellowing and shuddering system of coke-fired radiators. There were coal-holes and boiler-rooms down there, accessible from the basement locker rooms. Tom furnished himself in the village on a school outing, with a little oil lamp on a rocking base called a Kelly lamp. He remembered, in the days when he had been Tom, pursuing the hiding boy through the underground pillars and vaulted arches of the South Kensington Museum. Tom was one of those lonely boys who imagines rapidly and easily that he is the only one of his kind in the whole community, that he is in a sense the unique butt of all mockery, bullying and ordinary spite. So it did not occur to him that other desperadoes might have been driven to take refuge here, amongst the shovels and brooms. But he did find traces of previous fugitives—a chalk drawing of a row of hanged boys on gibbets on a wall, a carefully folded travelling rug, and pillow, with a neatly buckled satchel, under a heap of sacking. There must be, or have been, at least one more like him. So he made his hidey-hole in a very cramped, unpleasant corner behind a roaring furnace, which belched out unpleasant fumes. Even other fugitives might not think first of this as a refuge. There he spread a blanket, put on a sweater, lit his Kelly lamp, and read *Tom Underground,* smearing the typescript with sooty fingers.

The travelling prince had acquired various companions, some human,

some inhuman, some of whom had stalked him for days before revealing themselves, some of whom he had himself tracked through burrows
and into crannies. One was a mine-spirit, who was of a kind known as
gathorns, and whose name seemed to be, like all his kind, Gathorn. He
was slender and pale, and could make cobalt-blue light shine from his
hair and the tips of his fingers. He described himself as timorous, but in
moments of danger showed a tremulous, but real, courage. There was a
scurrying salamander-like creature, as long as Tom was tall, like a small
dragon on bow legs, with ivory-coloured scales, and crimson eyes like
red coals. He had hissed and reared his crest when he saw Tom, but the
gathorn had soothed him, and co-opted him to the company. He could
always find fresh water, where it trickled down slate or sprang through
fissures in the shale. There was a thing that was sometimes there and
sometimes not there, which took the form of a huge, transparent tube,
rounded at both ends, with eyes and a mouth that appeared and vanished from time to time in random places on its body. It was known as
Loblolly and had dropped like a bead of amber into the prince's hair,
and then had swelled and expanded to line a whole cavern. It could flow
along the ground, or diminish to a heavy square of jelly that the young
prince could carry in his pocket. It warned of the three lethal damps—
Fire Damp, Choke Damp, and White Damp—and would spread its
own body as an impermeable tissue to prevent these horrors creeping in
through cracks and pinholes.

Other beings were met, and neither trusted nor distrusted. Cutty
Soams, very jolly, half-mansize, chipping away with a pickaxe in a
green and mustard glow, bared to the waist but wearing a ragged green
cap and a spiky beard, warning against going further on or deeper
down—*he* would never dare, oh no. He misdirected the Company,
sending them left along a level which ended with an impenetrable rock-
face. He may or may not have been helping the Enemy. They were
aware of spies. Little fluttering bats with eyes like minuscule rubies
and diamonds, touching hair with bony fingers, flickering away into
shadow. Worms of all shapes and sizes, quick and slow. Dancing lights
that they had the sense not to follow. A carved figure on a stone chair,
swelling out of the rock.

There was also the Wild Boy. It was possible—Tom in the story
entertained the possibility—that the Wild Boy was Tom's Shadow. He
was always glimpsed at a distance, at the other end of a tunnel, running
fast. He was ragged and dusty, barefoot and fleeting. Sometimes he

turned to wave, mocking or inviting, they did not know, before vanishing into the shadows.

They found him, of course. Hunter and his sidekicks, Blewett and Fitch, stalked through the boiler-room in dressing-gowns and slippers, shining a light into crannies and under ledges and pipes. They probably went on these boyhunts regularly, though this did not occur to Tom, who felt he was Tomallalone, unique, the single object of their mocking venom. Hunter's dressing-gown was scarlet, wide-skirted, the colour of judges' robes, with gilded braiding and a gold cord round his manly waist above his purposeful haunches. He had glossy beetle-black slippers, embossed with his crest, which had plumes and portcullises on it. The butts would clean the coal dust off the slippers the next day. Tom remembered, holding his breath, that he had himself performed that task, and was furious with himself for not seeing what it implied. They sauntered past his hiding-place, and he breathed again, and then, of course, they turned, and Hunter said "Let's just cast an eye behind here—now *what* have we here, a naughty little newbutt, out of bed, with a little lamp and a filthy heap of paper, and a blanket too, all mod cons. You will see me tomorrow, Wellwood, and I'll flay your buttocks for you. Now, show me what you're reading to yourself. Some smutty tale, I'm sure." He motioned to Blewett to seize the pages. Tom bared his teeth, like a rat, and cowered back, and panted.

"Bum-wad," said Hunter. "Read it out, Blue, let's hear what the little swine is masturbating with."

Blewett read. He read badly, halting and humpy, putting on a false, exaggerated squeak.

. . .

Then Gathorn said "We need to go still further in, however dark it is."

And Tom said "I would give anything, almost, to see the light of day. I am shadowless by torchlight and candlelight, I might as well be shadowless in the sun."

And the Loblolly hummed a little tune, and said that rats were nearby, he could smell them, thousands of rats, swarming through the tunnel.

And Tom said "I am afraid I may never come out of here alive."

. . .

"What sort of crap is this?" said Hunter. "Stories for babies, whining babies who need bedtime pap like this. You won't forget this in a hurry, Wellwood."

Tom croaked "Give it back."

"Did you write it yourself? It's pretty comprehensive rubbish, isn't it? And you know what we do with rubbish. We could cut it up for bum-wad. Or we could just chuck it in here," he said, opening the door of the furnace.

A flame shot up from the surface of the incandescent coke-bed inside the boiler. Blue flames rippled, gold flames flickered, dull red patches sprouted on the exposed lumps. The stench was asphyxiating. Fitch began to cough, and Hunter began to throw *Tom Underground,* page by page, clump of pages by clump, into the open porthole. The story writhed and shrivelled on its bed of fire. Tom seized his Kelly lamp, which he had turned off, and hurled it at Hunter's head. It struck his cheek, leaving a bruise and a blister, and poured lamp-oil down the scarlet gown, in dark stains.

"You could be sent away for this," said Hunter, mopping his cheek with a handkerchief. "You nasty little turd, you could be hurled up in front of the Head, you could be beaten in front of the whole school, you could be *finished.* You've hurt me, you bummer. Really hurt. I'll see you never forget it. I think you might *like* to get sent away, and I don't think you should get anything you *like.* So I'll stay mum, and make sure you pay—this hurts, I'll hurt *you,* make no mistake." He cuffed Tom about the ears; rhythmically, several times, so that Tom's head was a box of pain.

"Come and see me after school tomorrow. *Think* about it. Bring me the black cane, after school tomorrow. Don't forget, now, will you? And you can get the oil off my dressing-gown first thing tomorrow."

The next morning, Hunter waited in vain for his butt. He sent scouts out to look for him—he was probably shaking somewhere, in some hidey-hole, paralysed with terror, he had no guts. He wasn't found by class-time, and was marked absent in the register. He did not appear to receive his beating after school. He was not in the dorm at night. Hunter sent Fitch down to search the cellars, but he was not there.

. . .

The next day, the headmaster asked the whole school if anyone had seen Wellwood. Hunter had shown his bruise and cut to the Head, saying curtly that Wellwood had caused it, by throwing a hot lamp, when he was caught reading after lights out. The Head said the boy was probably hiding. In his mind was a sick memory of an earlier beautiful boy, swollen-faced and no longer beautiful, hanging from a hook in the coal-cellar. He told Hunter to set about finding Wellwood. He instituted a search of the grounds. After another two days, he called in the police, and telegraphed Humphry Wellwood.

Humphry and Olive got on a train, and went North. Humphry was partly annoyed to be missing a deadline for the *Evening Standard*. Olive was trying to hold on to several story-threads, from *The Outlaws* to *Tom Underground*. At the same time, exactly, as they experienced normal continuing irritation, they found themselves, somewhere else, alien, frozen by fear, staring at raw shapes through the window of smoke, steam, looming vegetables.

When they arrived at Marlowe Tom was still lost. Humphry counted the days during which Tom had been missing and he himself had not been informed. He expressed indignation. Olive said Tom's letters had been *perfectly placid*. With hindsight, too placid, not like Tom at all. They met Hunter, who assessed them insolently, curtly displayed his bruise and cut. Olive asked him how he had come by it. Hunter explained that Tom had been using a lamp to read a heap of nonsense in the dark, and had thrown the lamp at him, when discovered. A hot lamp is dangerous, said Hunter. He stared coolly, and apparently unperturbed.

Olive suggested, when Hunter had gone away, that it might be worth talking to Julian Cain, who knew Tom outside school, and might be in his confidence.

Julian was fetched, and said he knew nothing. He said, under questioning, that he thought Tom was finding it hard to settle in. He said cautiously, to Humphry, that Jonson's was famous for discipline, and newbutts—new boys, that was—sometimes found it hard, at first. Humphry understood the unspoken message, but it did not help. There was no sign of Tom, and after a few days in an inn, Humphry and Olive went home again, to their other children, and to wait in case Tom got in touch, which he did not.

Todefright became terrible. Phyllis cried a lot, and got smacked frequently. Humphry drank whisky, and talked to the police. Olive walked. She walked from end to end of the house, as a woman in labour walks, to use the contracting muscles to distract body and mind from the pain. After three weeks, walking, walking, occasionally sinking into the nearest chair and pulling at her fingernails and hair, she took some of Humphry's whisky, and then some more. At first late at night, and then, in small slugs, in the evening, and then in the day, still walking, walking. After six weeks, her bright black hair was dull and bushy, and her eyes—though she did not weep—were puffed by whisky.

Violet managed everything. Meals, letters to editors, the little children, who had not been told, though Violet knew Hedda knew perfectly well what was going on, although she did not know what Hedda thought or felt about it.

Dorothy went out. She didn't go to stay with Griselda, or to any of her lessons. She went out into the country and disappeared. It was odd that neither Humphry nor Olive noticed her absence, though they might have been supposed to be anxious about their other children.

Dorothy went to the Tree House, which was still well camouflaged by autumn foliage and bracken turning gold. She sat quietly on the edge of one of the bracken beds, and waited. After six weeks, she found a chipped pottery mug, and some mouldy crumbs, just inside the door. She began to stalk the Tree House, creeping up on it from behind, not approaching down paths, and by this method she was able, one day, to go in and find the ragged boy curled like an unborn child in the heather nest, with worn shoe soles, a filthy jacket several sizes too large, a satchel she recognised, a shock of long, dusty hair, full of all sorts of things, living and very dead.

Dorothy said "I knew you'd come here. I think I'd have known if you were dead. I thought you weren't."

Tom made a scratching, snuffling noise.

"Where've you been?"

"Helping a gamekeeper," said Tom. It was all the answer she, or anyone, ever got. It was like and unlike one of Olive's tales of fugitives. It took Dorothy two more days to persuade him to walk back with her to Todefright. She never, ever told Olive that she had known for two days where he was, without saying anything, for she would never have been forgiven.

When Olive saw ragged Tom she had to rush into the cloakroom to be violently and unromantically sick. She came back, her face white as plaster, and put her arms around her boy, who smelled of unspeakable things, and whose skin had no bloom. He stiffened, and instinctively pushed her away. She said "Where have you been?" She said "We were sick with worry." Tom did not reply. Olive put her arms again round his hunched, unresponsive shoulders and said "You will never go back there again." Olive wanted to tell him, in pain and grief and rage, what the days of waiting and *not knowing* had been like, and knew that his own state was too bad for her to burden him with hers. She had been there before, when the pit flooded, when the fire damp puffed its venom. She had waited and grimly known she was waiting in vain, had almost longed for certainty to replace the agony of uncertainty. Something in her—because of those earlier waits—had known Tom would never be seen again. And now he was here, alien and grubby. She said "My poor boy." She said to Violet "He must have a bath, and his own clothes." She said to Tom "You can tell me all about it, in your own good time."

But he never told her about it. Olive suspected that he was telling Dorothy, and interrogated Dorothy. Dorothy said, quite truthfully, that she knew nothing except that Tom had been helping a gamekeeper. Olive did not really believe that this was all that Dorothy knew. Tom said one thing, after a week or so. "I haven't got the story." Olive said "Never mind. I have a copy. Don't worry. I know all about it. It doesn't matter."

"It does," said Tom, and went and shut himself in his bedroom.

Olive felt shut out. Tom was part of her, and she was part of Tom, and the evil boy, Hunter, had severed the connection. She was angry with Tom, because of the waiting she had done, and his unawareness of the waiting. She was not given to introspection. She had "been through" something bad, and she dealt with it in her usual way, writing a children's story of an innocent boy set upon by bullies at school, and bravely defying them. She made a Gothic horror out of the neo-Gothic turrets of Marlowe and included a heartfelt appeal for schools to become kinder and more civilised places. Innocence should not be regimented and brutalised, like recruits to an army. We should care for our young, and teach them tolerance, kindness and self-reliance. This book, with the title *Dark Doings at Blacktowers,* was a huge success. Julian Cain read it in the Easter holidays of 1897 and said to himself that if he were Tom he would find the book unforgivable. By then Tom was apparently back to "normal," running wild in the woods, and still doing Latin with Vasily Tartarinov and English with Toby Youlgreave. Olive had given him a copy of *Blacktowers,* inscribed "To my dear son, Tom," but it was not clear to her, or to anyone, whether he had read it. He had developed a habit of simply not speaking about a great number of things. Olive did not write any more of *Tom Underground* until after the publication of *Blacktowers.* She rewrote the last section she had sent to Marlowe, with the company trapped in a shaft which was a dead end, and made them hear a silvery tapping on the other side of what had seemed impenetrable rock. Gathorn wielded his pick from one side, and the other pick echoed his blows, until the rock suddenly crumbled, and they were in a large chamber, lit by silver lamps, where a creature neither woman nor spider, but with features of both, was spinning long silvery threads . . .

Eighteen ninety-six was a gloomy year. William Morris died in October, as Tom was hiding in thickets and Olive was pacing her corridors. Prosper Cain, still grieving over the suicide of his Director in June, was harassed, both personally and professionally, by the sustained Press campaign against the military presence in the Museum. The military, accused of muddle and incompetence, hit back with statistics and oratory. A Parliamentary Select Committee was formed to go into it, which met twenty-seven times in 1897 and twenty-six times in 1898. It included Sir Mancherjee Bhownaggree, Conservative Member for Bethnal Green, where objects from the Museum were on display. It also included John Burns, the socialist MP for Battersea. The committee recommended that the whole Department of Science and Art be reorganised, and the duties of all the officials redefined.

All sorts of institutions were coming to life. The Tate Gallery opened on Millbank in 1896, the National Portrait Gallery moved from Bethnal Green to a site next to the National Gallery, in the same year. The Whitechapel Gallery, a solid and elegant Art Nouveau building by C. Harrison Townsend, and an offshoot of all the teaching, studying and social enthusiasm in Toynbee Hall, was built between 1897 and 1901. A Fabian Society member, incurably ill, committed suicide and left his fortune to the Fabians, to forward their ends. Sidney and Beatrice Webb decided that this could best be done by the founding of the London School of Economics, and in 1896 the rich Irishwoman Charlotte Payne-Townshend took the top floor of no. 10 Adelphi Terrace for the first students and lecturers—though this move was not wholly approved of by all the Fabians. The dissenting Fabians included John Burns, and Sir Sydney Olivier, who worked in the Colonial Office and had taught at Toynbee Hall.

There were other suicides: in 1897 Barney Barnato, the bankrupt Randlord, jumped overboard and drowned on his way back from the Cape to a monstrous party, in his newly built monstrous house in Park Lane, to celebrate Queen Victoria's Diamond Jubilee. In 1898 Eleanor Marx, socialist, new woman, trade unionist, Ibsen translator, poisoned herself on finding that her lover, Edward Aveling, had secretly married an actress, and needed her to sell her father's papers to keep her. The *Yel-*

low Book produced its last issue in 1897, destroyed at least partly by Oscar Wilde. (Aubrey Beardsley had made a cover, which was not used, for the first edition of the *Savoy,* in 1896, which depicted a naked putto pissing on the discarded *Yellow Book*. The cover, when it appeared, was without *Yellow Book,* and showed a putto innocent of cock and balls.)

In 1899, in May, the little old Empress of India, having been celebrated in flaming summer weather by a swelter of loyal emotion in 1897, was driven up in a semi-state open landau to perform what turned out to be her last public duty, the ceremonial laying of the foundation stone of Aston Webb's new buildings at what was now to be called the Victoria and Albert Museum. The stone was red Argyll granite, and the ornate trowel, with which, assisted by Aston Webb, she laid the stone, was kept by the Museum. She was too tremulous either to climb any steps or to speak, and handed her speech to the Lord President of the Council, the Duke of Devonshire, who had persuaded her to add her own name to her dead husband's. "In compliance with your prayer, I gladly direct that in future this Institution shall be styled The Victoria and Albert Museum and I trust that it will remain for ages a Monument of discerning Liberality and a Source of Refinement and Progress."

In 1899, in October, the High Commissioner in Cape Colony prepared to go to war with the Boers for the gold mines of the Transvaal and the Orange Free State. The Boers immediately invaded Natal and Cape Province, taking Ladysmith, Mafeking, and Kimberley. Prosper Cain did not think it would all be over by Christmas. He went to Purchase House, to talk to Benedict Fludd, having visited those sappers who were to embark for the battlefield, where they were training as bombardiers and explosives experts in the barracks at Lydd. They had invented an explosive, Lyddite, which was to be used in South Africa to blow bridges and destroy farmhouses.

Cain did not like the war. He was not sure it was a just war, and he was not sure it could be prosecuted successfully. He quoted Rudyard Kipling, with a sardonic smile, to Benedict Fludd.

Walk wide o' the Widow at Windsor
For 'alf o' Creation she owns:

We 'ave bought 'er the same with the sword an' the flame
An' we've salted it down with our bones.
(Poor beggars!—it's blue with our bones!)

Fludd said "A Black Widow indeed." He was paying little attention to the war, which he denounced as another evil in a Fallen World. Cain, with and without his children, visited Purchase House frequently between 1896 and 1899. There had been a time when, as a very young man, Cain had drunk with the pre-Raphaelite Bohemia to which Fludd briefly belonged, and had watched him disappear into the night— "in search of dissolution," he always said, holding up a pale hand to prevent anyone accompanying him. There had been rumours that he took pleasure in danger. Often he disappeared, in black moods, for weeks together, and his friends and companions canvassed the possibility that he was dead in an alley, or flotsam in the black Thames. He came back from one of these absences accompanied by his own Stunner, Sarah-Jane, whom he named Seraphita, and married. Prosper, by then a young lieutenant, was at the wedding, and could still, with increasing difficulty, remember the radiant, blithely innocent face of the young bride, her hair full of flowers, her garments spattered with them, like Botticelli's Flora. She had looked at Fludd with a slightly silly, but touching adoration, the lieutenant thought, not himself finding her desirable, for she lacked spice. He himself was twenty-three, then, in 1878, and he thought Seraphita was younger. He was in love, and married his elegant and secretive Italian Giulia later the same year, taking her briefly to Lucknow, which she hated, and back to London for Julian's birth in 1880. When he next saw the Fludds, which was not until after Florence's birth, and Giulia's death, in 1883, Imogen was four, Geraint two and Pomona one year old. By then, Seraphita had taken on the blank, listless look she still had. The children were prettily dressed and slightly grubby. Fludd, he discovered, was absent for days and weeks together. He had been making pots in Whitechapel, and had set a house on fire with a kiln disaster, after which he simply walked into the night, and disappeared. It was not Seraphita who told this to Prosper Cain. She offered him tea made without boiling water, and with insufficient tealeaves, and stared slightly to the side of his head. Prosper Cain found some connoisseurs to buy some pots and commission some more, and when Fludd returned, employed him as a ceramics consultant at South Kensington.

He had been doubtful about the recent renewal of Fludd's artistic energy, on the arrival of Philip. He had noted that the daughters—Imogen certainly, Pomona in an odder, jerkier, more effusive way—had taken on Seraphita's vacant look. He went back from time to time to encourage the firings and was surprised how long both the work and the marginal profit-making had gone on. He thought this was to be attributed to Philip Warren, whose own throwing and, later, glazes increasingly impressed him. He thought Philip was stolid—he saw to the flues and the packing of the kiln—and was surprised by the intricacy and delicacy of his designs for tiles and bowls. Fludd was bold and breath-taking. Philip was fine. Prosper Cain was both amused and encouraged by the unconventional commercial support the pottery had. Geraint, still in a rage to escape poverty, suborned traders and charmed great ladies. Miss Dace, Frank Mallett and Dobbin kept track of orders and dispatches—these were not numerous, but were increasing. Fludd disappeared from time to time, silently and without warning, in the old way, but Philip went on with the work, silently. The house was more like a house, and less like a wrecked barn, Prosper said to Olive Wellwood, with whom he went walking in the Marsh, occasionally, when they were visiting.

"Oh," said Olive. "That's Elsie. None of them could do anything without Elsie."

Prosper said he had hardly noticed her, which pleased Olive at some subliminal level, since Elsie had recently become very pretty indeed, almost beautiful.

"She doesn't try to be noticed," said Olive, fairly. "She gets on with fixing things, so that they work. You know, Prosper"—they were on first-name terms now—"you know, I don't think either of those two—Philip and Elsie—get paid a penny. I suspect she gets all her clothes from cast-offs or Patty Dace's jumble sale stuff. I think Dobbin looks after *him*. I think Seraphita notices *nothing* and no one dare speak a word to Fludd in case he goes into a gloom, or stops working, which they expect him to do, every day, although he's been working on and off for five years now."

Prosper Cain was shocked. Olive went on.

"I notice—a woman will notice. Curtains are mended and things are polished—sideboards and spoons. There are bowls of wild flowers on the dresser. The sink is clean."

"How old is that girl?"

"No one knows. She must be about twenty."

"Do you think—with some arranged assistance—she could look after a group of students from the Royal College of Art? The poor souls are much harassed by the building works at the Museum—I had the possibly over-ambitious idea of a summer school in the outhouses and meadows of Purchase House—with tents to camp in, and camping for the ladies in the haylofts—and with great luck a few master classes from Benedict Fludd."

"It *is* ambitious," said Olive. "It would delight Geraint. We could add other things—literary talks, and plays put on, and so forth."

"Fludd is the attraction, and Fludd the major hazard," said Cain.

Fludd was in rather a gleeful mood, having made some odd-shaped vessels with Black Widow spiders lurking in their depths, their spinnakers busy, their multitude of eyes glittering opal. He said "Why not, why not, let them all come, let them learn to see clearly and use their hands."

They were having a business tea, and Frank and Dobbin were present. Dobbin asked, respectfully, if Fludd was sure he wouldn't find a summer school—intrusive maybe, oppressive perhaps?

Fludd said "Don't be daft. A bevy of lovely young ladies is just what we need around us—and some of them may even have an inkling of what it's all about. I've been thinking of modelling women again. Let them come."

"We must talk to Elsie," said Frank, who was quite as aware as Olive was of the importance of Elsie.

"Elsie'll do as she's told. Elsie's a good girl," said Fludd.

No one asked Elsie what she thought or felt. Or, at least, with a youthful egoism which she had been forced entirely to conceal, Elsie believed no one asked or cared what she thought or felt. She had worked out her master plan from the moment of setting foot in Purchase House—or perhaps even earlier, in the dusty track across the Marsh, when she noticed that Philip was taken aback by her presence. She didn't go quite as far as thinking he didn't want her there, but she kept the possibility in mind. She saw something was missing in the house—a real woman, she told herself, looking at the three pale Fludd females. Elbow-grease, cunning, foresight, tirelessness. She had brought her mother's fine camel-hair brushes for Philip. And for herself she had kept her mother's sewing-truss, with its needles and cottons and wools, and a pair of sharp scissors that had never been pawned. She would rather have had the brushes. She had been learning to decorate fine porcelain, when her mother collapsed, muttering Philip's name. She thought she would use the needles and scissors as a weapon to make a space for herself. She made excellent soups, out of almost nothing, a hambone and a sheaf of peapods, slowly simmered. Scrag-end of Romney salt-marsh mutton, with onions and pearl barley. She was not, it should be said, naturally tidy or orderly or domestic. She wanted to go barefoot, and didn't really care if her underwear was in holes. But in this situation she needed to be needed, she needed to become indispensable, and she made herself so. She learned—for herself, no one thought to teach her—the embroidery stitches, cross-stitch, petit point, and unpicked and reworked where Pomona had gone wrong. She worked out how to deal with Philip. She loved Philip, and believed he did not love her. He had room for only one passion, she thought, and it wasn't his family. By all sorts of mute signs, and tactful withdrawals, she made it clear to him that she expected nothing, nothing from him, beyond not being sent away. He would have been shocked if she had said he did not love her, and she did not. And his mode of being was largely silent anyway. At first she asked Seraphita and Imogen if she might mend the bedspreads, or collect scraps to make a peg-rug, and they gave their sweet empty smiles, and said, by all means. So she turned to, and put sides to middle in old bed-sheets, and contrived storage systems, and found muslin to hang over jugs in hot weather. She moved around the house fast and invisibly—it was as though all the energy that drained from the three pale females had collected in her, like galvanism.

At night, very late, once she had installed an initial order that she could keep her hand and eye on, she crept into the pottery studio. She made, as she had told Dorothy, little pots. Fludd didn't have porcelain clay, but she mixed kaolin with earthenware, and made it lighter, lit a lamp and painted intricate little designs on tiny cups and saucers and platters the size of pen trays. She had been starving when she came, with a bony body and lank, dusty hair. Adequately fed, intensely busy, she became, as Olive had noticed, pretty, or more. Her hair suddenly took to curling and became a luxuriant mass, which she kept down with a kind of gipsy-scarf. Her waist narrowed, and above it and below it she rounded out and found herself tempted to strut, or twirl, and resisted, for who was there to see her? The obvious person for her to desire—the only visible person—was Geraint. He had energy, like her, but mostly used it to get out and about on a bicycle, far from Purchase. And if she let her hair out, or made a new shirt from a roll of blotched blue cotton, he showed no sign of noticing.

There were people, besides Olive, who did notice. One night, as she was working on the little pots, she was surprised by Benedict Fludd, who strode in, wearing a rough cowled garment like a monk's habit, in black. He was carrying a candle and his eyes glittered in the shadow above its flame.

Elsie gathered her little pots together like a hen with chickens. Fludd made a gesture like some kind of benison.

"Please continue. Don't be alarmed. Will it trouble you if I draw you at work?"

"No," said Elsie, stoutly, though her veins had stiffened.

"Just keep working. There's an interesting light from the lamp. I'll use charcoal. You have a very interesting face, you know."

"I'm sorry," said Elsie, confused.

Fludd laughed and began to draw.

He showed her what he had done, before they went back to their rooms. It was done with bold lines, and sweeps of shadow. It was a modeller's drawing, of the young flesh and bones of a girl who was, indeed, beautiful. He had done her hands, too, the competent fingers holding the clay and the brush. He had sketched in her sharp breasts, under her nightdress, and the barest possible indication of the folds of the cotton as it fell over them. Elsie said she was amazed. She said, too boldly,

"May I have it?"

"Certainly not," said Fludd. "I'm making myself a collection." And he leafed through his sketch-book, showing her drawings she had known nothing about, Elsie bending a brooding face over the dishes, Elsie poised over a pie with a knife, Elsie feeding the chickens, with the wind in her skirts. The chickens were a miracle of economic indications of movement, a strutting one, one with its head back to crow, one with flaring wings attacking another. He had caught her own motions as he had caught the nature of the birds. She felt exposed, and that something had been taken from her.

"I didn't know," she said.

"Now you do. I should like you to sit for a more serious study."

Elsie clutched her nightdress about her body. She said, somewhere between pert and indignant,

"And who will do the cooking and cleaning and shopping, I'd like to know."

"Certainly not my family of pallid silk moths. They float about and don't know how lucky they are. I do. Major Cain is bringing us a gaggle of lady students from the Royal College for this summer school they are planning. Would you consent to sit for all of us—myself and the lady artists? You are very unusual to look at. In a good way. Very."

He thought for a moment.

"I'm sure Dobbin, or Major Cain, or the Vicar, can find you an auxiliary when the school people come. Then you could model for us. Delectable."

When he had gone, Elsie, somewhat ruffled, thought he might have looked at her little pots, as well as her face, and other parts of her. He might have given her some encouragement.

She wondered if there was a career in being a model. It might not be respectable. Did she care?

They were rather lovely little pots. He should have noticed them.

19

The summer school took place. Humphry put on *The Winter's Tale,* with himself as Leontes, Toby as Polixenes, and Geraint and Florence as Florizel and Perdita.

Herbert Methley talked to Olive about sex. He sat next to her during rehearsals, when neither of them was needed. He took her for walks, along the rivulet, past the church, into the Marsh. His talk was at once theoretical and fleshly. Much of it was about what women desired. He said that until recently it had suited men to suppose that women felt little or no desire, were pure creatures or milch cows, that men treated as property. The ten commandments listed wives along with ox, ass, field, maidservant or manservant as things neither to be taken nor to be desired. Adulterous women were beheaded, in Semitic cultures, but not adulterous men. And yet, as a good student of Darwin, he believed that sexual desire was instilled in human beings—like other animals—by the needs of the species to propagate itself. Elsie Warren, trim and fine-waisted, in a linen hat, came rapidly towards them with a basket over her arm. Did Olive suppose, Herbert Methley asked her, that such a young woman—he studied her figure very intently as she went past, smiling politely at them—felt none of the stirrings young men felt at her age? It was very improbable. Olive herself, he said, drawing her hand through his arm, was both a wise woman, and like himself, a student of human nature. What did she think?

"I am mostly a student of inhuman nature—imaginary nature," said Olive, evading. "I tell fairytales to children. The prince always marries the princess. Or the daft young man gets the princess because of his good nature and because he is the third son. Or the prince becomes a roe deer, or a swine, and has to be disenchanted by the clever princess. I don't know what it has to do with what you call the needs of the species. All the tales stop off with marriage, or perhaps foretell a large number of progeny, undefined."

They were going past a fenced field with a herd of cream-coloured cows, heavy, muddy, staring cows. In a corner, under an elm tree, one female cow was busily mounting another, making the movements a bull would make, although unequipped, and provoking—they both noticed—a quiver of response (or irritation) in the strained area under the lower cow's tail.

"Does not that prove my point?" said Herbert Methley. "The poor things are deprived of the presence of a bull—who would in nature be there, guarding his harem and snorting defiance at other bulls. Yet they feel a need . . ."

Olive felt a blush mounting from her bosom to her face.

"I hope I have not shocked you. I did not mean to shock you."

"I think you did. But I am not shocked. And I take your point. Scientifically, your example—look, she has got down, and sauntered away—is evidence for what you say it is."

"When we can prevent the unfortunate consequences of following our instincts to what John Donne called the one true end of love—our society will be different, and we shall be transfigured."

"By sexual freedom? Instincts are one thing. Donne uses the word, love."

"Is not desire always love, whilst it exists? Whatever it may become. I sometimes think, there are as many ways of loving women, as there are women. And I sometimes think, if women were honest, there are as many ways of loving men as there are men."

"Ah, but a good student of human nature needs also to study indifference, and even revulsion and distaste. For these also are instincts."

Methley thought for a moment or two about his remark, and then attacked directly.

"I hope I inspire none of those in you?"

He laughed, not quite easily.

"Don't be foolish," said Olive. "We are not talking about ourselves. And we are good friends, which is yet another relation between men and women, hard to manage and rare to find."

When she got back to the inn where they were staying, she found herself shrugging her whole body with a mix of emotions. Of course such talk aroused some kind of—yes, sexual—pricklings in her. It had to. She knew what desire was, and what its satisfaction was. But she had no idea whether she desired Herbert Methley. The presence of his body aroused her own in some way, but it was not clear to her that what it aroused wasn't indifference, revulsion and distaste. He was not lovely to look at, as Humphry was. Though he had a kind of dreadful energy which is always—how did she know these things?—stirring, like a huge octopus quivering through water, or flailing on a slab and slipping back into the sea.

What was very certain was that she had had none of these thoughts at Elsie Warren's age. They were a grown woman's thoughts.

Benedict Fludd held classes in clay modelling in what had been the grand coach-house. Elsie had cleaned its little row of spider-webbed windows and Philip had brought tubs and buckets of clay and slip. There was a serious group of five young women from the Royal College, whose previous experience of ceramics had been painting tiles, and one or two young men also. Then there were locals who wanted to try their hands—Patty Dace, Arthur Dobbin, a schoolmaster from Lydd, and the new schoolmistress-to-be from Puxty, a young widow called Mrs. Oakeshott. Mrs. Oakeshott had come from the North, to make a new beginning, she said, after the tragic death of her young husband in a railway accident. She was accompanied by her small son, Robin, who would start school at Puxty in September, with the few Marsh children who attended—the whole school, from five to eleven, was only fourteen children. Frank Mallett, who was on the local education committee, had been delighted to find Mrs. Oakeshott, and was already afraid she would find the harsh weather and the loneliness unbearable. She had excellent qualifications and a mild wit. Her son had come with her to Purchase, accompanied by a kind of nursemaid, twig-limbed, diminutive, frizzy-haired, perhaps twelve or thirteen years old, called Tabitha. Mrs. Oakeshott had a thick, coiled plait of strawberry-blonde hair, golden, creamy, rose-tinged. She had a fine face, square in shape, placid but watchful, and a delightful smile, when she smiled. She wore glasses, which she tended to mislay, and which were returned to her by the young men, and by Dobbin, when they found them in clumps of grass in the orchard, or lying amongst the drying pots in the studios. She was good at modelling.

Fludd had prevailed on Elsie to sit for the classes, although she sat there running over in her mind what should be fetched from the farm and the market for the next meal. No one dared contradict Benedict Fludd, in case he should cease to be amiable and become moody or irascible. He was teaching them to model a head. No one was modelling Elsie below the neck. They were trying to render her flying hair, and sharp mouth, and wide eyes. Mrs. Oakeshott's effort was much the best. She had got the angle of the jaw and the neck right. The brows over the empty eyes were promising and lively.

Little Tabitha wandered about with the child, Robin, and came upon Violet Grimwith in the orchard, reading aloud to the assembled smaller Wellwoods, Florian, Robin and Harry. Hedda, rather sulky, was with this group but not of it. She was reading a book, lying on her stomach in the grass, thinking this was not enough for her, not enough, she would go mad with boredom.

Tabitha crept up to the very edge of the audience. Violet looked up. "Come and sit with us, if you like, why don't you? What is the little boy called?"

"Robin. I look after him for his mum."

She was older than Hedda, but smaller. Violet said

"Well, bring him into the circle, to listen to the story. We're reading *At the Back of the North Wind*. Do you know that?"

"No, mam."

"I do," said Robin Oakeshott. He sat down, next to Robin Wellwood. "I like it. Go on reading."

Violet gave him a measuring glance, and went on reading.

Mrs. Oakeshott offered her services to help with the play. She gave Imogen Fludd a hand with the costumes, and turned out to be deft with bits of glitter-braid, and abundant pleats for the pregnant Hermione. Olive liked her. Everyone liked her. It would have been hard not to.

Olive came upon Mrs. Oakeshott, in the place behind the yew hedge, where they waited to go on and off, adjusting the clasp of Humphry's regal cloak. She saw Humphry's hand, in the nape of Mrs. Oakeshott's neck, his clever fingers feeling for tension, and relieving it, as he did for Olive herself. She stepped back.

"All the same, Marian," said Humphry. "However sensible you

are—we are—the whole idea is simply foolish. I wish you would go home."

Marian Oakeshott rested her head—intimately—on Humphry's shoulder.

"It is hard," she said. And then, "I do love you, I do love you so very steadily, so very much, my dear, however hopelessly it must be."

And Humphry said "Oh well, I love you too, that can't be altered. But it can't *be,* and you know it, you have always known it."

And Marian Oakeshott put up her arms, and drew down Humphry's head, and kissed him, and he gave a kind of groan, and grasped her, and kissed her back. Olive saw the crown of hair tremble and sway. She thought of marching forwards, and retreated.

Hedda lay in the long grass, with her skirt rucked up above her knickers, and her lengthening brown legs stretched out. She was fortunate not to have hay fever, as Phyllis did. She was not exactly reading *The Golden Age.* I am a snake in the grass, she thought, a secret snake. Violet was sitting on the roughly mown grass in the orchard, at some distance, in a low wicker armchair, sewing. Hedda spent a lot of time spying on Violet, as a revenge for the fact that Violet spied on her, going through her private drawers and notebooks. Hedda, like Phyllis, was perpetually agitated by being left out of the group of older children, Tom and Dorothy, Charles and Griselda, and now Geraint. But whereas Phyllis was plaintive, Hedda was enraged. She was the traitor in all tales of chivalry and in myths. She was Vivien, she was Morgan Le Fay, she was Loki. She despised the cow-eyed and the gentle, Elaine the lily maid, faithful Psyche, Baldur's weeping wife, Nanna. She was a detective, who saw through appearances. No one was as nice as they seemed, was her rule of judging characters. She was the darkest of the children, with long black hair and very solid black brows, drawn in a frown more often than not, and long, black lashes which in themselves were beautiful, especially when she was asleep. She had no one to talk to about her investigations. Phyllis was an idiot. Florian was a baby. She had had hopes of Pomona, but Pomona was an idiot, too, of the same kind as Phyllis. Dorothy was who she hated, because she was older, and in the way, and got things Hedda didn't get. And because she had Griselda, and they were together, and Hedda had no one. But Dorothy didn't know what Hedda knew, or partly knew. She had even wondered about

Tabitha as a sort of friend—it was odd that she, at ten, was certainly a young child, whereas Tabitha, at twelve, was supposed to be in charge of Robin Oakeshott, and was a sort of nursemaid. She saw that Tabitha's simple manner was put on. Tabitha had her own thoughts, which she kept to herself. Hedda did not know what those thoughts were, and she saw Tabitha didn't want her to know. Tabitha was acting, and could not afford a crack in the surface.

Olive came through the orchard, running, clutching her skirts. She pulled up a chair near Violet, and leaned forward, and hissed to her in a desperate whisper. Hedda could hear perfectly from where she was, and kept very still.

"I've just discovered something frightful, Vi. I don't know what to do."

She was all atremble.

"Tell me," said Violet. Violet liked being told things, Hedda knew.

"That woman—that Mrs. Oakeshott—who is no Mrs. anyone—she is the same woman—she is Maid Marian."

"That was fairly clear from the outset," said Violet.

"What?"

"That was what I thought, myself. What has upset you?"

"She kissed him. He kissed her. I saw."

"That was stupid of you. Better not see. She's going away to be the schoolmistress at Puxty. What are you thinking of doing?"

"I am not made of stone, Violet, though you may think so. I have violent feelings. I feel—very angry, very—I can't stand the mess. I can't work if there's a mess. You know that. I can't afford to get agitated, I need to work."

"Well then, you must not get agitated. You are the goose who lays the golden eggs on which we all depend. Including, I imagine, Mistress Maid Marian. You'll be better off if you leave her to go earn her living at Puxty. You don't need any more dependants."

"He kissed her."

"Well, you know what he is and what he does. He won't leave us, all the same, you can feel safe on that count. Mistress Marian is the victim, not you, you goose."

"But I saw—"

"Well, take good care to see no more. You've had practice. Kiss someone yourself, there are those who would enjoy that, and you know it."

There was something going on, Hedda sensed, that she did not understand, over and beyond what she did understand.

Olive gave a little laugh.

"Mr. Methley has been lecturing me on the nature of women."

"He's another who can't keep his hands to himself."

"You've noticed that?"

"There's not much I don't notice," said Violet, with quick satisfaction. That was it, Hedda thought, she has to know everything, or she feels—smaller, lesser—

"So you think I should just go on—as though nothing—as though I'd noticed nothing—"

"Isn't that one of your great accomplishments?"

"Oh, you are hard on me."

"Rather the opposite," said Violet.

That first summer school was ad hoc and haphazard, from start to finish. Later schools took up deliberately a pattern that developed casually and at odd moments, in that first year, where one event—a lecture, a drawing class, a poetry reading, the Play above all—became connected to the others, so that Toby Youlgreave gave a lecture on Italian tales of abandoned babies who were returned as beautiful girls, whilst the textile and embroidery group were put to designing floral prints and weaves for the black and white wintry first act, and the spring festival of the second, where Perdita scattered flowers. August Steyning came over to help with stage effects—notably Olive-Hermione, as statue—and stayed to instruct the young Fludds and Wellwoods in theatre and costume design. He took from *The Winter's Tale* what fitted his version of the theory that marionettes were more profound in their presentation of human passion than clumsy or self-obsessed human actors. He instructed Florence in how to dance "like a wave of the sea," bending her body with his own hands, inducing a paralysis of self-consciousness and then, inexplicably, a new freedom of flowing movement. Florence said, flicking her wrists and ankles,

"What have you done? I feel as though my hands and feet don't belong to me."

"Good," said August Steyning. "Now, again, skip, skip, glide, make a full moon of your arms, let your fingers hold it—it is cold to the touch—so—"

Florence felt she was made of quicksilver.

Prosper Cain came when he could, when the business of the Museum allowed it. He gave a talk on the craft of art, and the art of craft, and of how—even in painting and sculpture—the two were inseparable. You needed design, and you needed basic physics and chemistry, or your paint would not dry under its varnish and your clay would not hold its glaze. And you needed also something—a sharpness of vision—which couldn't be taught, but could not be acquired, in his view, without incessant practice.

He went to a class where several students—professionals and amateurs—were designing *The Winter's Tale* series of alternating squares, tiles as it were, on stitched or printed fabric. Seraphita Fludd was ostensibly teaching this class, sitting at one end of the barn, and saying "very nice, very acceptable," to whatever was brought up for her to look at. Cain wandered, with Olive Wellwood, behind the chairs and easels, offering comments. His own children had produced very pleasing, very faintly parodic, floral forms, Florence's Dutch, Julian's a version of Sèvres porcelain. "Very nice," said Prosper Cain to his son. "Very competent, you mean," said Julian. "I can do this with one hand behind my back. It's a mockery. I don't have any of that sharpness of vision you were extolling this morning. It's not real, as I know you know."

"I wonder what it needs to become real?" said Prosper, accepting Julian's evaluation of his own work.

"I don't think art should be personal," said Julian. "In fact, I think it shouldn't be. And yet, what is wrong with my very nice roses, is that they're nothing to do with me. They don't need me, and I don't need them."

When they were out of earshot, Olive said to Prosper that he was fortunate to be able to talk to his children with such ease, to put them at ease, she meant to say—she wanted to say, how very well he had succeeded at bringing them up—at being—

"Both parents," said Prosper. "Male and female, both. It hasn't been easy. Soldiers are very male, by nature. Except that they need female skills, like sewing and polishing, for they live separately from women. In that sense, they are like the boys to whom Dr. Badley is diligently teaching needlework and cookery at Bedales. A concept that, as a soldier, I find attractive. Camps, and needlework for boys. And theatre. Come and look at Miss Fludd's work. It interests me."

There she sat, Imogen Fludd, in her imperfectly hand-sewn garments, that lacked both art and craft. She had designed one black and white square, and one small group of spring flowers. The black and white was frost-flowers on a window-pane, their petals outlined with meticulous strings of minuscule dots, a laciness that owed something to Beardsley's work for the *Yellow Book* and the *Savoy,* though Prosper Cain could not imagine this dumb girl understanding Beardsley's sly, sexual forms. The lips and clefts of her frost-flowers were surely innocent? Her spring flowers were in vanishing pastel colours, a hint of rose, a shadow of primrose, a blue stain like the vein in her pale wrist. They were trying to retreat back into the plane of the paper, they were blushing mildly to be present at all. He was about to say something anodyne and pass on when the shapes pulled together in his head, and he saw that she had, in a helpless way, exactly that sharp vision that Julian had rightly renounced. He said

"These could be good, you know. Why do your flowers lurk in the centre of the paper? As though they were going down a funnel. You should do what Mr. Morris always insisted on, extend the vegetable forms to the edges of the square so that they can grow beyond it—"

"I can't."

She didn't look up, her face was heavy.

"Well, then," said Prosper, on an impulse. "Define their limits. May I?"

She handed him her charcoal and her pencils.

He enclosed the frost-flowers in squared panes. And then he drew a circle round the spring flowers, almost as though they were on a plate, or inside the rim of a basket. It was surprising how the confinement brought them to life. He laughed.

"They needed to feel safe," he said.

"They needed to feel safe," she repeated.

He said

"Have you other work I can see?"

She handed him a portfolio. He found a series of drawings of little coloured fishes, springing and curling, blue and yellow and red.

"I was trying to illustrate *The Arabian Nights,*" she said. "The talking fishes. It's got no shape, like everything I do."

Prosper enclosed the fishes in an extempore frying pan, with two handles, bringing them to life in the same curious way.

"Not," he said, "that you can now say they are safer. But they are livelier. They have a purpose, if it is only to get out of the frying pan."

"Into the fire?" said Imogen doubtfully.

"Have you thought of enrolling at the Royal College?" Prosper said. "You have talent. You could learn a craft—"

"I don't know," said Imogen.

"You should think. I will talk to your father."

He saw her think of begging him not to do so, and then deciding to say nothing.

When they had left the class, Olive asked him why he had encouraged Imogen Fludd, and not his own children. Who were, she said, clearly much more accomplished.

"Accomplished, oh yes," said Prosper Cain. "But that girl has what you have, my friend—she knows the shapes of things, as you know the shape of tales. Look at her work. One artist should recognise another."

"I am not an artist. I earn my living by storytelling."

"That is nonsense, dear lady, and you know it."

So they came slowly to the performance of the play, and the end of the summer school. The theatre was the wild garden at the side of Purchase House, which had once been a formal garden, and had unkempt hedges which had once been clipped yew, and were now bearded and tufted and invaded by brambles and Old Man's Beard. Steyning commandeered some students and helpers, including Dobbin and Frank Mallett, to make papier-mâché statuary on wire frames, which in the winter scenes were stark and in the summer scenes were garlanded with silk flowers and real flowers, mixed. He had brought footlights, with lime-light, which altered the shadows on these forms, making them bald and sinister, or bright and clear. There was a goat-horned herm, with shaggy thighs, and a naked girl with falling hair, seen from the back. There were two squatting, cross-legged little fauns who grinned at the stage-corners in the harvest scene, and were absent in the Sicilian sculpted palace. Then there was Hermione's plinth. He was exigent about this object—he wanted the woman-statue higher than the cast and the audience, with the moon, which was full, silver and shadowy behind her. He wanted both stone mother and fleshly daughter to be chastely clothed in endless swirling pleats of white cloth, and exhausted Olive by rearranging both her standing place and her complicated garment over and over again. He pointed out that by moonlight, with her back to the moon, and a veil cast over her, she would glow in the shadows, the shape of the dark bushes and her mysterious cowled head against the moon would be magical. And she must move, when she stepped down, like an automaton. As though the force of gravity, not her own will, lifted each foot, bent each knee, held her arms in place.

"I don't know what to do with my arms."

"Practically, you will need to hold on to the pleats, whilst you're up there, or they'll come out. Your right arm across your breast, to hold the veil down at your left shoulder. The left arm around the waist to hold the cloth in so it doesn't swirl away when you move. You need white rings on your fingers, ivory or moonstone, I'll see what I can find."

Olive was not very good at gliding like an automaton, and became irritated by the constant repetition.

"You are related to the stone man in *Don Giovanni,* you are a sister of Pygmalion's ivory Galatea . . . Think of the stone music—"

"I am a woman of a certain age, who has borne a number of children," said Olive drily.

"You are a fine figure of a woman," said Steyning, who was still thinking in terms of sculpture.

So there she stood, on the first night, with the moon behind her, making shadows in her wound garments, which she clutched, pale-knuckled. She was surprised how very difficult it was to keep still, for so long. She thought about her body, under all its unaccustomed white sheeting— like a dressmaker's dummy, she thought, something vague and muffled. She was ageing. She was pleated across her stomach as well as over her shoulders. She was still in her time. Prosper Cain admired her. Herbert Methley desired her. Humphry wanted her, but she was cross with Humphry. She had cheered herself somewhat, going over Humphry's conversation with Maid Marian, by remembering that it was quite clear from what he said that he had not known either that Marian was the new schoolmistress at Puxty, or that she was coming to the summer school. It would go by, she thought, as other things had gone by. She made what she hoped was an invisible adjustment to her stance, as her ankles were both numb and strained.

A woman on a plinth can see over a hedge she is designed to protrude above. There in the lane behind the yew hedge, their heads bent together, were Humphry, in his royal robes and hose, his red hair artificially whitened by August, and Marian Oakeshott, in a pretty dress with forget-me-not sprigs on cream. She was brushing the white powdering from his hair off the velvet shoulders of his cloak. It was a very wifely gesture. When she had brushed it away, she patted his arm, in an even more wifely way. Rage gripped the statue, who nevertheless must remain motionless. Rather deliberately, she thought of Herbert Methley's investigating fingers. Involuntarily she remembered the ludicrous and alarming cows. She was her own woman.

At the moonlit garden party to celebrate the success of the play, Olive stood with Humphry in a circle of admirers which included Marian Oakeshott. Everyone praised Olive's impassivity and stillness as the statue. Mrs. Oakeshott commented intelligently on the brilliant verse-speaking of Hermione's passionate self-defence in Act I. She was even able to quote felicities of stress. Olive was confused by this and turned gladly to Herbert Methley, who made several remarks about the character of Hermione as Woman, and spoke of how few of Shakespeare's female characters were women, since they were mostly to be played by young boys who were better at young girls. He had always wondered how a boy could create Cleopatra. He would like to see Mrs. Wellwood undertake Cleopatra. He kissed her hand, and held on to it too long.

And so Olive found herself in a bed with Herbert Methley. It was a bed in an inn called the Smugglers' Rest, on a bit of coast looking out at the Channel. It was a bed that sagged, and seemed likely to creak, in a bedroom with an uneven wooden floor and an ill-fitting window, with a crocheted curtain with fish on it. The inn was run by a somewhat unctuous and over-friendly fat woman, who had fed the lovers on plates of shellfish and day-old bread and butter. Methley said he took a room there from time to time when he needed to be alone for inspiration. Olive thought "be alone" meant "not be with Phoebe" since otherwise he was reasonably solitary on his smallholding. It had taken a surprising amount of fixing to be together here. Lies had had to be told. Olive had set off on the London train to see a publisher and had got off at the next stop, which was why she was rather formally dressed, with a large hat, and gloves.

It would have been better if they could have fallen impulsively into each other's arms in a hayloft, but that was impractical, they thought, surrounded by art students and miscellaneous children. Methley had repeated, with gratifying urgency, "You must come to me, you must come, it is meant to be." And he had his arrangements, pat, when he came to propose them, with an ease which Olive felt it better not to question. Over lunch, with a certain bitterness and jealousy he had criticised August Steyning's "bloodless" theories of impersonal acting. Bloodless and soulless, said Herbert Methley. There is too little passion in the world for it to be removed from the stage, where it should flourish, without hindrance. Olive felt it was all embarrassing, to be sitting eating oysters, and discussing Kleist and marionettes, looking into the eyes of an intended lover. It was all too deliberate, and not spontaneous. She thought there were women who would have enjoyed this aspect of things—but she was not one. She thought about how to say she had made a mistake, and must go home, and could not frame the voice or the sentence. So she ate her strawberry tart with cream, and followed Herbert Methley up the narrow wooden stairs.

Inside the bedroom, he bent to lock the door, and lifted his hands to remove her hat. She stood awkwardly, like a statue. He said

"You are thinking you have made a mistake, and should go home. You are embarrassed to be committing adultery out of a kind of revengefulness. You feel this is all mechanical, not passionate. I can read your thoughts, you see, I know you." Olive laughed, murmured "A palpable hit," and relaxed a few muscles.

"I am a writer, I know what people are thinking. I put my mind into their bodies. I love your body, and you will love mine. This is—as sex always is, my dear—both ludicrously comic, and passionately important. We shall know each other, as the Bible says. What could be more amazing?"

He was taking off his clothes as he spoke, and folding them, and putting them on a chair. Olive looked sidelong at his body. It was not pale with red extremities, like Humphry's. It was a kind of tanned yellow-brown, all over, owing to the naked sunbathing. She gave a snort of laughter. Bodies are ludicrous, she thought, he is very clever to say so.

" 'To teach thee, I am naked first. Why then
    What need'st thou have more covering than a man . . . ,' "

he said. She could not place the quotation. He undid her belt and began on her buttons.

"All the same," she said, finding her voice, "you are right, I do think this may be a mistake, I am embarrassed."

"Of course you do, and of course you are," he said, removing her dress and beginning on her underwear. "But I mean to make you forget all those thoughts, soon, very soon now."

And she plunged naked into the bed, with her hair pinned up, so that he should not scrutinise the slacknesses and scarring of her skin.

He talked a lot, during the sexual act. Humphry didn't, Humphry was silent and manful and lordly. Methley was intimate, curled round her, she thought, like a snake, like a salamander, murmuring in her ear "Is it better like this? Is it better here—or here—? Is this not delicious . . . ?"

Her body liked what he was doing—most of the time, and he noticed so quickly when it didn't, he changed tack, he corrected himself. She looked at his "thing" which was narrow and brownish, unlike Humphry's thick one. She must not think about Humphry.

"Don't think, stop thinking," said Herbert Methley in her ear, "now is the time to stop thinking, my dear, my darling," and she did stop thinking, and came to a quivering climax such as she had never before known, with a full-throated cry, which she felt must be audible all over the inn.

"I told you, I know you, we fit together," said the voice in her ear, and she saw that it could be hard to forgo a second experience like this, and yet she was, yet she was—not ashamed—embarrassed—by the difference of it all, and her own involuntary motions.

. . .

When Olive was disturbed, she wrote. She wrote as she might dream, finding the meaning, or abandoning the images, later. She wrote to get back into that other, better world. When she was back in Todefright, after *The Winter's Tale* and the Smugglers' Rest, she wrote a long description of a passage in which the travelling company came upon a tall, swathed object, a pillar or a prisoner, something, she wrote, like a plaster sculpture, wound in dripping bandages, which were hardening into a permanent form. It was greyish-white, a more than life-size cocoon. The young prince advanced on it fearlessly, as he always did. He was warned by Gathorn. "Don't touch it. Those are the webs she weaves, and they are poisonous." The prince approached, in the dark passage, with his little lamp, and caught the glitter of living eyes in the woven hollow eyes that spoke, though the mouth was covered and the lips only a soft mound. "It's alive, we must free it," said the brave boy to the good goblin.

Here she was briefly foiled by her own ingenuity. How could he unwind her, if her bindings were poisonous? He did it with his magic blade, which hissed where it came into contact with the liquid, and chipped away at the bits that had solidified. She could see it now. The bindings lay in writhing little strips, and solid stuff like clay or porcelain, like broken fingernails. When all the wrappings were removed, she stepped out of her shroud, a white-haired woman with a bent head, and hunched shoulders, who looked for a moment too old and exhausted to survive her release. She stumbled forward, and the young hero caught her in his arms, and steadied her, and suddenly found that she was a youthful fairy, her snowy hair full of unearthly life and light, her emerald eyes glittering with magic. And then again, she was old, white-lipped, her skin drawn over her bones.

She told him she was a powerful fairy, who had gone Under the Hill to help those whose shadows had been stolen, and had been snared by the dark Weaving Queen down there, and bound in dead shadow-matter, sucked dry of life by the Weavers. If there had been enough to cover her eyes, she would have become as they were. But she still had a little power, in her look.

Olive stopped, dissatisfied. The image was a good image, but the Underground story was not the right place for it. And the presence of this— apparently adult—fairy seemed to her to weaken, not to strengthen, the conflict between the white Queen of Elfland and the dark Queen of the Abyss. She had somehow been unable to put in female characters who were not those two. They would not come to life, boy readers would find them sissy, they messed up the thread of the narrative.

Nevertheless the idea of the good creature bound in dead shadow-matter was too good to lose.

So she rewrote the passage, taking away the height and age and beauty of the fairy, and substituting an air spirit, fine-limbed, with hair like pale gold sunlight (and no visible sex, she referred to it as an it). She was fascinated by the Paracelsian earth spirits—sylphs, gnomes, undines and salamanders. But as she had begun consciously to craft Underground, she had taken to excising any words or images that too easily made short-cuts to classical mythology and aroused all sorts of lazy, facile responses she didn't want her readers to make. She wanted her readers—Tom first, but she was very vaguely thinking of others—to see her air creature, as she had invented it. She made its hair spiky, as though the wind was in it, transparent as ice, but warm with sunlight. She gave it veins and sinews with blue of the sky and gold of the sun coiling in them. Its bones too were transparent. Its eyes? Uncanny yellow-gold eyes, with a black sunspot in the centre. She thought about it, and wondered, if she called it a Silf, whether getting rid of the Greek y and ph would steer away the classical associations. Silf was close to Elf, an English word, softened.

The Silf neither staggered with helpless age, nor lay like a ripe woman in the boy's arms. It danced about like a marsh light, celebrating its freedom, and warned the Company of unexpected dangers lurking in the next passages. It said that if it were Tom, it would go back whilst it could, and thought he could subsist perfectly happily without his shadow, in a perpetual noonday. It said "Maybe your Shadow won't want to come up to the air. Maybe it will want to stay with the gnomes and salamanders." Tom said "My shadow is mine."

"Maybe it no longer thinks so," the Silf said, and Olive wondered wildly what were the implications of that remark, which she had inserted on an impulse from nowhere.

20

At the turn of the century, the young were about to be adults, or some of them were, and the elders looked at the young, with their fresh skins and new graces and awkwardnesses with a mixture of tenderness, fear and desire. The young desired to be free of the adults, and at the same time were prepared to resent any hint that the adults might desire to be free of them.

Prosper Cain's family appeared to be unproblematic, indeed hopeful. Julian went to Cambridge in December 1899 and took the entrance exam for King's College, where he was awarded a scholarship. He would start in the autumn of 1900. Florence was studying for Cambridge higher certificates in several subjects, and was talking of studying languages at Newnham College. The newly named Victoria and Albert Museum was in a turmoil of building and a turmoil of reorganisation; arguments raged between those who saw the museum as a "collection of curios," and those who saw its primary task as the academic education of craftsmen and teachers. The Royal College of Art, which had replaced the National Training School, of which Walter Crane had been Principal in 1898–9, was now ruled by a Council of Art, four experts from the Art Workers Guild, full of Arts and Crafts idealism. W. R. Lethaby became the first Professor of Design at the college, and the course was energetically rearranged for "Art Teachers of both sexes," "designers," and "Art Workmen." There was a Matron for Women Students since there was no woman teacher, and a large body of young ladies.

Prosper Cain had been watching Imogen Fludd. He could not, he told himself, stand the sight of her mooning around Purchase House looking something between a draggled goosegirl and an incarcerated princess. By 1900 she was twenty-one, or thereabouts, and had neither husband, nor profession, nor sensible life at home. But she did, he thought, have a delicate but real artistic talent. He was sure she should get out of Benedict Fludd's aura, and the miasma of Seraphita's inactivity, and learn to do something. He spoke to Walter Crane, who admired Benedict Fludd's pots, and was well aware of the vagaries of his temperament. Prospective students had to take a rigorous series of exams in architecture (twelve hours for a drawing of a small architectural object); a six-hour modelling exam of—say—in charcoal the mouth of Michelangelo's David; drawing (a life drawing of the head, hand and foot); ornament and design—a drawing from memory of a piece of foliage, such as oak, ash or lime; and lettering by hand of a given sentence. Prosper Cain did not know whether Imogen had skills enough— or courage enough—to enter these public competitions. He persuaded Crane to allow her to attend the college classes as an amateur observer. They would see how she developed. There could be a polite fiction that she was "visiting" the Keeper of Precious Metals.

Cain went down to Lydd in the late autumn of 1899 and put this idea to Imogen, whom he took for a walk along the beach, having rather firmly and rudely rejected Seraphita's hints that Pomona would like to come too. This gave him a ridiculous feeling that he was behaving like a suitor, when in fact his feelings were quasi-paternal. Imogen wore a long hooded cloak, held together with two beaten silver clasps which he thought were very ugly. The hood would not stay over her head, and the whole garment blew and flapped in the wind coming off the sea. When the hood was down, her hair blew about too. It was caught up in theory, by a plaited strand which held it in a mane behind her head, but the whole thing, he thought, was a dreadful mess. She should see a hairdresser. She should have a hat with some style to it. She looked downwards, with cast-down lashes, at her serviceable but very worn boots, and reached, with hands draped in fingerless lacy mittens, to hold down the blown bits of her clothing. She had, he thought, a very sweet face, an innocent face, that should not have had the quality of lifelessness he perceived in it.

"I wanted to catch you by yourself, which has proved difficult. I have an idea I should like to put to you."

"I don't think—"

"Please, hear me out, before you refuse me."

That sounded very like a suitor.

She went on looking down.

He put his plan to her. He explained that after the period of apprenticeship, and learning the ropes, she could take the entrance exam, and become a craftswoman, or a teacher, as she chose.

"Why?" she said. "Why are you doing this for me?"

"I don't like waste. And you have talent."

"There are all sorts of reasons," she said into the wind and the spray, "why this can't happen. It can't."

"Would you like it, if it could?"

She bowed her head. The hood flopped forward.

"I shall speak to your father. Today."

"You can't. I mustn't . . . they need me, Mother and Father, Pomona . . ."

"And what do you need? Your brother hasn't felt he must stay here."

Geraint had indeed taken himself off to the counting rooms and telegrams of the City of London, where he was rapidly becoming successful in Basil Wellwood's bank.

"I believe I have some influence with your father. I shall convince him you will be safe, for I shall invite you to stay with myself and Florence, whilst you learn the ways of the college. How can he object?"

"You don't understand—" said Imogen, dully. He stopped, and took her by the shoulders, and looked into her face.

"No, I don't understand everything. But I believe I understand enough to put a case to your father."

And then, suddenly, she flung herself into his arms and buried her face in his shoulder. He could not hear what she was saying, nervously and rapidly, into his jacket, but he held her, and patted her back, and felt her sob between his hands.

He approached Benedict Fludd himself with an anxiety he concealed completely. He went to see Fludd in his study—the room that had once been a scullery, and was now full of drying pots and drawing pads, in the midst of which was a Morris & Co. Sussex armchair, in which Fludd was sitting.

He said

"I have something I want to say to you—a proposal I want to put you. About Imogen."

Again, that lurking, parodic sense of being a suitor.

"What about Imogen?" said Fludd, ungraciously. Prosper Cain said that he had been impressed by Imogen's talent, and explained his plan for her immediate fortune.

"She's very well where she is," said Fludd.

"She's lonely and unemployed," said Cain.

"Her family needs her, I need her."

"You have Philip Warren and the inestimable Elsie. You have your wife and Pomona. I think it is time to give Imogen her freedom."

"Ha! You think I imprison her."

"No. But I think it is time for her to leave."

"You are an interfering pompous military bastard. And you know, none better, that there's no money to pay for her keep in the filthy city."

"I propose that she lives with me as a visitor until—as I believe she can and should—she wins a scholarship to the Royal College. And then she will be enabled to earn her own keep. If she doesn't marry. She doesn't meet many young men, here."

"You believe I don't know what my duty is? And *her* duty is to care for her parents."

"Not now, not yet, however you look at it. Old friend, you are behaving like a tyrannical father in a story. I know you better than that. I know you love your daughter—"

"Do you? Do you know that?"

"Too much to part with her easily. But she will love you more freely if you can bring yourself to let her go. And I'll bear the cost of her move if you'll let me have that oxblood jar with the smoky snakes on it, which I've had my eyes on for a couple of years. It ought to be displayed in the collection, and you know it."

"You don't know anything."

"I know I don't know. But I have watched Imogen, and you haven't given one good reason why she shouldn't come to London."

"Oh, take my daughter, and take my jar, and go to the Devil, Prosper Cain. Have a brandy. Look at Philip's dandelion heads on these plates, with the seeds blowing. He's a bright lad."

"He's a young man, too, as Imogen is a young woman. May I take some of the dandelion work to show to the Keepers, as well?"

Imogen came to London, and Prosper said to his daughter that something must be done to get her a decent hat and dress, but he didn't know how. Florence said "I'll find a hat—you know how good I am at hats—and I'll tell her it's mine and I can't wear it. She's too tall for my dresses. I'll think of a way."

"I do love you, my Florence. Will you always be so sensible?"

"No. I quite expect to become very silly as I grow older. Everyone seems to."

. . .

In the Cains' house inside the Museum, apart from the crashing and trundling and dust of the building programme, Imogen did indeed seem to settle into a more cheerful normality. She turned out to have an unexpected flair for architectural drawing, she made a few silk rosebuds and forget-me-nots for the simple hat Florence found for her, and she set out of her own accord to restructure her clothing into a usual shape for a lady art student. In the Fludds' house, things were less cheerful. After Imogen's departure, Pomona began sleepwalking again. She ended up, several times, in Philip's bedroom, on one occasion wearing no clothes, and wrapped only in her excessively long, not very clean, golden hair. Philip and Elsie talked about this. Elsie thought Pomona was play-acting. She told Philip that Pomona was throwing herself at him—literally—because he was the only young male person anywhere in reach. She said Pomona was hysterical and was putting it on. Philip said no, she wasn't, she was deeply asleep, he could tell when she touched him. He wanted to tell Elsie that Pomona's cold, naked flesh, pressed against him, did stir and disturb him—he was only human—but at the same time as being most desirably creamy-white, with firm little breasts and soft pale pink nipples, she was somehow inert, meaty, kind of dead, he said to himself, so deeply asleep she was. Elsie did not tell Philip of an odd conversation she had had with Imogen, the day of Imogen's departure. It was so improbable, that when she tried to remember it, she wondered if she had made it up. Imogen had embraced her warmly, which was uncharacteristic, was indeed the first time she had embraced Elsie, whom she always held at arm's-length, in every way. She said to Elsie that there was something she must say to her. She drew her into the kitchen, in the pretext of checking supplies.

"If he asks you to—to pose for life-drawings, don't. That is, don't take your clothes off, even if you feel it's all right, don't. Do you understand me?"

"Yes," said Elsie, feeling perversely that she would take her clothes off if she liked, whereas if she had been asked ten minutes earlier whether she would ever pose nude for an artist, she would have laughed sharply, and said "Not on your life."

Things in the Wellwood families were less happy, and more contentious than in the Cains'. Basil Wellwood's children were both opposed to the futures their parents desired for them. Charles, or Karl, had done moderately well at Eton, spending parts of his vacations secretly attending meetings of the Social Democratic Federation with Joachim Susskind, and (also with Joachim Susskind) attending meetings of the Fabian Society where his uncle was speaking. The Fabians were going through a contentious period themselves, which divided the Imperialists, who supported the British army in the Boer War, and believed in spreading the virtues of British democracy throughout the world, from the gas-and-water socialists, who believed in concentrating, at home, on the public ownership and management of utilities and the land. The society had voted on a motion which expressed "deep indignation at the success of the monstrous conspiracy . . . which has resulted in the present wanton and unjustifiable war." The motion was narrowly defeated. Sydney Olivier, although a senior Colonial Office official, was incensed at the war: his wild daughters burned Joseph Chamberlain in effigy on Guy Fawkes Night in 1899. The Webbs thought the war was regrettable and "underbred." G. B. Shaw argued that the Society should sit on the fence, and wait till the war was won and demand nationalisation of the Rand mines and good working conditions for miners. A further vote was held in November, and won by the Imperialists. A flock of Fabians then resigned, including Ramsay MacDonald, Walter Crane, the head of the Royal College, and Emmeline Pankhurst, leader of the campaign for the rights of women.

Charles/Karl and Joachim were excited. Charles wanted to go to the new London School of Economics, then in its sixth year of teaching. Basil Wellwood, who had not been to university himself, wanted his son to be at Oxford or Cambridge, and insisted that he sit the entrance exam. Charles asked for time to make up his mind, at least. He thought he might like to travel, to see the world. He thought, though he did not say this, that he might visit the German socialists, with Joachim. It was usual for English gentlemen to travel. All he asked, said Basil, was that Charles should ensure his place at Cambridge before his travel. Charles agreed to sit the scholarship exam in December 1900. He went back to Eton, and did the minimum of academic work.

Griselda was already threatened with a Season as a debutante. She and Dorothy were sixteen in 1900 and were studying—more slowly, more haphazardly than if they had been boys—for their school certificates and Highers. Katharina gave little dances for Griselda already, with selected young men, a harp and piano, fruit punch and lobster salad. Griselda begged Dorothy to come to these. "I am paralysed with shyness; if you are there we can look at it from outside, we can smile at each other, I won't be alone." Dorothy said dancing was no part of her plan of her life. She came, however, on occasion. She did care for Griselda. Griselda was altogether too pale to be beautiful, but she was striking in a fragile way. Dorothy was the opposite, dark-haired, golden-skinned, lithe from running in the woods. She told Griselda she hadn't a party dress. Griselda gave her two of her own—an ivory silk, a deep rose chiffon. Violet adjusted them. Dorothy glared at her, and insisted that she strip away much of the ornamentation. This had the effect of streamlining Dorothy, so that she looked well-shaped and attractive. The boys pressed damp hands on her waist, and talked to her about hunting, and about other parties. Dorothy tried to talk to them about the war, and was rebuffed. She developed a fantasy which bothered her of anatomising the most clumsy and spotty ones in an operating theatre. If she said she meant to be a doctor, they said things like "My sister took a course in nursing until her children were born." They seemed to think she was confused about the medical profession. Whereas they were confused about her.

Griselda asked her if she had ever been in love. No, said Dorothy, oddly she hadn't, though perhaps she ought to have been, everyone appeared to be. Griselda said that sometimes she thought she herself was in love. This surprised Dorothy, and slightly annoyed her. She was the clever one. If Griselda was in love, she should have noticed for herself.

"Anyone I know?" she asked, too casually.

"Oh yes, you know him. Can't you guess?"

Dorothy ran her mind over the boys at the dances. Griselda treated them all the same, making gentle small talk, dancing elegantly, not joking, not flirting.

"No, I can't. I'm shocked. Tell me."

"You must have noticed. I love Toby Youlgreave. It's hopeless, I know. But things happen to me when I see him. I go to his lectures just to hear his voice—well no, not just—what he says is amazing—but when I hear it, I feel a jump, inside me."

"He's old," said Dorothy flatly. She said it too vehemently, because she had prevented herself from saying "But he's in love with my mother."

"I know," said Griselda. "It's totally inappropriate," she said lugubriously. She added sententiously "It doesn't matter how old he is, because at our age it would be a disaster to meet *the one,* because it would be the wrong time. Since it has to be hopeless, he can be as old as he likes. Well, is. As old as he is."

"I think you're making fun of me, Grisel."

"No, I'm not, I'm not. There's a sensible watching bit of me that knows I'm making use of beloved Toby, to practise being in love, in safety so to speak. And there's an irrational bit that goes swoony and dissolving when I see him. Doesn't that happen to you at all?"

"No," said Dorothy, staunchly and truthfully. They began to laugh, for no good reason, and were soon weak with laughter.

Prosper Cain was pleased with his children. The Wellwoods were anxious about Tom. He had become solitary in a way that was unexpected and did not seem quite natural. Charles had passed his Highers comfortably. Tom had not. He had done well in geometry and zoology and had failed everything else, including English, which was hard to do. Humphry and Olive were surprised, as were Toby Youlgreave and Vasily Tartarinov, who had both expected him to pass with better results than his cousin. Tom remarked briefly that he felt he hadn't been concentrating. He had found the whole situation—writing all that stuff—time-restrictive and unreal. What did he intend to do? Humphry asked him. Tom didn't know, apparently. He was always occupied. He spent his days on foot, in the woods, on the hills, never really considering going outside the bowl of English countryside between the North and South Downs. He didn't seem to mind being alone—Dorothy, to whom he had been close, lived as much at Griselda's houses as her own, and was concentrating furiously on physics, chemistry and zoology. He made friends, in a remote way, with gamekeepers and farmers' boys— he was good at leaning on fences, for long periods, asking questions about rabbits, pheasants, trout and pike. He sat on river banks with a rod and line, observing the weeds and shadows where the fish hung in the current, or lurked under a stone. He practised approaching rabbits and hares as Richard Jefferies recommended, putting his feet down softly and steadily, without a two-legged rhythm, keeping his arms close to his sides—human arms, Jefferies believed, alarmed wild creatures as teeth and claws and scent did in other predators. Tom got to be reasonably skilful at approaching recumbent hares, or keeping quiet in a wood at twilight and waiting for the badgers to emerge, snuffling. He could pick up their scent as though he was himself a wild thing. He spent hours rigorously training his imagination to understand the needs and limitations of the body of a bee, or a redstart, a slow-worm or a moorhen, a laying cuckoo or the enslaved foster-mother of its monstrous changeling. He made inventories of the varieties of grasses in the edges of the ploughed fields, or the numbers of nesting birds in one hedgerow, or the pond life in the clay-lined pond where the cattle slobbered with their lips, smelling of hay and dung and milkiness. He didn't consider all this a preparation for any particular way of life. He didn't want to "be" a naturalist, and had no professional interest in being either a sportsman or a gamekeeper. He read perpetually—there was always a book in the satchel he carried—but he only read two kinds of writings. He read books by naturalists—particularly Jefferies, whose very rooted mild English mysticism about the English soil seemed to Tom to be part of his own body. And he read and reread William Morris's romances about tragic lovers, monstrous dangers, and infinite journeys; this included *News from Nowhere,* with its ideally happy craftsmen in their stone cottages, with their rich crops of vegetables, flowers, vines and honey. There was much that he did not read. He shied away from sexual intrigues, feeling what he characterised as boredom and disgust, and secretly half-knew was a kind of fear. He did not read, as did many Fabian children, and upper-class renegades like Charles/Karl, the angry descriptions of the condition of the working class, in Manchester and London, Liverpool and Birmingham. Nor, which is perhaps more surprising in a boy with his inclinations, did he read travels and explorations outside England. India did not inhabit his imagination, nor did the North American plains and the South American jungles. He knew there was savage fighting in the Veld in South Africa, he knew there were stubborn and sturdy Boers resisting Imperial Britain, but his imagination did not partake in gallant battles, or suffer wounds and setbacks. Still less did it reach out to the original black or brown inhabitants of those remote places. It burrowed into the chalk with solitary wasps, and sky-blue butterflies who laid their eggs in ants' nests. He read Darwin's work on earthworms, and accepted—without thinking too hard— Darwin's views of the natural world, including human animals, as a perpetual violent striving and struggling for existence and advantage. Sex interested him in English creatures—he knew about the domestic lives of stoats, and the breeding of champion hounds and horses. Love interested him as something far away and hopeless in the world of romance. He walked over the earth, noting things like a scout or a hunter—a newly broken twig, a disturbed heap of pebbles, an unusually dense clump of brambles, the slotted footprint of a fallow deer, the holes stabbed in turf by predatory beaks. He seemed to be there just— simply—to take all this in, and know it. Underneath the earth, in an imaginary realm of rock tunnels and winding stairs, the shadowless seeker, with the trusted Company, never growing older, never changing their intent, travelled on towards the dark queen weaving her webs, and snares, and shrouds.

Olive Wellwood, visiting Prosper Cain in his London house, thick with the dust of building works, shaken by the sound of sledge-hammer and cranes, told the Keeper of Precious Metals, in confidence, that she was troubled about her son. She knew that Cain found this motherly concern attractive; she created, deliberately, a feeling of warmth and helplessness; it was also true, as she recognised with a slight shock of fear, that she *was* worried about Tom. He had been such a sunny child, she said, so sweet-tempered, so bright. And now he seemed to moon around, aimlessly, and had no friends. "I feel I don't know him any more," she said. Major Cain said that that was perhaps usual with parents and children. Children grew up, they moved away. Yes, said Olive, but Tom didn't exactly move away, that was partly what she was saying. He had moved, she said finely, into himself.

She took Prosper Cain's hand between her own.

"I wondered if Julian—he and Julian seemed to like each other— I wondered if Julian might come and—say—take a walk with him, talk to him?"

Cain thought it was always tricky, enlisting one member of a generation against another. He said cautiously that he knew that Julian had felt badly when Tom ran away from Marlowe.

"That was when it all began," said Olive. "I don't want you to ask Julian to interrogate Tom, that would be most unwise. Just to come and walk with him, talk with him."

So Julian wrote to Tom and asked him to accompany him on a walk through the New Forest. He wrote, which was true, that he needed to get away from London and academic work. He thought they might mix sleeping out of doors with staying in pubs. Tom took time to reply, and then sent a colourless postcard saying he would be very pleased to come.

When Julian saw Tom again he knew he had always been in love with him. Or knew, for Julian was always double-minded, that he needed to indulge in the fantasy that he had always been in love with him. Tom at eighteen was lovely in the way he had been lovely at twelve, with the same rapid, shy, awkward grace, the same perfectly proportioned face, the same—for Julian was now experienced—lovely buttocks in his flannels. He was still like a carving, with his mass of honey-hair and his long gold lashes almost on his cheek when he blinked. And his mouth was quiet and calm, and the odd fact that he had become very hairy, on both face and body, only complicated the carved effect by veiling it. Men who loved boys, Julian thought, simply loved beauty, in a way men who loved girls did not. There were beautiful girls who had the same pure effect as beautiful boys, but girls were to be assessed as mothers-to-be, they were not simply and only lovely. He had no illusion that kissing Tom, or simply touching him, would have anything to do with communing with Tom's soul. Tom's body was opaque. If there was a soul animating it, Julian felt that it would be both presumptuous and possibly unrewarding to try to commune with it. He watched the light in the hairs on Tom's forearm as he swung his pack to his shoulders. He felt— apart from a stirring in his trousers—as he felt when his father showed him a gleaming mediaeval spoon, when the wrapping fell away. He thought to himself that Tom had done well to leave Marlowe so precipitously. If he had stayed, he would have become prey to the hunters and possibly learned to be a nasty flirt, as happened to so many. This Julian thought along with many other things, as they strode along the field-paths and round the woodlands, for Tom was not given to conversation, only to companionable pace-keeping, so Julian talked to himself, in his head. Julian decided wryly that he had to be on his best behaviour, because Tom had been foolishly entrusted to him by their elders.

Tom did not look at Julian, almost at all. He poked with his stick in hedgerows, or stopped, raising his hand, to listen quietly to birdsong and rustlings. Julian knew that he himself was not only not beautiful, he was not even handsome. He was slight and wiry; his mouth was long, narrow and mobile; he was slightly knock-kneed, and he walked circumspect and hunched, unlike Tom's habitation of all the air around him. Because he had the sense to say nothing for a very long time, Tom did begin to initiate conversations. They were about hedges and ditches. He pointed out good places to set snares. He found an orchid—"quite rare." He discussed good and bad coppicing.

And at night—they slept out, on unrolled blankets and a waterproof—he talked about the stars. He knew them all, the planets and the constellations. Bright Venus, almost aligned with red Mars, Mercury faint on the horizon. The head of the Water-Snake, "just to the left of Canis Major" just below Gemini. The gibbous moon, waning.

He did not talk about himself. He never said "I want . . ." or "I hope . . ." and only rarely "I think . . ." He did express an impersonal grief at the vanishing of certain predatory species, exterminated by gamekeepers, the hen harrier, the pine marten, the raven. He speculated about why the weasel, stoat and crow had proved more cunning and more pertinacious. Julian said

"Perhaps you should be a naturalist? Study zoology and write books, or work in the Natural History Museum."

"I don't think so," said Tom. "I don't write."

"What are you going to do? What do you want to do?"

"Do you remember at the Midsummer party, they asked us all what we wanted to be? And Florian said, he wanted to be a fox in a foxhole?"

"Well?"

"I have some sympathy with that."

"And since you can't be a fox in a foxhole?" said Julian lightly, lightly.

"I don't know," said Tom. His face clouded. "They go on at me," he said. "They want me to go to Cambridge. They make me sit exams. And so on."

"Cambridge isn't bad. It's beautiful. Full of interesting people."

"Cambridge is all right for you. You like people."

"And you don't?"

"I don't know. I just don't know what to do with people."

The next day was hot. They found a river, and Tom said they would swim in it. He put down his pack, stripped to his skin, folded his clothes neatly and put them on the top of his pack. Then he waded in, through the reeds on the bank of the river: Julian sat on the bank, amongst the buttercups, and watched him, entranced. He would never, he thought, forget the vision of Tom's penis against his hairy thigh as he bent over his clothes. He would never forget the sight of those thighs, striding through brown-green water into something suddenly deeper, so that he vanished and rose again with floating duckweed scattered like confetti in his thick hair. Tom was not only sunny, he was sunburned. Everywhere exposed to the sun had been painted a ruddy-tanned colour, with paler hairs gleaming on it. The V of his shirt-neck, the bracelet of colour-change on his upper arms, various zebra-gradations of gold on his calves and thighs.

"Come on in. What are you doing?"

"Looking at you."

"Well, don't. Come and feel the water, the delicious water. It's hot on top, and cold and clammy under. I've got mud and tiddlers between my toes. Come on in."

Oh, and how I would like to come into him, Julian thought, undressing, patting down his own member with precautionary fingers. I can't believe he knows as little as he appears to know. He ought to be a dreadful bore. He would be, if he wasn't beautiful. No, that isn't fair, he's nice, he's nice through and through, whatever that useless word means. A nice young man. But sad, I intuit, sad under. His own knees were going under, and then the embarrassing appendage. Tom splashed him—from a distance, always from a distance—with great rainbows of water, and then swam off, upriver, like a trout.

"I'll show you where the pike would hide themselves," he said. "I know." He said "This is good, this is good fun."

"Yes," said Julian, enjoying the water as substitute sensation. "It is good fun."

Tom said, when they were sitting in the sun to dry themselves

"What's your favourite poem?"

"Just one? I could say ten. Busy old fool, unruly sun. Shall I compare thee to a summer's day? 'Ode on a Grecian Urn'? 'Caliban upon Setebos'? What's yours?"

> "What was he doing, the great god Pan
> Down in the reeds by the river?

"I can say all of it. I often do."
"Say it."

> "What was he doing, the great god Pan
> Down in the reeds by the river?
> Spreading ruin and scattering ban,
> Splashing and paddling with hoofs of a goat,
> And breaking the golden lilies afloat
> With the dragon-fly on the river . . .
>
> "He cut it short, did the great god Pan
> (How tall it stood in the river!),
> Then drew the pith, like the heart of a man,
> Steadily from the outside ring,
> And notched the poor dry empty thing
> In holes, as he sat by the river.
>
> " 'This is the way,' laughed the great god Pan
> (Laughed while he sat by the river),
> 'The only way, since gods began
> To make a sweet music, they could succeed.'
> Then dropping his mouth to a hole in the reed,
> He blew in power by the river . . .
>
> "Yet half a beast is the great god Pan
> To laugh as he sits by the river,
> Making a poet out of a man:
> The true gods sigh for the cost and pain,
> For the reed which grows nevermore again
> As a reed with the reeds in the river."

21

At Purchase House, things deteriorated. Benedict Fludd had always had swings of mood—there were days when he worked beside Philip with furious energy, and times when he sat for days together, motionless in his chair, snarling if Philip asked him for information or money, sneering at Seraphita if he spoke to her at all. After Imogen left for London he immediately went into a black depression, sitting and glaring at his picture of Palissy, or hunched with his head in his hands, as though it hurt. When the period of slump was over, he did not now return to work, but shambled rapidly, and without warning, out of the house and into the marshes, hatless and jacketless even on wet, windy days. On one very bad day he swept a whole tray of newly glazed pots to the ground, muttering that they were ugly abortions.

They were not, and Philip was almost angry at the waste of so much good work. But Philip was canny about what he could afford to feel, and he could not afford to feel angry with, or contemptuous of, his master.

He did say to Elsie, it's getting worse and worse. They both knew what "it" was. Elsie said she had tried to talk to Mrs. Fludd, but had got nowhere. Mrs. Fludd had said that her husband had things on his mind, and had a difficult temperament, and that Elsie already knew that.

One day, at Dungeness, in mixed, squally weather, where achingly bright patches of light off the water were succeeded by whipping winds and draggled clouds streaming over the sun, Philip, on one of his solitary walks, collecting driftwood, shells, and odd stones, saw Fludd at the water's edge, flailing his arms and roaring inaudibly at the sea. Philip thought he would give him a wide berth and hope not to be noticed. Then he saw that Fludd, in boots and cord trousers, was over his ankles in the rising tide. It is not easy to walk fast on sloping shingle. Philip changed direction and set off towards Fludd. The pebbles ground and whinged under his feet. Fludd shook his fist at the horizon, and took several steps forward, moving his arms like a windmill. He was now over his haunches in seawater, and splashing his hands in the blown crests of spray. Philip had never ventured into the water off this bank. He believed, without knowing why, that the steep slope continued, and plunged rapidly beyond a man's depth, into treacherous currents. He began a blundering run down towards the potter, who took another two or three grinding steps forward, and was waist-deep. Philip could not swim. He began to calculate what would happen if he lunged at Fludd and fell over himself, into the sucking water. He scrambled down to where Fludd was, and howled into the wind "Come back, sir. Come back home now."

For a moment they stood there, the old man swaying in the tide, and slapping at the surface with his great hands, the young man calculating furiously about balance and grip, moving forward always with both feet stable.

"Benedict Fludd—" he howled.

Fludd did turn round, his mouth snarling amongst his draggled hair, his torso lurching.

"Go home," said Fludd, and fell sideways with a sluicing sound, onto the sea. He rose again, obviously on his knees on the shingle, and slipping down the slope of the beach, shouting at Philip that he was a pest and a fool. Philip walked forward, mincing safe step by step, and took hold of the sodden flannel shirt.

"You'd best come out now. You'd best come home."

"Leave me be."

"How can I?" said Philip, betraying crossness. "I've got to get you home. Help me."

Benedict Fludd gave a kick—whether to help Philip, or free himself of him was unclear—and pebbles rolled thickly down under the water. Philip put his arms round the bulk of Fludd and pulled.

"You've got to help me," he said with furious reason. "You've got to help yourself. Come on, now."

And somehow they were scrambling together, and both on the dry land, which was not dry, but wet with the water that ran off them, and with the whipped water blown in the wind.

"You should have let me go on," said Fludd, mildly enough. "I had the idea of just walking on and down and in. You did wrong to stop me."

"Why?" said Philip. "Why are you like this? You are a great artist. You can do things most men can't dream of."

"It leaves me. I can do nothing. I think, I shall be unable—unable—unable for the rest of my life. And then I think, why drag it out?"

"That is just a mood. You've had it other times, the black mood. I've watched you. And then you've made amazing things. The sun and clouds pot, remember? And the one like flaming damask. Remember? Those pots wouldn't be, if you'd drowned yourself."

"You care more about the pots than about me."

"And if I do, it's because I'm like you. And this time, you nearly drowned both of us, which was unjust."

It did not strike Philip as odd that he had made no appeal to Fludd to save himself for the sake of his wife and daughters.

Philip was glad to see Arthur Dobbin, one day when he was in Lydd, buying provisions. He told Dobbin that Fludd was "very depressed" and this appeared to be a result of the departure of Imogen for London. He asked if Frank Mallett might call. Dobbin cycled back to Puxty, and told Frank, who got on his own bicycle and went to Purchase House. Fludd was not in—he was out tramping in the Marsh again—so Frank was able to talk to Philip, who described Benedict Fludd's frightening behaviour, and said that he was at his wits' end, for he could not watch the potter all the time—that might drive him to further extravagances—and more-over, he needed to work, or the household would have no money. Philip said Fludd couldn't abide to see a doctor—that was no good. Maybe Frank could talk to him. He added, on a sudden impulse, that Pomona was sleepwalking. "Mostly into my bedroom," said Philip. "It's embar-rassing. I know what you think, but she is deep asleep, deep. Elsie won't believe me, but you might."

"The family puzzles me," said Frank Mallett. "You and Elsie have saved it, so to speak. Major Cain may well have saved Imogen, but he has deranged the others. How is Mrs. Fludd?"

"I never know," said Philip. He said "Sometimes I see her, when I'm trying to get Pomona back to bed. She comes down in a dressing-gown, with her hair down, and drinks brandy. She looks like a washboard."

"A washboard?"

"Sort of crumpled and ridged. With no expression on her face."

"To be truthful, I am a little intimidated by Benedict Fludd. I shall speak to him, of course. I shall also write to Major Cain."

"I had hoped you might." Philip frowned. "When he is working, he's dangerous—pots are slow things, they need calm, they need ease—and he does everything at double pace. But he does it well at double pace, better than I ever shall, Mr. Mallett—he smashed a whole batch of good pots I'd made and painted—he swept it away."

"He makes you angry?"

"No-o," said Philip slowly. "I love him, in a way. But he puts the fear of God into me."

Benedict Fludd grinned evilly at Frank Mallett, and said he had no need of his ministrations—yet. "I am not long for this world, young man, and I shall need you to shrive me. But you may as well keep away till then. I did not ask you to come here. I require solitude."

"You are not alone in the house, Mr. Fludd."

"And what do you mean by that? It is my house."

"I came to visit Mrs. Fludd. And Philip Warren."

"Oh, get out, before I throw something at you. I am in an evil temper, and best avoided."

"It is hard on Philip."

"I know that."

When Prosper Cain received Frank Mallett's letter, he was planning one of several visits to the Grande Exposition Universelle de Paris, which had opened, with many of its palaces and pavilions unfinished, in April. There was a political frost between England and France, owing to the Boer War. The Prince of Wales, who was president of the British section and had overseen the construction of the British Palace, had refused to set foot in Paris in 1900. Several loyal British exhibitors had withdrawn, but the Victoria and Albert Museum was in constant communication with the experts in the decorative arts in France, Germany, Austria, Belgium and other countries where the "new" art flourished and was on show. Prosper Cain was interested in the new jewellery, both the French work of René Lalique and the exquisite Austrian work of the new Wiener Werkstätte and Koloman Moser. He had travelled to the new Museum of Decorative Arts in Vienna, and was excited by *Jugendstil* there and in Munich. He was due to make an extended visit in June, and conceived the idea of taking Benedict Fludd with him, to see the new styles of ceramics, and to take him out of his marshy desolation for a time. Some of Fludd's great bowls and slightly sinister vessels were on display in Edwin Lutyens's British pavilion.

Cain went to Purchase House and tempted Fludd with the sight of some of his "Paradise" ware, intricately covered with birds, beasts, fruit, angels, and naked humans, which he hadn't seen for twenty years since they had been bought by a Belgian collector. He said Fludd would like to see Gallé's work, and inspect the Art Nouveau. Fludd glared and grumbled, and said he hadn't been to Paris for twenty years. It was a pother of a city which would be worse with the stinking crowds of garlic-eaters there would be. But a glint of interest appeared in his eye as he contemplated these horrors, and he agreed to come.

Prosper decided he would also take his son, as he hoped he might follow him into his profession. He told Julian to bring a friend, and Julian said he should like to take Tom, if Tom would come, which he imagined he would not. Charles Wellwood, it turned out, was intending to go. Julian asked Charles if he would ask Tom.

Charles walked over to Todefright to ask Tom in person. The Todefright Wellwoods were sitting in the garden, taking tea in the midsummer sun. Charles said Prosper Cain was getting up a party to go to the Great Exhibition, and Julian would like Tom to come. Tom opened his mouth to say without thinking that he'd rather not.

Phyllis said "He won't come. He never goes anywhere anymore."

Hedda said "Tom's a recluse. Tom is growing odd, you know, Charles. I wish you'd asked me."

Tom closed his mouth, and his eyes. Then he opened them again, and said he would be delighted to go.

He was becoming odd. He did not want to be odd. He wanted to be invisible.

Charles said that Prosper Cain had persuaded Benedict Fludd to come with them. Tom said he supposed Philip Warren would be coming too—Philip needed to see all the new art.

It turned out that nobody had thought of taking Philip. When they considered the idea, they saw it was good. Philip was exactly the person who would be inspired by the new world of arts, crafts, and social hope embodied in the Exhibition. So Fludd told Philip he was going to Paris, and Cain bought him a new suit to go in.

On the deck of the packet-boat, midway across the Channel, Philip realised, with sudden shock, that he had no idea what France, or Paris, or Europe was. He had seen the French shoreline, on clear days, white cliffs with a difference, or vague solids melting into mist, which fascinated him. He was always fascinated by transparent films and substances that half concealed, and half revealed, other, different objects. He saw the French coastline as an analogy of glazes. He had been out on the Channel waters, fishing for mackerel—mackerel skin, like mackerel skies, was another endlessly fascinating structure. He tried to calm himself, when he realised he needed calming, by looking at the transient, repeated blades and arrows in the water ploughed back by the prow. Bottle-greens, greens chock-full of silver air, what cream and white, what a darkness under. Fludd was standing next to him, his arms on the rail, staring equally intently into the water. Philip knew they were seeing the same thing. Behind them, the three young men chatted and laughed. Julian was telling a story which entailed mimicry of a Frenchman. Charles was laughing. Prosper Cain was reading what appeared to be a catalogue. Philip realised he was both excited and afraid. Another country, other people, other habits, strange food. He was the only member of the party who had never travelled.

Julian had been to Paris several times before. He knew the museums and galleries: he had been in cafés, and ridden in a rowboat on the Seine. Charles had stayed in the best hotels, and ridden in the Bois de Boulogne. Tom had been on a family holiday, some time ago with Violet in charge, and had a vague recollection of Notre-Dame and aching feet. Fludd had spent time in attic lodgings in his misspent youth, drinking, smoking and exploring women.

Only Prosper Cain was at all prepared for the effect of the Grande Exposition Universelle.

The Exhibition could be seen as a series of paradoxes. It was gigantic and exorbitant, covering 1,500 acres and costing 120 million francs. It attracted 48 million paying visitors, took over four years to build, and included the elegant new Alexander III Bridge, arching over the Seine, the glass-roofed Grand Palais, and the pretty pink Petit Palais. But it had the idiosyncratic metaphysical charm of all meticulous human reconstructions of reality, a charm we associate with the miniature, toy theatres, puppet booths, doll's houses, oilskin battlefields with miniature lead armies deployed around inch-high forests and hillocks. It had the recessive pleasing infinity of the biscuit tin painted on the biscuit tin. It was forward-looking, containing new machines and weapons, and images of craftsmen, clearly enjoying their work. It contained a reconstruction of mediaeval Paris, with troubadours and taverns, picturesque beggars, and ladies in bumrolls. There were new facilities—plentifully scattered different public conveniences, from the basic to the luxurious with running water and towels, telephone kiosks, moving staircases and a moving pavement, travelling at three different speeds. There was a palace of mirrors, and a complete fake Swiss village, complete with waterfall, peasants, mountains and cows. Along the left bank of the Seine were the palaces of the nations, some with mediaeval towers, some baroque or rococo. The USA provided telegrams, iced water and Stock Exchange prices for businessmen away from home. The Kaiser himself had supervised the napery, glassware, silver and china in the restaurant of the German pavilion. He had also sent a collection of the complete range of Prussian military uniforms. The Italians had reconstructed St. Mark's Cathedral. The British had commissioned Edwin Lutyens to make a perfect replica of a Jacobean country house, which they then filled with paintings by Burne-Jones and Watts, and furniture and hangings by Morris & Co.

There was a Palace of Electricity, with a Tower of Water in front of it, a hall of dynamos and a hall containing hundreds of new automobiles, in every shape and size. The Tyrolean Castle was juxtaposed with the Pavilion of Russian Alcohol, the Palace of Optics and the Palace of Woman, next to the pretty sugar comfit-box Palace of Ecuador, which was to serve later as a municipal library in Guayaquil. In the Place de la Concorde, where you bought your tickets, stood the astounding and unloved Porte Binet—a monumental gateway, like something out of *The Arabian Nights,* decorated with polychrome plaster and mosaic, studded all over with crystal cabochons. It was flamboyantly artificial but was based on living forms in nature, the vertebra of a dinosaur, the cell-structure of beehives, the opercules of madrepores. On top of it stood a monstrous effigy of a woman—La Parisienne, huge-bosomed and fifteen feet tall, modelled on Sarah Bernhardt and dressed in a negligee or a dressing-gown designed by Paquin himself. On her head she wore the crest of their City of Paris, a prow, like a peaked tiara. She was generally disliked and jeered at.

The two largest exhibits in the whole Exposition were Schneider-Creusot's long-range cannon and Vickers-Maxim's collection of rapid-fire machine guns. The Kaiser had not been invited to his, or any other, sumptuous displays. His advisers and the French hosts were both afraid that he would say something disconcerting or incendiary. If British troops were killing Boers, the Germans were engaged in combat, in the outside world, with the Chinese. The Kaiser had reprimanded Krupp for equipping Chinese forts with cannon that fired on German gunboats. "This is no time when I am sending my soldiers to battle against the yellow beasts to try to make money out of so serious a situation."

The Chinese, despite murder, rebellion and war, had nevertheless constructed an elegant and expensive pavilion in the shining Parisian microcosm. It was carved in dark red wood, with jade-green tiles and pagoda roofs, and an elegant tea-room. It stood in the exotic section, side by side with a Japanese pagoda and an Indonesian theatre.

Art Nouveau, the New Art, was paradoxically backward-looking, flirting with the Ancient of Days, the Sphinx, the Chimera, Venus under the Tannenberg, Persian peacocks, melusines and Rhine maidens, along with hairy-legged Pan and draped and dangerous oriental priestesses. Some of its newness derived from the deep dream of the lost past which informed both Burne-Jones's palely loitering knights and porcelain-fine maidens, and Morris's sense of saga-scenes and bright embroidered hangings. But it was radically new also, in its use of spinning, coiling, insinuating lines derived from natural forms, its rendering in new metal of tree-shapes newly observed, its abandonment of the solid worth of gold and diamonds for the aesthetic delights of nonprecious metals and semi-precious stones, mother-of-pearl, grained wood, amethyst, coral, moonstone. It was an art at once of frozen stillness, and images of rapid movement. It was an art of shadows and glitter that understood the new force that transfigured both the exhibition and the century to come. Electricity.

The American Henry Adams visited and revisited the Exposition whilst it was open, driven by a precise and ferocious combination of scientific and religious curiosity. He wrote a riddling chapter of *The Education of Henry Adams* and called it "The Virgin and the Dynamo." He saw where the centre was, in the gallery of machines, in the dynamos. He began, he wrote, "to feel the forty-foot dynamos as a moral force, much as the early Christians felt the Cross." The dynamo was "but an ingenious channel for conveying somewhere that heat latent in a few tons of poor coal hidden in a dirty engine-house carefully kept out of sight." But he found himself comparing it as a force-field to the presence of the Virgin, the Goddess, in the great mediaeval cathedrals of France. "Before the end, one began to pray to it; inherited instinct taught the natural expression of man before silent and infinite force."

The dynamo that drove the exhibition was on the ground floor of the Palace of Electricity. At first it failed to work. In front of it was a Château d'Eau, designed to be brilliantly lit by a rainbow of light. There were tiers of fountains, like the fountains at Versailles, and the palace was covered with stained glass and transparent ceramics, surmounted by a statue of the Spirit of Electricity, driving a chariot drawn by hippogryphs. When all this failed to come to life, there was an uneasy black cavern, a gaping hole, at night. But workmen attended to it, oiled it, polished it, stroked it, like a beast being urged out of inertia. Adams was right: a bunch of fresh flowers was placed on the back of the cylinder as an offering. Its pulse was felt as it shuddered into life. And when it worked, it transformed the façades of buildings into rubies, sapphires, emeralds, topazes, and the dark cloth of the night into a tapestry of shimmering threads. The Water Tower ran liquid diamonds, shot with changing opal and garnet and chrysoprase. The Seine itself became a heaving, dancing ribbon of coloured lava, where variegated threads intertwined, sank, and rose again, changed and relumed.

Wonderful illuminated portals, curving like the vegetation of an artificial paradise, led down to the flashing electric serpent of the new Métro. The whole exhibition was encircled by a moving pavement where citizens could travel at three different speeds, squealing with amazement, clutching each other as they moved from strip to strip. There was incandescent writing in magazines about the "fairy electricity."

The Palace of Electricity was set about with warnings. *Grand Danger de Mort.* It was a death without tooth, claw or crushing. An invisible death, part of an invisible animating force, the new thing in the new century.

22

Prosper Cain's party had rooms in a hotel called Albert, in Montmartre. Cain had work to do—he visited the Bing Pavilion to study the delights of Art Nouveau, and the Petit Palais to look at the rich collection of historic art. He went repeatedly to the German decorative section, where the new elegance of Munich was displayed in rooms decorated by von Stuck and Riemerschmid, in their new young style, the *Jugendstil*. He went to the Austrian and Hungarian rooms, audaciously swirling with linear curves, round simple but luxurious furniture, with a lurking wickedness and suggestiveness.

When the young men went out in the morning, ready to get into the omnibus, covered with a striped awning and drawn by four horses, a figure appeared out of a side-alley and raised his hat to them. It was Joachim Susskind, who said he was surprised and delighted to see them there. He himself was attending a congress, but had already visited a great deal—by no means all, that would take months—of the Exposition. He was afraid they would find the German pavilion ostentatious. But there were things from his native Munich of which he was proud.

Julian thought immediately that Susskind was not there by chance. He was there by arrangement with Charles. Julian's imaginings were sexual, not political. He considered Susskind's hay-coloured moustache and did not think it would be pleasant to be kissed by him. He considered Charles's sharp blond slimness, and decided that Susskind was probably in love with Charles, as teachers tended to be in love with self-assured, eager boys. His smile of greeting had been both self-effacing and hungry, Julian thought, pleased with his own perceptiveness. Because he had been watching Susskind he had not been able to notice whether Charles appeared to be abashed, or confused, or gleeful. When he did look at him, he saw he was blushing, with what was certainly the self-consciousness of having engaged in a subterfuge—but what else was there? Julian was intrigued. But he was more interested in the possibilities this opened for himself.

Julian asked casually, when they reached the exhibition space, what everyone wanted to see. Tom said he should like to go on the travelling pavement, and ride on the Great Wheel. Charles looked at Susskind and said he would like to see the Hall of Dynamos and the motor cars. Julian said he himself wanted to see the Bing Pavilion, with the decoration which his father had said he must not miss. They agreed to meet later in the day in the Viennese tea-shop and eat cakes.

When Charles and Joachim Susskind were out of earshot of Julian and Tom, Susskind said, with some excitement, that there was a young woman he wanted Charles to meet. She was lecturing on anarchy and the sex question. She was here, in Paris, as he was, to attend the Second International Anti-Parliamentary Congress. She was also a delegate to a secret gathering of Malthusians, who wished to discuss birth control, which was outlawed in France. Her name was Emma Goldman. She had come from America, where she was a great Anarchist leader, and she was earning her keep, by showing American tourists round the Exposition. "She will certainly know what we should most like to see and learn about," said Susskind. "But you must be very discreet, and not repeat what I have told you. I said we would meet her outside the Palace of Woman."

Julian was planning a campaign to come close to Tom, without being at all sure what he wanted, finally, to achieve. He was himself very strung up, his nerves full of electricity, a state he intensely enjoyed. He had looked at himself in the hotel bedroom mirror, before they set out, trying to see his body through Tom's unimaginable eyes. He was slim, and looked agreeably wiry inside his cord jacket and egg-blue shirt. On the other hand he was—small, short—there was no good word for it. He had his Italian ancestors' olive skin, and dark line of moustache. His eyes were deep-set. His hair was slick, that was how it liked to be. How did he look to Tom, who was red-gold and casual, and sculpted where Julian was drawn with pen and ink?

Julian was good at being in love. He had needed to know about sex. He had needed, precisely, to know what an emission felt like in contact with another body, as opposed to his own hand and sheet. But he was clever enough to know that what he really liked about being "in love" was the state of unconsummated tension. Public school made one a connoisseur of beautiful boys, boys in surplices with angel-faces, always deliciously veiled in sweat as they toiled after a football or swung a bat, boys anxiously kneeling at the toe of one's boot, polishing a shoe. The beauty of them was the danger—even more, in some cases, the impossibility— of touching them. Their grave or gentle or mischievous faces hung in the half-dark before the imagination as one wrote one's clever essay on Plato's Forms of the Good, or as one snuggled one's head into one's solitary pillow and slept. Of course, one had to believe that these lovely creatures were, *in potentia,* the longed-for intimate friend, from whom nothing need be hidden, by whom everything would be understood, forgiven and admired. But Julian was clever and observant enough to see that love was at its most intense before it was reciprocated. "Love is a standing, or still growing light / And his first moment, after noon, is night." "What will it be, when that the watery palate tastes indeed / Love's thrice repured nectar?"

Did he really want to know?

He sometimes thought, he chose to love people like Tom, who seemed simple, good in some way, and opaque, so as to preserve some essential loneliness, or solitude, in himself, that he needed more profoundly than any human contact. He liked to make Tom smile. He liked to give him things, and see him flush with pleasure. But he liked this best when he had got back into his solitary bedroom, and could look at himself taking pleasure.

That was not the morality anyone taught him. Love is the highest thing, the books said, the teachers said. He had to think it must be. Or might be. So he would love Tom, and see how it felt, and suffer, delectably, the distance between them.

They left the omnibus and stood in a queue in the Porte Binet to buy tickets. They travelled on the moving pavement past various attractions and the windows of Parisian houses, some decorously shuttered, some offering glimpses into foreign drawing rooms and balconies. Each strip of the escalator had regular posts with brass knobs, to steady those changing speed. Women giggled and gripped their skirts as they made the little jump. Gentlemen and pickpockets offered arms to steady them. Julian and Tom, indulging in boyishness, gripped each other's arms and made several rapid transitions. There were thousands of people, from hundreds of towns and countries, carrying bags of food, elegant canes, parasols, parcels. There was a smell that was foreign. Julian knew it was garlic, added to cheese. Tom didn't. He sniffed it, like a hunting dog in a field.

They went on the Great Wheel. They sat side by side in the sunlight in their little cart and rose into the blue sky, next to the erect iron cage of the Eiffel Tower and the belching chimneys of the powerhouse. They saw the river and its bridges, the imaginary palaces along its front, the huge Celestial Globe inside which you could whirl around the zodiac.

Julian remarked lightly that he was afraid of vertigo. Tom touched him with a reassuring hand, and said that the secret was to look out, not down. He said he was happy up there, and confessed that he was more worried by a kind of choking feeling in crowds. He said he was unsure whether he could ever live in a big city. What did he want to do, Julian asked. They were still mounting. Julian remembered the Donne quotation again. At the very top, at the apex, he should touch Tom. Tom said he liked being up on the downs, and didn't know what else he might want, though he supposed he had to want to do something. They both laughed at the idea of thinking, up above Paris, in the sky, of being "up" on the "downs." They began to descend, and at that exact moment Julian swayed against Tom, as if by accident. Tom shrugged comfortably in response. There was no electric prickle.

Prosper Cain was very busy, on behalf of the Museum, and on his own account. He was exchanging information and advice with the new Austrian Museum of Applied Arts. He was interested in purchasing new metalwork, from the Scandinavians. He was concerned by the enthusiasm of one of the jurors at the Exposition, George Donaldson, who had purchased a collection of examples of the new Art Nouveau furniture, which he was to present to the Victoria and Albert. Cain himself took pleasure in the company of the designers from Austria, Germany and Belgium. The fact that he was a military man produced social awkwardness in certain French contexts. He felt he was judged guilty of the whole military adventure in South Africa, of which in fact, both as a soldier and as a political animal, he disapproved.

He also had problems with French military men over the Dreyfus affair. It had always seemed likely to him that the unfortunate Jewish officer, condemned six years ago for treachery and sent to Devil's Island, was innocent. With the fury of his supporters, and the investigations of the brave, and the suicide of his principal accuser, it became a certainty that he himself had been horribly betrayed. Last year, a decrepit shadow of a man, he had been brought back and retried. And found guilty again. This had appalled Cain as much as it had appalled Dreyfus's French supporters. Dreyfus had now been offered a pardon, to avoid an international incident, or national violence in the streets, on the occasion of the Exposition. That was rich, Cain thought, a pardon for a crime he had never committed.

Tensions ran high between the French and the English. The French published wicked caricatures of the Widow at Windsor, resembling a demented and malign spider or witch with bulging eyes. There was talk of international tension leading to a war between France and Great Britain. Cain smiled at the fierce dedication of a vase by Gallé, mounted in silver, bearing a ragged flamboyant iris in appliqué, and a quotation from Zola on Dreyfus. *"Nous vaincrons. Dieu nous mène."* A similar vase had been presented to La Bernhardt, who was also a passionate Dreyfusard.

Julian had arranged to meet his father in the Bing Pavilion, and went early, so he could saunter with Tom through its delights. Julian was suspicious of English aesthetes. Wilde he found silly and sordid, without knowing his work very well, and Aubrey Beardsley delighted and alarmed him with glimpses of a malign naughtiness which he liked to see but did not wish to share. He did not know, at nineteen, who he was going to be, and was acutely aware of this. But he was not going in for mascara, pot pourri, and green chrysanthemums. Like Kaiser Wilhelm and Prosper Cain, Julian secretly liked the mixture of opulence and severity in a well-cut military uniform. But he had no intention of joining the army, that was one thing he knew. At the Exposition he discovered a European self who needed to think precisely about the new European elegance. He found his velvet jacket sitting more sharply on his shoulders. He thought he might buy new shoes.

Siegfried Bing, from Hamburg, had introduced Japanese art to French connoisseurs, and had a gallery in the rue de Provence where he showed very modern paintings—not only the Impressionists, but the Symbolists and the dreamers. His pavilion was a make-believe small mansion. It was later transported to Copenhagen. This was another aspect of the Exposition that resembled Russian fairytales of flying houses, or Arabian tales of palaces transported overnight to lands beyond the oceans and deserts. This sense was in turn made more intense by the Palace of Mirrors, which from inside was a false infinity of exotic Middle Eastern vistas, in which you yourself were endlessly repeated from every angle, over and under, advancing and receding, or hanging in the void. And as well as that, there was the Upside Down Palace, in which, as in a tale for small children, you could plod across the ceiling and stare up/down on the tables and chairs. On its façade was a fresco showing two darkly slender young females with black-gloved fingers, fine waists, rounded small buttocks visible under their clinging garments, and swirling skirts or peacock tails. They stood in front of a fairytale house in a forest. They looked back invitingly over their shoulders. Julian was unprepared for Tom's comment, which was to regret that his mother couldn't see them, she would have liked them so much. They had transparent shawls floating like wings from their shoulders.

Inside was a series of various furnished rooms, all different, all rich and simple together, with shining woodwork, mottled and inlaid with other woods, with fabrics woven from stiff damask and spider-light threads, with tapestries and burnished copper, with glass, and fine ceramics, and touches of gilding that glittered in dark corners. Julian took a secret pleasure in "framing" Tom in these unlikely stage-sets. He looked as if he had wandered into the citrus-wood and damask off an English village green, having just put down his bat. He looked also like a Greek statue of a young athlete, who would not have been out of place here, naked but crowned with filigree vine-leaves.

They went into what was perhaps the most beautiful room, a dressing-room by Georges de Feure, all in moony colours, with furniture of dappled Hungarian ash, decorated with silvery copper inlay, hung with a shimmering silk tapestry of blue and grey formal flowers, shifting shape in the light, woven on a woof of silver threads. The chairs were covered with blue-grey cloth embroidered with white silk roses. Julian thought he would have liked to see Tom in a silk dressing-gown, standing in that room—he imagined the gown in midnight-blue, he imagined it in dark pewter, he combined the two, whilst Tom strode around with genuine curiosity and repeated that it was a pity his mother could not see it. "It would give her so much for her work," said Tom. He pushed his hands through his fair thatch, making temporary horn-stubs. They moved on into a bedroom, where a great bed was spread with an embroidered cover in every muted shade. Julian tried to imagine Tom spread naked on it, whilst Tom stood a little stiffly taking an interest in the bed-curtains. A large number of fashionable ladies and gentlemen came into the little room and exclaimed over the fittings, and made aloud several observations about inhabiting the bed. Tom said suddenly that he was tired, he felt oppressed, he should be glad if they could sit down.

They sat in an adjacent café, waiting for Prosper Cain. They ordered *citrons pressés,* and Tom deranged his hair with his fingers a little more. Julian couldn't think what to say to Tom, and Tom said nothing, so Julian said

"Doesn't it seem odd that Herr Susskind turns up, just like that?"

"Does it? Everybody in the world seems to be here. I can't get my breath for being crushed by people. I admit there are so many, the chances of meeting any particular one can't be very high."

"I think he fixed it with Charles. I think he knew we were there. Maybe he has a thing about Charles."

"A thing?"

"Maybe he's in love with Charles. He seemed excited."

"I wouldn't have thought of that. It's odd, though. I bumped into them together, once, in Hyde Park. I was going through with Papa. They pretended not to see us, and we pretended not to see them. Papa said it was gentlemanly to look the other way. I didn't quite know why, but I could see everyone was embarrassed."

Julian said "Have you ever been in love? Really in love?" Tom looked down at the table. Julian immediately thought he had gone too far. Tom was in fact thinking that Julian was sophisticated, and would mock the true answer. Nevertheless, he said

"Only in the imagination."

"A mysterious answer. What do you mean by that?"

Tom was dumb. Then he said "I don't know why I said that."

"Do you mean love in the imagination with real people you don't love—in the flesh, so to speak? Or in the imagination with ideal people you don't know at all?"

Tom looked up, and flushed. Julian was looking at him with a quizzical, but amiable grin.

"More the second. But they get mixed. You wonder what it would be like, you know—"

What Tom meant by "what it would be like," was in fact a reference to knights and damsels riding together through forests, heading from the city into the vacant and the unknown. He had had a habit since childhood of inserting his imagination into Sir Gareth, in Tennyson's "Gareth and Lynette," who had been bidden by his mother to be an anonymous kitchen-knave in the ashes of King Arthur's Hall, and who had ridden on his first quest with the scolding and jeering young woman, who said he smelled of the kitchen, like a foul agaric, but had slowly come to know how strong and gentle he was, who had been sorry, and watched over him like a mother in his sleep. He had no idea why he had picked on Gareth, and not the more complicated and passionate Lancelot.

Julian said

"I suppose we try it out in books, or on beautiful boys at school. Until we find something real—"

Tom flinched, and Julian remembered what he imagined had been done to Tom at Marlowe.

They sipped their *citrons pressés*. Julian said "Don't you find it rather heavy, to have everything really in front of you—all the people who are going to matter, whom you haven't met yet, all the choices you are going to have to make, everything you might achieve, and all the possible failures—unreal now? The future flaps round my head like a cloud of midges."

"When I think that thought," said Tom, "I think of caves of ice, I don't know why, with things frozen into weird shapes, and tunnels all bored into it—"

"They talk as though youth is carefree, and at the same time, ever so subtly, they try to mould you, into a gentleman, or an empire-builder, or whatever. I don't want anything to do with the Empire. I don't ever want to rule anyone, or order anyone to do anything."

"What do you want?" It was Tom asking, now.

Julian said "After seeing all this—all this lovely stuff people have made—I think I do want what my father wants for me—which is very banal and unorthodox, to agree with one's father, one ought to be in—manly rebellion. I wouldn't mind being a collector, or a dealer, in beautiful things. And I want to love, of course, someone. To love and be loved."

He looked straight at Tom, who had his chin in his hand and was staring, unfocused, at the beckoning ladies on the outside of the Bing

Pavilion. Julian wondered if Tom was putting this distant innocence on. He thought not.

He said to himself that he had never met anyone so virginal.

Karl Wellwood was finding out about sex in a quite different way. Joachim had hurried him to the Palace of Woman, an elegant modern building, in whose entrance hall stood figures of women of achievement, with the Byzantine Empress Theodora side by side with Harriet Beecher Stowe. There they met the famous Cassandra, the anarchist Emma Goldman, who was just bidding goodbye to a group of earnest American tourists. She was a serious-looking woman, with cropped dark hair, deep-set eyes and a black bow at the neck of a striped shirt. She kissed Joachim Susskind, and shook Karl's hand, saying that anyone trusted by Joachim was a friend of her own. They had heard her speak passionately against the South African War, earlier that year, in London, dealing wittily with hecklers, arguing lucidly. Her good sense and passion for justice and tolerance, like those of Peter Kropotkin, who spoke with her, were part of what excited Charles about anarchy, although, still the son of a successful businessman, he could not help feeling that these individualist idealists would save no one without better, and more, organisation.

They strode swiftly away to the boulevard Saint-Michel, where Susskind and Goldman were staying in the same hotel. Goldman told Charles she was earning her keep by being a cicerone at the Exposition and by cooking lunch on an alcohol burner for a group of friends in the hotel—"I am a good cook, you will see, I invite you to lunch, and you may pay what you can." She was, she said, irritated to desperation by the prudery of the American schoolteachers, who were embarrassed by naked statues in the Louvre—"What, I ask myself, do they make of the women for sale on every pavement—but I dare not ask them, for I must smile and smile and earn my loaves and fishes. I would truly like to guide them round the circles of a hotter place. Have you seen Rodin's *Gates of Hell*? You must—more than once, it is a masterpiece. That man knows how much sex matters, in the modern world, in any world."

She talked away about sex, with wit, indignation and a kind of social fervour that was new to Karl. She had argued with Kropotkin about it, she said, as they rode the travelator, and had been forced to tell him he underestimated it because he was no longer young. He had the grace to laugh and to concede the point, she said. She told Joachim in an under-tone that the Malthusian society was meeting in secrecy—she would tell him where and when if he was interested, but the police were snooping, and she had no wish, at present, to be imprisoned in the cause of birth control, because that was only one part of the larger mission, the whole vision.

They came to the hotel on the Boul' Mich' and ate Russian beet soup, and a beef hotpot, with boiled potatoes, concocted on the burner. The room was full of smoke from Russian cigarettes and French Gauloises—everyone's outline was blurred in Charles's eyes, and the gathering spoke many languages, apparently at random, French, Russian, Italian, German, American, Dutch. Joachim in this company looked smiling and wild, his hair ruffled, his shirt-neck open. He sounded meek and thoughtful in English. In German he sounded excitable and harsh. They were talking about someone called Panizza, who had been imprisoned in Munich for blasphemy and was now released and in Paris. Emma Goldman said that Panizza had called on her—she had been moved and excited—and had invited her to dine with Oscar Wilde. "Dear Hippolyte," she said, turning to her lover, had recalled her to ethics—it was the night of the comrades' session—but she would so very much have liked to meet Wilde.

Karl looked curiously at Hippolyte, who was small, agitated, ele-gantly dressed and had bandaged hands. He was a penniless Czech, who had ruined his skin cleaning boots for a living. As an example of "free love," he was uninspiring. He fussed. He said something in either Rus-sian or Czech about Wilde, in which the tone was disparaging. Some-one else, a grey-haired Dr. somebody, said he was surprised at Emma Goldman, a good woman, defending a man like Wilde, a pervert, and a perverter.

This led to an animated discussion of the right attitude to inversion, perversion and "sex variation." Most of it was in German. Karl had learned German, as his German mother wished. He thought Susskind knew that he knew German, but for some reason, he had kept quiet about it. He found he had an instinct to be secretive. He took pleasure in having a secret life, and within his secret life, he took pleasure in keep-ing secrets. He listened to the fierce discussion of Panizza's ideas about masturbation, rape and perversion with the blank face old Etonians knew how to put on, courteously imperceptive. He was both excited and alarmed by the world he had entered. If you were a German free-thinker, you could be imprisoned for blasphemy, like Panizza, or for *lèse-majesté,* like Johann Most, or shut in an asylum and declared insane. He stared, watchful, through the swirling smoke at the intent faces, and listened to the voices, earnest, bitterly ironic, gleeful. He was there and not there. He could always walk home, and close his respectable door behind him. But he was not playing, he told himself, he was in earnest. Something had to be done about the horrors of society.

The conversation had moved to Emma Goldman's forthcoming lecture on Trafficking in Women. This discussion was in English. What other ways of earning their bread did most women have, other than selling their bodies, Goldman asked. How could you blame a woman who was a servant kept to herself in a cellar, or a labourer at a factory bench, for wanting human warmth and better nourishment, yes, and pretty clothes. Wages were so low that married women sold themselves too. With their husband's connivance, often enough. The men who used these women went home and infected their wives—whom they had also bought—with syphilis. It was not the men who were punished by the state and its police and doctors, of course, oh no. It was the women. Women must take control of their lives and their bodies.

A thin woman in a grey dress, with a regular little cough, asked whether the supplies of rubber had arrived. Was it true that the Americans meant to demonstrate these things at the congress?

Goldman said she hoped so.

Charles felt himself vaguely excited. Not in quite the right way. Later, as he walked back to the hotel, he looked intently at all the women they passed, the little groups of smiling and beckoning girls in pretty skirts and prominent corsages, the elegantly strolling *demi-monde.* He had never seen a naked woman, except those sculpted in marble or bronze. He had an idea of apertures and protuberances he needed to know about. It might be a good thing to buy this knowledge—he would be contributing to a solid meal—but precisely because it was incumbent on him to see the strolling, signalling, smiling creatures as people in need, it became hard, perhaps impossible, to bargain with one. It was all a lie. Moreover, as Goldman had insisted, there was the question of disease. Panizza's condemned play, *The Council of Love,* Joachim told him, had presented God and Mary and Jesus in heaven as a degenerate enfeebled family who gave the Devil licence to introduce syphilis to the world to punish the Borgia popes for their orgiastic excesses. Joachim would never have talked like this in England. Karl wondered for the first time what Joachim did about sex. He could not think of a way to ask him.

He dined with the Cains, Tom, Fludd and Philip. Everyone talked of what they had seen at the fair. Charles did not mention Emma Goldman, and did not discuss streetwalkers. Cain said he supposed it was encouraging that people at war with each other—the Germans and the Chinese, for instance—could coexist in this imaginary city. Benedict Fludd, who seemed alternately excitable and grumpy, said perhaps Cain had not seen the papers? An anarchist had stepped out of a crowd with a revolver and shot point-blank at the King of Italy. They missed him three years ago with a knife, said Fludd. This time they got him. He's dead. What do they hope to achieve?

"Chaos," said Prosper Cain. "They are mad." Karl kept his polite public-school face at this moment also. He was in a moral knot that he was beginning to recognise. Belonging to something, believing in an idea, meant perhaps conceding assent to things that were, outside the belief, ludicrous or horrid. He had tried being Christian, and had tried to force himself to believe in the Virgin Birth and the Resurrection. He found the anarchists compelling and arousing. But he could not—he could not—accept that a symbolic killing of this or that muddle-headed or insulated old monarch would really advance freedom or justice. And then he tried to see it from the anarchists' point of view. He formulated an idea: they are more sane, and madder, than other people. They have a better idea of human nature, which is perhaps only an idea. But they are serious and real, and this hotel is not, and this soufflé is all airy nothing, and the women in evening gowns at the next table are bought and sold.

It was, however, a delicious soufflé, elegantly put together with Seville orange and Grand Marnier. It lingered on the tongue like a blessing.

Philip had spent much of his time alone. Fludd would refuse to get out of bed, or would sit in the hotel gloomily drinking coffee and cognac. He told Philip to get out and educate himself. Philip walked for miles, looking at the lights, translating things seen into ideas for pots, failing miserably. It was all too much for him. His own art seemed small and provincial and far away, and he felt he was a lout and an ignoramus.

He found the ceramics stands on the Esplanade des Invalides. He was attracted to the special exhibition of the Gien Faïencerie by its principal exhibit, an awesome ceramic clock, towering more than three metres, and standing on a carved pedestal. He thought it was a silly shape, and was in awe of the extraordinary technical skill that must have gone into its construction. It was shaped like a very tall vase, decorated with gold underglaze he had never seen before, and sprouting, at its shoulders so to speak, spirals and pendants of green and turquoise blue foliage, out of which, like strange fruit, peeped and poked a bunch of spherical electric lights. Above this, three naked cupids knelt sportively, and supported a clock in the form of a pale blue celestial globe, studded with stars, and telling the time with a mechanism contained in its depth, showing the process of the hours in an opening in the equator. Another Cupid, with little wings, squatted on top of the globe and clasped a torch, which also contained a powerful electric light.

Philip started to make a drawing of it. He had learned his dislike of pouting cupids and what he called "pottery frills" from Benedict Fludd. He thought he might be able to tempt him out of bed with this monstrous vision. The visitors jostled him, and occasionally asked to see what he was doing. A young man, about his own age, in a workman's overall, came from inside the stand, and asked to see what Philip was drawing. He commented on Philip's draughtsmanship in French, of which Philip understood not a word, but the tone was both friendly and admiring. Philip said, in English, that he didn't speak French. He put down his pad and pencil, and demonstrated with mime that he was a potter, running his fingers inside the imagined cylinder of imagined clay on an imagined wheel. The Frenchman laughed, and mimed the painting of fine flowers with a fine brush on a close surface. Philip pointed to himself and said "Philip Warren." "Philippe Duval," said the Frenchman. *"Venez voir ce que nous avons fait."*

He showed Philip soft-paste porcelain vases, with copper flambé glazes, and spindle-shaped, or pillar-shaped, vases, painted on biscuit, one with peonies, one with bellwort. Philip took notes and copied the bellwort into his sketch-book. There were all sorts of new uses of metallic glazes, making surfaces like a shot silk, or silk brocade—he mimed admiration of this, and Philippe said in French that these were fiendishly difficult, which Philip understood. There was also a very good attempt at the secret Chinese red—"Chinese," said Philip. *"Oui, chinois,"* said Philippe. And crackleware in silver and gold. It was all very *dressy,* Philip thought.

And then Philippe brought out from a hidden corner some quite different pieces, the earlier and famous Gien reproductions of Renaissance Italian majolica, and Philip fell in love. He loved the colours—sandy yellow-gold and indigo-blue and a sage-green glowing on a black ground, or delicate on a white glaze. He loved the creatures who were entwined and climbing and gesturing on the surfaces, horned Pans with high pointed ears and pointed beards, whose shaggy hips below the waist ran into formal foliage, blue, gold and green. He liked the formal spiralling fronds of golden apple boughs and fine threaded tendrils and trumpets. There were lithe golden boys with wicked grins and blue dragons with fish-tailed children—not fat putti, laughing yellow-gold boys—and fauns, and dolphins, all swiftly done, all bright and glowing. He was put in mind of his sheaf of drawings of the Gloucester Candlestick, with the men and monkeys and dragons, and had the glimmering of an idea of a way he could make new patterns of his own, combining both on the branches of an eternal tree with space for everyone. He asked Philippe for time to draw one or two. "Arabesques," said Philippe. He drew for Philip an image of a different clock, decorated with these creatures, and showed him the very interesting design on the base of this—a Greek wave-fret, a wild-strawberry hanging.

They took a cup of coffee in a small café and communicated by drawing, taking turns—Philip drew the patterns on his Dungeness tiles, the Old Man's Beard and the fennel, and Philippe drew more creatures, and bowls with handles like dragons and harpies entwined with rinceaux. Philip drew Fludd's tadpoles but couldn't think how to explain Fludd. So he drew a master-potter at a wheel, and an apprentice with a broom, and identified himself as the apprentice, and with much pointing explained that he was going to find Fludd—he mimed snoring—and bring him to the stand. Philippe had black hair, and a very clean-cut, pointed face. "I'll be back," said Philip. *"Au revoir, donc,"* said Philippe.

23

Tom sat in the sombre library of the British Pavilion, in the late afternoon, when it was closed to the public. Guests of the Special Keeper of Precious Metals at the Victoria and Albert Museum were allowed in. Tom could imagine himself in the seventeenth century, surrounded by leather books and glowing tapestries of the Quest of the Grail. In front of him was Burne-Jones's painting of Lancelot's dream at the Grail chapel. The clearing in the forest was desolate and moonlit. The light was pale moony-gold, shining on the rump of the tethered horse, and the faces of the sleeping knight and watching angel. The knight was half-recumbent, his elegant mailed feet crossed like an effigy, his young, fine face expressing not rest, but absolute exhaustion. His shield was propped in a twisted, leafless bush: the moon glinted on his long sword and the helmet on the ground by his feet. The expression on the angel's concerned little white face was almost one of terror or horror. Thorns grew round the foot of the chapel wall. Tom was deeply moved by all this. He wanted to go home. He took the latest instalment of *Underground* out of his bookbag, and wrote a letter.

My dearest Mother,

Thank you for sending the unwrapping of the Silf. It is one of the best things you have done, I think, very exciting and disturbing. I hope we shall see a lot more of the Silf—is it a "she" or an "it"—you seem undecided. I think you are quite right about the spelling. Silf is much more mysterious than sylph, and gets rid of all sorts of airy-fairy associations.

I am having a very good time here, seeing lots and lots of amazing things, some entertaining, some instructive, some beautiful too. I have been up the Eiffel Tower and on the Great Wheel and have ventured into the new Underground Railway, the Métro, which has gates like the gates of fairyland. Everything is driven by electricity—it all hums and buzzes—and there are forests of lights twinkling and glittering everywhere. I don't know if it is more like Vanity Fair or Camelot or even at times Pandemonium. I am not very good at living in all this noise, I really am not, I think often of a quiet walk on the Downs in the early morning, with the dew on the turf and the sun rising. I really do wish you were here. You would make more of all this enchantment and artifice than I can. It is like that story you wrote of the palace inside the palace inside the palace. You could make stories out of almost everything.

Julian is very good to me, and I hope we are really friends. But he is so sophisticated and so—I can't find a word—sardonic? Not quite—you will know what I mean—that I'm never quite at ease with him, and daren't say what I feel, in case he thinks it's silly. Major Cain has been wonderfully kind, and explains the art objects to us. You would love to see the jewellery. Mr. Fludd is a bit mysterious—he seems to stay in bed a lot—Philip looks after him, I suppose. We hope to see someone called Loïe Fuller dance. I think there is all sorts of food for your imagination here. As for me, sometimes I really enjoy things like moving pavements, and sherbet in little glasses, and the Russian diorama. But sometimes—mostly I think—I do want to be at home and sit in the garden with lemonade, and read about the Silf.

Your loving son
Tom.

Prosper Cain came to the modest hotel where Benedict Fludd and Philip were staying. He found Philip, who said that Benedict Fludd was still in bed and had said he was not to be disturbed. Cain said he was to be disturbed, and immediately. He was to visit the Lalique stand, and he was to lunch with Siegfried Bing in the Pavillon Bleu, as he knew very well. Philip said drily that he did not think he dared disturb Fludd.

"I dare," said Major Cain. He considered Philip. "How are you finding the Exposition?"

Philip detailed his visits to the ceramics exhibitions, and pulled out his sketch-book to show Major Cain the monstrous clock.

"Have you seen anything except the pots, Philip?"

"I'm finding my way around them, sir. I made a French friend at the Gien place. He doesn't speak English. He's a decorator."

"You should be having fun and broadening your mind. Have you seen the jewellery? Have you seen the Bing Pavilion?"

"No."

"Benedict should be showing you things. I wanted to show some of the dealers here some of your work. You could come and draw for them. I might need you, if Fludd's out of form."

. . .

Benedict Fludd was under a wine-stained sheet, with his head entangled in a serpentine French bolster.

"Get out," he said to Cain.

"I won't. You are lunching with Bing, as you very well know. Get up. You owe it to Philip Warren, to show these folk his work, as well as to yourself. Bing is interested in your pond bowl. Very interested. Get up. In the army we had very nasty ways of making people get up. Get up and get washed. Horrible man."

Everyone, therefore, gathered at the Lalique stand. It was yet another imaginary dwelling, with pleated gauze hangings. Shining white moiré bats swooped in a highly arched window, and there was a screen, sinister, delicate, lovely, made of five naked bronze women, with huge, skeletal wings like the bronze veins of moths, hanging below and beside them. The most prominent exhibit was a large ornament, in the form of a turquoise woman's bust rising out of the mouth of a long, long dragonfly, its narrowing gold body studded with shimmering blue and green jewels at regular intervals, diminishing to a tiny sharp gilt fork at the base. The woman's head was crowned with an ornament which was a helm, or a split scarab, or the insect eyes of the metamorphosing being. From her shoulders hung what were at once stiff, spreading sleeves, and the realistic wings of the dragonfly, made in the new, transparent, unbacked enamel, veined in gold, studded with roundels of turquoise and crystals. The beast had huge dragonlike claws, stretching either side of the womanhead, on gold muscular arms. Round this piece were lesser jewels in the shapes of insects and flowers. Philip asked Fludd if he knew how the transparent enamel was done. He said to him "Look" at a brooch made of two completely realistic stag-beetles, their heads locked, the pitted horny roughness of their wing-cases perfectly reproduced.

"Hmn," said Fludd. "Another French wizard who moulds from life, I imagine. Like Palissy."

Fludd was coming to life. He took out an eye-glass and peered at the tiny tourmaline eggs which crusted the rumps of the insects, at the blood-red stone they clutched between them.

Julian pointed out to Tom that the heart-shaped form of another jewel with two dragonflies conjoined was in fact an exact reproduction of copulation. So it was, said Tom, with a naturalist's interest.

"I meant to surprise you," said Olive Wellwood, floating up to them under a creamy hat clustered with butterflies and silken bees. "Now be surprised, my darling. I couldn't resist, after your lovely letter—"

She was accompanied by Humphry, looking casually elegant, and August Steyning, wearing moth-grey and a peacock-blue cravat.

There were exclamations and kisses. Olive was lovely and excitable, with a hectic flush on her face. She was carrying a rose-coloured silk parasol, which, out of doors, made her shadowed face dark rose in pale rose. Tom had a feeling he immediately remembered, though he had never learned to expect it. Olive in the flesh, Olive perfumed with attar of roses, was not the secret sharer of the otherworld, to whom he wrote letters. That was a kind of second self, who wrote him and inhabited his dreams. This was a lively, sociable woman in creamy broderie anglaise, over whose fingers Prosper Cain was gallantly bowing his head.

"How pleasant to see you, dear Mrs. Wellwood. Just the right setting, among the peacocks and damselflies. I did not know you intended to visit the Exposition."

"I did not know myself. It was an impromptu decision, prompted by a letter from Tom—now I am speaking nonsense, impromptu can't be prompted—a letter describing all the enticements and enchantments so that I was irresistibly drawn to them. And we discovered that August Steyning had already planned a visit, so we attached ourselves to him. You must tell us everything, you must show us all the beautiful things . . ."

She is overdoing it, thought Tom. What he could not know was that Olive's coming was the effect of a move by Herbert Methley, who had insistently and even fiercely tried to coerce her into performing a sexual thing she found disgusting. She had blushed like fire. Tears had started from her eyes. She had no idea whether Methley was a monstrous pervert, or whether she herself was—as he accused her of being—naïve and cold, not to understand, not to respond. She suddenly couldn't stand the smell of him, struggled out of his arms, and out of the hired bed, and thought blindly "I have got to get away." She was so pleased to see Prosper Cain, whose admiration for her was old-fashioned and gallant. And Tom, of course, she was pleased to see Tom, Tom loved her more than anyone did.

Prosper Cain was buying jewellery. He liked buying small pieces, and was looking for the perfect gift to take home for Florence. He had bought her one of Lalique's horn combs, with carved sycamore seeds, and was hesitating over an unusual anemone brooch, in which the lovely flower was denuded of all its petals but one, made of pink enamel, set amongst twining ivory roots, through which strange faces peered. But perhaps you didn't give an image of fall and decay, however beautiful, to a young girl? He found a *pliqué-à-jour* enamelled poppy— "like a thin, clear bubble of blood" as Browning said of the wild tulips—and bought it to pin on his daughter's dark hair. He then examined another, paler piece, which combined transparent enamelled honesty seed-cases with a sumptuous thistle, made of enamelled silver and frosted glass. Olive, who was touching the jewels with a gloved fingertip, holding a snake-bracelet against her wrist to admire it, suddenly wondered if the second piece might be an offering designed for herself. It had a soft, fairytale gleam. Cain watched its wrapping, and put it, with the poppy, in his pocket. He thought he might give it to Imogen Fludd, if that would not embarrass her. She had become interested in jewellery design—the small scale, the precise craft, the rigour and delicacy of it suited her temperament. But London was full of ladies doing bits of enamelwork and stringing beads. If jewellery was to be her means of independence she must do it well, very well.

It was a mistake to try to visit the Grand Palais in a large group. There were thousands of paintings in the Décennale, which showed work from the last ten years of the century, from all the exhibiting countries. August Steyning said in a forthright way that they should all proceed at their own pace and follow their own interests until it was time for lunch, when they should forgather—"for a reason"—in front of Jean Weber's painting *Les Fantoches*. They strolled in ones and twos— Steyning, Cain and Olive, Tom and Julian, Charles and Joachim Susskind, Fludd and Philip. Philip was oppressed by the size and weight and insistent dark meaning of much of the work. He was appalled by vast paintings of clumped dead and dying naked humans, strewn with snakes and surveyed by tiny winged angels. In one painting, entitled *Towards the Abyss,* a woman in modern dress, with huge batwings and a wind-blown bonnet, strode forward against the wind, followed by a crawling crowd of nudes, geriatric and bearded, female and glaring, all *in extremis,* some already expiring. Philip timidly asked Fludd what it meant.

"Dunno," said Fludd. "She might be Woman, but she is not very taking, looks like a mad governess. She might be Capitalism but she looks like a miserable vampire. Or the Church, she might be. Or syphilis. Very French, she is. I prefer pots. They don't have to be weighed down with meaning. They are what they are, earth and chemistry."

Julian, by now an eager student of Art Nouveau and the artists of the Secession, hurried Tom away to look at Klimt, whose delicious *Lady in Pink* shone palely out, and whose ambitious allegory of *Philosophy* glittered with elegance. Joachim Susskind and Charles were arrested by Rochegrosse's *The Race for Happiness,* a mad conical heap of humans in frock-coats, evening gowns and workmen's striped jumpers, who climbed up and over each other, so that a bunch of desperate arms, black-sleeved, or silk-gloved, protruded like stakes into the sky, against a background of chimneys. Susskind said it was impressive as an image of capitalism. He thought for some time, and then said that maybe a very expensive painting that must have taken years of work wasn't the best instrument to bring about a just society.

There was more naked female flesh in *Les Fantoches* where they met. It showed what looked like an artist's garret with a long couch in the mansard corner. The light from the six glass squares of the window illuminated the naked body of a woman who lay diagonally across most of the canvas. Her head lay at an awkward angle. Her arms were open, and bent, with pathetically clenched fists. Her hair was dark, her eyes were closed, her expression might have been a pout or a scowl. Her legs were splayed, her tiny slit visible, though there was no pubic hair. One foot rested awkwardly on an embroidered cushion on the floor, one was equally awkwardly clinging to the embroidered cover of the couch. She looked both very uncomfortable and completely inert, her flesh like putty. Behind her sat a bearded, handsome man, his face intent on a delicate doll, or puppet, whose waist was circled by his two hands—the two seemed to be conversing. The rest of the painting was peopled with dolls, or puppets, shining out of the gloom—a Javanese figure, a Byzantine queen, erect and tiny and full of presence, a floating Rapunzel in the foreground, all long hair and huge wistful eyes. A jointed doll with no sex lay face down at an angle to the naked woman's knees. A kind of Punchinello was draped over the man's knee. The Punchinello had the peculiar lifelessness of unanimated cloth, which is different from inert female flesh.

When August Steyning arrived, they saw why he had picked this painting. He was accompanied by the puppetmaster from Munich, who had performed at the Midsummer party. Anselm Stern was soberly dressed in a black frock-coat and a wide-brimmed black hat. With him, thin and wiry, wearing a beret and a pale blue cravat, was a young man who was obviously his son, and was introduced as Wolfgang. They were neither of them tall: both had large dark eyes and sharp noses and mouths. Humphry asked Steyning and Stern to explain the painting, please.

"We can't agree on anything. Is she alive, is she dead? Is he ignoring the flesh for art and if so is he culpable or to be admired? Could he animate the dead woman if he gave her the attention he's giving the pretty doll? She looks damnably uncomfortable, as though she'll skid off that couch any minute."

Steyning laughed.

"It's about the borders between the real and the imagined. And the imagined has more life than the real—much more—but it is the artist who gives the figures life."

Olive said it was a pity more women didn't paint allegories about the imagination. This woman was like clay in a stocking.

Everyone looked at Anselm Stern.

"What one gives to one's art," he said, in slightly uncertain English, "is taken away out of the life, this is so. One gives the energy to the figures. It is one's own energy, but also kinetic. Who is more real to me, the figures in the box in my head or the figures on the streets?"

"You could see this artist as a vampire," said Steyning provocatively. "He has sucked the life out of that poor girl and is giving it to wooden limbs and painted faces."

"He has a good face," said Stern, smiling slightly.

Philip pulled at Fludd's sleeve and pointed out in a whisper that the draped Punchinello was the reverse image of the draped human woman.

"The message is," said Stern, "that art is more lifely than life but not always the artist pays."

· · ·

It was not clear for some time whether Wolfgang Stern spoke English. Joachim whispered to Charles that Anselm Stern was an important figure in Munich's artistic life—and a sympathiser with the anarchists and the idealists. "He is not your English Punch-and-Judy—he dines with von Stuck and Lehnbach—his work is discussed in *Jugend* and *Simplicissimus*. This I know. I do not know his son."

Philip was the odd man out amongst the young men. He found himself frequently alone. Wolfgang Stern found him sitting on a bench, drawing, and sat down beside him.

"I may?" he asked. Philip nodded. Wolfgang said "May I see? I speak only little English, I read better."

"I had a long talk in pictures with a Frenchman," said Philip, flicking the pages back to his dialogue with Philippe; drawings, the Gien faïence, and the little grotesque figures of the majolica urns and dishes.

"You are artist?"

Philip made his signature gesture of hands inside clay cylinder rotating. Wolfgang laughed. Philip said "And you?"

"I hope to be theatre artiste. Cabaret, new plays, also *Puppen* as my father. Munich is good for artists, also dangerous."

"Dangerous."

"We have bad—bad—laws. People are in prison. You may not say what you think. May I see your work?"

Philip was trying to work out a new all-over pattern of latticed and entwined bodies, part-human, part-beast, part-dragon or ghost. He was making impossible combinations of the Gloucester Candlestick's warriors and apes, the majolica satyrs and mermen, Lalique's insect-women, and, more remotely, the naked women who sprawled and smiled and died on all the huge symbolist paintings. The drawing he was working on combined the limp puppet with the limp woman from *Les Fantoches*; he was paying too much attention to the female breasts, and the proportions were ugly. Wolfgang laughed, and touched a breast with a finger. Philip laughed too. He said

"I saw your father's puppets in England. Cinderella. And one about an automatic woman. Sandman, or something. They come to life—and don't come to life. Uncanny."

"Un-canny?"

"Like ghosts, or spirits, or gnomes. More alive than us, in some ways."

Wolfgang smiled. He said again

"I may?"

and took Philip's pencil, and began to draw his own trellis of forms—little grinning black imps, and bat-winged females. "Simplicissimus," he said, which Philip failed to understand.

They went to the Rodin Pavilion in the Place de l'Alma. Here were gathered most of Rodin's works in bronze, marble and plaster; the walls were hung with large numbers of his drawings. Vast forms of sculpted flesh and muscle loomed. Delicate frozen female faces emerged from rough stone, or retreated into it. Everywhere was appalling energy— writhing, striving, pursuing, fleeing, clasping, howling, staring. Philip's first instinct was to turn and run. This was too much. It was so strong that it would destroy him—how could he make little trellis-men and modest jars, in the face of this skilled whirlwind of making? And yet the contrary impulse was there, too. This was so good, the only response to it was to want to make something. He thought with his fingers and his eyes together. He needed desperately to run his hands over haunches and lips, toes and strands of carved hair, so as to feel out how they had been done. He edged away from the Wellwoods and the Cains. He needed to be alone with this. Benedict Fludd too had edged away. Philip followed him. Fludd was considering *The Crouching Woman,* who squatted, clutching an ankle and a breast, her female opening displayed and lovingly sculpted. He spoke to Philip's thought. "Shouts out to be touched," said Fludd, and touched her, running his finger in her slit, cupping her breast in his hand. Philip did not follow his example, and looked around apprehensively for guards, or angry artist.

The artist was in fact in the pavilion, which he treated as though it was a studio. He was talking to two men, one of them tall and very shabby, with greasy long locks, muffled in an overcoat despite the warm weather. The other too was shabby and had wild jerky movements. They were standing in front of the ghostly white plaster cast of *The Gates of Hell,* and Rodin, red beard jutting, blue eyes glittering, was explaining it to them, showing them the grand design with sweeping and stabbing gestures.

"By God," said Steyning, "that is Wilde. I've heard he sits in the cafés here and takes tea from Algerian boys. He hasn't got any money, and people cut him in the street. He hides behind a newspaper so as not to embarrass his old acquaintances."

"We should say good morning to him," said Humphry. "He has paid a terrible price, and it is paid."

Anselm Stern said that the other man was Oskar Panizza—"our own notorious writer of—obscene plays and satires—in banishment here in Paris. He is an alienist, a madman who studies the mad."

"An anarchist," said Joachim Susskind, "who believes all is permitted. We should say good morning to him also."

Olive felt warm with admiration for Humphry as he strode forward, with August Steyning, to greet the great sinner. He was magnanimous. She loved him when he took risks. But she did not go with him.

The overpowering sensuality of the work had had its effect on Olive, too. She had managed to crunch, or tuck, her bodily memory of Methley's unpleasantness into a kind of compressed roundel of brownish flesh, which could be avoided when it rose to consciousness—ah, that again, look the other way—but things like *The Crouching Woman* re-animated it, like a frozen snake warmed. *The Danaïde* was lovely. She was white and gleaming, her back arched in despair, her face against the rock, and her marble hair flowing down over her head in frozen white waves. She was a denizen of the underworld, damned with her fifty sisters for stabbing her husband, damned to attempt for ever to carry water in a leaking sieve, the image of eternal futility. But she was breathtakingly lovely. Olive touched her ear timidly with a gloved finger. Tom concentrated on her beauty. He wanted nothing to do with Oscar Wilde.

Julian would have liked to meet Wilde, though he did not like the idea of Wilde. He stood a few steps behind Steyning and Humphry Wellwood, as they shook the wanderer's hand. They also shook Rodin's hand, which he would have liked to do. Wilde looked appalling. His skin was covered with angry red blotches, which he had unsuccessfully tried to cover with some sort of powder or cream, or both. When he opened his fleshy mouth, he displayed a black space where his front teeth were gone, and had not been replaced by a plate. He said he was touched to be recognised by Steyning—"you have still great things to do on the stage, whereas I am rattling like dead leaves in the wind." He introduced Panizza—"a fellow *poète maudit,* who is surprised by no human habit, and has studied them all—" When Rodin and Panizza turned away

Wilde came close to Humphry and breathed in his ear that he would be infinitely obliged by a temporary loan—his funds were much diminished and not reaching him. "He smelled horrible," Humphry later told Olive. "I gave him what was in my pocket, because he smelled so bad that I felt guilty of his stink. There he stood, foul, in front of the Gates of Hell. He shuffled off—receiving embarrassed him horribly—muttering about sipping mint tea. His mouth itself is a Gate of Hell."

They looked at *The Gates of Hell*. None of them saw the same thing as the others. The Gates were a ghost of what they would become. Many of the great forms of the beautiful and the damned were not yet fixed to the two white slabs, which had an almost abstract look, with mysterious swirls and rough spirals of plaster. But the rising columns of the frame and the receding space of the tympanum were full of swarming human forms attached to each other in all sorts of predatory, desiring and revolting ways. Julian knew Dante, whom he read in honour of his lost mother. He looked for the Circles of Hell which were not there, and got lost in the turmoil that was. Tom was puzzled that there were so many dead babies in Hell. Olive was grimly appalled by the figure of an old woman—a very old woman—rising or falling along the left pillar, with every detail of her fallen flesh remorselessly and lovingly recorded—flat, flaccid breasts, withered thighs, hanging bag of a belly. A dead child trampled her head, another pressed its face into her stomach. Olive stood there, in her pale pink dress, and her hat with roses, and gripped the pommel of her pretty blush-pink parasol. She felt anger with the sculptor for having observed the descent of flesh with such indifferent glee, neither love nor hate, she thought, but a pleasure in mastery, of every kind. And so she felt mastered, but stood there, pink and charming. She, like Charles/Karl, had observed the midinettes and the street-women, and had said to herself with Northern realism, there but for the grace of God, and her own lucky face and figure, and Humphry's magnanimity and eccentricity, went she. She caught the sculptor looking at her out of the corner of his eye. Undressing her? What did he see, this man who could model gauche passion, and shame and shamelessness and voracity in women? She turned her face modestly down in the shade of her hat-brim, swung her bottom under her skirt, and moved off to talk to Prosper Cain.

Philip could not bear the Gates. They were more unbearable than *The*

Crouching Woman, because they, like what filled his mind, were a pattern of interlinked human figures. He could not discern or analyse the pattern, though its presence was overpowering and annihilated him. He wanted to tear up his sketch-book, but instead he doggedly got it out, and began to draw the one rhythm he was sure he could see, a dance of repeating rounds in the tympanum, breasts and buttocks, cheeks and curls, intermingling with grinning death's-heads and grotesques. He thinks with his fingers, close-up, Philip knew. And one form gives him the idea for another, even before he is finished with the first. Is he ever at a loss for a form? I think not, I think he fears he will never get it out and down.

Drawing calmed him. He squatted on the edge of a plinth and devised a notation to get it down quickly. They would probably drag him off to eat French food, and he would not have seen.

A shadow fell across the paper. He looked up. Rodin was looking down at him, peering at the drawing. Philip grasped his sketch-book to his chest.

"Je peux? Ne vous inquiétez-pas, c'est bon," said the sculptor. Philip's face was red and damp. Benedict Fludd came to join them. Rodin turned the paper. *"Ah bon, c'est intéressant. Un potier comme* Palissy.*"* Philip understood "Palissy." He looked up at Fludd, and then automatically held out his hands to the sculptor, and made the airy shape of clay on the wheel with his fingers. Fludd laughed a deep laugh, made the same gesture, and said "Benedict Fludd, *potier, élève de* Palissy, *épouvanté par* Auguste Rodin. *Anglais.* Philip Warren, *mon apprenti. Qui travaille bien, comme vous voyez, je pense.*"

Rodin said he knew Fludd's work. He tapped the Gien-majolica-candlestick men with his clay-ingrained finger, and said they were interesting. Wait, he said, and opened a cupboard, and brought out a large celadon-coloured greenish jar, with a twisting female figure incised in the glaze. These, he said, he made himself at the Sèvres porcelain works.

"There is much to learn, in all forms of the clay," he said. And to Fludd, "I know your work. You are a master." Fludd ran his fingertips over the porcelain as he had run them over *The Crouching Woman.* He was in a good mood, alert and benign.

Out on the moving pavement, he began to look at the women, and comment to Philip in an undertone on their shapes and attitudes. He asked Philip if he was enjoying himself—and do look at that lovely sulky little visage, the one with the shiny little hat—are you widening your knowledge of the world, would you say?

"It is all a bit much. Too much too good too new, all at once."

"And too stimulating, I suppose, with all this flesh sailing past on the fast strip?"

"Sailing or standing," said Philip with a sigh, "too much."

"I think I should do my duty and see to your education," said Fludd. "I'll take you out tonight. Just you and me."

Benedict Fludd—that is to say, Prosper Cain on his behalf—had sold a very large midnight-blue bowl with a miasma of pale gold dragons to Siegfried, sometimes Samuel, Bing. He had French money in his pocket. He led Philip through streets alternately dark and flaring with lamp-light, alternately silent and shrill with voices, to a narrow street of tall houses, where needle-strips of brightness showed on the upper floors at the edges of shutters. Fludd knocked imperiously at one of these, and the door was opened, after a time, by a trim servant in a dark dress. Fludd said, in French, that Madame Maréchale was expecting him. He said that Philip was his apprentice, a word that had only recently crept into their relationship, which Philip recognised in French.

They climbed a narrow, carpeted staircase, and were ushered into a room with many tiny bright lights under etched glass shades, wine-red, strawberry-pink, topaz. It was inhabited by women, in various states of dress and undress. Some had elaborately knotted hair, and some wore it loose, like young girls. They wore ambiguous gowns, somewhere between morning gowns and dressing-gowns, open to display the swing of their breasts and sometimes more. There was a confusion of smells— orris root, which Philip had never met and found sickly, attar of roses, wine, cigarette smoke and an undertone of human bodily odours. He made out faces through drifts of smoke, faces weary, faces laughing, faces middle-aged and faces very young. The fully and fashionably dressed lady of the house hurried forwards to welcome Benedict Fludd. Champagne was brought, and Philip, now sitting gingerly on a sofa facing a watchful row of ladies, had his first taste of it. It steadied him. He was excited and afraid. More champagne was brought. He was studied and discussed in incomprehensible French. Benedict Fludd sat in an armchair decorated with cabbage roses, with a young woman on his knee, a girl with her hair down, meekly dressed in white cotton, barefoot, and, Philip could see, wearing nothing under the cotton. The ladies who were assessing him were older and more assertive. They smiled, professionally, but amiably enough. "Take your pick, Philip," said Benedict Fludd. "They can teach you a thing or two. They are good girls. I know them well."

Philip did not think he could know them very well, since he spent his life stamping around the Marshes or tending the furnace. He was suddenly homesick for the Romney emptiness, and the marsh grass. He had had too much of too many bodies, all these last days, and he did not know if he was overexcited or surfeited. He remembered *The Crouching Woman,* and primitive desire stirred in him. He drank more champagne and looked at the women. One had a bony face not unlike Rodin's squatting figure, and a big, sharp mouth. She was wearing a crêpe de Chine dressing-gown, with the kind of silvery crinkle over Japanesey flowers that reminded him of the clever crackle-glaze on the Gien pottery which he admired but did not like. He did not know how you went about "picking" a lady, so he asked her, in English, what her name was. Rose, she said, my name is Rose.

She took him upstairs, to a little room with an ample bed, a huge mirror and more shaded lights. He was curious, and afraid. He knew about the danger of disease. He might be killing himself. It was odd that he felt compelled to go on—Fludd expected it, his manhood was in question, there were things he needed to know. She took off his clothes, and sat beside him on the bed, exhaling tobacco. The skin of her face was quite thickly painted, and did not breathe. She looked kind, he thought. She began to teach him the parts of the body, in her language, pouring him more champagne, dabbing his fingers and chin and eyes with it, naming them in French, and licking away the champagne. Chest, navel, cock and balls. His body answered her touch. His fingers, with which he thought, set about her body, feeling the difference between flesh and clay, the weight of a breast, the warmth and damp of her, underneath. Briefly he remembered cold naked Pomona, pushing under his blanket in Purchase House. Cold and white like marble, like *The Danaïde.* Rose had clever, coercive fingers, with which she too thought. Philip, who was growing up fast in every sense, thought that the naming of parts must be a routine she went through with all foreigners, and then thought he didn't care, it was all perfectly sensible and efficient. Rose was generous to him. He got overexcited and came quickly, and she then revived him and showed him subtler ways of pleasure, slower rhythms, until at last he was thinking with that part of him, as happened occasionally when he was pleasuring himself. He thought Rodin must think a lot in this way. He had an obscure vision of a church window, on the Marsh, showing the Fall of Man, the woman handing the man the round apple from the tree of the knowledge of Good and Evil, and the fork-tongued snake staring with satisfaction. It had never made any sense to him, and he didn't believe a word of it, but suddenly as he pushed into the compliant Rose, clutching her breast, he saw it in his body, the round apple, the tough sinuous snake, the knowledge of nakedness and good and evil.

"*Bon?*" said Rose, with professional concern.

"*Bon,*" said Philip, drowsily, feeling the damp of sex like the slip on the clay.

August Steyning invited everyone to see Loïe Fuller perform in her own theatre; they went back to England the next day, so the dance was the finale of their visit. Loïe Fuller's image was pervasive in the Exposition—her whirling figure crowned the Palais de la Danse, and stood above the entrance to her own theatre, with her floating veils solidified into plaster. Bronze figurines and statues of her were on sale there and elsewhere. Philip said to Fludd that there must be better ways of making images of floating cloth than these solid blobs which reminded him of melting butter. The theatre itself was low and white, and its front wall, modelled to resemble a skirt or shawl with a frilled hem, resembled, Philip also thought, an iced cake before it was trimmed. There was a low portal, like the entrance to a grotto or cavern. Inside were huge butterflies and flowers and a grille of Lalique's bronze butterfly-women. "That is the way to do it," said Fludd to Philip. "With veining and empty space." Lalique had designed the electric light fittings also, in gilt bronze. Laughing imps were cupped round the mysterious face of an enchantress, above whose head the electric bulbs were suspended in delicate, snowdrop-shaped flowers on fine stems.

Fuller's dances depended on two things—furling, unfurling, billowing lengths of cloth, and electric lighting, in magic lanterns covered by different coloured gelatines. Her body was half-glimpsed through coils transparent, translucent, opaque. She deployed her veiling with the aid of supporting batons. They saw "The Flight of the Butterflies," and "Radium," an iridescent shimmering confection dedicated to Pierre and Marie Curie. They saw, finally, the Fire Dance, in which the dancer was lit from below, through a lantern using an intense scarlet light. The moving silks became a stream of volcanic magma, they became the rising flames of a burning pyre, they became the oven of a holocaust. "The Ride of the Valkyries" sang out, and the woman gyrated in a cocoon of fire—like red clay, like white marble luridly lit, smiling in the conflagration, stepping through the fires of hell-mouth incandescent and unconsumed. They were all entranced. Julian wondered if it was vulgar, and then got lost in the silk fringes. Tom was happy with that happiness that comes from being shut in the unreal box of the theatre. Olive was reminded of the uncanny feeling she had had as Hermione, wound in marble folds of grave-cloth or wedding dress. She remembered the flowing marble hair of Rodin's *Danaïde,* and felt that everything was of a piece, that the dancer, and the carved woman, and the glassy lit surface of the river outside with its threaded slivers of emerald, opal, amethyst, peridot, hissing and crackling with electricity, electricity, a river of life, a river of death, were all one. It made her want to write, as things delightful and things threatening, both, made her want to write.

When they were safely back in Todefright, Humphry sat down to write an article on Exhibitions and the Arts of War and Peace.

Olive wrote a tale in which, at night, the silky ladies and resplendent peacocks, the manikins and marble men and maidens, the puppets and the glimmering butterflies and dragonflies and fishes in the tapestries, came to life and held their own market of magical goods in the shadowy spaces and the sumptuous uninhabited chambers of the Bing Pavilion.

24

The hot summer days were long in the Marsh. In the absence of Benedict Fludd and Philip there was less for Elsie to do, and Seraphita and
Pomona did nothing anyway. Sometimes they sat in the orchard with
their embroidery. Elsie cleared up, and shopped, and did sewing of her
own. She had reached an age where every surface of her skin was taut
with the need to be touched and used, and all she had to occupy her was
a dusty old house and two mildly crazy women dressed in flowing floral
gowns. She herself was also dressed in clothes constructed from altered
hand-downs, covered with faded golden lilies and birds and pomegran-
ates. What she wanted was a sleek, dark, businesslike skirt and a fresh
white shirt with a collar, that would show off her narrow waist. She had
no money, and did not know how to ask for any, for she knew there was
very little in the household to cover the bread and milk and vegetables.
She also had a problem with handed-down shoes, none of which fitted
her exactly. She had red rubbed places on what she knew were pretty
feet, scraped heels and bruised toe-joints. She tended to walk around in
basketlike sandals that were too big, but didn't hurt. More than anything she admitted to herself that she wanted, she wanted new shoes,
her own shoes. Shoes that wouldn't destroy her feet. More than anything, in fact, she wanted to be made love to, to have hands gripping her
waist and stroking her lovely hair. She burned, but it was no use repin-
ing, or even admitting to herself that she burned. She set about remedy-
ing what little she could, taking dressmaking shears to the Morris & Co.
fabrics, and converting the loose aesthetic robes to neatly shaped skirts,
with darts and seams. She had seen in a shop window in Rye a soft, dark
wine-red leather belt, with an arrow-shaped clasp at the front, that she
desired passionately, as a substitute for hands, as a provocation to eyes.

Seraphita said nothing about the skirts. She stared vaguely, like a
china doll, or a garden goddess, Elsie thought. The house now had few
secrets from Elsie. She knew where Seraphita hid bottles, brown bottles
of stout, little blue bottles of laudanum, amongst her wool-baskets and
hairbrushes. She never touched or moved these bottles; she thought,
indeed, of offering help with procuring them, but Seraphita had a trick
of not hearing anything that was said, and must have had a satisfactory

system already in place, though she never looked awake enough to contrive one.

Elsie knew she ought to be sorry for Pomona. The girl liked to follow her around, never offering to help with the housework, though sweetly admiring of Elsie's achievements, such a delicious soup, such a pretty flower arrangement, such clean windows as there had never been, the sun had never come in so brightly. Pomona did touch Elsie. She stroked her, timidly, when Elsie sat down to sew, she asked if Elsie was happy. She said "We aren't very lively here, now Imogen is gone," and Elsie replied tartly that there was plenty of work to be getting on with. Somebody ought to be educating the girl, taking her out to meet possible husbands or teaching her a trade, Elsie thought, not very sympathetically. She wished Pomona would keep her distance. She preferred sitting alone to sew. She was making a not-bad, reasonably sober skirt, covered with willow boughs.

She went, when she could, into the potters' studio. The balls of clay were damp-wrapped, the buckets of slip were tempting, and she ran her fingers through them, just to get the feel back. She took some clay—it wasn't stealing, it could be squeezed back to nothing—and made several tiny figures, figures of women, sitting with their arms round their knees, or standing proudly naked, balanced on elegant legs.

She was curious about the locked pantry. She told herself that she had cleaned everywhere else, and should clean there, but knew that it was really the ancient challenge of the one locked door. The drawing of Bernard Palissy from the Kensington Valhalla was nailed to the locked door, one corner, she noticed, covering the keyhole. Without exactly setting about it, she looked for unattributable keys, telling herself at the same time that if the pantry held a secret, the key might be somewhere else altogether. Then, one day, standing precariously on a stool to reach a high shelf, she picked up a grim salt-jar, in the shape of a griffon with a threatening beak and lifted crest, and heard a metallic rattle. The jar was pushed back in the shadows. Elsie retrieved it, and brought it to earth. She tipped and the creature disgorged a fine iron key. Elsie put the key into the pocket of her apron, and smiled to herself, catlike. She replaced the jar. And then she waited. She waited two days, until Frank Mallett invited Seraphita and Pomona to a summer picnic at the Puxty vicarage. When she had the house to herself, she took out the tacks that held Palissy in place, and uncovered the lock. The key slid in easily, and turned easily, as though oiled. The pantry was indeed a pantry. A stone shelf ran round three of its walls, above and behind which were other shelves, rising to the low whitewashed ceiling. There was a small barred window, with a wire net to keep out flies, covered with dust.

On the shelves were pots. Elsie had expected something secret and different. One or two were largish plump jars, but most were small, and glimmered white in the shadows, white-glazed china, unglazed biscuit. When Elsie went nearer to make them out better her feet crunched on broken shards, as though someone had dropped, or thrown, a whole carpet of fragments to the ground.

The pots were obscene chimaeras, half vessels, half human. They had a purity and clarity of line, and were contorted into every shape of human sexual display and congress. Slender girls clutched and displayed vaselike, intricate modellings of their own lower lips and canals. They lay on their backs, thrusting their pelvises up to be viewed. They sat in mute despair on the lips of towering jars, clutching their nipples defensively, their long hair falling over their cast-down faces. There were also clinical anatomical models—always elegant, always precise and economical, of the male and female sexual organs, separate and conjoined. There were pairs of figures, in strenuous possible and impossible embraces, gentle and terrible.

Some of them had Imogen's long face and drooping shoulders: some of them were plump Pomona. The males were faceless fantasms. Elsie crunched towards them over the destruction of other versions, and saw that the wavering arms and legs, the open mouths and clutching hands were not all the same age, went back years, into childishness. There were so many, Elsie thought they resembled a coral reef, thrusting out stony thickets underwater. It was hard for Elsie to look at them, in the state of bodily need which already possessed her. Something inside her own body responded to the opening up, the penetration, the visual shock of these. But under the sexual response, and stronger, was terror. Not terror, exactly, of what the girls had been made to do, or maybe only imagined as doing. Terror of the ferocious energy that had made so many, so many, compelled by a need she did not want to imagine. She backed away. She had the presence of mind to take off her hated shoes and wrap them in her apron to be brushed clean of traces. She did not think that the maker of this display would take kindly to any hint or trace of her own discovery of it.

She did not know if she would have told Philip, if he had been there. She had a strong need to tell no one, as if silence would unmake the shelves, and the gleaming white things, and the dusty light. It had the opposite effect. She was haunted. When Pomona returned from the tea-party, Elsie's unwilling brain undressed her cream-skinned body, opened her legs, so that when Pomona next stroked Elsie's arm, Elsie, for the first time, slapped away her hand, said sharply, "Don't!" and turned away from Pomona's face, where distress flickered and calmed itself.

At the August Bank Holiday weekend Geraint came home to see his mother and sister. Basil Wellwood took him into Kent in his new Daimler. He had formed a godfatherly affection for "young Gerry" as he was now known, which Gerry reciprocated, asking intelligent questions about mines, bonds, and markets, which Charles had never done. Geraint was now working as a clerk in Wildvogel & Quick's currency department. He had lodgings in Lambeth, and strode daily across London Bridge in a crowd of black-clothed men, hurrying and intent, like army ants, or a tidal stream like the grim river beneath. It was a huge change for a ragged boy, "dragged up" aesthetically in an impoverished marsh. He preened himself in his new clothes, signs of a total metamorphosis, a grub become a dragonfly. He found the hum and murmur and heat and scent of the human crush the most alarming thing but he was resolute that he must not only get used to it, but learn to like it. He was amiable to other clerks, and learned to join in japes, and outings, where to be enthusiastic, where to hold back. He was canny, deliberately rather than instinctively canny. His handwriting was precise and beautiful—he had inherited something of his father's eye. He discovered he had a facility for accurate calculation, and took intense pleasure in it. It was of no use in a dusty old house in a dismal marsh.

He was frequently bored to exhaustion, but never yawned. There were things to learn. He looked around to learn them. He was going to have a country house, and servants, and champagne, and—much more vaguely—an elegant wife in fashionable gowns. He had a double vision of the City and the Stock Exchange. He loved its conformity, its narrowness, its pure drive to money-making. He learned to love its dun air, in which floated a fine haze of soot and grit, an air which was thick, like the sediment on dusty windows, a colouring at once a respectable toning-down, and a kind of vanishing, like the drab breast feathers of dunnocks scurrying under hedges. And it came to him vaguely that what was at the centre of it all was both a thing, and a symbolic key or clue to all other things, the gold that lay quietly in sovereign pieces and stacked ingots in the vaults of the Old Lady of Threadneedle Street, and the strong-rooms of Wildvogel & Quick. For the figures he scribed and arranged in his elegant ink columns, the telegrams and the bankers' drafts, were also symbols of things, whose solidity delighted his imagination. Things like bicycle-wheels, dynamos, thick cement, bolts of silk and bales of wool and pyramids of dusky bright carpets, tin-lined cases of tea and sacks of coffee beans, trawlers, steamships, typewriters, wines and sugar, coal and salt, gases in carboys, oil in flasks and barrels, spices sealed in lead caskets. It was all full of a curiously lively dust, which drifted and rose and fell. Dust from the cinders of thousands of chimneys, mixed with a sediment of spice and sugar, mixed again with the imagined glimmer of gold dust.

Once these things had been held in huge vaulted warehouses along the Docks, but this was changing, as Basil explained to him. The warehouses were becoming echoing empty sarcophagi, through the influence of telegrams and steamships. The Baltic Exchange, Basil told Gerry, received three telegrams every minute. Each could result in the dispatching of a ship which would take only a week or so from the States and only four or five weeks from Australia and the Orient. The great holding-merchants must change their ways or die out.

Geraint saw the turning globe in his mind's eye, with its vast red Imperial patches, its shifting frontiers, criss-crossed by the invisible threads of the telegrams and the visible furrows of the great iron ships forging steadily through flying foam and mirror-calm seas.

In the Daimler, on the bright Bank Holiday Saturday, Basil Wellwood talked about gold. Gold was needed to fight the war in South Africa, which Humphry had written against, describing it as a war in the interests of the London gold market, the bullion reserve, and the speculators. Basil was unsettled, because the Chancellor had chosen that day, at the beginning of the Bank Holiday weekend, when the Stock Exchange was closed and the city was empty, to announce a War Loan designed to replenish the depleted stocks of gold coins and bullion held by the Bank of England. Investors were disadvantaged. Trains would not run on time because of the holiday and time was vital at this delicate point. It was unfairly done. Geraint nodded agreement. He mentioned the South American mines—Camp Rind, Crickle Creek—where venture corporations were looking to replace the supplies which had thinned with the closing of many South African mines since the outbreak of war.

He was handling correspondence about these matters. His work was more interesting than it might have been, because four of the clerks from Wildvogel & Quick had marched away with the City Imperial Volunteers. Such patriotic young men had, of course, been promised that their posts would be kept open for them. There had been a most unpleasant incident when the *Daily Mail* had accused another German bank of telling two such clerks that they would have to leave. The paper had not named the bankers, but the City knew they were Kahn and Herzfelder, and Maurice Herzfelder had been closed in on, jostled, baited, brought down and kicked about his body and face by angry inhabitants of the Kaffir Circus. No one had been brought to book. The Stock Exchange was a place of anarchic gathering crowds, with wild emotions. Gerry had been in place on May 18th when the Relief of Mafeking was announced. Everyone marched and howled and sang, waving flags and blowing trumpets and singing anthems, accompanied by coaching horns. Gerry too, marched and sang. "Rule Britannia," "God Save the Queen." His mind was hooked into the communal mind. It was new to him, he had never known anything like it.

The Bank Holiday weather was golden. Basil and Gerry sat behind the chauffeur and looked out benignly at hopfields and cornfields. When they came to the Wellwood country house, Basil, in an excess of friendliness, invited his young clerk in for a glass of sherry, and then ordered the chauffeur to take the young man and his bag through the country roads to Purchase House. It would be a fine surprise, for his family, to see him turn up in an automobile. They would not be expecting that. Geraint was a little worried because he was not sure they were expecting him at all—he had meant to surprise them. He was agitated in his mind about what to do about the chauffeur—would the man expect a tip, should he be invited in, how would he negotiate this? They wheeled and chugged out of the Garden of England and into the Marsh, and drove up the long drive to Purchase House. No one stirred. They came into the stable-yard, which was empty and full of heat, like a vat. Nobody came out to meet them. Geraint said he could perhaps find a beer to refresh the chauffeur, who refused politely (he had his own beer in his lunch basket, he wanted to get back to his own family, he was aware of Geraint's social predicament, and only residually interested in showing off the automobile to the inhabitants, if any appeared, of Purchase House). Geraint stood in the yard with his bag, and watched the chauffeur crank up the engine and reverse out of the yard, with a series of spluttering and petroleum farts.

Elsie Warren came out of the dairy-studio just in time to see the high back of the car disappear between the trees. She greeted Geraint civilly, and expressed the right amount of surprise, both at his appearance, and at his conveyance. She said she had seen one or two in Rye, they were quite startling. She said she would make him up a bed, and that his mother was taking a nap, as she usually did in the afternoon. She did not know where Pomona was. She might have gone out with a bicycle. Was he hungry?

He was very hungry. Elsie produced, in a very short time, an excellent lobster salad and some fresh brown bread. "There's a fisher-boy," she said, "who brings me a lobster or a crab now and then as an excuse to hang around."

Geraint looked at her with mild curiosity. So she had a follower? He saw her see what he thought—she smoothed down her skirt over her hips, self-consciously. He saw that she had become extremely pretty, that her figure was just as it should be, and her face full of life. He observed her observing his observations. They both decided to say nothing. He looked at her reconfigured arts and crafts garments. They did not hang perfectly. He remembered shouting at Prosper Cain that no one had seen fit to pay Philip. He did not know if Philip was now paid—he was at least being taken on an educational trip to Paris, so Imogen and Florence had told him, when he called in at the Museum. He wondered if Elsie was paid. He thought if he didn't find out, no one would. Someone—the invisible fisher-boy?—would be after Elsie Warren, would want to take her away, make love to her, make a wife and mother of her. This would be both right and very inconvenient. He thought he must talk to Elsie.

Pomona came in and rushed into his arms, kissing and hugging him. He told her, as he had not told Elsie, that she was becoming a beautiful young woman, and she tossed her mass of pale hair and cast down her eyes. Imogen had asked him to look out for Pomona. She herself was taking a course in jewellery, and making drawings of designs for small silver and enamel pendants. She seemed calm, which made Geraint aware that in earlier days she had not seemed calm, only dulled, or dimmed. She said she worried about Pomona, who would have, she said obscurely, to "bear everything" now that both she and Geraint were gone. Geraint had looked anxiously across at Florence Cain, who was pouring tea. He was a little in awe of Florence, who was seventeen, two years younger than he was, one year younger than Pomona, and a good four years younger than Imogen, but seemed wiser and more assured than any of them. He thought Florence was beautiful, like an Italian painting of a saint. He thought she was "just right," without analysing her dress, or the way she managed a tea-tray. Imogen said "Don't mind Florence, she's a friend," and it was Geraint, not Florence, who blushed as their eyes met. He remembered Florence as he took in Pomona, bundling herself into his embrace, stroking his face. Her eyes were wet. Geraint said

"Have you been all right, Pommy? Are you missing us? Do you have plans?"

Seraphita came sleepily downstairs at this point, and was duly astonished to see her changed son, in his new linen jacket. She asked vaguely if Elsie had "seen to" him, and he said Elsie had. Elsie began, briskly, to clear up the salad plates. Seraphita sat majestically and smiled. Pomona said "Tell us about . . . tell us about . . ." but could not think what question to ask about a life of which she knew nothing.

"I came in an automobile," said Gerry. "Mr. Wellwood sent the chauffeur to bring me here. He is very considerate to me."

He was never going to be able to tell these two about bullion and loans, about telegrams and dust.

The holiday ticked on, in a sunlit haze. Geraint got in some good solitary walks across the Marsh, and some bicycle rides with Pomona. Elsie produced delicious dishes of fried sprats and dressed crab and potato salad with mustard. Herbert and Phoebe Methley called, and were given tea, and asked all the questions about life in the City which his family had not asked. He described the hurrying march of men over London Bridge, the hurly-burly in the Stock Exchange, the celebration of the Relief of Mafeking. Herbert Methley said it was generally believed that Money was soulless, but this was not so. Mammon was a great spiritual power, and perturbed both angels and demons. Mammon was conducting this horrific killing in the Veld. Gold had made the war, and gold kept it in motion. This disquisition annoyed Geraint. He knew gold was a kind of living force, but the personification weakened and sentimentalised it, which he sensed, without being able to put it precisely into words. He saw gold in his mind's eye, bright ingots, a hot flood from a crucible. He wanted no moth-eaten demon. Pomona said "We had no idea it was all so exciting. We thought it was dull and—and mechanical." So it is, said Geraint. Dull, mechanical and exciting. Elsie whisked past with fresh scones she had made, and a pot of excellent gooseberry jam.

He liked breathing the air of the Marsh, he felt stronger in his body; but he was not unhappy when the time came to leave. Before that, he had his little talk with Elsie. He asked her to step into the orchard, he wanted to talk to her. They paced between the trees. "Do you need anything?" asked Geraint. "You seem to perform small miracles with loaves and fishes—I feel I do need to ask, have you enough—enough money— to manage? My mother is not practical."

Elsie surprised him. She sat down on a grassy hump and stretched out her legs. She took off her bulky sandals.

"Look at my feet," she said. Her feet were not pretty. They were pinched and bruised, they had corns and lumps, they bled a little. She said, dry and intense,

"I want shoes of my own. I can't get about and do everything I do with these feet. I get hand-downs from Frank Mallett, none of them fit, I have thin feet. Look at them, Mr. Fludd. Look at them. They are old woman's feet. They are being smashed into old woman's feet. I shall truly be more use with shoes of my own."

"I have to ask—forgive me—are you being paid?"

"I don't see why you need to be forgiven, and I think you know the answer. No, I am not paid, I get board and lodging and hand-downs. I don't complain, I know money is tight, but I do need shoes."

"You don't—intend to leave, to go elsewhere?"

"Listen. I always swore I would never, never go into Service, whatever I had to do. I would have stayed in the Potteries and decorated the ware, it would have been a trade I would have had. Like my mam, who is dead. I came to look for Philip, when she died, because she wanted me to. I love Philip, Mr. Fludd, he's all I love. And I know he's right and has always been right—he's got a real gift, and he's driven. This is his dream-world, because your father is a great master. He is learning what he might never have hoped to learn. I don't think he's more than half pleased I'm here—he'd got away, into another place, and I remind him of what he'd left. But as long as I make things here comfortable for everyone, Philip is free—he can make pots, he can invent, he can work. I never meant to be a housekeeper. I had my own little ambitions. I can't bear the fecklessness here—forgive me, that's rude—I do enjoy tweaking things, mending and making do, and brightening a bit."

She was working herself up. She spoke rapidly, drily, furiously. She said

"And I feel a fool in all this flowery cloth and embroidered bits and pieces, I'd like the Reverend Mallett to see me in ordinary respectable boring things, I'm not a puppet or an Aunt Sally. I'm sorry, I shouldn't complain about that, I didn't mean to. But, you know, Mr. Fludd, the saying is a true saying—my feet are killing me. I'm sorry. Now I'll shut up. I am sorry."

Geraint sat down on the grass beside her. To his own surprise, he took one of the hot feet in his hands and bent over it.

"How much do shoes cost?"

"I don't know. You must know that better than I could. You've got ordinary clothes now—handsome clothes, I should say—good shoes."

His City shoes had cost a month's wages. He looked after their glowing leather like his own skin, and they were indeed smoother than that, as it tended to erupt. Geraint Fludd had only recently had money of his own, earned by his own efforts, in his pockets, and he was what Elsie would have called "close," very close with it. But he fetched out his purse now and counted four silver half-crowns into Elsie's hand.

"This should buy some shoes for you. When I come back, I shall expect to see you striding about comfortably, and going on long walks." He hesitated. He wanted to say that he would come with her, to choose the shoes. He was rearranging in his mind the little luxuries he would forfeit for the shoes and a magnanimous glow filled him at the thought of the fine toes wriggling comfortably in new leather. But there was something intimate, something improper, about going to a shoe shop with this young woman. Either he behaved as though she was—was a kind of vassal, of whom he was lord and master, or he behaved like an almost-lover, making gifts, which might expect a return. He said, a little stiffly,

"I do know how much more you do for my family than you need, or they—we—really appreciate. I do know."

Elsie smiled ruefully. She would have liked someone to be with her, on her momentous shoe-shop visit. Maybe she should wait for Philip. But her feet were killing her.

Geraint went back to Vetchey Manor in the dog cart, and in a day or two Elsie walked across the Marsh, and up the hill into Rye. There were two or three boot and shoe shops, in the window of one of which—Jas. Plaskett, estd. 1872—was the red leather belt with the arrow clasp. Elsie stood on the cobbles, staring into the window, calculating. She did not want her first pair of shoes to be workingwomen's clodhopping boots and she knew, with fatal realism, that if she bought herself any shoes remotely shapely, or almost dressy, she wouldn't ever be able to bring herself to wear them, for what she needed, trotting across the yard, running up and down stairs, walking into Lydd. She should buy something sensible, which, if assiduously scraped and polished, would look acceptable below her plain skirt, when she got it. She hoped for a moment that Geraint might have given her enough to buy both shoes and the red belt. She calculated. As long as she didn't go into the shop, she could imagine owning the belt.

"I have been wondering what you are dreaming about," said a pleasant voice behind her. Elsie jumped. "I didn't mean to startle you," said Herbert Methley. "I've been watching you thinking for maybe twenty minutes, and I couldn't resist, in the end, asking about *what* you are thinking and frowning and murmuring to yourself. You don't have to answer, I know I'm impertinent."

Elsie laughed. "Shoes. I'm thinking about shoes. For the first time in my life I'm buying new shoes, for me. I can't make up my mind. I don't know how to decide."

"And as long as you *don't* decide, all the shoes are yours to think about," said the writer.

"Yes, and the smart red belt with the arrow there. I could just about manage the belt if I bought cheaper boots—but I don't need the belt, I need shoes that don't hurt."

"This is indeed a momentous decision. I am a storyteller, you know, and I do need to know how it will come out. I think you must try on the shoes—as many as you can, so that you may see your feet in every possible light and every possible form. You will certainly find that some of the shoes that look good in the window, that promise comfort and prettiness, will turn out to be deceivers, will pinch your heel or hurt your great toe. And others, that look like nothing much sitting there on the stand, will turn out to feel like gloves that were made specially with your feet and your elegant ankles in mind. In an ideal world you would be buying walking shoes, and dancing shoes, and everyday housework shoes, but you need to find one pair that can be all these at once, I assume, and that isn't easy. I hope you will let me help you. I do have a good eye for women's feet, I have always been told. I really want to know how this tale will come out—"

So they went into the dark, leather-scented shop, and Elsie sat on an upholstered chair, with Herbert Methley kneeling on one side of her and the shoe-shop boy on the other, bringing more and more shoe-boxes from his store behind his counter. Methley stroked her feet as she inserted them carefully into black shoes and brown shoes, shoes with little heels and shoes with punched trimmings, and serviceable brogues. He was uncannily accurate about which shoes would prove to fit her feet comfortably, rejecting those that were too heavy, and also those that might prove to pinch. He made her walk in the shoes, and turn her body round so that he could see from all angles, and asked where the tips of her toes reached, and whether her heels scrubbed. It was oddly intimate. They had it down to two pairs, long after Elsie on her own would have made a rushed decision for the cheapest and ugliest, out of a sense that she didn't "deserve" to have anything better.

"They need to feel like gloves, Elsie. They need to support all those tiny little bones that do so much work in the arch of your foot, and you need to be able to move all your toes, without feeling you're wearing a shoe-box instead of a shoe. I myself like this black pair with the little heel best. At a pinch—or *not* at a pinch—they have a certain elegance— severe but fine—and yet I am sure they will be serviceable."

Elsie agreed to buy those shoes and was prepared to walk back to Purchase House in them. Methley told her she must not. "Wear them every day for a short time, until you and they know each other. You need to warm and stretch them, little by little. To make them yours. May I walk back to Purchase House with you? I was out for a stroll anyway, and should like the company."

Elsie was confused. Herbert Methley was, in her eyes, old, part of the father's generation. Maybe his friendliness and—and—*assiduity* were fatherly, though she didn't think so. He was much uglier than Geraint, and much more interested and interesting than Geraint. She had change from Geraint's half-crowns, though not the price of the red belt. She said she would be glad if he walked back with her, and then he produced, like a conjuror, a small parcel, tied with string.

"For you," he said. "Open it."

It was, of course, the red belt.

"I *can't*."

"Why not? It isn't often that one can surprise someone with their heart's desire. And you are quite right, you have excellent taste, it is a lovely belt."

It was shaped to sit on the hips, and point downwards, like an arrow, between them. Herbert Methley insisted on fastening it round her, his long hands, very briefly, echoing its form, lingering a few seconds, pointing down.

After this they walked back, over the Marsh, side by side, aware of each other. Methley said

"I wonder if you would mind very much if I put your feet—and your shoes—into a novel I am writing? They are just what I need as a solid example—"

"Example of what?" Elsie asked, neither pleased nor displeased.

"It's a novel about—about what's wrong with women's lives. Women's clothing is a form of oppression and confinement."

Elsie considered the jump of subject from shoes to freedom. She said she'd never had occasion to think about these things. She had too much to do, she almost said, and restrained herself, for she felt the sentence would sound silly.

"But you should think, Elsie. Why should your brother be in gay Paris, and you here as a domestic slave, with no shoes?"

"He's a real good potter. I'm not."

"Have you ever thought what you might be, if you had a real choice?"

"There's no point," said Elsie.

She thought about her discontent, making ends meet for those feckless and aimless females in Purchase House. She thought of the pantry, full of lascivious pots. There were several in which the female figure lay back with her fingers between her legs, at the spot towards which the arrow on the new red belt was pointing. She was aroused and disturbed—not entirely pleasantly—by Herbert Methley. He stirred her up, as Geraint, and the fisher-boy, did not. She needed to keep her head.

"And what is to happen to your—your character with no shoes? Does she end well?"

"She works out her own freedom, and is able to dance barefoot," said Methley. "She learns to live."

Elsie did not ask who would teach the barefoot girl. She made a remark about the view across the Marsh, and the larks singing. Methley followed her lead, and they sauntered on, demonstrating great interest in wild flowers and marsh sheep, in windblown trees and the Royal Military Canal, along whose deliberately designed bank they walked for some way. Methley turned off the road before it turned towards the drive to Purchase Hall. Elsie thanked him, with some constraint, for his help and for the belt. He said "I think you should come to a public meeting about the rights of women that Miss Dace is organising in Lydd. I think you should take an interest. Women's lives are about to change utterly. You—you yourself—need to think about that."

Elsie said she would need to think about whether it could be managed.

"My wife and I will be there. You would be among friends."

"I shall need to ask," Elsie said, already a little mutinous at having to *ask* Seraphita for anything.

"Maybe Mrs. Fludd would also consider coming? We need to speak to all women."

Elsie did not know how greatly Seraphita Fludd feared that Elsie herself would leave as suddenly and mysteriously as she had come.

25

Miss Dace had booked a kind of glorified wooden hut, in Lydd, known vaguely as the Club Hall, though it did not belong exclusively to any particular club. The army used it, for lectures and social events. The Chapel used it for bring and buy sales. The University Extension Lecturers used it in the evenings, for workers' education. Miss Dace had put up posters advertising a full day of discussions on the general theme of "The Woman of the Future." There were five speakers, beginning with Miss Dace herself, and ending with Herbert Methley. There was always the risk that the number of the audience would only equal the number of speakers. Miss Dace enticed the Theosophists and the sewing circle with promises of a very good cold lunch to break the day. She spoke to a major's wife who was a Theosophist, and asked her to encourage other wives to come. The colonel's wife was known to be a vehement Anti-Suffragist. She might even come—or send a minion—to heckle. The Vicar of All Saints in Lydd could not be expected to come, though some independent women from his congregation might do so. Frank Mallett and Arthur Dobbin would come, because they were good disciples of Edward Carpenter, and because one of the speakers was the schoolmistress at Puxty, Mrs. Marian Oakeshott.

The family at Purchase House were sent a flyleaf. Seraphita put it listlessly down on the kitchen table. Elsie said, slightly too firmly, "I should like to go to that, if that's all right."

Seraphita put her head on one side and looked as though she was considering objections, with difficulty.

"Do you think you will go?" Elsie asked Seraphita.

"Oh, I don't think so. I don't believe in all this agitation about votes, which is what I suppose it's about. I don't see how votes could change anything important. Women are . . . women must . . ."

She left most such sentences trailing unfinished.

"I will go with you," said Pomona. "It will make a change of scene." She yawned, prettily. Elsie was briefly annoyed. She had wanted to do something on her own. But Pomona was right—she did most desperately need a change of scene.

They set out across the Denge Marsh. It was a hot, still morning. Elsie had dressed carefully. She wore a white cotton blouse, her willow-bough skirt, the red belt and the new shoes. She had made herself a hat, on the base of a broken-crowned straw hat retrieved from Frank Mallett's hand-ons. She had stitched it together, and trimmed it with some ends of red braid, retrieved from Seraphita's sewing, and a kind of flower-form she had twisted out of bits of lace and gauze. It was the first time she had gone out in public in a hat. Pomona wore a flowing shepherdessy smock in apple-green, liberally embroidered with butterflies and blossoms. She was hatless. Her pale hair flowed over her shoulders. She looked as though she might be going to comment on Elsie's appearance, and in the end, did not.

The hall was one of those wooden structures with windows too high to see out of. There was a platform, on which the speakers sat, and rows of wooden chairs, of which maybe the first six were taken, the heads of the women sitting there quite invisible under the great dishes and wheels of their hats, their shoulders a mixture of decorous spinsterly dove-colours and brighter greens and purples. There were six men, including Herbert Methley, who was on the platform next to his wife, Frank Mallett and Arthur Dobbin, and Leslie Skinner, who had come to support Etta, who was also speaking. There was one soldier, an explosives expert, who had come with his wife, who was a member of Mrs. Humphry Ward's Anti-Suffrage League. There was one grocer, who was bookish, and went to the evening classes of Mrs. Marian Oakeshott, who was also on the platform.

Elsie and Pomona sat down two or three rows behind the last occupied row. From the platform, Herbert Methley smiled down on them, approving their presence. Elsie gave a tight little smile in return. Pomona folded her pale hands in her flowery lap, and turned her face to the light from the dusty window.

There were five speakers, three before lunch and two afterwards. Miss Dace spoke first. She was precisely eloquent about the injustice to women of being unrepresented in Parliament, unable to vote on matters which concerned their lives, their work, their health. She noted drily that when the words "Woman" or "Women" appeared in the names of laws, these were always laws which made the condition of women less free, more uncomfortable. Voters were householders and taxpayers, but women who were both must pay their taxes without any right to have their views, or needs, consulted or represented. Elsie tried hard to listen carefully. She liked Miss Dace's dry, ironic, passionate tone. She managed to work out what "suffrage" meant, having always vaguely thought that it was to do with women suffering. It must be like that bit of the Bible "Suffer little children to come unto me, and forbid them not." But Miss Dace wanted Parliament to suffer single householders and taxpayers like herself to vote in elections, and a kind of anger welled up in Elsie, for she was not sure how this helped a penniless young woman, *camped* in a house with a pantry full of beautiful, obscene female jars and vessels, who was full of bodily needs she could not describe, and was certainly suffering. But Miss Dace was a *good* woman, she put things straight, she was a reasonable woman, as far as she went.

When Patty Dace had come to her conclusion, the colonel's wife rose to speak. The country was fighting a terrible war, in a distant country, she said, and the British Empire entailed military responsibility in far-flung places which British housewives could neither imagine nor understand. Let women guard the Home, and the values of the Home, and leave armies and economics to the men whose work they naturally were. Miss Dace replied that those intrepid women who had visited the *concentration* camps in which the Boer women and children were kept by the British army might be thought to have contributed to the moral well-being of the army and the well-being of the suffering Boers. There was rustling and tapping in the room. Elsie didn't know what a "concentration" camp was. Miss Dace turned on the colonel's wife and asked her, would she then *remove* women from the local government and Poor Law Boards to which they could now be elected and on which they worked efficaciously? No, said the colonel's wife, she admitted they did competent work.

It is always so, said Miss Dace. So far, and no further. Your movement would be going against *any* such employment before it was tried, and now, like King Canute with the tide, you cry, so far, and no further. But the tide will flow in, it will rise, you will see.

The next speaker was not Herbert, but Phoebe Methley.

Elsie took a good long look at Herbert Methley's wife. She had been an attractive woman, Elsie thought, using the past tense a little harshly. She wore a plain dark skirt and a white shirt with a black and green bow at its collar. Her hat was black trimmed with a green ribbon. She looked mild and competent. Her subject was "A Woman's Place." She began by saying that she was grateful to the last speaker for having raised the subject of the sacred values of the Home, for it was of the Home she wished to speak. When it was mentioned in this way, she thought, everyone had a pleasant image of a woman in a sunlit house with a garden, and a warm fire in winter, surrounded by plump and smiling children, a baby perhaps in her arms, her mind full of little comforts for her husband on his return from an arduous day in the office or the club. Such a woman's head would be full of delicious new receipts for cakes and jellies, delightful new covers for cushions and original decorations for hat-brims and corsages. Women in this happy state were in fact few. Rich women did not mind their children, might go days or weeks without seeing them, delegated the care of their health to nursemaids and the care of their minds to governesses, and sent them away, as soon as they could, to schools where they might well be homesick or bullied. And then, such women suffered from boredom. Women could not use minds which had been fed on nothing but sugar flowers and cream soup and hatpins. And the vast majority of working women—and there were thousands and thousands of working women who not only earned the household bread but did what sweeping they could and spread the bread with what grease they could scavenge—they did indeed value the Home and keeping it together, however many adults and children slept in one room—for one step beyond such homes was the Workhouse, which was a mockery both of home and work. The "values of the Home" was an abstract paper phantom.

And let women not think that their sense of duty, their influence in their proper sphere, in the Home, counted for anything in the face of the law. A woman who shielded her children from an unreasonable or violent father had no chance of taking them with her if she fled from unhappiness. Such a man could claim that outside his Home she was unfit, not only to care for, but even to see or to visit, her children, who had been her life, though her heart might be breaking. Under the sweet sentiments about the domestic sphere of happiness, lip service paid to the wisdom of motherhood, lay cruelty. It was true that a young woman, seduced by a plausible man—an employer, an employer's son, maybe—if *unmarried,* was alone responsible in law for the welfare of her unhappy child. But a married mother, separated for whatever reason from her husband, ceased at that moment to have any rights as a mother.

. . .

Elsie's spirit drew back as Mrs. Methley grew more passionate. She was right, of course, but she *cared too much,* Elsie wanted to stop watching her caring. The Methleys surely had no children.

Elsie thought of her own mother. She had worked. She had been good at her craft and the air of the kilns had made her ill. She had tried to make a home for them. They had had a geranium in a pot on a window sill. They had had a Minton plate—it was a second—hung on a nail on the wall. They all knew what these things meant. They meant they were respectable. *Just* respectable. She tried to think she wouldn't so much mind being trapped in a gilded cage of a comfortable Home—she had done a fair amount of substitute Home-making at Purchase House, not so much out of a desire for homeliness as out of a powerful dislike for mess, and shoddiness, and discomfort, which was unshared by the Purchase women. All this talk about what women did, or should, or might want was unsettling to her. She had wanted shoes and a belt and she had them. She wanted—she wanted—she wanted—to *live.* But it was beginning to irritate her that she had thought so little. If she had sat up all night reading, who would she be now? She raised her face under her gallant hat, to look at the women on the platform, who got so much out of both *thinking* and being dissatisfied. She saw that Herbert Methley's dark look was turned in her direction. A very discreet smile lurked under the fronds of his moustache, and in the corners of his intelligent eyes. Elsie's face went hot. She looked down, although she would have liked not to. She touched the arrow of the red belt. He could not see her hands from where he sat.

The third speaker was Mrs. Henrietta Skinner, representing the Fabian Society, and speaking bravely and directly about Women for Sale. She spoke in praise of Josephine Butler, whose courage had brought about the repeal of the Contagious Diseases Acts, and of W. T. Stead, whose—perhaps sensational but efficacious—exposure of the Maiden Tribute had exposed the trade in virgin female children, and caused Parliament to raise the age of consent to sixteen. Elsie thought Mrs. Skinner looked like a pie with a frill—her round head, under a plain, "rural" straw hat, was perched on the mound of her Liberty clothing, which hung in bronze-green folds like a tent. Her hands, too, were little, pale, and plump. She used them to make very precise stabbing gestures to illustrate her uncomfortable points. She made no apology, she said, for using words that polite society was more accustomed to conceal behind euphemisms and hints, which were themselves part of the oppression and harm they avoided. She would speak of prostitution, she would speak of venereal diseases, she would speak of the damage done to women's bodies by unfeeling and unnecessary medical examinations to which they were subjected. She hoped no one would feel they should leave the room when she spoke of such things. Ignorance killed. Men—husbands and fathers—with what they thought of as "natural" urges and needs—went out and contracted diseases from sick women, and passed these diseases on, not only to other so-called "fallen" women and girls—or children—who had been bought, certified as virgins, and sold—but to their own innocent and ignorant wives, and to the generations to come, the infant son in his cradle, the daughter singing to her doll in the nursery. No one had suggested subjecting these men to medical examinations. It was unthinkable that they would submit.

And who were the "fallen women" who the popular imagination believed led these men, with their natural urges, astray, painting themselves with rouge and henna, showing pretty ankles and covering themselves with exotic perfumes? They were working girls and mothers as often as not, who could not feed their children on what the sweat-shop paid them, whose husbands had had accidents that left them unable to bear burdens or wield picks and shovels. They were young servant-girls, seduced by the master of the house, or his son, and turned out without a character when they were found to be with child. Men must regulate their urges, or be made responsible for the consequences.

Pomona's hands were clasped defensively in her lap. She was trembling a little, although her facial expression was one of detached attentiveness, like the child in the schoolroom who is really thinking about something other than the lesson. Elsie stopped listening to her own body and considered Pomona. What had been done to Pomona, what did Pomona know, whose white thighs were curled and spread in modelled china forms? Did she model for them, or did he *guess*? Elsie didn't want to know. She didn't think he guessed. She imagined, briefly, his fingers at work. She remembered families in Burslem where someone's little brother or sister was generally thought to be really her child by her brother or father. They slept so close there, flesh to flesh. Here she had her own bed, and tossed in it, consumed by undirected desire. Did Elsie care about Pomona? She didn't want to. She wanted. She wanted. She did not think anyone could ever really have desired Etta Skinner, so what did Etta Skinner know of all this from the inside? She looked at Professor Skinner, handsome in profile in the dusty light, and thought—does *he* have these urges, does he do anything about it? Does he clasp all that hummock of flesh in his arms? She smoothed her skirt over her hips.

The members of Miss Dace's club had prepared a salad luncheon for speakers and audience. Elsie was hungry. She advanced on the table with the plates and teacups, followed by Pomona, who clung to her as though they were connected by magnets, so close that she kept almost falling over Elsie's feet. Frank Mallett noticed them, and said he was pleased to see them. He asked if they had found the morning helpful, and Pomona said breathlessly "Oh yes, very." "And you?" said Frank to Elsie. Elsie repeated the word "Helpful," trying to work out what exactly the speeches were meant to help her *with*. Frank smiled. He said the world would be a better place if more women took an active interest in these matters.

Elsie said "It makes me see how ignorant I am. It makes me see I don't know enough and don't think enough."

Her tone was resentful.

Herbert Methley behind her said "Oh, but you *will* know enough and think enough. I am so glad you took up my suggestion. I am very happy to see you—and looking so *well*," he said, smiling in the direction of the belt and shoes. "I am speaking after Mrs. Oakeshott, this afternoon," he said. "I shall be interested to know what you think."

Elsie had been wondering whether to ask Frank Mallett about the pantry—not now, but some time. It weighed on her. But Frank had slid away to greet other women, smiling courteously. Herbert Methley said

"You will enjoy what Mrs. Oakeshott has to say. You may even be persuaded to come to some of her evening classes on the drama. I'm sure she would be delighted to see you."

He was looking directly at the red belt. Elsie was embarrassed, and wanted to slap Pomona for crowding her, for stopping her thinking clearly. She wished Pomona would just go away. Pomona, however, said blandly that she too would be interested in literature classes.

. . .

After luncheon, in what is always the dead time for speakers, when digestion takes place, Marian Oakeshott spoke of women's education. She was handsome and golden: her hat had English meadow flowers on brown linen, her pale coffee-brown linen dress was trimmed with creamy lace. She had a pointed belt not unlike Elsie's, and a row of little bright silk flowers round the neck of her dress. Her voice was warm and rich. The talk was a series of simple tales, which moved Elsie. The tale of Elizabeth Garrett Anderson, who with consummate persistence and courtesy became a doctor by attending lectures, and surgical demonstrations, from which everyone sought to exclude her. Two years ago this pertinacious lady had been elected President of the East Anglian branch of that very British Medical Association which at first had debated whether women could pursue rigorous medical studies.

She spoke of Millicent Garrett Fawcett, the doctor's sister, and leader of the women's suffrage movement, who had worked tirelessly, not only for the vote, but for the cause of women's higher education in Cambridge. Mrs. Fawcett had had the honour and delight of seeing her daughter, Philippa, studying mathematics at Cambridge, placed *above the senior Wrangler.*

Elsie did not know what a wrangler was, and could not imagine Cambridge. She was astonished by the resentment this aroused in her. At just that point Mrs. Oakeshott began to tell stories of women—real and imaginary—who, to use the Christian parable Mrs. Methley had so efficaciously quoted, had buried their talents in the ground. It is not easy for a woman to study. If a family cannot send all its children to grammar schools, it will send the sons, and keep back the daughters to wield the mangle, the needle and the poker, to make the Home comfortable for the boys to study. "Duty" is a word that only too often acts like restraining magic, to make a woman deny an important part of herself—and thus, only too often, to deceive and disappoint her husband, by her triviality, her inability to meet *his* mind. They were not to think that many women were not defeated. Much fashionable nervous illness was, she was convinced, a result of the festering of unused intelligence. Women needed to have the right—and the expectation—to study in groups of like-minded people. For this reason, among others, she had begun her reading group, which would study not only *The Mill on the Floss* and *Jane Eyre* but Mr. Ibsen's *A Doll's House* which had been both admired and reviled. She herself had not thought to see in her life-time so subtle, so terrible, a dramatic representation of those lies of the soul that reduce a grown woman—an intelligent woman—to a puppet and a doll, jerked about by the strings of a failed concept of duty, in a Home that was truly a Doll's House. She hoped, if there were actors in the vicinity with the courage to do so, to put on a performance of that controversial work.

Elsie read better than Philip, though she had the same stunted and trun-cated education. She picked up books at Purchase Hall and tried to make sense of them. She recognised well enough the hunger for something more than housework, of which Marian Oakeshott spoke. She was thinking much faster than usual, and reflected sardonically that those hungry-minded women, those frustrated female thinkers, of whom Marian Oakeshott spoke, would always need her, Elsie, or someone like her, to carry coals and chop meat and mend clothing and do laundry, or they wouldn't keep alive. Someone in the scullery, carrying out the ashes. And if one got out of the scullery, like a disguised princess in a fairytale, there always had to be another, another scullery-maid, to take her place.

Nevertheless, she would like to get out.

It was perhaps unfortunate that Herbert Methley was the last speaker.

Herbert Methley spoke about sexual freedom, freedom of the body, particularly for women. He did not say that this was what he was speak-ing about. He said he was going to talk about the Woman of the Future by comparing the imperfect, accidental condition of the Woman of the Present with that of women in uncivilised worlds and in earlier and other civilisations. He spoke of undifferentiated protozoa, constantly breeding and transforming, he spoke of herding animals, warm-flanked cattle, intelligent elephants, whose children were cared for in common. He spoke of earlier civilisations which had valued women more, set them higher than men, made goddesses and lawgivers of them. He talked of Mother Right as an organising force of society, and the pow-erful human loveliness of the naked ceramic goddesses who had been unearthed in Helen's Troy and Pasiphae's Crete. He spoke of Roman matrons and vestal virgins and sacred temple dancers.

He came to modern women, who were, in the world he described, both the victims and the corrupters of men. The symbol of all this was "dress"—such women spoke of "dress," not of clothing. Women "dressed" at once to stimulate and repel the natural attentions of men. They scented themselves, they besprent themselves with flowers and feathers and furs taken from other living creatures. They submitted to torture from whalebone cages to cramp their bodies into shapes that could show off their "dress" that was the blazon of their separation and servitude. They wore ludicrous shoes that crushed their toes and distorted their stride, not so very far away from the abominable practices of the Chinese footbinders. All this "dress" labelled, invited and repelled, in equal quantity. The women of today were as gaudy as the peacock or the male bird of paradise—gaudy with these male symbols of domination and combativeness—but they lurked like captive lovebirds in the cage of their adornment.

Women should be able to meet and speak as equals to other human beings, of both sexes. They should wear simple but lovely clothing, and there should be no false shame. A woman's ankle is a lovely thing. It is no scandal to ride a bicycle in a garment which is practical for the purpose, even if that natural part of the body may be seen.

He looked up and across to the back of the hall.

"There is no reason why rational dress should be shapeless, severe or ugly. A young lady with a trim waist, in the future as much as now, must be expected to take pleasure in a pretty belt. There is no necessary connection between rational behaviour and ancient, prudish Puritanism. We should remember that a woman is a woman, not a sofa, or a cake."

26

A family, and a human being inside a family, put together a picture of their past in voluntary and involuntary ways, carefully constructed, arbitrarily dictated. A mother remembers one particular summer gathering on a lawn, with iced lemonade in a jug, and everyone smiling— as she puts in the album the one photograph where everyone is smiling, and keeps the scowling faces of the unsuccessful snapshots hidden in a box. A child remembers one scramble over the Downs, or zigzag trot through the woods, out of many, many forgotten ones, and shapes his identity round it. "I remember when I saw the yaffle." And the memory changes when he is twelve, and fourteen, and twenty, and forty, and eighty, and perhaps never at any of those points represented precisely anything that really happened. Odd things persist for inexplicable reasons. A pair of shoes that never quite fitted. A party dress in which a girl always felt awkward, though the photographs are pretty enough. One violent quarrel of many arising from the unjust division of a cake, or the desperately disappointing decision *not* to go to the seaside. There are things, also, that are memories as essential and structural as bones in toes and fingers. A red leather belt. A dark pantry full of obscene and lovely jars.

And there are public memories, which make markers. They were all Victorians, and then in January 1901, the little old woman, the Widow at Windsor, the Queen and Empress died. All Europe was full of her family, whose private follies and conceits and quarrels shaped the lives of *all other families*. When she began to fail, her German grandson, Kaiser Wilhelm, cut short the celebrations of the two-hundredth anniversary of the Prussian Crown, and got into his special train to cross the Channel. No notice, he said, should be taken of him in his capacity as Emperor. He came merely as a grandson. His own people felt he should have respected their hostility to the war against the Boers. His aunt by marriage, Princess Alexandra of Wales, who hated Hohenzollerns, felt he should keep away. The Channel was brilliantly sunny and furiously stormy. The Prince of Wales, dressed in a Prussian uniform, met his nephew at Victoria. Deathbeds, like weddings, create dramas, both comic and terrible. The Kaiser took over this deathbed. He sat beside his grandmother, propping her up with his one good arm, with her doctor on her other side. "She softly passed away in my arms," he said. He made himself the hero of the funeral procession too. He rode beside the new King on a huge white horse. In Windsor the horses pulling the gun-carriage with the coffin came to a standstill. William leapt down from his pale horse, and reharnessed them. They moved smoothly away. The English crowd cheered the German Kaiser. His yacht, *Hohenzollern,* was now moored in the Solent, and the royal families celebrated his birthday on 27th January. He seemed reluctant to go home. He proposed an alliance of the two Teutonic nations, the British guarding the seas, the Germans the land, so that "not a mouse could stir in Europe without our permission, and the nations would, in time, come to see the necessity of reducing their armaments."

The Prince of Wales carried out his own family rebellion, and let it be known that he proposed to reign as King Edward. Victoria and Albert had named him Albert Edward, but he chose to follow the six earlier English Edwards. "There is only one Albert," he said in his Accession Speech "by universal consent, I think deservedly, known as Albert the Good."

He was not, in Albert's way, a good man. He was immediately named "Edward the Caresser." He liked women, sport, good food and wine. Hilaire Belloc wrote a poem about the Edwardian house party.

> There will be bridge and booze 'till after three
> And after that, a lot of them will grope
> Along the corridors in *robes de nuit*
> Pyjamas or some other kind of dope.
>
> A sturdy matron will be set to cope
> With Lord —— who isn't "quite the thing"
> And give his wife the leisure to elope
> And Mrs. James will entertain the King.

There was a sense that fun was now permitted, was indeed obligatory. The stiff black flounces, the jet necklaces, the pristine caps, the euphemisms and deference, the high seriousness also, the sense of duty and the questioning of the deep meanings of things were there to be mocked, to be turned into scarecrows and Hallowe'en masks. People talked, and thought, earnestly and frivolously, about sex. At the same time they showed a paradoxical propensity to retreat into childhood, to read and write adventure stories, tales about furry animals, dramas about pre-pubertal children.

Olive Wellwood became, not very willingly, a matriarch. She had constructed her own good picture of the Todefright family, which was innocent and comfortable. There were sons and daughters and babies in various stages of creeping, crawling and tottering, there were children having real and imaginary adventures in the woods and on the Downs, there were informal gatherings round the fire in winter, or the lawn in summer, where old and young mingled and discussed things with laughter and serious common sense. There was the steady scratch of the pen nib in the study, parcels of manuscript Violet took to the post, the satisfactory cheques that arrived with the admiring letters of readers, both children and adults. This she had made, as surely as she made the worlds of fairytale and adventure which were nevertheless often more real to her than breakfast or bathtime. She and Violet alone knew that both worlds were constructed against and despite the pinched life of ash pits, cinders, rumbling subterranean horrors, and black dust settling everywhere. The woods, the Downs, the lawn, the hearth, the stables were a *real* reality, kept in being by continuous inventive willpower. In weak moments she thought of her garden as the fairytale palace the prince, or princess, must not leave on pain of bleak disaster. They were inside a firewall, outside which grim goblins mopped and mowed. She had made, had *written,* this world with the inventive power with which she told her stories.

She could not, and did not, imagine any of the inhabitants of this walled garden wanting to leave it, or change it, though her stories knew better. And she had to ignore a great deal, in order to persist in her calm, and listen steadily to the quick scratch of the nib.

At the time of the old Queen's death, she had a popular success with a collection of tales, which included the tale of the wraiths and puppets at the Grande Exposition, and the sinister and sly tale of *The People in the House in the House,* in which a child imprisoned some tiny folk in her doll's house, and was in turn imprisoned by a giant child.

A fashionable magazine sent a young woman to interview Mrs. Wellwood, and a photographer, who posed her, sitting by the fire in a rocking-chair in a velvet gown, reading to the assembled younger children, from Phyllis, now fourteen, and Hedda, now eleven, in smocked dresses and black stockings, their long hair, Phyllis's fair, Hedda's dark, shining on their shoulders, to Florian, now nine, and Robin, now seven, and Harry, now five, in sailor suits. Violet handed round cocoa and biscuits, and did not appear in the picture. The interviewer, whose name was Louisa Catchpole, wrote reverently of the shining heads of the listeners—"you could have heard a mouse squeak, or a beetle scurry," she wrote, entering into the style. She asked the children which was each one's favourite tale, and was slightly baffled by their answers. This meant that Olive found herself explaining that each child had his or her very own story, which was continually added to, and kept in the glass cupboard in a specially decorated book. Louisa Catchpole said this was a *charming* idea, and begged to see the books. The photographer took pictures of the cupboard, and of the imaginatively decorated covers of the individual tales. Miss Catchpole said to the children that they must feel they were very special people, having their *own* stories in this way. It was Phyllis who replied solemnly, oh yes, they *did* feel special.

The interview and pictures appeared under the headline "A Modern Mother Goose." The article spoke of Mrs. Wellwood's calm motherly presence, and her expressive voice, spicing the stories with mystery, thrills and dangers, all by the flickering firelight, in which more magical creatures could be seen. Mrs. Wellwood, Miss Catchpole said, held strong beliefs about the imaginative lives of children being just as important in education as verbs and triangles. Her grateful family extended far beyond the pretty children clustered round her, into all sorts of homes, privileged and plain, wherever a book of tales could be bought or borrowed. People in the present age, she opined, did not leave their childhoods behind them, as the earnest Victorians had done. Tales for children, like Mrs. Wellwood's, were read and discussed with delight, by old and young. There is an eager young child persisting in every lively grown-up, and Mrs. Wellwood knows how to address these children, as she knows how to entrance her own.

THE PEOPLE IN THE HOUSE IN THE HOUSE

THERE WAS ONCE A LITTLE GIRL *who was very kind to little creatures. She used to make nests and put them out hoping that birds would find them. She went fishing in the park for tadpoles and kept them in a big jam jar, and cried bitterly, when they all died. She made homes in matchboxes for caterpillars and ladybirds. And she had a beautiful doll's house, in which there lived a family of dolls with tiny china faces and stuffed bodies.*

She made lovely little meals for the dolls in the doll's house. She made jellies with individual bits of blackberry in them, and currant buns with one currant, and tiny tarts which slightly overlapped the pretty china plates in the doll's house. She put out tiny glasses of ice cream with red-currant jelly on top, and little biscuits with icing flowers on them. The awful bit was when the food went limp and had to be disposed of—in case it attracted mice, or other nasty creatures, like beetles and silverfish, her mother said. Her mother was keen on hygiene.

Her name was Rosy. Her mother liked roses. The doll's house was decorated in a variety of rosy pinks. Rosy sewed quilts and blankets and rugs for the dolls. She had tried clothes, but her sewing was not fine enough and the dolls looked ridiculous in the hats and jackets she made. So she made more and more sheets and blankets. Some of the dolls had ten or twelve each.

She pretended that the dolls made their own beds and cooked their own meals, and went to school, and slept, but she wasn't very good at pretending, and knew very well that they depended on her sharp fingers for every movement.

One day, going to the park in the city centre to look for creatures, she thought she saw a beetle running under a tree root. She laughed aloud because it looked like a little old lady in a stiff coat. Then she saw it was a little old lady in a stiff coat, waving some sort of stick in front of her, which Rosy had mistaken for the beetle's horns. So she sat down, very quietly, not too close—she was good at watching creatures—and after a time she saw two more little people run across the grass—sheltering in the shadows of leaves and pebbles—dressed in the same kind of stiff, tubelike brownish clothes. Their heads were encased in round black shiny hats. It was as though they were trying to disguise themselves as beetles.

She came often to watch them, after that. She saw that they had paths, as ants do, along which they always scurried. She brought a magnifying glass her uncle had given her, and studied the roots of the trees, when the little folk had gone into the ground. She found cupboards and larders, with rough, hardly visible shelves containing parcels and packages wrapped in dried leaves, and fine, fine little hooks from which dangled fine nets full of seeds—beech mast, thistledown, sunflower seeds. Under another root she found a barely visible covered market, with baskets made from nutshells set out on trestle tables made from twigs—all cleverly disguised to look randomly stacked, to the human eye, or the questing eye of a puppy. There were minute clay jugs and pannikins full of a fluid a little thicker than water, that might have been juice, or diluted honey. There were chestnut shell platters of what looked like new chopped meat, but she could not tell what kind of meat.

She watched their comings and goings, and learned the rhythm of their gatherings. They danced on a Tuesday, under the highest arch— their music sounded to her like nothing but a whisper and a scratch and a squeak—she could see their fiddle-like instruments, and their straw pipes, but not the string of the bow or the holes for the fingers. They did not go to market every day. They went twice a week, all jostling and—cheeping, like chickens, almost inaudibly. She put a few tiny glass beads around the roots, to see what they would do with them. They avoided them.

She thought how amazed they would be, to move out of their drab, furtive world into the rosy, silky comfort of her doll's house. She persuaded her mother to buy her a fine butterfly net—with a small diameter for close work—and took it down to the park, with a couple of jam jars, with strings and lids. Then she waited until their dancing was at its liveliest, put the mouth of the net over the arch of the root, and stirred vigorously amongst the dancers with a stick, so that they leapt into the air and dispersed every which way. As she had hoped, a few of them made the mistake of fleeing into the mouth of her net. She scooped them up—she had caught about eight—and carefully decanted them into the jars. She held the jars up to her eye, and peered in. She had three old ladies, two children, a young woman and two men of indeterminate age. They were all flat on their faces, under their cloaks, trying to look like dead insects or fallen leaves. But she knew better.

When she got them home, she opened the mouth of the net to the doll's house door, and shook the net, so that they would run in. They did not. So she had to prod them with a knitting needle, which looked a bit cruel, but was for their own good. Then they crawled and scrambled into the house and collapsed on the sitting-room floor. Rosy, considerately, drew the little pink silk curtain across the window, so they could recover in shade and privacy. Then she latched the front of the house securely and went away. They would recover, she thought, and settle in, and play with her. When she went back, they had drawn back the curtains, and their beady little faces were pressed against the windows, peering out. When they saw Rosy, they retreated, creeping under the dolls' beds, and behind the pretty sofas. Rosy put her presents in through the door—tartlets and sponge cakes, icing sugar flowers and hundreds and thousands, a pile of little party dresses and velvet jackets from the dolls' wardrobes. She noticed, of a sudden, that the little creatures had dragged and heaped the resident dolls into a kind of rubbish heap in one corner of the kitchen. She gave them some dolls' teapots full of lemonade in case they were thirsty.

They would not play. They were worse than the dolls, for they made sick little screaming sounds if she tried to pick them up and dress them, and one of them bit, or stabbed, her little finger, which developed a nasty sore. They didn't touch the pretty food, and they tore up the pretty dresses and made a kind of nest of them, on the beds and the sofas. She knew what she should have done, but she was stubborn, and lonely, and meant well, so she sat and whispered into the keyhole, and down the chimney, that she only wanted them to play, to enjoy the nice things in the house, she would give them all sorts of things they hadn't got, wheelbarrows, chests of drawers, even a little omnibus, if they would play with her. They pretended to be dead. She thought they might be starving, and hit on the idea of giving them dolls' pans full of porridge oats, which were more like the food they sold in their market.

She began to feel, without realising it, that she was gross and monstrous. Her chubby hands seemed to her like legs of ham, and her fingers were like rolling-pins.

She said, "Please, play with me, it is such a lovely house."

Now, it is necessary to know that Rosy's house was on the edge of a meadow, by a cold stream that had come leaping and rushing down the side of a mountain, and spread out into still pools across the flat grassland, under willows and white poplars. In the old days this side of the river had been known as the Debatable Land, and no one had built there, because over and beyond the mountain was a strange country where no one went, and from which strange things and creatures occasionally came. There were tales of wild wolves, flowing in grey clouds along the hillside, and tales of the fairy folk, in green cloaks, and soft boots, selling strange foods that melted in the mouth and drove young women to death and starvation, for they refused all other food after tasting these pale wafers and sharply sweet berries. There were also tales of giants, who had put huge legs over the ridge, and came down into the plain, filling their pockets with cattle and sheep, pulling up whole trees, and leaving sandy pits, which were their footprints. Rosy had been told these "fairy stories" and liked to hear them. Like all children, her nature was unsatisfied by what she could immediately see and touch. But also, like all children, she enjoyed the comfort of knowing that dragons and witches, giants and wood demons, are real only in a different world, where the mind, but not the body, can travel. "Over the mountain" changed colour, shape and topography constantly, as Rosy made it up, with little thrills of delight and safe fireside terror.

But perhaps we only dream such things because somewhere, some time, they are and were as we imagine them? Rosy told no one about the little people in her doll's house, who were solid enough, and cross enough, to be independently real. But they were not to be shared, in case, despite being solid, they vanished.

One day Rosy was lying on her stomach, gazing in at the window of the doll's house. Her mother had crossed the river to shop in the village. She heard a heavy sound, like a hammer on a road, or in a forge. Thud, thump, thud, a regular crashing. The floor of her house trembled, and Rosy trembled on it. The windows of her house darkened. She heard a great wind, sighing and soughing in the chimney. She lifted her head, and tried to look out of the window, and could not at first make out what she saw. It was black velvet dark, ringed with concentric splinters of palest blue, mixed with silvery threads and emerald-green lights. The circle of splinters was surrounded by something whitish, between blancmange and the white of a soft-boiled egg. It was an eye. It was an eye that was as big as the window. There was an enormous gruff grunt, like an oak tree falling. Then her house began to sway from side to side. And then to rise, as though some vast creature was pulling it up by the roots, which was indeed what was happening. Rosy felt very sick and held on to a stool, which didn't help, as the stool shot across the sloping floor and back. The house was lifted, shaken, and dropped, falling with a muffled sound into soft dark. Then it rose again, and began to move, jerk by jerk—huge jerks—stride by stride. Something, someone, had dropped the whole house into a monstrous sack, and was making off with it. Rosy began to cry. Finally—because the striding went on so long, she fell into something between a faint and a sleep.

Later she peeped cautiously out of the kitchen window of her house. She saw huge carved posts rising out of sight, and realised that they were the legs of a vast table, whose surface was out of sight. She made out a bucket as big as the house she was in, and a lot of overlapping coloured blankets, which she understood to be the edge of a rag rug, the size of a lawn. Then she heard thudding again, and saw a shiny shoe with a thick high white sock in it, a little girl's shoe, on a huge foot. There was a rustling and thumping, and the eye was to the window again. The front door opened. Rosy cowered against the kitchen wall. The giant child began to murmur and growl what Rosy could see were meant to be soothing sounds. A plump hand, the size of a sofa, squeezed in through the door, twisted, and reached with bolster-like fingers in Rosy's direction. Thumb and finger closed round Rosy, who was dragged, resisting, out of her own door and swung up in the air. The giant child was sitting on the rug, in a heap of scarlet skirts like the folds in a hilly landscape. She pinched Rosy's middle, and held her up to her eyes, frowning as she stared. She had a lot of thick shiny yellow hair, standing out round her head like the sun. Her breathing sounded like bellows. An eye that size is a terrible thing—wet colour round a black space *that opens into an unknown intelligence. There were more booming, sooth-ing sounds.*

Rosy twisted and squirmed and spat, like an angry kitten. She bit the finger that restrained her as hard as she could, which caused the giant child to yowl so loudly that Rosy thought her ears were bursting. She went on struggling and scratching and biting. A huge tear brimmed on the lower lid of the giant eye, flowed over, and fell, a heavy liquid sphere, and splashed on the hand that held Rosy. Another followed. Rosy found herself thrust back inside her door; the fingers extracted her key, fumbled, and turned it in the lock, from the outside. Then the shutters were pushed, from the out-side, against the windows, and Rosy's world went dusty dark.

She did not even think about the little people in her doll's house. She was reminded of them when the giant child opened the front door and pushed in a platter the size of a tea-tray full of chopped-up fragments of some fruit or vegetable—turnip or pear—with a sickly smell she couldn't bear. She had food, for the time being—the kitchen and the larder were stocked with biscuits and cheese. But her revulsion at the giant food made her suddenly full of misery about what she had done to her own captives. She knelt down by the doll's house, with tears running down her cheeks, and opened the hasp that kept the front wall closed, and said in a whisper, "I'm sorry, I'm so sorry. I would let you out, I should never have shut you in, but now we are all prisoners. I don't suppose you understand a word I say. I want to say I'm sorry. I'm sorry."

The little people had been crouching in the nest of toy bedclothes. One of the little old ladies stood up. To Rosy's amazement, she spoke. Her voice was high and scratchy, like a cricket sawing away with its legs. Rosy had to stop breathing to hear her.

"We do understand. That is, we understand your language. We don't understand why you took us prisoner and we don't want to. We want to go home."

"Oh, if only you could. But something—someone—has carried away me and my house and we are locked up in a giant kitchen. Come and look."

She took the old lady up, very carefully, and placed her on the table, so that she could see out through a crack in the shutters. The old lady com-

manded Rosy to fetch the others. She asked them, very politely, to step into her sewing-basket, and in this she lifted them all up to the window.

It was clear that they could make no sense of what they saw. Rosy said "That's a table-leg, and that's the edge of a rug. This is a dish of food it put in for me to eat, but it's loathsome and smells quite horrible. You have to believe me. It took the key and locked the door on the outside. It is a monster."

"You are a monster," whistled one of the little men, severely. "We know a monster when we see one."

"Oh I am so sorry," Rosy said again, beginning to cry. Her tears splashed into her sewing-bag amongst her captives, and one of the little children was hit full in the face by a balloon of salty liquid.

"You see," said Rosy, "we can't get out."

"You can't get out," said the little man. "We can. We can squeeze and scramble under your door, which doesn't fit perfectly. We can escape easily, but to what and to where we don't know."

At this point they all fell silent, as they heard the crashing footsteps of the giant child. The cracks in the shutters were full of the red light of her skirts. The monster looked to see if its offering of food had been accepted, and sighed heavily when it saw it had not. It spoke, incomprehensibly, booming like an organ in a church. Rosy stayed mum. The door closed again, and the key turned.

Rosy said

"When it's dark, you could all get out and run away to somewhere. I should think you're so little the monster can't even see you. You can run away like spiders."

The little old woman then said something surprising.

"If you—Miss Rosy Monster—can push the key to the floor from inside the house, we can slide under the door, where the step dips, and take with us a string, a rope, which we can tie to the key, so that you can pull it back to the inside, and open the door, and go out."

Rosy was dumbfounded.

"Why should you want to help me to get out?"

"Well," said another woman, "we could say practically that your legs are a great deal longer than ours when it comes to making our way home. Or you could say we don't approve of locking people up and making them into toys. Or you could say both." She added "Don't cry. It makes us damp."

Rosy said "Even if I get out, I don't know where we are, or how to get out of this kitchen."

"That's as may be," said the little man. "One thing at a time. First we get out, second we hide and hide—we are good at hiding, we can give you advice—then we work out the way home."

"We must have come over the mountain."

"Then we find the mountain, and cross it. Some advice, young monster. You will be dreadfully visible in a bright pink dress. Find yourself some clothes the colour of shadows and dead leaves before nightfall. And make yourself a satchel of food you can eat, and put in some oats for us. We can travel in this basket and hide amongst the bobbins of thread. Think what you will need on a journey. Something to cut and stab with. Something to drink from, for you and for us. Now go and find string, to make a rope to pull in the doorkey."

Rosy did as he said, and they waited till nightfall and all went as they had planned.

How they made their dangerous way home over fells and fens, how the large child helped the small people, and how they helped her, must wait for another tale . . .

27

No child, it is said, has the same parents as any other. Tom's parents had been younger and wilder than Robin's parents would ever be. Harry had never known a family where there were not older children who seemed free and powerful, came and went mysteriously, were not confined to the nursery. The little ones experienced the family as a flock of creatures who moved in clutches and gaggles, shared nurseries and also feelings and opinions. Tom and Dorothy were old, and separate enough to have started thinking of their own futures, away from Todefright, full of tenuous hopes and fears, and in Dorothy's case a rigorous and sometimes dispiriting ambition. Tom, at the end of 1900, was eighteen. His parents had a plan for his future—he was to sit matriculation exams in the autumn, and present himself as a candidate for a scholarship at King's College, Cambridge, at the end of the year. They had engaged tutors—Toby Youlgreave and Joachim Susskind. Beyond that they did not think very often about what was, or was not, going on in Tom's head. Olive continued—at intervals—to elaborate the adventures underground, and Tom read them, feeling, as the year moved on, an increasing unease, almost a *guilt,* for being still so caught up in a tale. He had a fit of vehement anger when the journalist came, and was shown the secret books, even though everyone knew about them, they were not *real* secrets. He said you didn't display that sort of private family thing to the public, as a kind of boasting. It wasn't *nice*. Olive said she hadn't intended to do it, it had just happened. They patched up the quarrel, but Tom glowered for two or three weeks.

Neither Humphry nor Olive really knew what subjects he was studying for matriculation. Humphry was away, much of the time, writing and lecturing. Olive sat in her study and scribbled. Violet made steak and kidney pie, and darned socks, and gave Tom biscuits and milk at bedtime when he looked tired. It occurred to both Toby and Joachim that Tom was possibly going to fail to matriculate. This was partly because he sometimes failed to turn up for lessons—he had gone for a long walk, had slept out in a tent, had forgotten, he was sorry. Joachim and Toby did not tell Humphry and Olive about these absences. They joined Tom on country walks and discussed Shakespeare and botany as they went.

Tom's exam results in the autumn were, in a way, both odd and shocking. He gained a distinction in elementary botany, but failed general elementary science. He failed Latin, and scraped through in English. He passed elementary sound, heat and light, and failed maths, which Joachim could not understand. It was all somewhat embarrassing for the tutors. The tutors also felt that Humphry and Olive should have been more perturbed than they were by the patchiness of the results, by the evidence of Tom's lack of interest or application. But they said, never mind, he can sit the exams again at the same time as the Cambridge exam. He will find a way to do it, said the parents, without any real evidence to justify this view.

In the months leading to the Cambridge exam Tom went out more and more, striding away in all weathers. He took his books to the Tree House. Dorothy, who was worried about him, didn't know how often he opened them. What she did know was that he had made friends with the gamekeeper with whom he walked the woods, tracking down predators and poachers, looking for illicit snares and traps. The gamekeeper had been hostile at first—gamekeepers don't like wandering children, or picnickers—but this one seemed to accept Tom as a serious apprentice. Tom showed Dorothy, one day, the gibbet on the black tarred wall of a forest hut. There they hung on nails, rows of dead beaked things, and things with sharp teeth opened in agony. Some were fresh—a staring owl, pinned by the wings, a broken-necked jay, a couple of stoats. Some had been rotted in wind and weather to no more than scraps of mouldered skin and the odd adhering bone, or tooth, or battered quill. Dorothy said it was horrible, and Tom said no, it was the way things really were, it was how the real world worked. Dorothy said lightly "Maybe really you'd rather be a gamekeeper?"

Tom said "Oh no, I've got to go to Cambridge, it's expected, this is just—I *like* finding things out from Jake, I like knowing new things—like woodwork—"

The week before the Cambridge exams, Tom went out at night, not with Jake, but alone. He didn't come back. Search parties set out—rather belatedly, as he'd been expected to return as he always did. He was found, unconscious, with a broken wrist and blood in his hair, in a shallow quarry. His ankle was still entangled in the wire snare he had caught it in, tracking poachers along the rim of the quarry, by moonlight. He didn't regain consciousness for two days, and when he did, appeared a little crazed, and couldn't remember what had happened to him. Violet brought him nourishing broth and fed him with a spoon. He lay bandaged among his pillows, staring mildly at the window and the sky.

It was, of course, quite impossible in the circumstances, that he should sit the Cambridge entrance examinations, or even, with a broken wrist, resit his failed matriculation exams.

Dorothy thought that at some level, he was *smug* about this.

Tom and Dorothy noted hidden and shadowy things in the family, and then, on the whole, did not think about them. They heard Olive operatic behind closed doors, or saw Humphry pack his bags and leave in a sudden hurry, and they took stock of these events, and stayed silent. They were both afraid of uncovering things they were better not knowing. Hedda had no such inhibitions. Hedda was a finder-out, a sleuth, a discoverer and uncoverer. In 1901 she was eleven, and belonged neither with the elder nor with the younger children. She had spent hours of her childhood lurking outside the Tree House, trying to overhear conversations to which she had not been invited. It was Hedda who pricked up her ears when Marian Oakeshott was meaningfully and casually mentioned at table, and Hedda who knew Mrs. Oakeshott's handwriting on letters, though she had never gone so far as to try to read one. She was a light sleeper, and padded about the house, at night, lurking on the back stairs, standing in shadows of tallboys on the landing. She knew that the grown-ups crept about the house at night. She knew—and had so far not shared her knowledge—that Humphry Wellwood visited Violet Grimwith in the small hours. He always closed the door with velvet softness. She had never had the nerve to listen at the keyhole, though she wanted to.

Then, one night, there was more than a susurration or a chuckle from behind that door. There was a storm of weeping, passionate and audible, and broken murmurs and shushings from a male voice. Violet wailed, and Hedda crept up, because she could hear the words in the wailing, and she could sense that the two inside were too locked in some sort of argument to be listening out for creeping children.

"It is possible that you are mistaken," said Humphry's voice, trying for calm.

"I wasn't mistaken before. I am only just past forty, it is perfectly *possible*. I can't go through it again, I can't, I can't, I can't. The pain and the fear and the hiding. I shall die. And *she* will kill me this time, she will . . ."

"Hush, little flower," Humphry improbably said. "I'll look after you, I always have, we'll sort it resourcefully, we always do. We are clever creatures, you and I. We mean no harm."

"She will kill me this time. And I cannot abide any more hiding and lying. The children of my body don't know they are mine—though in some sense they are *all* mine, *all,* who is their mother if not I? Oh, Booby, we can't start again, on concealing and pretending and contriving, I'm too tired, I'd rather die, I might do away with myself—"

"And where would all your lovely family be then? Keep still, keep calm, breathe deeply. I'll go down and fetch you a flask of brandy."

"Better gin," said Violet's voice, in choking sobs. "Better a great glass of neat gin."

Hedda stepped hurriedly into the shadow of the tallboy and flattened herself against a wall. The trim figure of her father whisked past her and flew down the back stairs. She was side-tracked in her thoughts by the silliness of the nickname. "Booby" diminished her clever and elegant father—just as the revelation of his relations with Violet diminished him. This was altogether less pleasant than his mistake with Marian Oakeshott. And Hedda didn't like the idea of Olive—whose greatest failing so far in her eyes was abstraction—a want of attention—being ready to "kill."

It was only then that she realised she had been told that some of the children—an unspecified number—were, as Violet had put it, Violet's children "of my body."

Who? Who was not who they thought they were?

What did it mean?

Hedda heard her father coming back, creeping in his slippered feet. She waited until he had gone back into the room, carrying a bottle and two glasses, and then she retreated. She had been changed, and she did not know how.

Hedda called a meeting of the elders in the Tree House. She had never done this. Meetings were called almost always by Tom, sometimes—when there were practical problems to discuss, like birthday presents—by Dorothy. The elders were Tom, Dorothy, Phyllis and now Hedda. She told them they had *got* to come, it was something very important, and it was secret, secret, secret.

. . .

They sat on their wooden stump stools, in the hidden interior crackling with brown bracken. Tom poured lemonade from a bottle into a mixed collection of enamelled mugs, blue, white and black. He said, a little lordly,

"Well, what is it?"

Hedda suddenly did not know how to begin. Once it was out in the open, it would start to *act* amongst them. At the moment, it was only eating at her.

"I've found something out."

"You're always finding things out. You shouldn't snoop."

"This is an *important* thing. It changes everything."

Tom had a vision of bankruptcy. Dorothy had a vision of her father leaving for good, perhaps joining Mrs. Oakeshott. Phyllis sat even more still than she had been. She had a great capacity for not moving, somewhere between composure and inertia.

"Spit it out," said Tom. "Now you've started, you'd better get on with it."

"I saw. I heard. He goes into Aunt Violet's bedroom late at night, and stays. I've seen him before. You can hear them. You can tell what they're doing."

"You don't *know* if you haven't seen them," said Dorothy.

"They make cuddling noises." She blurted out "He calls her, little flower. And she called him Booby."

This revelation upset everyone, and made them all angry. They were angry with Hedda for making them know this, rather than with Humphry and Violet for what they did and said.

"Last night she was crying a lot. She said she was sure about something, and that she hadn't been wrong before. She said she wished she could die. She said she was frightened."

"Well?" said Tom, his imagination recoiling. Hedda looked at Dorothy, who was going to be medical. Hedda's brow was creased with pain and rage.

"She was *saying*," said Hedda, "that she was going to have a baby, that's what she was saying. And she said—she'd had babies before—she said—I heard—some of us are really *hers*. Children of my body she said."

The melodrama of the phrase felt improbable to Tom and Dorothy, just as the word "Booby" had done. But once it was *said* it was in the world. Their irritation with Hedda increased.

"So?" said Tom, with a little spirit. If there was one thing in the world he was sure of, it was that he was his mother's son. "I don't see what you think we can do."

"If we aren't—who we think we are—it might be good to know."

"I don't think so," said Phyllis, flatly. "What good would it do? We are still the same people, in the same house, with the same family."

Dorothy's thoughts were whirring. She didn't look like Tom, she had always felt only precariously attached to the group life. Different. All children felt "different," she had always supposed. She felt that she had always irritated Olive. She had thought that was perhaps because Olive loved Tom too completely to have enough love left over for her. But maybe . . .

The story Olive wrote for her rose up in her mind's eye. It was about shape-changers, scuttling, bustling little people who hung up animal skins on the hooks in the kitchen, and then put them on, and became half-hedgehogs, to go out into the bushes and ditches.

Violet was a scuttling, bustling little person, whose nature was domestic, like the aproned hedgehog-women in the underground kitchens of Dorothy's tale.

Dorothy wanted *not* to be imaginative. She wanted to measure chemicals and mend limbs and organs. But her imagination was just and fierce. If anyone *was* Violet's child, she herself probably was.

She did not say any of this to anyone. She said to Hedda

"I could shake you till your teeth rattled."

"I don't know why you're all so cross with *me*. You should be cross at them."

Some sort of deep prohibition prevented all four of them from making any effort to imagine the emotions, the predicament, the delights and terrors, of Booby and little flower. Their minds were busy with rearranging the family patterns in their heads, like chessboards which suddenly lacked a bishop and had too many knights, or where the queen ran amok in zigzags.

Knowledge is power, but not if it is only partial knowledge and the knower is a dependent child, already perturbed by a changing body, squalling emotions, the sense of the outside world looming outside the garden wall, waiting to be entered. Knowledge is also fear.

Tom dealt with Hedda's revelation by absconding on a long walk, stomping along the Downs, carrying his bedding on his back. Walking fast is a good way of channelling all sorts of emotions: fear, desire, panic.

Phyllis rearranged everything in her chest of drawers and her little desk. She mended a torn apron. Violet said she would have done that, and Phyllis said she *knew,* but she could do it herself.

Hedda thought bluntly that more knowledge would reduce the menace of the knowledge they had. She listened to every sentence the adults said to each other, and decided that, since they had been so deceived, she did after all have a right to read people's letters, when the opportunity presented itself.

Dorothy looked at everything as though it might vanish. The bright daily pottery, the spice-jars, the sweep of the staircase, the pigeons in the stable yard. What had been real was now like a thick film, a coloured oilcloth, spread over a cauldron of vapours which shaped and reshaped themselves into shadowy forms, embracing, threatening, glaring.

She looked at Violet. She had always reproached herself for not liking Violet. Violet was pernickety and small-minded, Violet was the female fate she meant to avoid by having a profession in the world. She had, she now saw, slightly despised Violet for minding another woman's children. That must be revised. Violet had once said to her that they, Violet and Dorothy, had "the same eyes" and she had wanted to say, no they didn't, and had had to admit that they did. Dorothy took to looking furtively at Violet, which made Violet shrug as though a mosquito was buzzing. Dorothy still could not manage to *like* Violet, and was only abstractly sorry for her.

She stopped reading her fairytale, in its leaf-green notebook. It was only added to occasionally when the mood took Olive to think about wild things and little people. It was not like *Underground,* whose tale flowed compulsively on through the tunnels and corridors. After a time, wryly and crossly, Dorothy realised that Olive had not *noticed* that she was not reading it. It confirmed her cynical perception that Olive wrote for Olive, and was most complete in the act of reading and writing herself.

There were secrets also covered over in Purchase House, though perhaps there the covering was more frayed and threadbare than in Todefright. Philip had come back from Paris full of new knowledge about how his body worked, and new fears that he might have caught madness and death from his tutor. He was lucky. His body remained healthy and was only tormented by the dull ache, and the feverish greed, to do it again. He was edgy and wary with Benedict Fludd, who went into what was for him a good-humoured flurry of inventiveness, and needed constant assistance. He felt distant from Elsie, the stay-at-home in the kitchen. He did not notice her new shoes, or the red belt. He found it much—much—harder to be phlegmatic when Pomona sleepwalked and made her way into his bedroom. He did not particularly desire Pomona—there was something marbly, or even soapy, about her firm young flesh. But he desired *someone* so much that Pomona's slippery, sleepy embraces became a torment.

Elsie's mind had been full of the modelled jars and obscene nymphs. But for a long time she did not show them to Philip. At first she was afraid of Fludd, who might notice that the key had been moved and used, or might suddenly appear and catch her, looking, *in flagrante delicto,* but in the spring of 1901, on a day when Fludd had gone up to London to see Prosper Cain and Geraint, when Seraphita and Pomona were out to tea with Miss Dace in Winchelsea, she said to Philip that she had something to show him, and something to tell him.

She fetched the key. They stood in the cobwebby shadow of the locked pantry and stared at the whitely glimmering forms, the breasts, the vulvas, the chaste flower-shaped containers that, seen from another angle, were swollen female bellies. Philip, like Tom and Dorothy with Hedda, felt embarrassed and irritated by the revelation. It would have been more seemly, he vaguely felt, for Elsie to pretend to have seen nothing. He said "Well?" meaning "So what?" but it didn't ring true. Professional curiosity overcame both his sexual stirring and his distaste. He picked up one or two vases, turned over a reclining girl-child and found a swollen, almost man-size, clitoris. He remembered Fludd's fingers on Rodin's creatures.

"It's them," said Elsie. "He makes pots about *them*. It isn't right."

"Of course it isn't. But they might not know. It isn't our business. We should lock it up."

"I think they know. But I don't know what they think about it. Perhaps he—"

Perhaps he puts himself inside them, she wanted to say, and couldn't, but Philip heard the meaning of the silence.

"It isn't our problem. *You* shouldn't be thinking about such things."

"I have something to tell you. I'm going to have to go away. You'll have to do without me."

Philip turned to her, still holding the girl-on-her-stomach. He stammered. Had she got a job? Was she thinking of getting married?

No, said Elsie. She was going to have a baby. She would be cast out. If you looked at—all this—it would be unfair to turn her out, but that was what would happen. She would have, she said, in a steely way, to find one of those places for Fallen Women that the do-gooders talked about. She needed Philip to help her to do that.

Philip tried to say that someone must be responsible, and ask who he was. Fludd, Geraint, the fisher-boy?

"I'm not saying any more, and you won't make me. Just help me to go away, without a lot of scenes and shouting. I can't abide to be told off and shouted at. I can't and won't abide it."

She was terribly on edge. Philip put the china girl down and put his arm round his sister.

"I'll think of something," he said, rather hopelessly. He didn't know how he could or would, or what he would think of. But, in the event, he did.

He felt he could talk better to a man, and decided on Frank Mallett. He walked over to Puxty and said he needed to talk to the vicar in private.

Frank Mallett was not a judging man. His own temptations, made so much more comfortable by the sturdy openmindedness of Edward Carpenter, made him generous to the differing temptations of others. He listened to Philip, who was both worried and censorious, and remarked mildly that a person was about to come into the world in difficult circumstances, and needed the best possible start. It would be a good thing, he said, if it could all be managed without too much blame or punishment. *Gently,* said Frank Mallett. Did Philip know who the father was? Was marriage possible or desirable, was there likely to be any support, moral or financial?

"She won't say," said Philip. "She's hard as a rock. She's not going to say. So I don't think she's getting married, and I don't think she's expecting help."

"Don't take it too hard yourself," said the vicar. "I don't know how the family at Purchase House could manage without your sister. I can't see any help in appealing to them—they'd be baffled, merely. In different ways."

"They don't pay her a penny. It isn't really right, but they've made a good sort of—well, not a home—place to be, for the pair of us."

"I *think*," said Frank Mallett, "I shall consult the good ladies of Romney Marsh. But I shall consult them privately. I shall not put the case to the Home for Fallen Women, or the charitable trusts. No, I shall invite the imaginative ones to tea. Miss Dace, I think, who is practical and generous. Mrs. Oakeshott, who knows what it is to bring up a single child. And maybe Mrs. Methley, who has become a friend of Miss Dace, and is anxious for employment. I shall ask for their help."

"I don't want them to lay into Elsie or talk down to her. Even if she's been daft."

"I think with the best will in the world you won't avoid a little talking-down. You could even argue it would be *deserved*. But I think they'll find practical steps to take."

Frank's tea-party—to which he invited neither Philip nor Elsie—went well. It produced some interesting insights into the feelings of the three ladies. They were brisk, and they were practical, and they were kindly disposed. Miss Dace knew of a nursing home which would look after the young woman when the time came. She said that she and the Sister in charge of the Forget-me-not Home had together arranged several successful adoptions, quite quietly. Marian Oakeshott remarked mildly that it was always possible that Elsie would want to keep the child. Though she needed to be able to keep her job, if possible, and her board and lodging.

Phoebe Methley had said little. She said suddenly, with passion,

"It is a terrible thing to separate a mother from her children—from her child. We are fighting the injustices of the law on this—we should be careful not simply to grasp at a young woman's child and take it away." She paused. "Love," she said. "Love. Romantic sweeping-away, and loss of self. The trouble with the sex instinct is its power. It deranges you and makes you mad. But true love—true steady love—is what a woman feels for the child in her arms, for the sight of its head, bobbing on the lawn outside the window. You can't take that from her, without being very sure you're doing the right thing."

Miss Dace put her head on one side, and smiled, dryly, but with friendship. Marian Oakeshott said

"Of course I agree. Of course I know—"

She looked at Phoebe Methley. Both women thought they knew who was the father of Elsie's child.

"We are all friends here," said Phoebe. "It must be clear that I feel this personally. I have three children in Yorkshire whom I had to leave because—because of my great love for Herbert. There is not a day—not an hour—when I do not *feel* their absence and distance as a perpetual pain. I may never see them again. I envy you your Robin," she said to Marian, "whenever I see him. I admire you so greatly for what you have been able to do—to have your son, and to work, and to be independent."

"It occurs to me," said Marian, "that I myself may be the solution. Elsie Warren may wish never to see this unborn child again. I do not know her state of mind. But I employ a young woman to mind Robin, who could easily undertake the care of another child, whilst its mother worked—and then the child could return to its mother for weekends and holidays—"

"Someone," said Frank, "would need to talk to the people at Purchase House. They cannot do without either Philip or Elsie. They should, in my view, be paying both of them good wages for everything they do. They could be talked into seeing their own best interests, as well as their charitable duty—"

"If—if the father of the child is not in that family," said Miss Dace, blushing.

"He is not," said Phoebe Methley. "I am certain of that."

She too was blushing. Frank handed round a plate of shortbread. He said

"First, we must put this—this very satisfactory and generous plan—to Elsie. Then, one of us must talk to Mrs. Fludd. I am never quite sure that she really hears what I say, or remembers it. Who shall we send?"

The three good fairies looked at each other. Which of them could be most calm, most reasonable, most pragmatic?

. . .

In the end they decided they would all three speak to Elsie, and deputed Frank to ask Philip to bring her to Miss Dace's little house. They were enjoying each other's company—each felt—in the discussion of this intimate problem, that they had discovered new, real, friends.

Elsie came into Miss Dace's drawing-room and stood to attention, looking angry. She was wearing her hat, and one of Imogen's loose mediaeval gowns, neatly darned and patched. Miss Dace begged her to sit down, and gave her a cup of tea, some cubes of sugar, a slice of fruit-cake. They had agreed that they must not frighten the young woman with moral lectures. She sipped her tea, and drew her head back, like, Marian Oakeshott thought, a frightened snake ready to strike. Miss Dace spoke. It was her drawing-room.

"We know about your problem, Elsie, your predicament, and we haven't asked you here to lecture you, but to tell you how we intend to help you. I myself know a respectable—and kindly, very kindly—lady who will help with—with the birth of the child."

"We don't know," said Marian Oakeshott, "what you will want to do when the child is born. I should like to say that—if you so wish, if you want to . . . if you like . . . I would be happy to ask Tabitha to take on its care so that you could continue to work for Mrs. Fludd and to be with your brother."

Elsie was silent, her head still back. Marian said

"Then you could come to the child, or he could come to you, in your time off—you would not be separated."

Elsie said nothing.

Phoebe Methley said "We propose to speak on your behalf to Mrs. Fludd, and make the arrangements clear and satisfactory."

Elsie said slowly

"There's been a deal of talking about me behind my back."

"You are in a situation," said Marian, "where that inevitably happens. We are truly trying to help."

"I came to your meeting about women. I suppose I'm a single woman, and a Fallen Woman." She paused. She said, looking pale, "I really don't feel very well. I don't know as I can go on, anyway, hauling buckets and hanging over stoves."

"I shall ask my good doctor to examine you," said Miss Dace. "He will tell you what you may and may not do, in your condition, and give you tonics to help you, things like that."

"I *am* grateful," Elsie said slowly and flatly. "It's more than I could hope for."

"But—" said Marian Oakeshott, "there is a *but* in your voice. You may speak freely to us, we should prefer it."

"I never meant to go into Service, ma'am. *What I do not want* is to slave in someone else's kitchen and wash their clothes for the rest of my life. I didn't and don't want that. And now it seems my only way forward. I thought it was temporary, till Philip got to know his craft and got well known, as he *will,* and has the help here he needs. My mother was a paintress—she was a good paintress, the most delicate with her brushes of any in the studio—she died of it, of the chemicals in the air. She wasn't a skivvy, she wasn't a scullery-maid, she was an artist. You care about women's work, I've heard you talk. All of you. So I'll admit to you, I don't have Philip's talent. He has a *right* to expect to be an artist. I don't. But that don't mean I want to be a skivvy."

A sudden moment of involuntary spite came over her.

"And that lot are so useless and helpless and don't pay me a penny. And I've got this *lump* in me, that turns about and about, and will come out and need vests and caps and milk, and how can I make do, when I get *nothing*—"

"Don't cry," said Marian.

Elsie gulped.

"I shan't. I daren't. I've got to keep myself together."

Phoebe Methley said "What you say is true and moving. But you must admit—you are in this situation because of things you have done—about which Philip tells us it is no good to ask, so we are not asking. You are probably not the most guilty person in this muddle, but we are talking about help, not about guilt. And there is *one* entirely innocent person, who is not yet born, and must be cared for."

"Will you agree to us talking to Mrs. Fludd?" asked Miss Dace.

"I don't seem to have much choice. No, don't listen to me, that's not fair of me. I *am* grateful to you ladies—I couldn't have expected so much—I am, I am. But I am scared stiff, too. I've always been a strong one."

The three good ladies became more frank as they grew more intimate over the moral problem of the fate of Elsie Warren's baby. They held, and enjoyed, a long discussion of how best to approach Seraphita Fludd. They agreed that they had little idea what she thought or felt about anything. "Never have I met a woman so determinedly *vague,*" said Miss Dace, whose disposition was the opposite of vagueness. They imparted to each other what was common knowledge about her history. Her name was not Seraphita. She had been separated from her class by her great beauty. She had been, in late Pre-Raphaelite, early Aesthetic days, a "Stunner" and had modelled for Millais. The ladies agreed that she was still a lovely woman. The proportions of her facial bones were perfect, said Marian Oakeshott. "And all that mass of hair, hardly faded," said Phoebe Methley. "She doesn't look you in the eye, ever," said Patty Dace. "It isn't that she's devious, it is that she's *absent.*" They agreed comfortably that she had no idea how to run a house, or how to bring up children. Geraint had run wild, and the poor girls—though lovely to look at, as their mother was—had no social *nous,* no common sense even. They had heard that Geraint was doing well in the City, having thrown over the whole pastoral aesthetic.

Marian said it was quite possible that Seraphita had come from much the same world as Elsie, but she entirely lacked her common sense or her willingness to make do.

Patty Dace said that that fact could make her harsher with Elsie's predicament, or more sympathetic, there was no way of knowing. She might feel she had to keep up appearances.

"*What* appearances?" asked Phoebe Methley, tartly. "They're all darned and draggled, or were before Elsie took over."

"And Elsie seems to be saying that she isn't *paid.*"

"That isn't right."

"It's not. Is it our business?"

"What about *him* in all this," asked Marian Oakeshott. "He's another, you don't know what he thinks, or feels, or what drives him, except the making of beautiful pots. For which it appears he needs Philip."

"I do not know them well," said Phoebe Methley. "But I have to say, I have never seen him address one word to his wife. Not one word. Once I had noticed this, I observed him a little. He may have married her for her beauty, but his eye passes over her as though she were a jug, and not a masterwork of ceramics, but a common earthenware crock."

They were overexcited by their own openness. Miss Dace did not feel able to speculate about anyone's sex instinct or sexual behaviour.

Indeed she preferred to ignore such matters. But Marian Oakeshott, daring, said to Phoebe

"I saw him brush against her on the lawn. He flinched. And she turned that head of hers *the other way*."

"Are we any nearer to knowing what to say to her?" asked Miss Dace.

"Has she any substance to oppose to our decisiveness?" asked Marian. "Can we not overwhelm her with our calm certainty about what is best to be done?"

The day they went to speak to Mrs. Fludd was a bright spring day. They found her sitting in the orchard in a sagging basket chair, working—or about to work—on a circular tapestry frame, with a basket of wools open in the grass at her side. Marian Oakeshott, who had seen some Impressionist paintings, thought that Seraphita resembled a painting by Monet or a painting by Millais. The apple branches cast dappled shadows over the chalky face, which gave the impression of being blurred, as though rapidly and sketchily filled in. She was wearing floating dove-coloured muslin, which again appeared brushed-up, in the half-shadow, and her long fingers and long neck were insubstantially slender and very slightly textured, shantung, not smooth silk. Her large eyes were surrounded by slatey skin, slightly puffed, with liquid under it. The skeins of wool in the basket were bright jewel colours, emerald, amber, jacinth, sapphire, ruby. They were precise and sharp amongst the floating cloudiness. She greeted them without rising. It was delightful to see them, she said. Where was Elsie? Elsie would bring more chairs, and make tea. Marian said Elsie had gone into Rye, and that she herself would find more chairs, which she did, dragging them in from other parts of the orchard and garden. They had something particular to say, said Marian. It was no accident that Elsie was out.

Seraphita dropped her frame into her lap, and had to hunt for her needle. She said she hoped Elsie had done nothing bad.

"Have you noticed nothing—about Elsie?" asked Phoebe.

"No," said Seraphita flatly, her eyes widening.

"Elsie is expecting a baby," said Miss Dace. "In the summer. She hasn't seen a doctor, it is not precise."

There were several long moments whilst Seraphita took this in, and

seemed to decide what to say. Her face creased up, with thought perhaps, although it looked as though she was about to cry. She said in a
faint voice

"Who . . . ?"

As she didn't finish the sentence, none of the ladies felt a need to
answer.

Seraphita next brought out

"I should send her away . . . ?"

This exasperated all three ladies, who all knew that Elsie cost
Seraphita nothing, and saved her a good deal. Marian, more kindly,
noticed a plaintive hint of social fear in the wavering voice. Seraphita
was afraid of being judged for *not* sending Elsie away. Marian said

"We came to discuss with you the possibility of *not* doing that, Mrs.
Fludd. We are very aware of the importance of Elsie's work to the comfort of this household—you and your family," she said, lying, "have
often told us so. And it is a very happy circumstance that both Elsie and
her brother have been so welcome here, and contributed so much.
Philip confided in the Reverend Mallett, who consulted us, as, so to
speak, busybodies or good fairies, we hope. With your agreement, we
can make arrangements for the lying-in, and for the care of the child,
should Elsie wish to keep it, and continue to keep her place here."

Seraphita went white, which might have been thought impossible.
Even her lips blanched. She breathed a series of unachieved phrases,
kind, too kind, such a shock, so unexpected, and again who . . . ? and
the whispered word "responsible"? Marian could see her trying *not* to
think of either her husband or her son in connection with that word.
Unlike Phoebe Methley, Marian did not have a clear idea of the unmentionable male, and had wondered about both Benedict Fludd, and the
lively and handsome Geraint. She answered obliquely

"I am sure if Elsie feels that there is no obstacle to her staying here,
you need not worry, Mrs. Fludd. And we have talked to Elsie, who
accepts our plans, or appears to."

"She doesn't feel very well," said Miss Dace. "I hope you will
encourage her to work less hard for a few months. I am arranging for
her to see my doctor."

Seraphita did not offer to pay the doctor. She was beginning to tremble. She said

"Do as you think best . . . infinitely grateful . . ."

She said, in a different voice, staring into space,

"It is a terrible thing to be a woman. You are told people like to look at you—as though you have a duty to be the object of . . . the object of . . . And then, afterwards, if you are rejected, if what you . . . thought you were worth . . . is after all not wanted . . . you are nothing."

She gave a little shrug, and pulled herself together, and said "Poor Elsie," in an artificial, polite, tea-party voice, though she had not offered, and did not offer, to make tea.

The secrets in the house in Portman Square were of a more innocent kind, which might be thought odd, since Basil and Katharina Wellwood inhabited the fringes of the new, naughty social world of the pleasure-loving King. Both children, Charles/Karl and Griselda, were secretive, which distressed their parents, who nevertheless did not bring the subject up. Katharina Wildvogel had inherited a great deal of money, and employed a large number of servants. Her secret was that she was temperamentally a hausfrau. She would have loved to bake and sew and discuss clothes with her daughter, and perhaps even advise her son on affairs of the heart. She herself had no pretensions to beauty—she was slender, and carried herself well, and chose her hats and shoes and jewellery with taste. She saw Griselda as the being who would do, rightly and easily, everything she herself had had to struggle with, contrive, approximate. Griselda at seventeen was indeed—in her pale, fragile way—almost a beauty, with a pretty figure and a clean-cut face under her white-blonde hair. She was, or said she was, not interested in dressing-up. She spent as much of her time as she could with her cousin Dorothy. They were trying to become educated women, though in both cases their parents were only half-hearted about the education, and had to be badgered and pestered to arrange classes at Queen's College, or tutorials with Toby Youlgreave and Joachim Susskind.

Dorothy's path was harder—she did not live in London, and had to travel up by train, or stay for days together in Portman Square, aware that Katharina, though she liked Dorothy well enough in herself, deprecated her influence on Griselda's ambitions. Dorothy got moral support from Leslie and Etta Skinner, who arranged for her to attend demonstrations and experiments at University College. But she was aware that the Todefright Wellwood family income fluctuated alarmingly, and dared not ask for too much. The life of the mind was easier for Griselda, who sat curled in the window-seat reading—at great speed—histories, philosophies, poems and fiction. Griselda felt both pain and pleasure over being secretly in love with Toby Youlgreave. Of course he must never know, but the tingle of imprecise desire delighted Griselda whilst she felt vaguely frustrated. And it meant she saw herself as set apart. She did not have to worry about Charles's friends flirting, or her mother's preoccupation with suitable dancing partners.

They were troubled, as intelligent girls at the time were troubled, by the question of whether their need for knowledge and work in the world would in some sense denature them. Women worked, they knew, as milliners and typewriters, housekeepers and skivvies. They worked because they had no means, or were not pretty or rich enough to attract a man. The spectre of imaginary nuns haunted them. If Griselda did manage to be admitted to Newnham College, in Cambridge, would it be like entering a nunnery, an all-female community, mutually supporting intellectual desire and ambition which the world at large still saw as unnatural, and frequently as threatening? Griselda's quiet love for Toby reassured her on this front also—she had ordinary womanly feelings, she was not a freak, or a withdrawn contemplative. She just wanted to be able to *think*.

Dorothy was sterner—she had to be—the path she had chosen was still into hostile country, even though there were now a respectable number of qualified women doctors in the world, and a new women's hospital. The life of the mind, and the truly useful life of medicine, would doom her, too, to the inhabiting of an all-female community. Women doctors treated only women, and worked with other women doctors. One side of her nature would have to be denied, in order for her to become the professional person she meant to be. It was not so for males. Men doctors married, and their wives supported their surgeries, and comforted them when they were tired. In low moments, late at night, Dorothy asked herself if she was some kind of monster. But she went on, at least partly because she could not imagine confining her life to frills, furbelows, teacups, gossip. If women only, better the operating theatre than the sewing-circle. But it wasn't easy.

Charles's secret, his political opinions, caused him paradoxically to live in the frivolous, parasitic way those opinions condemned. He didn't want to commit himself to university, and kept telling his father he needed time to work out what he really wanted to do and be. He went on European cultural journeys, frequently to Germany, since he was, after all, half-German. He talked Joachim Susskind into accompanying

him for tours of six or eight weeks—thus putting a great strain on
Dorothy's instruction and disrupting her planned progress. Susskind
was originally from Munich, and liked to go back there and talk anarchism and other forms of disorder—sexual, theatrical, religious—in the
Café Stefanie, and in the Wirthaus zum Hirsch in Schwabing. Charles/
Karl was introduced to a psychoanalyst, wild Otto Gross, and the social
anarchist Gustav Landauer. He went to satirical cabarets, which he did
not follow, because his German was not idiomatic enough, and his local
political knowledge was nonexistent. But he loved the smoke-filled air
and the smoke-stained ceilings and the air of serious, witty wickedness
and idealism. He would have liked to be a writer or a painter, but was
not sure he could write or paint. He bought a sketch-pad and drew some
secret cows and naked women, both of which were so wooden that he
tore them up. Munich was full of serious, laughing women, painting in
the open air. He loitered behind them, and watched their wrists turn
as they put the strokes of paint on the canvas. He said to Joachim that he
would like to stay long enough to take lessons in art or design. Joachim
said complacently that München was a cauldron of creativity.

28

Prosper Cain was troubled by his responsibility for his motherless daughter, who was becoming a young woman. He feared she was in love, and he feared the love was hopeless. Before Julian went to Cambridge, he and Florence had been very close, reading the same books, taking walks together, arguing about the nature of things. Now Julian was at King's he had moved into the penumbra of the secret society, the Apostles, and was being watched by young men like Morgan Forster, to see whether he would be a suitable embryo, to be propagated and "born" as a member, on the sacred hearthrug. The sponsor of an embryo was, in the occult language, his "father." The members of the Society were Reality: everything else was merely Phenomenal. An older student, Gerald Matthiessen, a brilliant Classic, had taken an interest in Julian, with a view to potential fatherhood. He had invited him to breakfast, and taken him on long walks across the Fens. They had discussed Plato, the Aesthetic movement, the nature of virtue, the nature of love. They mocked each other, intently, like sparring partners in a gymnasium. Julian had at first thought that his own penchant for irony, his belief in the dangers of seriousness, would put off Gerald, the passionate thinker, the moralist. Gerald was handsome, in the way Julian himself would have been handsome—fine, narrow, dark, slightly evasive, even sly. Julian's ideal lover was still someone blond and outdoor and innocent: Tom Wellwood. He was aware that Gerald was interested in him. Many of their conversations turned on male love, and the sublimation of base desires. *Tamen usque recurret,* murmured Gerald, one night over port. Julian, feeling like a girl, looked down at the cheese and grapes on his plate, and smiled a secretive smile. He rather thought he was putting up with the motes of sexuality in the light from the windows, the sensuality breathed like cigarette smoke and thinning out into the general air, just in order to be able to talk so intensely. But then again, maybe it was becoming his natural atmosphere. He invited Gerald to stay in the South Kensington house—"you will find the quarters cramped, but we have courtyards and staircases and secret cupboards to dream about."

. . .

Prosper Cain was a connoisseur but not a university man. He had spent his life in the army, which was also a male enclave, and he knew the value of intense comradeliness, even though he knew nothing at all about the Apostles. He also, with deep alarm, saw that Florence was studying the male couple wistfully, was standing outside the *pas de deux* wanting to be let in. She could not fall in love with Julian. Nothing more natural than that she should fall in love with Julian's other self, totally eligible, totally at home in the world she had grown up in. Simply because she was female, Florence was the creature Prosper Cain loved most in the world. He loved his son very nearly as much, except for the extra slight rage of protectiveness. He was offended to see his poised Florence with an expression of anxiety, or wistfulness, or looking lost and left out. He talked amiably to Gerald about majolica and putti, about Palissy and dried frogs and toads, and wanted to stab him in the heart for ignoring his daughter. For Gerald did not see Florence, except as a generic girl. He also did not see Imogen Fludd.

Imogen was doing good work as a jewellery designer. The small scale, the precision, the concentration suited her. She made some delightful asymmetrical silver pendants, decorated with drooping threads of tiny pearls like water-drops on spider-webs, and some elegant horn combs, to wear in the hair, inlaid with slivers of ebony, mother-of-pearl, and enamelled copper, one of which she gave to Florence. The art students liked her, but she was intimate with none of them, and did not appear to expect to be. She went only occasionally back to Purchase House, never alone, with Geraint, or—once or twice—with Florence. She had her mother's long neck and large eyes, and might have been beautiful if she had been more animated. In 1901 she was already twenty-two. At Easter she presented Prosper with a little jewelled egg she had been working on in secret, midnight-blue outside, pure milky white inside, studded with little moons and stars and crescents made of fine slivers of gold and pearl. Inside the egg was a gold charm in the shape of a phoenix, with crimson eyes and flaming crest. When she handed it to him, the blood flared up her neck and cheeks. "I owe you *so much*," she said, in an almost-whisper. Cain put his arms round her, and felt the liveliness of her spine and the soft weight of her breasts. She needed a husband, he thought. She needed love, and a life of her own.

He conceived the romantic idea of giving a dance—a dance for Florence and also for Imogen. He would have given it on Midsummer Eve, but he wanted to invite the Todefright Wellwoods, and it would not do to clash with their annual festivities. So he decided on May 24th, the birthday of the late Queen, which fell on a Friday. He discussed the matter with Olive Wellwood, when she was visiting the Museum and checking gold and silver treasures. It was hard for him, he told Olive, to bring up a motherless daughter as he should. His Florence was eighteen, and should be thinking about things like "coming out," he supposed, though she also talked about following Julian to Cambridge. He had the idea of giving a supper and dance—not too formal—in the Museum itself. He thought a small orchestra—the Regiment could make one up—could play in the tea-room in the evening. It would be very pleasant to see the young people dancing amongst the ceramic work of the students, and between the Minton pillars. And the Morris Green Dining-Room could be used as a kind of retirement room, where guests might sit and chat, or eat sorbets.

Olive was enthusiastic. It would be wonderfully romantic, she said. Like the dancing princesses in the hidden palace under the lake—it would have the pleasure of being secret and impossible. The Museum was impossible, in many ways, at present, said Major Cain. It was full of dust from the huge building works, it was not peaceful, as the hammers crashed and the drills howled. But in the evenings the tea-room was quiet and the dust had settled. He was in need of a fairy godmother to help organise everything. He did not think his company sergeants would understand romantic dances for young ladies. He wondered . . .

Olive Wellwood, like very many women who have risen from the lower classes, felt a primitive terror, a gulf opening at her feet, when asked to deal with social complexities she had never learned. She could not do it, she saw immediately, she would betray herself again and again. And yet, the delight of working with Major Cain, of being confided in, of exchanging confidences. Her mind whirled, frantically in her head, like a rat in a cage. She could give socialist, unconventional parties in her own garden. She made her own rules, and Humphry could carry off anything. But something semi-military, in the Victoria and Albert Museum, is quite another matter. She said

"You know, I think you would do best to consult Katharina Wellwood, my sister-in-law. She wants so much to give parties and buy dresses for Griselda, and Griselda retreats into books, and says she wants to study at university. Griselda and Dorothy are quite naughty. They won't join in. But *here*—she would be in her element—it is just what she most wants—"

Katharina was delighted. She discussed catering and flowers with Prosper. She recommended dressmakers and shoe shops. Griselda submitted to being measured for a new, grown-up party dress. Dorothy was to have her first real evening dress and Florence her first grown-up dance dress. They were like princesses in fairytales who had been given magic walnuts or acorns, which they cracked, and out floated beauty.

Florence's dress was white lace over dark pink silk, with a silk rose in the low neck, and elbow-length lace sleeves. Griselda's was made of Liberty silk, in grass-green strewn with floating white and gold flowers, lilies of the valley, pale primroses, bluebells.

Prosper Cain would have liked to give Imogen Fludd a ball dress—an elegant, modern, shapely ball dress. But he felt it would not be proper. He deputed Florence to ask her what she would wear. He had invited Benedict Fludd, Seraphita and Pomona to come to the party, and had found lodgings for them in a house near the Museum, with a retired sergeant-major and his wife. Florence repeated that Imogen had said that Purchase House was full of stunning embroidered silks and linens, all baled up and folded away. She suggested they both go down to the Marshes, find something possible, and bring it back to be refashioned by Katharina's dressmaker into something less mediaeval and more up-to-date. What about Pomona? Florence asked Imogen. "She will just have to wear what Mama puts on her," said Imogen. "She's very pretty, whatever she's wearing. She doesn't seem to notice things like that."

When they went to Purchase House, things were more than usually chaotic. Elsie was nowhere to be seen, and Benedict and Philip had just lost a whole firing of porcelain bowls. Seraphita was limp and pale, and Pomona scorched some grilled fish and boiled vegetables.

Imogen took Florence into a closed room, where dusty leather trunks full of folded materials and barely worn dresses were piled on top of each other. Pomona crept after them, and stood, large-eyed, half-in half-out of the room. Florence noticed that the sisters seemed to have nothing to say to each other. Imogen, resourceful and deliberate, turned over garments, shook out folds. She found what she was looking for—a dark green and ribbed silk, embroidered with pink and white daisies. It was shaped like a mediaeval gown, with a high waist and a little train. "We can do something with that," she said. "And it will look good in the Green Dining-Room with the Burne-Jones panels and the Morris paper. It will blend in."

It was Florence who asked Pomona what she would wear, if they could help . . .

Pomona replied flatly that her mother spent her life sewing, it was what she did, she would put together something, as she had done before. Her face was lovely, her voice was vanishing. Florence asked, where was Elsie?

"She went away to have a baby. She's coming back, it's all arranged."

She did not invite questions. Florence asked lightly whether Pomona, too, would come and study at the Art School, and noticed that the question distressed both sisters, in different ways. A look went between them. Pomona said she thought not, she was needed here, in Purchase House. She looked down at the dusty floorboards. Imogen said they must go, they must go back to London, now.

In the train, on the way back, she said suddenly to Florence

"I'd be happy if I never had to go back there again."

"Why?" asked Florence, lightly.

"I can't bear to be so *odd* and so hopeless. It's a place without hope. Well, the pots are hopeful, when the kiln doesn't melt down. But— but—I cannot tell you how grateful I am to you and your father."

Florence dared not ask what Imogen thought about Elsie's baby, or whose it might be. She did not dare raise the question of what was to happen to Pomona, though she didn't know why. They went back to South Kensington where a delicious dinner, and the secretive, grave young men awaited them.

Violet said she would make Dorothy a dress. Humphry was told to bring ladies' magazines from London, and Violet looked at the photographs and drawings. She said it wouldn't suit Dorothy to wear a girlish colour—Dorothy was handsome, but not pretty. It should be deep rose, perhaps, or dark blue, maybe in shot taffeta with a glow in it. Dark blue like the midnight sky, said Violet, and insisted on taking Dorothy on an excursion to London, for if she was to have a grown-up dress she must have some sort of shaping bodice. Everything this year, in the magazines, was lacy. She had the idea of making a lacy jacket—not in bright white, in some silvery thread—with short sleeves and a collar that would stand up when Dorothy had put her hair up.

Dorothy found the expedition, and the subsequent sessions of fitting and pinning, both stressful and alarming. Before Hedda's revelations, she had found Violet's proprietary motherliness rather sad, when she thought about it at all. Violet was a spinster aunt whose role was to free their mother for her creative work. It was natural that she should insist on her affection, perpetually require that they repay it, that they love her, that they should be grateful for her life, which she had given them.

But now, Violet seemed, and felt, different. She moved around Dorothy's hem on hands and knees, her mouth pressed tight over bristling pins, her thin hands tugging at Dorothy's skirt, or tweaking and clasping her waist. Dorothy looked down into Violet's tightly drawn scalp and the knob of her dark hair on her narrow neck. It was true, her body was more like Dorothy's was going to be, than was Olive's maternal amplitude. Dorothy, who was going to be a doctor, who had to keep telling herself she was going to be a doctor, since everyone was paying half-attention, at best, to this fact, had made it her business to inform herself thoroughly about how babies were born. She had cut open dead pregnant rats, full of tiny, pink, blind, beanlike sleepers. She had looked at a midwifery textbook, with a fat, full-term baby curled in a diagrammatic womb, the crown of its head in the pelvic cavity, the umbilical cord floating and twining in the fluid. She had stopped short of imagining either such a creature inside herself, or herself blindly waiting to be ejected from Olive, *down there*. But now, as Violet fussed over her, and admired her, she involuntarily had a vision of a Dorothy-puppet—snug or stifled, which?—inside Violet's lean stomach. She did not feel a flow of filial warmth. She felt repelled. She stood in her midnight silk, in its stiff rustle, and wondered what had happened to the baby Hedda had been so sure was on the way. Violet was as flat as a board. As she always had been. It would be nice if Hedda was lying, or had deceived herself, but Dorothy did not think so. Hedda believed what she said, and what she said was convincing. *Either* Violet had been wrong about her condition, *or* she had been trying to upset Humphry, *or* she had done something to get rid of this unwanted brother or sister. That seemed the most likely. And yet here she was, her mouth full of pins, skinny and sexless, making "mmn" noises of satisfaction over Dorothy's waist, over the bodices that gave her, for the first time, pushed up and into shape, a pretty little bust.

She ought to feel kind to Violet, indeed, indignant on her behalf. She did not. She was embarrassed and irritated to the depth of her soul.

Violet said "You're growing into a good-looking young lady after all, my love. You were scraggy as a little 'un but you are going to blossom after all. You must put your hair up, and I'll make you some silk flowers to put in it. Or maybe moons and stars on some frothy bits of illusion. To go with the sky. How do you feel?"

"Whatever you think."

"*I* think you are going to be the belle of the ball. You must stand up straight and not slouch. You'll surprise them all."

The note was—possessive? Fierce beyond what was needed?

"What are you going to wear, yourself?"

"Am I invited? I think I may not be. It is a supper dance for young things. I'm not the mother, even if I do a lot of the mothering."

The obvious irony hurt Dorothy, who did not know what to think or say.

Dorothy had no one to talk to about what Hedda had said, or about what she felt about it. Tom had closed it out as though it had never happened. Phyllis was "too young"—younger sisters are always too young to be talked to. She had not discussed this matter with Griselda, with whom she discussed almost everything. She felt that anything she said, any speculation she voiced, even to Griselda, would immediately become hard fact, out in the world. And then she might need to *do* something, or at least begin to *be* something she hadn't known she was.

On the day of the supper dance, which the Wellwoods called the Ball, Prosper Cain persuaded the Museum, which was open until ten in the evening, to close the Refreshment Corridor early, so that the rooms could be decorated with flowers, and a dais built for his regimental music-players: a fiddle, a cello, a flute, an oboe, a clarinet and a horn. Food was prepared in the Grill-Room, and fragile gilt chairs were scattered around the Centre Refreshment Room. This had been designed to be washable, or possible to swill out, with the result that it was set out entirely in ceramic tiles. It was a light room, with huge arched windows, of light stained glass. There was a domed ceiling, supported by immense majolica pillars made by Minton, in peppermint-green and creamy white majolica, with dancing putti, supporting a crown of coat-hooks, at shoulder height. The floor was tiled in chocolate, the dado was faced with dark tiles, between maroon and umber, and the walls were tiled in yellow, green, white, with strips and stripes of complicated running designs, a text from Ecclesiastes, in cream pottery on a red-brown ground: "There is nothing better for a man than that he should eat and drink, and make his soul enjoy good in his labour—XYZ." Amorini cavorted and gambled along the dado. More decoration had been woven in, in more styles, than might seem possible. It was sumptuous and utilitarian, a cross between a fairy palace and a municipal dairy, with electric globes on gilded stems hanging from the ceiling.

The Royal College of Art backed onto this corridor, and Prosper Cain had judiciously invited both teachers and students from the College to make up his numbers. They came to the Refreshment Rooms from various directions, the guests, some through the great golden doors, which were originally designed to be the entrance from the Cromwell Road, some having wandered through those courtyards and corridors that were still open. There was a sullen background noise of thumping and slicing, from closed-off areas where Aston Webb's prize-winning quadrangles and courts were at last being constructed. Olive held on to Humphry's arm, and said that what with the dust that inevitably flew about the floor from the workings, and the dust-sheets that were thrown over various displaced glass cases, like palls over coffins, you felt you had entered both the palace of the Sleeping Beauty and the tomb of Snow White. The visitors to the gallery looked at the young women in their dance dresses and velvet cloaks as though they were a wedding-party, or an irruption from some other world.

In the dark, warm Grill-Room, with its blue and white tiles, and its ceramic panels of the Four Seasons, food was cooked and offered, patties of shrimp and trout, cups of consommé, confections of cherries and meringue and cream, a fruit punch shimmering and hissing icily in a great glass bowl, champagne with the bubbles wavering upwards in fine threads in misted, frosty glasses. In the Green Dining-Room the mothers and fathers could sit on more comfortable, Jacobean-style chairs.

Other military officers were there, with their wives, and Basil and Katharina, who was elegant in a gown with a lace overdress over black silk, with roses at her waist, and a short train behind. Seraphita was there, without her husband, who was, she said, packing a kiln with Philip. She was wound in a reddish-brown, flowing garment which by accident or design matched the twelve figures by Burne-Jones, representing the months, or the signs of the Zodiac with the sun and moon, no one was sure. She looked as though she belonged inside the dark green wallpaper with its woven willow boughs and dotted cherries and plums. Olive, on the other hand, was dressed for the dancing in the pillared hall, in a simple dress in a rich fabric, a darker green than the Minton pillars, with borders of gold and silver braid.

Prosper opened the dancing with Katharina and complimented her on Griselda's beauty. Then he danced with Seraphita, who was taller than he was, and managed to be simultaneously graceful and ungainly, making exaggerated swoops, not on the beat. The young were clumped in separate clutches of males and females, talking distractedly and looking across the room. Julian and Gerald Matthiessen were there, leaning against the dado in a darkish corner. Prosper wandered past them, having returned Seraphita to the Green Dining-Room, and said he relied on his son to get the young people dancing. He went to speak to the orchestra, smart in their uniforms and shining buttons.

Julian looked around the Refreshment Room, which he secretly rather liked, but knew Gerald despised for its cluttered detail and congeries of styles.

"We shall have to dance. Who would you choose to dance with, out of all these beauties?"

"I couldn't ask him, alas," said Gerald, *sotto voce*, barely indicating Tom, who was standing alone in his formal suit, his fair head bent over a group of amorini on a pillar. Julian was both pleased to have Tom's beauty recognised, and briefly, ludicrously, jealous on his own behalf.

"That's his sister," said Julian. "She's changed. She was a tomboy."

"I shall ask *your* sister," said Gerald. "Then we can talk about you. That will be easy."

"I hope you don't," said Julian. "I don't know what she might say."

Gerald strolled over towards Florence, who was standing with Imogen and a few female art students. Geraint Fludd, from the other side of the room, was making his way towards her a great deal more decisively. He had secured her hand by the time Gerald got there, to Florence's distress, though she was able to write down a dance for Gerald later in the evening, in a pretty little book with a hand-painted cover, made by the Royal College calligraphy class, who had contributed a collection of these, all original, to the festivities. Geraint felt a sense of awe, and a rush of blood, as he put his hand in Florence's, and took hold of her waist. Florence did not notice. She was wondering what, if anything, Gerald would have talked about. Julian told Gerald to ask Imogen Fludd. "The pater wants her to have a good time. She's his protégée."

"I see."

"No you don't. He's a good officer. Cares for his men. Students count as men."

"These aren't men," said Gerald, with comic regret. He did as he was told, and asked for Imogen's hand. For some time they sailed round the pillars in stately silence, occasionally getting out of step. Then Gerald asked her a few questions about silversmithing. It is a rule in Cambridge colleges that you do not talk professional shop on social occasions. Gerald thought it a foolish rule—he was a serious man, and did not really want to inhabit a world of clever banter. Imogen's face lifted into life. She talked almost animatedly about the innovations of the new Professor Lethaby, who had abolished the miserable copying of ancient drawings of watercress, and had given the students new live, recalcitrant clumps of the vegetable to look at closely, and study the form. "And then," said Imogen, "you really *do* understand how leaves grow on stems when it comes to formalising them in silver. I hope I'm not boring you?"

"No. I like learning new things. I mean that."

They both smiled. Julian saw the smile, and was irritated. He went to ask pale Griselda for a dance, but everyone had decided that she was the most beautiful of the young women, and students and teachers were clustered about her. So he wandered, in an accidental-looking way, after Tom, who was retreating out of the Refreshment Room into the Green Dining-Room. Tom was headed towards his mother, who was sitting in her chair tapping her toe to the music, every inch of her resenting her reduction to a sedentary dowager.

Tom liked the Green Dining-Room. It reminded him of his vision of sleeping Lancelot, an unreal world more real than stiff collars and shiny shoes.

"I can see you want to dance," said Tom to Olive. "I can see your toes moving. Come and dance with me, like we do at midsummer."

"You must go and dance with the girls, my dear," said Olive. "That's what we're here for, for you to dance with the girls. I'll dance with you when you've taken a turn with *two* of those pretty creatures, not before."

Julian joined them.

"*I* can ask you to dance, Mrs. Wellwood. I'm a kind of host, you can't say no to me. Come and dance. Tom is quite right. I know you would like to dance."

"Go along, Tom," said Olive, standing up, arranging her skirt and purse, giving her hand to Julian. "Ask a girl."

Olive and Julian progressed in an elegant way, pleased with the way their steps matched. Olive said

"I'm dancing with you because I'm at my wits' end about Tom. Is that dreadful?"

Julian thought it would only be dreadful if they were dancing, man and woman, as a couple, which they were not. He had a half-philosophical idea about the nature and the importance of formal dancing, in terms of that idea about who was, and who wasn't, a couple, a man and a woman. He thought about Jane Austen. "Whom are you going to dance with?" said Mr. Knightley to Emma. "With you, if you will ask me," said Emma. Julian thought that was a perfect moment. And would never—not *dancing*—happen to him. He said

"I know what you mean about Tom. He doesn't know what he wants."

At that moment Tom danced jauntily past them, flashing a mild smile at his mother. He had found a partner who was indeed a young woman. She was also his sister.

Olive said "You care about him, I can see. I can't tell if he is too contented, or somehow so discontented he's just floating. Nothing we suggest seems to—interest him. He doesn't take us seriously. He's the most *evasive* person I know, for all his attentiveness and charm."

"I know," said Julian. "I know."

Olive's hand patted his shoulder.

"Do try to make him take things seriously."

"I have enough trouble doing that, myself."

Tom told Dorothy that she had suddenly become a young lady. She looked very pretty, he said. Different.

"That's not very gallant."

"I don't have to be gallant to you. And anyway, you know what I mean, you're just being difficult. You're turning into a woman."

Dorothy, determinedly medical, considered she had been a woman, willy-nilly, since her monthly Curse began. She had been proud of the bloodstains, and also, despite her academic anatomical interest, dismayed by the speed of the changes in her body. She was also niggled by the fact that it was Violet, not Olive, who had taken upon herself to explain this momentous event—about which Dorothy, of course, was already informed, through reading books. She thought, as she and Tom stumbled more or less companionably across the tiles, that Tom probably knew nothing at all about the Curse. She was right. But she had not stopped to think about Tom's own reaction to puberty, which had tossed him about on waves of emotion, and rather disgusted him. He said, out of *The Golden Age,*

"You're turning into a Grown-up. Is it nice?"

"You're older than me. You should know."

"Girls grow up quicker. They say. I'm not sure it *is* nice."

The conversation was odd, rather formal, because they were in formal clothes, stepping formal patterns, between majolica pillars, to sentimental rhythms. Dorothy saw that Tom had chosen a daft moment to try to talk to her about something important. His hair was a shining mess. It was not parted and slicked down, like Julian's hair, and Gerald's and Charles's, and Geraint's, even though Geraint's bush showed signs of rebellion. She gave a twitch to the waist of her shapely dress. She was thinking of an answer when the music stopped. Charles, who had put his name in her little starry book, came to claim her. She said to Tom

"Do go and ask Pomona to dance. Nobody seems to, and she looks desolate. It would be a kind act."

Tom went over to Pomona, who was drooping a little, in a beautifully embroidered, less than perfectly tailored gown, white with a deep border of apple boughs, and embroidered strips of apple-blossom round waist, neck and sleeves.

Charles asked Dorothy if she was having a good time. He told her she looked quite the thing. He danced well—his mother had seen to that—and Dorothy followed, and they twirled cheerfully.

"*What* are you thinking?" Charles asked, after five minutes.

"Do you want the real answer?"

"I always do. There's no sense in telling fibs. What are you thinking?"

"If I tell you, you must tell me."

"Agreed."

"I was thinking about how I can't do quadratic equations, and how I never shall be able to, if you keep taking Mr. Susskind off to Germany on cultural trips just when I *almost* can. And I shall never matriculate, and never be a doctor."

"What a very unromantic thought. There must be other tutors."

"Well, this one knows what it is I don't understand."

A slow silence.

"You didn't tell me what *you* are thinking?"

"Oddly, dear cousin, I was thinking in a sort of way about the same thing. I was thinking how nice it is in Munich, and about going secretly to cabarets which would give my mater a *fit* if she knew. You see, I am being honest."

"Now we are at least talking *to* each other. What's good about the cabarets?"

Charles said they were very avant-garde. And smoky. And that the police sometimes invaded them. He said he needed Joachim Susskind to do simultaneous translation.

"Ah," said Dorothy, between fury and amusement, "but you don't need him as I need him. Dog in a manger."

Pomona's little hand was chilly in Tom's, and didn't heat up. He felt sorry for her, which was good for him. She didn't speak. He was looking into her mass of hair, which had embroidered flowers pinned into it. He said it must be wonderful to live in a magical place like the Denge Marsh.

In some ways it was, Pomona agreed.

Perhaps she was a bit lonely without Imogen, he ploughed on.

It wasn't really Imogen, Pomona said in a small voice. It wasn't very nice now Elsie had gone away.

Tom didn't know about this. He asked *where* Elsie had gone, and was told, in a kind of gentle hiss, that she had gone to have a baby, and was coming back when it was all over, but that nobody was very cheerful because of this, neither Mama, nor Philip, nor Papa of course either.

There was another silence while Tom dredged up a reply. He was not going to ask about the baby, that was not what he would do. He repeated that the place was magical, and heard the banality in his own voice.

Pomona said

"From outside it is. I feel we're under a spell. You know, behind one of those thickets in stories. We trail out to the orchard and back to the kitchen. And up to bed, and out to the orchard, and back to the kitchen. We sew. That's part of the spell. We have to sew things or something dreadful will happen."

If Dorothy had said all this, it would have been a joke. But Pomona's voice was amiably monotonous.

"Well, I suppose you could go to College, like Imogen, couldn't you?"

"And sew things? I don't think so. I don't think I'd be let go to College. Are you going to College?"

"I'm thinking about it," Tom said evasively.

They trotted on, dancing neither well nor badly. Tom said

"There must be other things, besides sewing."

"Pots," said Pomona. "There are pots."

Something in Tom evaded remarking stupidly that maybe she would get out and be married. He felt she was not all there, but then, there were moments when he felt he was not all there himself. Maybe, like him, she was somewhere else. He would have liked to get away from her, and this made him sorry for her, so he asked for another dance.

Gerald was enjoying the dance, against his expectations. He actually *liked* the physical exercise of dancing, which he had learned very thoroughly as a little boy in weekend dancing classes. There was no call to dance in King's College. He looked at the young women to work out which would be pleasurable to dance with, from this point of view. The best dancer was Griselda Wellwood, who moved elegantly, almost like a perfect mechanical doll. But her little book—decorated with lilies of the valley—was crowded. He booked what he could, and went back to Florence Cain. She had more space, having refused to give Geraint as many dances as he wanted. She was, in Gerald's view, the second-best dancer, less perfect in her movements, but also less mechanical, and, he discovered after stepping out with both young ladies, more responsive to his leading, readier to follow him in inventing variations on the steps. She annoyed him, at first, by what he saw as a tedious attempt to make conversation that would interest him. She discussed dancing in Jane Austen, she went on to Shakespeare and Dante. It took him quite some time, between the creation of steps-on-the-spot and sudden swirls, to realise that she was talking perfectly good sense—even wittily—about

Shakespeare and Dante, even if a supper dance was the wrong place. He answered with amusement, and twirled her again. Both Prosper and Julian observed her flush of delight with irritation, bordering on fury. They were too far away to see that her knees were trembling, and only she knew what was going on inside her, under her flowing skirt, as she swayed in time to the music.

There was a late arrival, when the dancing had been interrupted for supper. The young went to collect their plates and glasses in the Grill-Room, and came back to the Centre Refreshment Room to eat in groups at the tiny, but heavy, tables, made of ornamental ironwork with small grey marble slabs, encased in more ironwork. In the Refreshment Corridor were plaster bas-reliefs, depicting abstract craftsmen—Industrial Science and Industrial Art—and real humans. Arkwright inventing the loom, Palissy taking baked pots from a furnace. Tom pointed these out to Pomona, to whom he had somehow become permanently attached. She shuddered when she saw Palissy, and said "That's Palissy. You see, I can't get away from weaving and pots." Tom knew nothing about Palissy, and observed that he looked benign. Pomona said he might well have been, if you were interested in pots.

Geraint had managed to secure Florence for supper, since Gerald had insinuated himself into that place in Griselda's little book. Geraint deciphered the inscription on the porcelain painting on the Grill-Room buffet, and read it out in a funny voice.

"May-Day, May-Day, the Blithe May-Day, the Merrie, Merrie Month of May."

The Victorians were earnest, even about being merry, said the Edwardian young man. Florence laughed. But she felt a kind of loyalty to the ambition of the Museum, because of her father.

The late arrival was August Steyning, who went to join the elders in the Green Dining-Room, where waiters were serving supper on Minton plates. He was given a chair next to Olive. The table centre-piece was a large, glowing lustre bowl by Benedict Fludd, depicting that odd moment in the *Rheingold* when Freya is up to her neck in gold loot, the golden apples are turning grey and papery, and the two giants stretch out huge hands to take the young goddess. Fludd's depiction of the heaped treasure, in ceramic, was masterly—goblets, bracelets, glinting crowns, trickling coins and the shape of a young woman underneath the heap, hinted suggestively. On the other side of the bowl lurked, not Wotan struggling with the ring, but Loge, holding a very lively golden apple in a cloak of flame.

August Steyning was rehearsing *The Smart Set,* a drawing-room comedy by J. M. Barrie, with an edge of pain and irony. Olive asked him how it was going.

"The actors are good. It has a pretty pace. It is not without meaning, even though too much of it turns on undelivered letters and impertinent servants. But—dear Mrs. Wellwood, dear Olive—it isn't what I *want* to be doing. It's bread-and-butter work, and I do it to the best of my ability. But if I could have my way, all the tasteful furniture which makes the stage like an airless mirror of daily life would be *whisked* lightly up—sofas like flying elephants, tables galloping into the wings like wild ponies—and we should see *through* the looking glass into the world of dream and story. The stage doesn't have to reproduce drawing rooms with false balconies and unreal windows. We can put *anything* on the stage now, daemons, dragons, Worms, sly Elves, slow trolls, malign silkies, even the Brollachan and Nuckelavee. Instead of which I have actresses quarrelling over the waists of tea-gowns and freshly made egg-and-cress sandwiches every rehearsal."

"We all went to see *Bluebell in Fairyland,* with Seymour Hicks," said Olive. "The children loved it. The songs were pretty."

"But it wasn't fey, or uncanny, now was it? It was prettily whimsical, very English. The Germans know that otherworld creatures aren't pretty little misses with wings and flower hats. They know that things lurk in dark woods and deep caves. Things we need to remember. Look at that, Olive. The bowl. I long to pick it up, but I dare not for it would certainly slip through my fingers and I should be cursed by the wraiths of Victoria and Albert, and a very lively Major Cain. The man—Fludd—is a genius. He takes the great—perhaps the only— *Gesamtkunstwerk* of our time and produces a version in a chilly, still world—that went through the fire all flowing with elements and elementals, and *fused* into colour and form—a regular-shaped *bowl* holding passion. Look at Loge's wicked laughter. Please turn the bowl carefully, Major Cain, so that Olive may see Loge. See how the golden apples shimmer and fade, and the light is fiery and lucid and golden as the bowl turns. We need mystery."

"Your rehearsal has upset you."

"It has. This mysterious room restores my good nature. The eternal hounds, pursuing the eternal deer, under the dark eternal forest boughs. Those glooming Burne-Jones wodewomen. Prosper, your quails' eggs are dainty and delicious, and your champagne is a chilly fountain of youth."

"Why don't you put on such a play, yourself?" asked Prosper Cain.

"Because I haven't the imagination and can't write. I need a myth-maker. You, Olive, you could do it. You could write me an Otherworld. You have the true sense of what is beyond window and mirror alike."

After supper, they danced quadrilles. The elders mingled with the young. It was both more stately and more frivolous, more playful, than the waltzes and polkas. Olive and Steyning danced with Tom and Pomona: Humphry led out Katharina, and made a square with Dorothy and Charles. Prosper and Seraphita danced with Florence and Geraint.

Afterwards, as the evening drew to a close, fathers danced with daughters. Basil Wellwood claimed Griselda, clasped her firmly, whisked her round and round, and said he was proud of her, and she had made her mother very happy. Prosper danced with Florence, lightly, and said he hoped she had enjoyed her ball. She said she loved dancing and had danced every dance, and the Museum had been transfigured. Then he danced with Imogen, whose father was absent. She gave a little sigh, and settled into his arms as though she was comfortable there. She said he was a magician, who had conjured up a palace, which was, for her, an unexpected flight of fancy. She reported to him, as a daughter might, that Henry Wilson, from Jewellery, had danced with her twice, and had complimented her on her silver-work. "He said I understood both pennywort and silver," she said. "I am in hope of being able to earn my living." She rested her head briefly against his shoulder and he resisted the temptation to stroke her hair. Instead, he asked her whether she thought he should try and persuade her father to send Pomona to the Royal College, in her footsteps.

"She looks a little forlorn," he said.

"I sometimes think she would give anything never to see another work of art again," said Imogen. "But that isn't to say she does want anything in particular. She doesn't talk to me. She doesn't talk to anyone. She tries to talk to Philip but that isn't easy. I wish you could help her," she said, sounding not entirely sincere, "but I truly don't see how. She's been dancing, at least, some of the time."

"I wish your father had come."

"I don't." She opened her mouth to say something further, and closed it again. Her hands tightened on his shoulder. He held her with military firmness, and they turned a corner.

Dorothy was dancing with Humphry. Humphry was possibly the best dancer in the room. He said to her "Let me lead," and she let him lead, and they began to move as though they were a single creature, swaying and tripping, making tiny chasing and concentrated steps, floating dreamily. His hand was hot and strong in the small of her back: both halves of her body, above and below his hand, moved as he dictated. He went fast—she had the sensation she had when she was a little girl, on roundabouts and helter-skelters. He said

"Well, you've been having a good time, young woman."

"I have."

"Your dress shows you off. A great success."

He held her very close. They waltzed towards one of the great, full-length mirrors in the room, framed as though it were a door, in cast-iron painted as *trompe-l'oeil* sepia-brown marble. The mirrors were angled to give the illusion that the room was infinite, that you could step around an invisible corner into another shining space. It was clear that it was a mirror partly because a Greek or Roman nymph stood on a fat marble pillar with her back to it. She was modestly clutching, in her front, a sculpted flow of drapery, that covered her thighs, but not her bared breasts over which her hands were defensively clasped in an ancient, conventional pose. At the back, oddly, she was entirely naked. Her shoulder blades, fine waist, and rounded buttocks were exposed to the mirror, though not to the room. She distracted Dorothy, as her father whirled her towards the glass. She saw her own pale little face, staring dreamily over his strong shoulder, and her own small, female hand on his arm. She saw her unaccustomed high knot of hair, and the sleek, foxy red of her father. And then, as she turned, she looked back at the mirror, and saw the midnight-blue dress, and her bare back and shoulders, and the powerful hand planted on her waist, on the unaccustomed whalebone strips that shaped her.

"If you go on like this," said Humphry "you'll have them fighting over you."

He said "Perhaps it's true, what they always say, don't you think?"

She had no idea what he meant.

After the dance, the Todefright Wellwoods drove back to Portman Square, where they were staying with the London Wellwoods. Olive sat in the back of the carriage with Tom. Dorothy sat facing them, and put her head on her father's shoulder. They didn't speak much: they were sleepy and thoughtful.

Katharina sent the young people to bed, with a maid carrying milk, iced biscuits, and a small oil lamp with an etched glass shade. Dorothy always had the same bedroom when she came to Portman Square. It was small, and high up, looking out at the back over gardens. It was decorated in Katharina's taste, in a froth of white muslin, sprigged with pink. The bed was a nest inside prettily swathed curtains. There was a washstand, with bowl and jug decorated with pink rosebuds on a china-blue ground, but no writing desk. Another young woman might have found all this nostalgic femininity charming after the plainness and brightness of Todefright. Dorothy didn't. But she didn't mind it, or feel at a loss in it.

She slipped out of her ball dress, and her petticoats—she didn't need the maid to help, and told her so. Another maid would certainly be unhooking Griselda. She hung the midnight-blue dress neither carefully nor carelessly over a prettily upholstered dumpy chair, dropped her drawers on top of it and put on her plain, voluminous, white cotton nightdress, its bodice pleated by Violet. She thought she would read a little, before she turned out the light. She was trying to read fairytales in German to please Griselda. She was not a born linguist, and was ambivalent about fairytales.

Someone knocked at the door. She thought it would be Griselda, come to talk over the ball, and rather wished she wouldn't. But she said, come in. It was Griselda's house and she loved Griselda.

The door opened slowly and silently. It was not Griselda. It was

Humphry, her father, in a silk dressing-gown covered with coiling Chinese dragons. He looked around for a chair—both the fat chair and the dressing-table chair were covered with abandoned female garments. He sat down beside his daughter, sinking into her flowery eiderdown, and said

"I thought we might talk about things."

He was in an aura of whisky. Censorious Dorothy believed that both his wives—as she now thought of them—should do something to stop, or slow down, the whisky-drinking. She said

"I'm tired."

He put an arm around her shoulder.

"You are such a lovely girl. I never thought you were going to be so lovely. Queen of the Rosebud Garden of Girls. My Dorothy."

Dorothy stiffened.

"There are things I ought to tell you. But I wanted so much to tell you—to tell you"—he stumbled—"how perfectly *lovely*—"

He breathed hot whisky at her. She shrank back, and he gave her a clumsy push, which unbalanced her. She turned her face into the pillow, and muttered, in a child's voice, "Go away. Please. Get off."

And then he put his hand, unequivocally, inside the white cotton folds and touched naked flesh. Dorothy ceased to be timid and confused, and became very angry.

"*Don't do that.* Or I'll scream. Or ring the bell."

"I only want to play with you a bit. My darling."

His face wavered over hers. One hand worked inside her nightdress. One came over her mouth. Dorothy bit it. She bit with all her strength and she was strong. She bit the soft cushion below the thumb, and her mouth filled with blood. She shook the hand in her teeth like a mongoose with a snake.

"Bitch," said Humphry. He sat up. His hand was pouring blood on the white frilled bedclothes. He said "Have you got a hankie? We must stop this. That *hurt*."

"It was meant to. How *dare* you? Here's a hankie. It's far too small. Girls have stupid hankies. Go and get the hand towel. Then I'll tear something up and make a bandage. I haven't got much I can spare to tear up. Violet will be furious if I tear up this petticoat she spent so long on. You'll have to put up with knickers."

This word caused her to begin to shake. She said, drawing deep, sobbing breaths,

"You can't go back with any of the stuff from this room, that belongs to the room, as opposed to belonging to *me,* or everyone will know. So it will have to be knickers. You could get to them. They're in the drawer."

Her pillow was blood-spattered. So was the neck of her nightgown.

Humphry said with a ghastly laugh

"You've got blood on your teeth, like a stoat. And on your pretty lips."

"I shall have to say I had a nosebleed. You've got blood on your nice dressing-gown, too. Two nosebleeds in a night is a bit unlikely. You must cut yourself shaving."

She was trying to make a bandage strip from the knickers with an unsuitable pair of nail scissors.

Humphry said, stumbling over the words,

"Stop ordering me about."

"It's either be businesslike or collapse and scream, and I think even you would prefer the former. You're drunk. I need to think for you. As well as for me," she added, in a swallowed sob. She was breathing either too much or too little air.

Humphry said

"It's not what you think."

"I'm here, aren't I? You—you *attacked* me. I was there. It's not a question of thinking."

"Yes it is. There are reasons. This is the wrong way to say it. I was always going to tell you. When the time came."

"You don't have to tell me. I know."

"What do you think you know?"

"I'm Violet's daughter. Someone—not me—has been listening into things."

"Well someone has been garbling 'things.' You're not Violet's child. Phyllis is. And Florian. You're Olive's daughter. But not mine."

Dorothy clutched the coverlet to her chest like the naked nymph in the ballroom.

"*What?*"

"You aren't my daughter. So, you see, it wasn't—this wasn't—what you thought."

Dorothy sat like stone.

"I didn't mean to tell you this way. I do love you. Always have. Always will. My dear. Say something."

Dorothy said *"Who is my father?"*

"You met him one midsummer. He's a German from Munich. His name is Anselm Stern. The puppet-man. Things got out of hand at a carnival.

"You can't say it's made any difference," he added, foolishly.

Dorothy said

"You are being childish. You aren't *thinking*. Of course it makes a difference. I am not who I thought I was. Nor, for that matter, is Phyllis. You have muddled us all up. All of you, you and both of *them* have made this muddle. You can't just say it made no difference."

"I love you," Humphry repeated, clutching his bandaged hand in his whole one.

"Please go away," Dorothy said with desperate dignity. "I need to think. I can't think with you saying silly things to me."

"I handled it badly," Humphry said, with drunken ruefulness.

"You didn't even *handle* it," said Dorothy with scorn. "You just added a worse muddle to a monstrous muddle that already existed. Go away. Please. We have to sort out tomorrow."

"We can just go back to where we were, maybe . . ."

"That's childish. We can't. Go away."

Humphry went.

Dorothy sat on top of her bed, clasping her knees, thinking furiously. She was thinking in order not to feel, and her whole body was set and aching with the force of the thinking.

She thought she would not go home—go back to Todefright.

She tried to rearrange Olive in her mind, and failed.

She thought she would not think about Humphry.

She thought, slowly and reluctantly, that she was going to need to tell Griselda—something, she was not sure what, she would have to think of that. She had not told Griselda anything about Hedda's discovery. She had wanted to go on as they were, cousins and friends, and not let the evil creatures out of Hedda's Pandora's box.

She decided she must pretend to be ill, and stay here, in Portman Square. She would explain the blood-spattered sheets by a gushing nose-bleed. She would also tell Griselda to tell people—in confidence and untruthfully—that the Curse had come upon her early and with terrible pain, that she couldn't bear to move.

She was one of those beings who cannot bear uncertainty or indecision. She must act, she must make a plan of action. She must get away, she could not sit any longer in Todefright with horrible secrets bubbling up around her like hot geysers out of a lava-field.

Where could she go, and how?

Tom had run away. Running away was what children in stories did. There was no point in hurrying off to be a wild woman in the woods. She wanted to be a doctor. She tried to think of someone she could plausibly visit for a time.

She was getting tired. She allowed her mind to touch, tentatively, at the image of Anselm Stern, her blood father.

Incurably truthful, she remembered she had not much liked him, had been even a little afraid of him. Griselda had liked him, had talked German to him.

She remembered a slim, black, bearded figure, a bit like a demon. Putting Death into Death's own box.

His English was no better than her own clumsy German. His puppets had made her uneasy.

He was a kind of showman. Was he a serious person?

She thought a bit harder. Did he know she was his daughter? Did he know he had a daughter?

She felt, in a hot and angry way, that he should be *made* to know.

She felt, in an exhausted, tearful way, that she needed to know who he was.

Could she bring herself to tell Griselda?

In the morning, she did not go down to breakfast. She huddled under her eiderdown, and said to the maid who brought her ewer of hot water that she felt ill, really ill, and would be glad if Griselda could be fetched. The maid said she would speak to Mrs. Wellwood—either Mrs. Wellwood—and Dorothy said, no, she would be grateful if Griselda could come. Quickly. There was no need to bother anyone else.

Griselda came in, in a white shirt and green skirt, her hair knotted loosely on her neck.

"What is it? Aren't you well? What's wrong? Do you need a doctor, or anything?"

"No. I had a nosebleed. I'm sorry about the bedclothes. Something has happened, Grisel, something that changes all my life."

Griselda moved the midnight dress, and the petticoat, folding them neatly, and sat down on the stubby chair.

"Tell."

"I almost can't."

"We don't have secrets from each other. Only from the world."

"This is a secret that a lot of people know, which is a secret about me, and was kept from me."

"Tell me."

"My father—that is—well—he told me, I am not his real daughter. He had drunk a bit too much, and it sort of slipped out. He hadn't been *planning* to tell me."

Griselda's pale face went white.

"Did you believe him?"

"Yes."

"Did he say who your father was—is?"

"Yes. He's that German man with the puppet-show who came to the Midsummer party, when we were younger." She thought. "I don't know if *he* knows he's my father. I can't face asking my mother—anything—I just can't. I can't go home. I've got to think of a way to get away. You must help."

One tear rolled out of Griselda's blue eye.

"Grisel, you don't have to cry."

"We aren't cousins," said Griselda. "If it's true, we aren't cousins."

Dorothy had not thought of that.

They looked at each other.

"We're even more best friends," said Dorothy. "Help me. Where can I go?"

Griselda was thinking furiously.

"Would you consider telling Charles?"

"He isn't my cousin either," said Dorothy, with a brittle cackle of laughter.

"No—but—he keeps going on these cultural trips to Germany with Joachim Susskind. He goes to Munich, where he—Herr Stern—is. Do you think—just possibly—*we* could go, too? With Charles, and Herr Susskind, and maybe even with—with—Toby—do you think a grown-up brother and two tutors would be chaperone enough? Charles is good at secrets. He has lots. He does all sorts of secret things with Joachim Susskind who looks so respectable and gentle. He gets up to all sorts of things—revolutionary things, avant-garde art things—the parents would *die* if they knew. We could both go. I could speak German and study there. And if the tutors went, you could go on working for your exams. I'm sure they have classes in Munich we could go to. And you could think about seeing him—Herr Stern—your father. I liked him. I liked him very much. He's gentle."

Dorothy sprang out of the bed and flung her arms round Griselda. They hugged each other. Griselda considered the bloodstains on the nightdress.

"That was a *voluminous* nosebleed. Buckets of blood. You must have had a frightful shock."

"I did."

"Are you all right now?"

"I'm all right as long as I keep *doing something*. I shall have to lurk here, for a bit. *I'm not going back to Todefright.*"

"Won't your parents be upset? Will they let you go to Munich?"

"I need to make them frightened of what I will do if they don't. Tell everybody. Run away altogether. Kill myself. Waste away. Shout and shout at them. They wouldn't like any of those. Which do you think?"

"I think you should lurk here and be stormy and intimidating. Whereas *I* shall be persuasive and charming, and say if I can go and study in Munich for a bit, I will let them give a sumptuous ball for me when I get back."

"I don't think I shall ever enjoy another ball."

"Well, if I fix this for you, you'll have to promise me to come to that one. As moral support. We shall have to *tell* Charles or he'll never agree. But if we do tell him, I think he might, because he does love secrets and subversive things."

29

Elsie's child was born in an attic in Dymchurch, from which you could see the sea. It belonged to a semi-retired midwife, who was a friend of Patty Dace. The labour was long and terrible, and the bruised child— a very small child—was slapped and shaken into a quavering howl, just as the dawn rose over the Channel.

"It's a girl," said Mrs. Ball. "She's little, but she'll live." Elsie swam in and out of consciousness, like a mermaid in the sea.

"Do you want to see her?" asked Mrs. Ball, who had attended births where the mother turned away a grim, resolute face, and would not look. Elsie swam. Elsie floated. She heard a voice say

"Give me her. Let me see."

Mrs. Ball put the bundle in the crib, and raised Elsie's pillow, on the cast-iron bed.

"You must stay awake then, you mustn't drop her."

The sea poured in and retreated.

"Give me her."

The baby was swaddled in a piece of towelling, like a peg doll. Mrs. Ball put her in Elsie's arms. She had a creased little face, like an ancient wise monkey. She opened a tiny mouth, and mewed. Hair, of an indeterminate colour, was plastered to her head. She opened dark, dark eyes under bruised lids, and blinked, and then stared, letting light flow over them.

"*Oh*" said Elsie, catching her breath. Her breasts swelled and hurt. She said

"Her name's Ann."

"Did you think she might be a girl? Did you have a name ready?"

"No." Elsie gave a kind of sobbing laugh. "I can see her name's Ann. She's so small, it's a small name."

"She'll grow."

"I want to see all of her."

Mrs. Ball unwrapped the little body. Elsie touched the raw-looking feet, considered the swollen sex, put out a finger for the wavering hands to grip, and was gripped.

"Ann," said Elsie, shifting her painful body so that she could rest the nodding head on her shoulder. "Hey, Ann. Stay with me."

Mrs. Ball, who tried not to be sentimental, and failed, felt tears in her eyes, and a choke in her throat. It was not the first time, and would not be the last.

Philip came to see Ann. The whole business of her birth and begetting had shamed him, somehow. He felt sullen, and put out, and deeper than that, afraid of something that concerned him dreadfully and was out of his control.

"Her name's Ann," Elsie told him. Mother and child were clutching each other, Ann's face pushed into Elsie's breast.

"Just Ann?"

"Just Ann."

"It suits her. She looks—she looks all right."

"You're her uncle."

"I know that. You'll keep her."

"I don't seem to have no choice. I thought I might. I didn't know what I'd feel. I had an idea of turning me head away, you know. And then I saw she was mine."

She said "They're unbelievable, those ladies, they sorted it all, just like they said at the meeting about the women of the future, they said single women should be looked after, and they're looking after me. And Ann."

"Turn her face this way a bit. I want to draw her. She's got your brow."

Neither of them mentioned anyone else she might resemble.

Phoebe Methley came to see Ann, bringing a bunch of wild flowers for Elsie, and a blue vase to put them in. She also brought apples, and two little baby dresses, and a bonnet. She perched on the end of the bed, and watched Philip's pencil move on his sketch-pad.

She sniffed, and got out her handkerchief.

"I'm sorry, it's silly, I always cry when I see newborns."

"Her name's Ann."

"You'll keep her?"

"I couldn't give her up, I couldn't." A silence. "If it wasn't for you, and the other ladies, I w'd a had to. I can't ever tell you . . ."

Both women were weeping.

Phoebe Methley had a fairly clear idea about who was Ann's father, and could not, for some time, bring herself to look closely at her face.

She had had, she now understood, a romantic hope that Elsie would want nothing to do with Ann, that she herself might *have to* offer this child a home, in a house where her own unmentionable children would never come. This act might entail a generosity of which she would not be capable, she knew also. She said

"Anything you need . . ."

"You are too good to me."

"Women must work together," said Phoebe, with a healthy asperity.

That evening she said to her husband

"Elsie Warren has given birth to a daughter."

They were sitting at the dinner table. She served him a stew of haricot beans, simmered with onions and pork rind, and a spoon or two of molasses, and a trace of mustard, flavoured also with rosemary from their garden, and sprinkled with chopped parsley and chives. It was a slow-cooked, thoughtful dish. Herbert Methley sniffed it, and said that it was good. More than good, ambrosial, said Herbert Methley, not meeting his wife's eye.

"I went to see them. Her name's Ann. She's a very sweet, tiny little thing."

Herbert Methley did not like to talk of children, anyone's children. He said he had, today, made enormous progress with his new novel, it had finally settled into shape, and was flowing along like water in a river-bed.

Phoebe went on, sternly and bravely.

"We formed a little feminist committee of fairy godmothers to make sure Ann will be well looked after. I wondered if we might even have her here, a little—only now and then, you understand—Marian Oakeshott has offered to ask Tabitha to help—"

Herbert Methley stared distractedly out of the window. He said he thought this new novel might be his best—his best yet—might make their fortune—if he could have time and silence and absence of distractions to write it at its current speed, while the spirit moved him. He said he had a good title.

"Do you, Herbert? What is it?"

"It is to be called *Mr. Wodehouse and the Wild Girl*."

"Mr. Woodhouse from *Emma,* Herbert?"

"No, my love, though the connotation is present, and you have perceptively noted it. It is spelt, in this case, Wodehouse. There is a figure—a kind of Green Man, a kind of Wild Man of the Woods—who is known as Wodwose. I discovered, to my great delight, that country people still talk about Wodwoses but call them Wodehouses. It is to be the tale of a timid man who retreats to a cottage in the woods to live naturally—a man who at that stage temperamentally resembles Mr. Woodhouse from *Emma*—who coddles himself with woolly comforters and embrocations—and meets the Wild Girl who is living freely in the depth of the forest—"

"You said it was a wood."

"It is an English wood that *symbolically* takes on the properties of the deeper Forest—where he learns to walk free and naked in Nature—"

"What is she like, the Wild Girl?"

"I haven't wholly invented her. She has your eyes, of course. I cannot invent a—a beloved woman—who does not have your eyes. But she is hard for to tame. Yes."

"And how does it end?"

"I don't know that, yet, either. Wonderfully, I think. But, it may be, with a wonderful disaster. I need to find it out, I need to follow my instincts. Which is why I need *particular* peace and quiet in the next few months—such as you have always protected for me, my darling."

In June, a party consisting of Toby Youlgreave, Joachim Susskind, Karl Wellwood, Griselda Wellwood, and Dorothy Wellwood, set out by boat and railway for Munich.

Most of the persuasive talking had been done by Griselda. A child who has been brought up in a partly public space, surrounded by servants directly and indirectly concerned with the controlling and ordering of her own life, a child who has not been brought up in intimate contact with either of her parents, and who has been accustomed to meet them in formalised, public spaces, has had to learn to keep her own counsel, to create a private space for private projects, inside her own head and body. Many upper-class girls did not learn that, and went doll-like from nursery to dance floor to white lace in church and the unexpected fleshy horrors or delights of the bridal bedroom. If Griselda was not a doll, even though she had often been dressed as a doll, it was, in fact, because her father and mother loved her, with however much reticence, as a human being. She knew this—as indeed Charles/Karl also knew it in his own case—and now exploited it, with some cunning, on Dorothy's behalf. She did not know what it was that had so shocked her cousin—it was something appalling in the *way* she had been casually told about her parentage, Griselda surmised. But she loved Dorothy, and Dorothy was shocked. So Griselda went to Katharina, and confided in her. What she confided was a series of half-truths and serious fibs about Dorothy's unhappiness at home, about the lack of seriousness with which her flighty parents approached her steadfast ambition to be a doctor. Delicately, Griselda accused her mother of favouring Charles/Karl—*he* could command the attention of a tutor, and by travelling with this tutor as his companion, deprive Dorothy of lessons she needed. Dorothy was nervously depressed. She, Griselda, was restless. Why should they not, with each other for company, go with Charles and Joachim Susskind to Munich and perfect their German—

"You will not," interposed Katharina from Hamburg, "learn classical German in Bavaria—"

"Herr Susskind speaks classical German. And he has an aunt, Mama, who has a *pension* and gives classes in mathematics and biology to young ladies—mathematical genius runs in Herr Susskind's family—she is called Frau Carlotta Susskind—and we could stay in her *pension* and see the artworks, and study, and it would take Dorothy out of herself— I can't bear to see her so unhappy."

"Her unhappiness is very sudden."

"No, it isn't, Mama. She is very strong, and she hides things well. I can confide in *you,* she has given me permission—"

Katharina sometimes thought that Griselda and Dorothy were almost unhealthily bound up in each other. Griselda saw that thought pass across her thin face, though it was not articulated.

"And when we come back—you will give a dance, and I will be serious about coming out, and *after that* you will allow me to study in Cambridge if I still want to—"

Katharina kissed Griselda. She said

"There is something I don't know—"

"There is always something girls don't tell. But it isn't an *important* thing," said Griselda, lying splendidly. And Katharina smiled, and agreed to the journey.

Dorothy had formed the violent intention of never returning to Todefright. She would become an exile. She would go to Bavaria, where she had no particular wish to go, to find a father whom she did not particularly wish to see. But she was a practical being, and understood that she could not get away without going back. Clothes must be packed. Money must be discussed. Studies must be arranged. She asked Griselda to come with her. Together they were less approachable, less open to blackmail, or emotional invasion. She dreaded being in the same house as Humphry, and assumed he dreaded confronting her. Olive, too, had shifted in her inner landscape. She had done something, felt something, which had been kept a secret, which changed hugely who she *was* for Dorothy, in ways Dorothy had not yet worked out.

She stayed a few days in Portman Square, pretending to be ill. She did not say much more to Charles and Griselda than she already had. Any wrong things said, could only make things more dangerous, more precarious.

She dreamed about both her fathers. Her dreams were hectic. She dreamed of Humphry, walking towards her, smiling under his foxy moustache, across the meadow at Todefright. In the dream he stood in the sun, and opened his arms, and lifted her up to kiss her, as he had done when she was a child, and in the dream she understood she had made a terrible mistake—she could not remember what it was—but her father was holding her safe and all would be well. Then she woke up, and remembered.

Her dreams about Anselm Stern were more confused. She could not exactly remember what he had looked like, and in the dream confused him with his own marionettes, so that he advanced towards her swaying and gesticulating, with a fixed, silent, sinister smile. He was always black, as he had been when he came. He was a kind of spider. He floated towards her in many different, unknown rooms, and held out his arms with their fluid joints, to embrace her, and she wanted to run away, and knew she must not, and woke in a fright.

In Todefright, everyone tried to behave well. Humphry and Olive greeted them in the hall, and Humphry, smiling too much, told Griselda she looked very pretty, and welcomed Dorothy without looking at her. Dorothy kissed Olive coldly. Olive could feel a turmoil of feeling, by which she was baffled. Dorothy was closed and cold, and she didn't know why. This perturbed the writer as well as the mother—she liked to leave her world warm and smiling before she closed herself away with the typewriter.

Over supper that night Griselda explained the Munich project. She was so keen on going herself—Charles was always going there—the tutors had agreed to come—and she so wanted Dorothy to come with her, it was a wonderful opportunity before she had to concentrate on all those terrible exams.

Joachim Susskind's aunt had a *pension*. Charles had been there.

Olive thought secretly that she had not known Griselda was such a minx. Butter wouldn't melt in her pale mouth. Something had happened. Money was short at that moment in the Wellwood house. Travel to Munich and accommodation and tuition for a daughter who could very well stay at home were inconvenient to find. Dorothy, naturally truthful, trying to find a lie, said in an unnatural voice of enthusiasm that she had never wanted anything so much as she now wanted to go to Munich with Griselda and Charles and the tutors. Mr. Youlgreave was coming too. Humphry, also sounding unnaturally enthusiastic, said that in that case, the money must be found. Tom said he couldn't see why anyone wanted to travel.

In their bedroom at night, Olive turned on Humphry and asked him what had happened.

"You know *you* can't find the money to send the girl to Munich, which is to say that *I* must. And *I* can't work any faster. And we must do something about Tom. There's something going on, that I don't know about."

"I told her she isn't my daughter. It slipped out. I'm sorry."

Olive stood in her dressing-gown and looked hard at him.

"We don't *know* that she isn't."

"Yes we do. Be honest, Olive. We do."

"Why did you tell her? It wasn't your right."

Humphry, crestfallen, stared at the carpet.

Olive considered him. Reasons for his madness flickered across her mind and were rejected. The writer in her could have imagined a scene in which the secret had "slipped out." The woman in her felt both threatened and enraged. The woman needed to keep calm, or the writer would be unable to *work* tomorrow. The woman was afraid of age and loss. Toby was abandoning his devotion to her to go jaunting off to Munich with two blossoming girls. She hadn't heard from Herbert Methley for months. He had besieged her, and then had abruptly retreated. She looked coldly at Humphry who was sitting on the edge of the bed, with his arms folded round himself.

"It all seems very odd to me," she said, mildly enough. And added "It will do her good, to get away from here, for a time. She's growing up." She thought hard. "I shan't speak to her, myself."

"No need," said Humphry.

Olive knew that there was a need, and that she had not got the required courage.

On the day Dorothy left for the Continent, escorted by a debonair and smiling Toby Youlgreave, August Steyning came to tea with Olive. Humphry had shut himself in his study to write. Tom had vanished into the wood, as he did vanish. Violet was out with the little ones. Hedda was hanging around, when August Steyning's trap came up the drive. She looked angry and resentful. Olive came out on the step to greet the visitor, and saw Hedda kicking gravel. Everyone seemed to be surly, Olive thought. She said

"Go and find yourself something useful to do, Hedda. I'm sure you should be studying."

Steyning climbed down, and handed the reins to the stable boy. He took Olive's hands.

"I trust you have some time for me? I have sunk into a slough of despond, and need your strong hands to pull me out." He saw Hedda. "Good afternoon, young lady." He turned back to her mother. "I *need* you, my dear, I really need your help." His voice was light and cool, his emphases almost mocking. Hedda shuffled her feet.

"Hedda, do go away, I've already asked you to go away. I need to talk to Mr. Steyning and he needs to talk to me. Go and—go and read a book."

She said to Steyning that they would have tea on the lawn, and took his arm. They turned their backs on the glowering girl.

"Do you remember," Steyning asked Olive, "the appalling boredom of being that age? With nothing to do, and only oneself to think about? There are compensations to being older."

Olive sat in a basket chair and spread her skirts. She turned an eager face to her visitor, as he took his chair. Humphry was sulking, Methley had vanished, Toby was going to the station with Dorothy, laughing and insouciant. She flirted in a serious way with August Steyning, of whom she was slightly in awe. He was hidden a long way behind his quizzical smile and his narrow face. She thought he *really* liked her, but was not sure. She knew he liked to look at her, but did not think he felt desire, as Toby and Herbert Methley did. She did not know him well enough to know how he lived. She supposed he might, like the imprisoned Oscar, feel romantic love for young men. This was common in the theatre. She tried to be broadminded—she would have liked to be Bohemian—but felt in fact a squeamish distaste for the physical descriptions in the newspapers of the hotel rooms to which Oscar had taken his boys. She smiled at August Steyning who smiled back.

The maid brought a tea-tray, and set up a table. She poured tea. August said it always did him good to be in that garden. It was a hive of energy. He could feel Olive's mind, hovering and inventing in that garden, finding strange creatures in the shrubbery and drama in the bonfire. Did she remember their discussion of that fairy play? He wanted to suggest to her that she might write him a tale—a play—a real work of the imagination. Strange and wonderful, not pretty. Like the Austrians—like Hofmannsthal—or like the *Ring of the Niebelung*. He was so sick of tea-parties on the stage, and of cheeky servants, and soubrettes, and *jeunes ingénues*. He wanted to make people's hair stand on end. Adventure, danger, dark and light.

Olive drew him out and gave him sandwiches and iced biscuits. He talked about the mood in the world of the arts. Everyone, he said, was reading stories originally written for children—stories of magic, stories of quests, stories of half-humans who were still in touch with the ancient earth, of speaking beasts, and centaurs, Pan and Puck. He was quite sure she could write him a play along those lines—in that dreamworld that was more real than urban rattle—he wanted to do something delightful and complicated with mirrors, and lights, and wires . . . and shadows.

Olive said, her voice dragging a little, that she was writing a tale about a boy—a Prince—who lost his Shadow, and went Underground in search of it.

"How did he lose it?"

"Oh, it was snipped off his feet in his cradle, by a monstrous rat, with sharp yellow teeth, who rolled it up, and took it behind the skirting-board, and down horrible holes, underground, to the Queen of the shadows. His family—the King and Queen—try to keep him safe, in a walled garden—you know how these things always—but he meets the

Queen of Elfland who needs his help, and carries him away on her white horse with bells—through seas of blood abune the knee, of course—to the opening of a mine-shaft. And he has to go in, and further in, and further in—and meets all sorts of strange creatures down there, some friendly, some evil, some indifferent . . ."

"Does he get it back?"

"I haven't got there yet. It's an *interminable* story. I'm telling it for Tom. Each of my children," she said, in the charming voice with which she had spoken to Miss Catchpole, "has his or her own story, in his or her own notebook. They were bedtime stories, but now the children are older—or some of them are—they're a kind of game. I don't know why I keep that going. Sometimes it feels a little silly. You know what you have said, about stories under the hills, of old things and inhuman things, and magic that used to run through *everything* and has now shrunk to odd little patches of magic woods and hummocks? Toby Youlgreave talks a great deal about the Brothers Grimm and their belief that fairytales were the old religion—the old *inner life*—of the German people? Well, I sometimes feel, stories are the inner life of this house. A kind of spinning of energy. I am this spinning fairy in the attic, I am Mother Goose quacking away what sounds like comforting chatter but is really—is really what holds it all together." She gave a little laugh, and said "Well, it makes money, it does hold it all together."

30

They arrived at the Pension Susskind, in Schwabing, which was managed by Joachim Susskind's aunt, Carlotta. Katharina Wellwood, being
German, imagined this place as a severe and upright dwelling, spotlessly
clean, with dull and wholesome food served promptly at fixed hours.
"Lotte" Susskind she saw in her mind's eye as a tall figure in black, with
a châtelaine at her waist, an impeccable white collar, and a shiny knot of
greying hair. Olive imagined something more informal and rosy—her
vision of Lotte Susskind wore a fresh apron over a large bosom, and
baked sweetmeats for the lucky residents. In fact Joachim Susskind's
aunt was a young aunt, though she had two teenage daughters, Elli
and Emmi. She was bony and angular, dressed in flowing blouses and
sweeping skirts, with a mop of wild wiry hair, and a pointed, slightly
witchy chin. The *pension* was a rambling building, with balconies and
corridors joining structures which might once have been stables or
dairies. Dorothy and Griselda had adjacent attics under the eaves, minimally furnished, with little wooden box-beds, plain wooden tables,
muslin curtains and fat feather quilts. The walls were painted apple-
green, and the woodwork was mustard-yellow. Dorothy wondered if
this was usual in Germany. Griselda knew it was not. Charles had been
here before, and was greeted by Lotte as a returning prodigal.

The *pension* was amiably noisy. It was inhabited by very diverse people. There were two very large men with huge heads of hair and tangled
sprouting beards, one red, one dark. They sat in shirtsleeves, in a corner
of the eating-room, and argued—about the cosmos, Griselda thought,
trying to understand the southern German accents and eccentric termi-
nology. There were two very buttoned-up, precise men, with slick
black hair and small moustaches, who wore pince-nez with black rims,
and with tiny circular handles on the eye-pieces like moons on a planet.
They went in and out—to work, presumably—but over dinner joined
in the arguments about the cosmos. There were also three young
women—art students at one of the independent women's art schools.
The Royal Bavarian School of Art admitted only men. One of the
young women was clearly well off—she had many changes of dress, elegant hats and elaborately dressed hair. The other two were patched and
darned and serviceably clothed. All three laughed a great deal. There

was a perpetual smell of paint and varnish in the *pension*. Elli and Emmi, when they came home in the evening, turned out to be younger versions of these three. Both had their mother's bony and somehow rackety good looks, and struck up casual and amusing conversations with the other inhabitants. They had simple dresses under aprons streaked with spilled colour. They hugged Charles, as though he was a family member or old friend, and expressed surprise when he introduced Griselda as his sister. We didn't know you had a sister, said Emmi and Elli in unison, and laughed. Griselda felt awkward. Dorothy, who understood nothing at all of what was said, felt more awkward. The place was buzzing and humming with chatter and argument, and it is hard, when you are seventeen, in a foreign land for the first time, not to feel that the laughter is mockingly directed against you, and the camaraderie designed to exclude you. She had a moment, standing stiffly amid the clamour, when she wondered why on earth she had disrupted her life so furiously to come here and feel lost. She was rescued by Toby Youlgreave, also a stranger to this world, who could read German as a good folklorist must, but had no speaking vocabulary and also no acquaintance with Bavarians.

"We shall feel like old inhabitants in two or three days, I imagine," he said to Dorothy. "All this will come to seem quite normal and ordinary."

The *pension* was, it became clear, open to all sorts of café society—artists, Bohemians, students, wandering mystics and anarchists—at lunch time. In the evening the guests of the *pension* dined together, round a large table, from charming flower-rimmed plates. There was soup, full of cabbage, and sausages and large pork cutlets, and a heap of potatoes and a delicious pudding of red berries and cream. Much beer was served, in large earthenware mugs. Afterwards, one of the precise men produced a flute, and one of the art students sang, in a husky voice, whilst the guests tapped with feet and fingers, until everyone joined in, beards wagging, throats swelling. Toby drank several jars of beer and joined in, humming the tunes. Dorothy said she had a headache, and went to bed.

It is hard to get to sleep in an unknown room, with unaccustomed bed coverings. Dorothy shifted and stirred and dozed and jerked awake. She could see a thin, curved penknife of a moon, steel-bright on a blue-black sky. She heard a strange sound, a regular banging and flapping, banging and flapping, thump, thump, thump, speeding up as it continued, which it did for a long time. It was accompanied by a creaking sound of bed-slats, and also by a mixture of moaning and giggling. Then there was a wailing cry, and silence.

Dorothy knew well enough, in the abstract, what she was hearing. Unlike many of her contemporaries she knew how the sex act was performed, in principle. She had watched dogs and horses. They did not take all this *time* over it. That was interesting. What could be going on? The scientist in her took notes, and the tired, overwrought girl wished that her neighbours would speed up even more, and come to an end, and allow her to sleep. She could hear a murmur of voices, after the banging stopped. She dozed. And woke again, as the banging enthusiastically recommenced. That, too, was unexpected and odd. It was characteristic of Dorothy that she wondered, not *who* was banging whom, but how it was done, and why it had that rhythm.

In the morning the girls had two hours' lessons, in maths, in German, in literature. They were taught sitting on a little balcony overlooking a kind of farmyard and a vegetable and herb garden. Charles did not come to the lessons—he was a young man, not a schoolboy, even if his education was unfinished. Sometimes he slept in, and sometimes he wandered out into the streets, and sat in the cafés. Then they paid cultural visits to galleries and museums, and returned to the *pension* for lunch, beer, conversation and a siesta.

Griselda was aware that Dorothy was tense like an overstrung bow. When they found themselves alone, Dorothy would turn to Griselda and say, we must find him, we must look for him, it is what I came to do. She begged Griselda to ask Tante Lotte about a puppet show run by a man called Anselm Stern, and Griselda demurred. She was shy. She was reserved. She did not know how to set about it. But after a few days, during a particularly lively lunch, full of intense little eddies of argument and expanses of foreign laughter, Tante Lotte brought them apple cakes, and sat down for a moment to talk to Joachim. What have you seen, she asked him. The classical statues? The State Museum? You must take everyone to the new cabaret, the Elf Scharfrichter, it is very clever and shocking. What do the young women like to see?

Dorothy understood most of this. She pushed her finger into

Griselda's flank, surreptitiously. "Tell her," she said, "tell Frau Susskind what we want to see—"

"Once, in England," said Griselda, "we saw a puppet-show. The— the *Puppenmeister*—was called Herr Stern. Anselm Stern. He acted a version of E. T. A. Hoffmann's *Sandman,* and *Cinderella.* It was—very interesting. Do you know anything about him?"

"But of course," said Tante Lotte. "He is a famous artist. Marionettes and puppets are famous in this city. There is Paul Brann, whose work is witty and magical, and there is Anselm Stern, who has made his own theatre in a cellar—it is called Frau Holle's Spiegelgarten—he is more mystical and poetical—but all the artists admire each other, all exchange ideas, all came together in the Künstlerhaus to make a funeral feast for our great painter Arnold Böcklin. You have seen Böcklin? He had a wild imagination, a fantastic vision . . . you should visit the Spiegelgarten."

(A garden of mirrors, Griselda whispered to Dorothy.)

"Fräulein Dorothy is particularly interested in puppets?"

"She wishes to become a doctor. It was I myself who was entranced by the *Sandman.*"

"It will be very easy for you to find out everything," said Tante Lotte, rising. "Those two young men, over there, are Herr Stern's sons, Wolfgang and Leon. They are often here, Wolfgang studies art—not at the Munich Art School, he's too revolutionary in his ideas to stay there and paint cows and angels. He also helps with puppets—he is more satirical than his father—he has been working with the Scharfrichter on a puppet play about the European kings and queens—the Fine Family— in three Sensations and a Prologue—dangerously comical—Leon is still at school. He is a more serious boy. I shall introduce you."

Griselda put an arm around Dorothy, as Tante Lotte strode away to the other side of the room. In the early days—when they had been cousins—Dorothy had been the strong one, the protector, the unfazed. Now it was she who had to protect. To be introduced to two unknown and foreign brothers, with no warning and no preparation, was a shock. Dorothy had gone white, and was breathing rapidly. She whispered

"I didn't know . . . I didn't know he had children . . . I didn't know he was married . . ."

Wolfgang Stern was tall and gangly, with long, thin arms and legs. He wore a loose shirt and a large floppy bow tie. His brother, equally thin, was smaller and neater, in a dark buttoned-up suit that might have been a uniform. Wolfgang had unruly, long, black hair in a cloud round his head: Leon—who must have been younger than Dorothy, but not by much—had a precisely cut hairstyle and a neat tie. Both had large dark eyes, like Dorothy's. Both were, or so Dorothy in her wrought-up state immediately felt, *recognisable*. They were faces she knew. She stared, and then looked down, feeling how odd their intent gaze was.

Griselda talked, with nervous warmth. She introduced Dorothy, in her schoolgirl German, and spoke a sentence or two about how much, in England, some years ago, they had admired their father's interpretations of Hoffmann and the Grimms.

"Really?" said Wolfgang. He bowed over Griselda's hand. "He would be enchanted to hear that. And your name?"

"I am Griselda Wellwood. We are—cousins—"

"And one of you—you I think—must be the mysterious, beautiful sister of Karl whom we see in the Café Stefanie and the Scharfrichter— Karl has been rather quiet about his sister. I think he is rather quiet about many things."

"So I am finding out," said Griselda.

"We shall be very happy," said Wolfgang, "to take you to one of our father's plays. Maybe Karl and Herr Susskind would like to come too? And your other companion—Herr Youlgreave? My father would be honoured."

He could not stop looking at Griselda. This was not unusual. Many young men looked with excitement at Griselda's pale and beautiful face. What was unusual, Dorothy thought, noticing as always, despite her own agitation, was that Griselda was responding. She was looking equally persistently at Wolfgang. She was looking down at the table, and up into his eyes, and her lips were parted. Toby Youlgreave came over from another table, where he had been talking to Joachim and Karl, and also noticed the alert stares of both Wolfgang and Griselda. He knew that Griselda was in love with himself—he had known it for a long time, and never said a word. Recently, however, as Griselda had grown into her beauty, and Olive Wellwood had grown stouter and angrier, he had begun to wonder if . . . and whether . . . he was not entirely pleased to see the smiling German so eager to make friends. He agreed, in a reserved way, that they would all enjoy a visit to the Spiegelgarten. He spoke about what he remembered of Anselm Stern's work. The beautiful automaton in the *Sandman* was peculiarly fine. She was differently artificial, in a world where all the actors were in fact artificial. He said this in a mishmash of German and English, to which Wolfgang replied in a similar way.

"I have some pitiful in English," said Wolfgang to Griselda. "You must teach me more."

Leon, like Dorothy, said nothing, only looked on.

Later, in Dorothy's bedroom, the two girls discussed the Stern brothers. Griselda was overexcited. She said it was wonderful suddenly to have two such interesting brothers. Dorothy sat stony and tears stood in her eyes.

"It is not wonderful. I wish I had never come. I wish all this had never happened. I wish I was the same as I used to be."

Griselda was immediately sympathetic and said they need not go to the Spiegelgarten if Dorothy didn't want to. Dorothy said grimly that they *must* go.

"I can't bear mess and muddle," she said. "I thought if I *found out*—about him—I should be clear in my head. But I see now, it might all be *worse* mess and muddle."

Dorothy found it hard to sleep. Her feather quilt was heavy and hot. She felt a surge of homesickness for Todefright. Her mind fixed on her Todefright brother, Tom, and his golden, slightly maddening, innocence. Tom was part of an idea she had had of an English family, the children running wild in safe woods, in dappled sunlight, the parents smilingly there, when they came home, scratched and breathless, from the Tree House and its simple secrets. They had all been one thing, the whole graduated string of busy children, all the same, all different, as children are, and they had all been absorbed by daily life and ever so slightly confined and constricted by it—a feeling which she now sensed as a luxurious indulgence. She knew the garden and the staircases, her little bedroom and the Tree House, as she knew her own body, her hair under the brush, her thin feet, her wiry hands. Only nothing was what it seemed. Violet was not an old maid of an aunt. Phyllis was only half her sister, Hedda with her cross and nosy habits of investigation and suspicion turned out to be wiser than Tom and Dorothy, her elders and superiors, who knew nothing. She thought hard about Tom, in order not to have to think about Humphry and Olive, past and present, real and imagined. Long-legged Tom, running and running with purposeful absence of purpose. He had sensed that the Garden of England was a garden through a looking-glass, and had resolutely stepped through the glass and refused to return. He didn't want to be a grown-up. Dorothy had always known she was going to grow older, and had been slightly impatient to get on with it. Now, she thought Tom might get away with his unknowing, and almost envied him. The Downs were full of young, and not so young, men in breeches and tweed or jackets, carrying rods or guns, with linen hats flopping, striding from pub to pub and talking wisely about trout, and weather, and the diseases of trees.

Tom, she thought, as she almost wept over him, was no more and no less her brother than these two dark Germans, the flirtatious one, and the quiet one. Well, that wasn't true. She had shared her life with Tom. They had played at families in the Tree House. They had held out hands to each other as they climbed, rode or strode naked into deep ponds.

It was hard to admit that she was homesick for those two deceivers, Humphry and Olive, who had turned out to be snakes in the grass as well as Adam and Eve in the Garden. She let her mind get round to Humphry's "act" as she referred to it in her head. She remembered his hand in her nightdress, her own mixture of excitement and revulsion. "I love you," he had said, "you know I love you, I have always loved you." And she had never for a moment doubted that he did—all along the lie of their life together—and what was more, she was just enough to recognise that he did indeed love her—as a father should—and had always done so. They were a modern, liberal, Fabian family. He was no paterfamilial tyrant, no ogre, no invisible person who disappeared to Work and was unknowable—as his brother was, in many ways, to Karl and Griselda. He knew how to play with his children. He had played with all of them, laughing and inventive, and still did. She had ridden on his ankle as a horse, when she was tiny, she had later ridden behind him on a bicycle in the lanes, he had steadied her. And loved her.

She had always, perhaps naturally, loved her father much more than her mother. She sensed that Olive had attention to spare for only one of her children—and that was Tom, not Dorothy. From quite early, she had refused to play Olive's game—to live in a fairy story, not on the solid earth with railway trains and difficult exams. Olive wanted to love her as a hedgehog, and she wanted to be human and adult.

It is just my bad luck, she thought, wryly and tragically, to have a mystery parent who turns out to make fairy stories—and sinister ones—with automata and *dolls*.

. . .

They went to Frau Holle's Spiegelgarten together, Toby and Joachim, Griselda and Karl, and Dorothy. They had arranged to meet Wolfgang and Leon at the door of the house in the Römerstrasse where the marionette theatre was. Dorothy had thought of confiding in Toby about her reasons for coming, and had decided against it. She had an instinctive knowledge of his relations with her mother—she had not, unlike Hedda, wanted to investigate these—and this made him, in a puzzling way, into yet another father or father-substitute. She wished that Wolfgang and Leon did not have to be present, and yet—since it was impossible, obviously, for her to speak to Anselm Stern in their presence—they allowed her to defer the encounter. She would watch him, and think what to do.

The house was high and forbidding. It had runes—Toby said they were runes—painted on its doorposts and lintels, and a *Jugendstil* painting of an apple tree, with gold and silver fruit, in the architrave. The young men met them at the door. They went through a dark inner corridor directly to the back of the house, which was lit through a stained-glass window, with more runes, in ruddy gold on white, and a medallion depicting a figure in a circle of flames.

Through this door, they went into a high, bright courtyard, with painted inner walls and bushes in flower in tubs and pots. A tiny fountain splashed in the centre: it was carved with efts and lizards, butterflies and snails, which from certain angles could be construed as peering faces or outstretched fingers. Griselda exclaimed with delight: Dorothy stood back. The sunlight poured in, golden and quivering in the heat like liquid. The puppet theatre was in an outbuilding on the other side of the courtyard. Its door was flanked by two carved wooden figures, one winged, hooded and slender, one short, stalwart and bearded. *Elf und Zwerg,* said Wolfgang to Griselda. Elf and dwarf. He added something which Toby translated as "The guardians of the other world." How Mother would love this, thought Dorothy, grimly.

Inside was as dark as the courtyard was light. They were in a small theatre, they saw, as their eyes adjusted to seeing—the sudden change had blinded them, and filled the space with hallucinatory flashings and varied colours, intense, fading. They made out rows of benches, and on the walls mirrors framed with carved heads and foliage, some of them covered with black veils. The easiest thing to see was the high, gilded proscenium of the marionettes' stage, covered with a blue silky curtain painted with moons and stars. A kind of blackboard to the side of these announced "*Heute wird gespielt* Die Jungfrau Thora, ihr Lindwurm, seine Goldkiste."

There was a source of light behind the curtain, limelight mixed with rays of crimson, pink, sky-blue and deep green. Other members of the audience crept in and stood, getting their bearings. Music began, a faint high twanging, a wistful fluting. Wolfgang said to Griselda

"He never comes out before the play. The characters don't speak. It is all light and movement. Sometimes he comes out after. He waits for complete silence. He is exigent."

Leon said to Dorothy, who was on the end of the bench, "Are you comfortable?" He said it in English. It was the first thing he had directly said to her. Yes, thank you, she said, clasping her hands in her skirts.

The curtains opened. The *Jungfrau,* Thora, glided in. She was a delicate, lovely creature, with an exquisite porcelain stare and a mass of floating, silky, silvery hair. She wore a white dress and blue mantle, and her movements were thoughtful and precise.

She was presented with the glittering gold casket, by a kind of white-bearded, black-gowned wizard on bended knee. The set was a turret room, the starry sky visible through slits of windows, with high Gothic chairs. The Princess placed the casket on a table, and, when she was alone, bent over it and opened it. A tiny golden worm, sinuous and bearded, shot out of it like a firework, shimmered in the air, flew in circles, and went back to rest.

The story of Thora and the Lindwurm is the story of dragons and gold, Toby Youlgreave later explained. Dragons sleep on gold; a poetical kenning for gold is "*Wurmbett,*" dragon's bed. This dragon increased the gold in its casket and the size of its gold bed. The hidden treasure shone out of its box with brilliant ruddy light. The dragon grew, and outgrew its case. The curtains of the theatre slid together and reopened, and each time the dragon was larger, and fatter and more fearsomely bearded. Its eyes glittered ruby: its talons were silver: its mane frothed with coloured lights. It coiled itself round the box, tail-tip in grinning mouth between pointed, curving teeth. It coiled itself like a constrictor around the *Jungfrau* herself, who began to make movements of anguish and pain.

The old wizard reappeared, in another set, and prompted a series of princely, strutting puppets, booted, caped, with feathered hats and bright blades, to advance into the chamber and attack the creature. The set for these attacks was an antechamber opening onto the treasure room in which the beast was coiled up and the Princess constricted. They went in—some debonair, some a little tremulous, and were flung out in bloody pieces which spun in segments and fell. Children in the audience cried out with glee.

Prince Frotho appeared. He was a mild and workmanlike figure in serviceable moleskin brown. A serving-maid suggested in mime, he should consult the Mothers.

A new scene showed a bleak stone cavern in which Frotho threw herbs into a cleft in the rock. The Mothers rose slowly from Underground, three huge figures, swaying like growing plants, with veiled skulls for faces and hunched backs. Frotho mimed his problem, mimed the Worm, mimed the Princess. So much expression, Griselda thought, from so simple a collection of wires and china and clay and cloth. The Mothers turned their horrible fixed grins on Prince Frotho and invited him to embrace them. The audience knew he must not hesitate or recoil or he was lost. He stepped out decisively and kissed each creature—they had to bow their upper bodies to receive his kiss. When he had kissed all three, they spun around and around, and changed their appearance—instead of the skull inside the skin, they showed beautiful, dreaming female faces under the now translucent skulls. They stood up proudly and did a stately dance. They had rich hair under their dark veiling. They gave Frotho a blue flower—"*Rittersporn,*" whispered Wolfgang to Toby, who nodded knowledgeably, and whispered to Griselda that it was "knights' spurs," or larkspur, a magical herb.

Armed with the *Rittersporn,* Prince Frotho returned to the treasure chamber, now entirely filled with the coils of the Worm, between two of which, like a captive through bars, the *Jungfrau* peered whitely. Prince Frotho brandished his flower and his blade. He whirled it, and the gold head followed its movements. He stabbed—once, twice, three times—and the dragon disintegrated into golden segments, like great coins, which flew in the air and settled in a heap, like money in a vault, with the grinning head on top, and the tail dangling over the front of the stage. The Prince embraced the trembling Princess. The audience applauded. The curtains closed. The puppetmaster stepped out to take his bow. He wore a black gown, absolutely plain, buttoned to the neck, and a kind of square academic cap. Toby and Griselda were clapping vigorously. Dorothy frowned and stared. He had a pale face and a thin, clear-cut mouth. He looked something like one of his own figures, bowing with deliberate grace, unsmiling, lifting his hands, and making a gesture towards the invisible cast behind the curtain, that resembled the acknowledgement of a conductor to an orchestra. His hands were thin and fine. He wore a ring with a green stone. He was alien. He was not quite in this world, and this world was alien to Dorothy, it spoke another language, and lived by other rules and habits. How could she tell who he was? How could she *see* him? And yet, as with his sons, she "recognised" his face, though she did not know what "recognised" meant. He bowed again, amongst the folds of his gown, and stepped back into the dark.

Wolfgang said, as a dim light glimmered in the theatre, and the audience stirred, that they must all come back and meet his father. Griselda looked at Dorothy who said in a rush that she felt unwell, she really must go home, she was very sorry, another time . . .

There was some ambivalence as to how far Griselda and Dorothy might be allowed to wander the streets of Munich without a guardian or chaperone. Toby and Joachim took their responsibilities seriously. It was agreed that Karl was a good enough watchman, and the girls managed to persuade him to go "shopping" with them, the next day, and in fact take them as far as the Spiegelgarten. They found the door to the street open, and went in, as before—it was a bright morning, and the next performance was announced on a noticeboard for late that afternoon. Karl was happy to leave them, when they asked if he would. They arranged to meet later in the Café Bettina, unlike the Café Stefanie, a quiet place where women art students gathered to drink tea and coffee.

There was no one in the little courtyard, where the fountain chuckled perpetually. Dorothy and Griselda went into the auditorium, and waited for their vision to adjust. There was no one there, either. But they could hear movements behind the theatre, whose curtains were closed and still. A rattle, a swish, felted footsteps. Griselda whispered "We could call out—" Dorothy said "Come on," in the tense voice she had used since they came. She was terribly strung up, Griselda thought, following her. She was resolutely calm, and it was costing her.

Behind the stage was a space which was a mixture of a workroom, a storeroom and a wardrobe. Lifeless figures hung in neat lines from parallel rods, like clothes in a wardrobe, or, thought Dorothy with a pang, like those dead trophies on the wall of the gamekeeper's hut, which Tom had found. Chins sagged, hands and feet dangled. Griselda thought of gibbets. There was a glass case along one wall, full of faces, faces in wood, faces in clay, faces in painted porcelain, some with wigs, some without, grotesque and elegant, sweet and evil, all with that peculiar quality of great marionettes, which is to have one unchanging expression, one character, which can, in motion, mysteriously express many moods and passions, simultaneously fixed and serene, and purely expressive. There were neat piles of the black lacquer boxes in which the marionettes had travelled to Todefright. There were workbenches, with tools—chisels, screws and nails, files and knives—with jars of glue and boxes of silk, satin, felt, floss, illusion, sackcloth.

It was a dark room, but lit by a skylight. Under the skylight, on a kind of throne, padded with red leather, sat Anselm Stern, clothed in black—a velvet jacket, narrow trousers. He was sewing. He had a female marionette bent over one hand, her skirts flung forward over her face, and he was stitching somewhere between her waist and the fork of her dangling legs, which were made of stuffed cloth, but ended in pointed china toes. He seemed to stitch as a marionette would stitch, each push of the needle, each long pull of the thread, exquisitely performed. He said, without looking up

"*Wer sind Sie? Warum sind Sie hier? Das Kammer ist geschlossen.*"

"We—I—need to speak to you," said Dorothy. "It is important."

Griselda translated this into German. They stood together in front of his chair, like two schoolgirls before a master. Griselda's dress was duck-egg-blue and shining. Dorothy was in severe dark green. She clutched her purse. Anselm Stern spoke again, briefly.

"He says, if it is important, then tell him what it is."

"My father told me," said Dorothy, and stopped, confused. "That is, I have been told that—who I thought was my father is not my father. He told me that you are my father."

Griselda translated. The hand with the needle paused, and then pierced again.

"So I came to see you," said Dorothy, calmly desperate.

She had not known what she expected this father to do, on hearing this announcement. For a moment, he did not look up, but tightened his mouth and drove in another stitch. Then he laid aside the doll, carefully, and looked straight at Dorothy. It was a studying look, neither friendly nor unfriendly, but searching.

"Who are you?" he said.

"My name is Dorothy. Olive Wellwood is my mother. My—her husband—is Humphry. He seems to be sure of what he says."

"And you are how old?"

"Seventeen. Nearly eighteen."

"And why have you come here? What do you want?"

Dorothy found it hard to breathe.

"I want to know *who I am.*"

It was wildly absurd to be saying all this through Griselda's deliberately expressionless, gentle voice.

"And do you expect me to tell you?" asked Anselm Stern.

"I thought," said Dorothy with spirit, "that if I knew who *you* were, I should know more about who I really am."

"Indeed," said Anselm Stern. The sharp mouth smiled a wry smile. "And in your place, Fräulein Dorothy, I should have had the same thought, I think—so maybe, *vielleicht,* that tells us a little of who we both are."

He was silent, for some time, thinking. He said

"When were you born?"

"On November 23rd, 1884."

He counted months on his precise fingers. He smiled. He said

"What does your mother think about the fact that you are here?"

Dorothy looked to Griselda for help. Griselda looked blank. Dorothy began to speak fast, in her normal voice, not the unnaturally formal one she had been using.

"She doesn't exactly know, that is, it hasn't been openly discussed. But I think my father—I think that *he*—has told her what he said to me, because she seems—perhaps angry, with him or with me—she didn't try to stop me coming here, but we didn't talk about why—I think there was an unspoken—understanding. I don't think she meant me to know. I don't think she knew what to say to me." She paused. "It was a great shock to me. And difficult for her."

She listened to Griselda's soft German, following the rhythms of her English, half a sentence behind.

"So," said Anselm Stern. *"Ich verstehe."*

"I understand," said Griselda.

"You are an unusually determined and outspoken young woman," said the two voices, the German one both amused and judging, the English one hesitant.

"I like to understand things. To *know*," said Dorothy.

"So I see. Had you thought what this—this knowledge—would mean to me? I have a wife and two sons. What did you expect me to do, when you had told me?"

"I didn't know what you would do. That is up to you. You can tell me to go away. I think you believe what I say."

"I think I do believe you. You were born nine months after Fasching. There are many Fasching cuckoos in Munich."

"Fasching cuckoos?"

Griselda and Anselm Stern began to explain simultaneously.

"Fasching is Karneval. All is permitted," said Anselm Stern.

"Fasching is a great mad Shrove Tuesday feast, with dancing in the street," said Griselda, and broke off to translate Stern's explanation.

Griselda said, translating nothing,

"We have met your sons, Herr Stern. In the Pension Susskind where we are staying. They brought us to the performance yesterday. But we said nothing to them, and did not wait to see you, because of what Dorothy had to say."

"Translate, please," said Dorothy, excluded.

Stern said to Griselda

"And you, who are you?"

"I am Dorothy's cousin, Griselda Wellwood. That is, I am *not* Dorothy's cousin, but we have always been closer than sisters. My mother was born Katharina Wildvogel. You may remember—you were kind enough to explain the Aschenputtel story, at Todefright, when you performed it."

"I remember. Your German is better than it was at that time." He was silent for a few moments. He picked up the marionette he had been stitching, shook out her skirts, and looked into her painted eyes. He fingered the silky hair, which looked as though it was real human hair, tucking it into shape.

"I have always wanted a daughter. My sons are good sons, but I always wanted a daughter. What to do now?"

"I didn't want to embarrass you, or make your life difficult."

"This is Munich, this is *Wahnmoching,* this is the home of doctrinaire Free Love, where it is laid upon us to greet cuckoos as golden eggs. This is the city where you may say openly what you have just said to me, here in this inner room, and no one will think worse of you—no one that *matters* that is, of course, for the heavy burghers and beer-drinkers are only Matter, inessential, what they think is heavier than air. But you may not wish to say anything, on your own account. You may be ashamed, which you should not be, or embarrassed, which you have a right to be. You may wish to keep the secret you have been told and share it only with those who already know it, Herr Humphry, your mother, and the wise Fräulein Griselda here whom we must both thank, I think, not only for the bridge of language, but for the calm and philosophical atmosphere that comes with her. I could take you to meet my wife—"

Griselda blushed, and her voice faded, far behind. Dorothy continued to work for clarity.

"What would—what will—your wife think?"

"My wife is an artist. My wife models in clay and carves stone and teaches at the Damen-Akademie. Her name is Angela, and she is an Angel. She likes to be in the forefront of modern thinking. In principle, she would expect a family to welcome a discovered child. In practice, I do not know. How long are you in Munich? For if you are here for some time, we might proceed—delicately, soft-footed, sagaciously—"

Griselda was having more trouble with the translation as Anselm Stern—who chose his words carefully—began to use the slightly odd, poetical vocabulary his friends would have recognised.

"We are here for two or three months. We are studying. I am trying to learn German. I have to pass my matriculation. I am not gifted at languages, Mr. Stern. But I will try."

"Not gifted at languages? But serious, not a hausfrau. An interesting kind of daughter. What are your gifts, your inclinations, your hopes, Miss Dorothy?"

"I mean to be a doctor. The training is very hard. I should like to be a surgeon."

"Let me see your hands."

He put aside the limp puppet—his own hands seemed uneasy without occupation. Dorothy moved closer to him, and he took both her hands in his. Both pairs were thin, wiry and strong. They were the same kind of hands.

"Strong hands," said Anselm Stern. "Capable hands, delicate hands." He gave a dry little cough. "I am moved."

Dorothy went red, and then white. Tears threatened, and she held them in.

"You are tired, young ladies," said Anselm Stern. "A great effort has been made, strain has been endured. We should go and drink coffee, or chocolate, and eat a pastry, and talk calmly and generally, about Life and Art, and begin to know each other? Yes?"

That night, Dorothy said to Griselda

"His name suits him."

"Stern."

"Yes. He looks stern. Serious and stern."

Griselda gave a little laugh.

"*Stern* in German doesn't mean stern."

"What . . . ?"

"It's the German word for a star."

"Oh," said Dorothy, revisiting the imagined figure in her mind. "A star."

31

The events, so far, had been initiated by Humphry's lapse, and controlled by Dorothy's will. To her surprise—and in some ways, to her relief—Anselm Stern now took over the control of the story, which he began almost to direct as though it had been the structure of a play. He arranged meetings, of different kinds, in different places. He took his new daughter for walks in the Englische Garten, with Griselda walking like a shadow a few paces behind. He wore a swinging coat with wide skirts, and a wide-brimmed hat. In his pockets, it turned out, puppets were tucked, with strings and bars. A wistful female child, a wolfman with a snarling smile and a fur coat, a strange mooncalf, luminous green with huge eyes. He held them out and they tripped along beside him. Passers-by waved to them. Anselm said to Dorothy

"I do not know whether I believe they have souls, or temporary souls, or intermittent souls." He looked searchingly at Griselda. "*Du kannst übersetzen?* I think I believe that we are all fragments of one great soul—that the earth is one living thing, and the clay and the wood and the catgut these are made of are forms of life, as is the movement I lend them."

Dorothy nodded seriously, pink. She had a pretty straw hat with a midnight-blue ribbon.

"I have embarrassed you," he said.

"No."

"Oh yes. I knew I would. But I always walk here, with these creatures—these manikins—and I wish my daughter to know me as I am."

The little figures danced on the path, and stopped, and looked up at Dorothy.

"Take one," said Anselm Stern. "Move him."

Dorothy pulled back. Griselda held out her fingers and was given the mooncalf. Dorothy then took the wolfman. They sagged. Griselda twitched and adjusted and the mooncalf began a drunken dance. Anselm Stern put his hand over Dorothy's.

"Do not be afraid. Let him walk."

The strings were, after all, alive. Horribly alive. Once, with Tom at the brook, she had tried dowsing with a hazel fork, just for the fun of it, and had been terrified when the dead wood lurched at her fingertips, and pulled. She had dropped the thing and refused to have more to do with it. These strings pulled the same way. She let her fingertips listen, and the wolfman began to stride, and bow. He raised his paw. He threw back his head, to howl, or to laugh. Her fingers tingled.

"You said," said Anselm Stern, "you wanted to know who I am. I am a man who makes dancing dolls." Griselda was tangled and did not translate, but Dorothy understood.

"I see," she said, and halted the wolfman and handed him back.

Griselda would have expected the old, resolutely rational Dorothy to be worried, possibly even repelled, by the strangenesses and formalities. The garden walk was followed by an exploration of the cavern behind the stage, an introduction to all the hanging family, a disquisition on the character of every severed head, an exploration of the boxes in which they lay, decently, head to tail, all except Death, who lay back in his single casket until Anselm Stern raised him to bow deeply to Dorothy, to stretch out his arms to her, fold them, and lie back again. He talked only intermittently and Griselda could not translate all of it. The creatures had a purer, more essential existence than emotional beings. Griselda, the imaginative one, found it was she who was being half-sceptical. Dorothy wandered on in a listening dream.

It was not only serious metaphysics of marionettes. It was cream cakes and coffee in Café Félicité, with Anselm and daughter leaning on their elbows and staring into each other's eyes, and a long interrogation.

"Your favourite colour, Fräulein Dorothy?"

"Green. And yours?"

"Green, naturally. Your favourite smell?"

"Bread baking. And yours?"

"Oh, bread baking, there is none better."

He gave her little gifts. Things he had carved. An owl. A walnut. A hedgehog. She frowned over the hedgehog. It reminded her of Olive's Dorothy-tale, about Peggy and Mistress Higgle, the shape-changer, and in a way that appeared truly uncanny Dorothy received, on the day he gave it to her, a fat envelope from home, containing another instalment, a placatory peace-offering from the storyteller in Todefright, who did not know what Dorothy knew, who was afraid of what she was finding out, and could think of nothing better to do than to send a segment of fairy-tale. Dorothy meant not to read it. But did. Mistress Higgle's hedgehog-mantle—and with it her magic—had been stolen, Dorothy read. It had been folded away, in its secret drawer, and Mistress Higgle had come home to find the window open, and the spiny jacket nowhere. All the dependent furry creatures in the house—the mouse-people, the frog-people, the little vixen—had lost the power to change shape, because the thorny integument had vanished. Who was responsible? The story stopped there. Olive's accompanying letter was somewhat plaintive.

> *I'm not sure, my darling, whether you still want the stories—maybe you are a grown-up lady now, and past childish things—but I thought about you a lot, and since writing stories is what I do, I wrote the one I still think of as yours. You don't write to tell me how you are. We all miss you dreadfully. There is no one like you for good sense and understanding and getting things done. We are all a bit feckless and down in the dumps without you. And Tom is positively* dirty with nights out in the woods. *Please write, my darling. You don't have to read the silly story if you don't want to.*
>
> *Your bewildered and loving mother.*

There were now things Dorothy wanted to say to Anselm Stern without saying them to Griselda. She was picking up basic German but she could not speak it well enough to explain Mistress Higgle, or to ask him questions about her mother. She felt, in odd moments of solitude—like this one, sitting with the English schoolroom paper with writings on it about English furry creatures that were also human—that Anselm Stern had her under a spell. She was not happy now except when she was with him, or on her way to meet him, and yet she also felt fear, fear of a trap, fear of something unseen.

She handed him—they were sitting in his workroom—the sheaf of papers from Olive. She said, expressionless, in German

"*Ein Brief von meiner Mutter. Ein Märchen. Ich habe meiner Mutter nichts von Ihnen—von Dir—gesagt.*"

He gave her a long, sombre look, and picked up the papers. Dorothy was in that state human beings passed through at the beginning of a love affair, in which they desire to say anything and everything to the beloved, to the *alter ego,* before they have learned what the real Other can and can't understand, can and can't accept. Griselda sat pale and vanishing. Anselm turned over the pages, with their little drawings of hedgehogs and frogs and underground kitchens with rows of pannikins. He said to Griselda

"What is this?"

"Tell him—" said Dorothy. "She writes a story for each of us. This is mine. It is a whimsical story about magic hedgehogs."

"I can't translate whimsical." She looked at Dorothy. "Dorothy, don't cry. Why did you bring it?"

"She's in this story too. I brought it to *bring it together.* Don't translate that."

But he nodded, as though he had understood.

"Higgle," he said. "Mis-tress Hig-gle. What is Mistress Higgle?"

"Eine kleine Frau die ist auch ein Igel," said Griselda.

"Ein Igel," said Anselm Stern.

"An *eagle*?" asked Dorothy.

"No, no. *Igel* is the German word for a hedgehog."

" 'Hans mein Igel.' That's a story from the Grimms. He says he played it for her." She turned to Anselm.

"Für die Mutter?"

"Genau."

"So. Mrs. Higgle is Hans mein Igel. I have not played it for many years. The Hedgehog-human puppet is one of my finest, I think. We will find him out, and tomorrow I shall perform the story. I think she must have named you Mistress Higgle for Hans mein Igel. The story is strange. It is the tale of a woman who so desired a child that she said she would give birth to anything, even a hedgehog. And in tales, you get what you ask for. Her child was a hedgehog above, and a pretty boy below, and he revolted her."

Griselda had trouble with "revolted."

"So he slept in straw by the stove, and rode out into the woods on a fine cockerel, playing the—I can't translate *Dudelsack.*"

Anselm Stern mimed.

"Ah, bagpipes. He sat in a tree, and played the bagpipes and looked after herds of swine, and prospered. By and by he came to the attention of a king lost and bewildered, to whom he showed the way, and the king promised him whatever first met him on his way, which was of course, as it always must be, his daughter. And the daughter must marry the half-hedgehog swineherd, for promises in tales must be kept. And she was greatly afraid of his spines, and did not respond to bagpipe music. So we move to the bridal chamber and there in secret the hedgehog takes off his hedgehog-skin, and servants of the king rush in and burn it in a fire. This is a fine scene for puppets to play. And then he is wholly human, but black as coal. So they wash him, and dress him as a prince, and the princess runs into his arms and loves him—very much—mightily—and all is well. I think, Dorothy, your mother was thinking of the half-alien child, and the hedgehog—who is a trickster, a clever Hans, a German character—when she named your Mistress Higgle. You are the much-desired child who is half from somewhere else, a different child.

"In this story she sent, someone has stolen the hedgehog-skin. In *this* story, she needs it, it is magic, it makes her smaller, or invisible.".

Anselm Stern found out the old puppets from "Hans mein Igel," the spiny-coated changeling, the prancing red cockerel with his golden comb, the mother with her face that perpetually wept, two painted tears on her wooden cheek—first, because she had no child, and then, because her child was uncanny. A few days later he put on the old play, with Wolfgang as his assistant. This play was not silent—the two men spoke all the parts, and Wolfgang played a tripping tune on a primitive bagpipe. They all came—Joachim and Karl, Toby and Griselda, Leon and Dorothy. Dorothy had noticed that the artist was quietly disappointed if she was not at every performance in the Spiegelgarten. Light glistened on the half-hedgehog's lively spines. She thought, I shall never pass my matriculation, if I spend all my time in here, watching dolls dance. And yet, as the hedgehog came blackly out of the thorns, like a butterfly out of a chrysalis, and was washed white so he could bed his princess, she was moved to tears, she felt liquid inside, she was pulled about like tides by the moon. She had not bargained for all this.

Wolfgang, a few days later, caught at Griselda's sleeve as she was leaving the lunch table in the Pension Susskind.

"A word with you—" he said, in English. "Some quiet place," he said.

Griselda felt his fingers electric. She had been aware that he watched her—her skin was warmer in his searching stare. He was both a mocking and a serious young man. He made wry jokes about Bavarians and beer, about the Kaiser and his wardrobes full of uniforms, about King Edward in England, his harem of ladies, and the Boers suffering stolidly in South Africa. He was at home in this strange new world of satire, skits, innuendo and sudden plangent sentiment. He watched her, Griselda. When he saw she saw him watching, he curled his wide mouth in a deprecatory grin, and looked away.

She followed him out into the garden, and they sat at a table, under a vine sprawling over an arbour.

"I want you to see this," he said.

He handed her a large sketch-book. It was filled with drawings of female heads, very occasionally with bodies attached to them, seen from every angle, with every possible expression. They were done in charcoal, in pencil, in chalk, in ink.

They were herself and Dorothy. They studied their bones, their hair, their attitudes, their habits of mind.

For a moment, Griselda thought Wolfgang had done them. Then he said

"What have you done to my father? He is *verzaubert*—bewitched. Is he in love with you? People have been speaking—to me and my mother. He has never been like this, never. Have you made him mad?"

Griselda stared at him in horror.

"It isn't *that,* at all. Not at all." She thought furiously. "I think you must ask *him.*"

"How can I? He is my father. He has always been—rather serious, a little distant. How can I ask him if he is in love with one or two English girls? People have said—spiteful—things to my mother."

He looked gloomily at the table.

"We want you to let him go," he said, slowly.

"I only translate—"

"So it is the other, the Dorothy—"

Furies flapped in Griselda's head. The secret was not hers. She said

"There is a secret. It is not mine to tell you."

"What have you done?"

"Listen," said Griselda. "It is their secret. If I tell you, it will only be so as to stop you—thinking wrong things. It is a secret."

"So?"

"She is his daughter. She came to tell him she had found that out. He—he believes her, you can see. They—they are—you see how they are. I only translate," she was compelled to add, though she was covertly studying the repeated recording of her thin and pale beauty in the sketch-book. She said

"And you are her brother. Half-brother."

Wolfgang put his head to one side and considered Griselda. She said

"I think you should tell him you know. I think—"

I think it is all too intense, she wanted to say, and could not.

Wolfgang said

"I am glad you are not my sister."

"Why?"

"You know why."

Griselda flushed and looked away.

"Will you come with me, to him—?" said Wolfgang.

Anselm Stern, confronted by his son, his sketch-book and a deprecatory Griselda, was briefly taken aback. He had been controlling a story, and one of the actors had taken the strings into his own hands. Wolfgang asked, politely and implacably, whether what Griselda said was true. Then he said that his father must speak to his mother, because people had been saying unkind things. He had always intended to speak to her, Anselm said. He had wanted—time to himself, time to think how best to go on, what to say to his sons. He smiled ruefully at Wolfgang.

"Now you know, there is no further reason to hesitate."

"I'm sorry," said Griselda.

"Why?"

"It wasn't my secret." A child both spoiled, indulged and neglected, she had never before for so long been simply ancillary to someone else's drama.

"No, it is good," said Anselm Stern. "Now I reflect, I must thank you."

Angela Stern sent hand-decorated cards—with wickedly grinning cherubs—to the Pension Susskind to invite everyone—Joachim, Toby, Karl, Griselda and Dorothy—to supper in the Spiegelgarten. Dorothy looked at the cherubs and said that Frau Stern had a sense of humour. She put her hair up, carefully, for the occasion.

Frau Stern received them standing by the fountain. She was larger than her husband, in every direction, and seemed a little older, solid-featured, with a crown of greying fair hair. She wore a lace-trimmed blouse and a full grey skirt, nothing fancy. She shook everyone's hand, Dorothy's no longer than any other. She had one of those faces that in repose looks heavy, but can be transformed by a smile, or an eager sense of interest. When she smiled, she resembled Wolfgang, the same wide grin, the same concentrated glee. She served salmon and cucumber, sour cream and potato salad, accompanied by a choice of beer or Riesling. She said that the carvings on the fountain and the mirrors were her own work. Griselda watched her watching Dorothy, when Dorothy was not looking. Dorothy was sitting next to Leon, who said composedly that he had been talking to his brother and was happy to have his news.

When they had finished eating, Angela Stern invited Dorothy to come into the house and look at her work. Everyone—even, by now, the tutors—understood the importance of this. Anselm Stern brought the figure of a black cat out of his pocket and began to dance it on his knee.

"I shall show you my atelier," said Angela Stern, who spoke English, in her own way. They climbed steep stairs and went into a large, largely empty room, with an easel set up, and two tables of modelled clay heads, some in progress, some finished.

"These are my sons," said Angela Stern, pointing to three heads of very newborn babies. "Here Wolfgang, here Leon, here Eckhardt, who did not live. I love my sons, and I love my work, and I'm happy to see you in my house, Fräulein Wellwood."

"Dorothy?"

"Dorothy."

"It is kind of you to invite me."

"I do *believe* that we should all be free to love when—where—we must—that we should not be constrained. What we believe and what we feel, you will understand, are not always the same. I—I did not know you—you—existed. I met your mother when she was here. She is a beautiful woman, full of life. She was very unhappy, in that time. We tried to comfort her.

"I believe I *ought* to be happy to see you—Fräulein—Dorothy—and now that I do see you, I believe I *shall* be happy. Come to see us, often. I shall show you my work. This is the room where I am myself. I should like you to know me—me also. I think I need say no more."

"You are incredibly kind."

"If there is any fault, it is not yours. These are my sons, as cherubs, and here, beginning to be young men. This is Anselm. I could not model him without a model in his hand. I have never got his look to my own satisfaction. I also do caricatures, and there I do better, I can make a simplified—how do you say—edge—outline of his look—"

Thinking about this conversation, later, Dorothy thought that the older woman was determined both to behave well, and not to be left out. Later still, she came to see that there were many ways in which Angela Stern resembled Olive Wellwood. "This is the room where I am myself." Dorothy was at an age where she was still amazed to be able to describe to herself the movements of the minds and feelings of others. If you knew how somebody's mind worked, did it mean you liked them? She was not a person of fierce affections or spontaneous emotions. All this bubbling up of excitement and delight and fear over her found father perturbed her. Angela Stern's lovingly modelled heads of her boys were like Olive's family tales—a form of love, a form of separateness.

Good sense is both a curse and a blessing. Dorothy sat in Munich, and thought everything out. If she was to be a doctor, she must return to Todefright and matriculate. She thought briefly about trying to stay in southern Germany and become a doctor there, but German women had more restricted options for study than the British, at that time. And she realised she had no idea what her new-found family would say if she asked to be taken in. And then she realised that she did not want to stay, not yet, not really. She was homesick even if she was happy. She missed both the Tree House and the convenience of Queen's College, Harley Street and the lectures in Gower Street. There was also the problem of the tutors. Griselda and Karl knew what was going on and had accepted Wolfgang and Leon as proxy cousins. She made a plan. She asked Griselda to tell Toby Youlgreave, in very strict confidence, what had happened. And she asked Karl to tell Joachim Susskind, in even stricter confidence, the same story. They would be part of a circle who knew the truth about Anselm Stern and Dorothy Wellwood, and they would preserve the convention that Dorothy was indeed Dorothy Wellwood, and thus she could go home. She wondered what Toby would think, who had loved her mother so long—she was trying to rethink, revisit, what she surmised of the relations of those two. She rejected the idea that he might always have known that Dorothy was not Humphry's child. She would have noticed, if he had looked knowing in any way. He did not. He looked baffled.

And how should she prepare her return—to a certain extent, a climb-down—to Todefright? She wrote a letter to her mother. It took her a long time to write.

Dearest Mother Goose,

I was so pleased to have your letter and hear that all is well at home. I miss the children, and Tom, and the countryside, even though it is both beautiful and exciting in the city. I am learning a lot. Germans are very different from us, and you come to understand yourself better by seeing people who are different.

I don't know why you thought I might not want the fairytale. I always love to see it, and know what happens next. I showed it to Herr Anselm Stern whose theatre we have been visiting. He said Mistress Higgle might be related to Hans mein Igel (originally by the Grimms) and put on his own puppet play about Hans the Igel for all of us to see. We have become great friends with Herr Stern and all his family. Frau Stern is an artist. I don't know if you have met her. She is a very kind and welcoming woman and invites all of us—including the Tutes—to supper. Herr Stern's sons, Wolfgang and Leon, are very good friends of all of us, now. They talk to Griselda in German, and take Charles to cabaret theatres and cafés! I know you are sad we shall not be in Todefright for the Midsummer Party, but the Sterns have invited us to celebrate it—it is called the Johannisnacht Fest—here, with them, and we will think of you all. Everyone in Munich—that is, in artistic circles in Schwabing—dresses up in fancy dress on every conceivable occasion, so we shall have to think what to go as. Herr Stern has promised to do a version of Midsummer Night's Dream *with marionettes for the occasion. Everyone here loves to go out and see the* Bauerntanz—*the people dancing in the streets. Herr Stern says he can make the rustics in the* Dream *be like the German* Bauern. *I am learning German but very slowly. Griselda speaks it like a swan swimming in a river. But she too will be happy to come home. We all send love, to you, and to Father, and to everyone in Todefright.*

Dorothy.

Dorothy thought this letter was both a masterpiece of the disingenu-
ous, and a very useful lifeline, cast to Olive, if Olive wanted to grasp it.
She then sat down to think about her own fury at Olive, her wish to
close her out and punish her. What exactly was she punishing her *for*?
For a moment of passion (she supposed it was a moment of passion)
with the mysterious and intriguing Anselm? For her own birth? She was
glad she had been born, she was contented enough with who she was,
even if that person turned out to have a different origin from what she
had always supposed. For bringing her up in ignorance, as a Wellwood?
What else could a woman in that situation have done? She had not lied
to Humphry—possibly could not. They had both loved Dorothy, that
she had to admit. What angered her was the *lie*. Those who are lied to
feel diminished, set aside, misused. So Dorothy felt. But she was also
discovering that knowing about lies that have been told is a form of
power. She had power over both Humphry and Olive, because they had
lied to her, and she knew. And they did not know how much she knew,
and they were fearful. The letter she had written would make them
more fearful, more anxious. They *deserved* that. But the letter also, in its
naïveté and neutrality, left the door open for everyone to pretend that
nothing had happened at all—for them all to know they were pretending, and tell a story together. She pressed the envelope shut, licked the
stamp, and carried it to the post.

Charles/Karl was also preoccupied with his double identity. He saw
more both of the politically agitated and of the raffish and satirical sides
of life in Schwabing than the young ladies did. He sat in the Café Stefanie, in the thick smoke and the singing, and listened to psychoanalysts
and anarchists preaching ferment. He listened to slogans. "Unity is
princely violence, is tyrannical rule. Discord is popular violence, is freedom" (Panizza). Intense analogies were drawn between hidden destructive parts of the soul, and the excitement of peasants and workers in
mobs. It was dangerous to deny such impulses—violence, conspiracy,
revolution, murder became necessary and desirable as the tyrannical
state was opposed and overcome. It was a long way from the polite
lucubrations of the Fabians, and even further from the horse-racing,
shooting-party circles of the new King, at the edge of which Charles's
father moved—thanks to his German mother's fortune. Charles was
quite intelligent enough to see that he was able to be an anarchist
because he was rich. The Munich café thinkers were aesthetically

excited by peasant manifestations of energy—the charivari, the *Bauern-tanz*, the Karneval. Karneval and misrule went together, and were glorious. Joachim Susskind mostly listened. Wolfgang said little, though, like his father, he sketched incessantly, beards wagging in passionate dissertation, women's legs visible under their skirts as they leaned back, applauding. Leon joined in. He discussed the necessity of assassination, almost primly. Karl said he did not see that it was necessary—such detached Acts as there had been—anarchists had killed the President of France, the Prime Minister of Spain, the Empress Elizabeth and the King of Italy—had only led to more repression. There speaks an Englishman, said Leon, not unfriendly. You don't recognise oppression as we do. You cannot be put in prison for *Unzüchtigkeit*—"obscenity" Joachim translated—or for *lèse-majesté* as our artists regularly are. We are driven to put on our serious plays in private clubs and cabarets. And then, the police come in, and the artists are imprisoned, or banished. Oskar Panizza is in Switzerland and cannot return.

"We shall take you to the new artists' cabaret, the Elf Scharfrichter. Eleven executioners," said Joachim. "It's better in German—the sharp edge of the axe is the bite of the wit."

Karl was already amazed by the satirical poison and violence of the periodicals, *Jugend, Simplicissimus,* with their drawings at once elegant, wicked, obscene and lively. Black dancing demons. Bulldogs. Women like bats and vampires with black mouths. Leon invited him—as an English anarchist—to admire Simpl's cartoons on English matters. Leon explained to Charles/Karl that artists in Schwabing felt great sympathy for the oppressed Boers in South Africa. The cartoons preached "Shoot the English in the mouth, where they are most dangerous." There was a graphic and horrible image of King Edward and a colonial officer stamping on Boers in a concentration camp. "The blood from these devils is befouling my crown," said the King. "Strong, is it not?" said Leon. "English tourists have tried to get it suppressed. It mocks the Kaiser also. His endless uniforms. His journey to the Holy Land."

Karl was surprised—somewhat surprised—by his reaction to these images. He felt pure, chauvinistic *English* resentment and hurt, which he concealed from the Germans as he had concealed his anarchism from his family. Like Dorothy, he had moments of homesickness for a life more slow-paced, less intense, more ruminative. More polite. The English could not take such pleasure in giving offence. The cartoon would be funnier, less—less unpleasant.

. . .

They took him to see the Elf Scharfrichter perform. They took him on
a night when the puppets were playing, because Wolfgang had helped in
the construction of the cast, and was involved in the performance itself.

The Scharfrichter were eleven artists—including the playwright,
Frank Wedekind—who paraded in blood-red robes and hangmen's
masks, carrying executioners' heavy swords, and performed plays,
songs, puppet and shadow plays, using popular forms—which were
referred to as *Tingeltangel*—and comparing themselves to the workers
in applied arts—they meant, they said, to make songs to be sung as
craftsmen made chairs to fit people's bottoms. *Angewandte Lyrik* was
what it was about. They had a private stage in a tavern which held
eighty people, at nightclub tables. It was, when Karl went with Joachim
and Wolfgang, crammed full of spectators. The black walls were decorated with lurid and elegant posters from *Simplicissimus,* and with
pornographic Japanese woodcuts, which startled Karl, though he tried
to retain a studied English calm. There was a programme, on the cover
of which a gleefully naked woman was tossing out her long, blood-red
gloves. Inside the entrance was a totem: a solemn head of a bewigged
person, from the Age of Reason, embedded in which was an execu-
tioner's axe.

The executioners marched in, singing the song they always sang,
aimed at the Catholic hierarchy.

> *Ein Schattentanz, ein Puppenspott!*
> *Ihr Glücklichen und Glatten*
> *Die Puppen und die Schatten.*
> *Er lenkt zu Leid, er lenkt zu Glück,*
> *Hoch dampfen die Gebete,*
> *Doch just im schönsten Augenblick*
> *Zerschneiden wir die Drähte.*

> A shadow-dance, a puppet's joke!
> You happy, polished people—
> In heav'n on high the same old bloke
> Guides puppets from his steeple.
> For good or ill he guides their moves,
> Each doll an anthem sings,

But then, just when it least behooves
We cut the puppets' strings.

On this evening the executioners performed this song with gusto, and were followed on stage by Marya Delvard, a skeletally thin woman with a mane of flaming hair, kohl-rimmed eyes and a white skin, who sang, twisted in a long black gown, about sex and passion, suicide and murder, in a kind of low moan. She was lit by violet light. She had a vampire's mouth. After her came the puppet play *Die Feine Familie.* There was a pit between the audience and the stage, which housed both musicians and puppeteers. It depicted the crowned heads of Europe as a gang of squabbling children, quarrelling over toys—the Empire in South Africa, the palace in Peking. There were the uncle and the cousins, Edward, the Kaiser Wilhelm, Tsar Nikolas, roaring with rage like toddlers, conspiring with each other against each other. Karl sat very still and tried to follow the rapid patter. He did not approve of kings and royal persons. But, again, he became surreptitiously English. These strangers should not so easily mock England's green and pleasant land, even in the person of a fat, amorous, red-faced, droning person in ermine and a silly crown. He had a moment of wondering what the world would be like to live in, when the desired burst of violent outrage finally happened. He had a moment of wondering whether it would really be better to be ruled by the whims of masked executioners and raucous seductresses. He applauded the end of the play, and Wolfgang winked at him.

"You have this kind of work in London?"

"We have music hall. It isn't like this. It's—sillier, and—and more sentimental."

"We have sentimental things, too, in abundance. Schwabing has invented a word for them, a word I like. Kitsch."

"Kitsch," said Charles/Karl.

Another new theatre, Richard Riemerschmid's Schauspielhaus, had also opened that spring. They went there all together—the tutors, the Sterns, Karl, Griselda and Dorothy—to see Oscar Wilde's *Salomé*. The theatre was *Jugendstil,* and delicately, exquisitely beautiful. The auditorium was a hot red cavern or womb which was also an elven wood. Fine golden tendrils and stems spilled and clambered and tumbled every-where, irregular, linking balconies to stage, framing the actors. Wilde was dead, now. He had died shortly after Karl and Joachim had seen him in Rodin's atelier in the Grande Exposition. Karl did not enjoy *Salomé,* with its rhythmic moaning and sick sensuality. He had got rather attached to the new word "kitsch." He ventured to say to Joachim that he thought this might be kitsch, and Joachim was shocked, and said no, it was Modern Art, it was freedom of expression. Dorothy stopped looking after a time, and started to try to remember the bones of the body and their names. The actress playing Salomé seemed supple and boneless, like a snake-charmer and a snake, simultaneously. Wolf-gang said to Griselda that he believed the play had never been put on in Wilde's own country, in his own language. Toby Youlgreave, on the other side of Griselda, said it had been written in French and translated into English, but the Lord Chamberlain had stopped the performance. Ah, said Wolfgang. You too have a Lex Heinze. Toby said he thought the reason given was blasphemy, acting biblical characters, not obscen-ity. The text had been published with illustrations by Beardsley. Naughty illustrations. But clever. Wolfgang said he thought he had seen them, in the tone of one who has in fact no real memory of doing so. He then said Beardsley draws sex, but always coldly. Unlike our artists. The English are cold, they say. He looked quickly at Griselda, and away. Griselda looked at the rich red curtain, closed for the interval. A very faint flush rose in her white cheeks.

Finally, it was the Solstice again, it was Midsummer. In England, Olive presided as usual over a depleted gathering on the lawn. It was a grey day. The fairy queen wore a velvet opera cloak over her floating robes. The absent Youlgreave was replaced, as Bottom, by Herbert Methley, who had finished his novel and resumed his social and amorous dealings. Florian was Cobweb instead of Dorothy. Tom was still Puck. Humphry was still handsome, but there was grey at his temple.

In Munich it was altogether wilder. The artists and Bohemians of Schwabing dressed up whenever they could, celebrated all feasts with gusto, danced in the streets and in courtyards and gardens. Anselm Stern put on a version of *A Midsummer Night's Dream* for marionettes. The puppets, human and stumbling, and the fair folk with trailing wings, rushed through a painted wood, whilst flutes and bagpipes squealed eerily. The Mechanicals were dressed as Bavarian workmen, and danced peasant dances. Oberon had Anselm Stern's own thin face, Dorothy saw, and one of his characteristic looks of intent, almost dangerous, thoughtfulness. Puck looked like Wolfgang, with horns pushing through the unruly hair. Hermia and Helena were Dorothy and Griselda, expressions set in wide-eyed surprise.

After the show they roamed the streets. Midsummer in the south of Germany was warm, was leafy, was inviting. They crossed other groups, and stopped in taverns and cafés to take a beer, or a glass of Riesling. At one point Dorothy, who was dressed as a silver moth, and Griselda, who was dressed as an eighteenth-century lady, bumped into a Valkyrie, with breastplate and horned helmet, who turned out to be English. Her name, she said, was Marie Stopes. She was studying at the University. Dorothy was interested. She said she hadn't known women were admitted. They aren't, said Marie Stopes. In my department I am the only woman. I am a palaeobotanist. I study the sex of fossil cycads. It is very interesting. If one, then more, Dorothy thought. At this point Joachim Susskind joined them and recognised Miss Stopes, who had taken an unprecedented first-class Honours degree in Botany—in one year, moreover—at University College. Dorothy suddenly felt silly in grey silk and velvet. She should be in a classroom. But then, here was the successful Miss Stopes, dressed as an ungainly Valkyrie, and slightly drunk.

Anselm Stern and his family had built a balefire in their courtyard—a cheerful, flickering construction, not mountainous, not a furnace. They all danced round it, and, as it subsided, jumped over the ashes. Anselm had given them all blue flowers, *Rittersporn,* larkspurs, to throw into the embers—"And all your cares and troubles with them," he said.

Dorothy had two memories from that day which never left her. The first was of dancing with her new father, with Anselm Stern, a kind of fast whirling polka, round the Spiegelgarten. She caught sight of herself in a mirror—her hair had come loose—she looked wild—and she suddenly remembered waltzing in South Kensington with her other father, her new dress, his hand on her waist, and everything that had come from it. Because of that dance, this dance. She missed a step, and Anselm supported her. He looked down at her worried face, and, for the first time, carefully kissed her on the brow.

Dorothy's second memory was of going indoors to find a lavatory, and having found one to be occupied, searching for another. And she came upon two people, standing closely together. They were Wolfgang and Griselda. Dorothy saw that both of them had closed their eyes. They had not seen her. She went back round the corner she had just turned. She said nothing to Griselda, and Griselda said nothing to her.

III

THE SILVER AGE

32

Backwards and forwards, both. The Edwardians knew they came *after* something. The sempiternal Queen was gone, in all her manifestations, from the squat and tiny widow swathed in black crape and jet beads, to the gold-encrusted, bedizened, crowned idol who was brought out at durbars and jubilees. That pursed little mouth was silent for ever. Her long-dead mate, who had most seriously cared for the lives of working-men and for the wholesome and beautiful and proliferating arts and crafts, persisted beside her in the name of the unfinished Museum, full of gold, silver, ceramics, bricks and building dust. The new King was an elderly womaniser, genial and unhealthy, interested in oiling the wheels of diplomacy with personal good sense, in racehorses, in the daily shooting of thousands upon thousands of bright birds and panting, scrambling, running things, in the woodlands and moors of Britain, in the forests and mountains of Germany, Belgium, Denmark and Russia. It was a new time, not a young time. Skittishly, it cast off the moral anguish and human responsibility of the Victorian sages Lytton Strachey was preparing to mock. The rich acquired motor cars and telephones, chauffeurs and switchboard operators. The poor were a menacing phantom, to be helped charitably, or exterminated expeditiously. The sun shone, the summers broiled and were brilliant. The land, in places, was running with honey, cream, fruit fools, beer, champagne.

They looked back. They stared and glared backwards, in an intense, sometimes purposeful nostalgia for an imagined Golden Age. There were many things they wanted to go back to, to retrieve, to reinhabit.

They wanted to go back to the earth, to the running rivers and full fields and cottage gardens and twining honeysuckle of Morris's Nowhere. They wanted to live in cottages (real cottages, which meant old stone, mossy cottages) and grow their own fruit and vegetables, getting their own eggs and gooseberries. They wanted, like Edward Carpenter, to be self-sufficient on smallholdings, and also to be naked and dabble their toes in real mud, like him, having taken off real, handmade sandals, like him. They did love the earth. The chalk Downs and Romney Marsh are the ultimate heroes of *Puck of Pook's Hill,* published in

1906, the year of the building of HMS *Dreadnought*. Ford Madox Ford, living on a smallholding in Winchelsea, wrote movingly about digging the bones of a buried Viking out of the cliff at Beachy Head. Ford's bones in the cliff are like the human bones in Kipling's chalk, or the bones turned up on the Downs by rabbits in Hudson's *Shepherd's Life*. They are a dream of humans as part of the natural cycle, as they no longer seem to be.

E. M. Forster grieved over the invasion of Abinger by machines and the violation of Chanctonbury Ring. Bloomsbury coexisted in Bloomsbury and in simple farmhouses on the Downs, where they had servant problems and problems with plumbing. They loved the earth, but they loved it for something irretrievably lost, as well as for its smells and scents and filth and bounce and clog and crumble. Those great masters of the description of the English earth, Richard Jefferies and later W. H. Hudson, who can describe the whole expanse of the clean air, and the currents in it, and the rabbit-nibbled, sheep-cropped grass on the Downs, the close trees in coppices, the solitary thorns shaped by the wind, the fish fanning against the current, the birds riding the thermal flow, so that we think they are our guide to the unspoiled green and pleasant land—both of these are in fact men of a Silver Age, elegiac. They spend pages listing the species of birds and mammals erased from their land by pheasant-rearing gamekeepers. The goshawk, the pole cat, the pine marten, gone, gone away. Pike decimated. Trees tidied out of their wild shapes and habits. The Golden Age was when no humans interfered with anything.

English earth is confined, even where it is wild, by what Melville called the masterly and alien ocean. Its fields are confined, its copses are enclosed and managed, its footpaths are well trodden. Visitors from South Africa and the Far East feel odd on British earth. They have the sense that none of it is pristine, all of it has been trod and trod and trod, from the Stone Age on. Compared to the Cévennes and the Massif Central the wild Yorkshire moors are a pocket handkerchief on a tarpaulin. Poets, as well as peasants, deplored the enclosures of commons. It is a sad fact that military camps, like the one at Lydd, tend to preserve wild species, birds and plants, by excluding curious and loving humans along with human predators.

German earth is different, though Germans at this time, in a largely landlocked country, under its Kaiser with maritime ambitions, also felt the huge pull of earthly nostalgia. Germans, until the twentieth century, had lived in small walled cities, between which extended their *Wald*—not Robin Hood's hiding-place in the greenwood, but miles and miles of Black Forest, sombre forest, alien forest, haunted by creatures and presences altogether more dangerous and threatening than Pucks, boggarts and that squat nasty fairy, Yallery Brown, stuck in the Lincolnshire mud. Germans went back to the earth. They went hiking and singing up mountains, into the Wood. They were *Wandervögel,* going back to Nature (an ambivalent goddess). They too, camped by lakes and plunged naked into their depths. They became vegetarians, and wandered the streets of Munich and Berlin in earthy garments, wholesomely constructed by killing only vegetables. They worshipped the Sun, and the earth mothers who had preceded patriarchy.

The inhabitants of Schwabing retreated, or progressed, to the community of saints, artists, and nature-lovers on the Mountain of Truth, the Monte Verità, near Ascona, beside a Swiss lake. Here in 1900 came Gusto Gräser, a poet who played with his name, which meant grasses, and said he was in search of roots, the roots of plants, roots to eat, the roots of words, the roots of civilisations and mountains. He eschewed not only meat, but metal, which he believed should be left inside the earth, in its place, inside rocks. He lived in caves and slept in wayside chapels. His brother, also believing that the use of metal implied mines, miners, foundries, armaments, guns and bombs, made a house of wood, using its natural sproutings and forkings as forms. He lived there with Jenny Hoffman, who wore date stones, for buttons, on her clothes. They danced there. Rudolf Laban later led his chain of naked maenads celebrating sunrise by the lake, in the meadows. Lawrence and Frieda came there, Hermann Hesse and Isadora Duncan. The anarchist Eric Mühsam came and the psychoanalyst Otto Gross, whose father, a criminologist, wanted him locked up for lewdness and drugs. Everyone wore sandals, like pilgrims, like apostles, like ancient Greeks.

Max Weber believed that the modern world was an iron cage, *ein stahlhartes Gehäuse,* an engine casing. The *Naturmenschen* tried to break the bars, to go back. Carl Gustav Jung came to believe that the minds of humans were moulded not only by human inheritance, and individual history, but by the earth, the soil, which grasped their roots. *Deutschlands Boden,* German soil, was put to use by *völkisch* thinkers and believers in racial purity as well as by those desiring to go back to Nature and Mother Earth under the Sun. There was birth, and there was rebirth, enacted by the Sun Hero who returned to the tellurian depths, confronted the terrible Mother, or Mothers, and burst out again into the sunshine. Siegfried was a Sun Hero. So was D. H. Lawrence, a miner's son, reborn as a German sensibility after finishing *Sons and Lovers,* having read the letters of Otto Gross, Frieda Lawrence's earlier lover, and *The Meaning of Dreams,* by Sigmund Freud.

A concomitant, but not consequent, backwards stare was the intense interest in, and nostalgia for, childhood. The men and women of the Golden Age, Hesiod wrote, lived in an eternal spring, for hundreds of years, always youthful, fed on acorns from a great oak, on wild fruits, on honey. In the Silver Age, which is less written about, the people lived for 100 years as children, without growing up, and then quite suddenly aged and died. The Fabians and the social scientists, writers and teachers saw, in a way earlier generations had not, that children were people, with identities and desires and intelligences. They saw that they were neither dolls, nor toys, nor miniature adults. They saw, many of them, that children needed freedom, needed not only to learn, and be good, but to play and be wild.

But they saw this, so many of them, out of a desire of their own for a perpetual childhood, a Silver Age. One aspect of it was male clubbable behaviour, eating school suet pudding in gloomy surroundings, playing japes and jests on fellow house guests, retreating into boating expeditions, and hikes, and picnics, playing elaborate practical jokes on the unsuspecting, disguising themselves as Middle Eastern potentates (Virginia Woolf) or newspaper reporters (Baden-Powell in the army in India). They were good at playing with real children—H. G. Wells turning a nursery into a model field of war, or a series of railway junctions, Baden-Powell, again, amusing the children by pretending that his feathered helmet was a chicken. They used waggish school jokes in their letters: Tee hee! My wig! They wrote wonderful tales, also in letters, for their solemn children, of messing about in boats, of picnic baskets, of getting lost in the Wild Wood in the winter and finding a comfortable hearth underground in a badger's holt, of tooting horns in automobiles and making idiots of the Law.

Richard Jefferies wrote about Bevis in the 1880s. In *Wood Magic* Bevis is a small child who could speak the languages of the woodland creatures. He can speak their language, but his vision is schoolboy and lordly, unlike that more subtle forest child Mowgli. He knows spiders are male, and the thrushes he converses with kindly allow him to collect one egg, as long as he leaves one, and tells no other boys.

In *Bevis, the Story of a Boy* he makes a raft, and a camp, and plays at being an explorer in the deserts and jungles of the Empire. He plays at making stockades, like Jim in *Treasure Island* and Robinson Crusoe, and goes home for tea and bread and honey.

In 1901 James Barrie wrote *The Boy Castaways* for the Llewellyn-Davies boys, *Peter Rabbit* was published, and Kipling published *Kim,* the tale of a boy scout. In 1902 E. Nesbit wrote *Five Children and It,* a tale where resourceful, unwise children meet a sand-fairy. In that year Barrie published *The Little White Bird,* in which an embryonic Peter Pan, the little boy who wouldn't grow up, made his first appearance. This book was given by the sage naturalist W. H. Hudson to David Garnett, son of the publisher Edward Garnett, and Constance Garnett, the translator of Tolstoi, Dostoevsky and Turgenev. David Garnett, who did grow up, in some ways at least—he became a "libertine" on principle and attracted both men and women—found the book sickening, and returned it to the giver, saying he did not like it. *Peter Pan, or The Boy Who Wouldn't Grow Up,* was staged (in a primitive form) in 1904. Rupert Brooke went to see it twelve times. In 1906 *Puck of Pook's Hill* appeared, and so did *The Railway Children* and *Benjamin Bunny.* It was seriously suggested that the great writing of the time was writing for children, which was also read by grown-ups.

Kenneth Grahame, who wrote for the decadent *Yellow Book* in its golden days, published *Pagan Papers* in 1893, *The Golden Age* in 1895, *Dream Days* in 1898 and *The Wind in the Willows* in 1908. He had what might be thought of as a grown-up job; he was Secretary to the Old Lady of Threadneedle Street.

He married in 1899. He was forty and an archetypal pipe-smoking bachelor. His new wife turned up to the wedding in an old white muslin dress—"dew-wet from a morning walk," with a wilting daisy chain round her neck. She was a girlish thirty-seven-year-old.

He wrote to his wife in baby talk. "Jor me no more bout diet cos you are mixin me up so fritefly. I eets wot I chooses wot I dont want I dont & I dont care a dam wot they does in Berlin thank gord I'm British." His son, known as Mouse, had to be sent away with his nanny to the country because his favourite game was to lie in the road in the path of approaching motor cars, causing them to halt abruptly.

In 1905 Major-General Baden-Powell, in charge of the British army in Mafeking, was fascinated by *Peter Pan* which he saw twice. That year, Baden-Powell proposed unsuccessfully to Miss Rose Sough. She was eighteen. He was forty-seven. He finally married in 1912, when he was fifty-five and his wife "a girl of twenty-three," a tomboy who became a Lady Scoutmaster. He constructed camps for Boy Scouts and was moved by photographs of naked boys bathing. One of his interests was watching executions—he would travel many miles, and cross frontiers, to be present at them.

In Germany, there were theories of children and childhood. A child, according to Ernst Haeckel, was a stage in the evolutionary development of an adult, as a savage was a stage in the development of a civilised human being. A life recapitulated the history of the earth—the embryo in the womb had the gills of a fish and the tail of a simian. Haeckel had a religion of nature, finding the good, the true and the beautiful in the forms of life, from radiolarians to Goethe. Carl Gustav Jung took up this idea, and came to believe that the thoughts of children resembled those of ancient peoples. He drew a parallel "between the phantastical, mythological thinking of antiquity and the similar thinking of children, between the lower races and the dreams." The human soul was layered, from the roots of the mountain to the conscious tip. The child lurked and cavorted in the lower levels, occasionally rising like captured Persephone, to sport in the flowery meadows.

Meanwhile, in 1905, Sigmund Freud published his *Three Essays on Sexuality,* including one on infantile sexuality. Infants, he said, were polymorphously perverse. Thumb-sucking, ear-stroking, pleasure in the wind in your knickers as you swung rhythmically in a swing tied to a branch, pleasure in the speed of the motor car and the pistons of trains, all these were indications of a masked and active sexuality. Children desired their mother or father, wished to marry her or him, had fantasies of slaying the other parent. An Austrian bourgeois of his time, Freud felt able to judge these propensities. Children had not constructed mental dams against sexual excesses—shame, disgust, morality. "In this respect children behave in the same kind of way as an average uncultivated woman in whom the same polymorphously perverse disposition persists . . . Prostitutes exploit the same polymorphous, that is, infantile, disposition for the purposes of their profession . . ." Freud knew that children were not sweet, or gentle, or carefree. He knew they could hate. He quoted Bernard Shaw from *Man and Superman*. "As a rule there is only one person an English girl hates more than she hates her mother; and that's her eldest sister." In England, that remark is flippant, a drawing-room witticism, an Oscar Wilde shocking paradox. In Germany, where Max Reinhardt put on Shaw's plays along with Wedekind's *Spring Awakening* and Gorky's *Lower Depths,* it would be received with a difference.

Everyone went out into the tamed and changing earth, and made camps. From Ascona to Chipping Camden, where C. R. Ashbee had led his East End guild of craftsmen like Aaron into the Promised Land, and had immediately constructed a huge communal mud-bath of a swimming-pool, people went out into the air, built temporary shelters in tree roots, practised skills that in some cases were derived from the scouting and tent-building skills of Mafeking and Ladysmith. David Garnett camped with the four wild and beautiful Olivier sisters, Brynhild, Marjorie, Daphne and Noel, who climbed trees like monkeys and dived naked into rivers from ancient bridges. (Their father was a Commonwealth Office minister, Sydney Olivier, a founding Fabian who spoke out against the Boer War and was sent to govern Jamaica.) These combined with the perfectly beautiful Rupert Brooke to form the Neo-Pagans, along with James Strachey, who was hopelessly in love with Brooke. Later, the Fabians themselves ran educational summer camps, with lectures, and gymnastic drills. Baden-Powell made many rules, moral and practical, for Boy Scouts, and later, with his sister Agnes, for Girl Guides. He drew on American Native woodcraft and British military camaraderie, as well as Kim and Mowgli. There was a camp at Hollesley Bay Colony on the East Coast, visited by Beatrice Webb in 1905, where broken-down men were to be put together again. She went also to a Salvation Army camp in Hadleigh Farm, where they collected released convicts, tramps, drunks and vagrants, fed them, helped them and preached at them. There was also an idea current amongst anxious social thinkers about the undeserving poor, which said that the "concentration" camps invented by the efficient British army in South Africa might be used to segregate—even, it was suggested, to sterilise or put down—the irredeemable, the hopeless, the dangerous.

. . .

Time passed at very different speeds for all these people, between 1901 and 1907, when one event changed all their lives. For some it ticked like metronomes, for others it lurched giddily, for some—the little ones— it still resembled space, boundless and sunlit, boundless and shining with snow and ice, always threatening impossible boredom, always offering corners to go round, long, long roads stretching ahead. There were measures for some—menstruation, exams, parties, camps, pay days, cheques in the post, deadlines, telegrams, crises in banks. And for others, day after similar day. Some bodies got older rapidly—the babies, the menopausal. Some appeared hardly to change at all, from year to year.

Ann Warren changed most, and felt time, paradoxically, as something hanging and slow. She was a neat baby, a brown baby, like a hazelnut, Frank Mallett said, presenting her with a woollen jacket and knitted boots. She learned to sit up, and sat where she was put, and looked around Marian Oakeshott's cottage garden, seeing hollyhocks and marigolds she assumed were eternal. One day she stood up, and staggered from grass to border, crashing down amongst the delphiniums and knowing them now as an acrid smell as well as a blue series of towers. For Ann, aged two in 1903, a year was half a lifetime. She did not expect the second winter, and then, when it came, vaguely assumed it was eternal, until spring came, and summer came, and she understood that they had come "again" and began to learn to expect. She learned language, and faces, Elsie and Marian, Tabitha and Robin, who pushed her over and kissed her better, his red hair blowing in the breeze. She learned to expect sweets from Patty Dace and Arthur Dobbin and Frank Mallett, who made her daisy chains. Marian Oakeshott said to Elsie, as they walked with their children along the Military Canal in the summer of 1903, that she thought Ann was a very clever child, a noticing child, a thinking child. "Like you," said Marian to Elsie.

"Much good it has done me," said Elsie to Marian, not denying that she was clever.

"It's not too late," said Marian. In 1903 Elsie was twenty-four. She would be twenty-eight in 1907, which is almost thirty, and was no longer "young." She was already afraid in 1903 of being somehow solid- ified into resignation in 1907.

"It is too late," she said to Marian, whom she had come to care for. "I done for myself having Ann, you know that. So I must sit in this Marsh and slave for these silly women. I made my own bed. Or at least, I put the mattress down."

"I don't ask Tabitha to look after Ann so that you can settle down in a Slough of Despond. What do you *want* to do? You must want something."

Elsie wanted sex, but there was no one to offer it whom she would have touched, and Ann's coming had made her wary. She wondered if Marian wanted sex. Once, thinking about desire, which she didn't do for a good year and a bit after Ann's birth, she had said to Mrs. Oakeshott "I expect you still miss him terribly." And Marian had said "Who?" And Elsie had known, as Marian smoothly talked over her mistake, and said she missed him all the time—Elsie had known that Marian was in the same position as herself, that there was no Mr. Oakeshott, dead or alive. This made her feel less beholden—which was good for her—and protective, which was also good for her. She knew Marian knew she knew. She knew neither of them would ever mention her knowledge. She felt a kind of love for Marian's courage and resourcefulness.

She said now, with her usual sharpness, "Girls from my class, mam, are not encouraged to *want* things." The mam was a joke, they both knew. They walked on in silence. Elsie said

"I did want to make very small pots. Miniature pots. I still do sometimes, when Mr. Fludd and Philip are away. But then I squash them up again, almost all. It's hard having Philip around. I know what a really good pot looks like, and I know his look like that and mine don't mostly. They can exist or not, it don't matter."

"You'd be better off being a teacher than a sort of servant."

"Hah! And how should I be qualified to do *that*? I don't read too well."

"I shall teach you to qualify to be a teacher. I shall teach you—and two or three others—in the evenings. Once you've got some of the way, you can be a teaching assistant and go on to qualify. Then you'll be able to choose where to work and earn wages. I still can't fathom how the Fludds pay you."

"They don't, mostly. Philip does. He sells a few pots and he gives me some money. They give him some, sometimes, not regularly. What he really cares about is being able to buy clay and chemicals and fuel and things. But he sees me right."

"You're *all* mad and muddled. It's shocking."

"I'd like to try this teachering. I can bring Ann, can I?"
"That is my idea."

Between 1902 and 1907 Tom Wellwood changed from being someone who was about to settle down to be a student, to being someone who had not settled down to be a student. In 1901, when Dorothy suddenly went to Munich, Tom was eighteen. In 1907, he was twenty-four, a young man, not a youth. He had gone through broken-out skin and new stubble on lip and cheek, his voice had rounded out, his gold hair thickened and coarsened. He had gone through believing he wanted to go to Cambridge with Julian and Charles, to knowing, without allowing himself to know he knew, that he must avoid this, that it would destroy him. During these five years he went on walking holidays with Toby Youlgreave, and sometimes with Julian, and sometimes with Joachim and Charles as well. These were supposed to be "reading" holidays, and Tom was supposed to be learning. He read a lot. He read books of woodcraft, and books of knightly romance, and books about the earth. He knew a lot of lyric poetry. He had interesting conversations with Toby about Shakespeare and Marlowe, but when he did finally get into a schoolroom with an exam script before him, he had the odd sensation that he did not know who he was, that there was nobody there capable of setting pen to paper. Some kind of automaton in his place wrote some pages of banal nonsense. He failed. He was more afraid of becoming unreal than of failing to progress in his education, but that, too, he did not put into words. He wrote things in the Tree House, and burned them, in case anyone found them. He became secretive. Most of what he felt he really was, was incommunicable to his companions who were striding or sauntering into the social world. He knew the woods. He watched the trees age and thicken and spread. He watched saplings struggle and take hold, he saw the keepers axing the rotten beeches. He wanted, but he did not know he wanted, to be like Ann, to stay in a world, in a time, where every day was an age, and every day resembled the one before. Some of the time, he lived in the old story. He found himself muttering and murmuring with his back to an oak where Tom Underground had faced a pack of wolves with a flaming brand, or running easily along tracks as though he was himself a wild creature, a wolf.

This was both intensely satisfying, and sickly, like masturbation and its aftermath.

Tom might have been different, Dorothy thought later, if Dorothy's sense of time had not been completely the opposite of his. It began when she came back from Munich. She was seventeen, he was nineteen, they had been inseparable, she had followed him like a squire, like an animal helper, through furrows and thickets. But she did not tell him about Anselm Stern, and only casually mentioned Wolfgang and Leon, as exciting new acquaintances. Tom could have been forgiven for thinking Dorothy had fallen in love with one of these Germans, but his thoughts didn't run that way, love was something he sheered away from. He felt, simply, excluded. He was like a wild animal ranging round a stockade, or a forest house, trying to get in, to find a slit or slot, and failing.

This sense of Dorothy's distance was exacerbated, for both of them, by the artificial—that is, nothing to do with the weather and the earth—timetable she had set herself, or discovered had been set for her. The parents and tutors were not wholly helpful with this. The person who told Dorothy what she had taken on, how very much *work* was ahead of her, was Leslie Skinner, who took a fatherly interest in her, and once, involuntarily, stroked her hair.

She would need to matriculate, he said. She would need to pass Latin, English, Maths, General Elementary Science, and one of: Greek, French, German, Sanskrit, Arabic, Elementary Mechanics, Elementary Chemistry, Elementary Sound, Heat and Light, Elementary Magnetism and Electricity, Elementary Botany.

After successfully matriculating, there would be the Preliminary Scientific Examination, in Chemistry and Physics, and General Biology.

In order to get the MB degree she would need

1. To have passed the matriculation exam not less than five years previously.

2. To have passed the Preliminary Scientific Exam not less than four years previously.

3. To have studied medicine for five years after matriculation or four years after the Preliminary Scientific Exam, one year of the four to have been spent in a recognised institution.

    4. To have passed two medical exams, the Intermediate and the
       Final MB.

For the final MB she would need to have attended lectures, seen twenty certified labours (of women), practised surgery for two years, and medicine for two years, including a study of infectious diseases and lunacy.

She would need to specialise in medicine, surgery or obstetrics and be proficient in vaccination. To take the BS and become a surgeon, she must also have done a course in operative surgery and operated on a dead subject.

The London School of Medicine for Women was granted a Royal Charter in 1902 and was now a college of the University of London. So Dorothy's way was open. It was a very hard way.

Dorothy sat in Leslie and Etta's dark, polished drawing-room and worked it out on her fingers. At the earliest, she could qualify as a surgeon in 1910, which, for someone aged eighteen in 1902, who would be twenty-six in 1910, seemed to slice a whole segment, her youth, out of her life. She sat very still listening to the hooves and wheels in Gower Street, and thought about Dorothy Wellwood. Did she want to know all that? People were married at twenty-one or twenty-two. They had passions and dramas which she could not afford to have. She looked down at her moving fingers in her lap, and thought, after all, how *interesting* flesh and bone is, how *interesting* the growth of a child from a seed is—is knowing better than doing?

Leslie Skinner said "You are pensive."

"It's such a long time. So much of—of my life, of anyone's life. Particularly a woman."

"There are easier ways of helping people."

Dorothy continued to look at the skin, the knuckles, the slightly bitten nails, the lifeline in her palm. She said

"It isn't really *helping people*. It's *knowing*."

"A rare thing in a young woman."

"Why should women not *know* things?"

"It is generally believed that they prefer to feel, to care for others . . ."

"Are you telling me *not* to try to be a doctor?"

"I have been a teacher long enough to know when that is no use. Even if I have not taught many young women. And I have to say, those women I have taught are self-selected for willpower and—intent. The decision is yours. But I will help—I should like to help—if you feel you must go ahead."

Nothing is final, Dorothy thought pragmatically, and made a final decision.

Time passing, for most young women, was to do with finding a husband, or being sought as a wife. In 1902, Griselda, like Dorothy, was eighteen, Florence Cain was nineteen, Phyllis was sixteen, Hedda was thirteen, Imogen Fludd was twenty-three, and Pomona was twenty. Of all these young women, only one, Florence, was "in love," and she was in love with her brother's lover, Gerald, which was an unsatisfactory state of affairs for all three of them. It was possible, Philip Warren thought, that Pomona was in love with him. She followed him around, and once or twice began sentences with "When we are married . . ." which he pretended not to hear. He did not like her touching him, though she was beautiful, in her childish way. She might be what in the Potteries was known as "simple" but he thought also she might be acting a part. He didn't want to have to think about her. He wished Elsie would think about her, but Elsie thought about Ann, and house-cleaning, and her programme of reading. She simply didn't like Pomona, although she was perfectly polite. But politeness and dislike combined can be deadly. Pomona pretended not to notice, but made no advances to Elsie.

Phyllis thought less about being in love than about preparing to be married. Like many children of shifting, insecure Bohemian households, she had a romantic vision of an *ordinary,* comfortable household, that kept strict hours and was warmly predictable. She dreamed more of quilts and counterpanes and table-linen than of male bodies, or even chaste kisses. She didn't talk to anyone much—except Violet, who encouraged her hope of respectable domesticity—and no one told her something might be missing from her calculations. She—alone of the Wellwood children—had played with dolls as a little girl, and she now imagined babies, clean, docile, smiling, holding out little rounded arms to be cuddled, some blonde, some dark, some boys, some girls. She would be the maker of a world with no shouting, no insecurity, no danger. When they went camping, she was in charge of the pots and pans and made delicious hotpots for everyone. By 1907 she was twenty-one and no one in any camp had clutched at her, or trailed her, let alone suggested they might marry. She knew the wrong people, she thought, and did not know where to find the right people. She was sandwiched between two sisters with too much initiative. Violet said the right young man would come along and notice her, but Violet was not in a position to introduce her to young men. Phyllis tried calmly to believe Violet.

Hedda in 1902 was thirteen. She resented being female. She thought she had been born to suffer injustice, and subordination, and that she would rebel. In 1903 Mrs. Pankhurst and her daughters founded the WSPU, the suffragettes. Olive, like other successful women of her generation, had not involved herself in agitating for the Vote, although she accepted unreflectively that it was a "good thing," better to have a Vote than not. Florence Cain attended meetings of the NUWSS and heard Millicent Garrett Fawcett speak. It was Hedda who, between 1903 and 1907, became more and more obsessed with suffrage, with opposition, with action, with revolt. She followed, eagerly, the campaign of the militants, as they broke glass and set bombs, were imprisoned, and later took to hunger-striking and suffered forcible feeding (1909). She occasionally hectored her mother and sisters. The rest of the time she brooded darkly. She would Act. In the beginning was the Act.

The person whose timetable, during the early years, was directed towards matchmaking was Griselda. She had promised her mother that in exchange for her time with Dorothy in Munich she would take part in the London Season of dances and house parties. Dutifully, she did. For her, 1902 was measured out in dressmakers' and hairdressers' appointments, balls and dances, country-house parties, tea-parties, lists of dancing-partners in tiny books with pretty covers hanging on gold and silver threads. She received two or three proposals of marriage—her pale and elegant good looks excited admiration—and protested calmly that she "did not know" these young men, that she could not imagine spending the rest of her life with them. There were many other young men who sensed a remoteness, a wilderness of ice, inside her, danced with her because she danced well, and proposed to other, funnier, warmer girls. Griselda invited Dorothy, with gentle desperation, to come to dances with her as she had gone to Munich, and Dorothy, grimly facing the reality of the timetable she had imposed on herself, said she could not. She could afford neither time nor money. She loved Griselda as much as ever, but she had a *timetable*. She said also that Griselda had said she meant to matriculate and study. Griselda said, maybe she would. Wait and see. She wasn't as clever as Dorothy, she said, though both of them knew she was.

Julian Cain was at King's College, Cambridge, where he discussed both the Higher and the Lower Sodomy with Gerald and others. In 1901 he had been an Apostolic "embryo," invited to breakfasts and dinners, investigated to see if he had interesting or amusing ideas. In 1902 he went through the birthing ceremony on the famous hearthrug, received the essential anchovy toast, and became a full member of the secret Conversazione Society, or the Apostles. He gave a witty talk on the manifold uses made of museums by human beings, from cognoscenti and artists to tradesmen, policemen and naughty children, which was well received. The Apostles gently mocked German philosophy by referring to themselves as The World of Reality—everything else in the universe was only Appearance, and persons who were not chosen Apostles were dismissed as phenomena. Something similar was going on, but with more bombast and more edge, in Bohemian Schwabing where the anarchist Erich Mühsam claimed that Schwabing had no boundaries because nothing in it was normal, there was no norm, measurement was not possible. The members of the Schwabing exclusive society, the Kosmische Rundschau, referred to themselves as *Enorme,* or Giants, or outside the normal—and those who were not *Enorme* were *Belanglosen,* unattached, meaningless. The *Kosmiker* inclined towards nature mysticism, and racial mysticism, and were given to dressing-up as ancient Greeks and Romans, with vine leaves in their hair. They put on plays and pageants, as did that beloved Apostle, Rupert Brooke, who enacted the Herald in Aeschylus' *Eumenides* in 1906, lovely in boots, greaves, helmet and a military tunic and skirt so short that he was unable decently to sit down at the postperformance party in the Darwin house in Silver Street.

Julian talked easily to Brooke and to Bloomsbury but he did not belong. He was cynical about their high-mindedness, and more cynical about their cynicism. He wanted to want something, and did not know what it would be, or if he would find it. He knew it was not Gerald, though he loved him. He thought to himself that a love-affair, once begun, always envisaged its end. Time did not stand still. If Gerald could have loved Florence, as Arthur Henry Hallam, Alfred Tennyson's beloved friend in the days when they were young, and Apostolic, had apparently come to love Tennyson's sister Emily, there might have been a future, with the children Tennyson had imagined dandling on an avuncular knee. Sometimes, Julian thought, he would not much mind if he were told he was to die tomorrow. It wouldn't matter. When he felt like that he walked into the Fitzwilliam Museum and asked to look at Samuel Palmer's water-colours. They shone from an unearthly, too earthy, earth.

Charles/Karl decided for study, rather than immediate anarchy, and also went to Cambridge, a year later than Julian, and also to King's. He was neither observed nor selected by the Apostles, and did not know of their existence. He took part in the luncheons and talks the serious undergraduates of those days arranged for workingmen, and found himself tongue-tied and at a loss. He went, in the summer vacation, on a walking holiday with Joachim that happened to wander past the new clinic on the Monte Verità, and the encampment of the holy, the mad, the aesthetic, the criminal and the lecherous that lay around it. He danced amiably in circles, hand-in-hand with *Mädchens* and maenads, greeted the Sun, discussed the coming of a future state of total freedom, and went back to Cambridge. He discovered he was good at economics. He graduated in 1905 and went to Germany to visit old friends. The British Government appointed a Royal Commission to study the Poor (and appointed Beatrice Webb as a member). Karl decided he could help the poor better by studying them than by getting to know them, and enrolled as a postgraduate at the London School of Economics.

Geraint Fludd was in love, and making money. He was in love with Florence Cain, who smiled enigmatically and sadly when he told her so, and behaved as if he had said nothing. He found he needed urgently to know about sex and visited those who sold it. He coupled with street women, thinking of Florence, told himself he would not do that again, and did it again. Basil Wellwood, from time to time, found himself treating "Gerry" as the son he would have wished to have, interested in money, that most abstract of subjects, and in the ships and caravanserais and descending pit-cages and slow barges that took things, all sorts of things, coconuts, carpets, sugar cane, glass beads, ingots, wheels with spokes, light bulbs, oranges, apples, wine and honey and converted them into change and exchange, shares and hunting and fishing and house parties and golf.

Basil asked Gerry what he "would do" theoretically, in certain situations—the issue of Consols, the run on Kaffirs—and lent him small sums of money, like the landlord in the parable of the Talents—five guineas, say, which Gerry made into another five guineas. At the end of May, in 1902, it was clear that the war in South Africa was coming to an end. There was expectancy in the Kaffir market. Gerry made a quick profit on some shares in a project called "Geduld Deep" which was simply a hole in the ground unrelated to the respectable Geduld Proprietary Mines. He bought, and sold, before the bubble burst and the story was over. The *Financial News* downplayed the concentration camps—in April they say, there were only 298 deaths out of 112,733 inhabitants—2.6 per thousand, say 32 per 1,000 per annum. "English factory towns often get as high as that." Gerry had a straw boater and a selection of stiff collars. He felt slightly contemptuous of those, like Julian, Tom and his parents, who had no idea of the intricate beauty of gold and silver, the real things. But he was also lonely, and when invited to the summer camps by the river amongst the trees, he came, divested himself of suit and city boots, and bathed naked with the others.

Time moved as differently for the generation of the fathers, mothers and aunts. Humphry Wellwood welcomed the end of the war—it had been uncomfortable, even if gallant, being a pro-Boer. He wrote articles about mining scandals, including Geduld Deep, mocking the confidence men and the gullible alike. He became slowly obsessed by the way in which Alfred Dreyfus must have experienced Time, since time was the most terrible aspect of the long-drawn-out, cruel and confusing injustice done to him. He had been arrested and condemned, for a crime he did not commit, in 1894. His sword had been broken in front of him, and for five years he had been a convict, in appalling conditions, on Devil's Island. The real traitor—acquitted in 1898—had killed himself, and in 1899 Dreyfus's case had been reopened. His conviction was quashed by the Court of Cassation—he was still marched into court between guards, a convict—and then he was reconvicted, and sentenced to spend ten years in prison. Humphry had stood with the crowds and had seen him, a sickly, upright, grey husk of a man, with lightless eyes. (In 1906 he would be exonerated, and recalled to active duty.) He twined round Humphry's imagination. All those stolen years, all that time of meaningless horror in that place—how did it pass, what was in his mind? Was it sluggish, or a false eternity, or did it burn with the pain of injustice and solitude? Humphry wrote about it. He wrote an article in which he said it was everyone's duty to imagine, every day, that apparently endless, unreal reality of subjugation. Humphry wrote better as he got older.

He had hoped that his inconvenient need for new women would slacken with his muscles. Women his age were no longer desirable, why should he be? And yet, he was. He kept testing it—women lecturers at summer schools, youngish ladies in bookshops, Fabians, socialists, he excited them, and through them, himself. He visited Marian Oakeshott from time to time, and played with her Robin and young Ann, before catching her round the waist and complimenting her on her fine figure and lively intelligence. Her Robin was the spitting image of his other Robin, at Todefright. He felt everyone must notice this, but no one said anything. Marian did not love him, now, he knew. But he sometimes persuaded her into bed, because she had a need, which tormented her, for certain things he had taught her. "I hate you," she would say, clutching him, and he would murmur cheerfully, as he pumped, "Better hatred than indifference. At least we are alive." And she would laugh drily.

He had frightened himself by clutching at Dorothy. He did love Dorothy. He had always loved Dorothy, always knowing she was not his. And it was not that he loved, in her, the same things he loved in Olive for she was not darkly passionate but stubbornly practical, somehow wise in her independence. He was tortured by the rift he had caused. (He relieved the torture by seducing a female student from the LSE after a meeting on women's rights.) He watched her behaviour, when she came home. She spoke to him in public, drily, practically, much as she always had. He wondered whether she would ever allow him to speak to her in private again. Then, one day, she came to him, in his study—it was the summer of 1902, and she had sat some of her exams for matriculation, and was preparing others for the end of the year. The tutors were organising a reading party in a cottage in the New Forest, a romantic cottage, in a clearing in the trees, with a river running past. Dorothy said she was going, with Tom and Griselda and Charles, to read there—and Julian and Florence would come, and Geraint and maybe the Fludd girls. She said

"And my father is coming to stay with August Steyning, and his sons are coming with him, and I think it would be fun to invite them to the camp. Wolfgang and Leon, that is."

Humphry dared not ask any questions. He murmured, awkwardly, "That's good, that's good." Then, lightly,

"What do they know?"

"As much as they need to know. We don't really talk about it. But I like them. Very much. And they like me."

"Well, that's good. No harm done?"

Dorothy hesitated. Both of them remembered the urgently fumbling hands, the blood. Humphry wanted to say, please don't set one mad moment against a lifetime—well, your lifetime—of love. He stared at the floor. Dorothy said, judiciously,

"Not no harm, no. But it is all right. You are my father, that's a fact."

It was a warning, as well as a concession.

"I do love you," said Humphry, entering the forbidden ground. And Dorothy was able to say, lightly, practically, apparently easily, "I love you too. Always did."

Humphry put his arms briefly round her, and kissed the top of her head, as he had done when she was a little girl. And she kissed the side of his beard, lightly, lightly, as she had done as a little girl.

During these years Prosper Cain was preoccupied with the slowly rising, dangerous, dust-clouded new building, draped in a network of scaffolding, muffled, and mysterious. Under the scaffolding domes, pinnacles and a central crowned tower came into being. Inside the building there was dissension between those concerned primarily with the beauty of the objects to be displayed, and those concerned with their utility as teaching aids for craftsmen. There was a movement on the Continent to construct or reconstruct rooms and settings—panelled, or with stone pillars and lancet windows, in which beds, tables, chairs, carpets and ceramics could be seen as the museum designers imagined their makers might have seen them. In Munich the Bavarian National Museum was newly built to show—on its façade—every period and style of architecture—and inside rooms with ceilings, floors and pillars expressly designed to show off a collection of church furnishings, or a lady's boudoir. Photographs of these splendours were published in 1901, and the Emperor of Prussia expressed approval and delight.

Prosper Cain had failed to save the strange and lovely furniture, bought by one of the jurors at the Paris Exhibition and donated to the

Museum. It had been banished to Bethnal Green, and South Kensington had been sneered at as a "pathological museum for design disease" by those favouring order and logic. In 1904 Major Cain travelled with the Director, Sir Casper Purdon Clarke, and Arthur Skinner, who was to succeed Clarke, to the opening of the Kaiser-Friedrich-Museum in Berlin: they went also to the Kunstgewerbemuseum, and Cain went on to Munich, where the display impressed him. They went in 1901 to the opening in Paris, in the Louvre, of the Musée des Arts Décoratifs and saw that the display mixed "order and connection to facilitate study" with "sufficient variety to give the feeling of life: thus a piece of tapestry is seen, as it should be, over a bed, a chest or a seat, not placed in a line between an earlier and a later specimen." This was what Prosper Cain would have wished to achieve. But it was not to be. The Museum's fate was to be decided by a civil servant from the Board of Education, Robert Morant, who had tutored the royal family in Siam, and taught the poor in Toynbee Hall, before setting South Kensington in order. He believed that it was the duty of the curators to make an educational order—spoon after spoon, banister next to banister, dishes in rows and carpets side by side. He simply demoted Skinner—who died fifteen months later, in 1911 at the age of fifty, of a broken heart. Prosper Cain had admired Skinner and had shared his views. He kept his own post but felt detached from the new order. All this was still to come. Major Cain plotted and planned and projected in the first seven years of the new century. It ate up his life, but he took pleasure in it.

His children delighted and worried him. Julian seemed to have settled for the life of a scholar, for want of an urgent vocation. Florence, who had been so forthright and practical as a girl, became, he said to himself, "moony" as she grew into womanhood. He was distressed by her ability to cling on to a hopeless—indeed, he considered it an unreal—passion for a man who was not what she thought he was. He thought he should perhaps speak to her, but was profoundly shy, when it came to speaking of the heart. She would not listen to him if he *did* speak, and what could he decorously say? He assumed—he needed to assume—that Julian would grow out of what he, as an army man, saw as a normal phase of passionate male friendship. But the other—this Gerald—he knew in his bones would not. But you can't say that to a young girl. He considered appealing to Imogen Fludd but she, too, could not be decently approached on this subject.

He had his worries about her, also. In 1902 she was twenty-three and becoming an accomplished silversmith. He liked to watch her work.

The new Professor of Design, W. R. Lethaby, and Henry Wilson, the expert in silverwork and jewellery, newly arrived from the Art-workers Guild, had introduced new ways of working. The artists sat at French jewellers' benches, which were made of beech and had semi-circular holes cut, like a flower, under which hung leather sheepskins to catch every shred and filing of precious metals as they fell. Each worker had his or her own blow-pipe, and tall Imogen sat there patiently, her hair coiled behind her head, tending the sharp blue flame, making long silver wires for filigree work, beating silver plates finer and finer. She worked in soft stones—turquoise, opals. She used a delicate bow, an ash rod strung with iron wire, to slice opals, which had to be done very very slowly and precisely. Prosper Cain liked to look at her calm face as she concentrated. She wore an indigo-blue overall, full length, and tucked her long legs under the sheepskin. At first he had thought her inexpressive and slow, but he thought now that she was a masked woman, that underneath was another kind of creature, fierce, precise, determined, capable of beauty. He was surprised that none of the male students seemed to have discovered these qualities. They paid her little attention. Other women students were vivacious or sultry. Imogen Fludd was—as her teachers recognised—an artist, and committed to her art. But Prosper Cain felt she should have life, too. Her douceur was unnatural.

There had been talk of Pomona joining Imogen at the Royal College. She had come up to London, looking flustered and pink, and had taken the exams. She had failed. Neither her father's reputation, nor her sister's excellent progress, nor Prosper Cain's interest in her could disguise the fact that she had no talent, the examiners said, that the work was both childlike and childish. She seemed rather relieved, than not, when the decision was broken to her, and went back to Lydd. It was Imogen whose eyes were red-rimmed at supper that evening, but she said nothing.

33

The New Forest camp took place in the peaceful summer of 1902, when the war in South Africa had ended. There was a cottage in a clearing, with two bedrooms, a kitchen and a parlour, made of old, red, crumbling bricks. Its windows were unevenly glazed and slightly opaque. It had a garden, full of plants that love shade and were half-wild— foxgloves and mints, sweet woodruff and forget-me-nots. It had a rough lawn which turned into sandy earth, which ran down to a bathing place in the river, a deep pool, half sunlit, half mysteriously green under branches. Someone had built a rickety wooden pier, which extended over the water, and could be dived and fished from. You could also dive from a woody bank on the dark side (it was deeper there), crushing sorrel and campion between your toes as you arched up and out.

Toby Youlgreave and Joachim Susskind inhabited the bedrooms, and unpacked boxes of books onto makeshift bookcases constructed of bricks and planks. They came early, by train to Ashurst and then in a dog cart, carrying the heavy things, tents and kettles, cooking pots and jars of jam. Tom was already there. He had walked across the Downs and leapt out of the fringe of wood, to help with the unloading. Another dog cart brought Dorothy, Griselda and Phyllis. Hedda had been told she was too little, which at twelve she thought she was not. She had had one of her rages, which were beginning to worry her parents, and had deliberately broken a fruit dish made by Philip Warren. Phyllis, at sixteen, was going to cook. She had brought an apron. Florence Cain also arrived in a trap from the station. Julian had suggested she come along—he was coming with Charles/Karl from Cambridge, the next day. And Prosper Cain had asked whether they could not include Imogen. Florence had demurred—the invitation had been to *her.* Julian, when approached, asked Toby, who said "Why not?" So Imogen had come.

Toby and Joachim and Tom put up tents. There were four of these, two for males, two for females, erected, stretched and pinned down. The girls gathered armfuls of bracken to put under the blanket bags they unpacked. Julian was walking from the station with Charles/Karl on the following day, and hoped to meet up with Gerry who was catching the same train. Florence had written, lightly, to Julian, that he ought to bring Gerald with him, Gerald would enjoy it. Julian had already that summer joined Gerald at an Apostolic reading party in the Tyrol, which had strenuously discussed truth, friendship, moral obligation, ideal beauty, the working classes and other, naughtier things. Julian occasionally thought that enjoying oneself was a very strenuous occupation.

Dorothy and Griselda set off with cannikins to walk through the woods to the farm for milk. Imogen asked if she could go with them— she was always somehow in the position of asking, mildly, if she could join in—she was not, spontaneously, invited. Florence stayed in the camp watching Phyllis shelling peas and making jellies. She was listening. She was listening for Julian, Gerry, Charles/Karl and Gerald as though she was in suspended animation until they arrived.

Love—fantastic, unrequited love—distorts and tweaks time into terrible shapes. Through the uneven window-panes Tom and Toby seemed grotesque, their bodies changing shape, fatter and thicker, stretched like elastic. Imaginary Gerald, in Florence's mind, was precise and radiant and perfectly shaped. Several times every minute she imagined him sauntering through the wood, crossing the lawn, smiling his shy smile of pleasure at seeing her waiting for him. Her skin pricked at the sight of the fantom. She willed him to come.

"Here they are," called Phyllis, running out in an apron. They strode in—Gerry first, then Charles/Karl, and Julian lazily last. Gerald had not come. Florence knew immediately that she had always known he would not come—probably Julian had not even asked him, knowing that he would find their company childish, after his fine friends. And if she had *always known* he would not come, what had she been doing to herself, imagining? She was hot with shame, and turned crossly away when Geraint strode across to her—"like a puppy" she thought meanly—and said he was so glad she was there.

Later that day, the Germans came, Wolfgang and Leon, with green hats and sticks, having walked from Nutcracker Cottage with packs on their backs. They sang together—*Wandervogel* songs, songs from the *Winterreise* and the *Ring*. Like Imogen, they were outsiders—they had not shared a childhood. They made the young women self-conscious, and sang to them, and they all joined in.

Afterwards, they all said that they must remember this time, they must never forget what it was to be young, and alive. The sun shone down. The air was golden, and blue, and dark dark green and fragrant under the trees. They walked miles, one day, in a long string of purposeful, purposeless, striding bodies, and the next day they sat in the camp, and sang in German and in English, read aloud to and with each other, read silently lying in grass, or under the stars and moon. They bathed naked in the cool water, by day and by night, the girls behind the cover of the patch of yellow flags, the boys leaping from the high bank. They saw each other's bodies with the kind of milky curiosity—there would be time enough, they thought and knew, time was infinite and elastic. They laughed at the zebra stripes and chevrons where they had browned beyond cuffs and inside shirt-necks. They all stared at Tom. Tom leaped, and pranced, and hurled himself wildly in curtains of water-drops, stirring up mud and pondweed, trailing leaves and cresses like a savage embellishment. Tom was baked golden-brown *all over*. His hair was bleached and his body was like gilded branches. He must, Dorothy thought, have spent hours and hours getting sunburned at the Tree House, or somewhere else. They all laughed at him, and he laughed back, and then set off again, running, walking, leaping, diving, in perpetual motion.

They read plays—*Comus,* with Griselda as the Lady, Julian as Comus and Gerry as the Attendant Spirit, *A Midsummer Night's Dream,* with Wolfgang as Oberon, Florence as Titania, Imogen as Hippolyta and Charles, Griselda, Dorothy and Geraint as the confused lovers. Tom was Puck. Toby Youlgreave read Sir Philip Sidney and Malory, Joachim Susskind and the Sterns read poems by Schiller and Goethe, Julian read Marvell's "Garden" and Tom read Tennyson. Julian had learned conversations with Toby Youlgreave about Philip Sidney. Sidney had written what Julian believed was his favourite sentence—certainly his favourite this year. "Nature never set forth the earth in so rich tapestry, as divers Poets have done, neither with pleasant rivers, fruitful trees, sweet-smelling flowers: nor whatever else may make the too much loved earth more lovely. Her world is brasen, the Poets only deliver a golden . . ." He said he had been looking for a thesis subject, in case he decided to apply for a Fellowship at King's, and he rather thought there might be something there. "English pastoral, in poetry and painting—" Pastoral was always at another time, in another place. Even the green pool and the long walk, over the Downs, would not become pastoral until they were past. And yet, the sun shone on them, and the leaves and the water and the grass shone with its reflections.

. . .

Memory, too, can smooth nastiness and horrors into gilded patterns. A horsefly bit Julian on the buttock, and the place swelled and burned and pricked. Phyllis burned an apple crumble, and they all said they liked its caramel taste, but left it on their plates—it was too cindery. And another night, there were uncooked sausages. Sage Dorothy got badly sunburned, even though she wore a hat. Her crimson face puffed and glistened around her eyes. Cool Griselda had hay fever. Her mouth tasted of tin and dishwashing water, her pretty nose streamed and streamed, her throat swelled and constricted her breathing, her small stock of handkerchiefs was soaked and smelly, and had to be washed and rewashed and pinned down with big stones to dry in the steady sunlight. Charles/Karl tore a fingernail and bled all over his better shirt. Phyllis had acne. Florence and the Germans remained smooth-skinned and intact, browning slowly.

After the partly cooked sausages, they all had loose bowels, which is embarrassing when you are sleeping in rows in a tent, and there is only one earth closet, attached to the cottage. They had two quiet days after that, and made meek jokes about what had not been entirely funny. But their bodies were resilient. They were young.

The two heroes of this camp were Wolfgang Stern and Tom. They made friends. Leon and Charles/Karl sat and discussed utopia with Joachim Susskind, but Wolfgang charmed everyone, male and female. Dorothy, very sensibly, had drawn Wolfgang aside, and had said, flatly, "I have said nothing to Tom."

"No?" said Wolfgang.

"He wouldn't understand," said Dorothy, defensively. "He would change. I don't want that."

"So you arrange your brothers, to suit yourself, Schwesterchen."

"You are always laughing at me. You do understand, really."

"I shall be silent as night, and—I don't know the word, it is not cunning, which I do know—*taktvoll*."

"Tactful."

Dorothy was somewhat apprehensive when she watched Wolfgang set out to charm Tom. They went on little rambles together and exchanged names of plants—*Rittersporn,* larkspur—the spur is in both. He charmed the young women, too, paying carefully casual compliments to Imogen, Griselda, Florence and even Phyllis, finding them little gifts, stones and bunches of flowers. Julian, who was the same age as Wolfgang, envied him his ease. He was able to swing on the gate between youth and man, innocence and experience, back and forth, easily, with his dark, sharp, alert smile, at once youthfully silly, and slyly almost sexual. "What do you like *best* about me?" he said to Griselda, with whom he conversed in an Anglo-German babble.

"Oh, that's easy. Your *name*."

"My name? But I was simply given that, it is not me."

"You were simply given your long legs and your face, for that matter," said Griselda, resting her eyes on these excellent forms. "But you can't hear Wolfgang in English. It's terribly romantic. Wolf walk. Wolf pace. We don't have names that mean dangerous animals."

"Am I dangerous?"

"Oh yes."

But this was as far as flirting went, and he had much the same conversation with Florence, and with Imogen.

They waited until the very end of the camp to hold the daring bathing party in which they all went naked into the pool. Wolfgang said it was a ceremony to ensure friendship would last, a kind of pagan total immersion. They invited the tutors to join them, but neither wanted to come. Julian knew that this was because their bodies were already less than perfect. They came shyly out of their tents and took hands, and danced on the lawn, white and gold Griselda with high mediaeval breasts, thickset Dorothy, willowy Imogen, the one who was trying to cover herself, and could not, because Florence, gleaming like porcelain, and chubby Phyllis were holding her hands. They circled a bit, singing "Greensleeves," as they all knew the tune, and then the line peeled off, and one by one, resolute, laughing, looking furtively at each other, they ran, still holding hands, into the water, shrieking as it closed over their sexes, laughing as their hair tumbled under, and then chasing each other, swimming like ducks or fish. Wolfgang's hand closed around Griselda's breast and let go. Geraint managed to catch Florence, and hold her, before she wriggled away like an eel or a Rhine maiden. Tom leaped up out of the water, and somersaulted, and dived down in a curtain of mist and came up, and dived again.

Julian sat on the little pier, his sex lolling between his thighs, and looked on. He thought, we are such fools. We cannot imagine we shall grow old, and we shall grow old, year by year, all this pretty—more than pretty—flesh will be damaged and diminished, one way or another. He put his chin in his hands, and from below the water Tom pulled him down by the ankles, and, laughing wildly, smeared him all over with mud.

Time is cyclical. Time is linear. Time is biological—breasts change shape, mouths harden, hair loses a little gloss. Time is named in years and months. In 1903 they made an attempt to repeat the camp and its innocent pleasures, in the same tents, in the same garden, by the same deep pool. Dorothy was struggling with the Preliminary Scientific Examination. Tom, nearly twenty-one, had made a worse hash of his matriculation than in 1902, and knew it, though his tutors and family did not, for the marks were not yet public. He spent time avoiding questions about when he would go to university, and where. All this had added a studied evasiveness—still charming enough—to his carefree demeanour. Imogen had graduated, and needed to decide on the future. Florence was thinking about whether to study, what to study, where to study, and was in the interim reading and dreaming, in a generally accusing way, if these things can accuse. Gerald came less often to the Museum, but he still came, just enough, and talked intelligently to Florence, with easy good manners, just enough to prolong her torment. Julian had sat his Finals in Classics, and was also waiting for the results.

Spirits were lowered, in the group as a whole. It was possible that the camp might have restored them, but in the event, they were overwhelmed by rain, in what turned out to be the wettest summer ever recorded. They lay in their tents, night after night, listening to the beating of the water, and the flailing of the branches, and the hissing of the wet leaves and the trickling of mud under their groundsheets, around their tent-pegs. They mostly moped. Tom proposed a mud-fight, but the others could work up no real enthusiasm. They were clammy and uncomfortable. Then one night the wind got up, and the guy-ropes tore loose and the tents slopped and slapped over the grass. They crawled, soaked, out from under. The tutors tried to light a fire in the cottage, but spirals of rain soughed in the chimney and it sputtered and went out. They made tracks gloomily towards the back door, huddled under sodden blankets. A figure went past them in the opposite direction, racing and whirling. It was Tom, half-visible through the ropes of driving rain. He ran along the jetty, and dived into the pond, and came up again, blowing water like a triton, his hair plastered to his face.

"Come on," he cried. The rain beat in polka dots around him, and vicious whip-lashes of wet wind stirred up the pond's surface into crowns and ridges. "Come on," cried Tom, but no one came, and although he splashed vigorously for some time, they all felt—including Tom—silly, and humiliated. The next day, they went home.

Nineteen hundred and three was the year when the English King went to Paris with pomp, circumstance and amiability, to lay the foundations of the Entente Cordiale in 1904. In Germany the Social Democrats won an election and argued over the principle of wearing knee-breeches to pay an official call on Kaiser Wilhelm, who believed they were a gang of traitors. In 1903 H. G. Wells joined the Fabian Society with the intention of shaking it up. A lunatic penetrated the Bank of England and fired shots at the Secretary, Kenneth Grahame. Grahame left the Bank in 1908: the Bank seemed to think he was more interested in writing stories, and messing about in boats, than in the national economy. In Manchester Emmeline Pankhurst formed the Women's Social and Political Union. She was, the editor of the *Labour Leader* told her daughter Sylvia, "no longer sweet and gentle." Patty Dace was interested, but did not join. In London there was a Festival of the Music of Richard Strauss; Anselm Stern and his sons came over and accompanied Dorothy, Karl and Griselda to the performances. Griselda was excited by the music. Dorothy was not.

Herbert Methley published *Mr. Wodehouse and the Wild Girl*. This was a mystical, fleshly, atmospheric tale of the doomed passion between the solitary poet ("my name is a version of Wodwose, the Green Man, the Man of the Woods") and an earthy, even muddy, child of nature in Romney Marsh. It was briefly successful and had some good reviews, before the police and the censors descended on the bookshops and burned their stock. Phoebe Methley said to Marian Oakeshott that she knew she should be very angry, and that censoring serious literary work was wrong—"but I am glad, I have to say, that people aren't reading it and asking me questions. And that wild girl, in my view, resembles no one, living or dead, except the inner tremolo of Herbert's strung-up sensibility—but I wouldn't like to be anyone who thought it was based on *her,* even ever so slightly."

"Shall I read it?" asked Marian.

"I'll lend it to you. Wrapped in brown paper, wrapped in newspaper. Keep it in a drawer. You'll find you don't really want to read it in bed. Or so I imagine."

At the end of the year Dorothy had passed all parts of the Preliminary Exam except Physics, which she was to resit. Griselda had matriculated. Julian had his First—neither the best, nor the worst First, a gentlemanly First. Karl had passed Part I of the Maths Tripos. Tom had failed again. Philip was working on a new, silvery blue glaze.

34

When Geraint, or Gerry, Fludd left Purchase House he wanted, he thought to himself, deliberately using the cliché, to shake its dust from his feet. His mind was full of images both mocking and distasteful. The holes in the long dirty carpets in the corridors. The vacancy in his mother's large eyes. Pomona being skittish or girlish. Half-cooked fish (before Elsie came) and watery porridge. Clutter, as though the workshop was trying to infest the living space with drying knobs of clay and smears of engobe. He needed to get *out,* and he had got out. Now he was calmer, and had his own life, he began to feel he might have responsibilities.

This feeling was inextricable from his need to continue to visit the Cains, which was easy for him to do, because his sister was there. But after some time he began to be really interested in Imogen's future, as opposed to appearing to be so. She was good-looking, in an elongated, old-fashioned way, and her slow speech and gestures were less mannered, more natural. She appeared to have talent. She was worth helping. And if he helped her, intelligently, he would be helping those abandoned helpless ones in the Marshes. His father might be a genius but he was the exact opposite of a good businessman, even more a good salesman. He did not appear to want to part with anything he had made. And he might turn Philip Warren into a copy of himself. Geraint visited the Cains when Prosper came back from his visit to Berlin. He said he thought there should be a showplace somewhere in London, where Imogen's work could be displayed and sold—and the work of the Purchase potters also, and possibly other selected artists who had been at the Royal College with Imogen. Somewhere perhaps in Holborn or Clerkenwell. It could combine a studio with the display—so Imogen, perhaps, and a potter, maybe—could be seen working, and could explain the work to interested visitors. He had talked to Basil Wellwood, and Katharina, and they were interested in investing in the project. And he himself could help with managing.

Imogen said she had thought she should leave South Kensington and set up on her own. Major Cain said he hoped she would not—it was good for Florence to have her company—she should feel more than welcome to stay at least until this excellent idea had been put in place, and was running. Geraint looked at Florence, to see if she was happy. He did not think her expression was one of pleasure. Much of the smiling poised calm he had loved her for had vanished lately. But he still loved her, doggedly. He thought of her in the beds of the women he visited, and he remembered this now, as he looked at her, and flushed. "What do you think?" he asked her. She said it was a clever idea, and she wished she had a talent, as Imogen had.

The showroom was set up in a street in Clerkenwell where other artisans already worked and showed. It had a plate-glass window and display shelves and cabinets (made by furniture students) in elegant modern Arts and Crafts forms. There was a counter which was more like a long hall table, also in pale wood, and behind the counter, a recessed space in which Imogen's work table, with blow-pipe and leather bags, was set up, next to a wheel for a potter. Various young women from the college came and threw pots from time to time. Geraint brought in young men from the City and Basil Wellwood himself came, and bought large vases by Benedict Fludd, which Geraint had had transported from Lydd. There was argument over what to call the place. Geraint thought of "Kiln and Crucible," which Florence said sounded industrial. Imogen, who had been working on some small silver, walnut-shaped boxes, said "Why not The Silver Nutmeg?" and that was agreed on. They made a strange tree, from bronze and silvery wire, about five feet high, which they stood in a large jardinière, made at Purchase by Philip and Benedict, in a glaze shading from pale sea-green to deep indigo, painted around with a prancing dragon with fourteen legs, whose teeth closed on his own scaly tail. Imogen hung this tree with small gold and silver objects made by herself and other silversmiths and from the top branch she hung the Silver Nutmeg and Golden Pear, smooth and glowing.

Geraint liked fixing things. He believed he was the prime mover behind the summer crafts camp in 1904. One idea led to another. If there was a camp in and around Purchase House—a camp where people could come and make things, and other people could come and learn, *then* the carpets might be replaced, and the furniture spruced up, and the house full of talk and work instead of female lethargy and retarded tocking clocks. It came into being in his mind—tents in the orchard, for men and for women—classes in the empty stables, painting, weaving, Imogen at a table in the harness room, surrounded by a circle of eager learners, classes at all levels from elementary to masters, in making pots . . . He thought about the studio in the dairy, and his father in the studio. He was a man of moods, Benedict Fludd, many of them evil, more of them morose, some of them manic. In one of his *good* moods—by which he meant manic—his son thought, he might be got to agree. There would then be the problem of the mood he might be in by the time the camp was set up. Geraint quailed. He went to talk to Prosper Cain who suggested that the summer camp should be set up elsewhere—they might ask Frank Mallett and Dobbin and Miss Dace if they could suggest a site—but it should be set up *in reach* of Purchase House, so that Fludd could perhaps give a lecture on his work—or a demonstration—and so could Imogen. It would be good for Pomona to have something happening—she must be given employment.

The person who helped out—instigated by Dace, Mallett and Dobbin—was Herbert Methley. A neighbouring farmer had just died, and his widow was happy to let the run-down farm buildings to the proposed camp to make studios for classes. She would provide milk, bread, apples and cider. There was plenty of room in the meadows for tents, there was a farm pond even if there was no river, the bathing places of Dymchurch and Hythe were within reach. Methley proposed some lectures on the Art of Writing. Wood-carvers and landscape painters were suggested. Geraint went, with Prosper Cain, to Purchase House, where they ate a lamb pie, cooked by Elsie, and surreptitiously studied Benedict Fludd. They asked if he would, when the camp was in place, spare Philip to help with the pottery classes and perhaps even lend his kiln to fire the work of the pottery enthusiasts. Fludd said Philip was more than busy, and he did not propose to put his kiln in danger. But his mood was not savage. Geraint had spent a short lifetime calculating how savage his father's mood might be. His lip muscles were relaxed. Geraint looked from his father to Prosper Cain. He thought: I do not love my father. I have never loved my father. I wish I had a different father—a man like Cain who protects people, a man like Basil Wellwood who understands that I'm clever and ambitious. Benedict Fludd had loved his daughters in some odd way. But he rarely acknowledged the existence of his son.

"Imogen will be here," Geraint said. "Imogen will be giving classes in silver-working. You really should make the effort to come to London and see The Silver Nutmeg. We sold two of your Janus vessels. It's going well."

Fludd had been making two-faced vessels, benign and calm on one side, possessed by rage, or grief, or pain on the other. They were in dark ruddy earthenware, decorated with black, in the hair and beards. Geraint did not like them, but the cognoscenti appeared to.

"Imogen does not come here. She has left us."

"She will be here for *weeks* in the summer, for the camp. I wish you felt able to join in. Everyone would want to see you and your work. You could even work with Imogen—to make some things . . ."

Philip said he didn't mind directing beginners on how to wedge clay and how to centre pots and so on. But what was needed was a talk by Benedict Fludd, about the whole history of working with clay, about Palissy and majolica, porcelain and slipware . . .

"I might think about it. If the time was right—"

"And people could come—not every day, but once or twice—to see where you work—" said Geraint.

"I don't want people prying or messing."

"Imogen and Philip will make sure they do neither."

Fludd said neither no nor yes to this, which was more than could be hoped for.

The summer drew nearer. Geraint worked with those other organisers, Patty Dace, Frank Mallett, Arthur Dobbin and Marian Oakeshott, who said there should be someone to teach healthy exercises, and there should be drama of some kind. There should be theatre classes. This plan, too, burgeoned. Geraint was despatched to speak to August Steyning, who said that he had a master puppet-maker staying with him, who might be induced—he and his son—into giving classes on puppets and marionettes. And he himself might put on a performance—he had always wanted to make a hybrid work, with marionettes and fallible human actors.

And so it advanced, day by day. The Fabians and the Theosophists, the Anglicans and the craftsmen's guilds put up notices and offered services of hammer and chisel, teapot and cake, stage and workshop, healthy drill and movement classes. The original campers were rather put out—there was a lack of intimacy, a lack of spontaneity, an absence of the pagan and the sun-worshipping. But Geraint said persuasively it wasn't *instead of* the wild wood, it was *as well as*—it was an opportunity to create beautiful things and enjoy Nature, all at once. He started planning the day-to-day life of this so far shadowy world. They would build up to a climax, when Fludd would lecture, the play would be put on, and there would be an overnight firing in the bottle kiln, with everyone helping to carry wood, and midnight feasting.

Imogen acquiesced in all these plans on her behalf, but made no suggestions, either for activities, or for organisation. Florence Cain said she had no handicraft talents of any kind, but would stay in a hotel and drop in on the campers from time to time. She didn't want to be prancing about in gym slips and knickers, either, thank you. Geraint was briefly mortified—he had imagined her playing some unspecified role. He said Imogen would be disappointed. Florence said "I don't think so. I really don't."

A few days before the campers arrived, Prosper Cain went in a cab, one summer evening, to Clerkenwell, to collect Imogen Fludd and her tools. It was a very hot summer. The early evening light, though full of particles and floating debris, was gold in the grey. Prosper stood outside The Silver Nutmeg, and looked in. The tree shone with its perpetual fruit. The shelves were bright with precious metals and subtle glazes. Enamel work and threaded beads hung from ceramic branches on miniature ring-trees at either end of the long table. Between these trees was a pale mass, tawny hair, spread shoulders in a grey, Quakerish shirt. She had got tired of waiting—he was late, the streets were crowded—and had gone to sleep, he thought, looking with pleasure at the abandon of her limbs, usually so inhibited. He had done well, he thought—for the last time, as it turned out—to take her in, this companion for Florence, his motherless daughter.

He went into the shop. The pretty brass bell over the door trilled, and Imogen started. She did not lift her head. Prosper stepped across the room and touched her shoulder. He said he was sorry he was late, and did she need help, getting things together?

She raised her face to him. It was, briefly, the face of a madwoman, staring, puffed up, blotched with crimson stains. Her eyes were wet, and her face was wet, and even the collar of her shirt was damp. She caught her breath, heaving, and tried to say she was sorry.

"My dear—" said Prosper. He took two steps backwards, drew up the only other chair in the room, and sat down beside her. What was the matter? What had so distressed her?

"I can't," she said. "I can't . . ."

She wept. Prosper offered his own perfectly folded handkerchief.

"What can you not do?" he asked.

"I can't go there. I can't go back there." She paused and sobbed, and was more explicit.

"I can't sleep in that house. I can't, I can't, I can't."

Prosper Cain did not ask why she could not. He drew back from the answer, which he thought it was better for her not to give. He said

"Then you must not. We will make other arrangements."

Imogen murmured desperate liquid things about Geraint—and betraying Pomona—and dirt, dirt on the carpets, dirt in the kitchen. She began to wave her hands, agitatedly, and Major Cain caught them, and held them down, wet and hot, in his own.

"It must be possible for you to join the other young women, in the encampment? Or to remain with Florence and me in a comfortable hotel?"

"You don't know—"

"I don't need to know. You are part of my family. I care for you. I shall take care of you." .

"There is no reason. No need, not—not—not really."

"There is clearly a need if you are reduced to this state. Perhaps we should say you are ill, and cannot attend this summer school at all? Maybe we should take a holiday."

"*Don't*. I must stop this nonsense."

"You will soon be independent. Your work is good, as you know. You will be able to earn a living, and, I hope, find someone to love, and a home of your own, where you will be safe."

This caused renewed, quieter tears. Then Imogen said

"I must go away, now. But not back to that house. *I don't know what to do.*"

"I hope you will let me look after you, until you have found," he repeated his earlier phrase, "someone to love, to care for you—"

"I do love someone," said Imogen. Her eyes were closed. There was an infinitesimal silence of decision: "I love you." The silence went on. "So I must go away."

They sat still, side by side. Then Imogen put out her arms and cast herself from her chair into Prosper Cain's chair, her face against his, her body leaning into his.

His arms closed automatically around her, to save their balance. So long, so very long, without women, even though his small house felt full of them. He kissed her hair. He held her, and tried to stay stiff as a ramrod, which he found he was in a perfectly double sense.

"It isn't possible," he said, very gently. "For every reason we can think of. It is an impossible thing, in this world. It must be forgotten."

"I know that. So I must go away. And instead, everything is conspiring to send me back into that house—"

He found he felt violently that she should not go back into that house. He said

"I will take care of everything. Dry your eyes, and tidy your hair, and let us go home."

He did not know what he would do. But he imagined he would think of something, as he always did.

He found it hard to go to sleep, that night. He looked at himself in the mirror. A sable, silvered moustache elegantly clipped, a lined face, steady eyes, the right side of fifty, but not for much longer. And a young woman—a lovely young woman—had fallen into his arms and said she loved him. He stroked his moustache, and stood to attention. She was probably right, she should go away, but who would look after her, if he did not? He had made her happy, when she had been unhappy and at a loss. He was not her father. She had a father, of whom she was afraid. She loved him, he was sensible enough to see (he told himself) because she was afraid of her father. That could be described as a tangle, or a muddle. He was good at cutting through tangles, and smoothing muddles, in the army, in the Museum. But they were not *his own* tangles or muddles. He had had enough of self-scrutiny, and got ready for bed in his military cot. Who dares, wins, he said to himself drowsily, without knowing what he meant. He couldn't, he thought, ask Florence about this, as he had asked her about everything else. Damn that self-satisfied young animal, Gerald Matthiesen.

Cold water, he said to himself. Clean cold water, pour on it.

He had one of those terrible dreams in which things will not fit. In it, he found himself, as he frequently did, supervising the movement of furniture in the Museum, furniture swathed in dust sheets, shrouded and bound about and about. There was a large crew of beetlelike workers shifting an object, first in one direction, then in another. They were trying to get it through a door into the Crypt, and it was too large, it would not *go*. "You will scrape it," said Prosper in the dream, "you careless fools, try some other way."

Then he was back with the removal men, all boys, who were now struggling to move the piece of furniture round a sharp angle on a narrow staircase where it would not fit. They were carrying it down; it was suspended over the narrow banister. He said "Can't you see it won't go?" "Then us mun tek it up, see," said one of the men or boys, in the voice of a thick corporal whose life Prosper Cain had once saved when the lad made a silly error with a firing mechanism. He had gripped his wrist, and the boy had thought of aiming a blow at him and had thought better of it. In the dream, Prosper Cain was pleased to see Simms. He said "Use your head, Simms, it won't go up there, it's too big by far."

"You told us, sir, it mun go up," said Simms, and gave an almighty heave, which broke the bands on the shrouding, and caused it to flap to earth over the banisters.

The object was a huge, beautifully carved, ebony bed, fit for a sultan. "And all his harem," said Prosper's mind, as the beetle-men rammed the monstrosity into what he saw was his own wall, toile de jouy and all. The staircase began to disintegrate under the weight.

"You'll bring the house down," said Prosper to Simms, and, perhaps fortunately, woke up.

35

The presence of the Sterns, father and sons, in Nutcracker Cottage should have agitated—and to a certain extent, did agitate—Olive Wellwood. She had a sense, when she thought about it, which she tried not to do, that everything *unseen* in her household had shifted its invisible place. Things had always been behind thick, felted, invisible curtains, or closed into heavy, locked, invisible boxes. She herself had hung the curtains, held the keys to the boxes, made sure that the knowable was kept from the unknown, in the minds of her children, most of all. And now she knew that grey, invisible cats had crept from their bags and were dancing and spitting on stair-corners, that curtains had been shaken, lifted, peeped behind by curious eyes, and her rooms were full of visible and invisible dust and strange smells. She was rather pleased with all these metaphors and began to plan a story in which the gentle and innocent inhabitants of a house became aware that a dark, invisible, dangerous house stood on exactly the same plot of land, and was interwoven, interleaved with their own. Like thoughts which had to stay in the head taking on an independent life, becoming solid objects, to be negotiated.

She knew very well that Dorothy had gone to Munich to see Anselm Stern. She knew that Humphry knew that, and supposed, but had not been told, that he had spoken about this to Dorothy. She waited for either Humphry or Dorothy—or Violet, in whom Humphry might have confided—to say something to her, and none of them did. Dorothy went on just as normal—except that it was not, and could not be, as normal. She had become, her mother thought, disagreeable and domineering about this medical training of which she did speak, a great deal, in an accusing voice, or so Olive understood it. Humphry placated their daughter.

She did not think Tom knew any more than she did. He had most innocently made great friends with the unacknowledged German brothers. He was uneasy, yes, but this was because he felt people thinking he himself ought to be, or do, something.

A metaphor for herself came into her mind, which was the equivalent of her metaphor for Dorothy. Dorothy she perceived as a doorless, windowless hut, encountered by a lost soul in a deep forest in need of shelter. The quester prowled around and around, and the blind brick walls emitted no light or sound, and there was no way in.

Sometimes she moved the brick tower to a distant place on the plain. Surrounded—her mind worked busily—by the dried-up skeletons of those who had seen it as a refuge and arrived thirsty and starving.

Opposite it, on the plain, stood a building which was made of hard porcelain, which had once had the shape of a capacious wardrobe, and was now carapace, in which a living creature was enclosed, or self-enclosed, had perhaps excreted the shell, which had graded colours and ridges and frills, as a whelk might, or a monstrous hermit-crab.

There were things—many things—she did not wish to know, was appalled to think of knowing.

The porcelain was light, lighter than air. The wind took it over quicksands. The porcelain was painted with eyes, but they did not see as a peacock's tail does not see, or a moth's wing.

If she stopped spinning, the thing would sink.

Another part of the problem was Anselm Stern. When he had first come to England, she had treated him gracefully as an acquaintance, and he had accepted her lead. There was a sense in which he was no more than an acquaintance. They had met in masks, amidst music, in an unreal world where everything is permitted, which seemed more real than the real world, which was always happening to Olive, whether at Todefright, or in Munich, or anywhere, almost, except the Yorkshire coal-field. But now, he too had acquired a lacquered surface, like the faces of his puppets, with their single, fixed expressions to which the lights and shadows added meanings. She had seen him look at Dorothy—quick, quick, think of a story about someone who had a child they never knew they had—stolen away by a witch—would they recognise each other if no one told them, or pass unacknowledged in the street? It was a good story, but it made her profoundly unhappy to see the two smiling secretively at each other. She thought of a story of a puppeteer for whom all human creatures had strings to pull and batons to direct. That was a good story too, but its impulse was unjust. The damned couple were *happy*. They did not intend her to share the happiness.

There was a kind of relief, and a kind of anguish, to her, to understand that all principal actors intended to maintain this state of affairs.

She was surprised when August Steyning asked her to collaborate on a kind of pageant or play to be worked on during the arts and crafts camp. He had an idea for a play about magic that would use human actors and puppets—puppets moreover, of two kinds, both life-size, with a dark human moving them, and glittering small marionettes, with their own stage. He had in mind one of Olive's magical tales. Something like *The Shrubbery,* the human boy entering the land of the Little People, which could be represented by marionettes.

Mrs. Wellwood sat and stared at her teacup; she looked at Anselm Stern, to see what he thought, and he was looking out of the window, with a carved, motionless face, inscrutable. She liked August Steyning. She felt safe with him—he liked her *work,* there was no human mess or muddle.

"Mr. Stern?" she said, lightly, lightly.

"I think this idea of August is a very good idea. We might make a new art. An art of two worlds."

"I am so happy to be included," she said sincerely, sounding insincere, because she was in two worlds.

August Steyning, English and urbane, poured tea.

One advantage of putting on a play—or performance—at a summer camp is that it is possible to use a huge cast, and a large crew of wardrobe and props workers, without paying them. Indeed, Steyning said to Olive, they pay you. They sat down with Anselm Stern and Wolfgang at the dinner table in Nutcracker Cottage and elaborated a plan. Steyning's first idea had been to use the tale of the stolen child— or possibly of the stolen wet-nurse—who is spirited into the Fairy Hill, and needs to be rescued. This, he explained, would mean that you could "see into the hill" if the marionette theatre could be—a closed, curtained world—in the midst of the human theatre. Anselm Stern said that they might use those versions of the universal Cinderella story— Catskin, Allerleirauh—in which the princess, fleeing her father, finds a prince, only to have him spirited away by a witch, at the ends of the earth and put into a magic sleep of forgetfulness. He had always been particularly drawn to those tales of a resourceful heroine covering the earth in her search, asking guidance of the sun, the moon, the stars, the winds. Wolfgang said he was interested in making life-size masks and puppets. He had had an idea of making a whole audience of great dolls and scarecrows, who would be there at the beginning, and sit quite still, and then suddenly—dangerously—join in the action. Besiege the fortress, maybe. Maybe be invoked by the many-furred girl.

Olive said

"There is something in my mind. A search for a real house in a magic world. A search for a magic house in a real world. Two worlds, inside each other."

"*The Wizard of Oz,*" said Steyning.

"Humphry says *that* is an allegory about Bimetallism and the Gold Standard, with its road of gold ingots and its silver shoes."

"It has a little wizard in a huge machine," said Stern. "Which is good for marionettes, or other puppets."

"The fortress is like the Dark Tower in *Sir Roland to the Dark Tower Came,*" said Olive. "A lightless block."

"There is a lot one can do with lighting," said Steyning. "Even in a barn, without a conflagration."

"These small pieces of tales are like a kaleidoscope," said Stern. "Without end to be reshaped, differently ordered."

It was an odd play. It grew like a vegetable from its story-seeds, and the metaphors in Olive's mind. The early days of the camp were spent on construction and reconstruction. Marian Oakeshott appeared and took charge of an army of wardrobe workers, who brought old clothes and new bales, and cut, and stitched, and decorated. Wolfgang had a workshop for life-size puppets and mask-construction, in which he involved Tom, who was full of inventiveness. The workshop was in an old barn where bales of straw still stood about, and Tom began to make a strawman. This creature turned out not to be benign, like the one in *The Wizard of Oz,* but vacant, swollen and menacing. He had a huge boll of a head, with black tunnel-eyes and a mouth stitched with string, jaggedly. This head lolled and revolved above a larger-than-life-size bale of a body, with swivelling dropsical legs, and short, useless arms, no more than fringes of sticks at the shoulders. Wolfgang said it was full of horror, and should be one of the enemies met on the way. I'll act it, said Tom. It can burn up. It should burn up, said Steyning, admiring it, but we can't risk it, not in a barn full of children and dolls.

"*Blasebalg,*" said Anselm Stern. "I do not know the English."

"Bellows," said Steyning. "Of course. Straws in the wind. A small tourbillon, leaving nothing."

"And *I* shall be a Wolf-man," said Wolfgang. "Someone has brought a coat of fur and a fox with some paws, and I was going to use them for Allerleirauh, but I shall make me a wire Beast, with a hot red tongue and a how-do-you-say, *zuckender Schwantz,* and great tearing *nails.*"

"Twitching tail. Claws," said Steyning.

"*Ja,* claws. I shall be killed with a sword."

"Our heroine doesn't have a sword. She is a girl, not a woman."

"Why?"

"Because she has been promised to my sister Hedda, and because my sister Dorothy will have nothing to do with it."

"Cold iron," said Steyning. "Those who go out against the Good People, or the Pharisees, must go armed with cold iron. She takes a kitchen knife."

"I wouldn't like to face Hedda with a kitchen knife," said Tom.

Olive thought the final adversary should be a metal man, a machine-man. A suit of armour, said Steyning. Tom remembered the night-black rider in *Gareth and Lynette*. He recited, and Olive joined in

> High on a night-black horse, in night-black arms
> With white breast-bone and barren ribs of Death
> And crowned with fleshless laughter—

Wolfgang liked that. A helmet which was a skull, a skeleton which was a carapace. Ah, said Tom, but there is a twist. Inside there is a blooming boy. With a bright fresh face. Nothing bad. A part for Robin, said Olive. Florian can be the stolen changeling. Leon can move the Death figure, said Wolfgang. He's no good at making, but he is good moving.

Geraint enjoyed planning, he enjoyed finding the right person for a job, he was, in his City form, as good at compromise and consultation, as in his Marsh form of sulky boy he had been inept and sulky. He met an army quartermaster from Lydd in a pub near Old Romney, and arranged to borrow a number of tents and some cooking equipment, which amazed everyone. He drew up an agenda, a timetable. Gymnastic exercises and dance movements after breakfast. Excursions to churches.

Classes in embroidery, silversmithing, ceramics, theatre design, acting. A lecture at the end of most afternoons before the evening meal.

Benedict Fludd had to give one of the first lectures—so that all the aspiring potters could learn first principles from him. He would speak in the Tithe Barn, and Philip would sit at the wheel on the platform beside him, to demonstrate wedging, and fritting, and pulling, and building, and centring, and the rhythm of the wheel. Later they would return, and demonstrate painting and glazing. And at the very end of the camp they would examine the pots that had been made, and choose which were fit to be fired, and fire the great bottle kiln, for which the wood was being collected. At a much later stage in the planning, during an idle conversation with Wolfgang Stern, Geraint conceived the wild idea of dismantling the fairy tower—which itself bore an odd resemblance to a bottle kiln or oast-house—and carrying it through the lanes to add to the firing. Wolfgang said his fabricated audience—a mixture of sagging or rigid scarecrows and stuffed dolls, softly representing smiling women, with pink painted cheeks, or men in blazers and boaters—could rise up and pull it all down, and run through the landscape. The best drama, Wolfgang said, would be, if they put the *Puppen* in the fire door. It would be an amazement. But I do not know that I could support to burn so much careful work.

Burn the failures, said Geraint. There always are some.

Prosper Cain, and Florence, and Imogen were in the Mermaid Inn, in Rye. Geraint came to drive them over to Benedict Fludd's lecture. Geraint supposed, as the rest of his family supposed, that Imogen would then go on to Purchase House with his family. Over breakfast, Imogen had said, in a thick, swallowed voice,

"You do understand. I'm not going back."

"We understand. Florence needs you. I shall explain."

When Imogen had gone to fetch her hat, Florence said

"I wish you would not say I need Imogen. I don't. She may need me."

"She doesn't wish to return home."

"I know that. You consider all her wishes. There was no suggestion, when she came, that she would be here for ever."

"Oh, Florence." He looked a little helplessly at his rigid, rigorous daughter. "She won't be here for ever. She must find a way to make a living, and a home for herself."

"I'm sure her mother wants to see her," said Florence, who was sure of nothing of the kind. She said with passion

"I wish we could go back to Italy, to Florence. I don't want to spend my summers in dingy Dungeness where I have nothing to do."

Prosper Cain was about to put his arm round his daughter, who had been born in Florence, when Imogen returned with her hat, which was very pretty, huge-brimmed, covered with artlessly artful feathery flowers.

The Cains arrived at the Tithe Barn when the audience for the lecture was largely assembled. There was a raised platform at one end, on which stood a lectern, and next to the lectern a potter's wheel, and a table on which bowls, jars, models, stood, some perfect and gleaming with intricate design, some pale and matt, with unfired glaze, one or two blown into strange hobbling or deliquescent shapes by misfirings.

Benedict Fludd and Philip came on together, to mild applause. Philip was cleanly clothed as an apprentice, in a linen overall, his bush of hair smoothed down. Fludd was wearing a kind of overall-robe, in midnight-blue, with gold piping, streaked with clay stains, including a ghostly handprint. His full Victorian beard also had clay in it. He wore small, round spectacles, which gave him the air of a scientific eccentric. He stood quite still, staring out at the audience, checking, and then began to speak. His family was in a row—Seraphita in floating embroidery, Pomona in innocent muslin, Elsie in a round shiny black straw hat, fastidious Florence in brown linen, Prosper Cain in a summer suit, and Imogen, under her flowers. He nodded to them, and began to speak.

"Potters, like gravediggers, are marked by clay. We work with the cold stuff of Earth, which we refine by beating and mixing, form with our fingers and the movement of our feet and then submit to the hazards of the furnace. We take the mould we are made of and mould it to the forms our minds see inside our skulls—always remembering that earth is earth, and will take only those forms proper to its nature. I hope to show you that those forms are infinitely more extensive than most people may imagine—though not infinite, as earth is not infinite. We are chemists—

we must know metals and ores, temperatures and binding elements, weights and measures. We are artists—we must be able to be exact and flourishing together, with a brush or a cutting tool. We are like the alchemists of old—we employ fire, smoke, crucibles, gold, silver, even blood and bone, to make our vessels, our simulacrae, our fantasies and those containers necessary for daily functions, food and drink—which can be lovely, however plain, graceful, however simple . . ."

He went on. Everyone listened. He called on his assistant to demonstrate the mystery of the craft, and Philip silently, and skilfully, taking lumps of clay from baths and bins ranged beside him, made airless blocks, or rising coils, or, towards the end, a turning bowl, wavering up against gravity between his strong fingers.

There was much applause. Tea and sandwiches were served and Fludd made his way to his own family group. Prosper Cain told him the lecture was both earthy and fiery. He accepted the compliment. He moved step by sideways step to where Imogen stood, talking to Elsie in a self-consciously absorbed way.

"You came," he said. "You have come back to us. We are fellow workers, fellow members of the crafts. My dear."

He put his arms around her. Imogen stiffened. When he released her, she brushed down her dress, as though slivers of clay were on it. She said

"You spoke wonderfully. As always."

Fludd was bustling and smiling. Members of the audience crowded him, all complimentary. Philip, on the platform, was packing the exhibits into crates. Geraint joined him. He said, "That went well." Philip frowned.

"He's excited. When he's this full of himself, there's always a reaction. You know that. I'm bothered. He has set so much on—"

"On?"

"On her coming back. But it won't be for long. And then—"

When everyone else had gone, the Fludds remained. Benedict said to Imogen

"Come now. Everything is ready, Elsie has seen to it."

"I'm staying—with Florence," whispered Imogen.

"Bring Florence. Come."

"I'm going back to Rye."

Her father caught her wrist. He gripped and ground it.

"You are coming home. I'm here because you agreed to come home."

He stared, or glared, at her.

Florence took two or three little steps back, out of the group.

Imogen said, inaudibly,

"You know I can't."

Prosper said

"Benedict, you are hurting her. Let her go. Let her come back to the Mermaid, and we'll talk things over—"

Benedict turned on Prosper Cain.

"All this is your doing. You seduced her. You are keeping her from me—"

"Be careful what you say," said Prosper. "Be very careful."

Benedict hit him. Not with a clenched fist, with a flat hand, very heavily, across the cheek, leaving fingermarks that looked flayed, and clay on the tips of the moustache.

Prosper ducked the second blow.

Imogen began to shake.

Prosper said, very formally, to Seraphita, "You must see, madam, that she is a woman grown, and may choose where she sleeps. I shall take her back to the inn until we are all calmer."

"Philip—" said Seraphita. "Fetch Philip—"

Prosper Cain swept his ladies away. He had to support Imogen. Florence trailed behind them, treading with little stamps of her heels. Geraint, annoyed by the failure of his well-planned day, and anxious in some other dark place he did not wish to acknowledge, went back to Philip, and helped him to help Benedict, who appeared to be choking, into a pony-trap.

The Cain party had its own small breakfast room. Imogen did not appear the next morning. Florence and her father ate largely in silence. He said, once,

"We might go to Italy later this summer."

"Never mind Italy," said Florence, repressively, chewing toast. "What are you going to do now?"

"Do?"

"About Imogen Fludd."

Prosper Cain took a long time to answer. Florence observed

"They are all *impossible* people, all of them."

"Should you like to go for a drive this morning, perhaps."

Florence said she was going out to walk with Griselda Wellwood, who was also in Rye. She said her father would be expected at the crafts camp. She went out.

After a time, Imogen appeared in the doorway, dressed in travelling clothes, carrying a small portmanteau. Prosper asked her to sit down and drink some tea, and eat some toast at least. She did sit down, rather heavily. He poured tea for her. There was a silence.

"Where are you going?" asked Major Cain.

"I thought, to Geraint. He will have to help me. He is my brother, he is the right person."

"He is a very young man, and he works long hours in a difficult place, and lives in a lodging-house. Much better stay here, and we will think about what is best, together, sensibly."

Imogen sipped her tea. The tension in her usually calm face made it, Prosper thought, wild and beautiful.

"There are things you don't know," she said.

"The world is full of things I don't know, and shan't know. I know what I need to know when I am in a campaign, and I know what I need to know about how to run a museum department and buy gold and silver. I don't know what I need to know about young women. I am not well equipped, as regards young women. But I am very good at not seeking to know what does not concern me. Often it is best to remain ignorant for ever of painful things. I have known several people who have brought themselves to confess this, or that, or to complain violently of this, or that, and have regretted it for the rest of their lives."

He looked at her portmanteau.

"When I was a boy," he said, "I used to pack a suitcase, and form a project of running away. Sometimes the packing was enough. Sometimes I set out, and had to be brought back. Once I was away a whole night, and was savagely beaten, on my return, and then cuddled and kissed."

"I am not a child, and I do know I must go."

"I hope you will let me look after you."

"You can't. I see that, now. For every reason."

"My dear," said Prosper Cain, very stiffly, his back rigid, "I have not forgotten, and cannot forget, what you said to me in Clerkenwell."

"I didn't mean—"

"Did you not? It has made me see what I myself feel. For my own part, I can think of no greater happiness than making you my wife. And giving me the *right* to look after you. I am much older than you are. I know that. So do you. But in some timeless place, I do believe, we see each other as equals, face to face. I don't want to let you go. Perhaps I should, but I cannot. And will not."

He looked at her, almost angrily.

She looked at him. Her large eyes were steady. She said

"I love you. I do love you. Perhaps that is all that need matter?"

He thought of cross Florence, and raging Benedict Fludd, and knew it was not. He was a strategist, he would devise a strategy. He said

"Come here—"

She stood up and came. He took her in his arms and kissed her brow, and her neck, and then, gently, her lips, and then, less gently, her whole mouth, and he knew that she did indeed love him.

He said "We won't tell Florence, until we have thought things out, further. Or Julian, of course. I do not think that will be easy, but I think it may be managed. What I shall do, as soon as possible, with your permission, is drive over to Purchase House—no, my love, you will *not* come with me—and ask your father, very formally, for your hand in marriage. Everything else, we will plan calmly, and carefully. Do you feel able to go to the metalwork school in the camp? I could drive you there, on my way."

Elsie let him into Purchase House. She pointed across the yard, to the studio in the dairy. She opened her mouth to impart some information or other, and closed it again.

"He's in there. I saw him go in," she volunteered.

"Thank you," said Cain, and marched across the yard. Fludd was standing at a high table, modelling one of his facing-both-ways jugs. He was incising more sullen lines into the sullen side. The other was a blank oval.

"Who is it?"

"Me, old friend."

"Ah, you." Fludd turned round, at bay. Cain did a mental calculation about their respective ages. Fludd must be less than ten years older than himself. He was not yet fifty and Fludd was not, he thought, sixty, though he looked older, grizzled and heavy.

"I have come to ask you something."

"You have done enough harm."

"I don't think it's harm. It is—I agree—unexpected how it has turned out. I have come to ask you for your daughter. Who has agreed to become my wife."

"*Wife—*"

"I am older than she is, but she is happy to set it aside. She says I may ask you for your goodwill."

"I don't give it."

"Wait. Think. She does love me. I do love her, Benedict. I think in an odd way we have a chance of happiness. We are at ease with each other. I can make her comfortable, and encourage the talent she has inherited from you—"

"What have you done to her?"

"Nothing. She has been like my daughter, together with my daughter. And very recently things have changed—developed, one might say—"

"Stop making reasonable noises, for Christ's sake. You can't do this. That's final."

"She is of age, and I don't need your consent. But I do beg you to think for a moment of her—this *is* a chance of happiness for her— I have assured myself that—"

"She was happy here."

"I think not, Benedict. I do think not. But this is a new beginning."

"Howl," said Benedict unexpectedly. "Howl, howl, howl."

After a moment Prosper realised that this impossible person was quoting King Lear, as he came on stage bearing his dead daughter in his arms.

36

The important lectures were at the weekends, so that audiences might come in from outside, or even travel down from London. On the first weekend, in the late afternoon, on the Saturday, Humphry Wellwood spoke on Human Beings and Statistics: Changing the Condition of the Poor. On the Sunday, Herbert Methley spoke. His subject was Leaving the Garden: the Shamefulness of Shame. Miss Dace had asked him if he was quite sure about this title, and he had answered, flatly, "Yes."

Prosper Cain and Imogen Fludd were in a state of exultant tension. They smiled too much, and Florence watched them, and they watched Florence watching them. They touched hands, secretly, in doorways, and when they were sure they were quite alone, Imogen ran into his arms. He had not expected his intense, quasi-fatherly affection and concern to become blind physical passion, but that had happened and he felt reinvigorated and renewed. As for Imogen, the slight stoop she had had, the deferent low voice, the slow movements that resembled her mother's had turned to eagerness and quickness. Prosper knew he should tell Florence, and found himself taking intense pleasure in secrecy.

Things were complicated by the arrival of Julian and Gerald, who were on a walking holiday and had decided to walk to Lydd and hear Humphry's lecture. Gerald was trying to decide between becoming a moral philosopher and going into politics, if he could find a party that met his exacting standards. Julian had an idea for a thesis on English pastoral poetry and painting. He wanted to write about the bright, transparent visions of Samuel Palmer and the woodcuts of Calvert. Gerald was writing about Love and Friendship and the Good, when he was not talking late, or swimming in the Cam, or bicycling across the marshes, or climbing in the Alps. He thought Humphrey's Fabian socialist views on human nature were interesting. The young men arrived at the Mermaid in time for lunch, and were shown up to the family sitting-room, where they found Florence, writing.

"You could have *said* you were coming," she greeted them, taking in Gerald's beauty under his floppy linen hat.

"We didn't know. Then we saw a poster for this lecture, so we thought we'd call on you for lunch, and go to hear it. Where's Papa?"

"Silversmithing."

"Is he coming here for lunch?"

"He didn't say."

Julian looked at Florence, who was looking at Gerald. He said "Well, we can lunch with you, and cheer you up, can't we?" He saw that she needed cheering up. He said

"Are you not helping with the silversmithing?"

"I have no skill. And I don't want to."

Gerald had walked across to the window, and was staring out. Julian said "What's up?"

"You'll soon see," said Florence, darkly.

At the lecture, they found themselves in a row of old friends. Julian was on the end, and Florence was next to him, and Gerald was on the other side of her. Beyond Gerald was Geraint, and next to him the young woman from Purchase House, Elsie Warren, decorously dressed and looking severe. Next to Elsie was Charles/Karl Wellwood, who was thinking what to do at the end of his Cambridge studies, whether to go to the London School of Economics or to Germany, to be an anarchist or a socialist or some kind of worker. Dorothy and Griselda were not there. They had gone into the hay barn where the marionettes and life-size puppets were being constructed. Griselda wanted to speak German. Dorothy was watching Anselm Stern stitch a tiny costume on to a slender silken trunk. Wolfgang and Tom had made a lolling platoon of death-still scarecrow men and women, decked with hay and flowers, stretching out rigid arms of coat-hangers and hoes.

Humphry more or less bounded onto the stage, his red hair and beard darkly glowing. His wife was in the front row, looking queenly, and Marian Oakeshott was towards the back, looking thoughtful.

Humphry talked about the paradox of statistical surveys and individual human fates. The Christian religion, he said, which had formed our thought, insisted that each human soul was unique and valuable in the sight of God. Jesus Christ had advised the rich man to sell all he had, and give to the poor. He had also said that the poor were always with us. He had said that where every prisoner and sick man and pauper was, there He was also among them. He had urged charity on his followers.

Much had been done, much that was valuable, by those who had gone out amongst the starving and the derelict and had reported on crowded rooms in unsanitary buildings, dead and dying crowded together, the sickness of sweat-shop and lucifer workers. He read out a description of the appalling, rapid descent into penury and death of a good worker who injured his back.

He said that compared to individual witness and individual feelings, the compiling of statistics might seem dry. But those stirred not only the imagination but the reason, and the will to act. Statistics was a human science. It had begun, he rather thought, with Durkheim, noticing that the number of suicides in Paris did not vary from year to year. All of them different human creatures, all of them grim decisions taken that life was no longer bearable. The causes might be poverty, lost love, failure at business, humiliation or sickness. But the figure was the same.

In the case of poverty the compilation of figures touched the imagination in a way individual cases could not. The hero of this study was Charles Booth who had interviewed everybody—registrars, school attendance officers, School Board visitors, census-takers—and had produced, beginning in 1892, seventeen volumes of reports on the nature and extent of poverty in London. He had mapped it street by street, colouring the streets according to the data, and had come to the conclusion that a million people, over 30 per cent of the population of London, had not the wherewithal to subsist or continue living. This figure revealed an unjust society as individual descriptions alone could not. It was a prerequisite for putting forward constitutional and legal changes—the introduction of a pension for the aged in place of the foul and degrading Workhouse, the suggestion of minimum legal wages, and maximum hours of work, of help for the unemployed that was rationally administered and not a function of charitable impulses amongst the better-off.

Charles/Karl listened dubiously. He had been moving amongst those who believed that only a revolution of the underdogs would bring about any change in the gruesome system. Everyone bothered about the poor. His parents' friends truly held the belief that the undeserving poor should be sequestered in concentration camps and reformed, reconstructed or even—in the case of imbeciles and madmen—charitably put to death. In his college in Cambridge lunches were given for working-men, some of whom were crusty, some of whom were boys with sidelong glances under long lashes, some of whom were auto-didacts, socialists, or would-be poets. He did not feel he had got to know any of these selected and collected examples. He did not know what to say to them. He did not speak their language though he could communicate with intense small groups of German anarchists. He thought he might discuss the LSE with Humphry. The glamour of statistics had touched him.

Gerald kept making remarks to Julian over the top of Florence's hat, as though she was not there. He said once, with a sardonic smile,

"He who would do good must do it in minute particulars."

Julian drawled back "Not clear, my dear chap. Are you referring to particular people, or minute particular *figures?*"

Florence said "William Blake was mad, you know," but neither of them appeared to have heard her, and perhaps it was not a clever remark.

They gathered after the lecture, the three Kingsmen easy in each other's company, analysing good points, dismissing bad ones. Personal relationships, said Gerald, were the root of every virtue, couldn't be done without, a man could not spend his life on reducing other men to figures without damage. Florence said we are not all monads, and nobody answered. Charles/Karl said society did exist, it was not only a mass of individuals. Classes existed. And male and female said Florence, crossly. Indeed, said Julian politely. Geraint, who had joined them, said that new women's groups for agitating were very interesting. Gerald took the conversation back to human friendship.

He was embarrassing Julian, not because he was insulting Julian's sister, but because Julian no longer loved him, and was not ready to admit that, precisely because of the intensity of the Apostolic faith in friendship as a supreme value. Julian no longer wanted to kiss, or indeed even to touch, Gerald, who had—as often happens—become much more eager to touch, to hold, to grasp Julian as Julian withdrew. Julian had begun to think Gerald was clever and silly, and did not want to know he thought that, it was inconvenient, their group was so comfortable, their walks so companionable, Cambridge and the English countryside so lovely.

Geraint moved round the group to Florence's side. He said "I wish you had been able to persuade Imogen to go back home for a few days."

So did she, said Florence, repressively.

Geraint said she was looking beautiful. She broke off her intent frown to smile weakly at him, which encouraged him. He did not feel at home with the theoretical Kingsmen. Also he half-despised them for their lack of acquaintance with "real life" which he thought he knew better. He asked Florence her opinion of Humphry's talk and she said it did seem to suggest things that could really be done, and that it was absurd for the middle classes to live in fear, as they did, of the dirty and desperate armies in the sinks of their towns.

At this point, inopportunely, Elsie Warren approached them. She nodded to Florence, and asked Geraint, without urgency, if he had seen his father. Geraint had not.

"He's not at home. At least I think not. He's not at meals. Mind you, he often isn't."

"Probably recovering from his lecture," said Geraint. "A very small quantity of society makes him a recluse for days."

"That's what I thought," said Elsie. "Your mother isn't bothered."

"We shall need him at the end of the camp—for the firing."

"I think he'll come. He'll want to oversee it."

Geraint turned away from her rather abruptly, and asked Florence if he could walk her back to Rye. He expected her to say no, but she said yes. This was partly to claim independence from Julian and Gerald, and partly because she thought Geraint might have something to say about Imogen. But it was partly also that his feelings for her—his steadfastness and patience—were comforting. He was as much out of a men's world as the Cambridge men, but in his men's world, men liked women, women interested them.

"I need to talk to you," she said. "Something is going on, that's *odd*."

"I always like talking to you. About anything at all."

"I don't know about this—"

"Try me," said Geraint.

"It's Papa," said Florence.

They began to walk away, towards Rye.

Charles/Karl was left with Elsie Warren.

"You don't recognise me, do you?" she said. "I'm out of place. You've met me at Purchase House, carrying dishes and clearing up. We've not been introduced, so to speak."

He could not place her accent, which was not local, but he could tell that it was working-class. He considered her. She had made the best of herself, he thought. She had a pale grey high-necked shirt, with tight cuffs, and a swinging skirt in a dark grey cotton. She had a bright red belt, round a shapely waist, and a straw hat with a bright red ribbon and a dashing bunch of stitched anemones, red and purple and blue. He did not know what to say to her, or indeed, how to speak to her. He was also aware that she knew this, and was amused by it. Amusement was not a reaction he had expected.

"Did you enjoy the talk, then?" she said.

"It was of great interest. I am trying to decide whether to study these matters—statistics, poverty—at the London School of Economics."

"Or?"

"What you mean, or?"

"If you don't do that, what will you do?"

He could not say, be a good anarchist and foment a revolution. He blushed. "I might go to Germany."

"Might you? Nice to have a choice. I should like such a choice."

He looked at her and she looked back, intently. They saw each other clearly. She went on

"Being as I am both a woman and working-class, choice don't come into it, much, for me. I do what I must." Charles/Karl wanted to say he was sorry, and couldn't.

"I imagine you don't talk to many of us, as against studying us in bulk. The dangerous masses. To be put in camps, and set to work on projects."

"You are being unfair," said Charles/Karl. "You are mocking me."

"We can do that, at least, if we dare."

"Miss Warren," said Charles/Karl, "I wish you would not talk as though you were a group, or a class, or a committee. I should like to be talking to you as a person."

"*Can* you?"

"Why should I not?"

"For every reason. I am both working-class and not respectable. I am a Fallen Woman. I have a daughter. You don't want to be talking to me as if I were a *person,* Mr. Wellwood."

This information, far from shocking him, excited him. In Munich the goddess, Fanny zu Reventlow, was the mother of a lovely child with no known father. Desire should be free, they said in Schwabing, and Charles/Karl listened, and desired in the abstract, and agreed in principle. He could not—not now—discuss Fanny zu Reventlow with this pugnacious person with a narrow waist, in a red belt.

"Do you talk to everyone like this, Miss Warren?"

"No. I don't. Only to well-meaning persons like you."

"I should like—" said Charles/Karl. He would like, he realised, to undo the belt, and several of the buttons, and slap her and kiss her. He was astounded. He was also gratified to find such a spontaneous reaction in himself.

"What would you like?" asked Elsie, in a way that almost persuaded him she had read his secret mind.

"I should like to get to know you. I should like you to stop treating me as a representative of a class, and allow me to talk to *you*. I should like to be permitted to walk you home, if you are going home."

"I am. You can come, if you want. I really should be looking for Mr. Fludd, but if he don't want to be found, he won't be. He is a secret man."

They set off together. Motion made them easy with each other. He said "Do you think a man and a woman can be good friends, Miss Warren?"

"Elsie, why don't you. I suppose you call Philip, Philip."

"Karl."

"I thought it was Charles. Karl for Karl Marx?"

"You know a great deal."

"I have friends—women friends—who are teaching me. I hope to become a teacher myself. I do not fancy cleaning and carting for ever. And, in answer to your question, I think yes, a man and a woman can be good friends. But it isn't easy for them, being as no one else will suppose that that is what they are. And then, there's the problem of men and women being different sexes. You are not to laugh. It *is* a problem."

"I know that. What I do think—"

"What do you think?"

"I think if they are good friends—then whatever else they are—or are not—is better."

They went on walking. He said

"You will only laugh if I say you can be just as trapped in a house in Portman Square, and a public school and a university, as in the kitchen."

"Yes, I will. I will laugh heartily. I will listen, Karl, and I will laugh and laugh."

"I never talk to anyone as you talk to me."

"I shall teach you, Mr. Deprived-Rich-Man. I may even introduce you to my very little, very clever daughter."

She looked into his face to see if she had gone too far, had lost him.

"I should like that," said Charles/Karl.

Herbert Methley leaned confidentially out over the lectern. He told his audience that he was a workingman. He worked hard as a gardener on a smallholding in this county, the Garden of England, and he worked also at his desk, describing life in that Garden. But the fruits of his labours had been taken from him by the police in their boots and helmets, and had been cast into a fiery furnace, and consumed. He had been told that what he had written was shameful. But it was the men in gowns and helmets who had real cause to be ashamed.

He was a stringy sunburned man, with a crimson silk neckerchief round his prominent Adam's apple. He had that habit good lecturers have of letting his eye rove over the audience, looking for listening faces, or expressions of boredom. He saw Griselda and Dorothy with Tom and the two Germans, near the front. At the back, at the side, Julian and Gerald sat together. Florence was not with them. She was with Geraint, towards the front, in the centre. There was a row of older, judiciously composed women, Marian, Phoebe, Patty Dace, towards the back. Also near the back was Elsie Warren. Charles/Karl had seen that the seat next to her was empty, and had sat in it. She was sitting very upright, with her arms folded round her chest. Phyllis came in late, and sat down just behind Leon. Frank Mallett and Arthur Dobbin were there. Methley acknowledged them with a nod, before embarking on his attack on the clergy.

Where did the concept of shame come from? he asked. Our fellow creatures in the garden of earth do not know shame, though we persuade ourselves sometimes to feel it for them, to our shame. Shame began, we are told, in the Original Garden, when the innocent man and woman saw that they were naked, and were ashamed. What caused this? The wily serpent caused it, by making them eat the forbidden fruit, which he told them was the knowledge of good and evil. *Thus,* said Herbert Methley, insinuating that good and evil originated in those parts of the body that the shamed human beings now felt they must cover. Yet why should this be so? Are good and evil not much more—

infinitely more—to be found in cruelty, in humiliation of others, in selfishness, in abuse of power, in theft—I could go on in this way, said Herbert Methley—for the rest of this little talk. Good and evil do not reside in human flesh, in which we should rejoice, about which we should not—neither men nor women—feel shame. Every day in this camp the young folk come out and perform graceful, and strenuous, and delightful bodily movements. He smiled, imagining them.

Gerald whispered to Julian, with the grave naughtiness of the Apostles, "I think he emits some kind of musk. From under his armpits. He has well-developed armpits, you can see."

"Hush," said Julian.

The lecturer developed the Garden metaphor. He passed on to Blake and the Garden of Love, in which a Chapel was built, with

> Thou shalt not, writ over the door
> So I turned to the Garden of Love
> That so many sweet flowers bore
>
> And I saw it was filled with graves
> And tomb-stones where flowers should be
> And Priests in black gowns were walking their rounds
> And binding with briars my joys and desires.

He said much of the distorting shamefastness of the world we lived in was the historical consequence of the centuries of celibate priesthood. He looked at Frank Mallett, who looked blandly back.

The novel had suffered. In England it was written to be read aloud round the fireside of a married vicar or curate, with his wife gravely listening. In France the priests took charge of the women and children, and novels were written for the separate—and often salacious—male readers.

It was not possible in a novel to describe most of the world as it really was.

It should be. We need honest novels much more than we need moralising tracts.

His own novel *Mr. Wodehouse and the Wild Girl* had been about a modern man of the woods, a Wodwose, who had loved a woman as men do love women.

He believed, he said, in a pagan unity of nature. We are all *one life* which began long before there were any gardens, or any men in black gowns. Our feelings developed subtly, over millions of years, from the feelings and stirrings of jelly in the marshes, of slow, cold-blooded reptiles in hot swamps, of beings who clambered in trees that were now coal. It was possible, he said, to make a strenuous attempt to rediscover the strong, primal joy in being. One must go back to the roots of things. He quoted Marvell

> My vegetable love should grow
> Vaster than Empires, and more slow—

Gerald said "That's rich. Is he doing it on purpose?"
"Oh, I think so. Do be quiet."

Elsie's arms were still tightly clutched around her. Her mouth was set firm. Charles/Karl wanted to pull her fingers, to unwind her, and knew he must not.

Herbert Methley's eye wandered over the upturned faces like a bumble-bee over a flowerbed. He had a skill the younger men had not developed. He could tell which of the women were, as he put it to himself, in need, potential wild girls. Dorothy's dark face was judging him and made him uncomfortable. Griselda, blonde and peaceful, was weighing up the arguments—there was *something* alive there, and the face was lovely, but not in need. Phyllis was prim and pretty and undeveloped. He did not look at Elsie, though he had glimpsed the red belt. The agitated one, the one who breathed fast, and shifted in her seat, and looked about her for something, was Florence Cain. He took note of her.

After he had finished, some people left rapidly. Others came to talk to him. Frank Mallett said

"You have not given enough attention to the remarkable persistence of shamefastness. Men must need it very much if it is so tenacious."

"A good point."

"Marvell also said

> 'How happy was that Garden State
> When Man there walked without a mate.'"

"Indeed. There is a time for mutual love, and a time for solitude. I myself am solitary and celibate when pursuing my calling."

Out of the side of his eye he saw Florence leaving with Geraint.

There would be another time. Or another woman.

Florence and Geraint walked along a footpath by the Military Canal. Dragonflies skimmed the water. Moorhens paddled, and a rat slid out of a hole and swam busily away. The sun was still bright, though going down. Footsteps hurried after them. Geraint turned, irritably. It was Frank Mallett.

"I won't keep you, I just wanted to ask you—"

He joined them.

"Yes?" said Geraint.

"Have you spoken to your father recently?"

"Not for some days. He hasn't been around since his lecture last week. He tends to go into hiding after things like that. I was going to Purchase House when I've walked Miss Cain back to Rye."

There was a silence. Geraint said

"Have you seen him?"

"Not for some days, also." He strode along, looking at the water, and seemed to come to a decision. "No matter. No matter. When you do see him, please tell him I was asking after him."

He turned back. Geraint said to Florence

"Something is worrying that man. My father does worry people."

"I know."

There was a long silence. They moved on, companionably, walking at the same pace. Geraint said, not looking at Florence,

"I am probably an idiot to choose this moment. When we are going on calmly, that is. You needn't answer this, now, yet. *But*—I want you to be my wife. Don't speak. I have wanted it for years, you know that, I think. I don't have much to offer, yet—but I shall, for certain. I am doing well in the City, and Mr. Wellwood treats me as a son, almost. I am saving money. Also, I love you. I do love you. Don't speak for a moment. It couldn't be for a year or two. I ought not to tie you down. It may be only my fantasy. I have never seen—never—anyone like you. I think of you—you don't know how much of the time."

"May I speak now?"

"If you think it is even *possible*—I will ask again—later—if you—"

"May I speak? I was going to say—yes. Yes I will marry you. There."

They stopped walking and turned and looked at each other. Geraint said

"I haven't just *worn you out,* with waiting and watching?"

"I said, yes. I do know my own mind."

"I want you to be happy. You haven't been looking happy, lately. I want—more than I want anything—for you to have what you want. Of course, I should like it to be me."

"I haven't been happy, it's true. We can be happier together, I do think." She gave a small smile. "We can *try.* Stop worrying."

Very gently, he put his arms around her. She stiffened. He wished she had not, but he had learned patience.

"May I speak to your father?"

She gave a strange little laugh. "I shall be very happy for you to do that, yes. Then we can make plans."

Dorothy Wellwood had set off alone, for a walk across the marshes. She had given herself a sick headache, with studying anatomy, and told herself that it was for the good of her own health that she was going out. She had been having trouble with willpower. She wanted to be with the German father and the German brothers, who were making intricate things in the barn, and laughing together. She was somehow hurt that Griselda could laugh with them, in German, and make clever suggestions for scenes in the puppet play, whilst she could not. She did not want to, of course—somewhere inside her there was a puritanical rejection of imaginary worlds, that was tough and largely unquestioned. Nerves and tendons, veins and arteries, were both more real and more mysterious than wired joints and dangling strings. She knew Griselda was far from trying to steal her new family—she was, on the contrary, hurt when Dorothy went off to do her hours of study, angry as much because she, Griselda, had no calling of her own, as because Dorothy was abandoning her. She walked faster and faster, running over the articulations of her body in her head. She found herself at Purchase House, looking up the avenue of trees beside the shabby drive.

She suddenly thought it would be good to see Philip Warren. She walked into the drive. She did *not* want to see Seraphita, or Pomona, or even Elsie. So she went neatly and quietly round the house, and into the stableyard, and directly to the door of the dairy-studio. She thought, then, too late, that she might encounter the ogre, Benedict Fludd. She peered in through the dusty window. There was Philip, in a blue overall, his back to her. No sign of Fludd. She tapped on the upper half of the door. Philip opened it, and smiled widely when he saw her.

"I were about to say, go away, I'm busy. And then I saw it was you. Come in."

"I took a long walk, to think, and then I found I was here. So I came to see how you are getting on."

"I've been drawing seaweeds. Wi' things moving in them, with the water moving. Things like pipefish and cuttlefish and such."

"Show me."

He fetched his drawing pad, and they sat down, side by side, to look at it. There were some extraordinary images of bladderwrack, half-stranded, half-floating, its air pockets just above the surface of the shifting sea.

"First, I see how it looks. I keep looking, and see all the shapes as it moves in the different light. And then, a lot later, I make formal patterns." He frowned. "You see what's *chance*—little flips and flurries on th' water—and what's constant, what repeats."

"It reminds me oddly of *Gray's Anatomy*. I have to keep drawing veins, and muscles, and tendons, and joints. I could draw you different levels of what's moving in your hand as you draw. Muscles that tighten, and what they do to other muscles. How the blood runs like a tide along the veins and arteries. You could make the most beautiful designs from the circulation of the blood. Like currents in the water, and strands of weeds. Only I'm not good at drawing, like you. I have to do it, for all these exams, and I try, and I try. But I mess it up."

"Show me," said Philip, pushing the paper pad towards her, and handing her the crayon. Dorothy laughed. She drew a rough image of a hand—the palmar surface—with the strong pulling parallel bands of the muscles and the cross-gartering effect at the sheath of the fingertip. Then she drew an arm, with the main nerves blacked in like rivers and tributaries. Philip was following her crayon by touching his own hand and arm, locating the stresses and counter-stresses, the flow and return.

"Sometimes," said Dorothy, "I think I shall never get to grips with all of it. External cutaneous nerves. Deltoid. I sometimes feel I'd like to be free of it."

"Not really," said Philip. "It's *got* you. You've got no choice, I think." He took back the pencil and drew a more elegant version of the network of muscles. "Like me. I hadn't a choice, from before I could think about it."

"It means giving things up," said Dorothy. "Things like camp and the play, now. Things like parties. And more, probably. Women don't get to be doctors and have time to do the things women do, like getting married, even."

"No," said Philip. "It's like monks and nuns, work, I come to see."

"Show me your work. I like seeing it."

Philip fetched out some pots with seaweeds flowing round them, dark green on a marine green blue, with flashes of tawny yellow. He showed her some of the variations on the climbing creatures on branches, derived partly from the Gloucester Candlestick and partly from the Gien version of majolica, with capering grotesques. Dorothy was happy enough with imaginary creepers and creatures anchored so safely in cold earth, held by glaze, set in place by fire.

Philip said

"D'you want to make a pot? I've been teaching i' th' camp—it's amazing how people's aptitudes vary—I think you would throw a good pot, with a bit of practice. You've got good, strong, solid hands. With good nerves and tendons and things in the fingers, I should think."

So Dorothy sat down at the wheel, and Philip stood by her and made it move, and centred the clay for her. He showed her how to feel its texture, how to find a speed, how to hold the wall steady as it rose between her fingers like a cool, wet, living creature. Two or three vessels slumped and flailed, and then, suddenly, easily, she had a rhythm, a fat-bellied pot rose, widened, narrowed, and was cast off by Philip.

"Told you," he said. "You've got good hands. You have to see wi' your fingertips. Sometimes I think it's done wi' the whole body. The rhythm an' all. And the mind."

Dorothy thought of her future. Pulling blood-covered curled human beings out of another woman, making them breathe, cutting the cord. Cutting into flesh with scalpels. The only person she knew who understood the glamour and the terror of *work* was Philip. They didn't bother each other. They didn't *know* each other. But they understood some of the same things. She felt better for having come. She had not exactly set out to see Philip, but it turned out to be what she meant to do.

. . .

Griselda Wellwood and Florence Cain found themselves in the Mermaid Inn without their families. So they sat down and talked to each other, over a cup of tea and plate of scones. Griselda talked about the interesting aspects of the camp play or pageant, of the way it explored and exhibited so many unexpected talents, in such new co-operative ways. But she sounded a little wistful, and a little discontented. Florence did not say much at all, until Griselda had run out of commentary. She bit her sandwiches sharply and looked faintly disapproving.

"We are all so good at *playing,* nowadays," she said. "Like children."

"Oh, I think it's more than play. They are artists, Mr. Steyning, my aunt, Herr Stern and his son Wolfgang."

"It may not be play for them, but it is for most of the camp people. Physical exercises, creative snipping with scissors, fancy dress and so on. You wonder where the real world really is."

"You do," said Griselda. "I agree, about that. My brother worries a lot about the poor. He is thinking of going to the LSE to study statistics. He has always been bothered about what was real. He doesn't want the life my father planned for him."

"And what life did they plan for you?" said Florence. "As a woman?"

"Oh, they hoped I would go to dances and make a good match. I went to the dances, and was bored stiff by all the eligible young men, and now I don't know where I am. The future seems very *long,* don't you think? It *is* different for women. There's this huge *thing* coming—getting married—all the lace veils and stuff, as Mrs. Elton said—and then what? Choosing patterns, and menus, and telling servants what to do, and worrying that they won't or can't do it. What I'm trying to say is, you can't plan a future without making a decision about all that—which is hard to do, in the abstract."

"Do you think—if a woman marries—there can be any other future than what you just said?"

"I want to *think.* Just as much as Charles does, but no one cares what I want to think about, as they do with him, whether they are for or against what he thinks is important."

"I want to think, too," said Florence, slowly. "I want a life of my own, that I choose. I want to be *someone,* not someone's wife. But I don't know much about the someone I want to be."

"Nor do I. Dorothy does. She's got a vocation. She's got her future all planned out, general science exams, medical exams, surgical exams, a place in a hospital. It's like an iron corset, I think, but she seems to need it. I think she is prepared to give up on the marriage thing. I don't know that I would be. It would seem unnatural. But surely so does *not thinking*."

"Some women do both."

Florence had just agreed to marry Geraint Fludd. She felt a violent need *not* to confess this to Griselda Wellwood. Once it was out in the open, this engagement, it would become a different kind of fact.

"Not many women do both."

Florence said "Do you remember, the day we went to Todefright for Midsummer, and everyone—our age—had to say what they want to do in life? And both you and I said we would go to university. To Newnham College, or somewhere like that. I've gone on thinking about that. What do you feel?"

"I feel a lot of incompatible things. I feel I must *think* or I'll go mad. And then I think of those colleges full of women—knitting, I imagine them, and flower-arranging, and drinking cocoa. And I think, is it like taking the veil, which is an idea that's always given me the horrors. Unhealthy, part of me says. And then, part of me says it all is secretly exciting. *New.* Doing things women haven't done, aren't expected to do. Things brothers take for granted—look at Julian and Charles. One would be a new kind of human being—"

"It's not the same as Dorothy being a doctor."

"It's very clear what a doctor is. I've been talking to Toby Youlgreave. I'm going to do some hard work, and try to go there. Find out what I am."

"I started on my matriculation and stopped," said Florence. "I shouldn't have. Would Mr. Youlgreave take me on? I know my father would be positively pleased—"

"It would be wonderful," said Griselda, sincerely.

Florence was in a turmoil. She had promised herself to Geraint, and she was now promising herself to years of study. She did not think Newnham College would care for married students. She wished to disturb her father, at some ferocious girlish level, and felt—she was not really thinking—that the engagement would do that.

And yet—like Griselda, she did want to think. And she did see her future as, perhaps, the choice between thinking and sex.

. . .

Not only did *The Fairy Castle* change and develop as the campers worked on it during the days of construction—it went on developing during the performances in the Tithe Barn, for the ten days during which it was performed. August Steyning was in charge of both the set design and the production. There were two castles at the end of the barn, one in front of the other. The smaller was shining and gilded, a casket of a castle, in which the marionettes performed fairy feasts and transformations. Behind it, in shadow, rose the curiously kiln- or oast-house-shaped dark tower, made of wooden crates painted to look like mossy stone blocks, with no apparent way in, and no apparent way of looking out. The story was simple and complicated at the same time. It began with two children, playing in a clearing in a wood.

The clearing was in the centre of the barn. The trees were children, clothed in green and brown dyed cheesecloth, holding up branches. The children were Hedda, now fourteen, and Robin Wellwood, now ten, with his father's flaming red hair. The Girl went to sleep with her head against a stump. A crew of tiny goblins, with pricking whiskers and long tails, of stumping dwarves with boots and beards, and an imperious Elf king and queen moved in on the couple and held out enticing iced cakes and transparent beakers of shiny liquid to the Boy, who nibbled and sipped, and fell dramatically into their arms. They carried his rigid body through the barn, and behind the golden box. Lights shone on a white sheet that rose (held up by Phyllis and Pomona) and then, magically, a swarm of flying shadows of the tiny beasts, only infinitely tinier, whirled like a swarm of wasps, or a crowd of starlings, and plunged into the secret castle.

The Girl woke and was disconsolate. She waved her arms and howled. A cottage on twelve naked feet danced into the clearing, and swayed to a standstill. Out of it came a lame old woman on a stick, who asked the Girl for help picking apples, for water from the well, for a shoulder to lean on as she walked. She gripped and was heavy. Hedda stumbled with pain. The old woman then revealed herself as a serious and beautiful gold-headed child, who gave instructions as to how to find the stolen Boy.

"You must travel on, over the mountain, beyond the sun and the moon, to the Land of the Stars. You must not speak a word. You must offer help to all who ask it. Enemies can be unmasked and defeated with cold iron." She gave Hedda a large, slightly rusted kitchen knife, and went back into the cottage, which tripped out of the barn.

Hedda went on, and on, and on. Steyning did some very clever things with lighting, so that she seemed to be hurtling through snow-storms, and staggering across hot deserts, and treading through shining pillars of ice. She met, and defeated, the man of straw, the wolfman (in a pine forest) and the monstrous armoured death's-head man who turned out to be a blooming child—the other Robin, Robin Oakeshott, uncannily like Robin Wellwood—who told her how to penetrate the impenetrable fortress.

Hedda went behind the golden box, and flute music was heard. The puppet Hedda appeared as a shadow on the screen, and then in the cen-tre of the feasting in the castle. With strong gestures of her arms, and swinging of her hair, she refused to taste food, or sip drink, and bran-dished the knife at the creatures, who hissed loudly and collapsed into dislocated heaps of cloth and tangled limbs. The puppet Hedda bent over the sleeping puppet and took his hand.

In the dark tower, behind the golden casket, slits of light appeared between the building blocks, one of which fell forward, as the Girl stepped out, carrying her knife, holding the hand of the Boy.

Tom's big dolls sat in the audience. At the final performance, these creatures rose, and waddled, or rolled, or hopped, or trundled through the barn towards the dark tower. Two of them (Wolfgang and Leon, to be safe) carried away the golden castle, and the rest of the creatures fell upon the dark tower, and tore it brick from brick to shrieks of laughter from the audience, and a few tears from children. Tom had begged to be allowed to orchestrate this mayhem every night. He had said he would reconstruct the tower with his own hands, for the fun of bringing it down again. But Steyning said it was not to be risked, until the very end. So when the destruction came, it was thorough and savage. Things flew through the air, and lumps rolled into the audience. It was ghastly and comic. Everyone was exhausted.

37

The climax of the camp was the Firing. During the first half of the camp students and professional potters had been constructing vessels and objects and figures, some of which had been given a previous biscuit firing before being returned to their makers to be decorated in various ways. Geraint had prevailed upon his father, when the camp was only a project, to allow the Firing to take place in the big bottle kiln in the field at Purchase House. The kiln was wood-fired. The Firing would last forty-eight hours, more or less, and the cooling another day or more. At the end of the second day there would be a celebration for the workers, potters, wood collectors and campers. Benedict, in the euphoria which had led to his public lecture, had agreed to give a talk on the firing and management of the kiln. But he had disappeared, and the task fell to Philip, who was anyway more practical at packing and setting the kiln. He knew its hot places and its draughty places, the parts where the fire raged strongest, and the parts where it was cooler and more even. It was customary, given the size of this kiln and the infrequency of its use, to fire green, or clayshapes (biscuit) at the same time as the glazed shapes needing the hotter fire of a glost kiln. Philip had put a lot of thought and experiment into the packing. He had constructed saggars to hold the pots, which stood in carefully ordered heaps, or bungs, allowing the flames to rush and flicker between them. They stood on layers of quartz sand and were protected by fire bricks and tiles. Delicate ware stood on clay stilts in the saggars. Clay pugging was placed around the rims of the saggars. Fire-cones of clay which changed colour at certain heats were placed at spy-holes to be watched during the firing. Like all professionals Philip had his own refinements—a new form of stilt, a pacing of the baiting, or feeding, of the fire in the three fireholes.

There was a brief discussion as to whether the Firing should be called off because of Benedict's absence. But too many people expected too much, and Geraint, and to a certain extent Philip, were hopeful that he would reappear dramatically in time to set the torch to the timber. Philip sat for three afternoons at a trestle table in the stable yard, vetting the pots. An air bubble, a too-wet texture, an unevenness of shell could cause a pot to explode, or sag, or simply collapse during the firing, and bring down all its neighbours, or at worst, the whole kiln, the whole conglomerate of work. Young ladies were sent away with rejected vases, unbalanced dishes were rejected. Elsie helped him, in the absence of Benedict Fludd. She helped him also with the puzzle arrangements of pots in saggars and saggars in the kiln. She was not in charge of the provision and cooking of the picnic—that was left to Patty Dace and Marian Oakeshott. At the weekend of the Firing Dorothy Wellwood came to help, with Charles/Karl and Griselda.

On the day of the Firing, Prosper Cain had ordered a luncheon in the Mermaid Inn. He had invited the Fludds, and his own family. He had gone as far as discouraging Julian from bringing Gerald, who was still hovering around the camp and going for long walks along the coastline. Julian had assumed that his father was worrying about Florence. The luncheon took place in the parlour, with sunlight pouring in through the leaded lights of the Tudor windows, and shining on the white damask cloth and heavy silver. There were little nosegays of white and red rosebuds round the table. Seraphita and Pomona clattered up the narrow cobbled street in a pony-trap, dressed in embroidered party-dresses.

A place had been set for Benedict Fludd. Prosper was at the head, between Imogen and Seraphita. Julian was between Seraphita and Pomona, who was next to Geraint and Florence. The empty seat separated Imogen and Florence.

They ate whitebait and broiled lobster, samphire and Vichy carrots, followed by a Queen of Puddings in a porcelain dish. They chatted about the camp, and everyone praised Geraint for his organisational powers, his coup with the army tents, his imaginative ordering of events. Julian said it was always oddly disturbing to find one was living inside works of art, rather than observing them in museums. Seraphita made one of her rare contributions to say dreamily that life would be better if it were all artful. Florence observed that the word "artful" had a curious *double entendre*. Seraphita cast her look down at her plate, and speared a decorative shrimp, with some difficulty.

When they had eaten, Prosper ordered champagne to be brought. Everyone was given a glass. Prosper rose to his feet.

"At the end of the successful cooperation that made such a success of this camp—the meeting of art, craft, art teaching, practice and criticism—I should like to drink to Geraint Fludd, who had such good ideas, and put them into effect." They drank. Prosper did not sit down, though Geraint was stirring to reply.

"I am sorry my old friend Benedict Fludd is absent. I should nevertheless like you to drink to the happiness of Imogen, who has done me the honour of agreeing to become my wife. I have already asked her father for her hand and I believe we have his approval."

This announcement caused consternation. The first person to drink was Imogen herself, perhaps to fortify herself. She was white. Seraphita took a large mouthful, and could be heard to be murmuring either "My dear" or "Oh dear . . ."

Julian raised his glass and said "Of course we all wish you well. Long life and happiness!" he said awkwardly, and then flushed darkly. Imogen nodded at him, looking overwhelmed. Florence stood up.

"As it happens, we have not had time to ask my father, but I also should like to tell you all that I am engaged to be married. I have agreed to marry Geraint. I am telling you myself because I asked him to say nothing. But now, you all need to know, I think. The relationships of the people round this table have suddenly become very confused."

She gave a sharp little laugh. She went on, staring darkly at her father across the silver and white.

"So Imogen is to become at once my sister and my mother. It is like a Greek myth. Or those things in the Prayer Book you aren't supposed to do."

Pomona put down her champagne glass, and broke it. Her fingers were bleeding—not very much, but blood was on the white damask. A waiter came with a silver brush and miniature dustpan and moved round her, clearing the splinters. Geraint said, pacifically and practically, "We are all surprised by suddenness, I should think. But most of you must know that my feeling for Florence is not sudden. You must all have seen that I have loved her for many years, from boy to man. We didn't mean to say anything yet. I am not in a position to support a wife and household, and I mean to do it well. I cannot tell all of you how happy her consent has made me." He paused. "Imogen's engagement is—to me at least—very sudden. But for my part, I know just how many good things Major Cain has brought into her life already. He has already made her happy." He raised his glass. "I wish them well." He bowed to Prosper, and to Imogen, with an awkward grace, and sat down again.

Prosper Cain stood and faced his daughter, who had not sat down. Her face was full of energy and her eyes glittered. She had been, since she was born, the creature he loved most in the world, and he was partly angry that he had noticed no change in her, no softening or excitement that might suggest she was in love. He felt full of energy. He was a military man, faced with a difficult situation, out of which he must extricate everyone with no losses. He looked from his daughter to his beloved, who was looking at the tablecloth. He loved Imogen, he wanted Imogen. That was a source of power. He loved Florence, he would find what was best for her, which might or might not be Geraint Fludd, and because he loved her, he would find a way to open a path for her. It came to him, as he stood there, that he must marry Imogen *very soon,* as Imogen's position was anomalous. This delighted him. He raised his glass to Florence, and included Geraint in the gesture.

"I wish you both every happiness. We have much to talk of and think about. Now, if you are all in agreement, I think we should do as we planned, and make our way to the Firing. It is possible that my old friend Benedict is already at Purchase House."

And he more or less swept them all out of the parlour, and into the traps and dog carts that were waiting to take them to Purchase House.

The sun was setting. Over the wide, flat expanse of the Marsh, the sky was red and seething with brightness. There was a red light on the salty grass, and a strange fiery liquid dancing over the slate-dark liquid of the sewers and ponds they passed as they drove. They went past Rye golf course, where the players were silhouetted against the hot ball, black and two-dimensional, waving a club, trundling a buggy. Flocks of plovers wheeled and re-formed, and wheeled again. The few strips of cloud were purple, and violet, and mauve, and shifting in the light. Everything had a metallic sheen, like a lustre glaze. Even the fat sheep had radiant rosy patinas on their creamy fleeces.

The Firing was going, as far as Philip could see, smoothly. He had been steadily baiting the fire, controlling as best he could the amount of smoke and the evenness of the flames. He peered in through various spy-holes at the roaring scarlet holocaust, the odd swirl and spatter of flame, the brilliance, the dull edges. He had willing helpers with the baiting but he had to oversee what was fed into the fireholes. Ware irregularly fired, or fired with impure fuels, could become sulphured, discoloured, gloomy and dulled. Too much oxygen meant sulphur vapour; so did too little. He was keeping back the best wood for the finish. An enthusiastic helper was Tom Wellwood, who had carried many of the crates and boxes which had made up the Dark Tower in the play, and thrust them in at the fireholes. He had also brought his army of puppet-scarecrows—"They can go in at the end, into the fiery furnace" said Tom. Philip checked them for components that would contaminate the flame, or make it burn unevenly. Dorothy was there—it was the weekend, she was not studying—with Griselda and the Germans, who were helping to carry wood. Everyone was remembering the tale of Palissy, thrusting his own furniture into a firehole to complete the trial burning and testing of the new white glaze. The sun went down further, and the sky grew dark. Inside the chimney, light and heat sang and danced.

Frank Mallett was sitting with Arthur Dobbin, drinking a glass of ale and chewing homemade bread and crumbling cheese. A young man in fishermen's boots and a heavy jacket came and pulled him by the sleeve. Frank listened, shook his head as if to clear it, stood up and looked at the gathering. Seraphita was sitting in a glow of firelight from a bonfire on which potatoes were baking. She looked dazed, which was not unusual. Frank continued to look around, and saw Prosper Cain, who was bending over Imogen Fludd. Frank walked over to them, not too urgently, smiling at parishioners as he passed them.

"Major Cain. May I have a quiet word with you?"

They moved to the edge of the gathering, out of the light.

"I have just had a message from Barker Twomey. He's one of those line-fishermen, at Dungeness. He caught a boot. Hadn't been in the water long. He thinks it's Mr. Fludd's boot. Barker Twomey thinks someone should look at the boot."

"What are you suggesting, Mr. Mallett?"

"I have been disturbed by the absence—now the prolonged absence—of Mr. Fludd."

"His family and those who know him do not appear to be much disturbed."

"They do not. It is true he was always wandering off, just walking out, sometimes for weeks."

"And you think you have cause to think this is different."

"I am not a Catholic, Major Cain. I am an Anglican, of a liberal kind. Confession is not part of the way of my Church. It isn't a recognised sacrament. But people do tell me things. Things they expect me to remain silent about. I believe it is my duty to listen. And to keep silent."

"Why are you telling me this?"

"I am afraid Benedict Fludd may be dead. I am afraid he may have walked into the sea, down there at Dungeness, where the currents are thick and violent and the water is deep."

"And you think this for a particular reason?"

"He came to see me, just after his talk to the camp. He said he meant to do away with himself. I should add, this was by no means the first time he had expressed such an intention."

"He confessed to you, you are suggesting—"

"He was in the habit—fortunately not very frequently—of telling me things about himself—about his former life—about his *life*—I don't know much of the world, Major Cain, I suppose, professionally, I should be surprised by nothing human. I shouldn't say this, I know. I should keep quiet. But he told me things—he told them—not so that I might be able to offer him the Church's forgiveness—but so as to hurt me. I don't even know if what he said was true. I just know—it harmed me to listen to it. And it was *meant* to harm me. I'm sorry. I'm agitated. I do think he is dead. But we have one boot."

"I am going to marry Benedict Fludd's daughter Imogen," said Prosper Cain. "So this concerns me, as a member of the family, so to speak."

Frank Mallett's face worked, as though he was about to dissolve into tears.

"I have known old Fludd for many years," said Prosper. "*Nothing* he could do, or say, would surprise me. You are a good man, and a generous man and have done what you should—including telling me. Let us go to see this angler."

They went on foot, in the thickening last light. They walked past the military camp near Lydd and across the Denge Marsh, and then the bleak shingle banks of Dungeness, skirting the Open Pits where the birds were settling for the night on the islets. This stony, shifting land supports a colony of caulked wooden huts, for the most part sooty black, some with boats beached before them, some with curious agglomerations of winches and pulleys. Lanterns were already glittering inside some of the small windows. Frank carried a storm lantern himself, but had not yet needed to light it. They came to the lighthouse, striped black and white, with its oil-fired, mirrored shaft of brightness searching the dark. Barker Twomey, said Frank, would not have left his rod; that was why he had sent Mick. They crunched on, over the stones, paler than the sky, towards the high shingle bank on which the anglers perched, black silhouettes like the golfers, their lanterns, next to their stools, ready for complete dark. They were both fit, and went lightly up the ridge, into the air off the sea, full of salt and the sound of the incoming tide throwing wave after wave at the stones, sucking them, grinding them, turning them over and over. A line quivered against the creamy tongues of the incoming surf, tautening, dripping with spray. "That's Barker," said Frank Mallett. They looked to see what he was hauling in; it was neither human, nor manmade, but a live fish, arced in protest, turning on the hook. Barker Twomey caught its body in his hand, and killed it with a professional twist and crack.

"Mr. Mallett," he said. "Good evening."

He was weathered and oily, not unlike the boot, which he produced from under his bags of tackle. He wore an oiled sou'wester, and an oiled jacket with the collar up.

"I reckon I seen this on someun's feet, last week," he said. He turned the boot over. It dripped. Its laces were still fastened. It was old, but had once been expensive. Its tongue lolled.

"I think so," said Frank Mallett.

Prosper Cain took it in his hands and turned it about.

"I think so, too," he said. "God help us, it's got clay in its eyelets and under the tongue. And it hasn't been decently cleaned, it's cracking. I think we know whose it is. Any further findings, Mr. Twomey?"

"No, nor very likely to be. The current here is powerful strong. It would pull things—pull a man—deep under and away fast, round the Ness. You won't find by searching, too hard to know where."

"Where this came, more may come to the surface," said Prosper. "Can you ask your friends to keep their eyes open?"

He took the wet boot, rewarded the man, and set out to walk back to Purchase House. The Channel was darkening. The colour of the crashing foam was indescribable—you knew it to be white, but it was the ghost of white, light itself with silver sifted in, and the dark swell of the sucking water.

"I can see him," said Frank Mallett. "Just walking out into it. He knew how it would take him, what it would do to him."

They were walking back past the huts. They stopped, whilst Frank lit his lantern. Stars were showing, pale on the blue-black. The sudden beam of the lantern lit up a kind of clothes-line, stretched from the eave of one of the black huts to a mast-head, from which fluttered a narrow St. George's cross, on a pennant.

"What's that?" said Prosper.

It was shredded, and crumpled, and mangled. It was stained, and soaked, and it appeared to be the overall-robe Benedict Fludd had worn for his lecture. Flotsam, jetsam, retrieved from the sea.

"Mr. Mallett," said Prosper Cain, as they walked slowly back towards Purchase House with a brown paper parcel. "Mr. Mallett—these thoughts may be premature—though I think both you and I think not. If my old friend has done away with himself, we may yet find him. He could hardly have chosen a more final place to disappear. The uncertainty will be very painful for his wife and daughters, very. Now I, too, am confiding my private anxieties to you. I wish to marry Miss Fludd *as soon as possible*—this event has both made me more anxious to do so, and rendered it harder to arrange. I do not know what would be appropriate mourning for a dead man—where no body exists. I do know that his family would live more easily if I were in a position to look after them with a right to do so. I should like you to marry us, Mr. Mallett. Quietly, but not surreptitiously. With flowers in the church, and a decorous feast. How soon could this be done, do you think?"

"If—if nothing floats in to shore—if he does not suddenly walk up the drive—maybe in a month?"

They quickened the pace.

"A final suggestion, Mr. Mallett. Would you agree to say nothing of this to anyone else until the kiln is cooled and the festivity is over? All we have to convey is doubt, suspicion, uncertainty. If we wait, certainty may come. And if it doesn't, the uncertainty itself will be more of a certain thing—a *real* thing, if you follow me."

"Indeed," said Frank Mallett. "May I say, I am grateful to you for—for taking over the burden."

"I have known Benedict Fludd, God rest his soul, for a very long time. He had genius. He was excessive in everything he did. I am not surprised he tried to frighten you. Your response is commendable."

38

Prosper Cain was a man used to getting his own way. He was married to Imogen Fludd, in St. Edburga's Church, on Tuesday, December 27th, in 1904. Frank Mallett married them. There was still no sign of Benedict Fludd, although a second boot had been fished up, weeks after the first. So they were neither in mourning, nor not in mourning. The congregation was small—the Purchase House people, including Philip and Elsie, Julian and Florence. Arthur Dobbin was there, and Marian Oakeshott, and Miss Dace. It was extremely cold. The stones of the church were like blocks of ice, and the grass in the graveyard was crusted with frost. Frank had two woollen vests under his surplice. All the women had solved the problem of mourning by resorting to discreet greys and violets. Florence had a very smart slate-coloured grosgrain long coat over a blue-crocus-coloured dress; her hat was severe crocus-grey tulle, to match. She was not a bridesmaid. Pomona was the only bridesmaid, in a dark-grey velvet gown, decorated with violets. The same flowers were round the brim of her hat. Seraphita was wrapped in a feather-edged robe in a kind of thick complicated tapestry, purple and grey and silver, edged with dyed swansdown and ostrich plumes.

Geraint gave away the bride. Miss Dace struck some chords on the piano, and Imogen Fludd laid down the stone hot-water bottle she had been clutching, picked up her sheaf of hothouse lilies and walked through the church. She was wearing shimmering silvery velvet, very plain, with a high white fur collar, and big white fur cuffs. Florence turned to stare at her as she went to meet Major Cain. Florence had been thinking of Imogen with bad words. Sly. Insinuating. 'Umble. She thought her face would show false modesty, maybe, or irrepressible triumph, but she had to acknowledge—she was just—that what she saw was pure happiness, touched with fear. That Prosper loved Imogen, Florence acknowledged with some bitterness. She now acknowledged, also, that Imogen loved Prosper. She looked like the white wax of a candle, lit by a golden flame.

After the ceremony, Frank Mallett gave everyone hot drinks, or glasses of sherry, in front of his dancing fire. His housekeeper replenished the ladies' stoneware hand-warmers with kettles of hot water. Rugs were wound round them, and they all drove back to the Mermaid

in Rye, where Prosper had ordered a wedding breakfast. There was
a blazing wood fire in the hearth there, too. As the evening closed
in, ruddy light flickered over the pale faces, and lit the grey silks and
satins. The food was plentiful—soles with shrimps, smoked and roasted
salt-marsh loin of lamb, elegant custards, an iced cake, which the
bridegroom cut precisely with his sword. Geraint made a neat little
speech, and said that he and Florence hoped—as soon as feasible—to tie
further knots in the relationships of the families. Prosper replied,
briskly, warmly, and then raised a glass to the absent Benedict Fludd.
He wished, he said, that his old friend could have been there to share
their happiness. He wished, of course, that his friend would return—
as he had done before—from a journey. In the meantime—or, if necessary, in the long term—he himself was now part of the family, and
would hope to take on some of the practical burdens of the work, and
the house. The wind rushed and eddied up the cobbled street. The
flames swirled in the hearth, and Philip stared into them. Seraphita
stood up, and said, in a surprisingly strong voice that she would like—
personally—to express her thanks to Major Cain, now her second
son—and to say how much comfort the wedding had brought her, in
this trying time. Florence, who might have looked at Geraint, who was
looking at her intently, was still studying Imogen. The firelight ran up
the folds of her dress, and made a blush on that palely ecstatic, unblush-
ing face. I shall never be so happy, Florence thought. She could not
bear—the thought made her sick—to imagine her father taking Imogen in his arms, alone in the black-beamed bedroom. Everything was
going up in flames. Exultant, and dangerous.

Philip Warren had it in mind to make a memorial to Benedict Fludd.
He had been included in talks between Geraint and Prosper about the
future of Purchase pottery and sales through The Silver Nutmeg. He
had felt the subsiding of hope or expectation in himself as the bottle
kiln cooled slowly after the firing. He had waited alone, until the saggars were ready to be unpacked. Then he unpacked them, slowly. The
firing had been almost wholly successful. Some small pieces of student
work had crumbled, and one of his own seaweed bowls, to which he
had been particularly attached, lay in shards. But generally the treasure
gleamed and glistened. Pomona had crept quietly to his side and asked
to be allowed to help to take out and arrange the ware. She seemed, he

thought without considering the matter, less determinedly childish. She had tied up her hair. She said

"Do you think he's dead, Philip?"

"I don't know. He has gone off, before."

"I feel he's dead. I think I would know inside me if he wasn't."

"I know what you mean. I feel that, too. He's somehow gone."

She went on lining up slightly unbalanced amateur goblets. She said "Things will be different."

Philip had just begun on what might turn out to be Benedict Fludd's last warm pots, cooling under his fingers. A two-faced drinking mug leered at him. An elegant dragon spread its gold wings in an inky sky.

"You'll be wanting to study, maybe," he said to Pomona.

"I have no talents," she said.

The projected memorial was a globe-shaped pot, large and simple. It was to be layered, like the round earth, with fire beating up from its depths, with coal over the fire, with fossil forms in the coal, with dark sea-blue flowing over the coal, and over the sea, on an inky sky, with a moon in it, a tracery of white foam which should be both wild and formal in its movements, somehow Japanese. He could see it clearly in his mind's eye. It was fiendishly hard to conceive—all those glazes, welded together, the necessity for the difficult red to be simultaneously both bloody and fiery. He made drawings of lizards and dragonflies and snails, coiled in the jet-black coal. Sometimes he thought the moon should be full, and sometimes a hair-thin crescent, barely scratched in.

He thought—he was not much given to studying people's feelings—that Seraphita was relieved and released by her husband's death. She went out, spontaneously, to call on neighbours, to take tea with Phoebe Methley, who was kind to her. He was less sure about Pomona. She seemed both more ordinary, and stunned.

Then, one night, in the small hours he woke to hear footsteps in the corridor outside his room. He waited, irritably, for her to turn his door-handle, but the steps went past. They were hurried, and measured. He thought of returning to sleep, and knew he must not. So he pulled on a coat, and went down the stairs. He heard her unlock the kitchen door. And go out into the yard. He imagined her casting herself into the Military Canal. But she went into what he now thought of as his studio. There was a full moon. He lurked by the window, and heard a scratching, and a scraping. He was possessed by terror that she meant to break things. He crept up, and peered in. She was on the other side of the room, unlocking the forbidden pantry. He had not known she knew about it, let alone knowing where the key was hidden.

She came out with a white vase in the shape of a naked girl. She moved dreamily, mechanically, but he was now not sure she was sleep-walking. He followed, at a safe distance—they were both barefoot—into the garden. She flowed on, into the orchard. She sat down at the root of an apple tree, and took out a sharp trowel, from a space in its roots.

"I know you're there," she said. "Don't say anything. Just help."

He stepped forward, out of the shadows. She handed him the creature—lovely, with coiling hair, open lips in an ecstatic face, and underneath it an explicitly modelled vulva, spread wide, under its furry roof, with its delicate rounded lips. Pomona said

"I can't smash them. I can put them away. Under the trees."

"I could put them away for you."

"They aren't yours. I shall do it. One by one by one. When they are all—under—then—"

Philip found himself stroking the cold pot, out of a desire not to offer false comfort to the girl. He knelt beside her and took the trowel, and excavated. She brought out a piece of old linen, wrapped the image, and tucked it, neither kindly nor unkindly, into the cavity. Philip held out his hand to help her to her feet, and feared she would fling herself into his arms. But she held off.

39

On the day of Prosper Cain's wedding, *Peter Pan, or The Boy Who Wouldn't Grow Up,* opened at the Duke of York's Theatre, in St. Martin's Lane. It was late: it should have opened on the 22nd, and had been delayed by the failure of some of the complex machinery for its special effects. There was to have been a "living fairy" reduced to pygmy size by a giant lens. There was to have been an eagle which descended on the pirate Smee, and seized him by the pants to carry him across the auditorium. At the very last moment a mechanical lift collapsed, and with it racks of scenery. Much that was to become familiar—the Mermaids' Lagoon, the Little House in the Treetops—was not yet constructed. And there were scenes, on that first night, that were later excised. It had all been kept a darkly veiled secret. That reconvened first night audience—an adult audience, at an evening performance—had no idea what it was about to see. And then the curtain rose on an enclosed nursery, with little beds with soft bedspreads and a wonderful frieze of wild animals high on the walls, elephants, giraffes, lions, tigers, kangaroos. And a large black and white dog, woken from sleep by a striking clock, rose to turn down the bedclothes and run the bath.

Both August Steyning and Olive Wellwood knew James Barrie, and were part of that first audience. Their party filled a whole row: Olive, Humphry, Violet, Tom, Dorothy, Phyllis, Hedda, Griselda. The light flared in the fake fire. The three children, two boys and a girl, all played by young women, pranced in pyjamas and played at being grown-ups, producing children like rabbits out of hats, having clearly no idea at all where children came from. The audience laughed comfortably. The parents, dressed for the evening, like the audience out in front of them, argued about the dog, Nana, who was deceived by Mr. Darling into drinking nasty medicine, and then chained up. The night lights went out. The crowing boy, who was Nina Boucicault, another woman, flew in at the unbarred window, in search of his/her shadow.

Olive Wellwood's reaction to theatre was always to want to *write*—now, immediately, to get into the other world, which Barrie had cleverly named the Never Never Land. It was neither the trundling dog, nor the charming children, that caught her imagination. It was Peter's sheared shadow, held up by the Darling parents before being rolled up and put in a drawer. It was dark, floating lightly, not quite transparent, a solid theatrical illusion. When Wendy sewed it on, and he danced, and it became a thing cast by stage lighting climbing the walls and gesturing wildly, she was entranced.

The amazing tale wound on. The children flew. The greasy-locked pirate waved his evil hook. The Lost Boys demonstrated their total ignorance of what mothers, or fathers, or homes, or kisses, might be. Dauntlessly, they sunk their knives into pirates. There was a moment of tension when the darting light who was the fairy began to die in the medicine glass, and had to be revived by the clapping of those who believed in fairies. The orchestra had been instructed to clap, if no one else did. But timidly, then vociferously, then ecstatically, that audience of grown-ups applauded, offered its belief in fairies. Olive looked along the row of her party to see who was clapping. Steyning yes, languidly, politely. Dorothy and Griselda, somewhere between enthusiasm and good manners. Phyllis, wholeheartedly, eyes bright. Humphry, ironically. Violet, snappishly. She herself, irritated and moved. Hedda, intently.

Not Tom. You would have wagered that Tom would clap hardest.

The penultimate scene was the testing of the Beautiful Mothers, by Wendy. The Nursery filled with a bevy of fashionably dressed women, who were allowed to claim the Lost Boys if they responded sensitively to a flushed face, or a hurt wrist, or kissed their long-lost child gently, and not too loudly. Wendy dismissed several of these fine ladies, in a queenly manner. Steyning spoke to Olive behind his hand. "This will have to go." Olive smiled discreetly and nodded. Steyning said "It's part pantomime, part play. It's the play that is original, not the pantomime." "Hush," said the fashionable lady in front of him, intent on the marshalling of the Beautiful Mothers.

After the wild applause, and the buzz of discussion, Olive said to Tom

"Did you enjoy that?"

"No," said Tom, who was in a kind of agony.

"Why not?"

Tom muttered something in which the only audible word was "cardboard." Then he said "He doesn't know *anything* about boys, or making things up."

August Steyning said "You are saying it's a play for grown-ups who don't want to grow up?"

"Am I?" said Tom. He said "It's make-believe make-believe make-believe. Anyone can see all those boys are girls."

His body squirmed inside his respectable suit. Tom said "It's not like *Alice in Wonderland*. That's a real other place. This is just wires and strings and disguises."

"You have a Puritan soul," said Steyning. "I think you will find, that whilst everything you say is true, this piece will have a long life and people will suspend their disbelief, very happily."

In the New Year of 1905, on a frosty evening, Humphry and Olive went to dine with August Steyning at Nutcracker Cottage. The room was candlelit. A log fire was burning in the inglenook. It had been hard to light, and everything was veiled with smoke and smelled of smoke. Steyning gave them comforting winter food—a winter soup of dried peas and ham, roast pheasant, stuffed with a piece of fillet steak, Brussels sprouts and chestnuts, glazed with marsala sauce. The only other guest was Toby Youlgreave.

They discussed *Peter Pan*. Toby had seen it, and was enthusiastic. Nothing like it had been done before. He supposed the young Wellwoods had enjoyed it. Especially Tom.

"Tom hated it," said Olive, sadly. "I thought he'd like it. He always liked the stories more than any of the others did. But it seemed to make him angry. He said it was make-believe and cardboard. He didn't like the women playing boys."

"He refused entirely to suspend disbelief," said Steyning. "It was odd, and almost alarming."

Toby asked how old Tom was now. Olive said she thought he was twenty-two: Toby said that his history of failing exams, or failing to be fit to sit exams, was perplexing, given his intelligence. Humphry said maybe they should think of some other course. He could not do nothing for ever. Dorothy was only twenty and had passed her Highers, and the Preliminary Scientific Exam, and begun her medical studies. She was lodging with the Skinners in Gower Street. Phyllis was the home-loving daughter. He did not know himself what Tom did with his time. He was out of doors, for much of most days. Olive said doubtfully that he had said from time to time that he meant to be a writer. Humphry asked irritably whether she had ever seen any writing he had done. No, she said. No, she had not. He thought it was private.

"You can't make a living out of *private writing,*" said Humphry. Toby said Tom was a Wanderer. He meant that he had a vision of Tom as an inhabitant of woods and downs, something out of Hudson and Jefferies. Steyning said drily that maybe he disliked Peter Pan because he recognised something. Olive said indignantly no, it was not that, she was sure it was not that, he found the play simply unappealing.

Steyning said that Tom had seemed to enjoy being occupied with the puppet play in the summer. He had made some good lay figures. Maybe the theatre would suit him.

Olive looked into the candle-flame, and across at Steyning's long, pale, regular face, lit, with dark shadows, from beneath. For most of Tom's life she believed she had known in her body—as though held to the boy by a myriad spider-threads—exactly where he was, how he felt, what he needed. He had been part of her, part of her had gone running with him, she had *felt* his sleep after he was tucked up. Or so she thought she had felt. Lately, she had found herself using, and then rapidly rejecting, the word "coarsened" in her thoughts of Tom. He was bristly. He was sulky. He was automatically argumentative. He did not seem to read her needs, as before he always had. She thought she would be glad if he found something to do, and stopped, as she almost put it to herself, *lurking* in the bushes.

August Steyning said *Peter Pan* had renewed his interest in writing a different kind of magical play. *Peter Pan* had used children's make-believe—"slapstick" said August Steyning. It had drawn on the English pantomime, which was a connivance between actors and director and audience. He stopped for a moment and did it justice. "Not that it doesn't get under your skin, and infest your mind. It does. In ways I think that odd little person who wrote it can't conceive. He is both sweetly innocent and positively *uncanny* about mummies and daddies—and what are we to make of the identity of the daddy in the dog-kennel and the evil Hook? Who would have thought of casting the same actor? It's a work of genius, but the genius is twisted like a corkscrew."

He said "I want to stage a fairy play that shall be closer to Wagner's

Gesamtkunstwerk than to pantomime. We made a beginning in the Denge Marsh Camp. What is needed is new versions—but only *versions*—of the old, deep tales that are twisted into our souls. The dark Palace under the Hill, the guest, the lights dancing on the marsh. We could use stage machinery, yes—not to lift sweetly pretty girl-boys in pyjamas—but to make *dames blanches* float, and bats and lizard-dragons cluster on rocks and branches. I know things about lighting—and shadows—no one else in this country knows. There are Germans doing clever things with masks and puppets that would entrance an audience of children and disturb an audience of grown-ups, rightly deployed."

"If *Gesamtkunstwerk*," said Humphry, "will you not need singers?"

"It will not be an opera. It *will* have unearthly music. I envisage hidden flutes and concealed drums and tambourines. And wailing voices, singing in the wind."

He said "I am relying on you, dear Olive, to write me such a tale."

"It would be hard—"

"But you could do it."

"I have an idea . . ."

"Yes?"

"But I need to think about it. I promise I will think."

Florence Cain tried hard not to be depressed by the new, extravagant happiness in the Kensington home. She had watched, with Imogen, the new double bed on its way up the narrow staircase. It was a festive bed with a bedhead carved with cherubs, not the catafalque of Prosper's dream. It embarrassed Florence, though she tried hard to prevent it. They could not keep their hands off each other, Prosper Cain and his new wife, though they tried to do so, when Florence was present. She felt aggrieved—she was *de trop* in her own house, for reasons nothing to do with her own conduct. Imogen had tried, once, to open a discussion. "I can see it must be strange for you, now, now that I'm . . ." Florence snapped. "Of course it's strange. It doesn't matter. We needn't speak of it."

"But, I—"

"Just be happy. I can see you are."

"I—"

"I said, we needn't discuss it."

. . .

She also did not wish to discuss it with her fiancé, Geraint Fludd. Geraint came often, running administrative errands between Purchase House, to which its owner had not returned, The Silver Nutmeg and the V and A. He had managed to become a Member of the Stock Exchange during a brief period of easy admission in November 1904, before the rules were tightened. On New Year's Eve, in 1905, he came to dine with the Cains, and was received by Florence.

"I've brought you something," he said. He handed her a small box, wrapped in cherry-coloured paper, with a silver bow. Inside was a pretty ring, the work of Imogen's jewellery master Henry Wilson, with amethyst and moonstone forget-me-nots set in woven silver leaves.

"The silver is my own," he said. "I bought it in a warehouse, in the City. I bought the stones, too, from a mining man I know. I hope you'll wear it. I hope it is the right size. I asked Imogen."

Florence was startled. It was a very pretty ring. Not what she would have expected from Geraint. Though she could not see why she should not have expected it. She said

"The engagement isn't announced . . ."

"You don't like it?"

"How could I not like it? It's delightful. Only . . ."

"I'd be happy if you wore it on the other hand."

Florence said "I've decided to study at Cambridge, at Newnham College. I've sent in an application."

This was a lie.

"I'm glad," said Geraint. "I think—I think you would be happy there. For a time. I do believe in women studying and working. I could come to the College and take you out." He was a good man, Florence thought, and she was taking advantage of him. She thought shrewdly that women were tempted to think less well of men they could hurt, if they chose to. She thought: if I felt about Geraint what Imogen feels about Papa, I should put my arms round him and weep. She drew the pretty ring slowly onto the finger of her right hand. It fitted perfectly. Geraint, with courtesy and care, took hold of the hand, and kissed it. Then he kissed her smooth cheek. The vision flashed through his mind of a knot of legs and buttocks on the dishevelled bed of Miss Louise, whom he had lately visited, despite thinking he ought not to. Could

Florence ever come to behave like that? He thought how odd the huge, smoky gap was between what you were thinking and what you were doing. He decided to keep hold of the hand, but then Prosper and Imogen came into the room. They had clasped hands, themselves, and brushed a kiss, at the foot of the stairs. Imogen said

"Oh, the lovely ring—"

Florence would have liked to kill someone, but did not know whom.

In 1905 Dorothy began to do practical work in the London School of Medicine for Women. The students went on ward visits and began to dissect the dead. Dorothy was well liked by the other women, but she kept herself to herself and made no close friends, returning to the Skinners' house to study in the evenings, and visiting Griselda, or Florence, at the weekends. In September of that year both Griselda and Florence became freshers at Newnham College, Cambridge, and Dorothy felt doubly lonely, because those two were now such good friends, and because they were no longer in London. Griselda was to study Languages, and Florence had opted for History.

In the autumn Dorothy felt, unusually for her, dispirited and low. She enjoyed the Anatomy, but was fazed by the patience, and terror, and occasional bliss of the women in the gynaecological wards. The Hospital for Women made things comfortable for patients: they had pretty curtains, and stoneware vases of flowers, and brightly coloured bedspreads. The women's bodies were used. Dorothy's was not. It was covered in a long skirt—the female students, like the nurses, had to wear skirts with braided hems, long enough for their ankles not to be seen if they bent over a patient. Over the long skirt was a flowing overall. Their hair was tightly coiled on the tops of their heads, or in the napes of their necks.

Quite suddenly and farcically, she fell in love. She fell in love with a demonstrator, Dr. Barty, during a dissection class. He was showing her the human heart, and how to extract it from the cavity where it lay and no longer beat. There was a smell—a stink—of formaldehyde. The room was ventilated by a small opening in the end wall, with a gas jet burning to draw up the heated air. The hospital was a converted house—the space was cramped and full of women, twenty living, one dead, soft and leathery. Dr. Barty asked Dorothy to make the cuts to extract the organ, a cross-shaped cut in the pericardium, then, with a larger scalpel, slices through the six blood vessels going into the heart, and the two that went out. Dr. Barty—a muscular, youngish man, in a green buttoned overall and a surgical cap—congratulated Dorothy on the precision of her work. He told her to take out the heart, and place it in the tray for another student to continue. Dorothy put her hands round the heart, and tugged. She looked up at the bearded, severely smiling Dr. Barty, and *saw* him. It was as though time stopped, as though she stood there for ever with another woman's heart in her hands. She saw every lively hair of his black brows, and the wonderful greens and greys of his irises, and the dark tunnels of his pupils, opened on her. She saw the chiselled look of his lips, in the fronds of his rich beard, reddish-black, curling softly. His teeth were white and even. She must have been studying him for weeks, quite as much as the inanimate fingers and toes, tarsals and metatarsals he exposed to her.

Her helplessness made her furious. She took in a deep breath of tainted air and fell unconscious to the ground: the dead heart rolled damply beside her.

It was not unusual for the women to faint. Dorothy, however, had never fainted before. They carried her out, and fanned her, and practised hands held a beaker of water for her to sip. She came brusquely to consciousness, and insisted on returning to the class, though she took no further active part. She watched Dr. Barty, who was kind to her. He was one of the doctors who went out of his way to be kind to, and to encourage, the women. He was said to take a particular interest in slender Miss Lythegoe, whose work was better than Dorothy's, whose demeanour was grave.

Dorothy went back to Gower Street and crept up the narrow stairs as though she had no strength. She *did not want* this visitation. Her life had a direction, which did not include desiring or swooning over Dr. Barty. They all looked at him a little soppily, she had thought, and now she had caught it, like a bacillus.

She began to weep. She could not stop. After a time, Leslie Skinner tapped on her door. (Etta was out at a meeting.) He said

"Are you unwell, Dorothy?"

"I must be. I'm sorry." She sobbed.

Leslie Skinner came in and sat beside her. He said he had thought for some time she was overdoing it. She was burning herself up. She should take a rest. She should perhaps take a week or two off and go home to the country, out of the foul London air. Dorothy sobbed and shook. Skinner petted her shoulder. When she closed her eyes, Dr. Barty's face rose in the hollow of her head, full of life and smiling mysteriously. Leslie Skinner read aloud to her, from an article by Elizabeth Garrett Anderson, in the *Encyclopaedia Medica*. Anderson was, Dorothy thought, maybe the greatest woman who had lived. She had so neatly, so persistently, so patiently, so *successfully* fought to be a doctor, a woman doctor, when there were none. The Hospital was her creation. She was also a married woman, but Dorothy did not think many women could be both wife and doctor.

"In health, the nervous force is sufficient for all the ordinary demands made upon it. We work and get tired, we sleep and eat and are again as new beings ready for another day's work. After some months of continuous work we are tired in a different way; the night's rest, and the weekly day of rest, do not suffice; we need a change of scene—and a complete rest. With these we renew our force and are presently again ready to enjoy work."

The Skinners' doctor, when consulted, reinforced this message. He said he did not consider Miss Wellwood to be overtaxed or unsuited to study. He did consider her to be in need of a rest. She should go to the country, and read, and walk, and let her strength flow back. Dorothy's nerves were jangling and her head ached. She did not want to go back to Todefright—it was a form of defeat. But she went.

Violet Grimwith was sent to fetch her home. She helped her pack, and asked no questions. As they sat in the train, rattling out of Charing Cross, going south, out of the smoke, Dorothy, whose eyes were closed to preclude conversation, tried to think scientifically about Love. It was an affliction of the nervous system. It bore some relation to the aura that was said to precede epileptic fits. It was not self-induced. It was like a blow to the brain. It could be recovered from.

It was horribly undignified.

Was it the same as sexual desire, which she did not think she had felt? Can sexual desire be experienced *in the abstract,* almost? She didn't want to grab Dr. Barty, or to be grabbed by him.

He had got into her mind, and invaded it.

That was because Dr. Anderson was right, fatigue did strange things to you.

. . .

Todefright was no longer a house overrun by children. Hedda, now fifteen, and Florian, now thirteen, had been sent to Bedales School, where they learned farming, swimming, physics, chemistry and thinking for themselves. Robin and Harry (eleven and nine) were both weekly boarders at a preparatory school in Tunbridge Wells. Tom and Phyllis were the odd children who had not left the nest. Phyllis had been assimilated into Violet's housekeeping. She made cakes for Fabian picnics, and lace collars for bring-and-buy sales. She was now nineteen, and passively pretty. Tom was twenty-three. He wore his bright hair long, and his clothes were shabby and shapeless. He was pleased to see Dorothy, who put her head for a moment on his shoulder. He smelt of horsetack, and fur, and brambles, with a note of wild garlic. He said, now they could go for walks, the leaves in the woods were turning.

Humphry was not there, and Olive was writing. Her children recognised the rhythm of Olive's writing—in the early stages of the story, it could be juggled, put aside, boxed and coxed with tea-parties and excursions. Then there were intense periods when she forgot to eat, and worked into the night. Tom said to Dorothy that he was glad to see her because Olive was *sunken,* an old childhood word for late preoccupation. He did not ask Dorothy how she was, or how she came to be there. She thought, even last year, he might have asked.

Olive did not ask either. She kissed her eldest daughter, and said vaguely how nice it would be for Dorothy to be able to get out in the country, which was what Leslie Skinner said she needed. She said "I shan't be very good company, I'm sunk in a very complicated play, which seems to change every day." When Dorothy had been at home for a couple of days, Olive came down to lunch, and said that she and Dorothy must have "a little talk." Dorothy did not want to talk, but felt it was right that talk should have been offered.

It turned out that the talk concerned Tom. Could Dorothy find out what Tom thought he would do with his life? He had taken to earning bits of money as a beater, or helping out in stables, or harvesting, or hedging. She didn't know what he *wanted.* Did Dorothy?

Dorothy wanted Dr. Barty, though distance was fortunately making his dark face more abstract, more diagrammatic. She had no intention of telling her mother about Dr. Barty. She said, deliberately flatly,

"Maybe that's all he wants, just to potter." She asked, woman to woman, with a malice she didn't know she felt,

"Does he get on your nerves?"

"I worry about him," said Olive, with dignity. "I'd like him to have a purpose."

"I see," said Dorothy, still flatly. The little talk seemed to have ground to a halt.

Dorothy went into the woods, to the Tree House, with Tom. He loped along the paths, so fast she could hardly keep up with him. He showed her things, as he had when they were little—where the badgers were, where a hawk had nested, where there was a little crop of fungi that weren't supposed to grow in Britain at all. Magic toadstools, said Tom, with an irony that was hard to interpret.

They came to the Tree House. It was still wonderfully disguised with brushwood and bracken and ferns. Tom had cared for it—alone, she supposed. He let her in, and made a little fire in the stove, and ceremoniously made her some tea from blackberry leaves he had dried himself. He said

"I sleep here, as often as not." There was a blanket-bed, on a heap of dry bracken. "I like the sounds. The trees. The creatures. The creakings. The wind, coming and going. Sometimes, Dorothy, I wake up and think I'm not there."

"Frightening?"

"No. I like it. I'd like to be able to vanish into the hedge, like one of those things you can't see, if they don't move. The hedge sparrows. Moths. I'd like to be speckled and freckled like a moth. I try to write about moths, but I'm no good, I think."

"Can I see?"

"No."

"I fainted," said Dorothy. "I came home because I fainted. In an anatomy class. Holding a heart."

"Don't. I feel sick. You're all right now."

It was a statement, not a question.

Dorothy sipped the leafy brew. She said

"Have you ever been in love, Tom?"

He wrinkled his brow. His brows, Dorothy thought, were fair and innocent. What was it that *wasn't there*?

Tom said "Once I was in love, for about a month, I think. With a vixen."

He saw her look of puzzlement, and said

"Oh, a real vixen. A young one, very graceful, covered with soft red fur, with a thick brush, and a creamy white chest. She knew I watched her every day. She *showed herself* to me, all the graceful things she did, curving this way and that. They seem to smile, foxes. I thought I *was* her, and she was me. I don't know what she thought. She stopped coming, when she had cubs. I'm not telling you very well. It was love, that was what it was."

There was a silence. It was impossible to introduce Dr. Barty. Tom said

"I read a story about trees that walked. Sometimes, lying here, I think the trees are moving in on the Tree House, taking it *in*—"

Dorothy was suddenly very irritated with Tom. She said, "I think it's time to go back, now."

"But we've only just come."

"I've been here long enough. I'm not well. I want to go back."

She didn't sleep well. She walked at night, in the moonlit rooms, not needing a candle, looking for something to nibble, or something to read. One night in the hall, she heard someone else, skirt rustling, slippers sliding. She stood still in a dark corner, shrunk into shadow.

It was Olive, in her flower-spread robe, gliding towards the cupboard where the family tales were kept. She was carrying one large manuscript book; she unlocked the cupboard and replaced it. Then she went away again, not having noticed Dorothy.

Dorothy was the one who had taken little interest in her "own" story, about the metamorphosing hedgehogs and the uncanny root-cavity-dwellers. She wondered for the first time if Olive was still spinning particular tales for particular children. She opened the story-cabinet. There were books for Robin and Harry. Florian's was now quite fat. The one Olive had been carrying was Tom's—his story now occupied a series of books, taking up a whole shelf, dwarfing the others. Dorothy hesitated a moment, and then took out the Dorothy book, with the fairies and woodland creatures on its cover. She had no imagination of what it felt like to be a writer and spin stories. She assumed her own story would have petered out, somehow, long ago.

She turned to the last page.

. . .

So Peggy went on her travels, and saw many strange and wonderful sights, snow-covered mountains, and sunny southern meadows. She met interesting strangers, and rode on shining, smoking trains. She thought at bed-time of the other, secret world in the roots of the Tree, of its inhabitants who spoke with strange voices, hissing or chuntering, squeaking or whispering. She thought of the strangers she had helped when they were caught on thorns, or hurt by cold iron, the Grey Child and the Brown Boy, with their glancing, inhuman eyes. They had helped her, too. They had found things that were lost. They had sung to her. When she thought of them, they grew thinner, more transparent in her mind's eye, wisps and tattered fragments. But they were there, and she knew they were there, always.

When she finally came back, she wore a long skirt with a braided hem which brushed on the grass, leaving a trail in the dew, when she hurried out to the Tree. It seemed older, with more cracks and knobs. She knelt down and looked into the hollow, and it was full of the kind of undisturbed dust that had not been there before, for there had been busy brooms to sweep it. She turned over the heaped leaves in the hole where she had always found the hedgehog-coat, which shrank her when she fingered it, so that she could slip inside it. It was there. It was stiff and dusty. She bent over, and lifted it out and saw that it was not—it was and was not—her hedgehog-coat. It was a hedgehog, a real hedgehog, long dead and dried to leather. On its nose were dried drops of blood, and its bright little eyes were lidded.

Nothing more.

So she walked back along the path, in her long, heavy skirt, and the breeze through the trees was cold and aimless, the light was simply scattered and lit nothing in particular, and no birds sang.

. . .

Dorothy put the book back, as though it had stung her. Psychology was not her gift; she had set her will to being practical. She did not want to think about the feeling behind this coda. Her mind became full of an uninvited ghost of Dr. Barty. She started to cry. She was ashamed. She hurried back to her bedroom, and lay down, and wept. There was nothing for her here.

. . .

· She was saved, though she never knew it, by Violet, who sent a message to Vetchey Manor, just in case Griselda was there. Griselda was. The next day, Dorothy saw her pedalling up the drive, dressed in country tweeds. Dorothy went slowly—she didn't feel up to running—to meet her. They kissed.

"You look dreadful. I heard you were here, so I came over. Are you ill?"

"I fainted. I fainted in an anatomy class. I was holding a heart in my hand and I dropped it, and fainted. I was so ashamed."

"You've overdone it, as I always knew you would."

"They sent me here for a rest."

"Is it working?"

"No. No, it's not."

They went into Todefright, and Dorothy made mugs of tea. Griselda said that maybe Dorothy should visit her in Cambridge.

"Do you like it, there, Grisel?"

"It's not quite real, but in some ways it's better than real. I really like the work. I like *thinking,* you know, thinking about things that aren't myself."

So Dorothy packed her things, and went on the train with Griselda to Cambridge, and was given a guest room in Sidgwick Hall.

Newnham College was austere, graceful and comfortable. The buildings were red-brick and slightly Dutch, which is to say, domestic. There was a very large, beautiful garden, with an orchard where in the summer the young ladies swayed in hammocks, reading Ovid and John Stuart Mill. There was a hockey field where they covertly (their legs in shortened skirts must not be seen) played vigorous and enthusiastic matches. There was a croquet lawn. They were in the University on sufferance; the women's colleges were not part of the University, and the women, though they took the same exams as the men, were not awarded degrees by the University. They were free women, pursuing the life of the mind, professionally. Opposition to their presence was smouldering and occasionally broke out into violent polemic, or even hostile rioting. They were felt to be a temptation to, and danger for, the morals of the often rackety young men who *were* part of the University.

Their tutors and mentors reacted to this opposition by using supreme caution. The young ladies must be chaperoned wherever they went. They must not entertain men who were not fathers, brothers or uncles. There were male lecturers in the University who admitted them to classes—always with chaperones—and those who did not. Florence Cain was the single woman student at a series of economic history lectures in Trinity College, and had to be accompanied by one of the Newnham Fellows on a bicycle. The women felt themselves to be both demure and dangerous, determined and impeded. They found their situation both frustrating and from time to time wildly comic.

There have, throughout history, been communities of women, from nuns who had taken vows of chastity and sometimes silence, to the women paupers, ruthlessly segregated by the Poor Laws. These women were different. They had asserted their desire—indeed, their need—to use their minds, to understand the nature of things, from mathematical forms to currency and banking, from Greek drama to the history of Europe. This generation, in the first ten years of the twentieth century—was neither as austere nor as single-minded as the pioneers of the 1870s and 1880s. They worked less hard, frequently, and were often more frivolous, as well as more uncertain, in many cases, of what would be the outcome of what they were doing.

And as Virginia Woolf observed, in a book which began as a lecture in that College, they liked each other. They made friends. The friendships were based on things other than sex and shopping, clothes and mating. Or sometimes, most often, they were.

College life had its odd little rituals, in which Dorothy was included. The women lived in comfortable bed-sitting rooms, heated by coal-fires, which were often temperamental and had to be coaxed to burn. There were maids, who carried hot water night and morning, and washed up the china. Shoes were cleaned by a man who collected them. Beds were made, fires were laid. In the early days the College had been left money to provide a lady's maid for every five young ladies, but the ladies' maids were not wanted, and the money was used to provide half a pint of sterilised milk each evening for each student. This had led to the custom of giving cocoa parties, often very late at night. Invitations caused anxieties, jealousies, bliss and other emotions. There was a curious custom of "propping"—short for "proposing"—by which one young lady would suggest formally to another that they cease to address each other as Miss Simmonds and Miss Baker and call each other Cicely and Alice. Griselda received many such proposals; Florence, who intimidated people, fewer. Griselda had a distaste for what she called *Schwärmerei* and attracted a lot of it, with her pale, composed look. She said to Dorothy, on Dorothy's first evening, that she would find both fiercely independent persons and perpetual schoolgirls in the company, and so it proved.

Dorothy, used to the pressure of laboratory work and demonstrations, was surprised by how much students like Florence and Griselda were left to their own devices. Florence seemed to be largely responsible for her own reading and learning, and had a tutor who barely commented on her essays. Griselda, studying Languages, was better off. She took Dorothy to a lecture by Jane Harrison, the Classics don who was also a public personality, passionate, eccentric, with a reputation outside the College and outside Cambridge. She lectured in the College, dressed in flowing black robes with a shining emerald stole, which she used to gesture with, almost like Loïe Fuller, whom she also resembled in her dramatic use of magic lantern slides, made from photographs and drawings of Greek carvings and jars. The lecture was on Ghosts, Sprites and Bogeys. It dealt with Sirens, Snatches and Death-Angels, bird-footed man-eating women and Gorgons with evil eyes. It had the odd effect on Dorothy of making her want to return to the labs, partly at least because Miss Harrison reminded her of her mother. Several of the women, Griselda said, were in love with Miss Harrison, and jostled to sit next to her in Hall. She was said to be a great tutor to those she considered worth her attention.

They walked along the river, and went out in a rowing-boat, Griselda, Florence and Dorothy. They discussed the shape of their lives. Griselda said she half-desired to spend the rest of her life in this College—largely because here she could call her life her own, and do what she wanted to do, which was to think about a kind of German version of what Miss Harrison was doing. She wanted to study the relations between fairytales and religions, find out all the ways in which particular stories—say Cinderella—varied and repeated themselves.

"And for that," said dark Florence, sitting in the bow of the boat, letting the river run through her fingers—"for that, you would be happy to live on burned legs of lamb with bleeding interiors, and watery prunes, for ever and ever?"

"I don't want to have a house, and staff, and have to *order* legs of lamb and prunes, black and watery or not. It's *not enough*."

"But is *this* enough, all these earnest women, and timid girls and the artifice of a manless world?"

"You needn't worry," said Griselda. "You are engaged to be married." Privately, she was curious about Florence's capacity to appear to forget this fact. Florence said that that presented its own problems. They drifted on in silence.

"The truth is," said Florence, "that the women we are—have become—are not fit to do without men, or to live with them, in the world as it was. And if *we* change, and *they* don't, there will be no help for us. We shall be poor monsters, like Viola in *Twelfth Night,* or Miss Harrison's harpies and gorgons. Do you not think it might be harmful to ignore the sex instinct? Don't you think that after twenty years of studying Cinderella you might be seized by the idea of the children you never had?"

"Quite probably," said Griselda, lifting a dripping oar and suspending it, so that the boat swung in the current. "But after twenty years of childbearing and fever and confinement and being *shut in a house* I might be seized by the idea of Cinderella.

"You are very quiet, Dorothy. Can you see yourself falling in love, and marrying?"

Dorothy revisited her mental image of Dr. Barty. He had lost much substance whilst she was in Newnham. He had lost, she saw, precisely, sex. All that was left of him was a Cheshire-cat-like smile. She ducked, as the boat slipped under a weeping willow, accompanied by a slip of fallen leaves.

"I think it best to suppose that I shan't," she said. "But nobody can tell what will happen to them. Do you think getting the Vote would help?"

"It would remove one of the endless humiliating differences between women and men. It might make it possible—in some new world—for the sexes to talk to each other, like *people*. At the moment the agitation is just making the women more womanish and the men more grumpy and masculine. Of course we ought to be able to vote. But I don't know that having the Vote will affect the things that frighten me." Griselda paused. "Whereas, if I wrote a really good book, that might. Or if you invented a new surgical procedure, or discovered a new drug."

"Ah," said Florence, grimly. "A woman has to be extraordinary, she can't just do things as though she had a right. You have to get better marks than the Senior Wrangler, and still you can't have a degree."

Griselda feathered the water, elegantly, and turned the boat, and they went back to tea, and glazed buns, and muffins. Dorothy felt a sudden need for London, and the labs.

In 1906 there was a General Election. There was a Liberal landslide; fifty-three Labour members were elected, of whom twenty-nine were professed socialists. There was a savage and arcane argument about the nature of the House of Lords. John Burns, the working-class man, entered the Cabinet. The bristling, pugnacious Lloyd George was Chancellor of the Exchequer. H. G. Wells, also bristling and pugnacious, joined the Fabian Society, and read them a paper on the Faults of the Fabians. Those Fabians who were children of Fabians formed what became known as the Fabian Nursery, full of forward-looking, idealist young men, and determined young women. Fabian summer camps were instituted, with lectures, discussions, and physical jerks. Dorothy and Griselda occasionally attended the meetings of the Nursery. Charles/Karl went to Germany and went from Munich to Ascona, where he watched the wilder German young ladies dancing naked, argued about vegetarianism, and realised that anarchy was impossible. A bomb was thrown that year at the King of Spain and his English bride on their wedding day, killing twenty people. Charles/Karl was appalled, both by the hatred and despair that had caused the deed, and by the random waste of life. In January 1905 on Bloody Sunday the Russian troops had massacred the workers, who had come to petition the Czar, and in February the cruel Grand Duke Sergei was exploded in his carriage by a bomb thrown by a young revolutionary. Charles/Karl made his decision, and enrolled at the London School of Economics to work under Graham Wallas and J. A. Hobson on the causes and structures of poverty. He knew he could not kill anyone, and had come to believe that that was not the way. So he too joined the Fabian Society, and went to the camps.

Julian Cain was also doing postgraduate work, trying to define a subject for a thesis on English Pastoral, in literature and art. He too went along to the Fabians, with younger men like Rupert Brooke and James Strachey.

The fiery Wells published a strange fiction, *In the Days of the Comet,* in which, in some immediate future to come, the magnetic field of a passing comet completely changed the sexual nature of the human race, which became simultaneously promiscuous without guilt, rational and ready to bring up children at the expense of the state in communal nurseries. The books that were loved, however, were still written for children. E. Nesbit published *The Railway Children,* in which the children's father was imprisoned, wrongly, and had connections with the Russian liberals. She published, also, *The Story of the Amulet,* the first book in which children were able—after finding an amulet in an odds and ends shop—to visit the remote past. The remote past, and the English earth, came hauntingly and solidly to life in Rudyard Kipling's *Puck of Pook's Hill,* set in Sussex, full of fairytales and magic from under the hill.

Humphry was sadly amused and pleased by the final rehabilitation of Captain Alfred Dreyfus, who, looking pale, transparent and somehow mechanical, was given back his command in the French army.

Olive was writing. She was writing the play, in collaboration with August Steyning. They had tried this plot, and that, Elves and changelings, Grimm and Lady Wilde. And one day, Olive had raided the cupboard, and carried the books containing the endless Underground tale over to Nutcracker Cottage. She said, hesitantly, that of course it was long, far too long, but it contained things . . . Steyning would see . . .

He was alight with excitement. Here was what they needed. Mines, shadows, a journey, supernatural beings, a good Queen and a bad Queen, a travelling crew of magical creatures, the Gathorn . . . She had written it as though she had had his own staging skills—his use of lighting—in mind. And Anselm Stern and Wolfgang would be integral to the special effects, the making of the world. They wrote, and talked, and rewrote, all through 1906.

At the end of that year Tom went to the woods, and found that a gamekeeper had chopped down the Tree House. They were public woods, and he had thought the man was his friend. But there was the Tree House, hacked into a heap of logs and spars—even including those branches of the tree which had supported and concealed it. The contents—the little stove, his writings, such as they were, Dorothy's outgrown collection of rabbit bones and bird bones and dried skins—all this had been taken. As had his blanket-bag, his mug, his knives. His wooden stool was chopped into chunks alongside the log pile.

Tom had a few very simple beliefs, one of which was that we should not be attached to *things*. Other creatures were not. He had taken to wearing the same clothes until they wore out—though Violet grabbed them, washed them, and returned them, at intervals. He saw that these chopped things were not possessions, they were—or had been—parts of himself.

He had no one to tell. He thought of going to London, to tell Dorothy, and then thought, how would that help? He didn't know whether she had come to the Tree House since he told her about the vixen, which he had regretted, as though he had betrayed either the vixen or himself.

He stood very still, for a long time, like a man at a graveside, looking from pale plank to brown bracken to moss on the branches.

A shadow went over the sun, and it was cold. Tom turned round, and wandered into the wood.

40

In February 1907, Hedda Wellwood was seventeen. She was again at home in Todefright, having left Bedales School with a reasonable, but not scintillating, set of exam passes. She did not know what to do, and both Humphry and Olive were too preoccupied to help her. Humphry was deeply, and deliciously, embroiled in the crisis in the Fabian Society, brought on by the imperious ambition of H. G. Wells. He was also in love with the telephone—one had been installed in the offices of the Fabian Society, and he was seriously thinking of installing a private line in Todefright. Women were now a quarter of the Fabian membership, and Humphry suggested to Hedda that she attend meetings of the Nursery, which was more revolutionary and anarchical than its parent group. Olive, writing as she had never written—and writing in collaboration with Steyning and the Sterns—said vaguely that she had supposed Hedda would be applying to Newnham, or the LSE. Hedda frowned, and said she had a right to a bit of time to think. Violet said that she could make herself useful whilst she was thinking, like Phyllis. Hedda put on her coat and hat and said she was going up to London to see some friends.

Hedda's friends were workers devoted to Votes for Women. She had discovered the Women's Social and Political Union, and went to their new headquarters in Clements' Inn, off the Strand, where she helped with letter-writing, poster-making and fund-raising. Olive, like many successful women at that time, despite her Fabian membership, did not pay much attention to the agitation for the Vote, though, unlike Beatrice Webb, she had never been silly enough to support the petitions *against* the Vote organised by Mrs. Humphry Ward and other ladies. Dorothy, Griselda and Florence wanted women to be able to study and work as they chose, but did not see the Vote as representing an automatic open gate to intellectual and financial freedom. Hedda was named for an Ibsen heroine whose savage life was sacrificed to meaninglessness. She had a capacity for indignation, and, as was later to be discovered, by her and by others, for rage. The women agitators knew who they were, and knew what mattered. This mattered to Hedda.

The WSPU had organised marches on Parliament in 1906, when it was learned that there was nothing in the King's Speech about female enfranchisement. One hundred women invaded the House of Commons, and fought, with umbrellas and boots, to gain admittance to the Chamber. They were fought back by the police—with considerable roughness—and carried away dishevelled, leaving a trail of hatpins, hairpins and bonnets. Ten women were arrested, and refused to pay fines. They were imprisoned. When they came out, they were feasted by the other women. Hedda was intensely moved by all this. Here was something that *mattered,* a fight, a cause, a way to make oneself into a single-minded speeding arrow.

At first, she only helped in the office. On February 9th, 1907, the non-militant National Union of Women's Suffrage Societies organised a mass march from a Parliament of Women to the Houses of Parliament. There was a large gathering of women, composed of forty suffrage societies, including many who had come from the North and the Midlands. There were many fashionable ladies, in landaus and motor cars. They were dressed in black and carried banners.

The weather was foul. Heavy rain poured and swirled in a slapping, chill wind. The skirts of the women, rich and poor, were soaked and draggled. Their cheeks and noses burned as the cold sleet bit. Mud in the parks, mud in the gutters, mud liquefying the dung in the roads, sucked at them. They went on, in their thousands. Mounted police were used against them. They rode down the women on the footpaths, jostled them and shoved them under the hooves and wheels. The women went on.

Hedda felt as she felt, walking in the countryside, when the weather turned wild. First, you put your head down, and try to protect the dry places inside your damp garments. Then, as damp becomes drenched, and fingers and toes cool and numb, you put your head up, open your mouth, and *eat* the weather, tasting the sting of the air and the water. This was the Mud March. Hedda was young and strong and striding. A policeman shoved her. She kicked at him with a sharp boot. He skidded in the mud. She was blooded.

She learned to speak at meetings. She went to a meeting in Sutton where someone emptied a sack of live rats into an audience. Things were thrown, foul things, rotten eggs, cayenne pepper, blown towards the speakers from bellows. The opposition was implacable, ingenious and stronger than most women. It was adept at knocking the chair from under the speakers. Men at meetings clutched respectable women by the breasts, or pushed beer-breathing mouths into their faces, pretending the women had invited it.

Hedda was afraid. She was partly excited by being afraid. It made her sure she was alive, and that life had a meaning, which she had always been uncertain about. But the fear was very real, and grew more intense as she came to understand, and to see, just *how real* the dangers were, of being badly hurt, or worse. She stitched up her own torn dresses: she did not want Violet asking too many questions. She did not tell her family where she went. They thought she was sticking stamps, and collecting subscriptions.

Talk boiled, and intermittent marches and other actions surged into being around the condition of women, and the condition of the Poor. In Cambridge in 1907, an idealist Trinity undergraduate, Ben Keeling, resuscitated the Cambridge Young Fabians. This was remarkable for being the first university society to admit both men and women as members. Keeling was a socialist and invited Keir Hardie, trade unionist and feminist, to speak. He diverted a howling mob of rugger-playing university thugs by deploying two counterfeit Hardies, in fat beards and red ties. He had a poster in his room with the workers of the world advancing with clenched fists. Its title was "Forward the Day Is Breaking." A Newnham woman, Ka Cox, was treasurer, and the Newnham contingent not only came to listen, but spoke fluently. Amber Reeves, daughter of William Pember Reeves, soon to be Director of the LSE, made a formidable speech proclaiming the relativity of morals, and sympathy with the Russian bomb-throwers and bank-robbers. She was self-assured and beautiful and very clever.

Graham Wallas, one of the Fabian Old Guard, who had resigned because of a difference of opinion on Free Trade, and had—with some reservations—supported H. G. Wells's attempts to shake up and reform the Fabian Society, came to speak. He was teaching Charles/Karl at the LSE and Charles/Karl came with him. Wallas spoke on the irrational aspects of human nature in politics—the herd instinct, the bubbling up of the subconscious in crowds and groups. That explorer of the unconscious depths, Sigmund Freud, was hardly known in Cambridge. *The Interpretation of Dreams,* with its claims that male infants desired to kill their fathers and marry their mothers, although it had appeared in German in 1900, had not yet sold out its print-run of 600 copies. Charles/Karl knew of its existence, because he had met the wild and anarchic psychiatrist, Otto Gross, preaching Pan and Eros, amongst the bacchantes from Munich in the Mountain of Truth in Ascona. The Society for Psychical Research, home to serious psychologists and needy spiritualists, had also noted the *Traumdeutung,* believing Freud's dreamwork to be a new way of exploring the Soul, and maybe the Common Soul to which all humans should have access. The irrational bubbled up, and met the rational, which fastened on it with glee, apprehension and, in Cambridge, wit.

In the summer term the Cambridge Young Fabians decided to invite Herbert Methley to speak to them. They wanted him to talk about the relations between the sexes. Wells was trying to recover respectability, after *A Modern Utopia* and *In the Days of the Comet,* denying that he had ever advocated "something nasty called free love . . . a sort of utopia of salacious freedoms . . . the absolute antithesis of that regulated parentage at which socialists aim." Methley was writing columns in magazines over the pseudonym "Wodwose," about the need for a new Paganism, for "natural" behaviour, for "spontaneity" and "a proper attention to the Life Force." He wrote short stories about women who were the priestesses of Gaia, who understood the ancient goddess, Chthon. (He corresponded with Jane Harrison about this.)

He spoke at the Cambridge Young Fabians on the subject of "The Conventions of the Novel." This looked innocent enough as a title to pass the critical gaze of censors and critics. He spoke in a Literary Lecture Room in Trinity Street. Julian Cain went along to hear him, with some other Apostles, including the beautiful Rupert Brooke from King's, who was an enthusiastic Fabian. There he found his sister, Florence, in a smart blue dress, and Griselda Wellwood in silver-grey, as well as the other Newnham regulars. Charles/Karl was also there, having come to visit, and chaperone, Griselda, which he could do, as an elder brother who had graduated. They were all invited to dinner in Brooke's rooms, afterwards, where a more informal discussion was to take place. Methley's books had been censored: he needed to be circumspect in public.

He spoke very cleverly about how the conventions of the novel mirrored the conventional attitudes of society. Everything in a novel must end with a marriage—this was still so, although great novelists had already revealed that life, and love, particularly love, continued after marriage and were not confined by it. He said that intelligent young people who read novels came to see—as they lived their lives—that the world did not quite correspond to the world described either by novels, or by conventional social beliefs. On the one hand, the young ladies present surely did not really believe that their very existence and presence would be an intolerable provocation to the young gentlemen present, unless they were accompanied by chaperones? On the other hand, the young gentlemen were not all ready to turn the young ladies into idols, or goddesses, or visions of perfection? They had come to *talk to them* as was right and proper. They were grown-up people, in charge of their lives.

And then, subtly and disconcertingly, he changed tack. As they grew older, he said—"I have the advantage over you of some years of experience and observation, no other"—they must realise that they knew, and felt, and observed, *all sorts of things*—nuances of delicate feeling, strange little social observations, seeds of attitudes, and problems—which did not appear in novels. He must mention the sexual feelings, because not to do so would be dishonest. The character in a novel must put into a reverential, chaste kiss feelings that surged up from underground and—in a novel, perhaps in life—had to be repressed. You came, as a reader, to recognise coded descriptions—taking off a glove, let alone a stocking, conveyed *so much more* than those simple acts. He was always surprised at the description of scholarly, or intelligent, ladies, as bluestockings. For the word—in itself a lovely, mysterious word—caused people to think of precisely what they were being defied to think of—the human body, in all its energy and beauty.

He had said he must mention the sexual feelings. But to give the impression that they were the only, or most powerful, feelings would also be wrong. Women in novels were saints, sinners, wives, mothers. Sometimes they were actresses. They were *not* politicians, financial managers, doctors or lawyers, though they might be artists of what George Eliot called "the hand-screen sort." And yet modern women felt inside them the struggling towards the light of the repressed doctors and lawyers, bankers and professors, politicians and philosophers. There was more subterranean life, *nearer the surface,* feeling its way blindly through veins and tunnels, like roots, which move like animals. And if these energies broke the surface, or the skin, there were dowagers like the Duchess and the Red Queen, waiting to hammer them down with mallets and bind them with iron hoops, as Blake said or, to change the

metaphor, to reply, as the Fool did to King Lear, who cried "O me! my
heart, my rising heart! but, down!"

Cry to it, nuncle, as the cockney did to the eels when she put 'em
i' the paste alive; she knapped 'em o' the coxcombs with a stick,
and cried Down wantons down!

Suppressing natural feelings, Methley said, in the end distorted both
mind and body. And excluding them from the consideration of novelists
distorted the novel, infantilised it, turned good fiction into bad lying.

Rupert Brooke's rooms were much grander than the Newnham bedsit-
ters, and had a deliberate leathery shabbiness. The dinner party consisted of a few Apostles and a few Fabians, including some of the
Newnham ladies. They stood, and sipped sherry, and nervously discussed the lecture.

Rupert Brooke must be, Julian thought, the most beautiful man in
Cambridge. All his features had exactly the right generous proportions
in relation to each other, brow, chin, lips; shoulders, waist, long legs.
His skin was milky and his eyes—long-lashed—small and grey-blue.
He wore his hair long, parted in the middle, and was always tossing
it back. It was bright gold, with a shade of foxy russet in it. He did
not often meet your eye. His voice was less lovely than his face—
too high, too light, with a squeak in it. The Kingsmen fell in love with
him, one after the other, and he appeared not to notice. His election
to the Society, Julian thought, was because he looked like a Greek
statue—they *wanted* him—and was part of a trend to admit members
whose claims to be interesting relied on loveliness rather than intellect.
Julian was not attracted to him. He tried too hard, was too universally
amiable.

But his presence made Julian think critically of his fellow Apostles.
They were plain, the serious ones, knobbly and awkward, and above all
pale, like things come out from under stones, Julian thought. They
looked washed-out. Julian considered Herbert Methley's metaphor of
pale roots pushing blindly in the dark, and looked at the nerveless, long
Strachey fingers, the thin necks and hunched shoulders of his fellow
students. They were famous in this little world, but they were timid

outside it. He had fits of thinking he had had enough of all this earnestness and bawdiness. He was half-Italian. He needed red wine and strong cheese, not crumpets and honey.

He said, truthfully, to his sister, that the Newnham ladies made the gathering much more interesting. Florence asked him what he thought of the lecture, and Julian said that Methley was master of mixed metaphor. "But he is right," said Florence. She went across the room to where the writer was being questioned, and said, very clearly, that she believed he had said things that needed saying.

Methley held both his hands out to her. They were thin, strong brown hands, that took a grip on Florence, in one polite movement.

"Thank you *very much,*" he said. And then "I remember you. You came to my lecture at Puxty, and *listened to it*. A lecturer is always glad to see a face with real understanding in it. This is the second time."

He did not add that an understanding face is more highly valued when it is young, female and handsome. But his look implied it. Florence flushed, and then paled again. She asked him a question about one of his novels.

Julian found himself, when dinner was served, sitting next to Griselda Wellwood. He discovered that, like himself, she was considering a life devoted to scholarship.

"What do you intend to study?" he asked her.

"I am half German. I should like to study German fairytales. They've been much studied already—as examples of an old Germanic religion, the life of the *Volk,* going back to Aryan sources, all that. But that isn't what interests me. It's really all the ways in which fairytales *aren't* myths that interests me. The way there are so very many versions—*hundreds*—of the same odd tale—Cinderella, say, or Catskin—and they are all the same and all different. They work according to some sort of *rules* and I'd like to work out what they are."

Julian was interested. He asked, what rules?

"They seem to me like coloured mosaics, with separate little pieces that fit together. *Why* does the stepmother always say the heroine has given birth to a monster? And *why* does the king then order her hands to be cut off and hung around her neck, and put her in a boat and push it out to sea? And *why* can the hands always be miraculously grown back?"

Julian gave a comic shudder. He said it was all very bloodthirsty, and those who wanted to keep fairytales from children were quite right.

"That's another thing I want to study. I don't think the real tales do frighten you. I think you accept the rules. They work in a fenced world which isn't the real world, where nothing ever really changes. Witches get punished, and goose-girls become princesses, and what was lost is restored."

"I don't know. I was peculiarly horrified as a small brat by the eye-balls stuck on the thorns, or the dead men impaled on a fence round the glass hill, or the witch in the barrel full of nails."

"I would suggest it was a kind of gleeful horror. Whereas H. C. Andersen's stories *do* hurt the reader. The Little Mermaid walking on knives and losing her tongue."

"So you think you will settle in Newnham and investigate magic woods and castles, and fairy foam on perilous seas?"

"I *cannot* make my mind up. Sometimes I think a women's college is like the tower Rapunzel was shut in, or even the gingerbread cottage. I don't want to become unreal. Do you know what I mean? I think it is different for men."

"It may not be. I'm writing a thesis on English Pastoral—I wanted to compare the poets and painters. I wanted to look at the world of the *Faerie Queene* and the work of those painters who followed William Blake. Do you know Samuel Palmer?"

"I'm afraid I don't."

"He paints magic corn-stooks with golden light pouring through them. English fields. Seductive. Lovely. Innocent. If you are half-German I'm half-Italian, and I sometimes think this College is simply the apotheosis of the public school—it looks like an iced cake, and we sit in it like—like—"

The image that came into his mind was enchanted rats and mice, but he didn't know why, and he didn't utter it. He said

"Guinea pigs."

"*Guinea pigs?* Why on earth?" Griselda laughed.

"I don't know. Yes I do. Comfortable in a cage."

They smiled at each other. Griselda was thin and sinuous. Her face was pale, and so were her lashes, and so was her fine gold hair, so demurely knotted. But she wasn't pallid, like the poking-roots Apostles, she wasn't pale because she was in the dark. She had a fine waist. She was much more beautiful, Julian thought, than the rosy, creamy, pretty Brooke. He suddenly remembered that he had swum naked with her, at the New Forest camp, years ago, and had paid no attention, because he was looking at Tom.

"There is an old gentleman who works in the Fitzwilliam Museum, who has a collection of Samuel Palmer. And Edward Calvert. I should like to show you. You could come with Florence, then we should be quite correct."

"It is odd that we have to be so correct, when we have known each other so long. It is very silly."

In flaming June, some weeks after Methley's lecture, Charles/Karl put his bicycle on a train at Charing Cross, got out at Rye and rode out across the Romney Marsh, past East Guldeford, Moneypenny and the Broomhill Level, swerving between dykes and sewers, watching the plovers circle and hearing the geese honk, and the splash of a fish rising. He rode up beside Jury's Gut Sewer towards Pigwell, skirting the Midrips ponds and the Lydd Firing Ranges of the army. He came to a cottage standing by itself, in a windswept but flowery garden, with a painted board, Birdskitchen Corner. It was an old, brick building, with a porch, and bench beside it. The lawn was small, lumpy and drying out. A small girl was playing on the lawn, with an assortment of pottery mugs and plates and dishes, and a ring of seated dolls and animals. She had long fine brown hair, and a small, neat face. "If you're *good*," she said to a stuffed badger, "you can have two slices." She poured water from the teapot, and handed out dandelion heads. "Not that you ever *are* good," she said, and looked up, and saw Charles/Karl.

"Hello, Ann," said Charles/Karl.

She stood up, turned and ran into the house. She came out again, followed by Elsie, wiping floury fingers on her apron.

"I was just passing by," he said to her, smiling cautiously.

"It's not often people pass by here, seeing that the track doesn't really go anywhere."

"It's a track I've come to like," he said. "So I ride down it."

"Sit down," commanded Ann. "And I'll give you some tea and cake."

"May I?" he said to Elsie.

"I think so," she said.

So he sat on the bench, and was given a blue lustre cup of clear water, and a rosy plate with two dandelions and a daisy.

"Pretty cups and plates," said Charles/Karl.

"Philip makes them for her. Well, no, now I look at them, you've got a little dish I made myself, years ago."

They were silent for a moment. He reached into his haversack and brought out a parcel in green shiny paper, tied with ribbon, which he handed to Ann. She opened it. It was a book of nursery rhymes, prettily illustrated. Ann held it to her chest, and said to Charles/Karl

"I can read, you know, I can read all by myself."

"She can, too," said Elsie. "I taught her." She said "You can stay to dinner, if you want. There's cod, enough for three, and parsley sauce, and potatoes."

"I should like that."

So they went in, and sat at table, and talked peacefully, to and about Ann.

"Mrs. Oakeshott is away?"

"She's gone to a lecture in Hythe. And Robin's out with a friend. So we'd have been peacefully lonesome, if you hadn't come along."

Elsie was now a student-teacher, in Puxty School. She earned a little money, and lived in part of Marian Oakeshott's cottage. Charles/Karl, after praising the juiciness of the cod, and the freshness of the sauce, asked if the work was as interesting as she'd hoped.

"It's *interesting*," said Elsie. "It's good to be needed, and watch the little ones light up when they grasp how to read. But I'm not satisfied. I don't know that I'll *ever* be satisfied."

"I don't know why I so like to see that half-cross look on your face. It was the first thing I noticed about you, a kind of constructive discontent."

"Well, that's not likely ever to change, I think."

"I don't know . . ."

Elsie got up abruptly, and began to wash the dishes. Charles/Karl took a cloth, and dried them. Ann wandered away, and fell into a doze on a sofa. They went out, and sat down again on the bench, by the porch, looking out over the beds of reeds and strips of shingle. He said

"You are the only person in the world I feel quite comfortable with. Despite your being so prickly and unsatisfied."

"I like to be wi' you, too. But we're going nowhere. This is th' end of the road. That track gets to the shingle bank and just *ends*."

"I should like to be able to see you much more—to be with you. You're good for me."

"I'm good for no one but Ann. And the little 'uns at the school, I suppose. I've made one mistake, Mr.—Karl—and I'm not about to make any more."

"It wouldn't be like *that*."

"You don't know how 'that' was. I made my bed, I'll lie in it. I've got good friends. You and me—this is an imaginary tea-party, like Ann giving you flowers and water. We come out of two different worlds, and they don't mix."

"I don't believe in all that."

"I think you do. You couldn't ever take me home to your high-up family—don't pretend to yourself, you couldn't. We are no good to each other."

Charles/Karl answered this by putting his arms round her, and gripping fiercely. He had not known he was going to do this. Their heads came close. He said "I want you, I need you, I need *you*."

There were tears in her eyes. He wiped them away. He kissed her; they were both trembling; it was a careful, not a greedy, kiss.

"You'll do me no good. I must be *respectable*."

"Oh, my love, I know that. I do know."

Ann came out into the sunlight, and they drew apart before she saw them. Charles/Karl said he must be going. He said "I'll come back, if I may?"

"I can't stop you passing by, on this road that goes nowhere—"

"I'll come back. Soon."

"Thank Mr. Wellwood for your book, Ann."

He rode away.

41

Herbert Methley came back to Cambridge at the beginning of the Easter Term. The Newnham Literature Society invited him to give an informal tea-time talk, in the tea-room in North Hall. He spoke about the changes that were taking place, and would take place, in women's lives, as sensible politics prevailed. He did say that women had a right to fulfil all their needs, but he mentioned neither Free Love, nor Mr. Wells's proposal for nurseries run by the State. He seemed, Florence thought, to be speaking particularly to her, responding to her interest, skating away from what didn't interest her. She remembered the warm, lean grip of his hand in King's. She considered his face and body. He was ugly, for certain. His neck was strained and muscular, round the Adam's apple. There was too much of his mouth, but it was not slack, it was full of movement. His eyebrows danced, as he moved from pleasant to unpleasant themes. He pushed his hair back boyishly, but he was a man, not a boy. She remembered his grip, again. After the meeting, the women gathered round the writer and asked questions. Florence asked him if he thought marriage would disappear and he said he thought it would not: human beings, it appeared, needed a long-term nest and partners, like swans and some seabirds. But other creatures had developed other habits. He thought, looking round him at the students, that the idea of dress as a prison—unmanageable hats and trains, shoes you couldn't walk on—indeed feet that were painfully crushed and broken, in China—all this might well be superseded. Young women now rode bicycles, which would have been unthinkable. He shook everyone's hand before leaving. He held Florence's for too long. His fingers played on hers.

Back in her room Florence paced, unsatisfied, dissatisfied. She looked out into the garden at one or two women playing badminton against a grey sky—the flimsy shuttlecock seemed to be her flimsy life. There were aspects of Newnham that were like a prison. She was near tears.

He tapped on the door. She opened it. She took in a huge breath.

"It's all right," he said. "I told them I was a friend of the family, a kind of uncle, and had left behind something I needed urgently—and so I found you. Let me in, and shut the door."

She let him in, and shut the door.

He said "It was *you* I came back for, *you* I had lost and found. You feel it too, I'm sure of that."

She stood stock-still, and made a small sound, between a sob and a gasp.

He took her in his arms, and kissed her, softly, not invasively. He touched her breast, under her shirt, softly, and then less softly. He stroked her haunch and she responded, involuntarily, pressing herself against him. He was all overcoat and buttons. He stood back, undid the buttons, and shrugged off the coat. He said

"Now you can *feel* what I want."

Florence didn't speak. If she had spoken, it would have to have been to protest, and she was not protesting.

"Buttons," said Herbert Methley, "are a bore and a tease."

He undid some of Florence's buttons on her shirt. Then he pressed his face into the bodice, under the blouse. His moustache prickled. So did Florence's skin. He did not take off her skirt, but searched for her body, with his hands, through it. Her body became independent of her mind. It rose to meet him, it pushed against him.

And then he said "I must go now. Remember, this is *good,* this is *right,* this is *your right.* Don't have second thoughts, my beauty, when I've gone. I'll write. I'll think of a place where we can meet, and . . ."

He left her, and she stood there, unbuttoned, unsatisfied, every nerve fizzing and hot, not knowing how to imagine what she had been made to want violently. She did up the buttons and thought, this is dangerous, I won't get any further in, I won't answer his letter. Little currents of anonymous desire ran all over her, and contradicted her mind.

But when the letter came, amusing, tempting and urgent, Florence answered. It was mid-May, and sunny. She wanted a life of her own. So she went to lunch with Herbert Methley, unchaperoned and secretly, at a restaurant called Chez Tante Sophie, with a very curtained window in a passage in Soho. She wore a pretty green dress and a gay hat, with long ribbons. They ate whitebait, and poulet de Bresse, and crêpes Suzette, and drank rather a lot of white Burgundy. They talked about literature and about the Woman Question, and the agitation for the Vote. There was a novel to be written, said Herbert Methley, about a truly free woman, who was *not* a commodity, and chose her own life. Something in Florence was repelled by this—it was old-fashioned, in its daring, compared to the ideas of some of the Newnham women, who were sober about real difficulties. But she was resolutely kicking over the traces, so she smiled and smiled, and made an uncharacteristic girlish squeak of pleasure when they lit the brandy over the pancakes and it flared intensely blue.

It turned out that they were to take coffee and cognac in a little private room Herbert Methley had reserved. "It will be an adventure," he said obscurely, following Florence up a narrow, winding stair.

The private room was furnished with a couch, and low coffee tables, a silk spread with an oriental look, embroidered with feather patterns, and candles in pretty china candlesticks. It had no window on the outside world. It had a perfumed smell. It was not a room Florence would have chosen to spend time in, but there were things she had to know, and do. She unpinned her hat, and laid it aside; she accepted a large cognac; she trembled. Herbert Methley stroked her, as a man would stroke a nervous filly. He drank a large glass of cognac himself. He made a joke about adventures with buttons, and divested himself, and then Florence, of various garments. Florence wanted to know, but did not yet know what that meant. Herbert Methley, brown-skinned, bony, nervy, touched and touched her, and talked in her ear, not about love, but about desire, and need, and *right*. There were things he knew how to do that Florence had never imagined—places he brought into shivering excitement that had always been quiescent, or vaguely troubled. She drank more cognac, and thought, "I am being played upon, like a musical instrument." This thought was strengthening. The player, or conjurer, removed more clothing, from both of them. Florence whispered that someone might come, and he said confidently that all was safe, all was prepared, all was provided for this purpose. Florence drank more cognac. Her hair slipped from its moorings. She was in her petticoat and bodice and her body was being stirred by a myriad small fingerprints.

"Here is the place," said Herbert Methley. He stroked and stroked without removing her drawers. Within them, Florence began to feel like a fountain unsealed, like a geyser rising. When he saw this, he did remove her drawers, and said "I must come in. You must let me in."

Florence's head lay back on the cushions and the room went round and round like a waterwheel. He was much more in control of her body than she was. She felt him push, with his own body, against her private place, and then push hard, like a mining machine. She tore open, and convulsed, and cried out, and he made a low deflated moan, and everywhere was wet, with blood, and semen, mixed.

"Damnation," said Herbert Methley. "That was tight. You were a virgin."

"What did you think I was?" said Florence, sickly.

"I didn't think," he said, having lost his self-assurance. "This is a terrible mess. I shall have to offer to pay for this—this bedcover thing. I suppose. I imagine they must expect this kind of thing from time to time. I wonder how much they will ask?"

"There is some money in my purse," said Florence, tightly. She thought she was going to be sick, because of the cognac, and she wanted desperately not to be sick, she wanted control of one end at least of her body. She wanted to go home. She gulped. She tried to stand up, and fell back again. Methley pulled aside a little curtain and discovered a washstand, and a ewer of water. He began, rather uselessly, to wipe the coverlet with a wet handkerchief. Florence managed to stand up, stagger to the washbowl, and mop her reddened flesh. Back to back, and awkwardly, they replaced their clothes, all except Florence's drawers, which were impossible. She rolled them up and put them in the ewer. She rebuttoned her dress, and repinned her hat.

She stood in the restaurant doorway so as not to have to see Methley negotiating payment for the damaged covers. She thought she might die, standing there, in public, waiting. She sensed that Methley did not know how to deal with the owners of the café to which he had so confidently brought her. He looked a fool, and she would never forgive him for that. She noted that he looked as though he had had to pay more than was comfortable for him.

Outside, he hailed a cab, and had to ask her if she had money to pay for it to take her home.

"Yes, I told you," said Florence, in nausea and scorn. He ought to have offered to come with her, to see that she was all right, for she knew she was not, but by then she already hoped never to see or hear of him again.

The cab-driver took her, half-fainting, back to the Museum. She walked into the little house, and up the stairs. Imogen was in the drawing room and expressed mild surprise at seeing her there, in mid-term. Florence said that she had suddenly felt she must get away from Cambridge for a couple of days. She did not feel very well. She would go to her room and rest. Imogen bent her head to her book, and Florence went, with difficulty, upstairs. The next day she went back to Newnham, and worked harder than usual.

When she came back for the summer vacation, she found that Imogen had put aside her silverwork and begun to embroider—pink rosebuds and blue forget-me-nots, on nuns'-veiling fine wool. Florence watched her for some time in silence. Imogen looked dreamy, and plumper than before—a contented Pre-Raphaelite madonna . . .

"What are you working on?"

"A coverlet."

"It's small."

"It's to cover a small bed. I am expecting a baby." She pushed the needle in and out, resolutely, and did not look up.

"I am very happy for you," said Florence, mechanically. "When are we to expect the happy event?"

"At the turn of the year. Maybe even Christmas, which is a hard time to be born."

"How *strange*," said Florence.

"Is it not? I feel very strange. Everything is hazy and I am sick."

Florence didn't want to know. She had just understood that the child would be her half-sister, or brother. The idea was uncouth.

"Please—" said Imogen, and could not finish her sentence.

Florence said that she and Griselda had agreed to go back, more or less immediately, to Cambridge and keep the Long Vacation Term, which provided an opportunity for more intensive study. Imogen bent her head lower over her moving fingers.

Prosper Cain was much exercised in his mind by events in the Museum, where the battle was still in progress over how to arrange and exhibit the whole collection. The Director, Arthur Skinner, was being, in Prosper's view, brutally harried by the Civil Servants. Cain was sitting in his office, writing a memorandum, when Florence found him. He looked up reluctantly, frowning.

"I am to congratulate you, I'm told," said Florence.

"Oh, yes. It is a very happy—" He couldn't find a word.

"You might have told me."

"I left it to Imogen. Woman to woman."

"*You* are my father," said Florence. "She isn't."

"Oh, my dear, please don't be difficult. Please be happy."

"I shall try. I'm going to Cambridge tomorrow."

"Isn't it the Long Vacation?"

"Yes it is. I want to study. We are allowed to stay in College and study for some weeks. Griselda is coming."

Later, this conversation haunted Prosper Cain. He should have paid attention. Damn Robert Morant, and his browbeaten staff, and his lack of imagination and his interfering ways. Damn him. It was hard for him to imagine the unborn child. And now he had failed to imagine the grown child.

In Cambridge, Florence said nothing to anyone, not even Griselda. She found it hard to work. She imagined the baby, fat and smiling, and she felt a kind of disgust, mixed for some reason with shame.

She was tight-lipped and worked hard. She told Griselda, expressionless, about Imogen's expectations, and Griselda said, enthusiastically, "Wonderful," and reddened in the heavy silence that ensued. Florence felt sick, all the time. She worked through waves of nausea, which she accepted as a punishment for what she thought of as "that mess." She read about battles and diplomacy, and her stomach lumped and lurched. One day, Griselda came into her room and found her vomiting into the wash basin.

"Florence," she said, "tell me what's wrong. I think you should see a doctor."

"I can't."

"You've been like this for some time, now."

Florence sat down on the bed, retching a little. Her handsome face was white and silvered with sweat.

"I think I may be—I may be—"

Griselda's imagination supplied the word. She said

"We should write to Geraint. He ought to know. He could arrange things . . ."

"It wasn't Geraint. It was once only, and it was *dreadful*. It made me long for a quiet monkish life in this place, talking to books. Instead of

which, if we are right, I shall be turned out of here, out of Cambridge . . ."

"You should be looked at. You should see a doctor."

"Who? Not the College doctor. Not my father's regimental doctor. I
wish I was dead."

"Dorothy," said Griselda. "She's done all her midwifery and obstetrics, I know. She would look at you. She might know how to stop you
being so sick. She might know—"

She might know how to stop the pregnancy, they both thought, and
didn't say. How to get rid of it. They wrote a letter to Dorothy saying
they urgently needed her advice, and went down to dinner, their hair
smoothly knotted and shining behind their heads, one dark, one glistening gold and silver. They joined a spirited discussion of employment for
women, of what work, if any, they should be excluded from.

Dorothy came to visit. During the days the letter took to reach her, and
her answer took to reach them, whatever was inside Florence went on
growing, cell by dividing cell, on a string, in the dark.

Dorothy came, and was given a guest room. Late at night, when even
the most determined cocoa-drinker had turned in to sleep, the three
young women gathered in Florence's pretty room, with its "Lily and
Pomegranate" curtains and bedspread. The light of the fire and the
lamps flickered on the Venetian glass Florence collected, advised by her
father. They had enjoyed shopping together, comparing vases and
dishes, testing their eyes. Florence sat on the edge of the bed, her hands
clasped in her lap. She was mute. Dorothy turned to Griselda, who said,
hesitantly, "Florence thinks she is pregnant. We wanted you to—to tell
her—if she's right."

Dorothy had done her midwifery. She had probed other women
with diagnostic fingers. She had seen a dead child finally ejected from an
exhausted body. She had held a howling newborn in her two hands and
looked—the first thing he saw—into his opening eyes. She was socially
embarrassed by the idea of poking into the elegant Florence Cain.

"You do know how to tell, Dorothy?" said Griselda.

"Yes, I know. I'm a little embarrassed."

"We all are," said Florence. "But since the situation is *worse* than embarrassment I think we should forget that bit of it. There's only you I can trust to help me."

Dorothy took a deep breath.

"Right. Questions first. And can Griselda get some boiled water, and if you have antiseptic to sterilise my hands . . .

"How long, Florence, since you last had the Curse."

"Just after Easter . . . I don't recall exactly. Well before . . ."

"Yes." She asked about the nausea. She asked about sleep. And weight. She asked Florence to lie back, with a towel under her, on the pretty bedspread, and she felt her belly, with confident, firm, gentle fingertips, inside and out. Florence shivered. She said

"It bleeds. But it is only the—the periphery, so to speak."

"You got torn," said Dorothy, whose experience did not stretch to the defloration of young women. Florence, accepting Dorothy's authority, said "It was only once, in fact, just the once. There was so much—mess—it didn't occur to me that I might—"

"I think you are past the early stage when women often miscarry. I think there is no doubt about this. I think you should tell Geraint."

"It wasn't Geraint. I don't want to talk about it."

Griselda and Dorothy looked at each other across the recumbent Florence. They were both thinking that Geraint, nevertheless—who loved Florence . . . They felt queasy. Florence rearranged her clothes and sat up. She said grimly.

"I shall have to go away from here. Immediately, I think. You are saying—there isn't any way of—of *losing* this."

Dorothy hesitated. She said, half-way between agitated friend and calm doctor, "There's nothing you could do that wouldn't be horribly dangerous. I think you should go through with it. And then decide what to do . . ."

"I shall have to go and see Papa. I am horribly afraid of what will happen then. I had better start packing, *now.*"

Griselda said "No, don't do that, don't. I can pack, with the bedders, later, when you know where . . . I can happily do that. I'll make us all some cocoa. Settle your stomach with pasteurised milk and sugar."

They sat, companionably, and put more coal, and some wood Florence had collected, on the fire.

"I was always in two minds about this place," said Florence. "I thought it was a fortress of irredeemable innocence—and experience was outside, and was all shiny and tempting. Now I'd give anything to be able to stay here, and learn to think clearly. Which I obviously don't. I followed my feelings and they were bad, and worse, they were *silly*. So the angel will close the gates and wave me goodbye with her sword. I think it's a female angel, in a women's college.

"Griselda, I have a huge favour to ask of you."

"Ask," said Griselda.

"Will you come with me to face Papa? I am afraid of someone—Papa, me—saying something unforgivable, or doing something silly . . . mad . . ."

"Are you *sure*?" said Griselda.

"I think so. Would you anyway come to London, and see how I feel there?"

The two young women stood in Prosper Cain's study, amongst the fake Palissys and under a fake Lorenzo Lotto Annunciation. Prosper sat behind his desk and said it was a pleasant surprise to see them. He could see that whatever it was was *not* pleasant. He thought Florence must be in money trouble. He asked them to sit down. The room was small—he had to stay behind his desk, like a judge.

Florence said "I asked Griselda to come because I need—I need this talk to stay—to stay *formal*—I need you to *think*."

"It sounds very dreadful," said Prosper, lightly.

"It is," said Florence. "I'm afraid I'm pregnant." Prosper's face tightened into a mask. Florence had never seen it like this, though his soldiers had, once or twice. He said "Are you sure?"

"Yes."

"Have you seen a doctor?"

"Not exactly. I dared not. I asked Dorothy. She's passed all her exams . . . in that area . . ."

"Well," said Prosper Cain. "He must marry you. Now, immediately. If he's worried about money, I must help."

"It's not Geraint," said Florence. She added, miserably, "I must send his ring back. I should have done that already. I feel—I feel—"

"In that case," said Prosper, "who?"

He was a soldier. He knew how to kill people, and he wanted to kill. Florence saw yet another face she had never seen. Her own face tightened into a mask, not unlike his.

"I don't want you to know. It was only once. I don't want . . . the *person* . . . to know. I was very silly." She flinched. Her father, who had never done so, looked as though he was about to hit her. She watched him decide not to. Griselda, watching both of them, thought their hard faces were like masks in a Greek tragedy. Prosper gave a kind of gasp.

"I need to think. Let me think."

Things raced through his mind like hunted animals in a dark wood. He would stand by Florence. For most of his life she was the creature he had most loved and delighted in. This caused him to think of Imogen, and the expected child. He knew, without putting it into words, that the inconvenient child was there in some way because of the loved and welcomed child. He could not, therefore, *think* of—yes, of killing—this child who was, or would be, the grandchild of his Giulia. He thought: I must take her in, and face—expect her, expect *them* to face—the opprobrium, and worse. He thought, and then, almost in a whisper, said

"I must leave the Museum, and take a house in the country, somewhere quiet, where we can all—"

"You can't do that," said Florence. "I can't bear it if you do that. I'd rather be dead."

She said "What we must arrange, is for me to go away somewhere—until—and find someone to *take*—the . . ."

She could not say, child. Prosper's imagination chewed at the unmanageable facts. How could his daughter ever now be in his house, with his new wife and his new child? He did not want her to give away her child—it was his flesh and blood, and did not deserve to be pushed into the dark. He was at a loss. His new mask was that of an old man, indecisive.

Griselda said "Perhaps Florence could go abroad—to Italy, say—as a young widow maybe—to a clinic, until the birth—and then decide what to do? It is too hard to decide now what to do. But it does seem clear Florence should go away. People are always going away to clinics—Frances Darwin spent two years in one when she had a breakdown when her mother died. My brother is always going to Ascona where there is a whole colony of artists and philosophers who believe in free love and wouldn't ask questions. There is a new clinic there. It's a beautiful place. Mountains, Lake Maggiore, Italian farms. Florence might be peaceful there."

Prosper and Florence sat still and silent, as though exhausted. Florence said

"I'm sorry. You can't know how sorry . . ."

Imogen Cain chose this moment to tap at the door and come in, her waist already thicker under a loose dress. She took in the stricken faces and her smile died.

"I'm sorry. I'll go."

"No," said Florence. "Don't. You will have to know, so you may as well stay. I'm expecting a child. We are making plans for me to leave the country."

Imogen went white. She put her hand to her belly, protectively, opened her mouth to speak, closed it and began to weep, completely silently, huge tears falling heavily down her face and into her collar.

"My dear—" said Prosper, standing up.

"This is my fault," said Imogen, not dramatically, but flatly, as though it was incontrovertible.

"No—" said Florence. "It is me who has been stupid and me who should be punished. *I* did it, you didn't. And I—I should say—I haven't been very nice to you, lately. I've been unpleasant. I know it. I'm sorry. But you can't say you're responsible for what I do. *I* am. I shall go abroad."

Imogen went on weeping. Florence stared, stony. Griselda said to Prosper "I could ask my brother about that clinic. He says the place is an earthly paradise."

"I can't stay here," said Florence. "At all. Now. I must go away *now*."

Griselda said Florence could come with her, if Major Cain agreed. Prosper was standing, still behind his desk, like a stag brought to bay by three hunting nymphs. He came out, now, took out his handkerchief, and wiped his wife's wet face. Then he turned to his daughter.

"You will allow me to accompany you—on the journey. You will need . . . "

Much depended on her answer to this question. She gave a little sobbing sound, but did not weep, only relaxed her tense muscles ever so little.

"Thank you. That will make a great difference."

Prosper said to Griselda that he was grateful for her presence. She said she would make sure all Florence's things were properly packed in Cambridge and sent back to the Museum. She would take care of the glass. She said to Florence

"I'll visit you, in the vacations. You won't be quite on your own."

"What shall I do if Charles comes . . . and sees . . ."

"Well, he won't be disapproving. He's an ex-anarchist. And he can be told not to talk, which he's actually good at, he's spent his life not telling people things . . ."

Father and daughter travelled slowly, and mostly in silence, across Europe to the southern foothills of the Alps, to the town of Locarno and the village of Ascona. Prosper Cain was baffled and neither as precise nor as competent as he usually was. One night, in a hotel in Paris, Florence heard, or imagined she heard, muffled sobs from the hotel room next to hers. Having made enquiries about the clinic at Monte Verità, Major Cain had discovered that it was new, and austere, giving courses of sun-bathing, mud-baths, water and a strictly vegetarian diet, with no eggs, milk or salt. He liked the idea of sunbathing—as a soldier he had made sure his men exercised outdoors, whatever the weather. But he was not sure that a woman expecting a child should deprive herself of milk, or nourishing beef teas. When they reached Locarno, Florence became Signora Colombino, her mother's maiden name. A cottage was rented on the mountain slope, looking out over a meadow; a manservant was engaged, with a pony-carriage, and a string of young women were inter-viewed as housekeeper-companions. Florence and her father agreed that the best was a powerful, smiling girl called Amalia Fontana. Prosper vis-ited the new clinic, and found a doctor, who agreed to care for the young Englishwoman, who had lost her husband who must never be mentioned. I have got into a second-rate novel, Prosper told himself in a moment of grim humour, and added that second-rate novels sprouted out of repeated real disasters. His daughter was monosyllabic, acquiescent and heavy-footed, although her pregnancy was not yet visible. When he tried to comfort her, anything he could say appeared to be a reproach.

"I wanted you to have everything," he said once. "I wanted you to go to University, and be a free woman."

"You see what has happened," said Florence, with a grim little smile, and then flung her arms round him. "No one could have cared for me better," she said. "We have all been very happy."

But this genuine cry of love was also made bitter by their sense—both of them in very different ways—that the coming of Imogen had broken the circle, and left the ends flying. And the time came when he must go, precisely back to Imogen and her unborn child. He said "I'll come back, soon. I'll write. I think Griselda will come, in the vacation. You must tell me everything—"

"This is all my fault, you know, not yours," said Florence. Prosper looked weary.

"Some of it is certainly your fault. But I did not pay attention."

"I shall read and read and plan a thesis," said Florence, who had brought boxes of history books.

They dined late, by candlelight, the first night in Ascona. Prosper looked across the table at his daughter, and handed her a small box.

"I always meant you to have this," he said. "It is your mother's wedding ring. You will need to wear a ring."

The ring was slender, and gold, with finely worked clasped hands. Florence tried it: it fitted exactly.

"You are very like her," said her father. "Here, in Italy, you look Italian."

He began to say something clumsy and heartfelt about the ring protecting, or bringing luck. And then he remembered how Giulia had died, and would have taken it back, if he could. Florence turned it in the creamy light, and it shone.

"I shall take care of it," she said. "You have been so *good* to me, when I have been so wilful and bad."

But she did not read. The lethargy of pregnancy came over her, and she sat on her little terrace, staring out at the mountain, doing little. People came past. Respectable, black-shrouded Italian peasants, driving goats, or sheep. Strange nature-worshippers, bearded, smiling, spectacled, with walnut skins and bare shanks over homemade sandals under vaguely biblical tunics. Women in broidered robes with flowers in their hair. Travelling musicians, with lutes. Rapid purposeful priests. Fat curates. She could not understand much of Amalia's accent, and came to see that the young woman had put on an Italian, over her patois, in which she could say simple, and necessary things, but could not make conversation.

She went up to the clinic, at first in a pony-trap and then on foot, where she spent days purifying herself with vegetable juice, and water, and lying in the sun in a linen gown, on a long, slatted daybed. The doctor

had kind hands, and told her she should abstain from meat and prefer-
ably from any animal matter. He saw how it was with her, and, she
thought, judged her harshly. Depression set in, as how should it not?
And then, she met an unlikely saviour.

There were people in the clinic who were neither doctors, nor
patients, nor servants, but appeared to be helping out, in exchange for
psychiatric or medical help. Florence's doctor had asked if she felt she
would be helped by psychiatry, and she had, more robustly than she felt,
rejected the offer. Her autonomy was dreadfully threatened—by Methley, by the thing growing inside her, by her dependence. She didn't
want to talk or be talked to. She was a soldier's daughter. She stiffened
her shoulders. She felt she was dissolving into jelly, but did not mean
anyone to see.

One of the helpers had a huge mop of tangled golden hair, like a lion
or a dandelion, a reasonable beard he trimmed from time to time, and a
mild, blue-eyed, slightly vacant expression. He wore a kind of white
clinical gown, and sandals. He arranged cushions to prop Florence's
back, and got them in the right place. He noticed when she needed to
vomit, and he noticed when her stomach was settled, and brought her
vegetable soup, which could have done with some butter and salt, but
was palatable.

"Not so sick this week," he pronounced, in English. "It will be better
from now on."

Another day, he said to her, "You are lonely." If he had asked, she
would have denied it. But he stated. "You need bread," he said. "You are
hungry."

He was always right. His name, he told her, was Gabriel Goldwasser.
He was Austrian. "I was training to be a psychoanalyst," he said.

"And now?"

A smile lurked in his beard.

"I am recovering from training to be a psychoanalyst."

They became friends. Cautiously, courteously, they became friends.
"Here, you should be honoured," he said to her. "The sun-worshippers
in the village, they want to return to an ancient matriarchy. Away with
the bearded Fathers who are the root of all evil."

"I do not belong here," said Florence. "My mother was Italian, but
she died, when I was born."

She was briefly silent, thinking of death in childbirth. Gabriel Goldwasser answered the unspoken thought.

"The doctors here are good doctors," he said. "It is a good clinic. You are in good hands. Where, then, do you belong?"

"In a museum."

"You are young, not old."

"No, I mean it literally. I grew up in a museum. My father is a Keeper. He knows about gold and silver."

"An alchemist," said Gabriel Goldwasser. "So you will go back there?"

"I don't know," said Florence, and faltered. Prosper's strategic planning had not yet extended beyond the birth. "I don't know," she said again, turned her face away, and began to cry. "I think I can't," she said.

Gabriel Goldwasser looked into the distance. Florence lay with her face in her pillow. He put a light hand, lightly, on her shoulder, and said nothing.

She asked him, once, when they had been talking about the study of history, what he had meant, when he said he was recovering from training to be a psychoanalyst. He hesitated. He said

"You must understand. I need not to think, not to talk, about myself."

"Have you done something dreadful?" asked Florence, lightly, but with a genuine apprehension.

"I have done nothing, that is my problem." He smiled, mildly. "My parents were—are—psychoanalysts. In Vienna. They sent me to the Burghölzli in Switzerland, to talk to Herr Dr. Jung. They thought it was an essential part of living, to be psychoanalysed. I earned my bread there, as I do here, helping. I was telling my dreams to Dr. Jung and also to Dr. Otto Gross, who was telling his dreams to Dr. Jung and hearing Dr. Jung's dreams in return. They were angels wrestling, you must understand." He paused.

"I dreamed the wrong dreams."

"Wrong in what way?"

"I think they were—*timid* dreams, is that a word?"

"It is a good word."

"Quiet dreams, like a cow dreaming of grass, or a squirrel of nuts. They were judged as inadequate dreams. And by listening to my silly dreams, bit by bit, those two changed my dreams. I dreamed I was stepping down stone tunnels to hidden caves, full of dragons and lions and snakes. I dreamed of the seven-branched candle—which I also did in my timid dreams, I am a Jew, the candle to me means a meal with my family—though my family had been dreamed into flesh-eating monsters and petrified women to please those two."

"You are making me laugh, but it isn't funny."

"No man has a right to dictate another man's inner life—the furniture inside his skull. They made me into someone else. An acolyte—you say acolyte?—good—of a new ancient religion. We were all dreaming the same dreams, because they were the dreams that excited Herr Jung and Herr Gross.

"They had invented me, do you see?"

"I do."

"They had made me into a—into an unpleasant sculpture, or painting. I was trapped in my artificial dreams, and couldn't get out. And then, I got out. I have to admit—you must not mock me, Frau Colombino—it was a dream which showed me the way out."

"What did you dream?"

Florence turned her body, and its burden, on one side, and gave him her whole attention.

"I dreamed I was in a studio full of light. I was surrounded by canvases perfectly painted. They were all very *pale*. White on white, with minimal shadows, in full light. Vast paintings, of a cup with its saucer and a silver spoon, on an endless white starched cloth, with folds in it. Or white flowers in a white jar on a white ground—in a white window with white curtains—"

"As though you were dead and had gone to heaven."

"Do you think? I didn't. I analysed it for myself. It said to me—like a commandment—consider the surfaces. Care for the surfaces. Don't dig under."

"Did you? Can you?"

"It can be done. All that white paint was a surface—a visible skin, laid on a surface. I went out and saw the lake. I looked at the light on the surface. Something said to me, if you can see the surface well, you are in a right relation to the world in which it is."

"But the lake has depths. Trees have insides. So does the earth."

"We can know that, yes. But I know I must live by staying on the surface. Like those flies that walk on water. Like a painted flower on a plate."

"So you gave up being analysed?"

"Everyone said it would be very dangerous, but I insisted. Then there was a lot of trouble with Dr. Gross, and Herr Jung was preoccupied, and my parents sent me here to come to my senses, which I thought I had done, myself, quite adequately."

He laughed, and Florence laughed with him.

"You should found a school of painting," she said. "Or of philosophy."

"I think more, of rigorous contemplation. I should like to be a Buddhist. I do paint, but I cannot paint the surfaces I see. Living on the surface is *hard,* Frau Colombino."

Florence suddenly thought that her own surfaces were not the truth about her and the creature growing inside her. She looked away, and began to weep. He said

"I did not mean to distress you. Rather the opposite."

"I am in a state of permanent distress. It is tedious."

"You are not naturally a . . . superficial person. But as an exercise, it is good. Look at the wind on the surface of the meadow, and how all the surfaces of all the grasses turn in the light . . ."

It was absurd, and yet, when she turned her gaze on the meadow, it was somewhere between a wonder and relief. She looked at the surface of the juice in her glass tumbler, and how it appeared to be suspended between the walls, an oval ruddy-gold coin. She looked at the sun on Gabriel Goldwasser's hair and beard. She had sensed him as an incomplete person, not in the real world, and talked to him for that reason, because there was no threat in him. Now she saw how deliberate was this absence of threat.

On another occasion she said to him "I can't live like you."

"I think not, no, that is so," he said, calmly.

One bright day, some weeks later, he said "Forgive me, but I think I have a superficial answer to a superficial part of your problem."

"My problem?"

"I think you are an unmarried lady, expecting a child, and you cannot take your child back to your own country, because of social disgrace—for you, and for your esteemed alchemical father."

"That is so. If I tell you the whole silly—the whole mad—story, you will despise me. I have almost decided I must give away this—this child—without even looking at it. Immediately. But that is a hard thing to contemplate."

"You will harm yourself if you do so. As well as the child. Has it no father?"

Florence's face, which for the last weeks had been grave and somewhat vacant, puckered into tearful rage, which was then mastered.

"I dislike him. It's weaker than hatred, it's pure dislike. Do you understand? I made a very foolish mistake. It is horrid, the whole thing is horrid."

"But your father cares for you."

"He has a young wife. The same age—as me. She is expecting a child. They are very happy. Or they were, until I made my mistake. I have ruined their happiness and my own."

"These children will be born and will have their own lives. They are not ruined. But human children are helpless. They must be cared for until they can stand on their feet. I sound sententious. But you have forgotten this."

Florence was silent. Gabriel said

"I think you would be better if you had a husband?"

"I can't. I have to face that, too. No one will . . ." She said "I was engaged to be married. I sent the ring back."

Gabriel Goldwasser's silences provoked truth-telling.

"I didn't love him. I always knew that. I've ruined his happiness, too."

"Only if he allows that. You are not a Fate, Frau Colombino, but a young woman who has made one or two mistakes. If you had a husband, you could go back to your museum, with your child—"

"I don't know that I want to go back—"

"Or make a life somewhere. I want to suggest—to propose myself, as a suitable Austrian husband."

"But you—"

"I know it is odd. I am proposing myself because I am living on the surface. I shan't want to marry in the way people marry—for—passion, or for—social reasons. My best hope is to continue living lightly, on the surface. But I should like to give you—a viable identity."

Something appalling happened to Florence. She had a vision of Gabriel Goldwasser, like the angel he was named for, walking on the surface of the lake, scattering brightness from his sunny hair. She saw that she ought not to marry him, not because he did not love her, but because she might come to love him. And he was queer, and had secrets, which he was not looking into.

"What would you do," she said, on a dangerous impulse, "if I married you, and then came to love you?"

"I do not think that would happen," he said. "You are too intelligent. You know we love each other, in an—unusual?—way, and that that is all. It is a good reason for marrying. I need to help you."

Florence began to weep. Gabriel stroked her hair. The child inside stretched its frog-fingers and its stick-legs, and put a fine thumb into its unfinished ghost-mouth, and sucked.

Prosper Cain came back to Ascona, and Florence explained Gabriel's plan.

"I could be Frau Goldwasser. I could come home."

"And what would Herr Goldwasser gain from this? Does he need money?"

"No, no, he needs nothing, that is why I trust him. He says he needs to live on the surface. He is a kind of *monk*, Papa, he is quixotic."

"Don Quixote was anything but a monk."

"Don't mix me up. You always do. I know it sounds mad, but I do believe it may work. What did you think would happen to this child? I shan't lie on these sunbeds and drink juice for ever."

"I imagined it would be given away. No, Florence, don't, don't be angry. I thought you must decide. I thought that was what you *would* decide."

"I could not give away the child, Papa, and come home and see you and Imogen *dandling* one. How could I do that? This way, I can—I can plan my life—"

Prosper Cain met Gabriel Goldwasser and took to him. It was hard for him not to, though the soldier was trim and upright, and the Austrian was shaggy and bearlike. Prosper prided himself on being able to judge character: here was an honest man, who proposed a viable solution to the problem that tormented him. Frau Goldwasser and her child could return to South Kensington, and Prosper could protect them. He organised. The marriage could not take place in the Catholic village; he found a Swiss Protestant church in an Alpine valley and took rooms in the White Rose Inn. There was a wedding-party, of a kind. Griselda was visiting Florence, accompanied by Charles/Karl, Joachim Susskind and Wolfgang and Leon Stern. Of these, only Griselda knew Florence's secret: the others believed she was suffering from nervous prostration owing to the pressure of work in Cambridge. Florence had a cream-coloured linen coat and skirt, over a rose-pink silk shirt, and a linen hat with a severe ribbon in a blushing pink. The bridegroom was unrecognisable in an old-fashioned frock-coat and complicated grey silk necktie. Joachim was best man, and Griselda attended the bride. At the last moment it was discovered that there was no ring for this wedding. Florence gave her mother's ring to Gabriel, who gave it to Joachim, who remarked how elegant it was. They were married by a stolid pastor. Prosper gave his daughter to Gabriel, who put Prosper's ring back on Florence's finger and kissed her. Griselda wept. They all dined companionably in the White Rose. Griselda talked to Gabriel Goldwasser in German. His descriptions of the clinic, and the psychiatrists, made her laugh, with an uneasy pleasure. What was Florence doing? What was happening?

Nothing was happening, said Florence. Gabriel was helping out. She was now a respectable married lady.

There were many things Griselda could have said in reply, and she suppressed them all. Florence was relaxed and smiling: she had not relaxed or smiled since Dorothy had examined her. Griselda wanted to know what Gabriel Goldwasser really felt. Perhaps he was secretly in love with Florence? He appeared to be mildly friendly. Helpful. Smiling. Wolfgang Stern said patients often fell in love with their nurses. But the nurses were usually women.

42

In October 1908 the Ledbetter Gallery in St. James's Street, Piccadilly, put on an exhibition of the ceramics of Philip Warren. Philip had been working like Vulcan all summer; idea after idea had risen to the surface of his mind, and taken shape under his fingers. Successive firings were successful. Prosper and Imogen, visiting, went into the studio that had been Benedict Fludd's, and saw the work. Imogen said it needed a bigger space than The Silver Nutmeg, and Prosper said that Philip could be thought the equal of his master. He came back with Marcus Ledbetter, the owner of the gallery, who said this work must be seen.

Everyone was invited to the opening. Everyone included the warring factions in the Victoria and Albert, and also included the Todefright family, the Purchase House family, the Portman Square Wellwoods, August Steyning, Leslie and Etta Skinner and Elsie. Philip said to Imogen that he was sure Elsie would be too shy to accept her invitation but it was only right that she should be asked. He asked the ladies from Winchelsea and Dungeness, too. Elsie made herself a dress from a remnant of blue-black grosgrain, and a lace collar she found in a shop in Rye, which was old, and complex, and looked as though it was worth twenty times what she paid for it. She put one new blue silk rose on a plain hat and looked elegant. When she came into the gallery, which was hung with white silk and had black lacquered stands and shelves, Philip did not, for a gap of time, recognise her as his sister, and thought she looked unusually interesting. He was about, when he had come to his senses, to tell her this, but found she had turned aside to talk to Charles/Karl Wellwood. They were laughing together. Geraint Fludd was in attendance on his mother, who was looking fragile but beautiful. Griselda and Imogen both looked at him with curiosity and pity to see how he was taking what must have been a mysterious and sudden rejection. He was most elegantly dressed, and was drinking rather a lot of champagne. He must be doing rather well in the City.

Even Dorothy Wellwood was there. Her mother, handsome in dark red velvet, said to her

"There is Tom, *lurking* again in a corner. Do go and make him talk to people. He used to be so charming."

Dorothy thought of a retort, and then thought she did, after all, want to talk to Tom. He had a sweetly uncertain look about him. He was drinking champagne as though it was lemonade.

"Come and look at the pots, Tom. This is all your doing. If you hadn't found Philip, when he was hiding in the Museum, none of this would have happened."

Tom said he supposed Philip would have found a way. Philip knew what he wanted.

They walked round, looking at the work.

There were various clusters of pots. The central exhibit was a group of vessels—bowls, jars, tall bottle shapes, with formally abstract glazes, many of them with a dull hot red like molten lava at the base, bursting into a sooty black layer on top of which raged a kind of thin sea of sullen blue with a formal crest of white foaming shapes rearing and falling. Other pieces had intricately random glazes that raced and climbed and plunged and scattered like forces driving in the glassy curls of wild sea water. There were greens and greys and silvers like needles of rushing air in dark depths. Dorothy turned to speak to Tom, and found that he had disappeared, and the presence at her shoulder was Philip.

"These are for Fludd," said Philip. "In memory of. Some of them are his shapes."

"Yes," said Dorothy.

"The ones over here are my own."

The second group was glazed gold, or silver, or lustre shot with both. The pots were covered with a lattice of climbing and creeping half-human creatures, not the little demons of the Gloucester Candlestick, not the tiny satyrs of the Gien majolica, but busy figures—some bright blue with frog-fingers, some black, some creamy-white, with white manes tossing—unlike anything Dorothy had seen.

"Pots are still," said Philip.

"Nothing keeps still on your pots."

"I make things keep still. That don't, naturally, keep still. Sea water. Things in the earth. You need to hold the pots to see how it works."

He reached over and picked up a round golden jar, covered with silver and soot-black imps.

"Here. Hold that."

"I'm afraid to drop it."

"Nonsense. You've got good hands. Remember?"

Dorothy stood with the pot in her hands, which held the cool light weight of the shell. The moment it was between her fingers, she felt it three-dimensional. It was a completely different thing if you measured it with your skin instead of your eyes. Its weight—and the empty air inside it—were part of it. Dorothy closed her eyes, to see how that changed the shape. Someone said "Excuse me, sir, madam, you must put that back, it is not allowed to touch the exhibits."

A small man was pulling at Philip's sleeve.

"I can touch them if I like," said Philip. "They're mine. I made them."

"*Please,* sir. Put it back. Madam, please."

He had blond hair plastered to a red-hot head. He said "You have to understand, everyone wants to pick them up, the pots ask for it, and if you start . . ."

Philip laughed. "Put it back, Dorothy. He's made his point." He said to the attendant "This lady is studying to be a surgeon. She's got steady hands."

"Yes, sir. Even so—"

Dorothy returned to the pot to its stand.

Charles/Karl said to Elsie "We could go out and eat dinner."

"And how would I get back?"

"Back to where?"

"Me and Philip are in a hotel in Kensington."

"I can take you back."

"I can't. You can see that. I have to have dinner with Philip, and the—the other people."

Charles/Karl said "I could cadge an invitation. Then we could—"

"All this is no good, and you know it."

But he cadged his invitation, and managed to sit next to her, and they both felt hot, and too much alive, and desperate.

Julian was in love with Griselda. He had not known for very long that this was the case. He liked keeping it quiet, a secret even from the beloved, unlike the simmering male gossip and endless speculation at King's. He was keeping it quiet, too, because he detected no signs that his love was reciprocated. Griselda enjoyed his company, because he knew a lot, and understood her if she said things that would puzzle most people. But she was *too* cosy with him. There was no quickened consciousness. He discussed Philip's work with her.

"These are turbulent pots. Seething pots. Storms in teacups and vases. Creatures running through everything like maggots in cheese. Stately vessels with storms raging on them."

"You get things right. You are very clever."

"I wish I could make things, instead of being clever about other people's things. I remember finding Philip when he was a filthy ragamuffin hiding in a tomb in a basement. I only wanted to stop him trespassing."

Griselda laughed.

"And now they've bought that big bowl with a flood on it, and that tall jug with the creatures climbing, for the Museum."

"That's a good story."

"Rags to riches."

"Well, to works of art, anyway—"

Dorothy went back to Todefright for the weekend. She got up early, and found Tom eating bread and butter.

"Let's go out for a walk," she said. "It's a bright day."

Tom nodded. "If you like."

"We could go to the Tree House."

"If you like."

They walked through the woods under turning leaves, yellow and yellow-green, lifeless as green leaves, not yet crisp and brilliant as russet or scarlet leaves. Now and then, one dropped through the branches, resting on a twig, falling a bit further, eddying aimlessly, reaching the mulch under their feet. Dorothy tried to talk to Tom. She did not talk to him about her work, because she sensed a determined lack of interest in it. She talked about the pots, and about Hedda's school exams, and about Violet's problems with the bones in her ankles, which she had not known about, and thought must be more serious than anyone appeared to realise. Tom said almost nothing. He pointed out pheasants, and a rabbit. The wood smelt of rich, incipient rottenness. They turned a corner, to where the Tree House used to stand, camouflaged and secret.

"It's gone," said Dorothy. The neat heaps of chopped-down wood were still there.

"Yes," said Tom.

For a moment she thought he had done this himself, in an excess of depression or madness.

He said "It was the gamekeeper. He had no right, it is public land, not part of his coppices."

"You didn't tell me."

Tom said, meekly and meanly, "I didn't think you'd be interested. Not really. Not much."

"It was the *Tree House*. All our childhood."

"Yes," said Tom.

"I'm sorry," said Dorothy, as though she had hacked at the walls herself.

"Not your fault," said Tom. "There it is. Where shall we go now?"

Olive called Dorothy into her study, before the pony-cart took her back to the station.

"I wish you'd come home more often. I'm worried about Tom."

The study had changed. It was full of odd dolls, and papier-mâché figures, and stage-sets in miniature, and puppets with strings perched on bookshelves. Anselm Stern's work, thought Dorothy, piqued that her real parents appeared to be working together behind her back. She said

"What do you think is wrong with Tom?"

"I don't know. He's hostile to me. I can't reach him."

"Maybe you don't try," said Dorothy, and wished she had not. Olive put her head briefly in her hands. She said with a weary spite

"*You* certainly don't. You never come home. I know you mean to save lives and work wonders, but you're too busy to notice your family, or be kind to them."

Dorothy picked up one of the puppets—a small grey, ratlike puppet, with a gold collar and stitched-in ruby-beaded eyes.

"And where do you think I learnt *that*?" she heard herself ask. "Look at you. Tom looks *sick,* and your room is full of all these stuffed dolls—"

"I'm writing a play. With August Steyning. We've just got the lease of the Elysium Theatre next year. There's never been anything like it."

"Well, I hope it's a very successful play. I really do. But I think Tom is sick. And you're his mother. Not me."

"Ah, but he loves you, and trusts you, you were always so close."

Dorothy set her teeth, and started to run over a list of all the small bones in the human skeleton, one by one, in her mind. Work. Work was what mattered. Olive's work was hopelessly contaminated with play.

"Someone should make Tom grow up," said Dorothy.

"He *is* grown up," said Olive, and then, in a small voice "I know, I know."

"I've got to go. I'll miss my train."

"Come back soon."

"I'll see how it fits in," said Dorothy.

43

Olive dreamed that a theatre was a skull. She saw it loom in a foggy, sooty street, pristine white and smiling. There was nothing surprising in this shape. She floated in, somehow, between the teeth, and was in a dome full of bright flying things, birds and trapeze artists, angels and demons, fairies and buzzing insects. She was supposed to do something. Sort them, catch them, conduct them. They clustered round her head like the playing-cards in *Alice,* like a swarm of bees or wasps. She couldn't see or breathe, and woke up. She wrote down the dream. She wrote "I see I have always thought of the theatre as the inside of a skull. A book can be held by a real person, in a train, at a desk, in a garden. A theatre is something unreal everyone is *inside.*" She was both entranced, and sometimes exasperated, by the exigencies of August Steyning. He had a skeleton of a theatrical performance to which things must be fitted. There needed to be curtains at the end of acts, there needed to be development, and a climax. "Your story is like an interminable worm," he said to Olive. "We must chop it into segments and reconstitute it. We must see what theatrical machinery we have, and we must use it. There must be music."

Anselm Stern said what was needed was music like Richard Strauss. No, no, said Steyning, something English and fairylike, something between "Greensleeves" and *The Ring of the Nibelung.* There was a young musician collecting English folk songs who would know what was wanted.

The play was to open with the shadowless boy meeting the Queen of the Elves—who would also have no shadow. The lighting was complicated. They argued over whether they should dramatise the Rat taking the shadow, and decided to save the Rat for a later encounter. Steyning named the boy Thomas—he was to evoke True Thomas, he was not a fairy prince, or a prince of any kind, said August Steyning, and Olive concurred. He would wade in blood, which could be done with red lighting, and the Queen would give him a silver apple branch, as a talisman, and as a source of imperishable food, as happened in Celtic myths.

She would also give him a coal-ball which would protect him in his hour of need. It is a pity, said Steyning, that we can't make the ferns and trees in the coal come magically to life again. He drew the back wall of the stage as he saw it—he drew it in charcoal, he rubbed in the coal dust to make his effects. The backcloth was a stratified black and grey series of ledges, going diagonally down. He discussed with Anselm Stern the possibilities of making animated creatures and tiny folk dance and run along the ledges. Stern said a puppetmaster could stand behind and move many, successively. They could appear and disappear. Steyning drew ferns and dragonflies with his charcoal, grey in grey. Olive said that the plants in the coalface did sometimes come to life—or death— they exhaled the gases of arrested decay. This was the horror called Choke Damp which killed quite suddenly. *Dampf,* yes, said Anselm. I know of that. And then, said Olive, there is White Damp, which is said to smell of sweet flowers—of violets—in fact it is carbon monoxide. And the third, and worst, is Fire Damp—which also comes from the decaying ancient vegetables—it comes seeping from the rocks or hissing out from fissures.

She stopped, remembering bad things.

Steyning was drawing. A demon made of flowers, a demon made of twisting ropes, a fiery devil with a flaming crown on a flaming mane.

"I could make those," said Wolfgang.

"There is the Fireman," said Olive. "The miner in soaked white linen, who holds up a long rod with a candle, to burn off the Fire Damp."

"It is like a ballet," said Wolfgang.

"Life-size puppets," said August. "And a real man, a dancer, in wet white linen—All the same, I should like the flowers to come to life."

"There must be," said August Steyning, "a heroine. At the beginning, you have the White Elf Queen, and at the end, the Queen of the Shadows—we need a female lead." He considered Olive's story as she had summarised it for him.

"You have this very good character—the Silf—who gets unwound from spider-webs and then doesn't do much. I think in the play we'll unwind her much earlier—almost immediately after Thomas enters the mine—and then she can go with him, as part of the Company. I like the Gathorn. I see him as a kind of underground Puck, or goodfellow? A trickster, but helpful. And I like the creamy salamander, which Anselm and Wolfgang can make so that it can run along the shelves and into holes in the tunnels. But we do need a female lead. A young woman. Can you write her in?"

She was a sylph, said Olive. One of the Paracelsian four elementals—sylphs in the air, gnomes in the earth, undines in water, salamanders in fire.

"The creamy salamander could glow with real light when danger is near," said Wolfgang.

"She'd be terrified of going deeper," said Olive, beginning to imagine. "She'd need to get back to the air."

"Splendid. Work on her. Give her things to do. Make her quarrel with Thomas. Make her faint in the underground atmosphere."

The end was easy to choreograph. Olive had never reached the end of the tale in Tom's book, which was constructed to be endless. The end was the meeting with the Queen of the Shadows, spinning her complex spider-webs in the deepest pit. They had a long and satisfying argument about whether she could be played by the same actress, and decided against it. She would have an entourage of bats, and whiskery sharp-toothed gnomes, and rats. They had another satisfactory argument about whether the rats should be actors or marionettes and decided they should be both. Tom's shadow would appear. He would be under the spell of the Shadow Queen and he would not want to go up to the air and be reattached to Tom. Olive said she could not see her way out of the narrative impasse, since the shadow was in fact in a better state running independently in the dark. Ah, said August, but that is where the Silf comes in. She describes the upper air to him, and colours and grass and trees.

"There must be magic," said Anselm Stern. "For the Finale. You can't come to an ending on an argument."

"*This,*" said August Steyning, "is where the coal-ball and the flowers come in. Can you, Herren Stern, make me a black knot of roots and leaves that can be made to burst open and let free an amazement of silk flowers and threads? And," he said, getting carried away, "the coal-ball and the silver bough would emit light, light would be in the darkness."

Wolfgang said that in *Peter Pan* they had wanted to use a large magnifying glass for the fairy in the glass and had failed. But he thought it could be done. The *Peter Pan* people had wanted to diminish a human being. He wanted to magnify a coal-ball. It was easier.

"In the light," said August, "the dark queen's face is a queasy grey-green, in the light."

Olive was worrying about the shadow. She had an idea. He could make a bargain—like Persephone—and be allowed to return underground in the white snowy months. Among the roots, he would journey, said Anselm Stern. Myths have a habit of winding themselves round us. And the Silf would come to visit him, underground, among the black diamonds and the veins of ore.

August was drawing the Silf, a thin, fine thing with white hair standing up and blown about as if by the wind.

They had been inventing this world, in this way, for months. But, unlike Olive's usual tale-telling, it needed to be made solid, it needed wings and flats, costumes and shoes, lighting and trap-doors and flying machines and wind machines and hiding-places for those who pulled the strings. August found money, and Olive persuaded Basil and Katharina Wellwood to invest. There came the day when they sat in the crimson velvet seats in the auditorium in the Elysium, and watched auditions, for Elven Queens, for rats and Gathorns, for the Silf and for Tom.

It was only at this point that Olive realised that August Steyning intended to cast a woman as Tom.

She was, in those days, slightly drunken, very tense with the excitement of collaboration. Writing stories, writing books, is fiercely solitary, even if done by housewives in snatched moments at the edge of the dining-table. She had come a very long way, from Goldthorpe in the Yorkshire coalfield to this gilt and velvet palace with the laughing and serious companions with whom she worked. She loved them all, and fought them fiercely when they appeared to misconstrue a narrative thread, or to take possession of her people and change them unacceptably. For she had lived with these shadows in that solitude, and had loved and hated and watched them do as they did, unconstrained.

She was not really a playwright. The auditions taught her that. A true playwright makes up people who can be inhabited by actors. A story-teller makes shadow people in the head, autonomous and complete.

The worst thing about the auditions—apart from the visceral shock of seeing Tom as a woman—was bad acting, wrong "interpretations."

Simpering misses making the sharp Silf sugary in dulcet tones. Gathorns who were neither lithe nor clever but playing for laughs and self-admiring. Queens of Shadows like society ladies, intoning. Rats who were *too* ratty, which was difficult, in principle. There was also the opposite problem—*good* actors, who twisted *her* people, the Elf Queen, the loblolly (who was only a voice attached to a jelly-serpent and lights).

But the worst thing was the women who auditioned for Thomas. Olive had tried to quarrel with August Steyning. If he was auditioning male juveniles for the Gathorn, why not for Tom?

Because of the pantomime tradition, said August Steyning. Olive appealed to the Germans. They said, shiftily, that the work appealed to many traditions, from Wagnerian opera to the puppet theatres. It had balletic elements and elements from the *commedia dell'arte*. They liked the idea of a central figure with a clear voice, neither broken nor childishly piping.

Olive was a woman who imagined male characters and male creatures. The travellers underground—Tom, the Gathorn, the salamander, the loblolly, were male, as Tom's angrily detached shadow was male.

Steyning said a woman could better do the element of mask, of *übermarionette,* he wanted.

Olive needed to please Steyning.

The audition piece was the meeting between Thomas and the Gathorn. A series of variegated Puckish boys talked to a series of boyish women, interspersed with divas. Olive's medium was words. She thought Lucy Fontaine might do, and imagined Gladys Carpenter as thickset. Sylvia Simon sounded hopeful, whereas Daisy Bremner and Glory Gayheart sounded girlish or unreal.

The women auditioned in skirts. Lucy Fontaine had a pleasant, clear voice and sizeable breasts and hips. Olive shut her eyes, and heard

"I'm lost, and I fear I shall never get out of here alive. I don't know where I'm going, let alone how to get there. I have this small light, and a sketchy map."

And the Gathorns. "It's not so bad. I live here. You can delight in the dark, if you understand it. It's full of unexpected riches."

And the boys/women. "Who are you? How do you live down here?"

"You can see in the dark, if you get used to it. There are creatures down here who shine their own light. You need to meet a loblolly."

"I've seen things glowing, or whisking along, in the distance."

"The mine is full of spirits. Some kind, or fairly kind. Some are tricky. And some are downright nasty."

"I didn't ask to—to go on a quest. I just wanted to be in the fields."

Stop, enough, Steyning would call at this point. Olive tried closing her eyes and simply hearing voices. She learned things. Her hero was more afraid, and less brave, than most heroes. Glory Gayheart, who was skinny enough, had a rich voice, a confident contralto. Lucy Fontaine got exactly the right mix of bleakness, light clarity, friendliness. *"Zu viel Brust,"* said Anselm Stern. Daisy Bremner was eager and girlish, Glory Gayheart was operatic, Sylvia Simon was scared and not good-looking, though Olive thought she knew what she was doing. Gladys Carpenter was tall and thin, with cropped white-blonde hair. Her face was bony. She had the luck of having by far the best Gathorn, a boy called Miles Martin, with a huge mouth which he curled into a variety of smiles and grins, a husky voice, a curly mop of hair and large eyes. He had worked out a crouching and skipping set of moves but when Gladys spoke, he *listened,* and she spoke to him. Olive shut her eyes again. The voice was sexless and silver. It was brave and full of the fear of the dark. She opened her eyes. This upright girl had crept into the skin of the boy she had imagined.

"I fear I shall never get out of here alive."

Matter-of-fact, dignified, desperate.

"She'll do," said August. "The only one without too much expressiveness."

They rehearsed. The Sterns worked on the puppets, the marionettes, the salamander, the loblolly, the coal-ball. Steyning designed and redesigned the sets. He rehearsed the masked groups—White Damp, Choke Damp, Fire Damp, the Fireman in white linen with rod and candle, rats, bats, shadows, spiders. New scenes were written to make more happen. The Silf—a girl of nineteen who looked fourteen and was called Doris Almond—was wound and unwound with cobwebs. They changed the material the cobwebs were made from, to something that shone, a little, and caught the light. The turntable that rose from under the stage broke and ground to an unbalanced halt. It was mended.

Puppets were discarded as too small, or ineffective. Wolfgang Stern designed and redesigned the coal-ball. A curtain was made, painted with black ferns, black dragonflies, black monstrous millipedes. Programmes were printed. The play opened. Steyning had given it a title: *Tom Underground*. Olive had not told Tom, either that they had adapted his story, or that they had taken his name. She had not thought about Tom whilst the work was going on. Names impose themselves on writers, and will not be changed, and come to be facts in nature, like stones, like plants, that are what they are. Only another writer, Olive thought, now it came to telling Tom Wellwood about the play, would believe her if she said that, about names. It was possible Tom would be *pleased* that his name was at the centre.

Steyning sent out invitations to the first performance. They were elegantly printed, with a silver bough and a coal-ball. "Olive Wellwood, August Steyning and the Management of the Elysium Theatre invite you to *Tom Underground,* a new form of theatrical drama."

Tom opened his at breakfast. Olive was watching him. He read it out, to Violet, Florian, Hedda, Harry and Robin, all of whom had similar envelopes. Humphry was away, in Manchester, but would be back for the First Night. Olive knew she should say—should already have said—something.

Violet said "So the hero's called Tom. That's nice, Tom."

"Yes," said Tom, "that's nice." His voice was unemphasised, toneless, not, Olive thought desperately, unlike Gladys Carpenter. He said

"I wasn't asked. Or told."

Violet said "It was saved up for a nice surprise."

Hedda said "Lots of people are called Tom. It's a common name."

"What's it about?" asked Robin.

Violet said "That's saved up for a nice surprise, too."

44

The First Night was New Year's Day 1909.

Humphry and Olive were in the box of Mr. Rosenthal, the impresario, with his wife, Zelda, Sir Laurence Porteous, a theatrical knight, and some Liberal politicians. The Sterns were behind the scenes, directing, deploying and manipulating the life-size puppets, the stringed marionettes, the loblolly and the salamander. Steyning was in the box with the Wellwoods, unusually fidgety. He felt that only he could get the lighting precisely perfect—the flood of blood, the White Damp, the Fire Damp, the brilliance surging out of the coal-ball. He was next to Olive, and at one point gripped her silver sleeve, and then muttered an apology.

The Wellwood children, with Violet, had a box of their own. Dorothy had not come. Tom was not in evening dress, but he was cleaned up, and had a clean shirt and an acceptable jacket. He was between Phyllis, in a golden caramel-coloured dress, made by Violet, and Hedda, in sea-green silk with a lace collar. Violet sat the other side of Phyllis. She wore black, trimmed with mauve, and a cameo brooch at her neck. She had set her pretty gilt chair back into the shadows.

The younger boys, Florian, Robin and Harry, now sixteen, fourteen, and thirteen, were grouped beyond Violet, washed and brushed.

Tom leaned his chin on the velvet rim of the box and stared out. The box was in the upper air of the dome, which was rich midnight-blue and star-studded. Gilded angels with silver trumpets sailed across it. There was a huge chandelier, a waterfall of crystal droplets, containing and scattering brightness. Tom looked out into emptiness, paradoxically crowded, with gargoyles under the boxes, and dreamy cherubs sitting above the curtained stage, which was a deeper emptiness.

Hedda said "You always feel as though you ought to jump, don't you?"

"Don't be silly," said Violet.

Hedda insisted. "It sort of pulls you, to fall into it."

"You're making me feel sick," said Phyllis, smiling. Tom put his head further into the cradle of his arms.

The orchestra arrived, and shifted and shuffled and made the usual discordant scraping and peeping tuning noises. Then they played. The music had light-footed dances in it, and whirlwinds scattering leaves, and a kind of dark, downward sucking drift from the clarinets and bassoons. The curtains with their floating bats and spiders drew back, and revealed a walled garden in the sun, on which an artificial sun shone brightly and evenly, across which a man-size rat scampered and danced to flute and drum music, carrying in its teeth, which were sharp and glittering, a limp smoky-grey web, which it spread out, using its forepaws, to reveal an elongated human shape, uniformly ash-grey, lifeless. And it rolled it up and jumped out, over the wall.

And the shadowless boy came into the garden. He sat on a bench, and played a recorder. He sang a ballad. He was a woman. Tom was disgusted. She wore doublet and hose, and had shapely legs. She had a cropped cap of silver and gold hair. She had red lips and polished fingernails. She moved her hips like a boy but they were women's hips. Another boy— a real one—came into the garden, and they played, and talked and the second boy said "Look at my shadow," and threw it across the lawn. And then Tom, its name was Tom, discovered it was single and had no shadow.

The story wound on. Tom knew, and didn't know, the story. His skin crawled. The Elf Queen came—she too had no shadow—and talked to Tom. The scene changed. It was a bare heath, with a crack which was a door in a wall of rock which was the backcloth. Red light poured blood from the wings. The orchestra played bloody sounds. Tom remembered Loïe Fuller in Paris. He refused grimly to suspend disbelief. The woman-Tom was up to the knees in the bloodlight, and staggered dramatically.

Tom cradled his head in his hands. Phyllis tapped him reproachfully on the shoulder. "You've got to look," she hissed. "I *am* looking," Tom mumbled. The dark cavern swallowed the woman-Tom. Cardboard, Tom thought, and lantern-slides, and smoke puffed with bellows. He did not think it out, but *knew* he was undergoing a trial or test. He must not for one moment, not for one second, *believe*. The test was not to be taken in by glamour, by illusion. The Tom-thing found something like a stalactite or stalagmite, a white pillar in the dark, which whispered incomprehensibly, to muted drumming from the orchestra in the rhythm of a heartbeat. The boy-woman and the person personating the Gathorn found a crack in the pillar and pulled. The stage was full of billowing white scarves. Flutes and piccolos shrilled. The Silf came out of her wrappings, whiter than white, with outstanding white hair. She danced, spikily. Her face was white, like her hair. Again Tom put his head in his arms and again Phyllis tapped on him. Violet said "Sit up properly, Tom." Tom shrugged and sat up. Violet was now permanently stiff with disapproval, or something darker. She talked to him as though he was ten years younger than he was.

The interval came and the audience applauded vigorously and there was a buzz of talk. Hedda said "It's brilliantly atmospheric. The puppets are so clever. It's sinister, don't you think, Tom?"

Tom excused himself, and blundered out in the direction of the lavatory. He stood in an anonymous line of males, and went in and pissed into the porcelain and tried not to think, which he had trained himself to do, or not to do.

He went back to the box. He was both not-thinking, and not-believing. Something had been taken from him, certainly, but in these lights, against this backcloth, it was something fabricated and trivial, which it made no sense to mourn.

The end came. Light, and silken ferns in multifarious transparent greens and golds, flowed out of the coal-ball.

The audience, in the same way, erupted into cries of approval and hands beating hands.

"You ought to clap, Tom," said Phyllis, clapping prettily.

Tom clapped, so that she would stop talking. They could see into the box where Olive was. People were applauding and pointing. She came with August Steyning, to the rim of their space, and inclined her head to the calling and clapping.

Tom thought, we are all shut up in these boxes and we can't get out.

He knew he was prohibited from thinking about his mother. He was shut in a box, and there was nothing he could do.

"Must get out," said Tom. "Air. Need air." He pushed his golden chair back, found the door in the red throat of the box-trap, and stumbled out.

So that when Olive came with Humphry, to be kissed and congratulated by her children, Tom was not there. She was dazed with success; her hair was coming loose, she had to put it up, again and again. She had not looked into the cupboard in her mind when she had locked away any anxiety about Tom Wellwood and Tom Underground. It would work out. Things worked out. Violet said "I trust you are happy" and

Olive then looked round her children, kissed them all, and said to her sister, lightly, "Where's Tom?"

"He went out to get some air, he said."

"It *is* very hot," said Olive. "I hope he enjoyed the play."

"Everybody did," said Violet. "And so they should."

Olive was given a large bouquet of red roses, lilies and stephanotis, in a silver holder, the size you have to cradle in your arms, which made the control of her hair even harder. She was wearing a black stiff silk skirt, embroidered with gold flowers, and a silver shirt, with a ruffled neck. Humphry had given her a double row of amber beads. It was a present for the First Night. There were insects trapped in some of the beads: one was a lace-winged fly, millions of years old, which had left traces, in the hard translucent bead, of its struggle to escape the oozing sap. Humphry had said "I thought it was appropriate. I couldn't give you a coal-ball." Olive kissed him. "I love you, Humph," she said. "We have come a long way from the *Dream* in Hackney." "A long way and no way," said Humphry, and kissed her again.

People came to praise. James Barrie, saying he was moved, and Bernard Shaw, saying she had managed to please the multitude with intelligence, which was hard to do, and H. G. Wells, who called the play an allegory, which caused Olive to frown. Fabians came, and the Portman Square Wellwoods, though Griselda and Julian Cain were not there, were coming with a party from Cambridge the following weekend. Prosper Cain was absent: his wife was near her time, and unwell, they were told.

Olive said "Where's Tom?"

"He kept dozing off," said Hedda, remorseless.

"Not really dozing," said Phyllis. "More resting his head."

"Where is he?"

"You know he doesn't like crowds," said Violet. "He'll turn up."

There was a party. There was champagne, and high excited laughter. People asked the Germans how they did it and were told it was an old German art made new. People embraced the Germans and embraced

Olive, again and again. Her beads were tangled in her flowers, and her hair came right down, and Humphry said she was the White Queen, removed the flowers, and found a theatrical make-up person to put up the hair again, with a red rose knitted into it. Steyning was criticising the timing of some of the lighting. Olive said

"Has anyone seen Tom?"

No one had. Violet repeated that he didn't like crowds, and would turn up.

Tom put on his overcoat and slipped out of the theatre, where the enthusiastic audience was spilling out into the lighted Strand. He began to walk. He walked along the Strand and down Whitehall, and came to the Houses of Parliament and Westminster Bridge. He walked on to the bridge, and stopped for a moment, leaning his head on his elbows, and squinted down at the river, which was high and on the turn, black, glinting, moving fast. He remembered Hedda, in the theatre, saying one was always tempted to throw oneself over, or outwards. He looked at the black surface—he didn't know how long. Then he moved on, over the bridge, and turned south. He walked along well-lit streets, and shady ones. Now and then an electric tram passed him, making a groaning sound and full of yellow light, but he did not think of boarding one. It did not matter where he went. All that mattered was to move, to be on the move, to use his body and not his mind. He wove erratically across the south of London. He found himself crossing the flat expanse of Clapham Common, with its ponds sullen in the meagre light, and its trees black. You knew you were out of London when the bark of the elm trees ceased to be thick with soot. London was a creature that grew busily and decayed busily: terraces and houses went up and came down. Cranes stood skeletal against the glow of the streetlights; there were huts in the road for the diggers of drains and of channels for cables. The air was nasty in his lungs. He went on, and came to Dulwich Village, which was pretty, though encroached upon by the tentacles of the city. He headed for Penge, avoiding Croydon. He did not have a plan. He meant to get out of the dirt, and the noise, and the dense population, and head for the North Downs where he knew where he was. At this point, he thought he was heading for Todefright, and home. Where else should he go? He went fast, in a long, loping, even stride. I am, he thought to himself, an expert in not thinking.

. . .

Olive and Humphry read the reviews over breakfast in London. They were ecstatic. *The Times* pointed out that like *Peter Pan, Tom Underground* had used old theatrical forms—the pantomime, the ballet—in new ways. *Peter Pan* was a children's play with hidden depths revealing hidden truths about childhood and motherhood. *Tom Underground* was for grown-ups, although its form was that of old fairytales, the places "Under the Hill," combined with images taken from Wagner's black dwarves and from contemporary coal-mining. This play had the magic of *Peter Pan* combined with something dark and Germanic, the bright black intentness and craziness of the world of the puppet and the marionette. The reviewer even quoted Kleist's essay on the superiority of the marionette and its pure gestures. Something of that had been experienced that evening by a bewitched audience.

"You are a heroine," said Humphry, and kissed her.

"I wonder what happened to Tom."

"He's always going off on his own. He doesn't like crowds. He'll surface."

"I think so, yes."

They went back to Todefright, by train.

Tom had reached the edge of the city, at dawn. He saw the stars, as he saw the edge of the London pall of smoke, and passed beyond it, and saw the sun come up, over the North Downs, as he began to climb. He knew the drovers' paths, and the wooded abandoned roads of the Downs and the Weald. He stopped beside a horse trough, and filled his hands, and drank. The water was very cold: it was early in the year, but there was no frost, and the ground was dry, not clagged with mud. He was on the road home. It would take him a day or so to come there. He bought a lump of bread in a shop near Badgers Mount.

A woman journalist had come from *The Lady* to interview Olive. She wrote about Todefright in the winter sunshine.

She lives in the perfect house for a writer at once so enchanting and so down to earth. I suggested to her that there was something witchy about the name Todefright and she immediately put me right. Todefright comes from the amphibian and an old Kentish word for "meadow." No death or spectres! And it is such a mellow pleasant house, with bright, unusual pots and plates, with hand-crafted modern wooden furniture that looks centuries old. There is a pleasant lawn for children to play on, which borders a satisfactorily mysterious wood. Mrs. Wellwood has seven children, ranging from young men and women to schoolboys, all of whom have been the privileged first listeners and readers for Mrs. Wellwood's spellbinding tales! The house is full of their presence—bats and balls, models and exercise books, no question of these children being banished to a nursery, seen and not heard.

We discussed her wonderful inventions, the Silf and the Gathorn, and the splendid acting of Miss Brettle and Master Thornton in those parts. Had she enjoyed the challenge of working with nonhuman actors, with life-size figures and tiny marionettes? She spoke enthusiastically of Mr. Steyning's innovative lighting, and the skills of the Stern family from Munich.

The interviewer did not want to leave the charming house. Violet gave her coffee, and Humphry drove her to the station.

"Where do you think Tom is, Vi?"

"He's walking about somewhere. That's what he does."

"That woman wanted to talk to him."

"That's probably why he's not here. He's not so unworldly that he doesn't think of lying low, at the moment."

Tom had suddenly come to a temporary stop. He had found a barn, at the edge of a coppice, in stubble fields, and had come in and found heaped logs and bales of straw. So he lay spread-eagled on the straw, and heard the mice scampering and the rooks cawing in the wood.

He went into a dreamless sleep and woke not knowing quite where he was, or why. A man with a grey-and-white woolly beard and a squashed hat was looking at him, gloomily.

"I'm sorry," said Tom. He found it was odd to hear his voice. "I haven't done any harm."

"I wasn't about to say you had."

"I'll be on my way."

"And where is that?"

They went out onto the downside, and looked up at the skyline.

"Over there, I think. Todefright."

"Over there. Aye. Take the track by the woody bits and bear right, and you'll come to the road, with luck. Are you hungry?"

"A bit," said Tom. He had meant to tire himself out, and was pleased at how slowly he thought, and how his hunger seemed not to be part of him. The old man offered him an apple, a red and yellow and juicy apple, which Tom bit into. The old man then offered him a broken-off piece of pasty, containing mostly vegetables, a bit of turnip, some carrots, some onion.

They went out onto the track in the bright light, and Tom set out again, over the chalky track and the short grass of the downland, up towards the skyline.

The easy way home was to join the main road which skirted Biggin Hill and ran south to Westerham. He stood on a ridge, with the cold wind in his hair, and looked about him.

Then he turned left, not right, towards Downe, and then he continued to go east into the heart of the North Downs.

He meant to exhaust himself. His body was something he observed, loping along, muscles pulling and ripping.

He thought, As for my head, there has never been much in my head, not really.

Full of an unreal world, he thought, maybe a question of a mile further on. A creature tried to materialise in his head, a boy-woman with a gilded cap of hair, shapely legs in black tights, an improbable Sherwood Green doublet with an elegant wide leather belt, with a silver buckle. He fought back. He imagined it bleeding, covered with blood. He tried to stop imagining.

He did this by concentrating on his steady feet, and this caused him to stumble.

He saw a hawk overhead, and that made him briefly happy. He didn't ask himself where he was going. It didn't matter. He was not going home. The Downs were empty and he was empty. He was possessed by energy and even thought of running.

Olive sent a letter to Dorothy. She persuaded Florian to cycle to the railway station to make sure it went quickly.

> *I wonder if you have seen Tom? He went out of the theatre after the play—everyone was talking, he doesn't like crowds. It seemed quite natural he should slip away but it's now three days and he hasn't come home. I remember when he disappeared before, you found him in a sort of hiding-place you had in the woods. Do you think he could be there? When can you come home? It has been very exciting here, with all the commotion about the play, but I'm worried about Tom. I hope your work is going well.*

She sat and chewed her pen. She wrote

> *I should say, and haven't said, how much I admire your determination and hard work. You said you got it from me. I should like to be able to believe that.*

She sat a little longer. She stared out of the window, at the quiet lawn.

She wanted to say *why* she was so worried about Tom. Dorothy was the only person who knew Tom. But she could not tell Dorothy that she had not told Tom the whole truth about the play. He had nodded and closed his face when he saw the title of the play on the programmes and then on the posters, but he had come along quite quietly to the opening.

He was doing what he always did with difficulties, persuading himself they didn't exist if he didn't name them. She knew him, he was her beloved son. It was *she* who had named *Tom Underground*.

It was only a fairy story.

It wasn't.

. . .

Dorothy answered.

*I don't think Tom can be in the Tree House, in fact I know he can't,
because he took me there and showed me, the gamekeeper had cut it down
and made it into logs. He didn't seem upset, but then, he never does.*

*I haven't seen the play yet. We got the tickets you sent, and I was
going at the weekend with Griselda and Charles and Julian Cain and a
medical friend of mine. But perhaps I had better come home instead.
What do you think?*

Olive answered. "Please come home. There is still no sign of Tom. Violet says it is a storm in a teacup but then she would say that."

She sealed the letter, and wrote several answers to letters from friends and the public about the originality of *Tom Underground*.

Tom had got onto the heights of the North Downs. He walked. He found himself crossing what he believed must be the London Road—he went across, looking neither to right nor to left, and saw a slow cart going south, and a sputtering, grinching motor car, with its heavily veiled and scarved passengers, going north. He came to a junction with a signpost, faded, and hard to puzzle out. It said he could go down Labour-in-Vain Road, to Labour-in-Vain. He liked the words, so set off along the track, to what was hardly a settlement. It took him a little further south, and then he went east again and found he had met up with the Pilgrim's Way, the old path where the Canterbury Pilgrims had travelled to the shrine of the murdered Thomas à Becket. That pleased him too. He tramped north-east and then followed the Way along the Downs until he came to Charing Hill and Clearmount. The Way then ran along the south side of Frittenfield Woods, at the end of which he turned south-west, seeing a sign that said Digger Farm. From there he went towards Hothfield Common and Hothfield Bogs. This brought him to the railway that ran from Sevenoaks to Maidstone. He scrambled down the cutting, and stood for a moment on the line, between the shining tracks. He heard a train, coming from the north. He thought he could simply stand there, and let it. Then he found himself on the other side, and waited to watch the engine, with its steam, and fiery grit and busy, clattering piston. He remembered all the talk about the end of Stepniak. He could.

He went on, crossing the Weald, south-west. Hothfield, common and bogs. Across the Great Stour river at a place called Ripper's Cross. The Weald was made of intractable, heavy clay, and was still covered with a mixture of ancient oak woods and gnarled copses of ash and thorn. He had walked most of it, over the years. Indeed all he had ever done with his life was walk about in this ancient bit of England. The Pilgrim's Way and the bogs reminded him of Bunyan, and the Slough of Despond. He had read that over and over, as a little boy, maybe once every two weeks, living the walking to heaven, not understanding a word of the theology. Walking over this earth was like being in an English story. He had read *Puck of Pook's Hill,* which Mr. Kipling had sent with an admiring note to Olive. He had read the Dymchurch Flit, where all the Pharisees, the People of the Hills, streamed over the midnight beach to leave the country which no longer believed in them. He knew—it was the kind of thing he troubled himself to know—that Purchase House was not a religious reference to the redemption of sinners, but an old word for a meeting-place of pucceles, little Pucks. Or maybe, he thought, it was both, the English language works like that. It mixes things up. He was on a kind of pilgrimage through English mud, and English chalk, and ancient English woods.

He didn't quite ask himself to where. He took signposts to places whose names he liked. He did now have in his head an image of a story. Not more than the skeleton of a story, a walker walking through England. The odd thing was, that he saw it (he always *saw* stories in his head) only in shades of cream, and white, and silver, a bleached, leached, blanched story, the colour of the skeletons of seaweeds, or indeed, of humans and beasts.

Hoad Wood, Bethersden, Pot Kiln, Further Quarter, Middle Quarter, Arcadia, Bugglesden, Children's Farm, Knock Farm, Cherry Garden, Maiden Wood, Great Heron Wood, and then, suddenly, he was faced with a line of water he recognised was the Royal Military Canal, built to add to England's defences against invasion by Napoleon. He was quite suddenly on the edge of the Walland Marsh. The canal ran East–West, inside deep banks. There were dragonflies, and long fat frogs. He walked east along it, crossing it and turning south on a road that ran to Peartree Farm, passing Newchard, down to Rookelands, Blackmanstone, past St. Mary in the Marsh, and on to Old Honeychild. He was now in the marsh proper, criss-crossed by waterways. South-east of Honeychild he crossed the New Sewer. He went between Old Romney and New Romney, over earth that had been steadily thrown in by the workings of the sea, and made habitable for sheep by the digging of dykes. Galdesott, Kemps Hill, Birdskitchen. He skirted Lydd and the military camp with its rifle ranges and ordnance targets, set up on the bleak pebbled forelands. He found a way out of Lydd, across the Denge Marsh, past a place called Boulderwall. The surface of the earth was huge, flat, ripples and ridges of pebbled shingle, with strips of grey-green lichen clinging to the sides protected from the wind. He went across the shingle of the Denge Marsh, between the black wooden huts, the rusty boat machinery, the upturned, beached, fishing boats. He went past the Halfway Bush and the Open Pits, on which seabirds floated and called. He went on, out to the point of Dungeness, beyond the place where the single-track railway line simply ended in pebbles, below the coastguard's hut.

You have to think about walking on pebbles. Every time you put your feet down, the pebbles impress themselves, hard and recalcitrant, through the soles of your shoes. They slide treacherously in front of you, to your side, you bow and recover yourself, you lean your body forward into the wind, which is usually fierce onto the shore, which takes your hair back over your head, which goes in and through the spiralling channels of your ears, feeling for your brain. Tom liked the pebbles. They were fragments of huge boulders from the cliffs at the edge of England, boulders which had been soft chalk and hard flint, and were now rounded by the water throwing them up and grinding them together. They are all the same, and none of them exactly the same, Tom thought, pleased with this idea, like human beings, innumerable as—was it innumerable as the stars, or innumerable as the sands, and where did it come from? It didn't matter. This was a satisfactorily hard place. He went on, and climbed over the crest of a high ridge of the pebbles, and heard and saw the sea. This was the end of England. He had come to the end of England.

It was late afternoon. He sat down, still in his theatre-going shoes and coat, both now dusty and clogged with clay. In his head, the white pilgrim sat down on a creamy couch of pebbles.

What now? said Tom to the pilgrim, though he knew the answer.

He would sit until the sun went down.

He examined some pebbles. A broken one with a marbly sheen on its fragmented facet. A pale one that was almost perfectly round. One with a hole—these were, or once were, magic, you could see the unseen world through the hole. It was a lumpy stone, mottled grey with rust-coloured stains and pale, bald patches where the chalk still adhered. Inside the hole was fretted like a beehive, and also chalky. Tom picked it up and looked at the sea through the hole.

The sea at Dungeness is not a placid sea. The pebbles shelve down and down, and the waters of the English Channel come whirling and whistling in, throwing up breakers, crowned with fine spray, that whip back and are sucked back through the pebbles they rattle. The water was noisy, the wind was noisy, the pebbles were noisy. Tom sat in the noise and stared at the waves—the tide was coming in—which were, like the pebbles, all like and unlike each other.

Under the waves is a current like a whirlwind, that sucks and drives, round the point, out into the English Channel.

Tom watched the sun go down, over the land towards Beachy Head, into the Channel.

The stars were indeed innumerable, like sand, like pebbles.

He had tried very hard to exhaust himself and stop thinking, and had not quite, not yet, succeeded.

He did the next thing. He thought in an animal way, puzzled, about his overcoat and shoes. They would muddle it. They would drag. He took them off, and put the shoes on the coat. He didn't know whether the tide would come in and take them. He didn't mind what it did.

He started walking again. He walked down the shingle and on, without hesitating, into the waves and the lashing wind, the flying froth and the sinewy down-draft. He was still walking, in his socks, on the pebbles, soaked to the skin, when he slipped, and the wave threw him into the current. He didn't fight.

45

Dorothy and Griselda had both come to Todefright. Dorothy had told Griselda that Olive was anxious about Tom. She told her about the Tree House, whose fate, irrationally, made Dorothy herself anxious about Tom. Griselda said they had been invited by Wolfgang to go backstage after the performance, and see the complicated machinery that worked the puppets and marionettes. There would be another time, said Griselda. Dorothy thought, not for the first time, that Griselda seemed to know more than she did herself about Wolfgang and his doings, although he was Dorothy's brother. Half-brother, like Tom.

When they got to Todefright, Olive was pacing the hall, backwards and forwards, like a shuttle in a loom. Be still, said Humphry, watching. Violet made tea for Griselda and Dorothy. Everybody in the house was on the move and watching from windows: Hedda perambulatory, Violet in the kitchen, Phyllis and the younger boys in the nursery. Griselda, in a fading voice, said to Olive that the reception of the play had been extraordinary.

Olive said "What did you mean about the Tree House?"

"When I was last here, I said, let's go to the Tree House. He didn't tell me it was all cut down. He just took me there. I thought—I thought it was unkind of him." She paused. "But like him."

"Very like," said Olive.

Hedda said "There's a motor car in the drive. There's a driver, and another man, and a woman with one of those veils. They're getting out. It looks like Maid Marian."

She had picked up this way of referring to Mrs. Oakeshott by snooping when she was younger. It was possible that she would not have used it, if she had been less anxious. Humphry gave her a dark look.

The car turned out to belong to Basil Wellwood. The male passenger, unwrapped from his goggles and leather coat, was Charles/Karl. They came into the hall, and stood, mute. Marian Oakeshott said

"I had hoped—to be able to speak to you in private." She addressed this remark to Humphry. Olive said "We are all here—we are all here because. You can speak to all of us."

Violet took Marian's driving coat, and Charles/Karl's. Griselda looked at him with a bewildered frown.

"I was just visiting—" he said, "when. Mrs. Oakeshott has something to tell you."

Violet said "Why don't you all come in, and sit down?"

Humphry said "Tell us, Marian, please."

Marian Oakeshott said that a light overcoat—a town overcoat—and a pair of shoes had been found on the shingle at Dungeness point. There was no name on them. They had not been in the water. The overcoat had been made by a tailor in Sevenoaks. In its pockets were thirteen acorns, a horse chestnut, and half a dozen pebbles from the shingle. And a programme of *Tom Underground*. Folded and folded, as small as it would go. The coastguard had these things. She needed to add that Elsie Warren's daughter, Ann, had seen, from the window, someone walk past, in these clothes. She said he was a tall, fair, thin young man, who was walking, she said, these were her words, "too fast." All this may mean nothing at all. She said, we all remember Benedict Fludd. She said "I shall never forgive myself if I have worried you unnecessarily."

"I am afraid there is little hope of that," said Humphry.

Violet said "I really do think we should all sit down."

Dorothy took hold of Olive—awkwardly, on the forearm—and led her into the drawing-room. A pretence was made of an ordinary tea-party, with cake, on a plate made by Philip Warren.

Humphry said he would drive back to Dungeness with Marian and Charles/Karl, if Charles/Karl was agreeable.

Olive said she would come too.

Not on this journey, said Humphry.

I can't sit here, said Olive.

You must, said Humphry. You must.

It was not exactly like the drowning of Benedict Fludd. After two days, the body floated into a fishing-net near Dymchurch. Humphry, who had identified the coat and shoes and returned to Todefright, set out to go back to identify the thing. Olive tried to say she would come, and accepted meekly when Humphry told her she must not. When he came back again, he was white, and looked older.

"Not recognisable," he said to Dorothy. "Not—as a person."

I know, said Dorothy, who had studied death, but not her own dead.

Dorothy stayed at Todefright. There was an inquest, and a funeral in St. Edburga's Churchyard, conducted by Frank Mallett. Olive was subdued, and held on to Dorothy. There was a good, warm tea at the vicarage, and conversation, of a kind. Arthur Dobbin was about to congratulate Olive on the success of *Tom Underground,* which he hoped to see, when the name caught him short, and he did not pronounce it. Olive looked at him darkly, piercing. He saw she knew exactly what had gone through his mind. He said instead that this was a churchyard full of changing weather, and the poor woman—he thought of her as a poor woman—lost her glare, and smiled briefly. She did not say anything about Tom, from start to finish of the proceedings.

Back in Todefright, she still clung to Dorothy. "You are the one who *knows,*" she said to her. Dorothy stayed on. For two or three days Olive did things she had always done. She answered letters. She thanked people for their good wishes. She stared out at the wintry garden, and the frosted tuft of pampas grass.

Then, one day, Phyllis fell over Olive, unconscious at the foot of the stairs. She was carried up, and put to bed. She lay like a stone for another two days, and then tried to get up, and fell. She nestled back into the big bed, where she had sat with Tom and made up stories that wound along the counterpane.

She allowed herself to think of him, briefly. And suddenly the room was full of every Tom that had ever been, the blond baby, the infant taking his first, hesitant steps, the little boy clutching her skirt, the besotted reader in too low a light, his brows pulled into a frown, the adolescent with his skin broken out, the young man walking, always walking or about to walk. They were all *equally present* because they were *all gone.*

She remembered the tale she had told to herself of the young woman carrying the packet containing the deaths of Pete and Petey, the young woman walking endlessly in grim weather across the moors, with the unopened packet. There was no room in that packet, for this.

She thought of the forest of coeval boys, all eternally present, crowding her room, and the old Olive thought idly, this is a story, there is a story in this.

And then she saw that there was not. There would be no more stories, she thought, dramatically, uncertain whether this too was a story, or a full stop.

She gave a great howl, and Dorothy came quickly. She gave her calming medicine that the doctor had left. She smoothed the pillows.

Olive said "You won't leave me? You will stay, now? You are the only one."

Dorothy gave a desperate little shrug, and closed her body in on itself. She said stiffly

"I can't stay. I must go back to my work. You know that."

Silence.

"It isn't true that I am the only one. There is Papa, and Aunt Violet, and Phyllis, who is much kinder than I am, and Hedda, who wants to help. They all care for you. I care for you, but *you know I must do my work.*"

A long silence. Then Olive said "Close the curtains before you go."

Dorothy closed them. She kissed her mother, who did not respond. She went out, and closed the door. Olive lay in the dark, surrounded by a forest of sempiternal boys. They did not exactly see her, that was her hope. She tried to remember the woman with the package, walking . . . She had asked for the stone with a hole, and had it under her pillow.

46

There were births, also. *Tom Underground* opened on New Year's Day 1909. Tom Wellwood was buried three weeks later. Imogen Cain's labour began on the same day. It was long, and difficult. Nurses came, and a specialist obstetrician. A day of pain went past. The doctors brought chloroform, and Imogen struggled briefly under the mask. The small, pale girlchild was helped into the world with forceps, in a flood of blood, which was hard to staunch. She was a small child, frighteningly inert. The midwife cleaned, and slapped and shook her, and in the end she mewed and breathed. Imogen lay in her blood, white as alabaster. Prosper Cain, who had seen blood on the battlefield, who had been called because of unnamed fears on the part of the specialist, turned white himself, and swallowed, and took a deep breath, and took her hand. Her fingers fluttered in his.

Mother and child lay in a no man's land between life and death. Imogen's head was full of shadowy, greedy, threatening things. They showed her her tiny daughter, swaddled in a shawl, and she smiled, but was not strong enough to take her. Her hair was wet with sweat on her pillow. The nurse fed her water with a spoon.

They had agreed to call the child Cordelia.

Imogen was still in danger when Prosper should have set out for Ascona, to offer support to his lost daughter. He could not leave his wife. He asked Julian, who was at home, in order to work in the British Museum, if he would go out to Italy. He was a just man in great moral distress. Julian, having taken a distant look at his new sister, thought he would be hopeless and useless where birth and babies were concerned. He was writing an essay on the scarcely known painter Samuel Palmer, who had painted golden, English, paradisal pictures of apple trees, sheep and ripened corn under a harvest moon. It was a long way from all this mess and medical odours. He said, of course he would go. For the first time in his life he patted his father's shoulder.

"Don't worry," he said. "You must stay, *of course*. And I can do almost anything you could do, in Ascona."

· · ·

He arrived in Ascona to find Florence huge-bellied and somehow shining with complacency, which he had not expected. He said "I can't kiss you, I can't *reach*." They laughed. It was sunny on the mountainside, even in February. They sat together in the shelter of the terrace, and Julian started to describe Imogen's state, realised this was tactless, and cut himself off. Florence smiled. "Don't mind me," she said. "Talk to me like a grown-up person. No one here really does that, except Gabriel."

"I don't understand, about this Gabriel."

"He's a good man. In an odd way."

Julian supposed odd meant queer, in a Cambridge sense, but when Gabriel came to eat with them, he saw no sign of it. He was both monkishly detached from the world, and observant, for the sake of kindness. Too good to be true, Julian tried to think, but couldn't keep it up, as they talked about socialism, about psychoanalysis, about literature. They were learnedly discussing *Heinrich von Ofterdingen* when Florence gave a low cry. Then she gave a gasp. Gabriel was immediately out of his chair.

"It begins? May I?"

Cautiously, without deranging her dress, he felt the rippling muscles. Julian was both repelled and moved. He wanted to go a long way away and he wanted his sister—his dear sister—not to hurt.

"Ah!" she said in another gasp and cry.

"Mr. Julian," said Gabriel. "Two doors down is a pony-trap. Knock and ask the owner to come."

"Quickly," said Florence, red with pressure.

"Do not worry," said Gabriel Goldwasser. "A first child is always slow. You may find it easier to walk up and down. Have you things packed?"

She had not. They called Amalia, who packed a bag with nightdress and toilet things. Florence walked up and down. She said, between contractions, "How do you know what to do, Gabriel?"

"I am a trained doctor. From a good hospital. I have the sense to observe the—midwives, is it? I have seen all this before."

Florence gave a muffled scream. "I hope it is slow."

"If it is very slow, you will hope the opposite."

Julian returned with the trap. They all three got in, behind the driver. The horse set off up the mountain, straining its muscles. Florence's muscles conducted their own purposeful, involuntary dance.

. . .

It was not slow. The child was not born in the pony-trap, nor yet in the wheelchair in the clinic corridor. But she arrived, on a great crest of pain, with a loud, defiant wail, barely an hour later. Julian was not there, but Gabriel was. There was a nurse, whose observations he translated, and commented on.

"She says you have good muscles."

"I—have not—thought about—these muscles."

Florence had lived with the fear that "the child," when it arrived, would resemble Herbert Methley, and she would hate it. The nurse cleaned it, and Gabriel gave it to its mother.

"A daughter," he said, waiting to see if she was pleased. The child had a shock of dark hair—like Florence's own, like Julian's Italian hair. It had large dark eyes which it appeared to fix on Florence. And a character. There she was, all shocked with rushing into the world, and she pushed with her head, impatient for something. Years later, thinking it all over, Florence admitted to herself that she had recognised in the daughter a kind of excessive primitive energy she had responded to in the father. And responded to in the daughter. She took her, triumphant, into her arms, and kissed her hair. Julian came into the room.

"Meet Julia Perdita Goldwasser," said Florence, laughing a little wildly. Julian bent courteously and kissed the small new hand as it clutched its shawl.

"I do not know," said Florence to Gabriel, "what I should have done without you. In every way."

"It was destiny," said Gabriel Goldwasser.

He said later, to Julian, over a glass of apple juice, "She was not afraid. Most women are afraid. Or become afraid."

"She was lucky?"

"Oh yes. She will think of it as virtue, but mostly it is luck. *Salut!*"

"*Salut!*"

In June 1909 King Edward VII opened Sir Aston Webb's new buildings for the Victoria and Albert Museum. He opened them with a golden key, with a stem of steel damascened with gold. The long white buildings, which had emerged slowly from their wrappings of tarpaulin, and thickets of scaffolding, were judged to be rhythmic and lovely, were compared to symphonies and chorales. The opening was attended by a glistening crowd of courtiers and dignitaries. The Webbs were there, and Alma-Tadema, with Balfour, Churchill and the Prime Minister, Herbert Asquith. The workers who had made the building were there, in smart suits, with bowler hats or top hats; they read an Address, composed by themselves, at the monarch's personal request. The choir from the Royal College of Music, perched high in an arch, sang Dowland's piercing "Awake, sweet love" and the Irish Guards played in the background. Prosper Cain was among the party, elegant in his uniform.

He was, like many of his colleagues and many amongst the public, disappointed by the uniform whiteness and looming austerity of the inside of the new buildings. The Keeper of the Wallace Collection, Claude Phillips, wrote in the *Daily Telegraph* that he was "overwhelmed by the vastness, the coldness, the nakedness" of the new halls. The interior still resembled a warehouse, or a public hospital. Prosper Cain had been present when the then Director, Arthur Banks Skinner, had been harshly and suddenly demoted in a public meeting, called to announce a new Director, Cecil Harcourt Smith. Skinner was aesthetic. The new regime was orderly and utilitarian. The civil servant in charge, Sir Robert Morant, was a failed candidate for Holy Orders, who had tutored the royal children in Siam. Objects in the museum were displayed by the succession of materials: glass with glass, steel with steel, cloth with cloth, like with like, so that the craftsman might study the development of his skill, and the historian the changes over time. Claude Phillips wrote that the soul had gone, that beauty had vanished. The newspapers made grumbling comparisons with the imaginative arrangements in German museums, in Berlin, and Munich. Prosper agreed with them, and was distressed by Skinner's quiet, humiliated grief. He was detaching himself from his work, involuntarily and half unconscious of it.

He had had to move house, and was now in a pretty Arts and Crafts town house in Chelsea, with more space—not for his random collection of objects, but for nurses, nurseries, and vociferous babies. Frau Goldwasser had returned, with the energetic Julia in her arms, to find she had an airy bedroom, with a delicious French wallpaper and pretty electric lights. Prosper and Imogen had discussed things, and decided that one nurse and one nursery would do for two babies. The room was most beautifully decorated by the ladies from the Glasgow School of Art.

There was a frieze of flying, ephemeral creatures, and white tables and chairs of a severe yet delightful modern design.

Cordelia was six months old and Julia five. It is an age when a baby can sit up, but not an age when it takes much notice of another baby. They had a nanny and a nursemaid. Florence had breast-fed her baby at first. Imogen had not been able to do so.

Florence, with her laughing child, saw what she could always have seen, if she had cared, that Imogen was afraid of her. Cordelia was a quiet, watchful little mite, tentative even when she reached for a rattle. Julia crowed and bounced, and had brief fits of roaring rage. Florence found herself encouraging Cordelia to play, and then talking naturally to Imogen. Prosper Cain smiled wryly under his moustache.

Florence could not, of course, return to Newnham College. She went to see Leslie Skinner, and started attending lectures, and classes in History, at University College. Dorothy was still with the Skinners. Florence discovered that Dorothy was now an MD and qualified to practise as a doctor. She was continuing her studies: she wanted to qualify as a surgeon. She was working in the Women's Hospital. She invited Florence, with Griselda, who was a postgraduate student at Cambridge, to her graduation ceremony that summer. She said her mother was ill, and would not be able to come. This proved to be so. Dorothy looked serious in her gown and cap. Griselda and Florence wore frivolous dresses and sunny hats.

Olive took to her bed, most of the time, much of the time in the dark. She was not writing. She was depleting Humphry's stocks of whisky. Her hair straggled on the pillows, turning grey, a rather glossy, metallic grey. Humphry sat with her, and opened the curtains, and told her she had six other children, who needed her. Olive replied curtly that they frightened her. Once, when she had drunk a great deal of whisky, she said "If you know that you can kill a child—"

"You have killed no one. Don't be absurd."

Olive shrank back into the pillows. "You don't *know*."

"Tell me—"

Humphry did not really want to hear. She said

"You don't really want to hear."

· · ·

In the autumn of 1909 August Steyning drove over in his new motor car to see Olive. She usually stirred herself when he came, and sat at the tea-table, staring around as though she did not recognise the room. She listened to his account of the continuing success of *Tom Underground,* and when asked about cuts in the narrative, or changes in the cast, said "Do as you will."

Violet, coming in with cream cakes on a plate said "Ah" and fell forward, crashing to the ground with her face in the cream, on top of one of Philip Warren's early Dungeness plates, decorated with seaweeds and umbellifers. The plate smashed. Steyning tried to help Violet, but she did not move and was not breathing. Her cynical sharp face was red and twisted. She was quite dead. She was turned over, and wiped clean. A servant was sent for a doctor. Olive said

"Poor Vi. Not that it's not a good way to go, when your time comes. But I had no idea hers had. She did not complain. Though it is doubtful I would have heard, if she had."

This event also was not a story.

After Violet's funeral, Humphry asked Phyllis into his office and gave her a box, containing Violet's few pieces of jewellery: a jet necklace, a cameo, a small ring, with a polished bluejohn stone, which Phyllis put on. Humphry watched her in silence. He did not know what to say. Phyllis said

"You don't need to tell me. I know. She was my real mother. Hedda found out. She likes finding things out. I don't think I do. Nobody asked me."

Humphry said "I'm sorry."

Phyllis said "I think you should be. But it's too late, isn't it. I can look after the house, now."

Her pretty face was like a china doll. She said

"I'd be glad if you'd sack Alma, and get a new kitchenmaid. She doesn't like me, and won't do anything I tell her."

She said "Nobody asked her what she felt, when she was alive. Even *I* didn't, because of knowing what I'd not been told."

Humphry said, almost grumpily, "*I* asked her. I may have been at fault, but I did—care for her."

"Yes. Well. It's too late, now. For everything."

* · ·

Alma was sacked, and replaced by Tilly, who appreciated the finer points of Phyllis's household-management.

Olive went back into her bedroom.

Humphry went to Manchester.

Life—for the living—went on. Leached of much of its colour, still where it had been full of movement.

Phyllis tended Olive. She could have said, and didn't, that she knew Olive didn't like her. Olive could not be sacked. But she could be made to be grateful for kindnesses she did not want. Phyllis persisted.

47

In February 1910 Richard Strauss's *Elektra* was put on in Covent Garden. It is a drama of fated royal families stirring violently in bloody passion, matricide and revenge. Elektra took hatred to her bosom as a bridegroom, "hollow-eyed, breathing a viperous breath." The English critics were divided. *The Times* said the opera was "unsurpassed for sheer hideousness in the whole of operatic literature." Shaw diagnosed anti-German hysteria. He said *Elektra* was "the highest achievement of the highest art." "If the case against the fools and their money-changers who are trying to drive us into war with Germany consists in the single word, Beethoven, today I should say with equal confidence, Strauss."

The English were reading novels about the invasion of England, and the invaders were Germans, men in steel helmets who bit into the globular world with iron teeth. There was the legendary William Le Queux, whose tales were serialised by Lord Northcliffe in the *Daily Mail* and hugely increased its circulation. He began with *The Great War in England in 1897* which was published in 1894. In those nineteenth-century days the hypothetical invaders were French: they were driven back, with the help of Germany, when they besieged London.

In 1906 Le Queux wrote the *Invasion of 1910,* a futuristic tale of a *German* invasion of England's green and pleasant land. The places of German landings, and German battles with the English, were changed, before publication, to suit the readership of the *Daily Mail,* to the places where Lord Northcliffe had most readers, who would feel the most poignant frisson of armchair terror. Among Le Queux's innumerable other works was *Spies of the Kaiser,* published in 1909, a mock-factual series of descriptions of infiltrating Germans and dangerous new weapons. *The Secret of the Silent Submarine. The Secret of Our New Gun. The German Plot against England. The Secret of the British Aeroplane.* These plots were foiled by a "patriot to his core," a pipe-smoking barrister, with excellent taste in furnishings. There were emotive illustrations, depicting, for instance, the "execution of von Beilstein" standing blindfold in the Horse Guards Parade, facing an execution squad of guardsmen in bearskin hats, a white-surpliced priest, and two solemn English policemen.

. . .

The Kaiser himself sat in his study on a stool in the shape of a horse's saddle and wrote letters to his family, his uncle Edward, his cousin Nicholas in Russia, making and proposing many different treaties, against many different enemies. In September 1908, in concert with Colonel Stuart-Wortley, he had written in the *Daily Telegraph* on German–British relations. German diplomats toned down the passages about how unpopular Britain was in Germany.

The article claimed that William's "large stock of patience is giving out . . . You English are mad, mad as March hares . . . my heart is set upon peace." He claimed that he had sent his grandmother tips about how to win the Boer War and ended

> Germany is a young and growing Empire. She has a worldwide commerce which is rapidly expanding, and to which the legitimate ambition of patriotic Germans refuses to assign any bounds. Germany must have a powerful fleet to protect that commerce and her manifold interests in even the most distant seas.

This article pleased no one. The English press were "sceptical, critical and grudging." The Japanese were upset by the shrill remarks about the fleets in distant oceans. The Germans were furious with their Emperor; there was a political crisis, the Kaiser made a confused speech when honouring Graf Zeppelin with the Black Eagle for his airship, and there were calls for his abdication. He went away to go hunting in yellow leather boots, and gold spurs, wearing a cross of his own design— a combination of the Order of St. John and of the Knights of the Teutonic Order. He went to a fox cull with Max Furstenberg and killed 84 of the 134 slaughtered foxes. In the evening he was resplendent, with the Order of the Garter below his knee, the ribbon of the Order of the Black Eagle across his chest, and round his neck the Spanish Golden Fleece. He had signed a letter to the English First Lord of the Admiralty about naval competition between Germany and England "by one who is proud to wear the British naval uniform of an Admiral of the Fleet, which was conferred on him by the late Queen of blessed memory."

In May 1910 the Kaiser's uncle, Edward the Caresser, died. He lay in state in Westminster Hall, and Wilhelm, in another splendid uniform, doffing his plumed helmet, stood by the bier, holding the hand of his cousin George. He went back to Windsor, the old family home, "where I played as a child, tarried as a youth and later as a man and a ruler enjoyed the hospitality of Her Late Highness, the Great Queen." The English cheered him in the streets. He went home, and spoke in Königsberg of divine right.

"I see Myself as an instrument of the Lord. Without regard for the views or opinions of the day I go My way, which means the whole and sole well-being and peaceful development of our fatherland."

That winter he added a decoration of real dead birds to the hat he wore to shoot, along with the high, shining yellow boots, and the gold spurs.

In August that year, Griselda Wellwood was working as a research student at Newnham, like Julian Cain, whose study of pastoral was spreading pleasantly, but unconstructively, into Latin, Greek, German, Italian and the possibility of Norwegian, without acquiring order or shapeliness. He earned some money by supervising undergraduates, who liked him. Griselda did not have any teaching, but attended classes with Jane Harrison. She was working steadily on the folktale, starting out from the Grimms. In their work both Julian and Griselda found much overlapping and repetition: motifs of death and grief and springtime and ripeness: motifs of flesh-eating and punishment and exoneration and the triumph of beauty and virtue. Both of them had moods in which the Cambridge weather—the chill winter winds blowing in from the Steppes, the luscious summers with boats and willows and perfect lawns and May Balls—seemed like an enchantment, a spider-web from which they needed to break free in order to taste and touch reality.

They spent time together: they attended some of the same lectures and had coffee afterwards. They attended the Cambridge Fabian Society. They discussed their states of mind. Julian made self-mocking mutterings about wanting to join the army, or make money in the City. Griselda laughed at him and said he had put himself into the story of the parting of the ways, or the story of the choosing of the caskets, gold, silver and lead. He went on making notes on Andrew Marvell, who had written so little and so well. He was improving his Latin. It was much harder to discuss either Griselda's alternative lives, or what story she was in. You could not—not if you were a man, a young man—ask her if she had rejected marriage to devote herself to scholarship. It was hard for a man and a woman to be friends with no underthought or glimpsed prospect of sex. They wanted to be friends. It was almost a matter of principle. Julian was nevertheless in love with Griselda. She was as intelligent as any Fellow of King's—though he thought she did not know it—he was in love with her mind as it followed clues through labyrinths. Love is, among many other things, a response to energy, and Griselda's mind was precise and energetic.

He wanted to make love to her, too. She was now almost too perfectly lovely to be attractive. Her calm, clear face had a carved look, which could easily be read as a cold look. She coiled her pale hair perfectly so that one was led to admire it, rather than to want to ruffle it. He did not detect in her—and he watched her—any flash of the sex instinct. He managed to raise the topic by discussing her London Season as a debutante. She became animated. She said it was horrible. "All that eyeing each other, and pairing off. Like a cattle market. Horrid. I have *no small talk* and I never met anyone who had anything else. And it was noisy. They *bray,* the upper classes, about their titillations and curious ceremonies. They shriek. And you have to be dolled up with feathers in your hair. I was rejected and rejecting. Firmly, in both cases."

He had asked himself if she preferred women. She might. The Newnhamites had passionate friendships and flirtations: they proposed to each other, he had been told. She had been friends with Florence, who had rushed into an odd story he hadn't been told, and didn't understand. She was friends with her cousin Dorothy, who had just qualified as a surgeon, which he could not but think of as a male occupation, knives, lancets, commands.

Then she said "I didn't really mean to get me to a nunnery. I didn't really mean to live in a world of knitting and gossip and—oh—petty jealousies. I wish I was you."

"I don't. I like talking to you."

And then that silence, that was the end of that conversation, as of others.

He invited her to go with him to see the Marlowe Society, who were reviving their successful production of Marlowe's *Dr. Faustus.* The audience consisted mostly of a group of visiting German students, ready to see what Goethe had read. Because it was not term-time there was not only no strict chaperonage, there were women playing female parts—which were admittedly non-speaking and brief. There were no transvestite Kingsmen as queens or temptresses. There were the Fabian Nursery with Brynhild ("Bryn") Olivier, daughter of Sir Sidney Olivier, founding Fabian, and Governor of Jamaica, playing Helen of Troy, the "face that launched a thousand ships," in a low-cut dress, her hair powdered with gold. Francis Cornford, the classical scholar, was Faustus, Jacques Raverat (who was eventually to marry Gwen Darwin) was Mephistophilis, and some female Fabians were Deadly Sins. Rupert Brooke was the Chorus looking marvellous, and speaking the verse somewhat squeakily.

Griselda asked if he could get another ticket. A friend was visiting Cambridge—Julian knew him, in fact—he was Wolfgang Stern, from Munich. The Sterns were over in England, planning changes in the puppets and marionettes for the reopening of *Tom Underground* in the autumn. Julian got the ticket and Wolfgang appeared, looking a little Mephistophelian with a sharp black beard and jutting brow. They sat in the centre, a few rows back. Behind them the Germans commented in German, supposing they were not understood. Wolfgang turned round and told them to be quiet. They laughed, and attended. Griselda sat sedately between Wolfgang and Julian. Behind them were some more Darwins, Jane Harrison and her lovely student, Hope Mirrlees. Harrison must have come to see Francis Cornford, with whom she corresponded daily and rode rapidly about Cambridge on bicycles. There was a party afterwards, at the Darwin house on Silver Street, to which the three were not invited. Julian took them to a restaurant near Magdalene Bridge. It was French and cheerful, with checked tablecloths.

Wolfgang Stern said rather aggressively that the voices he thought were good, but none of these English people knew how to move. They stood like melting candles bending over. Their gestures were *polite* when something else was required. Griselda said that was most unfair. The Mephistophilis had been quite snaky in his movements. He was French, said Wolfgang, that was why. The English should—was it "stick to"?—*tableaux vivants. Charades.* He seemed quite cross.

Griselda said placatingly that she meant to ask him—Wolfgang—about an essay she was writing on the differences between the Grimms' two versions of the Cinderella story—"Aschenputtel" and "Allerleirauh," Cinderella and the Many-furred. She said she loved the word

"Allerleirauh," every kind of rough fur. Cinderella was persecuted by a stepmother, but Allerleirauh dealt intelligently with an incestuous father and a cook who threw boots at her. And somehow she was moved by the fact that Allerleirauh, hiding her gold, silver and star-spangling dresses under the skin cloak, became a furry *creature*—an animal—neutral in German—not an object of desire.

"Until she chose," said Wolfgang. "And then she blazed out like the sun and the moon—"

"The English and the French have sweetened Cinderella—"

Julian felt an electricity. It sparked and flickered between the other two. Their hands were just too near together. Griselda looked too intently or not at all at the German.

"And what does that mean?" Julian asked himself, and did not quite know.

He and Wolfgang walked Griselda back to her College, into which she had to be locked, although a grown woman, at a ridiculously early hour. She stood on the step, smiling at both of them. "A *lovely* day," she said. "Civilised," she added. It was, Julian knew, one of her highest words of praise.

He invited his newly discovered rival into a pub and bought him a brandy. The German was prickly, a man out of his place where he was easy. Julian talked about many things—theatres, Goethe, Marlowe—and on the third glass of brandy said

"Let us drink to Griselda. *Die schöne* Griselda."

"*Die schöne* Griselda. You don't speak German."

"No, I don't. I am learning. I need to read it, for my work."

"She is like a statue in a story. Or a marionette. She doesn't feel."

Julian said carefully "I don't think that is true." He did not know if he wanted to share his discovery with this edgy creature, who didn't seem to have made it for himself.

Wolfgang said "There is no good in coming to see her. She smiles and sees nothing. Such a nice English lady. Such a princess. All her hair is controlled on her head. No one has ever disturbed her. Maybe no one can or will. Forgive me. It is the brandy."

There was a long silence. Wolfgang said "I am sorry. Maybe you—maybe you yourself—"

"Oh no. Nothing of that kind."

Another silence. Damn it, it was only fair. And moreover, it had a certain narrative interest.

"I noticed," Julian said, and searched for words.

"You noticed I was—unhappy."

"No, no, as a matter of fact, not. I noticed *her.* I saw her look at you."

"Look?"

"I haven't seen her look at anyone else, like that."

"Look?"

"Oh, don't be exasperating. She's *interested* in you. Not in anyone else. That I've noticed."

"Oh." Wolfgang pulled himself together, and gave a somewhat demonic rueful smile, because that was the shape his face was. He said "I am an idiot. That idea makes it worse. You see—she *is* a fairytale princess. She has ingots and ingots of gold in the Bank and she must marry another such, or find a donkey that shits ingots, forgive me. I make dolls. I make artificial men move around."

"You could say you are an artist?"

"I could, but I should not be heard. I should have boots thrown at me and be ejected."

"I don't see why you give up so easily," said Julian. He added, with real venom, "It is hardly fair to *her* . . ."

"On the contrary," said Wolfgang. "That is what it is."

In September 1910 the Second International Workingmen's Association held its Congress in Copenhagen. Joachim Susskind and Karl Wellwood went together and attended groups on anti-militarism. Socialism was international, it crossed frontiers, it was the brotherhood of men and women. Susskind was also in touch with Erich Mühsam and Johannes Nohl's "Gruppe Tat" (the Group for the Deed) in Munich, a very Munich mixture of men of letters, workmen, revolutionaries. Leon Stern was passionately interested in this. So were Heinrich Mann, Karl Wolfskehl and Ernst Frick. The deliberations in Copenhagen concentrated on the possibility of calling an International General Strike, an act of defiance to prevent a war. The resolution was proposed by an Englishman, Keir Hardie, just returned to the English Parliament with an increased majority, and Edouard Vaillant of France. They recommended that "the affiliated Parties and Labour organisations consider the advisability and feasibility of the general strike, especially in industries that supply war materials, as one of the methods of preventing war, and that action be taken on the subject at the next Congress."

Hardie was supported by the Belgian, Vandervelde, and by the charismatic Jean Jaurès. He was opposed by the German socialists, who were established in the German government, and whose unions had money and investments which they feared to put in jeopardy. As large congresses tend to do, faced with demands for precise, planned actions, they passed another resolution, condemning militarism, suggesting that organised labour in member countries "shall consider whether a general strike should not be proclaimed if necessary in order to prevent the crime of war." Conditional verbs, and future decisions, said Joachim Susskind, still at heart an anarchist. Keir Hardie wrote to his lover, Sylvia Pankhurst

> *Sweet, nay but did you not promise to have no more imaginings. There was nothing, darling, only on the typewriter it seems to come easier.*
>
> *From 9 a.m. to 9 p.m. I have been at it every day. Today there is a pleasure sail to which I go not and so I write to you instead. Voilà! . . . I have accepted invitations to speak at two meetings in Sweden next week and from there I go on to Frankfurt on Main for a demonstration . . .*
>
> *After that is uncertain. I shall post card from place to place but dearie, do not expect letters . . . I am in splendid condition and thoroughly enjoying the work. With affection and bundles of kisses. Yours K.*

It was not clear whether, in the event of any war, the workingmen and -women would feel a greater loyalty to their comrades or to their country. It was, however, clear that the General Strike needed planning and organising, though the image of a spontaneous uprising moved many minds.

Charles/Karl Wellwood was working energetically at the London School of Economics. He went to the lectures of the founding Fabian, Graham Wallas, who, as a principled agnostic, had resigned from the Fabian executive when the Society supported giving state aid to religious schools. Wallas's book, *Human Nature in Politics,* analysed the psychology of politics. Human beings, he said, were descended from paleolithic men, and had preserved many instincts and inclinations which had helped their ancestors. Political philosophers had believed that humans were rational creatures. They had not studied the structures of impulse. He analysed the nature of friendship, the emotional response to political candidates and monarchs, the forming of groups, crowds and herds. He introduced students like Karl to the essays by Wilfred Trotter on the *Instincts of the Herd in Peace and War*. Karl learned to think that men acted from irrational impulses, and that groups, crowds and herds behaved differently from individuals. He himself was an isolated individual, despite having signed the Fabian Basis, despite his socialism. He wanted to help the massed poor, but he did not know what to say when he met them, most particularly when they were in a group, or crowd.

Nevertheless, he undertook to lecture for the newly formed National Committee for the Break-Up of the Poor Law. This body, Beatrice Webb's brainchild, had its offices between the Fabian Society's premises and the London School of Economics, all just off the Strand. Their members overlapped considerably—they were all working to the same end. They hoped to be more realistic than the socialists. Beatrice Webb said that the vision of a socialist could stand as a long-term aim, but in the meantime something must be done with "the millions of destitute persons which constitute an infamous and wholly unnecessary accompaniment to an Individualist State."

Individualist politics was difficult. There were meetings, conferences, summer schools, study groups and leaflets. There were sixteen thousand members, and branches everywhere. There were eleven paid employees and four hundred lecturers on call. The lecturers included, as well as Charles/Karl, Rupert Brooke, who travelled in a picturesque caravan from the New Forest to Corfe and back. He and his friend spoke engagingly on village greens and street corners. Beatrice Webb meant to bring about "a rapid but almost unconscious change in the *substance* of society." Rupert Brooke was euphoric about human beings and human nature.

> I suddenly feel the extraordinary value and importance of everybody I meet, and almost everything I see . . . that is, when the mood is on me. I roam about places—yesterday I did it even in Birmingham!—and sit in trains and see the essential glory and

beauty of all the people I meet. I can watch a dirty middle-aged tradesman in a railway-carriage for hours, and love every dirty greasy sulky wrinkle in his weak chin and every button on his spotted unclean waistcoat. I know their states of mind are bad. But I'm so much occupied with their being there at all, that I don't have time to think of that.

In 1910 also the Fabians held a summer camp. The camps were on the North Welsh coast—two weeks for the campaign workers who included a mix of Fabian Nursery, lower-class professionals, elderly ladies, teachers and politicians. These were followed by a conference of Fabians from universities. The University Fabians were high-spirited and the Cambridge contingent were camp. Rupert reported, to Lytton Strachey, late-night titillations and rampages. Beatrice Webb complained that they held "boisterous, larky entertainments" and were "inclined to go away rather more critical and supercilious than when they came . . . They won't come unless they know who they are going to meet, sums up Rupert Brooke . . . they don't want to learn, they don't think they have anything to learn . . . the egotism of the young university man is colossal."

Julian and Griselda did not go to this camp. Charles/Karl went to the camp for the campaign workers. The women wore gym tunics. The men wore flannels or breeches and stout socks. There were sensible shoes, and gymnastic exercises, and swimming. Charles/Karl had managed to persuade Elsie Warren to leave Ann with Marian Oakeshott and come to the camp. Elsie was reading and thinking with a speed and intensity much fiercer than Rupert Brooke's little dives into Elizabethan poetry. As though her life depended on it, said Charles/Karl. It does, said Elsie. She read Matthew Arnold and George Eliot, *A Modern Utopia* and *News from Nowhere,* Morris's poems and Edward Carpenter. She wrote down what she liked and disliked about her reading in an exercise book she did not show to Charles/Karl.

There was supposed to be no sex at Fabian camps. There was companionship, and purpose, and a clean mind in a clean body. Elsie asked questions, and questioned the answers she got. When she arrived, her accent was defiantly midlands. In fact she could, if she chose, neutralise it to a flat, nondescript intonation. Charles/Karl watched her engage battle and make friendships with a teacherly pleasure. There was also sex. Charles/Karl knew, he thought, that Elsie "liked" him. They had private jokes. They were at ease with each other. Too much, Charles/Karl thought. Much depended on the weather. On one of the sunnier days they took a walk together, and sat down on a hummock nibbled by sheep. I should like to kiss you, said Charles/Karl.

"And then what?" said Elsie, moving neither closer nor further, lying at his side and examining the earth.

"Well, and then we might find out."

"Find out what?" said Elsie steadfastly.

"Hurting you, in any way, is the worst thing I can think of."

"And losing my independence is my worst."

"You can give me an independent kiss."

"Can I? I don't think so. One thing leads to another."

"You can't say," said Charles/Karl, daring greatly, "that you haven't been led before. You know about it. I don't."

Elsie frowned. "You haven't met a real snake in human form, I don't think. A bird-charming snake with cold eyes and a *will*."

"I have a will. But I don't want to hurt you—"

"There's a lot of things you don't want to do, as well as that. Another thing I don't want, is not to be friends with you. It means a lot to me."

Charles reached for her hand. She let him. He moved his face towards hers, and she closed her eyes. And then snapped her lips shut and turned away.

At the end of the camp, Charles/Karl and Elsie set off a day early, missing a talk by Herbert Methley on "Art and Freedom, Social and Personal." Elsie said she didn't want to hear him, and Charles concurred. "We can change trains," he said, "and look at the countryside." He waited. "All right," said Elsie.

They ended up at a pretty pub in Oxfordshire, with a garden sloping down to a stream, and roses, and pinks, and forget-me-nots. Charles said: "Elsie, you are Mrs. Wellwood."

"No I'm not, and won't be. But you can say so, this once. Just this once. I've thought it out, and I owe you."

"Owe," said Charles. "Damn you. I want you to be happy."

"I'm not ever going to be happy. I've got out of my place, and not into any other. But here we can play-act, if you want, I said we could."

In the bedroom to which they were shown, he thought of kissing her, and thought he would not kiss her, and opened the window on to the lawn so that they could hear the river running. Midges flew in. He closed the window. Elsie, her back rigid, brushed her hair out, and put it up again, her back to Charles/Karl. But she saw him in the mirror, and saw his look of anxiety, and gave him a rueful grin as she stabbed in the last hairpin. He smiled back at the glassy Elsie.

They went down to supper, one behind the other on the shallow steps with their worn carpet. The dining-room had pretty wallpaper and flowery curtains. Elsie sat up straight as a ruler, and clenched her hands in her lap. She chose mushroom soup, and roast leg of lamb with green peas, and plum tart. So did Charles/Karl. He said

"That fellow, Methley, is an ass."

"He doesn't write about the real world, that's for sure." She looked at her plate. "He takes people in, though." She said "Mrs. Methley, she was very good to me, along with Mrs. Oakeshott and Miss Dace. Women who might have been prim and nasty. They saved me, really."

Charles/Karl said "All sorts of things are changing." He wanted to say something personal and reassuring about her past disaster, but did not know what. He saw she knew that. The soup came, and bread, on little plates painted with flying storks and rising storks and feathery reeds. Charles/Karl asked if there was wine, and was brought a short wine-list and ordered a bottle of white Burgundy. Elsie said

"Minton. The storks. My mum—my mother—used to paint the storks. We got one or two seconds. They weren't her favourite. Japanese-style, she said they were, and the storks were for long life. For babies, she said, in England, and she had too many of those." She paused. "She died of white lead. She were an artist, was an artist, if she could have had the opportunity. Philip got it from her. She died o' white lead and too many children. We had a daft song."

"Yes?" said Charles/Karl.

"Seven in a bed and one of 'em dead" said Elsie on a sort of rush. "Philip and me made it up. There was nowhere to—to put me brother when he died, so he had to stay there, wi' all of us coughing and like to go as well."

She said "I'm sorry."

"What for? I want you to talk to me. Tell me things."

"They're not nice things for this good meal on these pretty plates. It brought it back. You've been good to me, like Mrs. Methley and Mrs. Oakeshott. I'm grateful."

"You are saying that," said Charles/Karl, "to emphasise—to act— the class difference between you and me. Which we ought to forget."

"There's real cream in the soup. Just the right amount. That's an art, too. We can't forget the difference."

His mind was full of a picture of seven—dirty—people, crammed coughing into one bed, and one of them dead. He saw Elsie, wielding her soup-spoon, neatly. It was a strong face, indrawn with self-control, alert with curiosity. It was alien, partly because of the class difference, because of what she had lived, and what he had not lived. He said

"I love you, when you look cross like that, and set your shoulders."

The firm face quivered. "Don't make me cry. It would be embarrassing. I should embarrass you."

There was a silence. The lamb came and was eaten, whilst they talked of the summer school lectures and Elsie said Mr. Shaw could imitate anyone's accent and then iron it out. She talked about Shakespeare. She talked about Rosalind and Viola, dressed as men, having to take charge of things, full of hope. She asked Charles/Karl "How did he know?" and said there was no other man who wrote so well about women, so you believed he knew them from inside, so to speak.

"And then, there's Lady Macbeth, who suddenly says she has given suck to a baby. That's the only mention. She don't—doesn't—seem like a woman who has a baby and she only mentions it to say she'd tear it away from its feeding. It's terrifying. He meant it to be."

They analysed Cordelia, and Goneril and Regan, and enjoyed their talk. The plum tart had a delicious custard. Cream, again, said Elsie, good rich cream. Thickened with eggs and cream, not just cornflour.

There was no one in the world whose company gave him such pleasure. But he could not say, he was at ease with her. He could not say, he felt "right" or "at home" with her. He didn't. And then he thought, that was part of it, that drew him to her.

. . .

They went up to the bedroom. Charles/Karl said it was a pity about the midges. Elsie began to take off her clothes, in a practical sort of way, finding coat-hangers, aligning shoes under the bed, as though she was alone in the room. She hung her skirt, and blouse, and went, in her petticoat, to clean her teeth, still looking practical. He loved her muscles, as she bent to untie shoes or stretched to hang her skirt. She brushed her teeth fiercely. She said

"Don't just *stand*."

So he too began to undress, shoes, woollen socks, breeches, jacket. His feet were long and white. They looked unused. He brushed his own teeth. He brushed his hair, for no good reason, and Elsie laughed. So he walked over to her and began to undo her bodice, with slightly tremulous fingers. She put her fingers over his and helped him. All their fingers were electric. She stepped out of her petticoat, and out of her bodice and stood there in her drawers.

"What the butler saw," said Elsie Warren.

Her breasts were carved, like a goddess, he thought, and her nipples were brown, chestnut brown.

She turned, and bent, and lifted the cover, and slid into the bed. The cover was white cotton embroidered with white rosebuds and roses.

Charles/Karl took off both his rational vest and his Jaeger underpants. He thought, this sort of thing happens in most lives and always differently. He felt a little drunk, but was not.

He got into the bed, beside her, and did not know what to do, partly because he did not know what she wanted. Beside him, she slid out of her drawers and moved close to him. She stroked him, and he grabbed at her, and she wriggled and laughed, and took hold of him, and guided him—like *this,* just like *this,* said Elsie Warren. And she took his hand, and guided it down, between the curls and twists of their underhair, and then he, or it, or they knew what to do, and found a rhythm, and he said, on a caught breath, "Oh, are you happy now?" and she said "Yes. More now. Oh yes."

Breakfast was happy and sad. There were already things between them that they were not saying, not discussing, deliberately not thinking. He did not think about seeing that fine face over breakfast for the rest of his life, nor did he think of sleeping nightly with his hand on those carved breasts or between the lean, strong legs. He did say, they could find a place for another night, and she did say "I mustn't stay away from Ann, Ann needs me."

Walking across the gravel path to the cab, after paying the bill, he thought confusedly that he could now never marry, because he could not imagine wanting another woman. He had made decisions that had made . . . muddle . . . for everyone.

48

In 1911 King George V was crowned in Westminster Abbey on June 22nd in the middle of the longest hottest summer the country had known. The King took a measure of 98° Fahrenheit on his greenhouse thermometer. Neo-Pagans slid naked into cool pools in Grantchester, under hanging boughs, and hid giggling in the undergrowth, watching punts pass, full of tourists and dons. The royal yacht *Hohenzollern* carried the Kaiser and his family to the Coronation. Queen Mary wore a hat with cream roses and delicate feathers. In July the Kaiser sent the new German gunboat, *Panther,* to Agadir and was accused by the French and the English of interfering in French colonial affairs.

The Webbs, the driving force of the Fabian Society, had absented themselves from heat, gaiety and tension together, and had parted for Canada on a tour that was to take them a year. Work at the National Committee diminished in intensity. This was partly because the poor, the workers and their dependants, were stirring with discontent, dissatisfaction, determination and even rage, all over the country. There had been miners' strikes and railwaymen's strikes, strikes of woollen and worsted workers in Yorkshire and of cotton spinners in Lancashire, strikes by the Card and Blowing Room Operatives' Association. In that hot summer there was a wave of action beginning with seamen's and firemen's strikes in Poole and Hull two days before the Coronation. Then the dock workers joined the seamen and firemen. Agreements were reached, threats of military action were made, new demands arose amongst the workers. In August, there was a strike of the Transport Workers, who were joined by the lightermen, the stevedores, the carters, the tugboatmen, the crane porters, the coal bunkerers and the sailing bargemen. The Port of London came to a stop. Vegetables rotted and butter went rancid in casks. Frozen meat from Argentina, New Zealand and the USA went foul, green and noisome as the refrigeration ships gave up work, powerless. Starvation threatened. At this point the women of Bermondsey, led by Mary Macarthur, suddenly left their work and ran into the streets, shouting and singing. It was spontaneous: they did not have one overwhelming grievance; they had discovered that their lives were intolerable and the world they lived in unacceptable and unjust.

Commentators saw this human ferment of wrath and energy as an expression of a natural force, like a fire, like a hurricane, or as Mr. Ramsay MacDonald put it mildly, like the stirrings of spring.

"The Labour world responded to the call to strike in the same eager, spontaneous way as nature responds to the call of springtime. One felt as though some magical allurement had seized upon the people." A conservative writer, Fabian Ware, commenting on the new syndicalism in the union members and the socialists, a French import that implied the will to cause a revolution, said that this set of beliefs was "an assertion of instinct against reason."

Ben Tillett, the workers' indefatigable and charismatic leader, wrote

"Class war is the most brutal of wars and the most pitiless. Capitalism is capitalism as a tiger is a tiger and both are savage and pitiless towards the weak."

Charles/Karl, reading Wilfred Trotter on the herd instinct in humans, observed the marching, famished, furious men and their starving families with anxiety, and a feeling of human uselessness. Trotter was interested in groups, in "the aggressive gregariousness of the wolf and the dog, the protective gregariousness of the sheep and the ox, and differing from both these, we have the more complex social structures of the bee and the ant, which we may call socialised gregariousness."

But Trotter believed, and Charles/Karl understood him, that human beings had constructed a social structure no longer directly subject to evolutionary pressures and checks. Man was a creature who made beliefs and myths about the world, and morals, and treated them as *things,* not as words and thoughts:

> We see man today, instead of the frank and courageous recognition of his status, the docile attention to his biological history, the determination to let nothing stand in the way of the security and permanence of his future, which alone can establish the safety and happiness of the race, substituting blind confidence in his destiny, unclouded faith in the essentially respectful attitude of the universe towards his moral code, and a belief, no less firm, that his traditions, laws and institutions necessarily contain permanent qualities of reality. Living as he does in a world where outside his race no allowances are made for infirmity, and where figments, however beautiful, never become facts, it needs but little imagination to see how great are the probabilities that after all man will

prove but one more of Nature's failures, ignominiously to be swept from her work-table to make way for another venture of her tireless curiosity and patience.

Charles/Karl was losing his belief in Beatrice Webb's Individualist State. He found it perilously easy to hate the whole of his own class—his mind was full of visions of over-bred chows and borzois, Cochin fowl with useless feet and nattering voices. He saw the Coronation in Trotterian terms as a confection of human-invented unrealities, a small man in a foolish hat, in a building made to house a non-existent human deity, surrounded by fawning creatures who could barely move in their dragging garments. To believe in the Empire as a truth was to join in the fiction of calling an evolutionary fact—tooth, claw, cringing and triumphalism—by a solemn and poetic name.

And in the East End the crowds marched like one creature, stirring its huge length out of the sloth, or subjection, or lack of knowledge of its own power, that had kept it down.

But there was no place there for him. He couldn't dance, and he couldn't march, or not with any sense of common purpose, and abolishing the Poor Law was not going to undo Trotter's argument.

The Prime Minister, H. H. Asquith, went on August 17th to meet representatives of the railwaymen's unions. He offered them a Royal Commission on their grievances. He spoke from the height of his position. The alternative to the long deliberations of a Royal Commission appeared to be the use of force against the workers. They went away, consulted, and came back. They refused, flatly, to accept the Commission or to return to work. Mr. Asquith was distinctly heard, as he walked out of the room, to say "Then your blood be upon your own head." Winston Churchill despatched troops to stand by for trouble with the miners. Tension and boiling indignation persisted.

In the autumn of 1911 Richard Wagner's *Ring* cycle, in its entirety, was performed at Covent Garden. Bloomsbury had seats, and the Fabian Nursery had seats: Rupert Brooke and James Strachey and the lovely daughters of Sir Sidney Olivier juggled tickets and sat in rows together.

The black elves tapped their hammers in violent rhythms in Nibelheim, one-eyed Wotan and Loge the trickster, the fire god, descended to the underworld and tricked its king out of his gold ring of power, and his helmet of invisibility. Fire rose and shimmered around Brunnhilde the Valkyrie sleeping on her rock, and Brynhild Olivier applauded. Wotan had mutilated the World Ash to make laws and treaties for his dispensation, which, all too human, slowly foundered in its own inanity and inadequate beliefs about good and evil. Human beings were either corrupt, or deluded, or victims, although the Rhine and the music—and indeed the flames of fire—rippled and sang.

Griselda Wellwood went with Julian, Charles/Karl, Wolfgang and Florence. Griselda was interested in what she thought were Wagner's own adaptations of the myths in the Edda and the *Nibelungenlied*. She told Julian that there was no source for the cutting-down of the World Ash to set fire to the World and Valhalla. It was Wagner's own invention, his addition to the story. Julian said the singing made him feel impotent. Charles/Karl, still interested in groups and instinct, said an audience was a different animal from a man reading on his own. An audience—if the work was good—was a creature. Like a dragon, said Griselda. You can lull dragons with music. Julian said a dissatisfied audience was a creature too, its emotions were common, it *worked itself up*. Wolfgang said, be quiet, pay attention, the music begins again. And the dangerous sound hung in tantalising strands, and answered itself, and grew stronger, and wove itself together.

Margot Asquith, the Prime Minister's wife, wrote in her journal in 1906: "I have not one woman friend who knows or cares about politics—they love the *personal* aspect, the prestige, the Cabinet-making." She had written: "Women are d—d stupid really, and only have *instinct,* which after all animals have. They have no size or reason—very little humour, hardly any sense of honour or truth, no sort or sense of proportion, merely blind powers of personal devotion and all the animal qualities of the more heroic sort." She despised and feared the suffrage agitators, who spat at her at the Lord Mayor's Banquet and in 1908 threw stones through her windows in Downing Street, making her fear for her infant son.

"I nearly vomited with terror that he should wake and scream. Why should my life be burdened by these worthless, vicious, cruel women?

They say men would not be so seriously dealt with, what lies they tell! Men would be horsewhipped on every street corner."

She had great faith in her own feminine authority and intuition. In late 1910 she made an appeal to Lloyd George during the election campaign. It was a silly letter, sublimely unaware of its own silliness.

> *I am sure you are as generous as you are impulsive. I am going to make a political appeal to you. I say political against personal for, if you do not respond to my appeal, I shall be very unhappy, but not affronted. Don't when you speak on platforms arouse what is low and sordid and violent in your audience; it hurts those members of it that are fighting these elections with the noblest desire to see fair play; men animated by no desire to punch anyone's head; men of disinterested emotion able to pity and heal their fellow men, whether it be a lord or a sweep. I expect the cool-blooded class hatred shown for some years in the corporate councils of the House of Lords has driven you into saying that lords are high like cheese etc. etc. etc.*
>
> *If your speeches only hurt and alienated lords, it would not perhaps so much matter—but they hurt and offend not only the King and men of high estate, but quite poor men, Liberals of all sorts—they lose us votes . . .*

Lloyd George replied with steel irony

> *. . . I have undertaken in spite of a racking cold to address a dozen meetings before the election is over. If you would only convey to the Whips your emphatic belief that my speeches are doing harm to the cause you will render the party a service and incidentally confer on me a great favour . . .*

In November 1911 Lloyd George mischievously announced that he had torpedoed the Conciliation Bill, which would have given the Vote to a limited number of women. Instead there was to be a Bill on Manhood Suffrage Reform. The women, both the militant suffragettes and the calm and reasonable suffragists, were appalled.

In February Emmeline Pankhurst stated: "The argument of the broken pane of glass is the most valuable argument in politics." Women had discomfited the daily life of the nation, as it had been, with increasing wit and venom. "Votes for Women" was burned into the greens of golf courses and written in scarlet greasepaint on the Prime Minister's blotting pad. Respectable black-garbed ladies, under respectable black hats, produced from comfortable, large, respectable handbags claw hammers and large stones, and walked steadily down the great shopping streets of cities, rhythmically crashing down the plate-glass windows. Miss Christabel Pankhurst, in various disguises, pink straw hat, blue sunglasses, evaded the one hundred hunting detectives to the tune of the "d——d elusive Christabel." She finally slid away to Paris, from where she directed the increasingly extravagant acts of outrage, and took her small, pretty dog for walks in the Park. Her mother was, as she frequently was, suffering in prison.

In March Mr. Asquith, the silver-tongued, spoke in the House about the coal-miners' strike which was paralysing the country. He appealed to the miners and to the members of Parliament. He broke down in tears.

In March, also, Margot Asquith decided to intervene secretly. She wrote to a labour leader who had been invited to luncheon, and proposed a secret meeting. It was a very feminine plea.

The big question I long to ask a man of your ability, sympathy and possibly very painful experience is: What do you want?

I don't, of course, mean for yourself, as I am certain you are as straight as I am, and disinterested. It would be on far higher grounds than this that I would ask it.

Do you want everyone to be equal in their material prosperity? Do you think quality of brain could be made equal if we had equal prosperity?

Do you think in trying or even succeeding in making Human Nature equal in their bank books, they would also be equal in the sight of God and Man?

I am a socialist, possibly not on the same lines as you . . . People who get what they want at the cost of huge suffering to others I would like to understand more perfectly.

Just now I suspend judgement, as I don't really comprehend. I don't care what creed a man holds, but the bed-rock of that creed should be Love, even of your enemies, which is a hard creed to put into practice.

Having suffered greatly yourself, I expect you don't want anyone else to suffer, and this is what makes you a socialist. It is also my point of view,

*but I am only a woman. I don't like to see my husband suffer in his longing
to be fair, just and kind to both sides in this tragic quarrel.*

The letter continues on the same note, which Wilfred Trotter would
have been able to identify as a making of human moral structures into
tangible Things, where they are not. She received no answer. The
strikes went on.

So did the suffrage protests. Miss Emily Davison was arrested in Parliament Street holding a piece of linen, saturated with paraffin, burning
brightly, which she was inserting into the pillar box of the Post Office.
The Prime Minister and a gathering of friends and family, returning
from a Scottish holiday, were jostled at Charing Cross by a crowd of
shouting suffragettes. The party fought back: Violet Asquith "had the
satisfaction of crunching the fingers of one of the hussies." It was Violet, wielding a golf club, who had driven off a group of women
attempting to strip the Prime Minister of his clothes at Lossiemouth
Golf Course. Asquith wrote in a letter that he himself resembled St.
Paul at Ephesus "fighting with beasts—Gorgons and Hydras and Chimaeras dire—as Milton says somewhere."

In April, that year, the City was snared in the invisible strands of the
wireless. There were posters everywhere announcing that the new,
invincible wonder-ship, the *Titanic,* had struck an iceberg in mid-ocean.
The ship sent radio messages to the land, which after a time became confused and fragmentary and then ceased. A rumour began that the passengers were saved and the ship being towed into Halifax. The City
went to bed quite cheerful, and woke to disaster in the morning.
Among the drowned was W. T. Stead, the crusading journalist, who
had so long ago purchased a young girl for sex, and exposed a business
of procuration and abuse.

The Webbs returned from their global journey and took in the changing
world. The Committee for Reform of the Poor Law was wound up, and
replaced by the New Fabian Research Bureau. The Society moved
closer to the Independent Labour Party and campaigned for a national
minimum wage. Ameliorating the condition of the poor was changing
to a syndicalist ideal of revolt.

Individuals were in odd states of mind. Rupert Brooke had taken Ka
Cox to Munich and ended his heterosexual virginity, which he was

convinced was causing a nervous breakdown. They returned—Ka pregnant, nervously exhausted, Rupert on the edge of madness. Madness was cured by a drug to repress sexual desire and by a regime of immobility and "stuffing"—lamb cutlets, beef, bread, potatoes. Rupert wrote wild letters of anti-Semitic nausea to his friends, and told Virginia Woolf, also enduring a breakdown, also being "stuffed," the tale of a Rugby choir where

> *Two fourteen-year-old choirboys arranged a plan during the Choral Service. At the end they skipped round and watched the children enter. They picked out the one whose looks pleased them best, a youth of ten. They waited in seclusion till the end of the Children's Service. They pounced on their victim, as he came out, took him, each by a hand, and led him to the vestry. There while the Service for Men Only proceeded, they removed the lower parts of his clothing and buggered him, turn by turn. His protestations were drowned by the Organ pealing out whatever hymns are suitable to men only. Subsequently they let him go. He has been in bed ever since with a rupture. They were arrested and flung, presumably, into a Reformatory. He may live.*

The tone of this is not quite the insouciant tone of the Bloomsbury/ Apostles school of buggery chatter. And it was written to a woman temporarily mad. To his neo-Pagan friends he was writing diatribes against Lytton Strachey's filth and prurience, not unlike D. H. Lawrence's horror of the same group as black beetles creeping out from under. Brooke knew, almost certainly, that it wasn't funny. What did he think—who did he think—he and it was?

Margot Asquith was one of a social set called the Souls, who were clever with words and sporty with tennis and bicycles. Margot's set liked to be daring and unusual, unconventional and "natural." The children of the Souls, including Margot's stepchildren, Raymond and Violet Asquith, formed what came to be known as the Corrupt Coterie. Raymond was the king of this group, who indulged in "chlorers" and opium, impiety and black humour. Lady Diana Manners said "Our pride was to be unafraid of words, unshocked by drink, and unashamed of decadence and gambling." Diana was, Raymond Asquith said, "an orchid among cowslips, a black tulip in a garden of cucumbers, night-shade in a day nursery." They parodied the charades and theatrical tableaux of their parent Souls (the nomenclature has an odd echo of the private grades of the Cambridge Apostles, or the Munich Cosmic Circle, with their embryos, godfathers and Angels, their Giants and Peripherals). They had a particular game called Breaking the News. It consisted of acting out as comedy the breaking of the news of a child's death, to his mother.

In November 1912 the great "silver scandal" gripped the City and filled the newspapers. Messrs. Simon Montagu & Co. had been secretly purchasing silver for the Indian government as part of its currency reserve. There were accusations of corruption, and smears of anti-Semitism. John Maynard Keynes—who believed in the gradual elimination of the gold standard, and of a tangible currency reserve—published his book, *Indian Currency and Finance,* in June 1913. In November of that year there was a crisis. "The great silver speculation has failed and the Indian Specie Bank is bankrupt. What a tragedy!" wrote Sir Charles Addis, who was instrumental in forming a syndicate of bullion brokers who in December managed to avoid the disaster.

Geraint Fludd had become more and more involved in the currency and bullion work of Wildvogel & Quick. He bought Keynes's book and read it carefully. Basil Wellwood invited the young man to dinner in Rules restaurant one evening and fed him on potted shrimps, venison, Stilton and syllabub, with a bottle of very good claret. It had never been clear to Basil exactly what had happened to Geraint's "engagement" to Florence Cain, who was now Mrs. Goldwasser. He had noticed a difference in Geraint—a grimmer determination about his work, an unsmiling propriety. At the end of the dinner he said

"I wanted to tell you how much I admire the resolution with which you have worked over the past year or two. I think you have had setbacks to contend with, and have contended with them."

Geraint said that that was so. He observed that if things could not be mended they should be set aside in the mind, but that that could be hard.

Basil said that he had come to feel that Geraint was in many ways another son to him. His own son made no pretence of being interested in the drama and life of the City. In that sense, Geraint was his spiritual heir—a spiritual heir of material things. He wanted to advance him as best he could, as fast as he could. He had been very impressed with his work on the Indian silver crisis. What would Geraint feel about being sent out there, next year, to take a good look at the Bank's business in that country?

They raised their glasses. The room smelt of wine and bread and gravy, and the light was rich and dim.

Geraint didn't answer.

"I thought a change of scene . . ." said Basil. "A long voyage on an ocean liner. Full of hopeful beautiful women," he added, daring.

Geraint read Kipling. He thought of the mystery of India, the jungle, the light, the colours, the creatures. The complexities of the silver dealings. The distance. He was, he saw, in need of distance. And his imagination touched on the beautiful young women sailing across dark starlit oceans in search of husbands. A journey like that made you free, made you a different man.

"I should like that, sir," he said. "You have been very kind to me."

Basil said "It was a fortunate day for me when you came into the Bank. You are too young to be fixed by one setback. You have all your life in front of you. The world in front of you."

Geraint set his hurt against the pull of the oceans and the strange continent. He could feel his own energy stirring.

"I know," he said. "You are right. Thank you."

49

On Derby Day, June 4th, 1913, Herbert "Diamond" Jones rode the King's horse, Anmer, in his silks with the royal colours. He was a national hero. The huge crowds applauded him. Emily Wilding Davison, wearing a tweed suit, high-collared blouse and unobtrusive hat stood by the rails at Tattenham Corner, where the horses wheeled round, flashing colours against the sky. Inside her sleeve was a flag with the suffragette tricolour, purple, white and green, and another was wrapped round her waist. When the heavy pounding of the hooves was heard, and she saw Anmer leading the galloping herd, she stepped out, in front of the horse, raised her arms, and grabbed at the bridle. They all came down, jockey, horse, screaming woman, on the bloodstained turf. "Diamond" Jones lay still: he was concussed, and his shoulder was hurt. The scene was filmed: Davison can be seen, crumpled and dragged, like a damaged puppet, her skirts awry. Her head was smashed. They wrapped it in a newspaper. She was taken to Epsom Hospital, where her fellows hung her bed like a bier with purple, white and green bunting. She died four days later.

The fallen horse had risen, and cantered away. King George wrote in his diary "Poor Herbert Jones and Anmer were sent flying. It was a most disappointing day."

Queen Mary sent Jones a telegram, commiserating with him after his "sad accident caused through the abominable conduct of a brutal, lunatic woman."

Jones said, much later, that he was "haunted by that woman's face." He had little success on the racecourse after this event.

Emily Davison was buried with ceremony by the WSPU. There were ten brass bands and six thousand marching women. They carried purple silk banners embroidered with Joan of Arc's last words: "Fight on, and God will give the Victory." Davison's flag, stained with grass, mud and blood, was retrieved and became a relic. Some men, and some women, threw bricks at the coffin. Hedda Wellwood, who had sat up late at night embroidering and hemming the banners, marched with the women, and turned a white face, full of contempt, towards the hecklers. Her feet kept time, the music held the women together, they were a creature with a purpose.

The group held her: the strangeness of all this wild, inventive, dangerous activity by creatures who were expected to be docile, timid, domestic and loving. Hedda as a child had been a rebel. She had stood outside groups—the Wellwood family, girls at school, Fabians. She subverted structures, she found out awkward truths. She could not find a purpose. And then she found it in a community of rebels, an army with a cause, and a programme of destruction. She enjoyed marching, hip to hip, skirt to skirt, shoulder to shoulder with women who had subdued their own needs and movements to a larger cause. Group life held and perturbed her, for she was naturally claustrophobic. Every now and then she thought they would crowd and crush her, like the Red and White Queens and the flying jury in *Alice*.

An army needs a general, as well as a martyr. Emmeline Pankhurst was now fragile with suffering through hunger-strikes and force-feedings. When the campaign of increasing violence induced the press to report that she was a wicked old woman, she replied "We do not intend you should be pleased." Yet the army was increasingly, and paradoxically, directed by pretty Christabel, tending her pretty dog in her pretty apartment in Paris, arguing that a leader must remain safe, and out of custody, to plan strategy. Like many absolute leaders, she quarrelled with people, with the Pethick-Lawrences, Frederick and Emmeline, who had paid, planned and suffered for the women's cause, with her sister Sylvia, who lived amongst the poor, in the East End, and upheld her socialist principles, whilst Christabel courted the rich, the Tories, the coteries of the famous and "influential." She issued diktats. On Bastille Day in 1912, Emmeline's birthday, Sylvia had organised a spectacular display in Hyde Park, caps, banners, smaller flags, all decorated with scarlet dragons and decked with white fringe. It was a huge success.

Christabel telegraphed from Paris. Sylvia was to burn down Nottingham Castle.

She refused. She didn't believe in burning things down, or destroying works of art.

But there were those who did.

They wrote each other coded telegrams. "Fluff, feathers, wax, tar violets poppies powder." They bought and secreted cans of paraffin and petrol. They put cayenne pepper and molten lead through letter-boxes. They grew braver and wilder as 1913 became 1914. In the first seven months of that year 107 buildings were set on fire. They burned castles in

Scotland and set about the inherited culture of solid Britain. In 1913 they ripped valuable paintings in Manchester and smashed the orchid hot-house in Kew Gardens. They blew up Lloyd George's new house at Walton-on-the-Hill. They cut telephone wires and slid pebbles into rail-way connections, to derail trains. They showed less and less reverence—ancient churches were burned down, mediaeval Bibles mutilated, the Carnegie Library in Birmingham burned. Like the anarchists before them, they exploded a bomb in Westminster Abbey and flooded the great organ in the august Albert Hall. They themselves were bashed, bullied, defrocked by police and angry crowds. Their breasts were twisted, their hair torn out. They interrupted King and Prime Minister with determined harangues and the suffragette anthem, which was sung to the tune of the Marseillaise. Mary Richardson set out methodically to mutilate Velasquez's self-regarding, elegantly fleshly Venus, a painting she disliked. She waited until the watching detectives took a lunch-break (one was merely hiding his eyes behind a newspaper) and rushed at the painted woman, and her protective glass, with an axe. She got in one blow. The detective looked instinctively at the skylight. The attendant skidded on the polished floor. Four more blows were struck. German tourists helped to bring Miss Richardson down, by aiming Baedekers accurately at the back of her neck. And then she was back in Holloway prison, facing force-feeding.

These stories were circulated, in shocked whispers, with wild laughter. Emily Davison's sacrifice seemed to mean that all women were called to act. The idea of "doing something" crept insidiously into Hedda's mind. Sewing was not enough, marching was not enough, posting pepper and glue through respectable doors, or spreading tin-tacks on office floors, was not enough. An act was required.

The problem was, she was afraid. At first, the problem was to think of an appropriate act, and then, one day, when there was discussion of Emily Davison's life, the act rose in her brain, golden and gleaming, quite literally, in the dark.

Emily Davison—whose speeches had been long and rambling, whose presence had often been creepy and irritating—had become sainted. She had once had the very clever idea of hiding at night in the

House of Commons, and springing out—on the day of the census—to claim that Place as her address. She had been found in the broom-cupboard by a kindly cleaner, and given tea and toast and sent out to make her way to her real home. She had found other ways of making sure of prison. In prison she had leaped like an acrobat from a balcony, to what would have been certain death, if she had not been saved by wire netting. Carried upstairs, she had leaped again. And again, dashing herself on the iron staircase.

There were tales of suffering in cages, of force-feeding that amounted to torture—wooden gags between the teeth, or metal clamps, breaking them, the terrible tube forced in, whilst the warders held the struggling woman, by the ears, by the breast, by the hair, by the hands and legs. And the snaking pipe might miss the surging target, might enter the lung, might rupture the bowel—all this was known, and recounted, the tales of the heroines, women who went into their captivity looking forty and came out looking seventy. Sylvia Pankhurst had refused to eat or to drink, and had been hosed with water and fed with the foul tube. She had walked. All day and all night and all day and all night. Her eyes, Hedda had been told, had become suffused with blood, entirely. Her legs had swollen to bolsters. At night Hedda dreamed of this gaunt red-eyed figure, walking, walking, and woke up in a sweat.

Because she knew what she had to do, she also knew that she had to do it, or it would not have come to her. It came out of the true tale she had been told as a child, of the boy who had hidden in the basement in South Kensington—a tale told by Tom, and by Philip himself, of the way in through the van-loading bay, and the watching plaster casts, and the tombs. A woman could hide down there, and come out with stones, when all was quiet, and smash the cases with the cold gold and silver, and smash the metals to chips and dust.

She didn't have real friends. It must be done on her own.

There was no real need to smash anything.

There was an imperative call.

It was May 1914. She had sharp stones. She had gone on flint-collecting picnics with other WSPU women. Out of rage with her past life, which would now end, and the dreamy, comfortable, unsatisfactory muddled order of Todefright, she quite deliberately took a collection of stones—some of them rare, some of them collected from the endless shingle at Dungeness—old flints and chalk from the Weald (including one or two Stone Age knapped hammers), a chunk of Etna pumice (too light and springy to do any damage), a rugged chunk of the White Cliffs of Dover. These stones were in a big, stoneware bowl Philip Warren had made, which stood in Olive's study in lieu of a bowl of fruit. In amongst them—put there apparently casually, to get lost amongst its semblances—was the Dungeness stone with a hole that had been found in Tom's overcoat pocket on the beach. She took it deliberately, knowing that to take it would hurt Olive, and half-understanding that Tom had meant to—be revenged on Olive, evade Olive, free himself from Olive and being written about? Olive had been mildly in favour of the suffrage, as part of the atmosphere of Fabian lawns and Fabian firesides; she had not approved of the violent acts. She would take Olive's stone with the hole and throw it at the golden bowl.

She did nothing more, for days. She was afraid. She did not know how *afraid* other suffragists had been. Her teeth ached with fear and she dreamed that they all fell out and stuck in her breakfast porridge, like bloody pebbles. She waited for a sign and knew she had it when she read that Sylvia Pankhurst had drawn, on a prison slate, an illustration to

> Awake! for Morning in the Bowl of Night
> Has flung the Stone that puts the Stars to Flight.

She wasn't well. When she breathed out, she could smell her breath. She knotted her hair grimly, packed her bag, which looked like an artist's bag, and set off.

The way in was as Philip had described it, still accessible as it had been before Sir Aston Webb's lovely new curves and clinical new spaces had been opened. She slid in behind two men wholly preoccupied by a heavy crate, straw-stuffed and unwieldy. She passed like a black spectre behind a white forest of plaster casts. She went on, and in, past tomb-rails and brass fenders and suddenly came on the Russian tomb where Philip had slept on the empty plinth, under the doves and acanthus leaves. Here she stopped and rearranged her possessions, the bag full of stones, the packet of buns. When Philip had hidden there, there was no electric lighting. Now, as the light died in the roundels of windows, she saw switches and systems of wires. She sat in the twilight, and then in the dark, letting her eyes grow used to it. She had bound her hair in a dark scarf. She looked around for the staircase with the iron rail, and did not see it. She waited. Night and silence spread. Cautiously she switched on a light and hid behind the tomb. Nothing stirred. The light, under a green shade, illuminated the white-tiled Gothic vaults. She needed a thread: she was lost in the labyrinth. She scuttled out of hiding, moving bent and hunched along corridors. She found the stone staircase and went up. At this point, she realised she had been idiotic. The door into the gallery was locked. Philip Warren had found and kept a key. She had not even thought about a key. She was like Alice for ever shut out of the garden, peering through the keyhole.

Because the act required her to *do* it, she looked around, seeking out the answer there *must be*. And there was. There was a panel on the wall of the tunnel at the foot of the stairs, with a whole jumble of keys and screwdrivers hanging on tarred string and hairy string, all lengths. They were not labelled. She tried one and then another and saw she needed a longer and larger one. She found it. The door ground open.

And there in the moonlight were the cases of gold and silver, gleaming and glinting. Hedda went up to them. There was the reliquary, there was the Gloucester Candlestick. There was no sign of any guardian of the treasure.

If the breaking of the glass was not too loud a crash, she would have time to wreak real damage on the things. She was sweating. She was cold. She took off her coat, and wrapped a large sharp flint in it, and swung, cautiously. The glass held. Hedda was filled with hatred, and swung with all her strength. The sides of the glass coffin splintered and fell in. The blow was muffled but the shards rang out on the tiled floor.

She took one of the Dungeness stones and brought it down on a little chalice, which was scraped, but held its form. Hedda was still alone in the high hall. She bashed a delicate spoon, silently enough, on a velvet mat which masked the noise. She turned her attention to the Candlestick.

There it stood, unique, mysterious, with its writhing, energetic dragons and imps and foliage and helmeted warriors. She was feeling very odd. She remembered Tom, reading Tennyson aloud, in the Tree House. This thing was like the gate of Camelot.

> The dragon-boughts and elvish emblemings
> Began to move, seethe, twine and curl: they called
> To Gareth "Lord, the gateway is alive."

And Hedda did see shape-shifting, climbing, flickering movement on the object. She must destroy it. Instead, foolishly, she launched Tom's hole in a stone at it. That glanced off a beast which was being slaughtered by a gnome with a knife. Hedda sank to her knees, as the warders came rumbling and creaking, and pulled her up, not too gently.

She was shut up in a police station, and put on trial. She knew she exuded a stink of fear and stood upright in the dock, whilst tremors ran up and down her body as though she was giving birth to something. Some of the WSPU had come to support her, and their expectation of fearlessness was part of her torture. She had not asked to see her family. She was condemned to a year's penal servitude for damaging government property and taken to Holloway Prison.

In the cell was a Bible, and a book called *The Home Beautiful*. This caused her brief amusement. She had had a hot bath, which she needed, and had been given some worn, ill-fitting clothes, which she also needed, for her own were drenched by her body's terror.

She knew she must refuse to eat. She did not know if she had the courage to refuse to drink. She began to walk. Backwards and forwards, backwards and forwards. The walls closed in on her and she began to sob, and went on walking. She decided she would refuse to drink, thinking confusedly that in that way she might die, which she appeared to want to do. She walked. She walked. She fell and picked herself up again.

They brought her, as they brought all the hunger-strikers, a tray with a little jar of Brand's Essence of jellied beef, an apple, some fresh bread and butter, a glass of milk. She did not touch it. She walked.

. . .

They brought the tubes, the gags, the clotted fluid (Sanatogen, from Germany). She did not fight, because she was shaking too much, but subsequently vomited over a wardress, and was slapped like a baby, for dirtiness.

Once, which was the worst thing, she started thinking of the little jar of beef jelly as though it had the authority of the act she had performed. She *must* have the beef jelly. She must not. She must. She walked. To and fro, and then stopped and took up the spoon.

The taste was intense, through her furred tongue. She gulped down the whole jar, spoon after spoon. A woman came in and said—with what Hedda felt was contempt—"That will set you up a bit, that's the first sensible thing I've seen you do."

Hedda wept, retched and vomited, and was slapped. She knew now that she had disgraced herself and could not break her fast. She walked, the foul stuff was poured into her, she vomited, she walked. If you hold the funnel too high or too low the food is suffocatingly painful as it finds its way to places where it is not meant to go.

They let her out, in July, under the Cat and Mouse Act, to make herself well enough to be reimprisoned without danger of death.

There was a group of women, waiting for her. A group of suffragists who knew all about cleaning, and resting, and slowly feeding the recuperating martyrs. And her sister Dr. Dorothy Wellwood, who tried not to show her shock at Hedda's cracking lips, blood-suffused eyes, sharp bones almost breaking the skin.

"You nearly killed yourself," said Dorothy. "We must get you well."

Hedda was muttering about beef jelly. Would she like some, said Dorothy. Hedda wept. She said Dorothy didn't understand. "I messed it up."

"Only if you die. And I'll see you don't."

IV
❧ THE AGE OF LEAD

50

In May 1914 Diaghilev brought the Russian Ballet with music by Richard Strauss for a triumphant season in Drury Lane. They played *Ivan the Terrible* and Strauss's *Joseph*. Rupert Brooke went to see them; Bloomsbury was there; Anselm Stern and his sons went with August Steyning. On July 25th the last performance staged both *Joseph* and *Petrouchka,* ending with the pathetic death of the living puppet. That evening the Austrian Ambassador rejected the Serbian reply to his ultimatum, and left for home. The Sterns also went home. It was prudent, Anselm said. There was conflict in the air.

On July 31st Germany sent an ultimatum to Russia, and declared *Kriegsgefahr,* danger of war, and began to mobilise its men. The socialist world rallied round Jean Jaurès, who was still hoping for a general rising of workingmen against war. That evening, as he dined in the Café Croissant in Montmartre, he was shot with a pistol, by a young man who had been following him for a day. He died in five minutes. On August 1st, as his death was reported, the French army mobilised.

The City of London, troubled by dangers to the gold market, sent a deputation to Lloyd George, to say that "the financial and trading interests in the City of London" were "wholly opposed to intervening in the War." Nobody expected war. Nobody was prepared for it. The financiers had believed that they lived in a world of financial and economic forces, so constructed that political forces were subjugated to the economic structures of prosperity and growth. Lloyd George remarked that "Financiers in a fright do not make a heroic picture. One must make allowances, however, for men who were millionaires with an assured credit which seemed as firm as the globe it girdled, and who suddenly found their futures scattered by a bomb hurled at random from a reckless hand." The *Economist* advocated strict neutrality. The quarrel on the continent "was no more our concern than would be a quarrel between Argentina and Brazil or between China and Japan."

Saki, who had written so many stories of feral and irresponsible children mocking the respectable in English gardens, woods, and pigsties, had published *When William Came*—a grimly satirical tale of English society adapting very well to Hohenzollern rule. The story culminated with a planned ceremonial march of Boy Scouts past the German Emperor and the monument to his grandmother in front of Buckingham Palace. The Emperor waited. And waited. And no marching children appeared under the flapping flags in the Mall. English boys had cared for England's honour. The wild children had a mind of their own.

Colonel-General von Moltke was Chief of the General Staff of the Field Army of the German Empire. He had tried to refuse this position; he was sixty-six; he was, he thought, unlike his great uncle, too cautious, too reflective, too scrupulous, to make rapid decisions on which millions of lives and the fate of his country depended. The Kaiser had overruled his wishes. He would follow his uncle. He would direct the elaborate Schlieffen Plan, which required the German armies to march into Luxembourg and Belgium and seize their railways, in order to sweep round from the north and encircle Paris from the west. He did as he must and deployed his troops and trains.

On August 1st 1914 he was called suddenly to a war conference in the Berliner Schloss, with the Kaiser, generals, ministers. These men were jubilant. The Kaiser ordered celebratory champagne. Von Moltke was told that Sir Edward Grey had promised the German Ambassador in London that Great Britain would guarantee that France would not enter the war against Germany if Germany promised not to attack France. The Kaiser, full of delight and relief, told von Moltke that now they need only fight Russia. The armies could now advance to the East.

Von Moltke tried to explain that a million men, eleven thousand trains, tons of ammunition, guns, supplies, were already deployed, travelling west; patrols were already in Luxembourg; a division was behind them. The Kaiser rebuked him, telling him, with childish petulance, that his great-uncle would have given a different answer. Von Moltke could "use some other railway instead."

Von Moltke was humiliated. He recorded that, as he realised the ignorance and light-headedness of his leader, the childish failure to imagine the world as it was, something inside him snapped. "I never recovered from that incident," he wrote. "I was never the same again."

Time was lost: the Kaiser countermanded orders; von Moltke sat in despair in his office and refused to sign the new ones. Then at eleven in the evening, he was recalled, to the Kaiser's private apartments, where the head of state was half undressed, with a mantle thrown over his withered arm. He handed von Moltke a telegram from George V. The German Ambassador had been mistaken. Britain did not guarantee French neutrality.

"Now you can do what you like," the Kaiser told his commander.

And the armies marched.

51

Some of them joined up immediately. Julian joined his father's regiment and was sent to Officers' Training Camp in Suffolk. He was good with guns and rode well. The sun shone. He made friends with another Cambridge man. He felt fierce because what was being attacked was the English pastoral he was studying—the woods and fields, the wild things, the cows, the sheep, the shepherds to a certain extent, the gathering in of the harvest. They said it would all be done by Christmas. His temperament was ironic; he believed in duty but not in glory and thought he must go steadily on to the promised end. He liked his men: it was necessary to like them, and he really liked them. He noticed when they were anxious and told them when they did well. In 1915 he embarked for France.

Geraint went back to Lydd, and trained as a gunner in the camp on the shingle that he knew so well. He enlisted as a private, and then became a bombadier. He kept the little ring he had given Florence in the pocket of his tunic. He thought: when this is over, everything will be different, including me. The ocean voyage under the stars vanished like a mirage. Like Julian, in those early days, he seemed to see everything more clearly because it had all been called in question. He made drinking-friends in his platoon, one of whom had been an acquaintance when he was a boy running wild on Romney Marsh, a fishmonger's son called Sammy Till. In 1915 he crossed the Channel and went north-west, towards Belgium.

Florian and Robin Wellwood and Robin Oakeshott all joined the Royal Sussex Regiment. Florian was sent to France fairly quickly. The two Robins found themselves in the same platoon. They sat together amongst their gear in a shared tent. They had been together, or almost, at things like the drama camp when they were boys. They had the same red hair and the same smile. They did not know, being well brought-up, how to broach the subject of whether they were brothers.

Robin Wellwood thought it would be insulting and hurtful to Robin Oakeshott to suggest that his Oakeshott father was a fiction. Robin Oakeshott thought he might embarrass Robin Wellwood by claiming the relationship which was never mentioned. Both of them shied away in their minds from the role Humphry Wellwood must have played in their origins. No one likes to think of their parents and sex, even in quite normal situations. But they stuck together, and did things the same way, and came to rely on each other.

Wolfgang Stern was already on the battlefield, in the German Sixth Army, under Prince Rupprecht of Bavaria. He was on the left of the Schlieffen scythe, retreating deliberately towards Germany to draw the French army outwards, away from Paris. The French soldiers wore a uniform from the past, with red trousers, a long great-coat, broadcloth tunic, flannel shirt and long underpants, winter and summer. Their boots were known as *brodequins,* which was the name of an instrument of torture. They carried a rifle, a kit weighing sixty-six pounds and a regulation bundle of kindling wood.

The French officers believed in attack, and then attack, and then again attack. They believed they had been defeated in 1870 because of a lack of firmness and *élan.* They charged, heavily, drums beating, bugles sounding, their long bayonets held in their guns before them. They were very brave, and the German machine-gunners, including Wolfgang, mowed them like fields of grass. Wolfgang felt alien to himself, in his grey tunic and forage cap. But then, he had always been an actor. Now, he was acting a very competent machine-gunner. He was well fed and his commanders planned intelligently. The war would not last long. The Plan was working to perfection.

Charles/Karl, the ex-anarchist, the socialist, the academic student of herd behaviour in war and peace, found that his intuition when faced with anarchist "deeds" of assassination, that he himself could not kill a man, was just. He went to tell his father that he was joining up. Basil Wellwood said he was glad, and sorry of course, and would give any help he could. Charles/Karl said he was not joining the armed forces: he was joining a Quaker enterprise called the Anglo-Belgian Ambulance

Unit. These people provided stretcher-bearers to bring in the wounded and ambulances to take them to the hospital trains to bring them home. He said "It isn't a lack of courage, Papa. And I do feel that I must *do something* in all this. And the ambulance units help everyone, they don't discriminate . . ."

Basil answered the unspoken thing.

"Some of your mother's friends are refusing invitations. They don't call on her. Many of them don't."

"That would be better if I was a patriotic soldier. But I can't, you do see?"

"I try to see. You don't lack courage. You have my blessing."

Charles/Karl gave him an envelope, marked "To be opened in the event of my death."

"I'm not being dramatic, I'm being practical. And you must promise not to open it before . . ."

"Very well. I hope to hand it back to you very soon. All this should not last very long. Go safely."

Dorothy too had managed to join a new kind of unit, the Women's Hospital Corps. This was the work of two resourceful women doctors, Louisa Garrett Anderson and Flora Murray. Unlike the Scottish women doctors who had been told to go "home," they had quickly worked out that the War Office would simply turn them away. Both were suffragists and both had had long contentious dealings with the Home Office. So they approached the French Embassy, and the French Red Cross, and offered their skills, and medical supplies which would be paid for by their supporters. Money poured in, from suffragists and women's colleges. A uniform was devised, for doctors, nurses, orderlies and managers. It was greenish-grey, short-skirted, with a neat loose long tunic, buttoned high. There were small cloth hats, with veils and overcoats. The women looked smart and purposeful. They had learnt that women must do everything more competently, more carefully, with more unrelenting discipline than men. In September 1914 they went from Victoria and Dieppe to Paris, which was full of wounded men. "An excitable British Red Cross lady," said Flora Murray, "explained that nothing was any good here. The red tape was awful—all the arrangements had broken down. The sepsis was appalling. The town was full of Germans whose legs and arms had been cut off and who were being sent to Havre next day like that!!"

Griselda Wellwood was with them. Newnham College was supporting the doctors. Griselda—after a brief training as a VAD in Cambridge—went with them as a kind of liaison officer provided by the College, someone who spoke fluent French and German, and could help out with patients and authorities. Nurses with next to no French were asking wounded soldiers *"Monsieur, avec-vous de pain in l'estomac?"* Griselda helped both patients and nurses.

A hospital was set up in Claridge's Hotel, in Paris, allotted by the French. Rooms were cleared, wards were set up, sterilising equipment and an operating theatre were installed and wounded men came in, steadily, French, British, German, to be nursed, to be operated on, to be protected, by severe Sisters, from curious flocks of visiting elegant ladies. To die. There was a quiet mortuary, in the basement. The surgeons amongst them had previously operated almost exclusively on women. They learned quickly.

Dorothy became skilled at amputations. Griselda made herself useful when, at Christmas, there were parties, and entertainments. The men put up a Union Jack with the legend: "The Flag of Freedom." The suffragists were not amused. The men became aware of this and the flag was changed. "Freedom" became "England" and the doctors were told that the men were "all for Votes for Women."

They put on plays. Wounded, shell-shocked, bandaged, tremulous, they put on plays. Some were farces and some were not. *The Deserter* was a precise representation of the court martial of a deserter, with bullying sergeant-major, bounding lieutenant, relentless judge-advocate. The accused was the hero, and died courageously, on stage, in front of the firing-squad.

The wounded men applauded, from beds and wheelchairs. Dorothy touched Griselda's arm.

"Are you all right? You don't look well."

"It's the execution. I have a horror of executions. They did it so *matter-of-fact*. But their sympathy was with—with him."

Dorothy said, quietly and grimly, that if what they had seen, and what they had been told, was a true description of events out at the Front, most men would be driven to desert. She said "They said it would be over by Christmas. It isn't. They don't know now how or when it will end. I'm glad you're here."

Griselda said "What do you think made them put it on? Does play-acting help them look it in the face? Or cut it down to size? It is *gruesome*."

"We can't afford to think about what is gruesome. You take a temporary bandage off a wound, and what is under it is gruesome and there is nothing you can do. They mostly know, not always. You know, Grisel, I am simply not the same person I was last year. She doesn't exist."

"I'm glad we are with the women. They are so intent on—on managing perfectly—that they just go on. Most of us, most of the time."

"It's early days," said Dorothy.

52

Philip Warren was still in Purchase House. The gardener and the handy-man had gone to the war, and there were weeds in the drive and the grass was wild in the orchard. Seraphita sat in semi-darkness, semi-conscious, and waited for the day to end, coming briefly to life in the early evening, when safe sleep was on the horizon. Pomona had sur-prised both of them by going into Rye and volunteering to become a nurse. She was in a hospital in Hythe, changing dressings, emptying bedpans, smoothing sheets, which she did well. She turned out to be good at calming the dying, answering what they said, nonsense, rage, fear, calls for mothers, with a grave, gentle respect that was mostly help-ful. She was good also with the bereaved, or about-to-be bereaved. She slipped dreamily around and yet made things temporarily clean and wholesome. She said to Philip, when she came home for a day, and lay, physically exhausted, in the orchard wilderness, that she felt useful, and needed, for the first time in her life.

"It's unbelievably disgusting and when you can *do* it you feel—oh, I expect, like nuns used to feel, when they deliberately did horrible things. I've got good at knowing which muscles to lift things with."

She hesitated.

"You know, Philip—this house—my funny family—they feel like a dream and I've woken up. No, they feel like two dreams—one full of beautiful things—pots and paintings and tapestries and embroideries, and flowers and apples in the orchard—you know—and one full of interminable boredom and waste, and—things that were *not right* but were all that happened—I know you know. I've stopped asking you to marry me. I've woken up."

Philip thought that among her wounded men she might find some-one to love her. Because she made his bed more comfortable, and cleaned his body.

It was not because of Pomona that Philip decided to volunteer for the army. He thought about it. He looked at his work, at his drawings, at his jars and vessels, shining quietly. He had, over time, found many of Benedict Fludd's secret caches of receipts for glazes, in holes in the wall, interleaved in books, Palissy's memoir, Ruskin's *Modern Painters*. He had mixed them, tried them, varied them, adjusted them. It was long, and slow, work, it was patient and sometimes frustrating, but he was a man who knew something, a man with a craft, a man who had wanted something single-mindedly and had got it. There were not so many men in the world who could say that.

He was thirty-five. He was not an eager boy. He came from a class which was cautious. He knew there was a good chance of his dying, and the pots dying with him.

He went, he thought, because the world had become a world in which his work was no longer possible. This thing had to be shared and sorted out and *finished*. It was something he appeared to have no real choice about being part of. He did not—after all his reflections and searchings—really know why. That was how it was.

He went to see Elsie and Ann.

"I thought you would," said Elsie, when he told her.

"You might go and see Mrs. Fludd, now and then."

"She doesn't know who's there and who isn't. But I will."

Philip's medical was satisfactory. He went to training camp in Lydd, and in the autumn of 1915, went out to Belgium and the battlefield.

In the autumn of 1915 the two Robins were in trenches on what had become a static front line around the Ypres salient. Ypres was shattered; its houses burning, its ancient Cloth Hall in ruins. The grand attempts to advance on the enemy had given way to a life in dugouts and fox-holes. Shells came over, woolly bears and black crumps made craters and changed the earth from minute to minute. Fighting was mostly raids on the enemy trenches, from which many men did not return. They crept and flitted across No Man's Land, and were spotted by machine-guns and picked off. At night in No Man's Land, stretcher-bearers, including Charles/Karl, looked for the living in the sweet stink of the dead, and stumbled amongst severed hands, legs, heads and bloody innards. The living often begged to be put out of their pain, and Charles/Karl for the first time considered killing, and once, as a head with no face screamed weakly at him, did shoot.

The Robins were nimble at raiding and had a good company commander whom they trusted. They sat in the door of the dugout and ate Maconochies, a mixture of tinned meat and vegetables. They scratched; they were infested with lice; everyone was infested with lice. There was a smell of old exploded shells, and a smell of death, and a smell of the unwashed, and a sweet smell of dispersed lethal gas, British gas which had floated back to its source when the wind changed. The Robins opened letters from home, from Marian Oakeshott, and Phyllis, and from Humphry, who sent gossip about Lloyd George and best wishes to Robin Oakeshott, if they were still together. Robin Oakeshott said casually

"He visited us a lot, in Puxty. He used to laugh and laugh with Mother."

Robin Wellwood said "He's a good man, in his way." He added casually "Randy, though."

"I think he was—that is, I think he is—my father," said Robin Oakeshott.

"So do I."

They considered each other, with mutual relief and embarrassment. Robin Wellwood went into the shelter, to fetch cigarettes. There was a singing howl, and a shell exploded in the trench. A splinter of it took off most of Robin Oakeshott's head. Robin Wellwood took one look, and vomited. Men came running, stretcher-bearers, men with a blanket to cover up what they could, men with buckets and mops to cleanse the dugout. Robin Wellwood sat and shook. And shook.

He developed a permanent tremor down the right side of his face, in his neck, along his arm. His hand shook as he cleaned his gun. The commanding officer considered sending him back behind the line, to recover. Robin said tersely, in an unrecognisable voice, out of a constricted throat, that he was fine, thank you.

Two days later he stood up, in his new-fangled tin hat, which like most of the men he wore at odd angles, on the back of his head, like a halo. He was not the first, or the last, to be killed by the very skilful German sniper behind the stump of a ruined tree.

Later in the war, it was decided that brothers should not serve together, just as all the men of one village should not serve together.

Marian Oakeshott came again—by train and fly, this time—to see Olive Wellwood. Olive made tea. Tea for survivors who were not surviving well. Both of them thought, but neither of them could say, that grief felt different when it had to be shared not only with each other, but with mothers all over Britain. Marian Oakeshott had gone to see Frank Mallett, with the telegram in her hand. "The English don't howl," she said to Frank Mallett. "Maybe they should," said Frank Mallett. So Marian Oakeshott cried out, at the top of her voice "My son, my son, my son," and the church echoed it. Then, a little rigid, she went back to being a kindly schoolmistress. She went to visit Olive, but hoped to see Humphry. Humphry was shut in his study. Olive said "My letter says he was killed instantly."

"So does mine. So do they all."

And indeed, their letters turned out to be identical, with the same phrases of admiration, affection, for their boy, of sorrow and regret for his death.

"Go and talk to him," Olive said to Marian.

Marian stood outside the study door. From inside came sounds of sobbing. Marian tried the door, which was locked.

Harry Wellwood was twenty in 1915. His reaction to Robin's death was to say that he must join up. Olive, who had not wept for Tom, who had not wept for Robin, suddenly began to weep with extraordinary violence. She repeated two words. "No" and "Why?" Over and over. Harry, a gentle creature, scholarly and, since Tom's death, rather silent, said that everyone was joining up, he felt horrid sitting at home. Humphry, who had gathered himself together enough to go back to writing articles on the conduct and misconduct of the war, gave his son some figures. British casualties were so great that it seemed likely that conscription would be introduced, probably early in 1916. Harry would have to go then. He could wait. "Your mother needs you," he said, looking at Olive's wet, mottled red face. Harry did not reply "My country needs me," though the Kitchener posters were everywhere. He said "People look at me. People who have lost their sons. It doesn't feel *right* to stay here and be comfortable." Humphry said almost viciously that winning the war would solve none of the political problems of Europe and thousands and tens of thousands had already given their lives for no advantage. Harry said "There are no men my age in the village or in the town. I need to join." Humphry said "There are no individuals. There

are just herds and flocks. It takes courage not to run with the herd."
Harry smiled icily. "More courage than I've got."

He joined up. In 1916 he was sent, with the fresh conscripts and the
middle-aged reservists, with the British Third Army to the hills and
woods and pretty villages of the Somme. It was calm there. They were
known as the Deathless Army. Harry practised his French, and once, in
Albert, collecting provisions, he ran into Julian Cain, who was in the
trenches opposite Thiepval. He told Julian that the Robins were dead—
"killed instantly, within two days of each other," he said. Julian smiled
benignly. "Keep an eye out, young Hal," he said. He did not say, though
they all knew it, that they were building up to an important attack.
They were constructing railroads and communication trenches, with
good revetments and duckboards to walk on. They were practising
communication by field telephone and signals. They were exercising
their bodies, to make them hard and healthy. They would flow out of
the trenches, over No Man's Land, and take the Germans by surprise,
driving them back, and then there would be real warfare again, with
marching and galloping armies, charges and feints and acts of courage,
the generals believed.

Julian had taken to writing poetry. It was not poetry of despair, nor
yet—not yet—savage poetry of anger. It was not poetry about the glorious hour, the glorious dead, and the high calling, either of perfect gal-
lantry or of bugles and fifes. It was poetry about trench names, which in
themselves were poetry.

Harry's battalion was part of III Corps which, in the small hours of
July 1st got ready to attack. The British bombardment of the German
positions in the villages of Ovillers and La Boisselle had been loud
and heavy. The plan was to make a breakthrough in the German
defences through which the Cavalry would sweep forward. The gun-
ners of III Corps were cautious about their wire-cutting. They could
not cut distant wire, and had not enough ammunition to be sure of cutting what was nearer. Nevertheless, before the attack, the artillery gave
up on the wire, and began shelling more distant Germans, which was
part of their plan to make way for the Cavalry. Nevertheless the

brigades moved forwards. Between the two villages ran Mash Valley, which was No Man's Land. It was wide. It was eighty yards wide. A mine which was intended to bury the Germans in their dugouts and confuse their response to the attack had been discovered by the Germans, and the miners captured.

Harry waited. He was standing next to an old corporal, Corporal Crowe. Harry thought in bursts, and between the bursts was numb and placid, as though nothing was real. He did not think about the King or the Flag though he did briefly think of the quiet North Downs. He thought: I am young and full of life. His teeth chattered. Corporal Crowe patted his shoulder, which he did not like, and said everyone was frit, no exception. Very brave men, he said, had filled their trousers, a miserable thought which had not occurred to Harry and added to his alarm. I am young and full of life. I have a gun and a knife and must fight. Corporal Crowe handed him a water bottle which turned out to be full of rum, and told him to take a swig. Harry didn't like rum. It upset his stomach. But he drank quite a lot, and felt vaguer, and giddier, and sick.

They were told to advance. The German shelling was precise. Hundreds of men died behind their own front line, or struggled back to the medical post. Harry got out of the trench in one piece and so did Corporal Crowe. They started to walk forward towards the black stumps of a wood on the skyline. There was noise. Not only shells and bullets, whistling and exploding, but men screaming. They stumbled over the dead and wounded, over men, and pieces of men, and were reduced to crawling, so mashed and messed was the earth and the flesh mashed into it. After a brief time, Harry felt a thump, and found his tunic damp, and then soaked, with his blood. He tried to crawl on, and could not, and other men crawled past him and sprawled in the mud. He bled. He lay still. He knew in the abstract that stomach wounds were nasty. His head churned. He wished he had not had the rum. He wished he could die quickly. He did not. Men crawled round and over him and he came in and out of consciousness. He noticed when there were no more men, and he noticed nightfall, unless the dark was death. It was not. But he was dead by the time he was found by the stretcher-bearers, so they took his identity-tag, and looked in his bloody pockets for letters or photos—there was a publicity photograph of Olive, looking wise and gentle. Then they left him.

Corporal Crowe made it to the German wire, which was uncut. He was caught up in it, as they shot him, and he hung like a beast on a game-keeper's gibbet and died very slowly. In this attack three thousand men were casualties.

The 2 Middlesex Battalion had 92.5 per cent casualties. On that first day over forty thousand men were killed or wounded. General Haig remarked that this "cannot be considered severe in view of numbers engaged."

The Todefright Wellwoods received another telegram. Humphry said "It is bad news" and Olive said "What do you think I thought it was?" She sat in an armchair and simply stared. Humphry said "My dear?" She simply stared. After a time, she heard Humphry, in his study, weeping. It was a strange, childlike, whimpering sobbing, as though he meant to conceal it. She stood up, heavily, and went, and stroked his hair as he sobbed, with his head on his desk.

"It's like a knife. Cutting the world up, as though it was a cheese. Or butcher's meat, that's a better figure of speech. I do love you, Humph, whatever that means. If it helps. It may not. There isn't much help."

"I love you, too, if it helps."

Tragedy had become so commonplace that it was impolite to mention it, or grieve in the open. Olive had the useless thought that she should have protected them, that she had thought of Tom, and taken her attention from these boys, and lost them.

Julian Cain was in the fighting round Thiepval and Thiepval Wood in July 1916. It was a pretty wood before the battle. It was a hopeless place to attack through and men went wild and mad and were lost there. There was a pretty château, which the shells pounded, and there were trenches whose parapets were reinforced with the deliberately built-in bodies of the dead. Julian was blown backwards by the explosion of a shell and lost consciousness, lost his mind, he thought, when he found himself lying on the earth near a field ambulance and could not remember who he was, or how he had come there. He had a shallow wound across his skull, and scattered shrapnel embedded in his flesh. He said, when they came to dress his wound, "Who am I?" and the orderly went through his pockets and told him he was Lieutenant Julian Cain.

He remembered, for some reason, very clearly, the Wood in *Through the Looking-Glass,* where things have no names, neither trees, nor creatures, nor Alice herself. He lay there, swimming in morphine, and thought about names. The dead who were buried had their names on temporary grave-markers, which were often blown to bits in the endless gunfire. Their name liveth after them for evermore. He had a drugged vision of names, like scurrying rats searching the battlefield for the flesh they had been attached to, like the prophet Ezekiel's valley of bones. You thought a name had a life but men you met in the trenches were not solid enough to have a named life that went before and after in what they had always thought was a normal manner. Men and their names were provisional: he realised he learned their names with a kind of dull grief, because there were already so many he did not need, any longer, to recall, because they could not be recalled, they were spattered and scattered in the churned-up mire that had been green fields and woodland. You could write poems about vanishing names. He did not want to write poems about beauty, or sorrow, or high resolve. He would—if his wits held and he did not stop one—try to write a grim little poem or two about naming parts, and naming the battlefield. Thinking of Alice, some book lover had named trenches for the stories: there were *Walrus Trench, Gimble Trench, Mimsy Trench, Borogrove, Dum and Dee.* There was *Image* wood somewhere. Where had that come from? He had seen *Peter Pan Trench, Hook Copse* and *Wendy Cottage.* They were some other joker's poetry but he could weave them into cat's-cradles of his own, these ephemeral words in a world where nothing held its shape in the blast. You built your hiding-hole out of blocked dead men, and you called it *End Trench,* or *Dead Man's Bottom, Incomplete Trench, Inconsistent Trench, Not Trench, Omit Trench,* or *Hemlock Trench.* The medical orderly came past and said they were taking him to a field hospital. Was he trying to say something, perhaps. Names, said Julian. Names. Names are getting away from things. They don't hold together.

They gave him morphine. He wondered, as he drowned, if there was a morphine trench.

There was so much, so much of what was his life, that he wanted neither to name, nor to remember. Waking, he forced it down. In sleep, it rose, like a floodwave of dead and dying flesh, to suffocate him.

. . .

In the field hospital Julian thought from time to time about the English language. He thought about the songs the men sang, grim and gleeful. We're 'ere because we're 'ere because we're 'ere because we're 'ere.

> Far, far from Wipers I long to be
> Where German snipers can't snipe at me.
> Damp is my dugout
> Cold are my feet
> Waiting for the whizz-bangs
> To send me to sleep.

> I had a comrade
> None better could you find
> The drum called us to battle
> He marched by my side.

Poetry, Julian thought, was something forced out of men by death, or the presence of death, or the fear of death, or the deaths of others.

He started making a list of words that could no longer be used. Honour. Glory. Heritage. Joy.

He asked other men for names of trenches. They came up with *Rats Alley, Income Tax, Dead Cow, Dead Dog, Dead Hun, Carrion Trench, Skull Farm, Paradise Copse, Judas Trench, Iscariot Trench* and many religious trenches: *Paul, Tarsus, Luke, Miracle.* Many trenches were named for London's streets and theatres, and many more for women—*Flirt Trench, Fluffy Trench, Corset Trench.* Julian collected them in a notebook, and started stringing them together, but his head ached. They naturally formed into parodies of jingles

> Numskull, rumskull
> Hear the bullet hum skull
> Now I've got my bum full
> Of shrapnel tiddly um.

That was no good. But in that direction was something that could still be done. Rupert Brooke was gone, dead of an infected spot on his lip, in Greece, a year ago. He had written about Dining-Room Tea and about honey or some such thing in Grantchester, unimaginable now, and about war as a release from the life of half-men and dirty songs and dreary, and fighting as "swimmers into cleanness leaping." These children, Julian thought, had been charmed and bamboozled as though some Pied Piper played his tune and they all followed him, docile, under the earth. The Germans had sunk the liner *Lusitania,* and Charles Frohman, the impresario who had staged *Peter Pan,* had drowned with gallant dignity, apparently reciting the immortal line which had been judiciously cut from wartime performances: "To die will be an awfully big adventure."

Writing about mud and cold and sleet and lice and rats appealed to the real genius of the English language. It would be good to include shit and fuck and words current at schools and repressed in the unimaginable social life of respectable England. Maggot was a good English word. Someone contributed *"Bully craters."*

He recovered, and went back to his regiment. They went to take over the captured Schwaben Redout. Here were the deep German dugouts and the powerful fortifications, Schwaben Redout, Leipzig, Stuff and Goat (Feste Staufen and Feste Zollern) and the Wonder Work, or Wunderwerk, about which poems should be written. Julian went underground, and found, on a lower level, a little door in a wall, which led to dark galleries, packed with boxes of shells and equipment, and beyond that a way to two well-shafts, with windlasses and buckets, whose depths could not be gauged by the eye, and seemed to go down and down interminably. Julian walked through storerooms full of piled bombs and tins of meat, of black and gold helmets and leather mask respirators: he was briefly reminded of the storerooms under the South Kensington Museum, with their order and disorder.

He came to a spacious hole which was lined with gilt-framed mirrors and full of heaps of the thick grey overcoats whose stuffy smell was part of the pervasive smell of these trenches. The mirrors must be booty from the now-crumbled château. There were, in this room, books, stacked in upright crates as a bookcase. Julian took a copy of the Grimms' *Märchen,* for Griselda, who would like to hear that he found it in an underground hall of mirrors. He caught sight of someone else, standing quietly in a corner, a thin, grim-looking, middle-aged man with a scarred face and weary eyes. He raised his hand to greet him, and saw, as the other raised his hand, also, that he had failed to recognise himself. He found another way out, opened the door, and found that it was largely blocked by the bundled body of a very dead and decomposing German. He retreated, and found his way up to the air.

A few days later, he was sent out at night, with a patrol to attack a German strongpoint. As they lay in a crater under a steady thumping of bombs, he felt his leg crack. When he stood up, he could not. His men dragged him, limping and falling, back to another crater, and eventually to their own dugout.

This time he had a "Blighty one." He was invalided back to England, among the walking wounded. The bones in his feet were crushed, which he had not immediately felt, because of the cracking of his tibia. In the end, the British surgeons could not save his foot, and took it off. Months later, he limped into the house in Chelsea, where the two little girls were running to the door, and nearly brought him down. He was rather upset when both Imogen and Florence began to weep wildly. There were delicious smells—toast, roasting coffee, a bowl of lilies, lavender and, as he bent awkwardly to kiss his half-sister and niece, the smell of clean flesh, and washed hair.

He dreamed he was being buried alive in a dugout, and could not free himself from the weight of earth, steadily increasing. He dreamed of things he had packed away and forbidden himself to remember. Florence made him hot apricot tarts and Chinese tea, with jasmine and its own pale, mysterious, clean smell, in Chinese porcelain cups. They sat him in a chair with a footstool to rest his leg, and their eyes were always just brimming over.

Alone of Todefright's bright boys, Florian returned from the fighting. Phyllis prepared his favourite food, herb sausages and mashed potatoes, and a Queen of Puddings. Olive told herself that she must love him, steadily and well, because he was alive, and her sons were not. She faced, she thought, the fact that she might resent the survival of this one who was not her own, and put the idea resolutely away. She had a small glass of whisky before the fly came in from the station.

Florian was walking. His appearance was shocking. He was gaunt, and limped heavily, and his skin was puckered and stained and scarred all over. One of his eyelids drooped. His golden curls, which had been shaved off for the draft, were growing back only sparsely and in tufts, and what there was of them looked ersatz, artificial. Worst of all, he emitted a heavy, painful, wheezing sound, having briefly breathed in blown-back English gas.

Phyllis and Olive made themselves kiss him. He recoiled very slightly. Humphry put a hand on his shoulder, and said "Come in, old chap, you're home."

He had really nothing to say to them. He sat for hours in the window seat, staring out at the garden. Phyllis tried very hard to love him. They were Violet's children, and shared an unspoken anger that Violet's death had been so little marked, had been swallowed up in grief for Tom, as her life had been swallowed up in Olive's. Neither of them was comfortable discussing this. Neither of them had ever discussed feelings. When Phyllis tried—falling awkwardly over whether to say "Violet" or "our mother"—Florian did show signs of feeling. It was an impatient, sullen rage. She made him little presents of cakes and sweet things, which he ate greedily.

In the day he sat and sat. At night he walked. He could be heard, his limping leg thumping, his wheezing a steady, sinister sound, on stairs and in corridors.

Olive woke one night as he passed the door and felt pure hatred. It was like living with a monster, a changeling, a demon. Then she hated herself, worse than she hated him. Then she went to find the whisky, avoiding the returned soldier because it was so easy to hear where he was wandering.

They noticed he was cutting advertisements out of the newspaper. One day he said he had accepted a post as a teaching assistant at Bedales school. He was, he said, with a sad, grim little smile, good at making camps and things like that.

They said they would see him in the holidays, and he said, "Yes, probably."

Phyllis wondered why she didn't go too. She thought, perhaps she would. Perhaps.

From
ROLL CALL AND·OTHER POEMS,

by Julian Cain

THE WOODS

When Alice stepped through liquid glass
The world before her was deployed
In ordered squares of summer grass
And beasts, and flowers, and gnats enjoyed

The power of speech and argument.
Logic is fine-chopped, roses and eggs
Insult each other; legs of lamb resent
Imputed insults. Peppers and salts have legs.

Clouds scud above, and flying queens
Like startled birds, and sleeping kings
Snore unperturbed in serious dreams
Of knights and dinners—serious things

That come and go amongst the roots
Of little lines of sportive wood
Run wild, where no one ever shoots
To kill or maim, and beasts are good.

Alice skips serious from square to square
Hedges and ditches hold their form
And make a chequered order there.
No creature comes to serious harm.

Our English Alice, always calm
Interrogates both gnats and knights,
Reasons away her mild alarm
At bellicose infants and their fights.

The foolish armies do not die
They fall upon their stubborn heads
And struggle up and fall again
And when night comes, rest in their beds.

Reds clash with whites in the great game.
Their fights are dusty but have rules
And always end with cakes and jam
And Providence is kind to fools.

The woods are dangerous. You lose your way.
The sky may darken and the Crow
Make black the treetops, dim the day
Shatter the branches, blow by blow.

Crump of a tea tray, rat tat tat
Of nice new rattle on tin hat
Saucepan and scuttle flat in mud
As fire flings past and black smokes scud

And no shapes hold. I watched a wood
Mix the four elements so air was flame
And earth was liquid: nothing stood
Trees were wild matchsticks, wild fire came and came
Bursting your ears and eyes. And men were mud.
Were severed fingers, bleeding stumps between
The leafless prongs that had been trees. And blood
Seeped up where feet sank. Helplessly we trod
On dying faces, aimlessly we fell
On men atop of men ground into clods
Of flesh and wood and metal. Nothing held.
There was no light, no skyline, up and down
Were all the same. Our lifeblood welled
Out of our mouths and nostrils.

In another wood
Alice walked with a fawn. They had no name.
Nor girl, nor beast, nor growing things. Plants stood

Things flew and rustled. They were all the same.
Quiet was there, indifferent, good,
Stupidly good, like that disguised Snake
In the First Garden, where the First Man named
The creatures, and knew Sin, and was ashamed.
In Thiepval, for a time, and in a space
Extreme of noise made silence. Too much pain
Took pain away. I too was given grace
To know unknowing. I knew not my name
No name of any thing in that dark place.
I stared indifferent at the stumps of wood
And stumps of flesh and metal. All was one.
The man beside me rattled in his blood.
He coughed and died. And I knew I was done.

CALLING NAMES

Little scrubbed boys stand stiff. Their names
Are called. Archer and Bates. Castle and Church.
Adsum they pipe. Adsum. Adsunt. Young Field
Stands next to Devon Minor, Green, and Hill,
Meadows and Nuttall. They smell clean,
Soapy and damp, through ink and chalk and dust,
And polish. Outside English sun
Muffled in English cloud, rests on the panes
Of mud-smeared English windows. So to the end.
Waterstone. Wellwood. Scrape of chairs. They sit.
Scratch with their pens the tale of Agincourt.

The leering lords who promulgate the laws
Of arcane study secrets, call names too.
Answer, what are you? Boy, get your names right
Or you'll be beaten. Say, what are you, boy?
If you don't answer you'll be beaten worse.
A worm, a maggot? Those were last week, boy.
A smell, a scapegoat, a smashed snail, a toad
A broken teacup? Now I'll beat you, boy.

You still know nothing, get it wrong, you cur
You bumboy. Drop your trousers, bend
Over this chair, and whilst I slash the rod,
Say after me I'm null. I'm nothing. I'm
Zilch, nichts, don't wince, but bear it like a man.

And now, in a French field, the bugle sounds.
Shaven and scrubbed and polished, they salute
The First Eleven and the First Fifteen.
Lined neatly up for battle, hear their names,
Answer the roll call. All these were my men.
Smiling gold Fletcher, eager Billy Gunn,
Knight with long shanks and curly-headed Smith
Shone, full of purpose, and marched out to fight.

What are they now? Names on a marble slab
In a school chapel. Names on double disks,*
One red for bleeding flesh, one green for earth
In which the flesh is scattered, smeared and mixed
With other flesh, and lost. Names written out
On telegrams and letters, which strike at
The hearts of waiting women, hearing fists
Knock on the door they daren't unlock but must.

I learned them all with gladness, at the start.
I knew them all, the fearful and the bright
Impulsive boys and canny men I knew
And named and named. My head is packed with names.
Names of dead men. I cannot learn the live
Names that come late, boys to replace the boys
Who marched away.
They come, they go, they smile, they frown. I guard
My mind's door. Today they stand and smile
Numbered and nameless. And they march away.
And I count up more boys and send them on.

---

*These coloured identity disks are worn by the Australian soldiers who fought at Thiepval.

TRENCH NAMES

The column, like a snake, winds through the fields,
Scoring the grass with wheels, with heavy wheels
And hooves, and boots. The grass smiles in the sun
Quite helpless. Orchard and copse are Paradise
Where flowers and fruits grow leisurely, and birds
Rise in the blue, and sing, and sink again
And rest. The woods are ancient. They have names
Thiepval, deep vale, La Boisselle, Aubépines,
Named long ago by dead men. And their sons
Know trees and creatures, earth and sky, the same.
We gouge out tunnels in the sleeping fields.
We turn the clay and slice the turf, and make
A scheme of cross-roads, orderly and mad
Under and through, like moles, like monstrous worms.
Dig out our dens, like cicatrices scored
Into the face of earth. And we give names
To our vast network in the roots, imposed
Imperious, desperate to hide, to hurt.

The sunken roads were numbered at the start.
A chequer board. But men are poets, and names
Are Adam's heritage, and English men
Imposed a ghostly English map on French,
Crushed ruined harvests and polluted streams.

So here run Piccadilly, Regent Street
Oxford Street, Bond Street, Tothill Fields, Tower Bridge
And Kentish places, Dover, Tunbridge Wells
Entering wider hauntings, resonant,
    The Boggart Hole, Bleak House, Deep Doom and Gloom.

Remembering boyhood, soldier poets recall
The desperate deeds of Lost Boys, Peter Pan,
Hook Copse, and Wendy Cottage. Horrors lurk
In Jekyll Copse and Hyde Copse. Nonsense smiles
As shells and flares disorder tidy lines
In Walrus, Gimble, Mimsy, Borogrove

Which lead to Dum and Dee and to that Wood
Where fury lurked, and blackness, and that Crow.

There's Dead Man's Dump, Bone Trench and Carrion Trench
Cemetery Alley, Skull Farm, Suicide Road
Abuse Trench and Abyss Trench, Cesspool, Sticky Trench,
Slither Trench, Slimy Trench, Slum Trench, Bloody Farm.
Worm Trench, Louse Post, Bug Alley, Old Boot Street.
Gas Alley, Gangrene Alley, Gory Trench.
Dreary, Dredge, Dregs, Drench, Drizzle, Drivel, Bog.

Some frame the names of runs for frames of mind.
Tremble Copse, Wrath Copse, Anxious Crossroads, Howl
Doleful and Crazy Trenches, Folly Lane,
Ominous Alley, Worry Trench, Mad Point
Lunatic Sap, and then Unbearable
Trench, next to Fun Trench, Dismal Trench, Hope Trench
And Happy Alley.

How they swarm, the rats.
Fat beasts and frisking, yellow teeth and tails
Twitching and slippery. Here they are at home
As gaunt and haunted men are not. For rats
Grow plump in rat-holes and are not afraid,
Resourceful little beggars, said Tom Thinn,
The day they ate his dinner, as he died.

Their names are legion. Rathole, Rat Farm, Rat Pit,
Rat Post, Fat Rat, Rats' Alley, Dead Rats' Drain,
Rat Heap, Flat Rat, the Better 'Ole, King Rat.
They will outlast us. This is their domain.

And when I die, my spirit will pass by
Through Sulphur Avenue and Devil's Wood
To Jacob's Ladder along Pilgrim's Way
To Eden Trench, through Orchard, through the gate
To Nameless Trench and Nameless Wood, and rest.

53

Basil and Katharina Wellwood had an unhappy war. There was a huge upsurge of anti-German hatred. Katharina's friends and acquaintances ceased to call on her or to invite her to gatherings to roll bandages or knit for the British soldiers. The fact—insofar as it was known—that their son was a conscientious objector also cast suspicion on them. Their country neighbours were as venomous as their city ones. They were anxious both for Charles/Karl and for Griselda. Basil was also concerned for Geraint Fludd, who was his substitute son in the City. Geraint was somewhere with the big guns. He wrote occasionally—reasonably cheerfully from the Somme, more grimly as his guns crawled through the mud in Flanders. General Ludendorff ordered the German army to retreat to the Siegfried Line in February 1917. Word came back to Britain of his "Operation Alberich," named for the Nibelung who had abjured Love as he clasped the stolen *Rheingold*. Operation Alberich scorched the earth, hacking, burning, poisoning wells, slaughtering cattle and poultry, leaving nothing that could be used by an advancing army, French or British. A woman spat at Katharina in the street. Servants gave in their notice. Katharina, already thin, grew thinner.

The letter came. It had a Red Cross and was addressed to "Basil and Katharina Wellwood" in the Quaker style. The Friends' Ambulance Unit, it said, was greatly saddened to have to report that their friend Charles Wellwood was missing, and must be presumed dead. His courage had been exemplary. He had ventured into parts of the battlefield where many stretcher-bearers feared to go. He had brought in the wounded, English and German, had dressed their wounds and spoken to them with true gentleness. He had appeared indefatigable. He had been much respected, and would be much missed, by his fellow workers and by those whose lives he had saved.

"He is only missing," said Katharina, in a thin, exhausted voice. "He may come back to us."

"I don't think the writer of that letter thought he would," said Basil. He said

"We have the letter he gave us, to be opened, if—if he died."

"But he may not be dead."

"Do you want to leave the letter unopened?"

"No. No. I think it would be right to open it."

They were afraid of opening it. It would not simply contain assurances that he had always loved them. That was not like Charles/Karl, who knew they knew he loved them. The letter contained a secret they might not want to know.

My dear father and mother,

If you read this I shall be dead. I hope I shall have saved other lives before losing mine. You will know that I thought of you steadily, with great love and gratitude, not least for your letting me go my own way, and live a life of study that you would not have chosen for me.

There is a secret I have kept from you. I have a wife, whom you have never met. Her name is Elsie, and she finally agreed to marry me because I was going away. We were married by Frank Mallett in St. Edburga's Church. We should have told you, and shared this with you, but there was no time.

Elsie is the sister of the potter, Philip Warren. She is a student teacher and I would have hoped, if I had lived, that she could study more widely and deeply.

I am asking you both, with loving apprehension, to go and find Elsie, and take care of her, as my wife. She is very independent, as you will see, and taking care of her is hard, as I have found, myself.

She is not from our "class." I believe profoundly that this has no real importance. She—more practical—does not believe that you would want to accept or acknowledge her, for this reason. I have more faith in you— in both of you—than that. She does not know you, as I do. You are honourable, and generous, and just, and you will see her for what she is, as I do.

I end with love, again. I have no wish to die, and hope I may come home, and burn this letter, unread.

If not—please forgive me, and please look after Elsie.

Your son
Charles/Karl.

It was a week before they set out, in the Daimler, with an elderly chauffeur, for the cottage at the end of Dungeness. Basil had the idea that they should stop at Frank Mallett's vicarage, and ask him what he thought of this Elsie. Katharina said this would be unfair, from which Basil inferred that she expected to think ill of the young woman. They did, in fact, drive through Puxty, but the vicar was not home, and Dobbin was away on war work on the land. So they drove on, into the only English desert.

On the outskirts of Lydd they were stopped by sentries as they passed the army camp. They could indeed hear the artillery, practising on the range amongst the shingle and blown bushes. This was a military zone, said the soldiers. They must state their business. They could hear the guns. It would be best to turn back.

Basil was by nature inclined not to reveal his business. He said he had private business with a lady in the cottage, along the Ness. His hauteur annoyed the soldier who said he would need a permit to drive in these parts, these days. Basil said he was visiting the schoolmistress, and the sentry said the army had taken over the school and the teachers had moved out of the zone.

Katharina showed them the letter.

"Our son is dead, this letter tells us. We have found the schoolmistress is his wife. We must see her."

Katharina's accent was more suspicious than Basil's hauteur.

"How do we know you're not spies? You sound German."

"I am German. I have lived in England most of my life. I think I am English but that is no help. Please let us go through and look for this person. Our son is missing in Flanders. Presumed dead. It is bad, out there."

The chauffeur said, in a Kentish voice,

"You can see where we go. You can keep an eye. You'll see us come back. There's nowhere to go you can't see us, it's all bare."

So they drove on. Katharina imagined, not incorrectly, Charles/Karl on his bicycle, on the stony path. They came to the cottage.

A young woman was hanging out washing.

The chauffeur opened the door, and Katharina, in her veiled hat and driving-coat, stepped down.

"We are looking for a Miss Elsie Warren."

"Well, you've found her," said Elsie, finishing the pegging of a towel.

Katharina's voice trembled. She said

"Can we go inside? Sit down? Please."

"If you wish. Come in."

Basil stepped out of the car, bowed and caped. Elsie gathered her basket of clothes under one arm, balancing it on a hip, and opened the door. They all went in. Elsie asked if they would like a cup of tea, and Katharina thought she could not sit, with the weight of her news, and endure the tea-making. She asked for water, and Elsie brought water for all of them.

"We have received," Katharina said, "a letter. It tells us our son Charles is missing. It tells us we must think he is dead."

Elsie took a sip of water. She was rigid.

"We had a letter," Katharina said, "from him. For—for this time. He asked us—to look for you."

"It's true," Elsie said, in a thin, expressionless voice. "What he told you. We were married before he went out. The vicar could show you the register. You needn't worry yourselves. I don't want anything. I'll not bother you."

Katharina said "What he said. She is very independent. Taking care of her is hard, as I have found, myself."

"That's him," said Elsie. One tear rolled down her cheek. She said "I lived here with Mrs. Oakeshott and Robin and Ann. Robin was killed in France. Like Mrs. Wellwood's Robin. So Mrs. Oakeshott went to work in a hospital in Hove, when they closed the school. The military want to have this cottage—for their staff—but I need to stay here and mind Ann. Philip's in Flanders—my brother. Charles came back once, on leave, some time after Robin was killed, and left us some money. I need to find work. Ann is almost a young woman. She'll have to find work, too."

"Ann?" said Katharina.

"Oh no. Don't think that. Ann's sixteen. Ann's not—not your granddaughter."

"So you were married before?" said Basil Wellwood.

"No. No I wasn't. Ann was—a mistake. He didn't tell you about Ann."

"No. He didn't."

"Ann were the bridesmaid when we got married. He's very fond of Ann. *Was* very fond of Ann."

They sat there, and sipped water, in a fog of suspicion.

"It's all right," said Elsie. "You don't have to bother about me and Ann."

Katharina Wellwood surprised herself.

"It isn't only you and Ann. Is it?"

"I don't know how you can see. It doesn't hardly show."

Katharina said "It's the way you hold your hands, on—You have no right to keep our grandchild from us."

Another tear rolled down Elsie's face.

"You can't take it from me. It's all I got of him. You can't do it."

"Can't do what?" said Basil, slower than his wife.

"Can't take it and bring it up to be a snobby lady or a posh gentleman. Oh, please go away, I don't know what to do."

"You are very unjust," said Katharina Wellwood, "to think so badly of us. Charles/Karl—asked us to look after *you,* which is what we want to do. It is *not good* for expecting mothers to work in armaments factories, and we—I was going to say, we cannot allow you to, but you must understand I know you are a free agent.

"What I want—more than anything—is to take you—and of course Ann—back to our house in the country. To make you comfortable. Karl said—wait—I will read it to you—'She is a student teacher and I would have hoped, if I had lived, that she could study more widely and deeply.' "

Elsie began to cry in good earnest. Katharina said

"You know—Elsie, if I may call you Elsie—we *are* his parents. He is—he was—our son. Not so unlike each other. Please come with us."

"You don't understand. Your friends will despise me and laugh at you. I'm not in your class and shan't ever be, no matter how you dress me up."

"I have lost most of my friends because they despise me and sneer at me because I am a German. We can survive that. It is superficial and horrible. You are the woman my son married."

Basil made a croaking sort of sound. He said "She's right—um—*Elsie*—she's right. It will make us very happy if you come with us. And we shall be—hurt, yes, hurt, if you won't come."

"It isn't right."

"Stop arguing," said Basil.

He liked her for arguing.

Ann came in, thin, little, leggy, with a face like a will o' the wisp. She looked as though you could blow her away, or snap her like a twig. She smiled uncertainly.

"These are his—Charles/Karl's—mum and dad. They've invited us to their house."

Ann nodded seriously.

Katharina said "We can *try*, Elsie. And if you are unhappy, we will think of something else."

54

The Belgian landscape is flat and watery, polders planted with corn and cabbage, claimed from the North Sea by a series of dykes. Further inland there are fields and houses resting on a thick bed of clay. There is water there too, water in ponds and moats, water running into little *bekes* (rivulets), water in canals. The land floods easily because the water cannot penetrate the clay and drain away. In 1914 the Belgians, having offered unexpected fierce resistance to the advancing Germans, had retreated towards the coast. The Belgians opened locks and sluices and flooded the land, letting in the North Sea, and creating impassable water plains between the Germans and the coast. The villages around the sandy ridges that offered height to an army had been battered by the guns into dust, which was worked into the clay, by churning wheels and hooves, by marching men and limping, hopping, crawling wounded. In the summer of 1917 General Haig commanded his armies to advance. In the early autumn, when the generals agreed to make a push against the Passchendaele ridge, it rained. The sky was thick with cloud, and no air reconnaissance was possible. The rain blew chill and horizontal across the flat fields and liquefied the mud, and deepened it, so that movement was only possible along duckboard planks—the "corduroy" road, laid across it. The men at the front crouched in holes in the ground and the holes were partly filled with water, which was bitterly cold, and deepening. The dead, or parts of the dead, decayed in and around the holes, and their smell was everywhere, often mingled with the smell of mustard gas, a gas which lay heavily in the uniforms of the soldiers, and was breathed in by nurses and doctors whose eyes, lungs and stomachs were damaged in turn, whose hair was dyed mustard yellow. The peaceful polders had become a foul, thick, sucking, churning clay, mixed with bones, blood and burst flesh.

Geraint and his gun crew were manoeuvring their gun on the corduroy road, between snapped and blackened tree stumps, over mud and pools of filthy water. He had had letters from unimaginable England. Imogen wrote that Pomona had announced her engagement to one of her patients, Captain Percy Armitage, who had lost both his legs and most of his sight in one eye. "She seems truly happy," wrote Imogen. She had attached a photograph of her palely pretty daughter, from which she had, with inconsiderate consideration, obviously cut away another child, with scissors.

Geraint didn't much mind. He was thinking very slowly, in the racket of gunfire and shellfire, having had no sleep for twenty-four hours, and only two hours in the preceding night and day. Maybe because they were so tired the crew lost control of the mule that was hauling its end of the wheels on the boards. The gun keeled over in the mud. Geraint was under it, and was killed instantly, crushed into the slime. Nobody stopped to dig for him. There were orders not to stop for those who fell off the snaking boards.

As the landscape grew more and more to resemble the primal chaos, human ingenuity became more and more desperately orderly and inventive. Columns of bearers, at night, carried ammunition and water and hot food in insulated rucksacks to the men at the front. They resembled Christian, in *Pilgrim's Progress,* making his way with his heavy pack through the Slough of Despond. One of the cyclist regiments balanced an odd load—full-size flat images of soldiers, painted in England by women who had once painted bone china, with realistic faces, with moustaches and glasses under their tin hats. These were puppets. They had flat strings snaking over the mud, operated by puppeteer soldiers hidden in foxholes and craters, who made them stretch and turn, stand up and fall. They made what were known as Chinese attacks, deployed in hundreds, under a smokescreen, inviting the Germans to fire on them and reveal their own positions. A man in a shell-hole could operate four or five of these "soldiers."

The Women's Hospital in the Claridge's hotel in Paris had been closed in 1915: the women moved briefly to Wimereux and then back to London, where they opened a successful, much larger hospital in Endell Street. There were still ambulances and a field hospital, paid for by women's colleges and run by crews of women. Dorothy and Griselda had elected to stay. Dorothy believed that if men's wounds were dressed as well, and as promptly, as possible, there was a greater chance of their survival, and of the survival of damaged hands and feet, arms, legs and other parts. Griselda continued to talk to the wounded prisoners. One evening, when they were sitting in their shelter over a cup of cocoa— a thick taste and texture that recalled the quiet studies, the library and the rose garden of Newnham as surely as Proust's madeleine recalled his childhood at Cambrai—she said, casually, that this tent of prisoners were Bavarians from Prince Rupprecht's Army Group. One of them, she said lightly to Dorothy, claimed to have seen Wolfgang Stern, alive, and as well as he could be, a month ago. Dorothy said "Do you ask all of them that question?" Griselda said "No, not all, of course not. Only the ones who might know."

"I never knew how much you cared for Wolfgang?"

"It is so far away. And there is all this killing. I think I—did care for him. I sometimes thought he . . . Oh, what does it matter, when we are trying to kill him in all this mud." She laughed sharply. "It's hard to be half-German. My mother is having a bad time. She sent an odd letter after Charles/Karl went missing, saying she was going to look for his wife in Dungeness."

"His *wife*?"

"That's what the letter said. Mama didn't elaborate. I ask about him, too, but get no answers. The men don't hate each other, mostly. The walking wounded help each other. Once it's clear they don't have to kill each other. It's all mad. Mad and muddy and bad and bloody. I don't know if it's better to stop hoping about Karl. And Wolfgang."

They were about to go to bed when a new contingent of wounded men and stretcher-bearers plodded slowly, and painfully, towards the ambulance. The nights were rarely quiet: the long snakes of men and animals moved into the dark and were hurt in the dark as the shells fell and found them. On the stretcher this time was a man almost invisible in a case or coffin of thick clay, which was drying onto him. The stretcher-bearers said he had gone right under. A shell burst, quite close, and sent up a lot of the stuff and damaged the duckboards. This man had been carrying a large pack on his back and had lost his footing when the shell came down, and he had gone sideways into the mud, and under. His pals pulled him out. There's orders not to pull men out, if they get in, because they mostly can't be saved. And they hold up the line of night-workers. Men were swearing behind, and shouting, leave the bugger, excuse my language, ma'am. We was passing by, on the track we come back on, and the man we was carrying died as we went. So we had just dumped him when this one got pulled out, lucky for him. He lost his trousers, they was sucked off of him. They wanted to save his pack, o' course. It was hot rations. He's breathing. Shell-shocked, seemingly.

They did get the pack. With mud in it and over it, but the hot food was still in it and still hot, we hoped. I hope you ladies can take him, we need to get back out there.

So the clay-cased man was rolled off the stretcher, on to a temporary bed in the hospital. Dorothy looked round for nurses. They were all busy. She found a bucket and began to pick off the mud, which came off in bloody hunks, at first. Griselda helped. The face was the face of a golem: the ambulance men had made breathing holes and eye holes but the hair was caked solid and the eyebrows were worms of mud, and the lips were thick and brown. Dorothy picked and wiped. Griselda said "He's got shrapnel down here, where his trousers were, I've got his pants off, it doesn't look nice."

The man trembled. Dorothy said "There's a lot in his back, as well." She washed him, quickly but gently, and then again, as though the mud layer was inexhaustible, always renewing itself.

The man said "I always said you had good hands." His voice was clogged, as though he had swallowed mud. Dorothy said

"Philip?"

Philip said, with great difficulty, "When I went under, I thought, it's a good end for a potter, to sink in a sea of clay. Clay and blood."

"Don't talk."

"I didn't think they'd pull me out. They're not meant to."

Dorothy said "Can you move your fingers? Good. Toes? Not so good. Turn your head? Not too far. Good. There's shrapnel in your back, and in your legs, and in your bottom. It needs to come out, or it festers. You're lucky, this is an ambulance attached to the Women's Hospital, we have Bipp."

"Bipp?"

"It's a patent antiseptic paste. You put it on and leave it for ten or even twenty-one days. It seals the healing. And it is good for the healing not to be disturbed. You'll need a lot of Bipp. Some of the army doctors think they can sterilise needles and blades with olive oil. We are cleverer than that."

There was no other surgical emergency, so Dorothy sat by Philip's muddy body in the lamplight, picking out the pieces of shrapnel, delicately, precisely. He said

"The feeling's coming back. I was all numb."

"That's good, though you may not think so. I can give you morphine."

"Dorothy—"

She searched with tweezers for a deep scrap of metal, in his flesh.

"Dorothy, you're crying."

"I do, sometimes. All this is hard. You don't expect to find a friend in a cake of mud."

"I can't laugh, it hurts. What are you doing?"

"You've got a deep bit, here between the legs. I shall need to get it out under anaesthetic. That can wait till tomorrow. I'll get out all I can, and apply the Bipp. And give you morphine, and make you comfortable. I think your leg's broken, too. You'll have to go back to England."

Philip gave a great sigh. Dorothy injected morphine. She slapped on Bipp, where the shrapnel had been extracted. Philip said "I don't really believe you're here. I often wished you were. I mean, not in the mud, in the abstract."

Dorothy said "Not abstract. Concrete."

55

Après la Guerre Finie

May 1919. A cab drew up outside the house in Portman Square. A man got out, a skeletal man, whose cheap clothes hung on him like a coat hanger. He hesitated a moment or two, then rang the doorbell. A young maid answered and looked at him doubtfully. He went past her, like a shadow, and into the drawing-room, where he heard voices.

He stood in the doorway. The maid stood doubtfully behind him. He was puzzled by the group of people there. There was a man with a strapped leg and thigh lying on the chaise longue. There was a thin young girl in a smart short skirt. There was a nursemaid. There was an elegantly dressed young woman, with fashionable short hair, on a low chair, with her back to him.

Basil and Katharina Wellwood were sitting side by side on a sofa, admiring the baby the young woman was holding. It was not as he had imagined it. He cleared his throat. He said, as people all over the world were saying, "Did you not get my letter?" Katharina sprang to her feet like a wire uncoiled, all of a tremble.

"Karl. Charles. It is not."

"It is," he said. His father stood up. The red hair was almost grey. Basil said

"You need to sit down."

Katharina came unsteadily towards him. The fashionable young woman rose to her feet, still holding the baby, who had white-blond hair and well-defined features, not pudgy. He said

"Elsie."

Katharina pulled at his hand. "Sit down, sit down."

She could not say how deathly she thought he looked. Elsie said, matter-of-fact, "You've had a bad time." And began to cry. She said

"This is Charles. We all wanted to call him Charles, because we thought—"

He sat down on the sofa, surrounded by his family, and tried to work out the wounded soldier on the chaise longue. He was, of course, Philip Warren. The room had changed, not only because of the baby and the nursemaid, but because two great golden jars of Philip's were there, either side of the hearth, covered with twined, climbing, tiny demons.

"I can't really get up," said Philip. "I am glad to see you."

"Where did you get hit?"

"Passchendaele. I was saved—I think—by prompt medical attention from Dorothy. Griselda was there. They're in the Women's Hospital in Endell Street now. So is Hedda. She's an orderly. She saved my leg, Dorothy did."

Katharina said he must be hungry. She went away to order beef tea, and soft bread, and a milk pudding. Charles/Karl sat on the sofa and looked at his wife and son. Basil said

"Elsie and Ann—and little Charles—have been such a comfort to us. As you can see. We have looked after them, as you asked."

Charles/Karl could not say that by "looking after" he had supposed he meant setting Elsie up in a comfortable cottage, with an income. Basil said

"Elsie has been such a support to your mother. She has had a difficult time. Not to be compared, of course," he added, still appalled by his son's boniness and bald skin. He said "We must telephone the Women's Hospital. Griselda is an orderly. She works very long hours, but she may be able to come home. She must, at least, know—"

Charles/Karl stroked his son's hair with shaking fingers. His son smiled, pleasantly. Charles/Karl did not feel steady enough to take the baby. Elsie leaned over him and kissed his hair and kissed his hand in small Charles's hair. She said "Your people have been *unimaginably* good to me. And Ann. Ann, come over and say—welcome back—to—to—"

Ann came over and looked at him, and said

"Have you been in prison?"

"I was. There was no food. The guards had next to no food. Everyone is starving."

He could not describe the unspeakable. He said he had been burned in an explosion, whilst carrying a German soldier on a stretcher in No Man's Land. The soldier and Charles/Karl's companions had been killed. He had been picked up by some German soldiers—Bavarians, who had looked after him because he spoke German. He hesitated. He could not begin to describe the foul journey, the deaths and the dead. He said

"I ended up in Munich. There was no food and men were deserting, a few at a time and then all together. I walked to the Pension Susskind. Joachim and his sister were there. They fed me. They found a doctor. They . . ."

He was about to weep.

Ann said "It will be better now."

Charles/Karl looked across at Philip, who looked darkly back.

Basil said "We must telephone the Women's Hospital. We must tell Griselda."

Griselda was registering the visitors for the medical wards.

"Next please," she said, to the line of tense, anxious and fearful visitors, mainly women, carrying bunches of flowers and boxes of cakes. Next, this time, was a man, a tall, dark, thin man, in a caped overcoat too heavy for the summer weather, wearing a wide-brimmed hat, pulled down so that his face was in shadow.

"Your name, please. Who have you come to see?"

"You, I think," said the visitor. He said, in a low voice, "I am a runaway, an escaped patient. I want to see you and Dorothy before they lock me up again."

Griselda looked into the shadow under the hat. The queue of women was stolid and anxious.

"I am a prisoner in Alexandra Palace. There I had influenza and pleurisy so they sent me to the hospital at Millbank. The war is over, but we may not go home until they finish signing the peace. I have stolen these clothes. Friends—prisoners—had a story of a Valkyrie on the battlefield, asking after Wolfgang Stern . . ."

Griselda was speechless. Wolfgang said "I can sit and wait for you?"

"You'd better sit. You look unsteady."

"Oh, I am, I am. I may faint at any moment. Then you would have to admit me, which I should . . ."

Dorothy came hurrying.

"Griselda—a shock—"

"I know. He's here."

Dorothy looked rapidly round.

"He isn't here. He's in Portman Square." Griselda nodded in the direction of Wolfgang, hiding in his hat.

"There—"

"I don't know what you're talking about. Your brother is in Portman Square. He's alive. He was in Munich. He made his way home."

Griselda trembled.

"And *your* brother is here under that hat. He escaped. He was in the hospital at Millbank—"

Wolfgang stood up, began to shake and sat down again, grinning weakly.

"Find a cab," said Dorothy. "Find Hedda. Get him into the cab."

There were flocks of willing girls from schools for ladies, doing voluntary work. Two serious-looking ones from Cheltenham Ladies' College were despatched on these errands, and Dorothy went over to look at her German brother in the shadow of his brim. She took his hand and measured his pulse. "Far too fast," she said. "You should be in bed."

In Portman Square there was happiness, a little giddy, mixed with apprehension, as the two old-young men told the little they could bear to tell of the chaos that had engulfed them. The English papers, at first cautiously welcoming, and then alarmed, had reported the succession of governments in Bavaria between early November 1918 and May Day 1919. The monarchy had been dislodged by huge crowds of the starving and desperate—mutinous soldiers and sailors, radical Saxons from the Krupp armaments factory, Schwabing Bohemians and anarchists, thousands of angry women, and an army of enraged farmers led by the blind demagogue, Ludwig Gandorfer. These had all been enchanted by the oratory of the wild-eyed and shaggy bearded socialist Kurt Eisner, who trimmed his beard and formed a government which could neither govern nor feed the people. Charles/Karl had never really supposed he would see anarchists in power. In December Erich Mühsam, to whom he had listened in the Café Stefanie as he advocated free love and all goods in common, led four hundred anarchists to occupy a newspaper office. In January there was an election in which Eisner won less than 3 per cent of the vote. In February, on his way to the Landtag to resign, he was shot down by Count Anton Arco auf Valley, a part-Jewish anti-Semite, who was himself shot down by the guards.

The anarchists took power. They were led by the gentle Jewish poet Gustav Landauer, whose beard and rhetoric were flowing. The

"Schwabing Soviet" nationalised everything, closed all the cafés except Café Stefanie and put the students in charge of the universities. They searched houses for hoarded food and found none. There was no food and the Allies were blockading the borders. The Foreign Secretary, a mild man, wrote urgent letters to Lenin and the Pope, complaining that someone had stolen his lavatory key.

In April there was an attempted putsch by the government in exile, and briefly, a Bavarian soviet, led by another Jew, the Spartakist Eugen Leviné. The exiles, reluctantly, having hoped to regain Bavaria with Bavarian troops, asked for help from the federal German army. They took Starnberg and Dachau. The White Terror came next. Landauer was brutally slaughtered. Leviné was formally executed. The Ehrhardt Brigade, a Freikorps unit, wore on their gold helmets the primitive sexual symbol that had formed part of the blazon of the Thule Society, with its theories of pure and impure blood, the "ancient coil," the hooked cross, the swastika. They sang full-throated songs in its praise. Order was restored in the Bavarian capital.

The Reds fought bravely, especially in the railway station, where they held out a day and a night.

Charles/Karl, stiffly, asked Wolfgang and Dorothy if they had news of the Stern family. They said no news had come out of Munich, no trains ran, letters went unanswered.

Charles/Karl said that Leon Stern had been killed in the railway station, fighting for his ideas. Wolfgang bent his head. There was a silence.

Charles/Karl said he had been to the Spiegelgarten of Frau Holle. Anselm Stern and Angela were as well as they could be, though thin and hungry. They thought they would move to Berlin, as Munich was now not a good place for Jews.

It had not occurred to Dorothy to ask whether her father was Jewish and he had not felt a need to tell her. She said, slowly,

"Perhaps, when all this is over, they could come here."

They could make magical plays for a new generation of children. Angela could work, in London, in Kent, somewhere in peace. The idea seemed both possible and unreal.

. . .

They sat, the survivors, quietly round the dinner table, and drank to the memory of Leon. Ghosts occupied their minds, and crowded in the shadows behind them. They all had things they could not speak of and could not free themselves from, stories they survived only by never telling them, although they woke at night, surprised by foul dreams, which returned regularly and always as a new shock.

Katharina lit the candles which had been brought out for the occasion, and stood in silver candlesticks.

Philip sat at the end of a table in a wheelchair that supported his leg. He was next to Dorothy, who was opposite Wolfgang. Charles/Karl was sitting next to Elsie, and their hands touched. Katharina watched her daughter watch Wolfgang Stern. Griselda had become fixed, efficient and almost spinsterly as the war went on. Katharina was almost resigned to seeing her close herself into a college. Now her composed face was discomposed and hungry in a way Katharina had never seen. Katharina asked Wolfgang if he would like more soup, and used the familiar "*Du.*" He smiled, and his grim face was livelier. She gave more soup to her frail and bony son, and to his wife, who watched him fiercely and fearfully. She gave more soup to Hedda, who was tired but almost contented, having worked hard and usefully all day, and to Ann, who had become attached to Hedda. She gave more soup to Dorothy, who gave more to Philip, who said it was delicious. Delicate dumplings lurked beneath the golden surface on which a veil of finely chopped parsley eddied and swayed. Steam rose to meet the fine smoke from the candles, and all their faces seemed softer in their quavering light.

ACKNOWLEDGEMENTS

This novel owes a great deal to many people, who have told me about things, shown me things, and shared their knowledge. People always thank their patient partners at the end of their acknowledgements, but I want to thank my husband, Peter Duffy, at the beginning. He has shown me southern England, driven me to odd places, and shared with me his considerable knowledge of the First World War, including his books. He has found things out about distances, modes of transport and buildings, and checked (some of) my mistakes. He has also been patient.

I owe a great deal to Marian Campbell, who showed me the gold and silver in the Victoria and Albert Museum—and understood that I would need the Gloucester Candlestick. She also showed me the basement and its treasure. Reino Liefkes showed me the ceramics department, including works by Palissy, and early Majolica dishes. A pot in the hands is quite different from a pot behind glass. Fiona McCarthy sent me her copy of Anthony Burton's *Vision and Accident* about the Museum—I saw I needed my own, and bought one. Her work on William Morris has also been hugely helpful. I am grateful to Sir Christopher Frayling, who sent me books about the Royal College of Art and talked to me about it.

My daughter, Antonia Byatt, when director of the English Women's Library, helped me with the history of women's suffrage and introduced me to Anne Summers, and to Jennian Geddes, whose generous provision of information about women in medicine at the time of my novel was both fascinating and extraordinarily helpful.

Edmund de Waal invited me to visit his studio, and allowed me to put my hands into a wavering clay pot. He also gave me books and suggested more, and I owe him a great deal. I was also helped by Mary Wondrausch whose book on slipware—apart from being full of interest—was also full of technical information and delectable vocabulary.

My friend and translator Melanie Walz, who lives in Munich, showed me the city and took me to the puppet museum—and everywhere else—and shared her wide knowledge of German and Bavarian art and life, over many years. The book could not have been written without her. I am also grateful to Professor Martin Middeke who took me to the Augsburg puppet museum, and to Deborah Holmes and Ingrid Schram who took me to see the Teschner collection in the Austrian Theatre Museum in Vienna, and to the Museum of Applied Arts there, where I learned a great deal, with great pleasure, from Dr. Rainald Franz. And I would like to thank Dimitri Psurtsev and Victor Lanchikov for help with things Russian.

Dr. Gillian Sutherland shared her knowledge of the history of women in Cambridge, and of Newnham College in particular—and again sent books. I am very grateful. Professor Max Saunders helped me with the Rossetti anarchists and his work on the period was informative and elegant.

The books I have collected are too many to mention but I should like to acknowledge the pleasure and information I found in David Kynaston's great history of the City of London. Linda K. Hughes's *Life of Graham R.* is full of detail, and Professor Hughes herself answered arcane queries with generosity. I am indebted to Peter Chasseaud's splendid *Rats Alley,* which is a comprehensive description of the trench names of the Western Front. Andrew Ramen at Heywood Hill helped me at the very beginning of this work by collecting and suggesting books on puppetry and other things. I reread Jonathan Gathorne-Hardy's terrifying book on public schools, which helped, as can be seen.

Dominic Gregory went to look at inns near Dungeness and sent me a pebble with a hole in it.

My American publishers at Knopf have been, and continue to be, encouraging, meticulous and generous. I am grateful for Sonny Mehta's enthusiasm. I immensely enjoy working with Robin Desser, my editor at Knopf—I am very happy that we have now worked together for a considerable time. Steven Barclay, my American lecture agent, is both a good friend and extraordinarily competent and imperturbable.

My publisher at Chatto and Windus, Alison Samuel, and my editor, Jenny Uglow, to whom this novel is dedicated, have been supportive and imaginative. Patrick Hargadon discussed knotty narrative points beyond the call of duty. My agent in the States, Melanie Jackson, has been both wise about the novel, and precise about practical matters. My British agent Deborah Rogers has looked after me, in more ways than I could have imagined, and I owe a great deal to her and to her assistants, Hannah Westland and Mohsen Shah. Lindsey Andrews was diligent and helpful when she worked as my assistant. And I am as always very grateful for Gill Marsden's patient and faultless typing, and for her calm interest in the work.

Finally, I was amazed by Stephen Parker's beautiful cover design, and Gabriele Wilson's elegant American adaptation of it. They are exactly right and all I could have wished for.

A NOTE ABOUT THE AUTHOR

A. S. Byatt is internationally acclaimed as a novelist, short story writer and critic. Her novels include *Possession,* awarded the Booker Prize in 1990; the quartet *The Virgin in the Garden, Still Life, Babel Tower* and *A Whistling Woman; The Game;* and *The Biographer's Tale.* She has also written two novellas, published together as *Angels and Insects,* and five collections of shorter works, including *The Matisse Stories* and *Little Black Book of Stories,* as well as several works of nonfiction. Educated at Cambridge, she was a senior Lecturer in English and American literature at University College, London. She lives in London.

A NOTE ON THE TYPE

The text of this book was set in Bembo, a facsimile of a typeface cut by Francesco Griffo for Aldus Manutius, the celebrated Venetian printer, in 1495. The face was named for Pietro Cardinal Bembo, the author of the small treatise entitled *De Aetna* in which it first appeared. Through the research of Stanley Morison, it is now generally acknowledged that all old style type designs up to the time of William Caslon can be traced to the Bembo cut.

The present-day version of Bembo was introduced by the Monotype Corporation of London in 1929. Sturdy, well-balanced, and finely proportioned, Bembo is a face of rare beauty and great legibility in all its sizes.

Composed by North Market Street Graphics

Printed and bound by Berryville Graphics, Berryville Virginia

Designed by Maggie Hinders